I0831786

THE DARK AVENGER'S SIDEKICK

Books by John C. Wright

TALES OF MOTH AND COBWEB

The Green Knight's Squire
The Dark Avenger's Sidekick
The Mad Scientist's Intern
The Ghostly Father's Novice

THE UNWITHERING REALM

Somewhither
Nowhither
Everywhither

STANDALONE NOVELS

Superluminary
Iron Chamber of Memory
Null-A Continuum

ANTHOLOGIES

Awake in the Night Land
City Beyond Time
The Book of Feasts and Seasons

NON-FICTION

Transhuman and Subhuman

COUNT TO THE ESCHATON

Count to a Trillion
The Hermetic Millennia
Judge of Ages
Architect of Aeons
The Vindication of Man
Count to Infinity

THE CHRONICLES OF CHAOS

Orphans of Chaos
Fugitives of Chaos
Titans of Chaos

THE GOLDEN OECUMENE

The Golden Age
The Phoenix Exultant
The Golden Transcendence

THE BOOKS OF EVERNESS

Last Guardians of Everness
Mists of Everness

THE DARK AVENGER'S SIDEKICK

Moth & Cobweb Books 4-6

JOHN C. WRIGHT

The Dark Avenger's Sidekick

John C. Wright

Published by Castalia House
Kouvola, Finland
www.castaliahouse.com

Cover: Scott Vigil
Editor: Vox Day

ISBN: 978-952-7065-26-6

CONTENTS

DAUGHTER OF DANGER

CITY OF CORPSES

TITHE TO TARTARUS

Daughter of Danger

HERE *with an arrow, lo, I trace*
A magic circle ere I leave,
No evil thing within this space
May come to harm thee or to grieve.
Step not, for aught, across the line,
Whatever thou mayst see or hear,
So shalt thou balk the bad design
Of every enemy I fear.

Toru Dutt (1856-1877)

Chapter 1

The Nameless Girl

1. An Unblinding Light

She found herself in a blinding light that did not blind her. It was a dozen times brighter than sunlight, but restful to her eyes, filling her with golden warmth. Before her was a shining and beautiful young lady in a white robe and bright red mantle. Standing before the bright lady, point downward, was a heavy iron sword, and the lady rested her hand on its hilts. In this hand, between her fingers, were a white lily and a green palm frond.

In her other hand the bright lady lifted up a golden chalice from which a scent more fragrant and savory than any wine of earth stole forth. The light of gold came from this cup.

The lady spoke. Her eyes were fixed on some high point. "By highest Heaven's express, unalterable will, your lost life is to you this hour restored, that you shall serve the purposes of Heaven. All prior oaths are void, all vendettas forgotten: you are made new.

"The dawn of eternal light is come when the mists of forgetfulness and deceit are driven hence, and all dark things revealed, all truths uncovered. Therefore tell the Twilight people, who are neither wholly of the Daylight World nor of the Night World, that when eternal day breaks, twilight is no more. Then will all their deeds be laid bare and judged. That hour is at hand!

"Let not the soul of thy beloved be drawn into darkness."

The bright lady lowered her gaze, and her voice grew soft and sad. "I am sent, for those beset by sudden death are mine. Wake now, lest ye die. Those who seek your life are nigh."

2. Sickbed

She woke. Even before she opened her eyes, from the smells and sounds of disinfectants and hushed electronic beeping, she knew she was in a hospital room. She opened her eyes.

The room was dim and small. Indirect lighting gleamed against soundproofing ceiling tiles. The other bed was empty. Through the cracks in the Venetian blinds glinted the lights of skyscrapers and murmured the crawling street traffic, sounding like the growling voice of a beast. Opposite the window was a door with a square window leading to a corridor.

Green curtains hanging from a track in the ceiling cut off the rest of her view of the room.

She raised her hands. They were slender and well formed. The nails were unpainted. The skin hue was yellowish, between tan and very light peach.

She flexed her fingers slowly. Something felt wrong.

On her forefinger was a little instrument like a cap, glowing with an eerie laser-light. A band was taped about her wrist. Taped to the back of her hand was an intravenous needle. She looked up.

The intravenous tube led to a drip of saline solution. From the doctor's notes scribbled on the bag, there were no other drugs in the drip. She impatiently pulled the needle out and pulled off the cap. This made the little machine on the rack next to her buzz angrily.

She tossed the disinfectant-scented bedsheet aside. She was wearing a flimsy blue hospital gown which left her arms and legs uncovered, as well as everything from her spine to her hamstrings.

She sat up and scowled at the buzzing machine. She saw the volume knob and gave it a sharp twist, shutting it off. She pulled off the wristband and tossed it down.

She flexed her fingers again. Without the distracting sensation of foreign objects affixed to hand or wrist, she could feel a small, solid weight circling her right middle finger near the knuckle.

But she could not see it. There was nothing there.

She gingerly reached with the fingers of her left hand. She felt something cold, hard, metallic instead of her skin in that spot. It was a ring. She could feel the intaglio. It had some design or device mere blind touch could not reveal.

She pulled on the unseen ring. It did not come off. She held her finger close to her face. She could touch the metal band with her nose. A faint and unpleasant odor issued from it. The smell of blood.

She then caught a glimpse of a closet door with a mirror bolted to it. That was when she realized she did not remember what she looked like.

She was on her feet and over to the mirror in a bound, expecting to see scars, wounds, or bruises from whatever fight it was that landed her in the hospital.

Looking back at her was a girl of the classical beauty for which Akita Prefecture was famous: the pale skin, slender face, high cheeks, piercing eyes and narrow lips which was called the *kitsune*, or "foxlike" look. Girls from the southern parts of the island were famed for being wide-eyed and round-faced, and having a softer, gentler cast of features, called *tanaka*. Whereas hers was the delicate, cool beauty of the north. But the prize of Japanese notions of beauty was the hair, and hers was dark as India ink, shining black, straight and rich, falling to her elbows.

She blushed in embarrassment. "Am I vain? I must be, to think of my face so highly. What would mother say!"

She had spoken aloud in English, and the voice that came out was huskier than she had expected a girl's voice to be, tenor rather than soprano. Strange. Why had she not spoken in Japanese?

And why had she assumed she had survived a fight and not, for example, a plane accident? And why was she crying?

She looked at the mirror, at the tears she saw on the cheeks of her reflection. "Mother…" she whispered. And then she knew.

Mother was dead.

The sorrow in her heart had no other meaning. As she raised her hand to wipe the tears, she saw a flash of black metal, darker than midnight, on her finger.

She could see the an invisible ring in the mirror. In the mirror. She could see it, but not with her eyes. How was that possible?

The band of the ring was an unreflective black, an ebon hue that absorbed every aspect and nuance of light. The intaglio was shaped like a skull, maggot-eaten, jaws gaping, eyeholes agog. And the smell of blood issued from it.

A freakish, frightening sensation came over her without warning. She had the unmistakeable sense that someone was looking for her. She could feel unseen eyes gazing at her; hostile, dreadful, implacable, inhuman.

She slapped the light switch as she jumped into the corner and crouched down, eyes darting to the window, the door, the ceiling panels, looking for some clue from which to guess the angle of the incoming attack. With the lights out, the lines of parallel glare from the Venetian blinds seemed bright. The headlamps of moving cars far below made a wavering ripple of shadows across the blinds.

The unseen ring frightened her. She tried to yank it off, but she could not get it over her knuckle. She twisted it, trying to loosen it. She felt it turn. Once, twice, thrice, she turned it.

There was an eerie tingling in her finger as she turned the ring. She felt lightheaded. She turned it a fourth time. It felt looser. Again, she tried to yank it off. But it was stuck.

Her eyes flicked back toward the bed. Why had she torn off her wristband? Her name would be on it, the date of her admittance, the physician in charge of her case. And the clipboard at the foot of the bed should have details of what exactly had happened to put her in this room.

But now she was afraid to step across the open space between her corner and the foot of her bed, for anyone standing in the corridor looking through the window in the door could have a clear view of her when she moved.

Instead, silently and quickly, she drew a corner of the green curtain around her. There was half a foot of open space between the hem of the curtain and the floor, so it did not entirely cover her, but it made her position less obvious.

She gathered up her hair and tied it in a rough knot at the back of her neck, hoping to make it harder to grab and wishing she had time to braid it or for a tight cap to wear.

She looked around for something to use as a weapon. The headboard above the bed, now out of reach, contained a panel where electrical equipment, oxygen tubes, catheters, and so on could be plugged. A table on wheels stood next to the bed and held the oscilloscope she had turned off. Atop a smaller table, also on wheels, were the nurse call button and the remote control for the television. Two silent television sets with dark screens peered down from metal arms near the ceiling, one above each bed. There were a sink and some drawers near her and cabinets she had not opened. The metal stand holding the I.V. was about the only object in the room one could hit someone with, and it looked unpromisingly light and thin.

The door opened quietly. She heard the sound of a soft, stealthy footfall. The figure in the room slowly approached the bed.

She opened her mouth in the hope of making her breath less audible.

3. The Three Intruders

A strange, painful sensation of hope came across her then. It was like a sick, hot feeling boiling in the pit of her stomach. Maybe nothing was wrong. Maybe those who sought her life were not nigh. What if this were merely the night nurse, walking softly so as not to wake a sick patient?

She lowered her eye to the gap between the curtain hem and the floor. Her check touched the floor tile, and she realized it was linoleum. It was good for footing: resilient, and splinter free. And if she were horribly wounded, there would be no delay to getting her to a hospital, would there be?

That stray thought produced a second: where was the hospital staff? Who had brought her here? Why hadn't he stayed to look after her?

The sight of the figure bent over the bed drove all other thoughts away. He wore a red cap with a white owl's feather atop his shaggy head, and a long green coat over his broad back, but beneath the lower hem of the green coat were not sterile and comfy shoes favored by doctors. He wore knickerbockers buckled at the knee and was barefoot.

His seemed to have a skin condition: his feet were covered with clumps of hair, and strands were even growing up between his toes. His feet were too long and thin. She wondered if a bone disease in his feet had disfigured them. His toenails were an inch long, half an inch thick, and yellow as horn.

Not a nurse. Not a normal person with healthy feet.

He lowered his head toward the empty bed. She heard a soft noise. A snort. A snuffle.

He was sniffing. The stranger with the bad feet was sniffing her bedsheets.

She was waiting for him to be far enough into the room that she might have a chance to slip out behind him and race out the door.

That hope was quashed when she heard the rustle of two other people entering the room. She heard the creak of the door being eased shut, and heard a slither of steel and then the click of a padlock shutting.

She was locked in the room with three of them.

4. *Laignech Faelad*

Her mind went blank. There was no other exit, no escape.

The first man was still sniffing the bed. He spoke without turning his head. "The ring was here, but the scent is confounded! Phaugh! My nose be filled with starch and stink, ammonia and disinfectant!"

A second man stepped into her view. He was bald, stocky, and dark skinned, wearing a green leather motorcycle jacket and steel-toed workboots. In his hands he carried a chain. He held it with his hands apart so that the chain was taut and the links would not rattle. He also wore a red cap. "The moon is near the earth. Let us take up our true forms."

The second man shrugged out of his jacket, tossed the chain on the bed, and began undoing his belt and trousers.

The third was not a man. He stood on two legs and had arms and hands like a man, but his head was the head of a goat. His knees bent backward, and his hoof was split. He was over seven feet tall, thick of chest and broad of shoulder to match. Except for his own natural pelt of brown and black, he was naked. A barnyard smell came from the monster. Between his ram horns was perched a red peaked cap with a white owl's feather. In his hands was a long trident, whose tines scraped against the ceiling tiles.

The monster spoke in a strangled voice, like a man sounds when he speaks while breathing in. "Here as yet, I wager, missy? Here as yet?"

The monster clip-clopped to the closet and yanked open the door, brandishing his trident as he did so.

"We are come to crack your bones and lap the marrow!"

Inside were a small toilet and sink. The goat-man's ears drooped.

The butt of his weapon brushed against the wheeled bed stand and knocked it over. The remote control for the TV bounced on the floor and came to rest a foot or so from her hand.

The second man had his trousers about his knees and was scowling and unlacing his boots. His face turned darker and began to elongate, and hair sprouted from his bald head as well as from his cheeks, jaw, neck, naked back, and shoulders. His ears were getting larger and standing out from his skull, like the ears of a dog.

The first man, the barefoot one, was beginning to turn his head as he looked to the other corners of the room. He was about to turn his head far enough to see her. She pushed the red button on the remote.

The noise of the television overhead, and the light from the screen, were startling in the quiet gloom. All three flinched and looked up. The barefoot man stepped backward and thus was half a step closer to her.

It was close enough. Instinct moved her limbs. Before she was aware of what she was doing, she had vaulted toward the barefoot man, selecting him as the most immediate target.

She heard the echo of a voice in her memory: *In fighting a man, a girl is less in strength, reach, speed, and spirit. Your bones are more easily broken. Your heart more easily frightened. This does not mean victory is his! Use his strength against him. Use his speed against him. Use his skill against him.*

The first man turned and rushed at her. She saw that he was an amateur fighter, one who tries to punch or tackle before judging his distance properly. She stepped closer, inside his swing, bobbing her head. His fist flew past her ear.

She snap-kicked, using her shin rather than her foot to land the blow. His legs guided the blow to his groin, and his strong forward momentum gave it force. Had he been a weaker man, moving less quickly, he would not have injured himself. But he was very strong.

On the backstroke on her same kick, she drove her instep down his shin and brought the heel of her bare foot onto his strangely narrow foot hard enough that she heard a cracking noise.

The echo said: *If a man cannot walk, he cannot fight.*

He doubled over in pain. He tried to grab her, but missed.

While he was doubled over, she gripped her own wrist and twisted her upper body to drive the corner of her elbow into his temple. He stumbled and fell.

The second man, the one who had been bald but was now halfway transformed into a wolf-creature, swung at her with a limb that was neither a man's arm nor a forepaw. But because the limb was still in the midst of changing length, it neither struck nor clawed her.

She grabbed the hairy wrist with one hand and drove her palm into the elbow joint. It is usually an easy joint to damage, but the man simply grunted in pain and swung at her with his other hand. With his trousers binding his knees, he was off balance. But he still had quick reflexes and he was blindingly fast.

She deflected his blow with both her forearms and let the force of his blow pull her inside his reach. His reflexes had betrayed him: now she was inside his guard.

She straightened both of her arms and struck at his face, one hand to either side of his nose. The index finger was extended, and the other three fingers were bent underneath in support, lest her index finger break from the blow. The curves of the face naturally guide the blow into the eye sockets.

The echo said: *If a man cannot see, he cannot fight.*

When he instinctively drew his hand back to his face to protect it, she drove her knee into his floating rib where his arms were no longer in place to block.

He doubled over. She did an acrobatic flip across his back and landed on the bed, picking up the chain as she did so. A second somersault carried her to the strip of floor between the foot of the bed and the bathroom door.

She was close enough to the goat-man now to strike at his long nose with the chain. He tried to parry with the haft of his trident, but the chain wrapped around it and struck him on the soft snout. Breaking a man's nose in a fight prevents him from drawing air. She hoped this held true for goats as well.

The echo said: *If a man cannot breathe, he cannot fight.*

Before she could follow up, the goat-man struck at her with the butt of his weapon, and, moving unexpectedly fast for someone his size, he vaulted backward until his rear hoof touched the door. She blocked the blow with her knee, but his strength was such that even the partial blow had force enough to fling her, stumbling, across the room. She tripped, did a back handspring, and regained her footing but she had lost the chain, her only weapon.

5. Goborchend

Her gaze was on the goat-man's monstrous form crouching by the door. She now saw how they had locked the door with no lock. One of them had inserted a metal strip between the door and the jamb, and padlocked a sliding clamp in place. She did not like the fact that they had evidently prepared this attack.

The goat-man said, "You hurt my hounds! But you will find a Goborchend is not overcome so readily as the Laignech Faelad!"

She was trembling with fear and rage. The other two men were now both on the ground, in convulsions. She dared not take her eyes from the goat-man, but in the corner of her eye she saw—or thought she saw—hair turning to fur and spreading over their flesh, faces stretching, writhing and changing shape, and limbs shriveling from human hands and feet into wolf paws. Both were howling, but whether this was from the pain of their wounds or the rage of their transformation, she did not know.

She backed up. There was a lightweight chair next to her, and she felt the Venetian blinds brush her backside.

She picked up the chair in her hands and turned sideways, crouching.

Blindingly quick, the goat-man lunged with his three-headed spear. She parried with the chair legs, deflecting the tines high. The tines became tangled with the blinds, and he pulled the whole curtain rod off the wall when he recovered from the lunge. The three windows stood in one frame. They were old-fashioned, from the days before the invention of air conditioning, nothing more than glass panes held in wooden sashes.

She was sweating freely now. He was taller and stronger, she was backed into a corner. There was no retreat. He was tall enough, and his trident long enough, that he could strike her anywhere in the room.

The two others rolling on the floor now grew less agitated. The bed blocked her view of them.

The goat-man shifted his weight and struck again.

His forward hand, which was constantly in motion, weaving and bobbing, guided the trident, and his rear hand, arm and shoulder, gave weight to the blow. With three spear blades instead of one, he could strike three places at once. And with each twitch of his hands, he switched the trident blades from vertical to horizontal and back again.

This time, she managed to deflect the blow to her left. The tines penetrated the glass and stuck in the wood of the frame. He roared and yanked. The whole window frame came out of the wall and fell into the room in a spray of splinters, nails, and clouds of powdery dust.

She saw a narrow stone ledge, less than nine inches wide, flush with the lower lip of the sill.

The only way to overcome a more skilled opponent is by doing the unexpected, something for which his reflexes are not primed to counter.

The monster took a moment to kick the wooden debris free from the head of his trident. That moment was her only chance. Up she vaulted, and slid out the window, in one smooth and reckless move, nimbly as a gymnast.

6. *Take It Outside*

Now she was in the filmiest of gowns, shivering with fear and cold, and the wind shear tried to pluck her from the stone side of the building. The myriad lights from other skyscrapers looked down from above and up from below. She saw the winking red taillights and white headlights from motionless and honking traffic far below as well as the pallid glare of streetlamps.

With her back to the wall, she began inching her way along the ledge toward the next window. The cold wind pried and pummeled at her. The knot of her hair came loose, and now the long black strands were whipping her face, shoulders, and neck. She spat and blinked.

She looked back. One after another, two wolves larger than wolves should be were creeeping carefully out of the broken window and onto the ledge. Both of them wore red caps on their narrow lupine skulls, and the white owl feathers whipped in the wind. The one in the front was dragging his left hind leg as if his foot were broken. But he had three good legs still. The one in the rear was bleeding from both eyes and moved his head in a manner that blindness. But still he came on, grinning jaws agape, for his nose could guide him as well, or better, than his eyes.

She seemed again to hear an echo in her memory: *If a man cannot walk or cannot see, he cannot fight.* "Wisely said," she muttered. "But what about a wolf?"

The cold air hissing around the sharp stone corner of the building plucked and pushed at them. Both wolves crouched down on the unsteady footing, ears flattened, and unwilling to step forward. She took the chance to shuffle quickly back. Then, she felt the next window at her hip.

The window was dark; the room beyond was unlit. She knelt, her fingers searching frantically for some way to open the sash. But there was none on this side.

7. Thursday

She was drawing back her hand to strike the glass, hoping she could break it without the recoil toppling her into space, when the sash suddenly moved. The window slid smoothly up.

The goat-faced man leaned out, grabbed her by both elbows, one in either hand, and pinned her arms behind her. His stench was overwhelming, and his strength was immense.

She planted her feet on the sill to either side so that he could not draw her inside. She was horizontal, straining helplessly, high above a dark drop with nothing below, and the wind tossed her black hair like a banner.

He laughed in scorn. "By Cromm Cruach, are you the willful one! Be done with your antics, missy! My hounds will dine on your fair, soft flesh!"

She shouted, "What do you want?"

He laughed again and spoke in his strange, gulping voice. "We are anarchists. All law we scorn and all authority defy. The trinket you took is claimed by my master, the Man called Thursday! I see the name dazes you with terror!"

Actually, she could think of no name less frightening. She was not dazed. She was shivering because of the height, the cold, and the wind. But the goat-man seemed to be having trouble breathing, as his broken snout was beginning to swell. She kicked at his nose again, but he ducked his head, and her bare foot struck his horns.

He shifted his grip and took both her wrists in one massive, iron-hard hand, and now he pulled at her finger. Had the ring somehow become visible? He pulled, and she screamed, but instead of breaking her finger, he fumbled, twisting the ring. She felt like she was falling. She kicked at him, and kicked again.

Cursing, he leaned out further, and grabbed her left ankle with his free hand, folding her body in half. She felt dizzy, as if she had no weight. She was too close to use her other foot, but she was now at an angle where his horns were not in the way. She struck with her knee into his bloody nose and then did it again. He roared in pain, started to lose his grip on her sweat-slicked and slippery body, and leaned out even more. She twisted and kicked a final time, and then he toppled forward, slid across the ledge, and rolled out into nothingness.

The wall of the building seemed almost to leap up and fly in front of her. A blur of windows rushed past. She was still in his grip. They both plunged down toward the alley below, and the rushing air screamed in their ears.

It seemed so sad to her to know that she would die without ever learning her own name.

8. A Passage through Night Air

The goat-man's eyes rolled in his head until only the whites showed. His lips, ears, and fur were flapping loosely in the wind. Blood and spittle trailed up from his snout in red and yellow clouds. His grip grew lax, and he released her, as he fainted dead away from the sheer terror of their fall. Their two bodies spun away from each other.

She did not understand why the wind dropped, becoming quiet, or why the body of the goat-man sped away from her, shooting toward the ground with the speed of a rocket. How could he be pulling ahead of her? Didn't all bodies fall at the same rate, aside from air resistance?

He struck the side of a skyscraper building and rebounded, and his body fell onto the flat roof of a red brick condominium below, breaking chimney pots and utility boxes and leaving wide stains like inkblots across gravel. She passed below the level of the condominium roof, and the grisly sight was gone.

And where was the air resistance for her? It was quiet in her ears now. She found herself floating high above the street, slowly spinning. The lights below looked like candy. The great rectilinear lights of windows looming about her like canyon walls slid past with dreamlike ease, shining like a manmade Milky Way. She watched the streetlamps changing red and green.

She passed across the street, about thirty stories up and dropping with the speed of an autumn leaf. She saw a bright marquee and a theater crowd milling beneath it, men in dark suits and women in evening dresses, like something from an earlier and more elegant era. She saw a hotdog vender kicking a stray dog. She saw a huckster playing three-card monte with a chump, a sailor probably on leave, probably drunk, while the huckster's allies stood clustered around, pretending to be players or onlookers.

Then, the wind carried her between two dark buildings. She saw a body in the alley, lying on a steam grating, asleep or dead. The wind in the alley blew up sharply from below and spun her end over end. Now she was lower—perhaps only fifteen stories above the ground—and beneath her was a line of loading docks, silent as a graveyard.

At ten stories above the ground, the wind changed, and she was flung around another corner. Beneath her naked feet she saw spin by a line of shops and stores with wire mesh or iron lattices locked down over their glass fronts. A pawn shop and the Korean grocery next to it were still open, their neon signs bright. The windows of a Salvation Army outpost were lit and stood directly opposite a brightly lit magic shop whose neon-hued windows were offering palm-reading, séances, and astrological counseling.

A portly man dressed in a tuxedo and black silk top hat, perhaps a late-night theatergoer, was stepping out of the magic shop, walking stick in one hand and cigar in the other. He looked up when she passed over, and the tip of his cigar grew red as he drew in his breath.

At the same time, a tall young man in black with a narrow face and round eyeglasses stepped from the Salvation Army door. With him was a friar dressed as a Dominican: a white alb beneath a black hooded cloak. His hair was gray and fell to his shoulders, but his goatee beard was black. He and the youth stepped into the circle of light cast by a nearby streetlamp. The Blackfriar cast no shadow. The youth looked up and pointed in surprise when she drifted past overhead. The Blackfriar raised his hand and placed it over the youth's eyes.

The wind carried her to the next block. She wondered who those people were.

She noticed her flimsy gown had been badly torn in the fight. At five stories above the ground, she put out her hand and caught a passing flagpole. There was no one around, not at this elevation at night, to see her; she tore off the gown and tossed it away. Some owner who had not been a Boy Scout when he was young had left the flag flying on the pole at night. She floated there a moment, flung a leg about the flagpole, and unclipped the colors from the line. She wrapped the flag around her like a shower blanket and tucked it in. It was large enough to cover her from armpit to upper thigh.

Feeling more modestly dressed, she gathered her wild hair at her neck with one hand and held the flag shut at her bosom with the other. She put her knees together in a kneeling position and launched herself from the flagpole into space.

Down the darkened street she sailed. All the windows below were dark and all doors locked, except in one spot. Here a flashing sign reading COBBLER'S CLUB hung above a wide door, guarded by two burly bouncers, from which the flashing lights and roaring music poured amidst the fumes of heat and alcohol. Tough-looking young men and scantily clad women were gathered before the doors. She waved, but no one in line saw her.

The club slid past her like the ruins of a sunken city seen beneath the prow of a dark ship that sails by night.

It was dark underfoot. She made a smooth landing. Her bare feet slapped on the cold concrete.

She was once more on the earth, somewhere in an American city, wrapped in a red, white, and blue flag, without shoes, stockings, or undergarments, with no passport, no money, no friends, and no memory.

9. No Voice Commands

She saw a scraggly tree growing in a small circle of concrete next to a small park hemmed in by a fence of iron spears. Green buds were present, and a few early leaves had opened on the lower branches, but the crown of the tree was still but a cluster of dry and naked winter twigs.

Turning, she saw her reflection in a storefront window. The ring glinted a light gray, the hue of pewter on her finger of the hand she held at her breast. When she released her other hand, her hair floated upward like the hair of a pearl diver.

The intaglio was no longer a skull, but a fair woman's face. Her eyes were half-closed as if drowsy, and the sculptured hairs stood up as if weightless.

She twisted the ring once around her finger. The metal face flexed and changed, and the hue of the metal changed. Now, it was as white as burnished silver. The metal hair retracted and now lay flat to the sculpted mask's scalp, and the little metal face opened its eyes wide. The expression was wakeful, watchful, and tranquil.

The eerie sensation which earlier had been crawling along her spine, the sensation of hateful eyes in the darkness peering at her, was now entirely gone. She had not noticed the exact moment when the feeling had fled.

Curious, she twisted the ring once more clockwise. The little face changed again and became the face of an angel. The metal changed from silver white to an argent hue of some celestial metal. A light as bright and clear as the reflection from a diamond began to shine from the ring.

Alarmed, she twisted the ring counterclockwise. It was silver again and a woman's face.

"Hello?" she said to the woman's face in the intaglio of the ring. "I don't remember my name or what happened to me. Can you help me? Are you a magic ring?"

The face did not change expression or utter any reply.

"Do you have a help feature? An instruction manual? Phones can react to voice commands. Are you not even as good as a phone?"

The face remained serene and blank despite this criticism, but it still did not reply.

She sighed. "How did I know that about phones? Did I have a phone? Who did I call?"

She asked the same question in Japanese and then in French, Russian, Mandarin, Cantonese, Latin, and Greek. She put her hands to her lips, suddenly startled. "How do I know that many languages? For that matter, how do I know that not everyone knows that many languages?"

She twisted the ring counterclockwise. She noticed it was sensitive to half and quarter turns. The face changed slowly to a half-sleeping expression as the ring darkened toward gray hue of pewter. The intaglio changed according to how far it was turned, with the eyes growing more shut and the metal growing darker as she twisted it toward her palm and then facing outward again.

The floating sensation came over her, and her toes left the concrete. Neither by speaking, nor flapping her arms, nor kicking her legs, could she fly, but in a weightless state, it was just as easy to kick off the ground and to float to the top of a lamppost as it was to hook an ankle around the lamppost and to use it as a starting block to float back down. She found she could kick herself and swan dive for hundreds of yards before the air resistance slowed her. She also bumped herself badly trying to stop. The rules of inertia and momentum still applied. It was just the law of gravity that was taking a nap.

She put her hand through the handle of a trashcan and tried to will it into weightlessness with her. No good. Apparently, it was only herself, and any flag she happened to be wearing, that could slip free of gravity's grasp.

She went back to the storefront window and held up her hand. The reflection and what she saw with her eye matched up. She twisted the ring two full turns to what she now thought of as the flashlight setting. The brightness in the reflection was much, much stronger than the light she saw with her eye.

She quickly twisted it back to silver, which seemed to be a neutral setting. Then, she twisted it once more to pewter. She became weightless. The face was half asleep. Again she twisted, one full turn counterclockwise. The woman was fully asleep, and the ring was dark gray like cast iron, almost black.

She looked down. In the circle of light from the lamppost, she cast no shadow. The light was passing through her as if she were a ghost.

Darkness began seeping out of the ring, crawling up and down her hand.

10. No Unseen Eyes

She screamed and yanked at the ring yet again, ignoring the pain in her knuckle. To her surprise, it slid off her finger.

The shadow reappeared under her feet.

The black iron ring now rested in her left palm, and it grew clearer than glass and vanished from her sight. She could still feel the cold circle on her palm, however.

She held it up to her nose. It was giving off the smell of blood again, but nowhere nearly as strongly as the stench the ring have given off when she had first seen it.

In the reflection in the store window, she could clearly see the dark gray ring in her hand, with its image of a sleeping woman.

"An invisible ring that only turns *itself* invisible! What use is that?"

She pursed her lips and put the ring back on her finger, this time on the ringfinger of her right hand, which had a smaller knuckle. This was to prevent it from getting stuck again.

She turned it once more counterclockwise, not knowing what to expect. In the reflection, now the woman's face in the intaglio was dead, her eyelid sewn shut, her lips a horrid line, her cheeks sunken and parched. The dark gray ring turned black as onyx, shining and lustrous.

Gritting her teeth, she turned it again one full turn. Now, it grew sooty black as solid nothingness, and the face became as a skull with no flesh. The odor of blood was pungent and strong. But nothing was happening to her: she was neither invisible as a ghost nor weightless as a ghost.

A sense of fear came over her. Once again, she felt as if hostile eyes were watching.

She twisted the ring clockwise. Once, twice, three times, four. From uttermost, unshining black to onyx to iron to pewter to silver. She found her shadow beneath her feet. The ring was plainly visible. The sensation of eyes hungrily hunting for her ended immediately.

She squinted at the ring. Magic or not, it had a logic of its own. The emergency room had not removed her ring because the nurses had not seen it. The ring turned the wearer invisible when the face was asleep even though, to her own eyes, the only clue that she was now ghostlike was the fact that her shadow vanished. She was not invisible to herself. However, removing the ring while the charm was active allowed the effect to continue on the ring but broke the charm on the wearer. Ex-wearer.

Putting it back on did not revive the charm. The onyx death-head seemed to have no effect, nor did the utter black skull, no doubt because she removed the ring from her finger between twists. Apparently, one had to twist it back to the null setting, a white ring with a calm-faced figure, before twisting it forward again.

She was not willing to do that. In fact, she was not willing to stand in this spot in case whatever had been seeking her had gotten a fix on this location.

She started walking rapidly, her cold feet slapping on the concrete. The lower hem of the flag flapped against her hips with the energy of her rapid walk.

But she felt calm, hidden, as if the evil watching eyes had been warded off.

She looked at the calm woman's face in the intaglio with a finer appreciation. "You are not a null setting, are you? Are you protecting me from whatever is looking for me? I feel like some evil mind, a soul of darkness, is seeking me. If you do not say anything, I will take that as a yes."

The ring did not say anything.

She petted the woman's face on the ring. "Next question. Where am I going to get any food or any place to sleep?"

Again, the ring did not say anything.

Chapter 2

Rookie Magical Detective

1. Upper East Side

She walked, wishing she had shoes. "Well, wait a minute! Was I wearing any shoes before I was brought to the hospital? The nurses must have put them somewhere..."

She came abreast of a payphone on a pole. She stopped walking and stared at it, wondering. The light above the phone was on and buzzing. Three little flies were circling the flickering neon tube. The street where she stood had no streetlamps. Other than the phone kiosk, it was entirely dark.

She had no coins, but surely she could call an emergency number. Surely she'd be safe with the police.

She shook her head slowly. Just as safe as in a hospital room. Whoever was after her had sent agents walking casually into a crowded hospital without anyone noticing or interfering. They carried tridents and...

She frowned. Why did that not seem odd? On the one hand, speaking six languages seemed odd. That level of linguistic skill seemed unusual for one her age. But fighting opponents armed with a gladiatorial weapon from ancient Rome?

How odd that this did not seem odd!

She craned her head. She could not have fallen that far from the hospital. How many blocks had she passed? There was a yellow pages in the telephone book, which, surprisingly, was still unvandalized. From the street signs, she knew she was in the Upper East Side between East 74th Street and Third Avenue. She could not have been blown more than three or four blocks. How many hospitals could there be? There was a place called the Manhattan Minimum Invasive & Bariatric Surgery Hospital, which seemed to be about the right address, and, from the suite numbers, the building might have been tall enough to be the one she fell from. But what was Bariatrics? That did not sound like a disease involving memory loss.

She set out north. New York City is impossible to get lost in because it is laid out on a clear grid, with everything numbered in sequence. She was surprised at how dark it was, however, and how empty. Her mental picture was of a city that never slept. In the distance, she could hear the growl of crawling traffic, but not here. She wondered where she had gotten her mental picture from. Did that mean she was not a native New Yorker?

A wolf limped across an alley in the distance, momentarily visible when it passed in front of a lit window. He was dragging his left hind leg.

Common sense told her to flee. She ignored it and followed the beast.

He went into an alley. Now, she stopped. Her instincts told her it would be too easy to be flanked or surrounded if she went into the dark alley. She twisted the ring on her finger from silver to pewter, and her hair stood on end and swayed. She kicked off the ground and soared smoothly up and up toward the upper corner of the nearest building. She fumbled, banged painfully into the cornice, flipped end over end, and came to rest hanging in midair, with her flag beginning to unwind from her body.

She angrily tugged and tucked the flag more tightly around herself and, by quickly twisting the ring clockwise and counterclockwise, managed to give herself enough weight to start a downward motion, and then turned weightless again before she hit the ground. She estimated wrong and hit the ground hard, but an instinct surprised her by turning it into an acrobatic roll. She slapped the ground with her hands and came to her feet unharmed and in a fighting crouch, her hands before her, fingers curled. *Nekoashi*. She knew it, just as she knew it was called a cat stance.

And she also knew she was just where she should not be: an unlit alley where an attacker could come at her from any direction. She could see the silhouette of a fire escape above her to her right and the planks of a wooden fence across the throat of the alley ahead of her, blocking the way.

Another twist of the ring banished her weight again. Her long hair, floating freely, tickled her eyes and nose. First on her mental list of things to buy was a hair ribbon, or perhaps a bathing cap. Second was some sort of line and grapnel so she could catch herself and hook herself back down if she floated out of reach of an anchor. Third were elbow and knee pads.

This time, instead of leaping the fence, she pushed her feet against the ground in a skating, sliding motion so that she skipped like an astronaut on the moon in low, flat arcs toward the fence. She swarmed over it and down the other side, keeping her silhouette minimal.

Clinging to the boards of the fence head-downward like a lizard, she looked quickly to either side. Below her, she saw a shorter side-alley going left toward a dark truck bay feeding into the back of several establishments. The main alley ran at right angles to this and met a larger, brighter main avenue. She decided to go toward the lights first. She kicked and made a long leap to the top of a utility pole standing right at the corner of the alley and the main avenue. The streetlamp on the pole was below her: she was in the cone of the shadow cast by the lamp's cap.

About a story below her were a jeweler's, a dress shop, and a tailor's, all locked up. Then came an awning she remembered seeing from much higher up: the light sign said COBBLER'S CLUB. The line of patrons was gone, but the two bouncers were still manning the door, which was still open, and pouring the sound of pounding music out into the street. She doubted a wounded wolf would have come this way. On the other side were a French restaurant, a china shop, an antique shop, and three empty stores with bars of scaffolding covering over their fronts. Perhaps it was merely the contrast with the colored light and raucous music from the club, but the sight of empty stores selling luxuries seemed desolate.

The building on the corner holding the jeweler's and clothier's was only two stories, unlike its taller neighbors. She made it in one graceful leap and then astronaut-skipped across the flat gravel roof to look back at the truck bay up the other alley.

Now she heard the noise of a struggle. A shrill and panicked scream for help, a woman's voice, rose over the rooftops.

She dashed forward but misstepped and overdid it. She tried to hook her foot on the coping of the roof to arrest her forward momentum, and sure enough, she did slow down to the speed of a toy balloon drifting, but she also tumbled over the side of the roof and into mid-air.

2. Killer Instinct

She spread her arms and legs to slow her tumble. Cursing inwardly, she saw the dark side-alley drifting past her gaze unhurriedly below her. Square blocks of concrete faced large metal grates where cargo could be loaded or unloaded from delivery trucks. Two trucks were in the bays now.

She passed over the first truck. Now she saw the scene: Between the trucks were three figures struggling. One was smaller and slighter. A girlish scream rang out again. The call for help was not as loud as the echo of the noise of the club pouring out into the air one street over. The chance that anyone had heard was nil.

Nothing was within reach. The scene was only twenty feet below her, and she was about to drift past the second truck. There was no way to move!

She spat her hair out of her mouth. Of course there was a way to move. Down.

She twisted the ring sharply clockwise, not once, but twice. Weight returned, and gravity hurled her like a missile toward the ground. But light, diamond-bright, harsh, celestial, darted in a bright ray from her finger. She uttered her *kiai*, a screaming cry like a falcon stooping. The man immediately below her looked up, blinded and blinking.

He was a scruffy dark-skinned man in a dark coat and a red cap. She landed with her knees in position to strike both his collarbones with all her weight and use his body to break her fall. She rolled as he fell and came to her knees.

Before the man could move or rise, she grabbed the hair on his head and yanked it backward. With her other hand, she used her palm to break his nose upward. She then, while his throat was exposed, struck him in the Adam's apple with her knuckles. The diamond-bright light on her finger bobbed and swayed wildly with her swift hand motion. He went limp and lay motionless.

The other man was even rougher and more unshaven-looking than the first, and his eyes did not point in the same directions. Perhaps he was intoxicated, perhaps merely panicked. He was shivering, mouth open but making noise with no words, one hand before his face, blinking at the dazzle. Before she could roll to her feet, he turned and fled down the alley.

"*Cooin lhaim!*" the other girl cried out. "*My sailt!*"

3. Flight and Flight

The white light darting from the ring she had been playing over the fallen body, looking for something, a knife or bootstrap or belt buckle she could use to slit his throat. But now she turned the beam toward the other girl. "What did you say?"

"Help me! Please!"

The other girl was blonde, rather young and rather shapely. She was perhaps seventeen. Her hair was bobbed just below the ears and curled upward at the bangs, giving her a tousled look. She was wearing a trenchcoat that had been half-pulled down her arms. Beneath, she wore what looked like a dancer's costume: a green bodice with a plunging neckline, a green miniskirt with a handkerchief hem, and pointed-toed green slippers with fuzzy white pom-poms large as golf balls.

"You must save me!"

There was no blood, no sign of wounds. "What's wrong? Are you hurt?"

"I'm caught!"

The barefoot oriental girl stood, tucked her impromptu garb in place, tossed her black hair impatiently back, and shined the ray from her ring carefully across the blonde. She saw no rope or chain binding the blonde. She saw nothing trapping her. "Can you stand?"

The blonde smiled prettily and bounced to her feet. Her posture was a little strange: she stood with her feet together, arms by her side, and palms forward, and she tilted her chin up.

"You meant stand on my feet, right? Not my head?" asked the blonde.

It seemed an odd question. "I'm sorry…?"

"Can you get it off? They put it around my neck!"

"I don't see what– wait. Is this what you mean?"

Around the blonde's neck was a necklace of loose red thread. The pendant was an iron nail—an old-fashioned square-topped nail, smaller than a pinky finger. The nail hung down, resting lightly at her décolletage. But the red thread was not tight, not knotted around her neck, not fixed in place in any way.

"It is iron, cold iron, that is master of us all!" The smile vanished. Her large eyes were damp. Her lip trembled. "Get it off me!"

A loud voice in the distance cried out. It was a man calling. With the drumming reverberations from the music one street over, it was hard to tell distances from sound alone, but the voice seemed near. A second voice answered him. The ravenhaired oriental girl twisted her ring and shut off the light.

"They are coming back! We've got to run!"

"I cannot!" cried the blonde. "I'm caught!"

The ravenhaired girl pulled the loop of thread over the blonde's head. She had no pockets and no immediate use for a nail on a thread, so she threw it clinking to the pavement. "Down the alley and over the fence! Try to keep up!"

She twisted her ring from silver to pewter and soared down the side-alley in two or three long, loping bounds. The wooden fence was speeding past her. A second twist restored her weight, but now she was traveling too quickly. Again, an unexpected instinct came to her aid: she turned her too-rapid stumble into a flying kick, caught one of the vertical posts of the fence with her bare foot, bounced up and backward, struck the opposite post with another kick, and propelled herself over the fence in a smooth leap. She turned a somersault in midair and landed on her feet.

In the dim light, she saw, to her shock, ahead of her, on this side of the fence, the blonde in the green costume seated on a trashcan, legs crossed at the knee. She was smiled gaily and clapped her hands when the ravenhaired girl flipped over the fence and landed so neatly. "That was wonderful! Are you Miss America? Do you fight crime?"

The ravenhaired girl took the blonde's wrist and yanked her into motion. Down the alley they ran, bare feet and slippered feet making little noise.

There! A fire escape was visible above and to the left. The ravenhaired girl said, "I am going to lower the fire escape ladder. Get to the top as fast as you can, and I will pull it up after. Get it?"

The blonde nodded eagerly, grinning, her smile bright in the gloom. "Got it!"

"Good!" said the ravenhaired girl and twisted the ring from white to pewter. "And… uh… Don't worry if what I do looks odd!" Now her hair and body grew weightless, and she soared upward with a kick. She neatly hooked the railing of the lowest balcony of the fire escape as she flew, which yanked her about in a quick semicircle, and landed her in a crouch near the crank of the ladder. It had a quick-release lever which she pulled. The ladder slid downward. At the last minute, she caught the upper rungs as they slid past, hoping to prevent the ladder from clanging loudly as it struck bottom. Instead, she eased it down silently the last foot or so.

She peered downward. There was not much light here. She made a hissing whistle through her teeth and called softly, "Sss! Sss! Are you there?"

A voice from behind her and above said, "No, I 'm here!"

The ravenhaired girl turned. The blonde was seated with her rump on the railing of the fire escape balcony the next story up, hands on the railing to either side, idly kicking her legs in the air.

The blonde pouted. "You have a weird look on your face. You said as fast as I could, didn't you? I didn't break another stupid rule, did I?"

There was no time for talk. She could hear men, several of them, all cursing filthy curses, climbing over the wooden fence. If she used the wheel to raise the ladder, it would make a racket. Nimbly, she leaped to the balcony rail, took the lower lip in her fingers, and vaulted upward, doing a backflip and landing next to the blonde.

The ravenhaired girl pointed at a tall building across the street and down a bit. She said, "I am going to jump to the roof of that bank."

"Bank of what? You mean like a riverbank?"

"That building there. Thirty stories tall! Can you make it there before me?"

The blonde's eyes lit up, and she clapped her hands for joy. "A race! Ooh! I love races!"

The ravenhaired girl nodded, looking the blonde carefully in the eye. Yes, a race. But we are outracing our pursuit. They must be left behind and not see us. You understand?

The blonde tossed her head so that her tousled curls bobbed. Of course! I am a private investigator! We are shaking our tails! She wiggled her hips energetically as if to illustrate.

And with that, the blonde girl glowed with a thousand multicolored pinpoints of sparkling lights. Out from her naked shoulder blades sprung gossamer wing-shaped shimmers, polychromatic as the rainbows that dance on the surface of a soap bubble. The girl shrank down to a dragonfly-winged figure the size of a finger and darted away through the air in the posture of a speed skater, with two little trails of sparks winking in the wake of her slippers.

The ravenhaired girl stared in shock, wondering whether the world was insane, or she was. Maybe both. But the sound of coming pursuit did not give her time to contemplate the question.

She twisted her ring to weightlessness, flung herself in a long leap to the roof of the building above, then to a telephone pole, then to the top of the pole, and then across the street to the roof of a second building, and hand over hand up the wall of the bank building.

On the roof of the bank, once more fully sized, the blonde was seated atop the metal cube of a tall thrumming vent, drumming her little slippered heels against the metal panels.

The oriental tucked her flag around her once again and pushed her hair out of her eyes, spitting a stray strand out of her mouth. She stepped toward the other girl, who was grinning.

The ravenhaired girl, looking up, said, "Are you human?"

The blonde tilted her head. "Is that a trick question?"

4. *Introductions*

The blonde said, "Wait! We have not been properly introduced!"

The blonde girl hopped down from her perch, set her feet just so, took the little hems of her miniskirt in hand, and performed a graceful curtsey, bending her back leg so far, and bowing her head so deeply that her forehead almost touched the knee of her other leg, which was extended before her, toes pointed.

She straightened up, grinning. "How do you do? Fine, thank you! A pleasure to meet me, I am sure. Are you enchanted?"

The ravenhaired girl folded her right fist into her left palm and bowed deeply, so that her hair brushed her bare toes. "I greet you, and I am honored by your greeting." She straightened. "Please let all be well between us."

Then, the ravenhaired girl frowned at the position of her hands. She folded her hands at her waist and bowed again.

The blonde giggled and then composed herself. "I am Elfine."

The ravenhaired girl said, "I cannot say."

The blonde pouted. "Did I do that wrong? Did I break another stupid rule? Let me try again! Ready?

The ravenhaired girl said, "No, I mean I don't know."

The other girl was not listening. "I'll do it right this time! My family is Moth of the Ayre Moths of Ayre Sheading in Bride Parish! I am daughter of Iolanthe of Lurline, who is daughter of Ellyllon of Annwfm, who was shamefully outraged by Gwyn ap Nudd. My brother is Strephon, who was raised among mortals and married happily, whose children to this day my sisters protect. My father is Ayre Moth, who was banished to Troynovant with all his books when he won the nose from the face of Gwyn ap Nudd in a wager, his bride-price to Iolanthe's dam."

The ravenhaired girl merely stared in bewilderment.

The blonde continued in a rolling rush of words, "By slyness won he the game, using my cousin Arriety O'Clock as his queen, and moving her own moves, him merely resting his fingers on her and letting her draw his hand. She is a mistress of chess and once played Fynoderee of the Hairy Stockings to a stalemate and saved a town from drowning! To this day, the Nose of Nudd stands on my father's mantelpiece, and from the snorts and wheezes, he knows the comings and goings of ghosts and other hidden things: and no storm can harm his house."

The ravenhaired girl was impressed that the blonde did not seem to need to pause for breath.

The blonde continued. “The father of Ayre was Pururavas, son of Yla, child of Vaivasvata, and his mother was Urvashi the Golden, who was stolen from his side by the cunning of a celestial musician named Citraratha and an unfortunate flash of lightning! A similar curse parted my father and mother: an act of cruelty by Ethne the May Queen, Balor’s daughter of the Evil Eye, who despises that an elf should marry a mortal. So much melancholy has afflicted my family that my godmother, the Grail Maiden of Sarras, blessed me with the blessing that no melancholy would be left for me, and my blood is filled with sanguine and giddy humors. And so who are you?”

The ravenhaired girl drew a slow breath. “I have amnesia. There must have been an accident or something. The knowledge is gone from me. My folk and friends are lost. My life is lost. I am alone.” Her eyes stung with tears. She wiped her cheeks with the palm of her hand.

Elfine stepped forward and put her hands on the ravenhaired girl’s shoulders, peering up into the taller girl’s eyes. “Then it was good hap that you found me! I can seek what is lost and uncover evil!”

“How can you help?”

“First, I can get a name for you! What is Japanese for friend?”

“*Ami*.”

“Your name is Ami Nesia! Get it? Like in *amnesia*.”

“That’s kind of—silly.”

“Use it until I can find your old one.”

“You can? I mean, can you find it?”

The blonde stepped back and threw out her chest proudly. “I am a magical girl detective!” Then, her shoulders sank a bit. “More of a rookie, actually. And not much magic. I know the glamour to make things and people pretty. And talking to the wind. But I read about detective work in one of Daddy’s books, so I am hoping to train!”

And she spun in a circle, with her head thrown back.

The wind passed across the roof, and the ravenhaired girl shivered and hugged herself and said, “I am bruised and scraped and tired and cold and mostly naked, so if you want to help me, find me a place to stay, preferably with a change of clothes, a warm meal, and a hot bath.”

Elfine did a little caper with her slippered feet, so her pom-poms bounced. She winked and grinned and snapped her fingers. "I can put you up! Let's away!"

5. Accommodations

The ravenhaired girl who was not really named Ami Nesia traveled down Park Avenue for at least a mile, leaping from rooftop to rooftop, with Elfine darting ahead out of sight and returning to urge her on periodically. Ami descended to the ground by sliding carefully down the side of the General Motors building and landed on East 58th.

A doll-sized Elfine flew up to her, swelled to normal size, and took Ami's hand eagerly. "Here we are. 'Tis only a block hence!"

They went into a highrise. Elfine, pulling her by the wrist, crowded up behind a tall man in a cowboy hat who was at the door. Elfine waved at the doorman, who did not look up, but waved all three inside.

It was a titanic tower of glass. Inside was a vast open space of layered pink marble and yellow brass, reflected in walls paneled in mirrors. Escalators rose up endlessly, and a seven-story-tall indoor waterfall plunged endlessly down. They rode up two floors.

The upper lobby was a large, square space under a skylight, where a dozen upscale shops, closed for the evening, peered at the collection of sofas and potted plants.

A man in a uniform stopped them and pointed silently to a sign saying proper footwear was required. Elfine smiled at him and said, "She forgot her shoes! I was just going up to the room to get them! Can she wait here? I'll be right back!" And Elfine pushed the ravenhaired girl into a sofa, saying, "Wait right there!"

The guard looked suspicious. Ami, feeling a little conspicuous dressed in nothing but an American flag, sat up straight, crossed her legs, smoothed back her mussed hair, and smiled at the guard. "You mustn't mind my friend Elfine. She was attacked this evening near a club. She said I could sleep overnight on her couch."

He said, “Guests are not allowed to go up unless escorted…” But at the moment, the radio on his shoulder squawked at him, telling of a broken window on an upper floor, so he said, “Excuse me,” and stepped away out of her sight.

Ami looked around, listening to the silence of the empty lobby. The elevator door in the mirrored brass wall opposite where she sat made a chime of noise and opened. Elfine leaned out and waved. “Over here!”

Ami walked over. “The guard said I had to be escorted.”

Elfine said, “I’ll escort you! Come on!”

Elfine pushed the button for the sixtieth floor. When the door opened, Ami saw a beige hallway with tasteful décor.

Elfine skipped down the hall. “Over here! This is the one!” She tugged on the handle and frowned. “Oopsie whoopsie! Guess what I forgot!”

Ami stepped over to the door, rubbing her feet in the carpet. The carpet was so thick that Ami paused a moment, luxuriating in the feel and the warmth of the plush fibers on her feet. She closed her eyes to enjoy the sensation. “What did you forget? Did you forget your key? Was it in your coat?” She opened her eyes when she heard no response.

Ami looked left and right down the corridor. Elfine was not in sight.

The lock clicked, and the door opened. There was Elfine, who had gotten inside the suite somehow. In her hand was a candlestick with a lit candle. The blonde waved her hand in a large, slow arc. “Ta-DA! Come on in. I invite you over the threshold. May cure and comfort, rest and weal be thine while this roof covers ye!”

Ami stepped inside and was about to ask Elfine how she ended up on the inside of a locked door, but the sight and size and splendor of the suite of rooms distracted her.

Tall windows looked out over the panorama of the city. Central Park was spread below like a green carpet. The light from the windows and the buttery glow from Elfine’s candle shined on the polished surfaces of table and counter. There was a sunken area with chairs and chaise-lounge facing a wet bar. The kitchen was opposite the bedroom. Through an open door, Ami saw a walk-in closet that looked like something out of a department store, with special glass shelves to highlight the jewelry boxes and shoe racks.

There was a separate room for a vast flat-screen television, a butler's pantry, a foyer, a dining room with candlesticks on a wide table, and a smaller nook for breakfast.

Elfine was pouting. "You did it wrong!"

Ami gave her a puzzled look.

Elfine said, "Now you have to go outside and step over the threshold again. And when I bid you welcome, you have to call down a blessing on the house!"

Ami was not one to question the customs of her hostess. She obediently opened the door and stepped back. "What kind of blessing?"

"*Slaynt Vie as Maynrys er y Thie shoh.* It asks for good health and happiness on the house."

Ami repeated the words, and bowed and said "*Shitsurei itachimasu*!"

"Well done and thrice welcome!" and now Elfine grabbed her arm. "You said you wanted a hot outfit, a hot bath, and a hot meal! Are you hungry? I can have the servants bring you some food. That's how it works here."

Ami said, "You mean room service? At this hour?"

Elfine nodded brightly. "And light comes out of these glass things. They are like lamps. They work on lightning, so don't unscrew the glass and put your tongue in the socket. Never do that! Did you want a bath? Come here. Come here!" So saying, she tugged Ami into another room, floored in marble and paneled in mirrors, where a sunken hot tub gleamed. "The water is as warm as you like it! Use as much as you like! Do you want me to help you wash your hair?"

"No, that will not be necessary, but I thank you for the..."

But Elfine was not dissuaded, so somehow, not exactly against her will, Ami found herself luxuriating in the warmest and large tub she could imagine, with jets of bubbling water massaging her in from all directions, and with Elfine kneeling behind her, rubbing shampoo into her locks.

Elfine was chattering brightly about a family of foxes she had known on the Isle of Man and a lost cub she had helped rescue, and that led somehow into another story about the lonely cries she heard geese make in autumn, before their long journeys to far islands where Summer was rumored to reside when he departed northern lands.

"Some say the trumpet that calls Summer away is in the hands of the Hours, but Father says it is kept in a crystal closet above the stars. But from what beast could the Horn of Time be carved?"

That tale wandered into another about a penguin Elfine knew who kept the egg of his child on his feet all winter so that the child would not touch the ground and die of cold before birth while the wife went fishing and was absent for weeks at a time. "It was the season where night leads into night without dawn, and the wind came by to mock him, calling out *woe! woe!* And telling him that night and darkness always triumph, no matter what, for all strength fails. Isn't that a horrible thing to say?"

Ami let this drench of words run over her without paying much attention. But then came a chime, and Elfine leaped up and ran into another room.

When she came back, she had both hands full of packages, boxes, and parcels, rustling with crepe paper. "Change of clothing! I remembered your wish! I got you some clothes and shoes! I had to guess at your size. I hope you like it! I know you probably need a red, white, and blue bulletproof bathing suit to go fight crime and stuff, but I don't know where to get one of those. Also, no hat. I don't know what you like in hats. Because I just met you." She giggled and skipped out of the room. Through the open door, Ami could see her flinging open the parcels, and laying out a jacket, a blouse, and a skirt on the table along with a pair of dress shoes.

Ami rinsed and dried herself, wrapping herself in one towel and her hair in another. She looked over what Elfine had spread on the table and was a little taken aback. Elfine had very expensive tastes.

"Elfine, how can your family afford this?"

"Afford what?"

"What does your father do?"

"He thinks deep thoughts, does good deeds, and talks about old wars and lost kingdoms with his friends in the pub."

"That's all?"

"And he collects books, mostly."

"Does he work?"

Elfine looked surprised. "I don't know. I only spent this winter with him. Mother raised me. I told you my parents were forced apart. He is not allowed to see her."

"So this is your mother's apartment? What does she do?"

"My mother is very influential."

"I mean, what does she do for a living?"

"Sheds influences. You know, she tells parliament when to sit, for one thing."

"The parliament in England? She is in government?"

"Yes. She also organizes dances, allays curses, and receives petitions. Things like that. For a while she was in the same troop as Lulea of Burzee, but when Lulea exiled Nelebel to California, mother sought out Lurline of the Rhine, who is older and more powerful."

"The Rhine in Germany? What? Is your mother some sort of royalty?"

Elfine said, "Oh, I know. I know. You are thinking the old families don't have much influence any longer, what with how the world has changed! It is true. Nearly everything is decided at Troynovant, or Tir Ildathach, or Mommur, or Slievenamon. That is how it is back in the old country. America is different! Just look at how wonderful everything here is!" And she spread her hands and turned in a slow circle, as if to show off the lavish furnishings.

Then, she looked over her shoulder at Ami and winked. "Americans are richer than the Gnome King. Og of Glocca Morra says that the Americans grow their gold in Kentucky, which is why Fort Knox is placed there, but I say that is nonsense." Elfine snapped her fingers, as if a bright thought had struck her. "Say! He lost his memory, too, or so I heard. The Gnome King, not Og. He lost his gold and his powers, got baptized, and married a mortal maiden. Og, not the Gnome King. He drank from the Fountain of the Water of Oblivion, which is mingled with the Mist of Everness. The Gnome King, not Og, I mean. Could that have been what happened to you? His name is Ruggedo the Red. The Gnome King never will marry anyone because he is in love with Polychrome, who is my…" Elfine screwed up her eyes and counted on her fingers. "…my first cousin once removed. Her mother, Iris of the Rainbow, is my great aunt."

At that moment, the door chime came again, and food arrived. Ami stepped back into the bathroom to dry her hair using the blow drier she found there. But the smell of the food made her stomach rumble, and she realized how hungry she was, so she came out with her hair hanging limp and wet and black down her shoulders and back.

Elfine insisted it was proper to eat while wearing a towel, and in fact went into the bathroom, doffed her green outfit, and came out clad in nothing but a towel herself. "Now we are twins!"

It was a strange sort of courtesy, but Ami appreciated the gesture. The meal included a thick slice of salmon fried in butter and pepper on a bed of brown rice for Ami. Elfine sipped a few sips of tea and ate a spoonful of honey. Elfine also ate the mint leaf sprig used to garnish the teapot.

Fatigue came as suddenly as hunger, and Ami found her eyes falling shut of their own accord before half the salmon was consumed. Elfine led her into the bedroom and tucked her in.

Elfine said, "I can step away if you are going to say your bedtime prayers! I'm allergic, you see. You didn't say grace at the meal. Lucky for me."

Ami said, "I've forgotten everything. What if I am Buddhist?"

"Then you ask Saint Jehoshaphat for help! Scootch over!"

Ami was a little surprised when Elfine, as unselfconsciously as a kitten, climbed in and snuggled up to her. Ami started to ask a question but yawned instead, and Elfine yawned back, and then they were both yawning while Elfine giggled merrily, whereupon both fell asleep so quickly it might have been a magic charm.

Chapter 3

The Three Worlds

1. Half and Half

It was past noon before the girls woke the next day. Upon seeing the unwashed dinner plates still on the table, Elfine went into the kitchenette and searched in puzzlement in the cabinets, in the microwave, and under the sink.

Ami said, "What are you looking for?"

"Cream! I forgot last night. I am always forgetting rules!"

Ami pulled open the refrigerator door. She pointed. "What about half and half?"

"I hate it when people call me that!"

"No, I mean this. Half milk and half cream. For coffee. Didn't you buy it?"

"Nope. I hope it will do."

Ami asked slowly, "If you have a roommate, where does she sleep? Does someone else use your refrigerator?"

"Anyone can use one of these! It keeps things cold by magic. It runs on lightning, like the lamps. Remember what I told you! Don't they have them in Japan? A man is supposed to bring ice they cut from the lake in winter." So saying Elfine poured some half and half into a saucer, opened the door, and set the saucer carefully on the carpet in the hall.

Elfine came bouncing back while Ami stared. "Do you own a cat?"

Elfine said, "I don't know if anyone can own a cat. They are very self-possessed creatures. Can you speak to animals? Let me do your hair while you're eating."

There was leftover salmon and hot buttered toast with jam for breakfast. Elfine ate the petals off the rose that sat in a vase in the middle of the table and a cube of sugar. Ami's hair was a tangled mess.

Ami sat in a chair in the breakfast nook while Elfine stood behind her and brushed out her tangles. "It is easy to unsnarl elf locks," Elfine chatted, "Once you know the secret. It is all in the wrist. I have a cousin somewhere here in the city who has the knack of speech with animals. John Doolittle of Caundle Marsh Parish also had it; he was of Oberon's blood without knowing. It is a very rare gift!"

Ami was startled that Elfine could not only brush out her snarled hair without yanking on her scalp, but that, at the end, the hair was as dark, full, lustrous, and shining as something seen on a shampoo commercial.

"How did you do that with just a brush?" wondered Ami aloud, looking at her coiffure in the mirror. "You even got the ends to curl without using a curling iron!" Ami put her elbows in the air and began to fold plaits of hair together. "And, no, I don't talk to animals. Not that I remember. Why do you ask?"

Elfine said, "What are you doing?"

Ami said, "Last night I swallowed very much hair, and it was in my nose and eyes. I promised myself I would braid it or get a cap."

"Oh! Let me!" So Elfine did up her hair in a nice French braid and gathered tails into a bun at the nape of Ami's neck, which she tied in place with a big red ribbon. Elfine pulled out one strand to let hang by Ami's cheek.

In the mirror, Ami was amazed. She turned her head this way and that. She had not realized her hair could look so pretty.

Elfine said, "It is very stylish. You cannot have perfect hair, or else the goddesses get jealous, so you need one strand out of place. Let's do earrings next!" and she clapped her hands in excitement.

"No, thank you. They might snag. Besides, my ears are not pierced."

"A necklace?"

"Only if it is very fine. It should give way if tugged on."

Elfine returned from the jewelry shelf in the closet with a chain as thin as spider's silk, with a white pearl for a pendant.

Next, Elfine dressed her. Ami thought it was a little odd to have another woman helping her with her underthings, buttoning her blouse, and doing up her skirt, but she did not remember whether that was unusual, so she voiced no objection.

The jacket did not fit, so Elfine skipped into the walk-in closet, and brought out a sharp looking businesswoman's jacket with padded shoulders and a pinched waist. "This should fit you! It is not shame not to talk to beasts. Man lost the power to understand the beasts under his dominion when he broke fealty with Heaven. That was in Eden. Then, he lost the power to understand his neighbor at the Tower of Babel. And in Hell, each lonely soul loses understanding altogether so that all they can do is scream and hear screaming. No one talks in Hell. You haven't tried on the shoes! Did I forget stockings?"

Elfine went into the closet and starting looking on high shelves and under the bed, peering cautiously into the pillow cases. Ami pulled open a drawer on the bureau next to the shoe rack, where socks and stockings neatly folded and arranged by shade and hue were stored. "Elfine, do you not know where your own sock drawer is?"

Instead of answering, Elfine led Ami into the den and pushed her down on the couch. Elfine took out pen and notepad from a drawer under the phone, and threw herself down on the carpet to sit crosslegged on the floor with the pad on a low coffee table.

"Now we are ready! I will call this *The Case of the Cursed Crimefightress*! Or do you think *Confused Crimefightress* sounds better?"

Tongue between her lips, she scratched out and rewrote the marks she was making on the page. Ami did not recognize the form of writing Elfine used: it consisted of vertical and diagonal strokes of one to five marks arranged in rows.

"Tell me the whole story!" said Elfine. "Everything you remember that happened from the moment you woke up!"

2. On the Case

It took over an hour to go through the whole story and then more time as Elfine cross-examined her, asking questions that varied from the penetrating to the bizarrely irrelevant.

When they were done talking, Elfine snapped her fingers, leaped to her feet, and fetched something from the bathroom. "This is yours!"

Elfine handed her the American flag Ami had been wearing yesterday. It was neatly folded into a triangle.

Elfine explained, "I saw you rolling and sliding last night. Or was it this morning? If the colors touch the ground, you have to burn them. Let's do that later. There is no fireplace in here.

"Now, then, what is our first clue?" Elfine continued briskly. "You don't have any scars or bumps on your head—I looked when I was brushing your hair—so your amnesia may not be due to physical trauma. What do you remember of your childhood?"

"Nothing."

"A Mickey Finn—that is what they call it here in America, but he changed his name to Rufus—usually affects only short-term memory. The active ingredient there is chloral hydrate. It would leave childhood memories intact. That leads us to our next clue!"

"And what is our next clue?"

"I don't know! We'll find it at the scene of the crime!"

Ami stepped into the shoes Elfine provided. These were dress shoes with too high a heel, and Ami did not like the sensation of walking in them. They were too unsteady. She found that by turning the intaglio of her ring inward, halfway between silver and pewter, the high heels made no noise even on a hard floor, and she could move smoothly.

Elfine went to a closet and tried on one coat and then another, finally donning a long beige jacket that fell to her knees. It had a hood that she pulled up over her riotous mop of yellow curls. Then, she strode dramatically to the front door and yanked it open. "Let's go! We can talk as we walk. And talk as we walk. Both at once. A mute digitambulist has to do one or the other!"

Ami said, "Where are we going? Aren't you taking your notes?" For Elfine had left the notepad with the strange writing sitting on the coffee table.

"I don't need it. Fairies have photogenic memories."

"Photographic."

"That, too."

"And—aren't you going to clean up your dishes?" She pointed at the breakfast table.

"The servants do that!"

"You means the housekeeping staff here does dishes?"

"I forgot to feed them last night. But why did I forget? Because I was distracted! A phonographic memory does you no good if you forget to look at the photograms in your memory! But why did *you* forget? Aha! Why indeed! I think we can rule out mundane explanations, such as an emotional shock or head trauma. There are no signs that you are in a fugue state. You recall what things like dishes and beds and bathtubs are. This would imply it is dissociative amnesia: only personal memories are affected. It is most likely psychogenic rather than structural."

Ami nodded eagerly, looking impressed "Now, suddenly, you are making sense."

"Worldly memories are stored in the brain, which is material, but personal memories are stored in the soul, which is quintessential and immaterial!"

Ami stopped nodding. "And then, suddenly, less sense..."

"Off we go! Dayfolk tend to forget us, except for Irishmen, so talking to witnesses may not be fruitful. But there will be a record of your admittance at the hospital. Also a diagnosis. Skull X-rays. Name of next of kin. Humans love writing things down. They don't have phototropic memories."

"Photographic."

"Nor that, either!"

Ami looked at her sidelong as the two walked down the corridor toward the elevator. "That– actually seems surprisingly– ah– like a good plan. A good place to start. Have you done detective work before?"

"You are not my first case! I helped that fox cub I told you about last night! He had to find his home."

Ami frowned. "I am not sure these cases are the same."

"You are a lost little foxcub! We just need to find your den. It is the same. Don't worry. I know my way around the human world! I've got it covered. I've read about it in my father's books."

At the end of the corridor, Elfine raised her bare leg and pushed the elevator call button with the toe of her green slipper.

Ami sighed. "I am sure we will fit right in."

3. Familiar and Unfamiliar

On the way out, Elfine rushed up the to the doorman and gave him a kiss on the cheek. "Everything was wonderful! We had the most wonderful time! Just perfect!" The man looked a little flustered, but he put a finger to his cap and gave her a friendly salute.

Out on the street, it was hot and bright, and traffic was crawling just as slowly as it had been last night, except now there seemed to be more honking and cursing.

Elfine had a brisk stride, swinging her arms, and only every now and again skipping like a child, or cutting a caper like a tap-dancer, or twirling on her toes like a ballerina. Ami walked more sedately, her eyes in constant motion, up and down, and watching the hands, gait, and gazes of pedestrians coming the other way, treading warily when passing in front of doors or corners of buildings.

Elfine spoke as she walked. She said, "If you've never been in a big city before, there are some things you have to remember. When Man moved into cities out from the dark woods, he did not bring any ravaging beasts with him, so some of the men volunteered to act as beasts of predation, and they are hidden among the humans on whom they prey. The black-skinned ones are often more dangerous, but it could be any of them. They are Ethiopian, and were brought here as slaves in chains, and forever seek revenge against those who once were their masters, whom they hate."

Ami said thoughtfully, "You are not from America, are you?"

"No. I was raised in the Third Hemisphere. But I have read much about America! The shire-reeves here are called 'coppers' and dress in blue and carry billies, and they protect the humans, but the humans don't like them because the humans want to afflict themselves with alchemical potions that drive them mad, opium and morphine, and the blue coppers beat them and take their worldly goods. And everyone in America has rights, but no one has responsibilities because the elfs are in charge. The elfs rule here, and men are their cattle. It was different in older days. We want to avoid the coppers because they might report us."

Ami said, "Why? What have we done?"

Elfine said, "I don't know about you, but I am a smuggler."

"What do you smuggle?"

"Me. Elfine Luminiferous Moth. I smuggled myself into this hemisphere! I am a loveable rogue, you see."

Ami once again stared in confusion. "You're a what?"

Elfine threw back her head and pitched her voice to a lower octave. "Don't be too sure I'm as crooked as I'm supposed to be. That kind of reputation might be good business, bringing in high-priced jobs and making it easier to deal with the enemy." But then she pouted and bit on her thumbnail with a fretful look on her face. In her normal soprano voice, she said, "But you are a crimefightress. Once your memory is back, you might have to turn me in."

Ami said, "Elfine, don't take this the wrong way, but–"

"Yes…?"

"How do I know you are not a madwoman?"

"That is easy! On the night of a full moon, take a silver platter from a wedding feast that held the bridal cake. Sleep with it under your pillow. If you dream of me and see me in a vision wearing a funnel hat or straws in my hair, that proves me to be mad."

"That does not actually sound all that easy," she said, wondering when the next full moon was due."

Elfine laughed. "Easier to prove it the other way then! If I find out your lost name and nurture, kindred and kinfolk, and who cursed you, then sane I am. Aha! I have another plan!" Elfine clapped her hands as if applauding herself. "How clever I am!"

"Did something happen to the first plan?"

"We can do both at once! You thought it was odd when I explained how lightbulbs worked, didn't you?"

Ami nodded. "It sounded strange."

"That's a clue. Now, cross the street."

Ami put out her hand and took Elfine by the elbow, "Wait for the light."

Elfine craned her neck and looked up at the sun. "The light?"

"The red light. It must turn green."

"Oh! Another rule! No one else waits!"

By the time they reached the curb on the far side, Elfine was wreathed in smiles. Ami said, "What is it?"

Elfine said, "When you crossed, you looked to the left, not the right. See?"

Ami said, "You are always supposed to look before crossing the street."

Elfine said, "But in Japan, they drive on the left, so you would look right to see if a car is approaching. Looking left in Japan, you would only see the taillight of a car receding. That means you were here, or, at least, somewhere with motorcars that keep to the right, long enough to make a habit of looking left when crossing! By listing what else you find ordinary or extraordinary, we can deduce backward what kind of a place you are from! For example: how many bullets go into the clip of a revolver?"

"Um. Six?"

"No! None! A revolver has a cylinder, not a clip! So you don't use a gun. That is to be expected! I bet you use a lariat or a boomerang or a throwing star shaped like the stars on the flag. What is the capital of Texas?"

"Austin."

"No, it is Dallas. Capital of New York?"

"Is Albany."

"Nope! New York City! Everyone gets that one wrong. I bet you are not an American."

Ami said, "Well… maybe not. But all this looks and sounds very familiar." She pointed at a billboard and at the storefronts. "I have seen that movie. The one with the spaceships in it. And I recognize that perfume company."

"That movie is new, so you were here recently."

Ami frowned. "Is it?"

"It is still in theaters. Do you remember anything about the movie?"

"Only that it is not the kind of movie I like. I keep thinking that if the filmmaker liked spaceships so much, for the same money it took to make the film, couldn't you build a real space rocket? Do something real?"

"I mean, do you remember the plot?"

"What plot? It was just a bunch of robots and laser blasts and scenes of buildings blowing up. They made the hero a buffoon so that his girlfriend could solve all the problems. In the last scene, when they are on the planet that is about to explode and ram into the sun that is about to go nova and fall into a black hole, the girlfriend picks up a laser-sword she's never held before and beats up the dark warlord of the Omega Nebula. Her stance was terrible. He falls into the mouth of the planet-pulverizing volcano-beam weapon cannon just as it goes off. She should have turned on her jetpack, flown up, and shot him from a distance with her atomic-powered crossbow. From ambush. Or just gotten on the spaceship and left because the world was going to blow up. And the dead guy came back to life in the Lazarus Vortex, but the tiny little robot that sacrificed itself to save him, it could not be fixed, and stayed dead. How does that make any sense?" Her voice trailed off. "That's… strange. I am pretty sure I don't go to spaceship movies. Never." She scowled. "For that matter, I don't wear perfume. I wonder why I recognized both of those things… Why can I remember these details and not my name?"

Elfine said briskly, "Next question: What is the emergency number on a telephone?"

"Nine one one."

"But you did not call that number last night. Why not?"

Ami shook her head.

Elfine said, "I think you are one of us."

Ami said, "Us?"

"Half and half. Like the cream. You instinctively avoided drawing attention. We do not fit in man's world, and the elfs who treat men like cattle—well, we don't fit into their world either, except to flatter, fetch, and tote! Everyone sneers at us."

"Us? Us who?"

4. *Three-Fourths Fairy*

"We are the people of the twilight. Men and dolphins are Dayfolk. Theirs is the daylight world. Elfs and efts and their serfs, svarts, spooks, and pooks are Nightfolk. They are of the night world. We are neither.

"Now then!" Elfine waved her finger. "I don't mean a parallel dimension or anything like that. Nightlings and Twilightlings have dusk and dawn, winter and summer, same as humans. We just live in the Third Hemisphere, the one they don't see. There are other planets like Mars or the Moon, but they are haunted by dead races, and no one goes there, except one crazy boy who is a cousin of mine. My third cousin four times removed, actually."

Ami's eyes lit up. "That is amazing! I mean, going to the moon is…." Words failed her. She was awed. "He must be very brave, your cousin."

"Or crazy." Elfine shrugged. "In any case, there are four big clans of the Twilight Folk that were scattered after the Elf Queen was lost. First are the Moths, who are friendly to mankind; next are the Cobwebs, who are not; third are the Mustardseeds, who are friendly to the Summer King and can work the metals of Tubalcain for him, which elfs otherwise cannot touch."

"That is only three."

"Last is the Peaseblossoms, who are the smart and sneaky ones that no one trusts, so they are forbidden to leave the Third Hemisphere. I do not think you would be allowed to be here if you were a Peaseblossom. And they have a distinctive scent. Unmistakable."

"What do they smell like?"

"Like a sweetpea flower, of course."

"And… you are a Twilight girl?"

"I have a fairy mother and a human father. Half human. Yes."

"I see…"

Elfine held up her hand. "Wait, not half. Let me think. Daddy is the son of an *apsara* and a mortal king named Pururavas. My great-grandmotherfather Yla was both daughter and son to Vaivasvata. Vaivasvata was the child of the sun god and the goddess of the dawn but was born human. Later he was granted immortality because he survived the Great Deluge and preserved a remnant of mankind. So whether he counts as being a mortal or not is a tricky question." Elfine shot her a challenging look.

Ami said, "I– I don't really have an opinion."

"Where was I?"

"The Great Deluge."

"Yes! Since the world was empty of people, not to mention being really damp, Vaivasvata commanded Yla to marry himself to herself to carry on the bloodline. Which displeased the gods. Yla is both father and mother to Pururavas. Moth, disguised as the Moon, acted as best man during the nuptials and as midwife during the birth and therefore claimed the child as his own. You see, the old tradition is that the best man married the bride if the bridegroom did not show up. So my family is officially Moth, but I am either seven-eighths or three-quarters fairy, depending."

Ami said, "Depending on…?"

"Whether Yla really shared the marriage bed only with herself and himself or if the bridegroom was Moth in disguise all along. Ayre fled from Iran to the Isle of Man after his son Nahusha—my half-brother from an earlier marriage—who was being borne aloft on a palanquin by a thousand great *rishis*, touched the great sage Agastya, who was bearing him, with the sole of his foot, so for that lapse was turned into a serpent. Any questions?"

"If you are Iranian, why is your hair blonde?"

"I wished it blonde. It is one of my glamours. I have ninety-nine sisters, and they all look like me, so I wanted to stand out."

Ami said, "How did your, I think it was, great-grandfather, disguise himself as the Moon?"

Elfine said, "You have to do it during the hours at night when the real moon is not in the sky, or the moon will look down, see what you are doing, and strike you down with madness. That is why it is called lunacy."

Ami asked, "If I find my past, will it be as complicated and weird as yours?"

Elfine shrugged.

"And am I one of– one of you? Also a twilight girl?"

"Yes!"

5. Twilight Girls

Ami was so surprised at such a clear and definite answer that she stopped walking. "You seem very sure."

"I seem sure because I *am* sure! And I think you are a Moth, like me. Maybe. Not sure there." Elfine danced with impatience and made shooing motions until Ami started walking again.

"Why?" Ami asked.

"Why which?" replied Elfine, waving at some pigeons flying by.

"Why are you sure I am of the Twilight Folk?"

Elfine ticked off on her fingers. "One, you are wearing a famous magic ring."

"You can tell it is a magic ring?"

"Not when it is white. Humans don't wear such things. Not these days. Magic is unlawful for the Daughters of Eve. Even for us, it is not entirely healthy—well, we Halfways are sort of like loveable rogues.

"Two, you were sprained and bruised and scraped last night, but this morning, your skin is fresh and fair. Daughters of Eve do not recover so fast, not without prayer, and you didn't pray.

"Two and a half, when I told you my family tale, I watched your eyes and listened for when you expressed doubt. The mist would have mugged a human hearing such a tale and darkened your heart to disbelief. You looked skeptical at all the right spots.

"Three, you plucked a nail of cold iron, iron cold forged, right off my neck without flinching. No Daughter of Nox could have done that. Witches and mermaids, yes. Elfs, no.

"Four, I saw you eat bread this morning, so you are not a fallen angel, and you did not flinch or cuss last night when I mentioned the screaming in Hell, nor did you look scared.

"Five, I saw tears in your eyes. And I put you in the bathtub to look for suckling marks and to see if you displaced water properly. A witch could do some of the things you did—flying from roof to roof or throwing light from your finger—but they don't cry, not real witches who have signed the Dark Compact.

"Six—well, I am out of fingers. You are neither a Partholan nor a mermaid because I put a pearl from the sea around your neck, and it did not change or grow brighter.

"So I covered all the possibilities," Elfine concluded spreading her hands with a smile. "You are a Twilighter. A Halfalfar. A Demi."

"And why a Moth?"

"*That* case is not airtight, but I have my suspicions. You saved me when I screamed, and I was wearing a coat. You thought I was a mortal, and you risked your life for a stranger. And you were not even really dressed. No Cobweb would do that! Only Moths like mortals. Half the Moths are mortal anyway, poets and heroes and such. And Moth girls are the prettiest!"

Ami blushed. "What?"

"Prettier than elf-maidens! That's why demigods and dark elfs, owl-men and mer-men, hideous satyrs and handsome princes all want to marry us! All sorts of monsters! You're too pretty to be a Cobweb."

Ami said, "Monsters? What do you mean by monsters?"

"Monsters!"

"Goat-men? Werewolves? Are those what you are talking about?"

6. Not Real Monsters

Elfine shook her head. "Werewolves are not real monsters."

"That is a relief."

"Werewolves are an abomination made by black magic and a dark spirit that enters a man and makes him a beast. They eat corpses. They have to kill someone they love to damn themselves and seal the spell. Real monsters are born from mommy monster eggs in the normal way and look like their parents."

"What about the goat-man?"

"That could be a satyr or could be a pooka. Listen: it is very strange and very bad that you saw three monsters walking around armed in the human world! Very bad! And wearing red caps!"

"Why is it bad?"

"Because the Sons of Adam still have scraps of their father's authority. Monsters cannot enter their world, cannot cross the threshold, unless they are invited, and no churchbells are ringing in earshot. But the mist makes men not able to see monsters these days, not clearly. Now, the elfs keep men like cattle, right? Like sheep!"

Ami nodded. "I see. I think I see. You are saying humans cannot see monsters so could not invite them into the world, and the elfs would not. It would be like a shepherd asking a wolf to tear his flock. So who is inviting them in?"

Elfine said, "Our people. The Twilightlings."

"Why would anyone do that? And why send them after me?"

"You said. He said. The goat who fell, I mean. You said he told you that they are anarchists, which means they are against the world rulers. And they want your ring."

"Who are the world rulers?"

"Elfs," said Elfine with a dimpled smile. "Elfs rule men."

7. The Black Spell

Ami creased her brow. "That sounds familiar. How did it happen?"

"I am not sure when it started. Back in Eden, elfs helped Adam with his cattle and Eve with her fig trees and vines. When Adam broke faith with Heaven, the elfs broke faith with Adam. A pale queen named Sin entered Eden from the sunset, and her son, the shapeless wraith named Death was in the shadow she cast before her, and the elfs bowed and vowed to serve her in return for the bread, and wings, and all the kingdoms in the world, and the glory of them." Elfine peered at her face. "You don't know that story?"

"They sold their souls for bread?"

"They were famished because the manna, soma, and ambrosia on which they fed no longer sustained them. Once they ate bread, they could mate with the fair daughters of Eve. Adah and Tsillah were really attractive. So I heard."

"So they sold their souls and became the rulers of all the cities of men?"

"No, of course not. The pale queen cheated them."

"Then how did they become the world rulers?"

"Step by step. In King Arthur's day the Church was strong, and the elfs were driven back, their idols smashed, their hearts filled with malice. The elfs deceived the north with phantoms and pagan gods, and the south with a false prophet. Christendom was beset by Norsemen and Paynims as between an upper and nether jaw!"

Ami rubbed her temples.

Elfine said, "What's wrong? You have a funny look on your face."

"I am sure I know this story. Tell me what happened next."

"Well, time marched on in the human world, and it never stops to play and dance like it does in ours. The Greeks and Romans quarreled and split the Church in two, and the Crusaders rode, and conquered, and quarreled, and failed, and their great deeds were slandered by foul tongues. Constantinople fell to the Paynims. The Sons of the North split the Church, making divorce lawful, setting the miter beneath the crown, and scorning the Queen of Heaven. Then, the Anarchists arose and began throwing dynamite and shooting kings. The mist grew and spread, and men forgot more and more. Does that sound familiar?"

"Yes. There was a Crusade. A Last Crusade against the Anarchists! Is that in the story?"

"I don't think so. What else do you remember?"

Ami shook her head. "Was there a part of the story where a mighty prince seeks his wife in the underworld. Something like that? She agreed to embrace him if he promised not to light the lamp and look on her. But he broke the promise and saw she was a corpse, and from the worms in her rotting body she gave birth to hags and evil phantoms to rend him, and he fled back into the sunlight. Was that part of it?"

Elfine frowned. "Oberon with an army of ten thousand thousands entered Hell seeking his wife, but he alone escaped, and he is missing an eye. He changed his name to Alberec. Is that the story you mean? Saint Mary Magdalene offered to show him the way in and out, which her cousin Lazarus had shown to her, but Oberon was too proud to follow the advice of a harlot."

"That might be the same story." Ami said, "I remember someone telling me all his fellow knights were slain, and he alone escaped. What happened next?"

"After Titania was lost, her servants scattered and hid. That's us. Erlkoenig seized his father's scepter, and winter came into the hearts of men. The black mass and the burned sacrifices of the Prussians and the Russians spread the Black Spell from pole to pole, and covered all mankind.

"The Black Spell was complete. The Cobwebs were established as the manservants of the elfs and the goatherds of men and were given red caps to wear.

"Then Erlkoenig the Elfinking set his human servants, warlocks and assassins and sly deceivers and false bards, among the parliaments and academies of the day-lit lands and bent the minds of men into docility and worldliness, then to bloodlust, then to occultism, then to love of nothingness. The men give the elfs their children and their goods, and more and more of the riches Heaven gives Man are taken away."

Ami said, "So this rule by the elfs is recent?"

Elfine said "I don't know how men count recent. There was a great war among men, and all the kings were thrown down or turned into shadows of what once they were. The sighting of the Angel of Mons was the last time the mists parted. Men forgot that magic was real. The roads to elfland were hidden, the unicorns were driven into the sea, and the islands of the young were drowned. Poets were struck with madness and fled from all words fair and fine, high and noble, and wrote drivel and gibberish instead. Songs about patients being etherized on tables." Elfine shrugged. "That is what Father told me."

"What were those the creatures that attacked me? They wore red caps."

"The red caps are necromancy. They are dyed in the blood of an unbaptized child to grant the wearer the false appearance of the authority of Adam. It allows them to speak the speech of men and be seen. But the caps you saw were stolen. No elf would give such a cap to a werewolf! Elfs love and defend nature. Werewolves are against nature."

"You are sure?"

Elfine nodded, her certainty plain to see in her eyes. "If the gunsel shows you a policeman's badge, you know it is counterfeit. That is a very bad sign."

"A sign of what? What does it all mean?"

"It means the elfs have dropped the scepter. The Black Spell is breaking. If monsters are gathering in the world of men to prey on men, men will learn to see them. No elf glamour is strong enough to hide all the monsters! And when that happens, it means war, and turmoil, and the end of an age!"

Ami said, "I was told to tell you that when eternal day breaks, twilight is no more. Then will all their deeds be laid bare and judged. That hour is at hand. Those were her exact words."

"Whose?"

"I don't know. I left that part out. You told me to tell you everything that happened after I woke up!"

Elfine stopped walking suddenly.

Ami said, "What is it?"

Elfine said, "Look around!"

Ami turned slowly in a circle. She saw crowds, crowded streets, crowded traffic, crowded buildings, garish ads. "What should I be seeing?" Then her eyes fell on a large marquee, unlit during the day: COBBLER'S CLUB.

Elfine said, "This is where you saved me. An alley on the other side of that building. Where is the hospital you fell from? It has to be near. We should just start walking in an ever-widening circle, and ask any passersby where the nearest hospital is."

Ami said, "No need. I saw the address in the Yellow Pages last night. It is two blocks that way. I'll recognize it by the stonework around the windows."

Chapter 4

The Scene of the Crime

1. Reception Room

A general practice hospital occupied the top twenty floors of the building. The other floors were occupied by other clinics, specialists, and doctor's private practices, including clinics specializing in other medical arts.

Elfine and Ami stepped from the elevator into a corridor on the seventieth floor. Behind wide glass doors at the end of the corridor was a waiting room furnished in pale pastels. Soothing pictures of abstract designs hung on the walls. Behind a wide window was a nurse at a reception and admissions desk.

Ami looked sidelong at Elfine's green showgirl outfit with its plunging neckline, miniskirt, and green pointy-toed slippers with their white pom-poms. "Why don't you occupy yourself here until I am done talking to the nurse, Elfine?"

Elfine put her hands behind her back and looked down at the water fountain and then up at the air vent. "Do your best, but you won't get anywhere. The city folk are secretive, and no one helps those in need."

Ami frowned. "That is very cynical."

"Not really. They know predators walk among them in disguise."

There was an old lady talking in worried tones to the receiving nurse. Minute after minute went by. Ami sat in one of the chairs, waiting her turn.

Eventually, the old lady was escorted by a young orderly to another room. The nurse at the desk beckoned to Ami, "Yes? Do you have an appointment?"

"I am looking for my sister," said Ami. "She is about my height and weight. She's a year younger than me. Were any women matching that description admitted here recently? I am quite worried."

The nurse looked up sharply. Her eyes narrowed. She was staring at the folded American flag Ami was carrying. Ami casually tucked the flag under one arm.

The nurse said smoothly, "Yes, we did have someone matching that description admitted last night. What is your name?"

Ami's mind went blank. She was not going to tell anyone her name was Ami Nesia, but she did not have a falsehood prepared. The was a sign on the desk that said visiting hours were over by 10:00.

"Ten O'clock," said Ami.

"What?"

"Tina. O'Clark. Tina O'Clark. It is an Irish name."

The nurses eyes narrowed further, taking in Ami's skin, hair color, and the shape of her eyes. "You don't look Irish."

"It's my husband's name." Behind her back, she pulled the ring off her right hand and placed it on her left ring finger. Then, she brought out her left hand and displayed the silver-white band on her finger, smiling.

The nurse looked at the ring skeptically.

Ami felt a moment of giddy desperation. Into the silence, she let words rush out of her mouth without thinking, "His name is Sparky. Sparky O'Clark. We met in the park."

The nurse picked up the handset of the phone on her desk. "Wait a moment, Mrs. O'Clark. I am sure the director would like to speak to you. He may have some news about your sister." She pushed a button on the phone, waited a moment, and said, "Director? There is someone here who would like to speak with you about the Jane Doe we admitted. Yes. The one from Room Sixty Sixteen. Last night. Ah…? Yes, Doctor. Certainly, Doctor." The nurse hung up, and looked at Ami. The nurse's face was a careful mask, trying to show no emotion. "He will be out in a moment. Doctor Pillory is our Director of Forensic Patient Affairs. He wants to discuss your sister's case with you."

Ami said, "Has something happened? Is she all right?"

The nurse's mouth curled into an absurdly unconvincing smile. "No, Mrs. O'Clark. Everything is fine. Please sit and wait. It may be a few minutes."

Ami said, "Okay." She went over and sat in a chair near the door, and when the nurse turned to speak to the next person waiting, Ami walked casually out the glass doors and into the corridor.

2. Security Room

Elfine was not there. Ami took a deep breath in through her nose and expelled it slowly through her mouth. She did this a second and a third time, trying to calm her heart and clear her mind. What should she do if Elfine had abandoned her? She could walk the mile back to her apartment tower, but the building security would not let her into Elfine's apartment.

A tiny light like a lightning bug zipped past Ami's nose. It twinkled and flew under the door to the lady's room, and Elfine came out of the lady's room a moment later. She was missing her coat.

Ami said, "You were right. I spoke to a nurse who spoke to a doctor I did not see. I think he called the police. The coppers. Who are probably on their way here right now."

Elfine pushed the button to summon the elevator with her toe as before. The door opened. Two police officers were in the car. Elfine smiled and stepped aside for the officers to step into the corridor and then pulled Ami into the elevator car and pushed the button for the top floor.

Ami said, "Where are we going?"

Elfine said, "The security storeroom is on the top floor. I hope you found out your name?"

"Jane Doe."

"That does not sound like a Japanese name!"

"I am pretty sure that is not my real name. But I was in room Six Oh One Six. Why are we going to the security storeroom?"

"Well, what do you think an emergency room crew would do if an unconscious woman carrying a weapon were brought into the emergency room?"

"Why do you assume I was carrying a weapon?"

"How else would you fight crime?"

The elevator doors opened. This corridor was not carpeted, and there were no soothing pictures on the wall. There were a pair of vending machines to one side and a line of doors to the other. The first of the doors was metal. There was a keypad next to the door.

Ami walked up. "Should we knock?"

Elfine said, "There was no one inside a minute ago. Wait here." She dwindled to a bright speck and flew up into an air vent. A moment later she opened the door from the inside. "Come in!"

Inside was a desk with a computer on it. The room was bisected by a wall of wire mesh with a barred door in it and locked with a padlock. Beyond that was a row of upright lockers, labeled with tags. Two of them read JANE DOE rm 6016.

"Pot at the end of the rainbow!" cried Elfine. "Or two pots."

Ami tugged on the barred door, frowning at the padlock. Elfine dwindled to a speck and passed between the bars, swelling in a spray of sparks back to normal size on the far side. "This isn't a door I can open for you. But the lockers are not locked!"

And she pulled open the first of the two doors.

Inside the locker were a quiver of arrows and the most beautiful bow Ami could imagine. It was a Japanese bow called a *daikyu*, or great bow.

This one was not made in the traditional way, of hardwood with bamboo laminations, but seemed to be made of a white substance like ivory. In shined in the dim light like a bride in a gown. It was asymmetrical, with a grip of white leather two-thirds from the top of the bow. It was wrapped with fine black rattan and gilded with thin leaves of red alloy. Black, red, and shining white the great bow stood, a single perfect curve of grace and strength.

There was an ache in Ami hands. Ami rubbed her fingers and felt calluses between her first and second fingers. "It is *hamayumi*, an evil-destroying bow. Those two white arrows are *haya* and *otoya*. They are for killing hungry ghosts."

"And the red arrows?"

"For killing people."

"Is it is yours?" asked Elfine.

Ami said, "No. I am its."

Elfine opened the other locker door.

3. Fox Mask

On a hanger was a dark gray one-piece garment like a catsuit with a hip-length cape. Folded in the bottom of the locker were a pair of black thigh-high boots and a pair of black opera gloves and also kneepads, elbow pads, and leathers bracers designed to attach snugly to the gloves and boots.

On a coathook to one side was a wide golden belt consisting entirely of holsters, scabbards, and pouches. Below this was a plastron, like a shaped leather breastplate, designed to protect the bosom of an archeress against her bowstring.

On a coathook to the other side was a full-face stylized fox mask from a Noh play. The mask was dark red with black markings around the eyes, a white jaw and bib, gold eye-lenses, gold teeth, and gold earhairs shining the triangular ears. It seemed to stare at them with a sinister merriment. The back of the mask had a cowl attached, making exactly the type of snug cap Ami had been wishing for earlier.

Elfine said, "All of this is too large to fit through the bars."

"What happens if you shrink down while holding something?"

"Most things like staying the size they are. Green is the best color for shrinking."

"Does that mean yes or no?"

Elfine pouted. "It means there are rules. I am not a Daughter of Eve. I cannot just order nature to obey me!"

"So what is the rule?"

"Friendly objects will shrink if I ask."

"Friendly?"

"Suitable things. You know how some colors clash and some match. You can tell by looking. This?" she pointed at the black costume. "This is super-heroine gear for a ninja crimefightress. It's too dark and serious to look right on me. It's not the right…" she rolled her eyes, groping for a word. "…not the right *genre*. It's not mine."

Ami said, "Bring me the belt."

4. Utility Belt

Elfine brought it near, but the meshes stretched between the bars of the locked door were set too thickly for her to fit more than a finger between. Ami asked Elfine to hold the belt flush to the door, and Ami reached through and touched the differently shaped holsters, pouches, and compartments.

One by one they opened. The waist belt contained throwing stars and barbs, arrowheads, hypodermic heads, a flashlight that could also be tuned to UV or IR, ultra-small gas grenades, ultra-small flash grenades, two flares, bugging devices as small as coins, tracer devices even smaller, a first-aid kit, miniature binoculars, a wire-harpoon, or "wirepoon" gun, no larger than a derringer, that used a silent explosive to fire a grappling hook and line.

A narrow pouch held skeleton keys and a locksmith's pick. These were small enough to fit through the mesh.

5. Lockpick

Ami knelt down and began picking the padlock. Elfine squealed in delight, put the belt down, dwindled to firefly size, and skated through the bars so that she could look over Ami's shoulder and make helpful suggestions.

It was frustrating. It seemed to Ami that her fingers could remember what to do, but not her brain, so Ami basically had to try wiggling and feeling around inside the lock by trial and error, until some instinct made her fingers twitch correctly. She had to keep her mind clear in order to separate the true impulses from mere nervousness.

Elfine was on her fiftieth helpful suggestion with no end in sight. The fifty-first suggestion involved asking ant colonies for help. The fifty-second suggestion was to bribe the gremlin who lived in the air conditioner with a kiss. The fifty-third was to highjack a high-speed magnetic levitation train from Japan and drive it through the door as a battering ram.

Ami breathed in through her nose and out through her mouth, trying to sap the power of the frustration building in her.

Elfine was saying, "…maximum operating speed is two hundred miles an hour!"

Ami said gently, "Perhaps you could help in some other way, Elfine. Is there something else detective-like you could think to do?"

Elfine looked crestfallen. "Well, sure… I guess…"

Ami closed her eyes and cleared her mind. Without anyone talking in her ears, it was easy to let her hands work. She suddenly realized the hooked implement was a tension wrench. She applied a slight pressure to the bottom of the keyhole, inserted the pick at the top of the lock, and scrubbed the pick back and forth in the keyhole. She prodded each pin, testing its tension. The most stubborn pin to push would be the first one to set… then the next…

She lost track of time. It might have been a minute later, or ten, when the cylinder turned, and the padlock clattered open. Ami stared at the open lock in elation.

She looked over her shoulder. Elfine was sitting at the desk, tapping the keys on the computer keyboard idly, and sipping a soft drink from a can. When Elfine saw the door was open, she leaped up, squealing with glee. "Now we can dress you!"

Ami said, "Wait. What?"

"Aren't you going to try it on? You cannot store it here: that might compromise your secret identity. Don't you have a fortress of solitude or some sort of a cave where you keep it? A fox den?"

"But how do we know this is mine? Even if it is, I cannot just take it without asking!"

Elfine looked bewildered. "Why not? They took it from you! Without asking!"

Ami said, "We don't know they took it without asking. What if I told them to put it here before I lost my memory?"

Elfine stood and advanced on her menacingly. "Here! This is liquid sugar. It will clear your head." She pushed the can of cola into Ami's hand. Cold drops had condensed on the outside of the red and white aluminum can. "You're not thinking straight. This is the forensics patient department. Where they put criminals and other dangerous people who need hospital work done on them. Putting on your supersuit might remind you of something your brain forgot!"

Ami took a sip. It tasted terrible. She decided that she was not someone used to drinking soft drinks. The bubbles tickled her nose. She put the can down. "You just like dressing and undressing people."

"Of course! Who doesn't? A new outfit is magic! One never knows what new aspect of your soul will be revealed!"

Ami reached out and stroked the black smooth fabric of the catsuit. That decided her. She *had* to try it on!

Ami looked nervously at the door. "What if someone comes?"

"If a mortal sees you naked, turn him into a deer, and have his own hounds tear him to bits!"

Ami looked at her askance. "Can we do that?"

"No, but our ancestors could. Our powers fade year by year as each generation growers smaller, pettier, and crueler." Elfine said, "There is a swimming pool on the fifteenth floor. They must have a place for ladies to change in private! Americans are elf-struck, but they have not lost all vestiges of civilization yet."

6. Pop Quiz

The two gathered up the suit and gear in a trice, closed the grilled door, and relocked the padlock. Elfine turned off the computer screen and grabbed her half-consumed can of cola. They walked to the elevator, with Ami walking in a normal gait and Elfine sneaking on her tiptoes, her hands held before her, wrists high and fingers pointed downward, in an exaggerated pantomime of sneaking.

Elfine cried out a cheery hello to any one of the several people who entered the elevator at various floors, asking how their children or pets were doing, or asking their opinions of the weather or the next lunar eclipse. One or two of the men looked with curiosity at the seven-foot-tall longbow Ami was carrying, but when Elfine engaged them in talk, their eyes were riveted on her face and figure. One younger man plucked up his courage and asked Elfine for her number, and Elfine replied that it was forty-nine.

The various women with whom she spoke complained about their ailments, except for one fat woman who took out photographs of her Welsh Corgi, which she showed to Elfine, and both were wreathed in smiles, sighing and cooing with pleasure over how cute the photos of the little dog were. Ami looked on in astonishment and decided she must not be a dog person.

The two girls stepped off at the fifteenth floor and followed signs to the swim therapy pool.

Ami said, "You are drawing attention to us."

"What?"

"Just now, on the elevator. If there are police—coppers—here in the building looking for us–"

Elfine shook her head. "Unless they are poets, or lucid dreamers, or Irish, they won't remember us. Hey! Hold the door!" and she skipped down the hall to where an older gentleman with white hair was exiting the swimming room. When Elfine took the door from his hand, he said, "I think you are supposed to have a key card to get in."

Elfine said, "That's okay! I don't have one, but I am working on a case! My friend has lost her memory. She saved my life last night! In the flag! She smites evil!"

That answer, for some reason, seemed to satisfy him because he smiled at the two pretty girls and held the door for them.

The locker room was paved in white tile, with mirrors and sinks to one side and shower stalls and lockers to the other.

Elfine put her soda can carefully upright into the sink to cover the drain. "Let me help you change! I can make the new outfit look pretty on you. It's one of my talents."

Ami put the outfit and belt, the longbow and quiver carefully on coat hangers and drew off her shoes and stockings.

Ami was shrugging off the business jacket Elfine had loaned her, when something rustled in the pocket. She put her hand in and pulled out a scrap of paper, on which were written some names and phone numbers and items one might buy at a convenience store.

In other words, it was the type of list no one with a photographic memory would ever have need of.

Ami looked from the list to the smiling Elfine. Elfine's face fell. "Is something wrong?"

"Elfine, where did you get the soft drink from?"

She said, "From the vending machine. If you get small, you can go up inside and push this little metal thing aside, so the can falls into the hopper. The gremlin told me. Should I not have listened to him? He seemed so helpful. It's called *pop*! The drink, not the gremlin. His name is Tom Knock Niss."

Ami said, "The apartment we stayed in last night…"

Elfine smiled again. "Wasn't it *lovely*! You must admit I picked a good one!"

Ami said, "…who owns it?"

Elfine cocked her head to one side. "Owns?"

"To whom does that apartment belong? Who pays the rent?"

"I don't understand the question."

"How did you find that apartment?"

"A house-hob I let free out of the whiskey bottle of a fat magician told me how to find it. His name was Sly Jack Crookshank. The hob, I mean. The magician was named Willy."

"Who slept in that room last night before you and I came there?"

"Oh. Um. I didn't know there was going to be a quiz! Don't tell me! I can figure this one out!" She screwed up her eyes. "Her name is Sharon. It was written in her diary. She is worried about her fiancée, whom she thinks is in love with her best friend Ruthie because they both act weird around her. She is going to marry him in October. Unless she breaks it off with him, but that will break her mother's heart, who thinks she is too old to get married. So: Sharon! Did I get the right answer?" Elfine crossed both her fingers, raised both eyebrows, and looked hopeful.

Ami blushed with anger. "Then all this is stolen! You made me a thief!"

Elfine look at her with wide and innocent eyes, utterly empty of guile. "The servants gave them to me. The servants told me it would be charged to the room if I signed a bit of paper they gave me, so I did."

"That is fraud! The woman who owned the apartment is going to be charged hundreds of dollars, or thousands, for these clothes!"

Elfine's lower lip trembled. "But– but you told me to find you a hot bath and warm meal! And I did that! You could not sleep where I do, in a swallow's nest in Central Park, because you are too *big*! After you saved my life, I could not refuse to grant your wish." Now Elfine's expression changed, becoming cross. "You should have worded your wish more carefully! Now you are all mad at me, and I don't like that one bit!"

Ami scowled, her lips compressed.

Ami said, "And this costume, whatever it is..."

"Your supersuit!"

"...whatever it is, we cannot take it without permission!"

Elfine sniffed a bit, and looked over her shoulder at Ami. "If we give those clothes back to Sharon, you have to take them off. She can't wear them if you are wearing them! And then if you put your supersuit back to the security room, you'll be naked. And if you do that, you cannot go play in the fountain in the park! I know because a copper told me!"

Ami said, "Don't you know the difference between good and bad?"

Elfine said, "I know the difference between fun and glum. It's the same thing, isn't it?"

"If you are a detective, you have to know what breaking the law means!"

"I told you I was a *rogue*! A loveable rogue! You don't listen!"

Elfine was on the verge of tears, which meant that what she had told her about being immune to melancholy might not have been true.

Ami was angry, but did not want to see the younger girl cry. She also did not want to argue with the only friend and helper she had. The elfin girl had, after all, saved her from sleeping half-naked in the gutter. Maybe fairyland was different, and they did not understand about private property.

Ami breathed in through her nose and out through her mouth. She knelt down on the tile, eyes focused on nothing, simply breathing, clearing her mind, and waiting for all anger and dark emotion to depart from her. So she knelt for several minutes while Elfine looked on, puzzled, peering at her now from the left and now from the right.

Ami stood and spoke in a serene voice. "We must make right whom we have wronged, including Sharon, and anyone else on whom we have trespassed. Did you keep the receipts?"

"There were bits of paper in the packages with numbers on them. I can recite the numbers if you like. Why were you sitting so still just now? Are you all right?"

Ami said, "Pour the rest of that soda pop away. You can't drink it because it is stolen. Once we find a quarter, we can put it in the machine."

"Six quarters," said Elfine. "So! Now what? Are you going to try on the suit?"

As it turned out, Ami could think of no good reason not to.

7. Ninja Girl

It was amazing how quickly the suit could be donned. It was as if had been designed to be put on quickly. The material moved under Ami's fingers strangely. Once she had the suit on, running a finger along a seam made the fabric, of its own accord, shrink and cling tightly.

The halfcape likewise was able to change its consistency, becoming either hard and stiff as canvass or soft and smooth as silk depending on how she ran her hand up or down the hem.

Ami said, "It is some sort of smart material. It changes shape and consistency."

The elbow and knees pads, once in place, folded to invisible thinness, but any shock or jar touching the fabric inflated them into existence for the duration of the blow. They protected her joints without limiting their mobility. The plastron was the same way, becoming stiff or soft as needed.

Elfine said, "Only elfs and twilights know how to make variable substances folded into the mist. No human made this for you."

"*Was* it made for me?"

Elfine giggled. "Of course! Look at how it fits!"

The were no ornaments, but there were shoulder clasps to hold the cloak. The collar had a small disk that was a dial. Ami turned it. The suit, plastron, gloves, boots, and all changed color into a broken pattern of brown, gray, and black lines. Another click turned it jet back, darkening even the gold trim on her mask, and changing the boots from a shiny reflective black to a dull charcoal that absorbed all life. A third click made the suit into a pattern of green and black splotches. A fourth click, and the whole turned white. There were other setting beyond this.

Elfine said, "How pretty!"

Ami dialed it back to a gray suit with black gloves and boots. "It is camouflage, with settings for urban, jungle, night, and snow. I must have been some sort of soldier."

"Or a ninja!"

"*Kunoichi*."

"*Gesundheit*!"

"Girl ninja are called *kunoichi*, and not many girls in real life are practicing ninja."

"You must come from somewhere else, then. Not from real life."

8. *Arsenal*

The fox-mask had built in wide-spectrum vision goggles in the yellow eyes and breathing filters in the pointed snout. Radio gear was built into the ears. A hinge in the earpiece of the cowl allowed the mask to be flipped back up to the crown of the head so that the chin of the mask was like a visor over her eyes. It could be raised or lowered by a toss of the head.

The belt clasp her waist tightly, and the leg straps circling her upper thighs held two larger scabbards snugly against her hips.

The straps held pouches containing throwing stars and barbs. Fanny packs to her left and right held a weighted bolo and a weighted chain, called a *kusarifundo*.

The large scabbards contained what turned out to be to folding boomerangs made of a white material—not metal—which Ami did not recognize.

A scabbard that fit into the small of her back held what seemed to be a folding sword. She saw ribs of the same material lining the inside of the cape.

"I think these turn into paraglider wings…" said Ami. Her shoulders instinctively remembered the way to shrug to snap the cape into a larger and rigid form. The cape doubled in size and now reached to either side, large enough to brush the sinks and lockers opposite. However, to put the cape back to lie flat, she had to yank on each wing joint with either hand simultaneously, not a move that could be done accidentally in midair. There was an intermediate form the cape could take to act as a shield over either arm and another form where the hem or point could grow hard and sharp as steel, much like an overlarge fighting fan.

Now Ami spun, as giddy as Elfine, and ended in a lunge with the leading point of the cloak embedded an inch into a white tile of the wall. A flick of the wrist relaxed the tip of the capehem from rigidly steelhard to silky pliancy. She recovered from her lunge, and the cape retracted.

"Okay," said Ami. "It's mine. I am *so* keeping this!"

There was a pocket in the cape. Inside, neatly folded, was a silk *yukata*, a summer kimono, with long drooping sleeves. It was adorned with a pattern of golden moths, mulberry leaves, and red foxes playing with pearls. Folded neatly was a waist cord called a *koshihimo* as well as toe socks.

Ami said, "It is missing its *obi*."

She put the kimono on over the catsuit, folded it left and right and tied it in place. The catsuit was so tight that, once she removed the cape, the outer garment could lie smoothly, looking natural.

Ami said, "Why was I carrying this?"

Elfine said, "It is your civilian dress. For your secret identity!"

Ami said, "It would not fool anyone. I'd have to remove the cape, cowl, mask, gloves, and boots, and there would still be a six-foot-tall thirty-pound longbow and a quiver of arrows. Where would I hide them?"

Elfine said, "You would hide them in the mist. Everything is hidden in the mist. That is how your bow can fold up without losing its shape."

"What do you mean?"

Elfine handed her the longbow. "Unstring it."

Ami did so.

Elfine shouted, "Someone's coming! Quick! Hide it!"

No one was coming, but, by the time she realized that fact, the bowstaff had turned into a baton in her hands.

She did the same instinctive actions again, more slowly. Her thumb found a hidden switch on the shaft. The segments of the bow slid neatly into each other like a telescope even though the wood seemed perfectly solid. Ami now held a baton about the size of her forearm.

A second twitch of her thumb made the baton telescope out to the size of a longbow again, as if springloaded. Ami spent a moment folding and unfolding the longbow. She found the bow would not fold when strung.

The neck of the kimono was wide enough in the back to allow her to slide the baton into a pocket running along the spine of her black suit of the exact size to fit it.

Elfine said, "The quiver is made by mermaids. They know the art of making packages and packs to be bigger on the inside than on the outside. Here, let me."

Elfine closed the flap over the arrowcase, folded it again, and then a third time so that the whole thing was now half its height and as thin as a wand, with only the first arrow protruding. Elfine pulled that arrow. A second one clicked into place, offering its fletching. She handed the arrow and quiver to Ami. "It unfolds the same way."

"How is that possible?" said Ami, eye goggling.

"It works by elf geometry."

"But… how?"

Elfine said, "You were raised by humans, or some part of elfland very far from the sea, if you've never seen a mermaid folding a poke before. The extra volume goes in the same direction ghosts go—the direction our eyes don't see—into the mist. The light you shined from your finger will make it come undone, so be careful. If you shine your ring, your bow will pop out to full length. The sleeves in your kimono are built the same way, and I bet you can put your gloves and belt and other stuff in them without anyone being the wiser."

The spine of the catsuit under the kimono had a second sleeve parallel to the first where the folding pouch of arrows could be hidden. Ami could yank an arrow out of her quiver even when the quiver was folded and hidden: but she had to take out the whole quiver and unfold it to full height to put the arrow back.

The kimono sleeves had hidden pockets of just the right size to hold her fox mask, gloves, boots, and belt.

Ami said, "What about the cape? Where does it go?"

Elfine squinted at it. "Does it have another shape?"

Ami tugged on it one way and then another. It came apart like two magnets being drawn apart and changed into a bright red color. Ami said, "It is the missing *obi*."

Elfine said, "What's that?"

"Kimono sash."

"Hand it here. I'll tie it."

"You know how?"

"Sure," said Elfine. "I have relatives in Japan. Turn around."

Ami did. Elfine gave a little shriek and dropped the sash. Ami spun, her hands up, fingers tense, legs bent. "What? What is it?"

Elfine positioned her in front of the mirror. "Look over your shoulder into the mirror. See that?" Elfine pointed to a large emblem resting across the shoulders of Ami's kimono. It was a tawny yellow moth with black wing markings.

9. The Crest

"I see it," said Ami, "What does it mean?"

"Do you recognize it?"

"No."

But looking at it made her want to stand with her spine straight and her chin up.

"That is a family crest. *Antheraea yamamai*. You are a member of the Moth family. You are from the Silkmoths of Japan."

"What does that mean?" Ami asked in wonder.

"It means who you are. Kasumi-Himi no Mikoto is the daughter of Amaterasu of the Sun and the broken saber of Susa-no-O of the Impetuous Storm. She married Bold Moth, the son of Mwynfawr and Palatyne, the Riverwater's daughter. In older days, Kasumi was called Takiri-hime no Mikoto, Her Augustness Torrent-Mist Princess, and was worshipped as a goddess: but Saint Francis Xavier convinced her to abdicate that title. All the Silkmoths are descended from her."

Elfine smiled a warm, bright smile. She added, "There! I have found your kindred! And your name: it is Moth. We are cousins! We are close to cracking the case! And that proves I am sane. Now hold still while I tie your sash."

Ami inspected herself carefully in the mirror. "If this is my civilian clothing, where do I live? In a clothing store? No one in Japan dresses this way anymore, except at festivals."

Elfine said, "We age more slowly than humans, and our elders last longer. So fashions among us don't change much. Ready to go?"

Ami said, "Go where?"

Elfine said, "Where the next clue leads!"

Chapter 5

The Eyes of Hungry Ghosts

1. *An Other Exit*

The two girls, carrying a folded flag and an expensive suit of clothing, walked to the elevator, meeting no one.

Ami said, "First, we have to go make amends to Sharon. Do you have any money?"

"What's that?"

"Gold."

"Gold is a fairy metal! When humans trifle with it, it drives them mad. And no, I don't have any." Elfine added, "Besides, if we had any money, the coppers would take it from us."

"What coppers?"

At that moment, they reached the ground floor. The elevator doors slid open. Across the lobby could be seen a knot of blue uniforms. Half a dozen police were gathered around the doors to the street, questioning each person who entered or left. They were holding photographs of a young and pretty oriental girl's face.

One of the officers, looking up, saw Ami, looked down at the photo in his hand, looked up again, and shouted, "Excuse me, miss! Stop right there!"

Elfine waved cheerfully while pushing the button to close the doors, calling back, "Thank you, but not right now! We love New York! It's a wonderful town! The Bronx is up! The Battery's down!"

The door slid shut. Elfine pushed the button for the roof. "The copper's best bet is to put a man in every elevator car, coordinate by radio with someone watching the floor lights, and put a man in the stairwell. If anyone on an upper floor pushes the button for this car, it will stop, and they will catch us. Change into your supersuit."

Ami said, "What? Why?"

"Your civilian garb did not fool them."

As they had before, her hands remembered what to do and moved with sure, practiced motions. As rapidly as a fireman getting dressed, she donned the mask, drew the other gear out of her sleeves, draped it over her shoulders, yanked the kimono down to her waist, donned the belt, removed the sash, changed it into a cloak with a snap of her wrists, folded the kimono inside, and clipped it to her shoulder clasps.

"Don't put on your gloves yet!"

"What is it?" said Ami.

"Hand me your ring first."

She did. The gloves and boots were rolled and loose, easy to don in a moment and easy to unroll up her limbs. Once in position, they connected to clasps at shoulder and thigh and tightened as if of their own accord. The last step was to tighten the belt and leg straps.

Ami said, "Now what?"

Elfine took her left hand and slid the ring over Ami's middle finger. "It won't fit." Ami said. "With the added thickness of the glove…"

It slid easily and painlessly over her knuckle despite the extra layer of glove-material covering it. "This is a famous magic ring, made by Ivald. A magic ring is always the size it needs to be."

"Why couldn't I take it off last night?"

"Who can say? Maybe the ring knew you did not need to take it off."

Elfine peered at the elevator button panel, pouting. "There should be a… hmm… maybe this one." She opened a red panel labeled DO NOT OPEN and pushed the button inside. The car jerked to a stop, and bells started ringing.

Elfine dwindled to a size smaller than any Ami had seen previously, smaller than a speck, and flew straight up, a darting pinpoint of light. She slipped between two ceiling tiles and vanished. A moment later, one of the ceiling tiles was yanked up and open with a bang as Elfine opened the trap door in the ceiling of the elevator car.

"Come on up!"

2. Up the Wire

Ami twisted her ring to pewter, drew her wirepoon gun, fitted the grapnel to it, and affixed the carabiner of the line dangling from the pistol butt to a connector on her belt. When the connector was engaged, her suit changed of its own accord once more and formed parachute harness of padded fibers just below its surface. She fiddled with the magnification and night-vision settings on her mask's goggles for a moment, selected a metal I-beam far up the shaft as her target, and shot.

The hook clung solidly. She was much lighter than the spool engine was designed to haul, so she shot up out of the elevator like a cork from a champagne bottle. Ami kept her wits and kicked obliquely against the walls of the shaft to prevent herself from slamming into any. A thumb switch on the wirepoon gun, when she pushed it, made the grappling hook pop open like a broken umbrella and release its grip. The motor yanked the grapnel back into the barrel, cocked and ready for the next shot.

She flew up the shaft, calmly unturned the ring to regain mass, and slowed immediately. At the zenith of her rise, during the moment when she was weightless, she twisted the ring again.

She worked the clutch of the auto-spool in her wirepoon gun and changed to a different gear. Then, she shot the grapnel again and pulled herself at a gentler rate of speed up the shaft to another crossbeam, where she perched.

Her suit was not done surprising her: a quick-draw wrist sheath unfolded from her wrist. The wirepoon gun not only could be fitted in place there, but the whole sheath folded against her glove until it was as thin as a playing card. Tensing the muscles of her wrist made the sheath pop back into existence and shove the wirepoon gun into her palm.

She spent a moment flicking the gun into her palm out of nowhere, pushing it back into the holster, shutting it, and doing it again. Where the mass and volume of the gun went when the holster was shut, Ami could only wonder. "Elf geometry," she muttered. But her eyes glittered with pride and awe.

Elfine grew from mote sized to doll sized and landed on Ami's shoulder.

Ami said, "I love this suit! It had better really be mine!"

"Why did you stop? We are going all the way to the roof!"

This time, Ami twisted the ring a quarter turn, so she was a fourth her normal weight, and made sure the spool engine in her wirepoon-gun was adjusted accordingly. She went up ten and twelve stories at a time and found herself among the elevator machinery.

There was a crawlspace for the mechanic to oil and repair the machinery. The tiny metal door was locked, but now Ami slid a corner of her folded cape into the crack between the frame and the hatch and made the cloak go stiff. The pressure popped the latch free. Ami kicked open the door, slid through the opening, rolled, and came to her feet in a low-ceilinged, dark utility room with a concrete floor. A set of green metal stairs to her left led up to a door to the roof. The interior was crowded with machinery and a workbench.

Through the narrow openings of windows yellow with dust, Ami could see the sun near the horizon.

3. Losing Track

Ami pushed her mask back on her head and rubbed her eyes. "I must have lost track of time," she mused.

But it had been late afternoon before she woke, and Elfine's quizzing had taken at least an hour, and the walk here had taken longer. How much time had passed since then? She had spent at least twenty minutes merely loitering in the waiting room to speak to the reception nurse.

Elfine said, "Time in the mortal world is cruel and disobedient and always goes at the same rate, terrible as the drumbeat of a dirge. In our home, the happier hours linger and perhaps return. For us, the seasons dance, and time steps lightly."

Ami said, "If we leave from the roof during daylight, we will be seen."

Elfine said, "Why? The Ring of Mists is on your finger. It is one of the Thirteen Treasures of Lyonesse. You can walk unseen of men, and, if you go deeper in the mist than is wise, you can walk through walls like a ghost. It once belonged to Eluned the Fortunate before his untimely fate."

"Why? What happened to him?"

"He used the ring to escape the dungeon of the giant Ysbadden, and when walking through a wall, accidentally fell through the floor, the ground, the earth, and the roof of the underworld. He was dragged away, screaming, by many unseen hands."

"Then why was he called *fortunate*?"

Elfine pursed her lips thoughtfully. "I am not sure why. He did own a famous magic ring! Not everyone can say that."

"Now, about this ring. Why do you think…"

"…Except Gyges, Angelica, Brunello, Bradamant, and Melissa."

"Beg pardon?"

"Not everyone can say he owns a famous magic ring! Except for them, of course. Gyges of Lydia owned it before Eluned, and Angelica of Cathay owned it after."

"How did I come to have it?"

"Well, I am not sure. Brunello the Dwarf stole it from Angelica, Bradamant the Martial Maiden took it from him, and she gave the ring to Melissa the Sorceress. Melissa used the power of the ring to overcome a wicked enchantress, and was supreme among sorceresses until her grandfather, Merlin, told her to put it back in the Glass Tower. Glinda is supreme now, but she will never be tithed. Such is the will of Heaven!"

Ami said, "So you recognize this ring?"

"Who wouldn't? It's famous. It is one of the Thirteen Treasures that were torn from the hands of the Old Gods by Arawn of Annuvin, and after he was driven forth by Constantine, the treasures were scattered abroad, doing much mischief among men. Merlin gathered and stored them in Elfland after Arthur conquered the elfs and became the first High King. The treasures are held in a tower of glass, against the day and hour when Arthur returns, and England is burned red with the blood of saints and the fires of Hell. The children of men must grow in power and wisdom ere such treasures can be entrusted to them, lest they be tempted beyond their strength."

Ami said, "Each time I turn this ring, I feel horrid and hostile eyes on me, like the eyes of hungry ghosts. I would rather wait until sunset."

4. The Ring of Mists

Elfine sat down happily on a folding metal chair, leaned back, and crossed her slippered feet at the ankles atop a throbbing boxlike arm of the air conditioning machinery. She folded her arms behind her head, looking pleased.

"This is exciting, isn't it! When a fox is hunted, he never goes into a den that does not have at least two exits. So don't let them corner you! And when someone comes to beat you senseless and tells you to stay off the case, that is when you should get stubborn! Never get off a case someone tells you to get off! Now, when we leave the building, should we go east or go west and double back to throw off pursuit?"

Ami brushed a spot of concrete clean, drew her short sword, snapped it to its full length with a flick of her wrist, and knelt in a corner, where she could see the windows and door and hatch leading into this small room without turning her head. The sword was made of a white substance that looked more like ceramic than metal. It was a two-foot-long short sword of a type called a *kodachi*.

"Why are we going east?" Ami asked.

"We want to go to the headquarters of the Nineteenth Precinct building."

Ami said patiently, "And why are we going there?"

"Humans write everything down! I told you that. We want to see what they said about you."

Ami remembered the Elfine had been playing with the computer console in the security room. Perhaps it had been more than mere play. "What did you find out? Did you see my records?"

Elfine looked surprised. "Well, you told me to do more detective work! When you were picking the lock. Remember?" Then she looked worried.

"You are not starting to forget other things, are you? This was like, ten minutes ago. Tie a red string around your finger! That stops elfs from stealing memories!"

Ami said, "I remember! You didn't tell me what you found out. Detectives are supposed to report their results, aren't they?" Ami found herself blushing with shame. She had simply assumed Elfine to be incompetent and scatter-brained, despite a number of clever and capable things she had done. "How did you get the computer record open? Don't you need a password?"

"Tom Knock Niss did that for me. The gremlin who lives in the air conditioner. I bribed him with a kiss. He thinks I am sexy!" She giggled. "Gremlins are nightfolk who meddle with machines. They built a monster computer called the Intertube to put dirty pictures of naked women in everyone's desks and cellphones. The elfs want men to be weak and stupid and told the gremlins to do it. Filthy creatures, gremlins!"

"But you saw my records?"

"I sure did!" She nodded eagerly.

"And?"

"You were brought into the emergency room by an officer named Dom Damiano of the Nineteenth Precinct. You were covered in blood but showed no sign of wounds. Samples of your blood and the blood on your clothing were taken and packaged to be mailed to a lab in Berkeley, California. Because you are a crime suspect, you were placed in the forensic patient wing under Doctor Sinters Pillory. There was no brainwave pattern, so you should have been dead, but you were breathing shallowly, with a slow heartbeat. That was marked as an 'anomalous result.' Then, at midnight, your brainwave activity started again. You opened your eyes and were unresponsive to stimuli. Then, at one in the morning, your vital signs returned to normal, you spoke several sentences in an unknown language, and you fell asleep. They put you in a room to wait for you to wake up. During the shift change, you vanished and smashed out the windows. That was at four in the morning."

"Wait. I am a crime suspect? For what crime?"

"It did not say. But you *do* have a habit of killing people. So far, you have averaged about one per day: the goat-man and the redcap mugging me."

Ami opened her mouth to protest and then closed it again, frowning.

"Why do they wear red caps?"

"Those are Carabas caps, but dyed in human blood. It lets them touch iron and cross thresholds. The feather is a Strega feather, from an owl-hag. It overcomes the confusion of tongues and allows the monsters to speak human speech. The real ones come from the Elfking, Erlkoenig, the Prince of Winter."

"These were not real?"

"Of course not! The real redcaps are servants of Erlkoenig. The goat man said he was from the Supreme Anarchists' Council. Sons of Night don't have free will like Sons of Adam: we cannot just swear fealty to a sovereign and later denounce or deny that oath, not even in jest. Elfs are very careful about the wording of their oaths. We cannot break our word. Our lawyers always have lots of work!"

Ami said, "Have you? Sworn any unbreakable oaths, I mean."

Elfine said, "When any of us turn twenty-one, it is expected of all twilight creatures to swear fealty and obedience to the Elfin King. I have not turned twenty-one. I heard rumors that some of my cousins escaped this oath somehow and also escaped punishment. That is the reason why I smuggled myself here. I am detectiving them. Is that a word? They are in this city."

"But the goat did not swear. Why not?"

"I don't know. But the fact that your goat-man said he was an anarchist, by itself, and is walking the earth in the Daylit World is very bad news. We should tell the King!"

"The Elfking?"

"Not him!" Elfine scowled. "His is a bad soul, twisted and malign, and he is not to be trusted! His knights are cruel, lustful, grasping, and wicked! I mean the true King!"

"Who is that? Where is he?"

"He sleeps with all his knights and snow-white steeds beneath the mound at Alderley Edge. Mother said his kitchen page is at large in the world, with a magical black pot. He uses it to brew the truth, a stew that base and wicked knights, cowardly and false, must spew from their mouths, for while it is savory in their nostrils, it turns bitter as wormwood in their stomachs!"

A strange sensation tickled Ami's spine. She came softly to her feet. Her eyes were at the yellow windows. It was dark out. The sun had set. Ami tossed her head, and this snapped her mask down over her face. In the light amplification lenses in the mask, she could see a trio of police officers in riot gear, with black and faceless helmets and bulky bulletproof armor on chest and back, shotguns at the ready. They were emerging from a stairwell and onto the roof.

5. Night Flight

The roof was cluttered with antennae, vents, other machines, and fixtures, including more than one utility room with a roof entrance like this one. A man in brown overalls was trailing the officers, and he came forward and unlocked any trap doors or roof doors they directed.

Ami turned and opened the hatch leading down into the elevator machinery. The engine was grinding and complaining, and she saw the elevator car rising. In a moment, it would be at the top of the shaft. The elevator car filled the shaft. There was no escape that way.

Ami turned and beckoned Elfine to go out at the small door which led onto the roof. Fortunately, this door was on the opposite side of the utility room from the police. Emerging from that door would keep the structure between the girls and the eyes of the men.

Ami said quietly and quickly, "Head for the side of the roof and go straight down. Fly near the stone between the windows. If we get separated, meet me, um… in front of the club where I met you!"

Elfine said, "Not there! The redcaps might come back!"

"In the cathedral we passed on the way here. Saint Jean Baptiste."

"He doesn't like fairies! The high school next door to it! In the courtyard!"

There was no time to argue. "The courtyard! Fine! Now go!"

Elfine said, "*Try* turning invisible!"

Ami shook her head.

Elfine said, "But the police will surely see you!"

Ami wondered which course was riskier. What if the unseen eyes seeking her were not looking this way? She decided to try it.

Ami twisted the ring on her finger from white to pewter to a dark gray the hue of cast iron, almost black. The dark face closed its eyes. A dark mist spread out from the ring and swirled with sinister movements around her body. When the dark mist passed before her eyes, the shadows in the small utility room suddenly seemed darker, and the angles and spaces in the room were subtly wrong.

Standing in the corner of the room was a pale man garbed in black. His boots did not touch the ground, nor cast he any shadow. On his black surcoat was the image of a leafless white tree. On his head was a black crown from which a fierce and airless heat radiated, like the heat from a dark furnace. His eyes were empty sockets. His mouth was a lipless slash.

With dreamlike slowness the apparition turned his empty sockets toward her, and smiled, and raised a curved horn to his ghastly lips.

He winded the horn. A shattering noise rang out and echoed strangely. It did not echo from the walls in the room in which he stood but from larger unseen walls standing farther off. Howls of wolves answered the horn call. The baying was distant, but it came from more than one point of the compass.

Ami gritted her teeth to bite back a scream and twisted the ring back to pewter. The man vanished. Elfine was also not in sight. Perhaps she had fled, for the door to the roof was now hanging open. Ami did a midair summersault and kicked off the wall behind her with both feet.

She passed with the speed of a striking shark out into the darkness and across the gravel roof. Her arms were at her sides, hands at her thighs, minimizing her air resistance. The rough surface of the roof sped by, inches from the nose of her mask.

A loud voice from behind her called, "Halt! In the name of the law!"

But there was no stopping her forward momentum. She sailed across the roof. She shrugged her shoulders, and the cape unfolded into glider wings. The scoop of the air carried her upward a foot or two, just enough to clear the railing of the short wall circling the roof. She twitched her wrist, and the wirepoon gun slapped into her palm. The tines snapped open like the ribs of a naked parasol. She snagged the hook of the grapnel on the iron rail as she slid over it with an inch to spare. Then there was nothing below but a dizzying abyss of air and the lights of shorter buildings.

More shouts came from behind her, and the baying of wolves was nearer. The wire spool played out as she receded several yards from the side of the building. She then engaged the brake of the wire spool. The wire jerked taut and flung her in a semicircle sharply downward. It was as if the brink of the roof jerked itself upward to block the view of the policemen above and behind her.

She pushed the thumbswitch to release the grapnel from the wall. Like a stone from a sling, she sped now in a straight line tangential to the semicircle.

The side of the building was now rushing toward her like a giant granite flyswatter. She did a half-roll, one wingtip pointed at the ground and one at the zenith. She caught the wind in her wings, and she peeled off toward the left, neatly avoiding the corner of the building. She saw her own reflection in the windows she sped past. The alternation of glass and stone caused by her rapid passage made the reflection flicker like a strobe light. The sleek and shapely black fox-faced figure swan diving in the depth of the reflections turned her gold eyes toward her as if in surprise, and the little triangular ears were standing up like parallel exclamation marks.

The air slowed her. She twisted the ring to give herself partial weight so that gravity bent her flightpath toward the distant ground. Reaching up with either hand, she yanked on the wing joints to collapse them into a silk cape. The cape fluttered and clung to her form as she fell head foremost down the side of the building, arms at her sides, sleek as a torpedo.

Would the police think to run to the brink, look over, see her, and open fire? She dismissed the idea as absurd. In the normal course of events, girls who threw themselves off skyscrapers died. Besides, the streets below and buildings beyond were inhabited, and she had seen shotguns, not rifles with scopes, in the policemen's hands.

In order to avoid the normal course of events, when she fell below twenty stories, Ami twisted her weight to zero and snapped her wings open. The sudden jerk on her shoulders was unexpected, and she was yanked upward, or so her inner ear told her. She tumbled like an autumn leaf in a gale for a moment, dazed. The squares of light from building windows slid dizzily past.

She spread her arms and legs like a parachutist to steady her tumble. Now she was face downward and slowing. She came to a standstill about seventy or eighty yards above the street. She could see the glint of streetlamps and the glare of headlights, the flicker of neon signs. No lights were bright enough or high enough to shine on her. She shrugged and twisted the ring to give herself partial weight, and as soon as downward motion started, she angled the wings to carry her into the dark alley between the hospital and the lower red brick building next door, a condominium. Beyond the brick building she saw the high school below her to the left and the cathedral below her to the right. She lowered her weight to zero and let the wings slow her. She shot the wirepoon pistol into a tree in the courtyard she found, drew herself to the ground, spread the wings once more to arrest her speed, folded the wings, twisted the ring, and dropped neatly to the grass.

She turned the ring to white. A sensation of relief, like a warmth, ran up her spine. The eyes were no longer seeking her. She felt as calm as the metallic expression in the face of the ring. She looked down at her empty hands. In the excitement, she had left the expensive stolen clothing and the folded flag sitting in the elevator.

The calm did not last. Ami pushed the fox mask back up to the crown of her head and looked left and right. Where was Elfine?

Chapter 6

In the Narrow Pass

1. Rendezvous

Ami looked over the square of greenery. Surely this was the place Elfine meant: there was no other patch of green between the school and the cathedral other than this walled park. Here were grass, a walkway between the school and the church, some trees, and a few trestle tables. Where was Elfine? Even a firefly should have been visible.

Above the wall to the left, Ami could see the tall red brick condominium peering and, taller still and further away, the hospital. She eyed the height of the wall. Ami toyed with the ring, but the calm sensation radiating from the white band was one she was reluctant to undo. She was not sure what the forces seeking her were using to track her, but using the ring certainly seemed to draw them.

She left the ring as it was and vaulted the wall, kicking from one rough brick to the next and flipping herself acrobatically to the narrow top, hands out to either side to steady herself.

She could see a line of dumpsters, an abandoned car, and then a larger space, a small empty lot. The dumpsters were parked beneath a scaffolding of metal bars and wooden slats that blocked her view.

Ami leaped onto the scaffolding, surprised at how heavily she landed. She swarmed up the bars and crouched at the top. The noise she made and the heaviness of her own body seemed excessive. It was alarming how quickly she had adjusted to the weightless and half-weightless ghostly motions that the Ring of Mists enabled her to enjoy.

She heard the pitter pat of slippered feet echoing from the wall of the alley nearby. It sounded like Elfine's gait, coming from just around the corner.

The need for speed outweighed caution. She spun the ring to quarter-weight and leaped down. She landed at the corner, rolled, came to her feet, and headed down the second alley, a small and unsanitary space between a ballroom dance hall and the hospital.

The upper floor of the dance studio was lit, but everything below was dark. The building walls at ground level were dark to left and right, but the reflected lights from the main street formed a bright rectangle between them.

Ami tossed her head, which slipped her mask into place. The night vision showed it was Elfine, standing still, looking wretched and confused. She had her hands up as if she were a mime pretending to be trapped in an invisible box. Ami raced forward on long, silent steps.

Elfine turned and saw a dark, slender silhouette against a darker background with pointed fox ears and silent, flowing cape.

2. *Charmed Circle*

Elfine screamed something, hands raised as if to push Ami back out of danger.

Seeing this, before the words even left Elfine's mouth, Ami ducked and raised the cape on her elbow just as a wolf-headed man-thing launched itself out of a hidden doorway toward her neck.

The cape stiffened to metal hardness, and his teeth and forepaws landed on the surface without finding purchase. He was much bigger and stronger. In one motion, she drew her *kodachi* and thrust beneath the cape to let him run onto the point with his unprotected belly, unfolding the white blade into his intestines as she did so. His momentum bowled her over; she rolled, bringing up her feet, and kicking his body neatly all the way over and behind her. Upside down, bleeding copiously from a gut wound, the wolf-man fell straight into the surprised arms of another attacker coming from the other side, a tall man with a knife in either hand.

Ami rolled to her feet and jumped upward and to the left. At less than one fourth her normal weight, she was able to jump up two stories. She drew the baton from her back and snapped it into its full length, using the thrust from the untelescoping butt of the longbow against the wall of the dance studio to throw her against the wall of the hospital.

Here, she found a bricked-up window, but with sill and ledge still intact. She wedged herself into the non-window, foot against one sill and spine against the other, shook the blood free from her shortsword, sheathed it, and then used both hands and one foot to string her bow.

"Look out! It's a trap!" Elfine's words echoed off the dark walls and were almost lost in the howling uproar. It seemed odd how long it took for the words to reach her ear, but time seemed strangely to be running slowly.

Ami's fingers were shaking as she strung the bow. The wolf-man who had attacked her was horrifically strong, larger and taller than Ami. Dumb luck and fast reflexes had saved her. But there was no time to feel the fear she was feeling. Ami cleared her mind of words, of thoughts.

She did not have a free hand to adjust the lenses on her mask, so she tossed her head to slide the mask up. She scanned the area. The night air was cold on her face. The wolf-man she had gut-stabbed was writhing on the ground and making a terrible noise. Howls of wolves sounded both far away and near at hand. There were shadows moving at the mouth of the alley and also from the empty lot behind. They were coming from all directions. She tossed her head a second time to lower the mask back in place.

The second man, a tall fellow in a red cap with a knife in either hand, was staring upward, looking for her. During the moment when her mask was up, he must have seen a flash of her white face, for he pointed and howled. She sent three shafts into his chest. Down he fell.

There was a noise from below. She dropped a handful of flashbang mini-grenades among them. The stuttering, shocking, eye-searing light revealed the scene clearly, but only for a moment: at least a dozen shaggy wolves were in the alleyway, crouched and waiting. Coming from the open lot behind were three figures in red caps.

A fourth figure on an enormous horse was behind them, hidden in the shadows. He was on the edge of the zone of momentary light, and the horse reared, and she heard it whinny, but otherwise Ami saw no details.

Of the three closest to the horseman, one seemed a human: a dark-haired man in a black suit and tie and wearing dark glasses. The second was half-human and half-wolf, shirtless, standing upright with human hands, but with human trousers still around his flanks and tail and crooked legs. The third had a wolf's body except that it was the size of a pony. He had the face of a man, a grinning big-nosed fellow with a beard. Gold chains were around his neck, and five of his teeth were gold and set with diamonds.

Elfine was standing halfway between the two groups, shivering. She ran two paces to the left, two to the right, and back again. Ami saw a circle of red thread, four paces wide, had been set on the ground. Elfine was in the middle of it.

Then, the light was gone. Ami twisted a gold ornament at the temple of her fox mask. The light amplification lenses slid aside, and the infrared lenses rotated into place. She now saw the heat escaping the bodies below. She raised the longbow and sent an arrow into the spot she remembered where the thread lay, hoping to sever the string.

It must have worked because she heard Elfine whoop with joy and saw the heat signature of the slender humanoid figure shrink to a dot. It vanished from view. Maybe it was not large enough or hot enough for the mask lenses to pick up.

Ami heard the noise of hoofbeats clattering. The glowing heat outline of a horse and rider rushed down the alley and away.

Ami, meanwhile, shot arrows at the wolf-man and the man in dark glasses just on the general principle that creatures with hands, who could throw or shoot, were more dangerous at the moment. The wolf-man fell, but the man in dark glasses, showing a remarkable presence of mind and speed of reflexes, put an elbow around the neck of the wolf-man and held his squirming, bleeding compatriot before him as a shield. The heat outlines were not clear enough for her to strike his face peering over his dying friend's shoulder, but neither could he draw any weapon as both hands were occupied.

From the sounds and heat shadows, she could tell the wolves were now making prodigious leaps, ten and fifteen feet straight up, and snapping at her where she rested in the windowsill. More than mere muscle power was involved because the wolves were making taller leaps with each attempt, as if the howling and baying of the wolves gathered below increased their strength and fury.

She shot and shot. Two wolves with arrows in their hides fell back into the alley, yowling. This was not working. There were too many, and their leaps were getting higher. She raised a foot, unstrung her bow, and collapsed it into a baton.

At that moment a particularly ambitious wolf leaped higher than the others. She caught it in the chest with the foot of her boot and shoved. It fell back into the air, snarling and snapping as it plunged. She shot her wirepoon across the alley, unable to see where she was shooting because the wall was not giving off any heat. The grapnel snagged something.

She swung away from the snapping jaws and let the whining wirespool draw her rapidly upward. She tossed her head to raise the mask, and, in the glare of the upper story lights of the dance studio, Ami caught a glimpse of a tangle of transformers and electrical wires protruding from the side of the building. She was about to run into them.

She did a flip in midair and landed on a warm and humming transformer. She tossed her head to lower the mask and saw the heat signatures of the wolves in the alley. They were milling and howling, unable to reach her high perch. But the pony-sized quadruped heat-shadow suddenly grew bright and then brighter in her lenses, as if the monster had swallowed a furnace. The man-faced wolf reared back. In her view, the red mouth looked like a yellow flower with a blindingly white center. The monster vomited a spume of flame up toward her.

She drew her baton and short sword. She vaulted upward, using the power of the unfolding bowstaff to propel her, and slashing the electrical cables running to the box as she did so, clearing her path.

Her instincts must have been sure the nonmetallic blade was safe, but, even so, it was a reckless blow. Wires spat sparks and fell down among the wolves, who were packed closed enough together that if one were touching an electrocuted one, he was electrocuted as well.

Fire from the spew of the monster splashed across stone and glass and clung, as if it were burning glue, including the transformer box she was no longer atop.

The lights of the upper floor of the dance studio went dark. She soared straight up, sheathing her blade as she did. This time she was not blind, because the burning monster-spew splashed along the wall stones beneath her sent her shadow, in a jumping triangle, up the wall ahead of her.

Ami shrugged the wirepoon into her palm and fired at the roof above her. She did not have two hands free for archery, so she folded the bowstaff back into a baton and sheathed it. As the wire spool drew her rapidly up the side of the building, she drew and threw a boomerang whirling into the skull of the flame-breathing wolf-man. He staggered, howled, and ran around the corner. She threw a second boomerang and must have judged the angle right because the spinning boomerang curved nicely around the corner and out of sight, and the wolf-man uttered an agonized yelp that trailed off into a whine.

The churchbells began chiming on the cathedral next door. That, or the flash grenades, or the loss of their leader, must have panicked the wolf pack because the beasts howled and fled in every direction.

By the time Ami reached the roof of the building, the dim alley was too far for a boomerang or throwing star. She once more drew out, unfolded, and strung her bow. Three wolf corpses lay there in the light of the dying flame, two of them with human clothing tangled about their twisted limbs. But there were no targets left for her.

Ami heard Elfine scream again. The scream was coming from the alley between this building and the cathedral. Ami twisted the ring to full weightlessness, fired the wirepoon to catch the opposite lip of the dance studio roof, and yanked herself across the distance, regardless of the danger of such headlong speed.

3. *The Black Knight*

Ami shot across the space between the dance studio and the cathedral. Looking down, she saw the top of an awning. It blocked the scene. The sounds of hoofbeats hammering and Elfine screaming in panic came from below this awning.

From the sound of the hoofbeats and the motion of a light that she could dimly see through the awning fabric, it seemed the horseman carried a torch in his left hand.

The shadows cast from the torch were crisp and large. Under the awning, his shadow parallel to him on a wall, was the horseman, galloping in full career. Strangely enough, he had a butterfly net deployed before him like a lance, and in it was writhing a tiny glowing dot small as a firefly. The butterfly net was peeping out from under the awning, and Ami could see it directly, not just as a shadow. The horseman must have just then snatched the burning dot out of the air.

Three things happened at once. First, there was a sudden spray of sparks which made the shadows jump and scatter. The butterfly net ripped open, and Elfine in her green bodice and skirt was there, full sized, burning with colored sparks, with the ring of the butterfly net circling her waist and pinning her arms to her sides. Second, the horseman passed out from underneath the awning and into view. The horseman was yanking the trapped Elfine to him with both hands, dropping the torch as he did so, and he threw her body across his saddlebow. Third, darkness filled the alley.

Ami, looking down from above, could only see the silhouette of head and shoulders of the figure bent over and pinning down the brightly sparkling girl. The light was directly behind and beneath him, and his dark outline rippled as the sparks danced. The many-colored sparks hid all hues but revealed his shape: He was in a tall helm and billowing cape. There were shadowy suggestions of a sword and shield hanging from his saddle, but the barding and skirts on the horse were clear. This was not merely a horseman, but a fully armed and armored knight.

Ami's heart leaped with pain. If Elfine were afraid of one small metal nail, what must she think of a knight covered from head to toe?

Third, as part of the same motion as he captured the fairy girl, the knight casually put his gauntleted hand on the small of her back. All her sparks suddenly went out, so the shadows swelled and filled the alley with darkness. The sound of Elfine's screaming, the knight's triumphant laughter, and the horse's retreating hoofbeats filled the gloom.

All this Ami saw in an instant as she soared over. Ami somersaulted in midair so that her feet would strike the wall of the church and absorb her impact, but, to her surprise, when she struck the wall, her full weight returned, and she fell.

With an enormous clatter, her bowstaff snapped out to its full length, and the bowcase across her back was suddenly its full volume and weight, shedding arrows. Some of her weapons erupted from her belt pouches and flung themselves into the air. The wrist holster, elbow pads, and knee pads all jumped into their normal size and weight, and the sword blade was now protruding a foot beyond its scabbard at her back. The silk half-cape unfolded into wings and flapped awkwardly in the spinning air. Features she had not known, such a triangular blades hidden in the forearms of her gloves and the toes of her boots, jumped into being. A newly discovered snorkel absurdly flapped past her nose.

She had the presence of mind to fire the wirepoon into the statue of a saint as she fell. The wire yanked her arm and slowed her sharply, but then the wire shrieked and snapped in half.

Ami fell onto the awning, bounced, hit the awning a second time, and fell to the ground. Throwing stars and spilled arrows fell to her left and right, making a sad, small sound like metallic raindrops.

She rolled to her feet and flung aside her wings and belt, snorkel and bowcase, and anything else tangling her limbs or slowing her movements. She left the gear without a glance and ran toward the sound of hoofbeats.

Down the alley she sprinted, listening. She could see no horse or steed, but the clatter of hoofbeats was loud and unmistakable. It grew louder, passed right before her face, and receded back the way she had come, heading toward the brightly lit street.

Elfine called out once more, woebegone, frightened, and uttered a smothered squeal from her nose, as if her voice were muffled. The sound grew faint and distant.

Ami ran and ran. Eventually, she came out of the alley and into the broad avenue.

Here were normal-looking people walking in the evening, faces drawn and glum, eyes down. There was the motionless traffic, beeping and bleating. Ami drew down her mask and clicked through the different bands of vision her lenses afforded. The main street was too bright and too hot: she saw a confused blur of images. She raised the mask and grabbed for where her binoculars should be: her fingers brushed her waist where there was no belt. She looked left and right. She shouted Elfine's name again and again.

The humans plodded past, ignoring her.

Elfine was gone.

4. *Missing Person*

Shaking with fury and blushing with shame, Ami returned to the alley between the cathedral and the dance studio and began to collect her gear.

She had been sure something would have been stolen or rolled into a stormdrain or something, but everything was there. It took only a few minutes to fit everything back into place. The longbow and short sword folded once again into their impossibly small shapes. She donned her cape, which was content to fall as silk.

What had happened? Elfine had warned her that shining the light from the flashlight setting of the ring might have this effect. But Ami had seen no light. Could it have been something done by the black knight?

She looked at the Ring of Mists. It was a combination she had never seen before: the metal was white, but the face had half-lidded eyes, which had been the weightlessness symbol. Perhaps it was broken. She drew it from her finger. The metal darkened to pewter. She let go of the ring. It hung in the air without falling. She returned it to her finger, twisted it once clockwise, once counterclockwise, and once clockwise again. Now it was white, and the face was calm. Ami felt no eyes on her.

She returned to the next alley over, the one separating the dance studio from the hospital. The electrical wires were on the ground, buzzing. Three dead wolves were on the ground. Ami frowned, disappointed it had not been more. Ami went through the pockets of those with human clothing, finding nothing, not even lint.

She carefully drew three tracking devices from her utility belt and jammed them far down the throats of the three dead beasts. Then, she recovered her arrows, hunted around, and recovered both boomerangs. One was covered with blood. The other one was lodged in the brainpan of a fourth wolf larger than the others. He had fallen headfirst into a trashcan in the open lot behind the hospital, and his legs jutted pathetically up into the night air. She had to reach into the can to pry her boomerang free.

She was unwilling to summon light from her ring, so she drew the flashlight from her utility belt. She peered into the trashcan. His human face had changed in death to a long lupine skull of a wolf, which, for some reason, she had not been expecting. She could not reach his mouth, so she placed the bug inside one of his open wounds.

In the shadows above the street lamps, she found a high perch on the skull of an ornamental gargoyle protruding from the wall of the dance studio. It seemed an odd architectural choice for a dance studio, but perhaps this building had originally been part of the cathedral next door. This position allowed her to watch all four wolves, the alley, the empty lot, and the still-buzzing wires.

She toyed with the ears of her mask until she heard the steady beeping from the homing bugs. She found to her embarrassment that all along there had been controls inside the mask, meant to be worked by teeth or tongue, which could rotate the eyelenses through their various settings or control the ear radios.

Her instincts or buried memories had failed her. Ami felt another stab of shame.

There seemed to be no screen or dial which would have allowed her to get a readout of the bearing and distance from the bugs or a way to display it on a scrolling map. A modern phone could have performed such a convenient function or more. Ami wondered why elfin gear—assuming it was elfin hands that had made this supersuit for her—was more inconvenient to use than human technology.

The realization slowly and relentlessly seeped into her thoughts that her worry over her friend had tricked her into rushing in too quickly, when it would have been better to stand back, examine the situation, and avoid any confined area were she could be flanked or surrounded. She could have used the infrared setting to spot the wolves hiding by the alley mouth or the wolf-man in the doorway who had jumped her.

Ami cleaned her weapons, threw away a useless length of wire, and restrung the wirepoon spool.

Chores done, she knelt on the high perch in the dark night air, breathing slowly and calmly, accepting her failures, reviewing her errors, and resolving her will until it was clear and hard like a polished diamond, of which there is no harder stone.

Her breathing slowed. She watched and waited, without fidgeting or sighing, as silent and terrible as a pool of undisturbed gray water beneath the motionless ice in which a man is fated to drown.

Chapter 7

Wolves and Shadows

1. Hunting Blind

Ami thought that whoever had sent the wolves to watch the hospital would wish to avoid both the attention of the humans and the attention of the elfs she had been told were the secret rulers of the world. Hence, the redcaps should be forced to act quickly, before either the power department, or the police, or whatever servants the elfs might send came to the scene. She assumed the owner of the dance studio, if no one else, would report the downed power line hissing in the alley behind the hospital.

She was baffled when, about forty-five minutes later, four workmen in a Con-Ed truck arrived and set up yellow cones and tape around the area telling pedestrians to stay away.

One man climbed the utility pole, shut off the power, and disconnected the damaged line. He inspected the transformer that had been splashed with fire. He marked the transformer with tape but left it in place. The damaged lines were wound onto a large wooden spool by a second man. The other two men stood smoking cigarettes, chatting, glancing from time to time at the dead wolves in the alley, and voicing quizzical bafflement but not actually being curious enough to go to look at them.

There was a conversation over the radio in the truck. The four men stood around idly for quite some time. Later, a supervisor in a car arrived. The supervisor stared for a moment at the dead wolf in the transhcan and then at the other dead wolves. He spoke to another man, who made a note on a clipboard. They both shrugged. Then, they drove away, first the supervisor and then the men in the truck, leaving the wolves where they were.

Ami wondered how often humans came across clear evidence that the world was stranger than any simple tale they had been told, but instead of questioning their simple tales, they doubted their eyes. She wondered darkly how much of the elfin dominion of men relied on men willingly acting just like the sheep the elfs held them to be.

Like the sorrow that touched her at the mere mention of a mother, the burning anger—bright as a sword—that flashed in her spirit then was an echo of her forgotten life. At that moment, she knew she was not a mere bystander, nor was she a servant of the elfs, she was firmly on the side of the Sons of Adam and an enemy of their enemies.

She set herself again to wait.

2. *Whelan and Phelan*

Ami cleared her mind of thought and her heart of desire. The chattering monkey-like thoughts of regret endlessly replaying her mistakes in memory were eventually quieted. Absurd and excessive doubts and fears came next, and then whispered thoughts of overconfidence, retaliation, revenge. Stillness and silence eventually prevailed. She waited. Somewhere far above the lights of the city, the cold stars turned.

At midnight, two wolves came into view, moving furtively. One limped, putting no weight on his left hindleg. The other moved his head strangely, hesitantly. When he put his nose near the wolf in the trashcan and sniffed, the light from a passing car crossed his visage. He was blind. Both wore red caps on their narrow wolfish skulls. Both sported a white owl's feather.

The two wolves circled the area, noses to the ground.

The blind one said, "The one we seek. She was here."

The lame one looked up. Ami knelt where she was, motionless as a shadow, as the wolfish yellow eyes peered upward. He said, "She sat in a bricked-up window and shot. Then leaped across the gap to the electrical box."

The blind one said, "We've already circled the building. She came out of the cathedral, crossed the roof, fought here, and went into the courtyard. There, the trail ends. Perhaps she flew up into the air."

The lame one said, "She cannot fly."

"Oh? Say so much to Ghid Goborchend, mighty in battle, whom she plashed like a tub of red ale across the roof next door."

"Winged Vengeance flies. Not the sidekick."

The blind one merely snorted in derision.

The lame one said, "Whelan, come! Let us take the shapes and shadows of men, and find a way to the roof, and find the scent."

Ami, listening, knew that the wolves could not fail to find her if they did that. However, deep in her icy calm, she did not stir, but waited.

The blind one said, "No, Phelan. Speak no folly. We would be nude, and you cannot walk. And what if she has conjured the mist and turned herself invisible?"

The lame one said dubiously, "Perhaps we could catch her scent through the mist, by some good happenstance, or stumble on her."

"You think to find the unseen and hidden things by some good happenstance?" The blind one lowered his voice. "There are easier ways and darker powers. Thursday is not the sole voice which speaks for the Supreme Anarchists' Council. What of Sunday?"

The lame one, Phelan, shivered and crouched.

The blind one, Whelan, sniffed. "What? You balk?"

"I sold myself because I was promised rapine, murder, and revenge against the haughty Sons of Adam. My soul is dark enough! Will you go down a mineshaft ever deeper? There is no way back! I still want a life in the sunlight once again, once my debt is paid."

Whelan said, "My eyes are gone. Why should I fear the darkness now? You are as lost to the sunlight as I, but I see truth."

Phelan shook his head and growled.

The blind one said, "No one wears the wolfpelt who has not killed wife or child, brother or best friend. Are you too fine and nice for our work now? A small ghost follows you, to be your judge on Judgment Day. How will you beg for mercy? Will you, perhaps, use the very same last words your little victim said in life? You mutter those words in your sleep. Do you hope to go to Paradise and sit at the feast table of the bridegroom, with all those you have wronged seated to either side, smiling, showing with pride the wounds you placed on them? Can you tolerate *their* forgiveness?"

Phelan lowered his head, lower and lower, as he heard these words, until he was prone on the ground, whimpering. He rolled over and exposed his throat. He said, "Very well, Whelan. Tell me what to do."

3. Necromancy

Whelan said, "Weave a circle thrice widdershins. Bow to the north, where Fenrir is chained. To the west, bow to Tigernmas, father of us all. To the south, bow to the Black Wolves of Krishna. To the east we look not: it is the dayspring and dawnlight, our foes. Say the secret words as you were taught, but chant them backward! Sunday's servant must appear."

Phelan walked in three counterclockwise circles about the two of them, dragging his lame foot, and then crouched and lowered his head in three directions. The words he spoke were horrible and seemed to burn his tongue because he spat them and yowled.

A spot of light appeared in the vacant lot. It was the color one sees when pushing a thumb into a closed eyelid, and it illuminated nothing. Slowly, it came closer. It came into the edge of the circle Phelan had traced on the ground, and there it stood.

Whelan growled, "Not enough! Say it again!"

Phelan whined, but complied, and spoke the words once more. He coughed, and blood was on his teeth.

Now by the edge of the circle stood a king in black. His skin was pale as paper. On his breast was a white and leafless tree. The black crown on his head smoldered with heat. His eyes were pits, his mouth a wound. On a chain about his neck hung the hunting horn that had earlier called the pack of werewolves.

"I am the shadow of the Hunter King. Who dares call me, I who know no rest, no ease, no peace?" His voice was less than an echo, less than a memory. Ami heard it in her head but not in her ear.

Phelan crouched in fear, shivering, but Whelan, who could not see, said, "I speak with the voice and authority of Sunday of the Anarchists. In his name you are called. Where is the one we seek? Is she here?"

The dark king said, "I was once as you are now, and I knew sun and sky and all the joys and pains of life. Soon, so soon, you shall be as I am, and my vengeance on you for this affront shall be fulfilled. Euhemerus Cobweb binds me, but a deeper chain binds him in turn, forged by his hand and fettered on his limbs, and soon the river of Hell shall claim him. Do not ask me to seek your prey, you who breathe the breath of life. It is unlawful."

Whelan said, "Anarchists defy all laws! Is she here? Is she nearby?"

"Do not ask. The price is more than you can bear."

Whelan growled. "I do not want your pity, shadow of a dead man! Tell me! I charge and compel you by the name you carried in life! Le Maudit!"

"Thrice I warn, and thrice the warning you refuse! Your fate is one you yourself, eyes wide open, choose."

The figure turned its empty eyes upward, and Ami felt the ring on her finger grow suddenly heavy. Her sense of calm was not disturbed.

Its eyeless gaze passed over her.

The apparition turned its empty gaze toward the wolves. "I see none here nor near, save you, whom now I very clearly see. The hour is at hand when you shall enter this dark realm of woe, and, as I am now to you, be subject thou to me."

There came a sudden wind down the alleyway, and rubbish and dust were thrown into the faces of the two wolves. Whelan stood still, but Phelan limped backward and stepped over the circle he had made.

The dark king smiled cruelly and vanished like a snuffed candle.

4. Ahemait the Devourer

Phelan, the lame one, glared at Whelan and snarled. "You fool! You damned fool! To spare yourself the bother and pother of climbing a wall, you thought it would be easier and quicker to call the dead! He gave us nothing! All bargains with the dark are cheats!"

Whelan said, "Silence, murderer! The shade of Le Maudit confirmed she is not nigh. There is no scent of elf or eft, one-legged Fomorian or six-fingered Nephilim, in this place. It is safe to call the rough, ungainly beast to clean the spoor away."

Both wolves trotted into the avenue, outside of Ami's range of vision and howled.

The churchbell in the cathedral next door tolled once; the peal rang out into the dark night air and echoed from the walls of the tall buildings all around. Ami wondered if this were some mistake. Surely an hour had not passed?

She looked down. A man in a white robe with a dark hooded cloak over it was standing in the alley. His hair was white, and his goatee was black. On a thong around his neck hung a crucifix of silver and ivory. His head was bowed as if he were inspecting the ground where the dark king had been standing; or perhaps he was praying.

The tap of nails on pavement came from the mouth of the alley. The two wolves came back around, one trotting and one limping. The man in the black hood was gone as if he had never been there.

Behind the wolves, a large truck approached. Its headlamps were off. A man in a black leather biker's jacket, smoking a cigarette, dismounted from the cab, and tossed two packages down, one before each wolf. He had the straight black hair, dark skin, and the harsh features of a Plains Indian. He wore no red cap, so perhaps he was human, but he had an owl's feather braided in his hair.

Phelan sniffed the package. "What's this, Cheyenne?"

The Cheyenne said, "Pants and shirt. You are helping. Stand up."

Whelan answered with a curse. The Cheyenne answered in turn by kicking the blind wolf in the ribs.

The blind wolf swore and snarled at him. The man said, "Who has Thursday's ear, dog? The name of Kuckunniwi is high among the Anarchists, and yours is lower than snake belly dirt! I did not have my butt kicked by a butt-naked frail chinky-chick and then sat licking my butt while my boss was tossed out a window into street pizza. Shut your yaps, whelps, and give thanks all is not worse for you. Thursday does not cotton to whiners and failures!"

Phelan opened his jaws to say something back, but the Cheyenne kicked him in the head. "Stand up! Stand on two feet."

The two wolves transformed. It was horrible to see. Both writhed in pain, snapping and rolling on the ground, and their limbs snapped and stretched back into human shape. Fur and claws were forced down beneath the skin, and the wolves howled as if needles and knives tormented their hide and hands. The wolf skulls swelled and distorted, pulsing atrociously. A cracking and grinding sound came from their bubbling flesh, as if skull plates and bones were breaking and reknitting. Both wolves yowled as their knees joints were bent backward and reversed to become human knees. The howls turned into human screams and curses.

The large truck now backed carefully up to put its tailgate across the alley mouth. The Cheyenne stood behind the truck and guided the driver with motions of his hand.

The driver, a black man with earrings in both ears, emerged from the cab. He and the Cheyenne lowered the tailgate. Inside was some huge living thing whose breathing was like a diesel engine hissing a deep and endless bass note.

The four men now took up long chains affixed to whatever it was in the truck. At the Cheyenne's command, they all heaved.

A huge creature, larger than a hippopotamus, came lumbering down the tailgate, shaking the truck on its shock absorbers with each step. Its skull was a flat, wide triangle, and the grin on the creature split its face all the way back to its tiny, round ears. Its head was more like that of a crocodile than any creature Ami could name. It throat was a pendant bag like the throat of a pelican. Its eyes were small and black and were surrounded by squinting rolls of fat. Short curved tusks protruded from the lower jaw. Its neck was a horseshoe of thick fur worn across its shoulders.

Its body in the front was like that of a great hunting cat, and its forepaws were those of a lion. But its rear parts were bulky, squat, and rounded like a hippopotamus. The hindfeet were toeless stumps, and the tail was long and wide like the tail of a brontosaurus, and it was held high to counterbalance the massive spatulate head. Its hide before was covered with a mane of fur, but behind was rough and scabby, and clumps of bristles peeped here and there.

The four men drove the huge beast out of the truck. It stomped awkwardly over to the corpses of the wolves. There, it lowered its wide, grinning head and squinted its piggy eyes in confusion, nostrils twitching. The Cheyenne cursed and struck the great beast with a goad, shouting commands. The vast mouth opened like the scoop of a steam shovel. The lower jaw was resting on the pavement, and the upper jaw tilted up to point at the rooftops. The men, moving quickly, crouched near the lipless jaws and shoved the corpse of the nearest wolf into the huge, red maw. It swallowed like a goose, by throwing its whole head backward while rearing up on stubby legs. And like a snake it did not chew, but brought the mass in its mouth down its throat whole.

The second wolf corpse likewise was shoved down the gullet of the vast beast. When the third wolf corpse was being crammed down the throat of the beast, the driver made a misstep and got too close to the jaws, so he was caught in the monster's teeth, and swallowed instead. His screams rang out from the creature's distended throat sack while the Cheyenne cursed the driver bitterly and told him to die without so much noise. They made no attempt to rescue him but shoved the third wolf in after. The fourth wolf was pulled from the trashcan and thrust into the great beast's mouth as well. The struggle here was hard and long, and the ungainly monster kept spitting out this final wolf because the body was a large as a pony.

The beast spent a moment licking up bloodstains, and then, reluctantly, snapping nastily and kicking at the three men goading it, the monster let itself be driven back up the ramp into the truck.

When Whelan and Phelan stepped toward the cab of the truck, the Cheyenne cursed and barred their way. "Thursday would have you recover the Ring of Mists. You saw the handmaiden of Winged Vengeance without her mask. She is a sidekick! A serving girl! Twice you had her in your jaws and twice she slipped between your teeth."

Whelan said, "The scent ends at the cathedral, which is a mighty stronghold of the enemy. Call the humans. Call the Sons of Adam, who can pass the thresholds uninvited, break the doors, and slay the priests. Are there no Norsemen? Are there no Paynim?"

The Cheyenne struck the blind man sharply in the face. "Find her! Saturday of the Anarchists already prepares the Nautilus to sail! Four kings fall, and mere anarchy arises to consume the world! Our day is nigh, but your bungling delays it! Seek no rest until she is found!"

From the cab of the truck, the Cheyenne drew out and threw down a wrapped bag of clothing, which burst open when it struck the pavement. It was the expensive skirt, blouse, and jacket Elfine had bought by fraud and loaned to Ami, which she had forgotten and left behind in the elevator.

"Here is spoor!" said the Cheyenne. "It smells new. Find the shop that sold them, find who bought them and find where she lives. Start here and search the damned city block by block if you have to!"

And with that, he climbed into the truck, and drove off.

5. Seek No Rest

Ami scowled beneath her mask at the sight of Whelan kneeling to sniff the outfit. The trail would lead back to the innocent girl Elfine had robbed.

Phelan uttered a curse, staring after the departing taillights and rubbing his lame leg. "It seems, for all that, we will need to climb to the roof after all." And he looked up, and his eyes just happened to rest on the spot where Ami was perched. The truck, as it was turning, turned on its headlights. They splashed against the opposite wall of the alley, and the bright reflection passed across her like the beam of a lighthouse. There she was: a dark and slender figure in a black cloak and grinning black fox mask.

He opened his mouth to shout, and she threw a *kunai* into it. The throwing knife was a black seven-inch barb, weighted and streamlined for throwing. It struck him neatly in the open mouth. Blood and screams gushed from between his teeth, but no words. She threw throwing stars into his chest, drawing blood and roars.

Whelan turned his head left and right, sniffing, knowing something was amiss but not what. He began to tear at his shirt. His teeth grew long, and his mouth and nose were pulled out of shape. The skin beneath was beginning to distort and darken and shoot forth clumps of hair.

Phelan, whether from boldness or mindless ferocity, did not run away but frothed at the mouth, spitting blood, and he hopped quickly toward the alley wall, dragging his bad foot, and threw himself at it, fingers and toes seeking handholds and footholds to climb.

She shot three arrows into Whelan before he finished changing into a wolf and four into Phelan before he had climbed fifteen feet. The weight of the bow meant that her shafts did not sink very far into their hides, but Phelan fell, and Whelan collapsed. She waited, looking down with cold eyes, as the wolves bled.

Phelan changed back into a wolf as he died. In his wolf form, the wounds were not the same size, and now he gargled, choking and spitting blood, but he spoke. He said, "I see Le Maudit! He is here! A whip is in his hand!"

Whelan said, "The girl sits aloft and watches us die! I smell her!"

Phelan groaned, "Call to her! She can fetch a priest for us from the cathedral to shrive us ere we die!"

Whelan rolled heavily over onto Phelan, clamped his jaws on his neck, and with one last effort, Whelan jerked his head and tore out Phelan's throat.

"Not so," gargled Whelan, his jaws full of Phelan's blood. "Damnation is better."

With that, he breathed no more.

Ami slid down a wire to the alley, carefully slit Whelan's throat with a *kunai*, and recovered her arrows. She took up the package of clothing. It fit into the pocket of her cape, which turned out to have had the same magical ability to fold objects into space without volume.

She stuffed two tracer devices down their throats as well. It seemed a methodical thing to do, but she turned the volume on those channels down to zero, so that this noise would not be confused with the feed from the other trackers.

Ami turned her head left and right, listening. The beeping from the tracking devices was audible. She was not willing to turn the ring to any darker shade than white. So it was on foot that she set out.

Chapter 8

Hunters and Trappers

1. Catoblepas Shipping

When she could, she cut through back alleys and avoided well-lit streets. When she could not avoid it, she jogged briskly down the boulevard, a dark-garbed and sleek figure against a dark background, drawing the occasional stare from late-night drivers.

The truck went south, down Lexington Avenue, and then cut west through Hell's Kitchen. The signal got dimmer as the truck got farther from her, but traffic came to a halt more often than she did, so the signal would get stronger again as she closed the distance. She lost the signal entirely when the truck entered the Lincoln Tunnel.

Ami saw no other way across the river. She turned the ring to make herself weightless and then turned it again so that a black mist thickened around her, and her shadow in the cone of passing streetlamps vanished. She felt the sensation of cruel eyes watching her, but she saw nothing nearby to make her afraid.

She discovered another strangeness about the ring: her weight slowly returned as the black mist covered her. It was as if the ring, with each turn, moved her deeper into the worlds of the mists, but made her weightless only when she was half in one world and half in the other. Her theory was that when she turned invisible, her visibility was not abolished, merely moved.

Perhaps this was why she was still visible to herself. Invisible, she was in the same world where her weight was stored, so weight returned. Why that should be, she could not even speculate.

She turned the ring to pewter, used the wirepoon gun to mount atop a traffic light reaching across the tunnel entrance, found a place to perch, and turned the ring iron-gray. Then, she selected a likely looking eighteen-wheeled truck, jumped down, and used two kunai to cling to chains crisscrossing the roof of the load the truck was hauling.

In Weehawken, on the other side of the Hudson, the beeping in her ears resumed as soon as the truck she rode emerged from the tunnel and came into the night air again.

She noticed from the sign that to go from New York to New Jersey was no toll, but traffic the other way was charged fifteen dollars. It was ten times the amount of Elfines swiped can of cola. Ami scowled, wondering how a penniless girl could pay such a fee.

For that matter, was it legal to cling to a passing truck? Was that some sort of trespass, or a free rider problem, or something?

It occurred to her that not even the slightest twinge of regret followed her slaying of Whelan and Phelan. Instead she felt a quiet jubilation of a job well done, particularly since she had slain them from a high and safe vantage.

Indeed, ever since those two men first had entered her hospital room, when she had crouched in the dark like a frightened child, unarmed and half-naked in a flimsy gown, a trace of lingering terror had been as close to her as her own shadow. Now that shadow was gone from her soul.

Ami was troubled by the thought that she had no idea what she had been in her past life. An assassin? A murderess?

Well, in any case, she was a trespasser now. There must be some law against from roof to roof. She found she could travel swiftly by lowering her weight to zero, propelling herself by using the unfolding longbow as a pole-vaulter's pole, and increasing her weight only enough to allow the glider wings to bite the air. She could sail hundreds of yards at the time using this method.

At one point she lost the signal entirely, and so she began a search pattern sweeping out an ever-larger east-to-west arc as she went south.

The effort was wearying. Time passed, and she was tired.

She found the signal again, and followed the steady electronic beeping in her ears. She entered a warehouse district near the wharves fronting the Hudson. Here were endless rows of dark, squat buildings and piled stacks of transport containers as uniform as children's blocks.

The signal led to one warehouse two lanes over from the wharves.

Ami circled the building twice, moving from roof to roof of the surrounding warehouses, and studying the frowning black walls with binoculars, infrared, and night-vision.

The sign over the entrance read CATOBLEPAS DISCREET SHIPPING AND TRANSPORT.

The warehouse was a rectangle. Two sides abutted its neighbors. There was a large yard in the front with a crane and truck bay, opening up to an empty, unlit road. The yard had stacked shipping containers sitting to either side.

There was a narrow alley in the back running straight as a ruler between the line of warehouses, a strip of pale concrete darkened with grassy cracks and decades of litter.

The skylights were lit with dim, flickering, furtive, and yellowish reflections. It looked like firelight, perhaps from candles or coals, not light bulbs. A putrid smell, like the fume of a tannery, issued from vents on the roof. The roof was circled with strands of barbed wire.

Its lower windows were covered with metal plates. Its upper windows were a smoked, semi-opaque glass covered with grills. The red gleam of burning lights inside could be seen, but only as smeared shadows. These orange reflections moved. Ami could not see whether someone was moving inside or whether this was an illusion caused by fires leaping and flickering.

Infrared showed heat inside the warehouse—perhaps of living things, perhaps of fires. Warm air escaped from vents, and warmth radiated from the windows.

She was too wary to approach. The tracking devices were definitely in the warehouse.

Across the road to the east was a similar truck yard with stacked containers and a warehouse equally dark, whose sign read MR. VEGETABLE and was decorated with a grinning cartoon carrot dancing with an asparagus in lipstick. Ami crouched, motionless, peering over the top edge of the Mr. Vegetable sign, watched, and waited.

Time passed.

She heard the main doors of the Catoblepas warehouse trundle open. It was utterly black within. The night-vision lens brought only a gray and fuzzy image into her eyes since there was so little ambient light. Something large was moving out of the main doors and down over the concrete lip of the truck loading bay. The infrared showed the heat outline of the hippopotamic beast she had last seen swallowing dead wolves. It moved slowly, sluggishly, across the yard. It stepped to the southern side of the truck yard and squatted. The stacks of containers on the south of the yard now blocked her view of the huge creature. She could see only its tail and hindquarters. It seemed to be walking in a circle again and again, like a cat padding down grass to sleep, but with slow and ungainly movements.

A noise came from behind the containers. It was partly a choking gargle and partly a deep, wet, syrupy eructation, as if a vast throat were trying to clear some obstruction.

Ami looked carefully in all directions. There was no motion, no noise, up or down the empty street. She debated whether to move or stay.

She saw that if she moved from behind the sign and jumped down to stand atop the piled shipping containers on the north side of the yard, she could have a clear view of the beast, but anyone looking out the windows in the warehouse would have a clear view of her.

She gritted her teeth, telling herself the risk was foolish, but also telling herself she had to find Elfine. Ami twisted the ring to summon the black mist.

The world turned dark in her vision, and the distances between objects seemed subtly off, as if the boxes and windows were no longer precisely at right angles at their corners, the dark telephone poles no longer quite upright, the lanes and alleys no longer quite straight.

Shadowless, now she leaped to the top of the stack of containers standing at the north side of the Mr. Vegetable truck yard. She struck the top container without noise, rolled, and came to her feet in a crouch.

The beast did not look up. She could now see the beast was choking and puking. Three dead wolves were lying on the concrete in a heap before him, their fur coated with spittle and half burnt away by digestive acids. Even as she watched, he vomited up a fourth wolf, larger than the others, from his distended throat.

Then, the beast crawled in a circle around the corpses, pausing every three steps to bang his lower jaw into the ground. There was something nightmarish about the awkward slowness of the motions, as if the monster were in pain or being pulled by invisible strings against its will.

Ami wondered what these strange doings meant.

2. *The Captain*

A dapper man dressed in an ostentatious Cossack uniform like something from the Napoleonic era now came swaggering out of the doors of the warehouse. He had more braids than a band leader or a doorman.

On his head was a shako of wolf's fur; over one shoulder was a half-cape adorned with braid. Silver buttons were on his tunic and silver buckles on his boots. A pistol was holstered on one hip and a saber sheathed at the other.

His paused to light a cigarette, and in the glint of flame, Ami saw his face: handsome and lean, with a mustache like two crooked boomerangs and a tiny triangle clinging to his lower lip. One side of his mouth was slanting up, and the other slanted down, and his eyebrows crooked in parallel. He had captain's stripes on his sleeves.

The great beast pulled itself with a painful motion to twist its head and turn its piggy eyes toward the Cossack. The man gestured nonchalantly to the great beast with his cigarette.

The great beast bowed to the man and continued its painful steps.

Then, stopping to pant and groan, the great beast hunkered down on its belly. It opened its great jaws wide and wider until its nostrils were pointed at the zenith. A light flickered in its throat. Small and pale balls of illumination, like the glints of marsh gas that deceive lost travelers in a swamp, issued from its mouth.

The spots of light circled, hovered, and hesitated, and then each one landed on one of the wolf corpses. The dead bodies trembled, and the half-burned fur rustled and shook. The dim orange firelight reflected in the upper windows of the warehouse grew bright, and the fumes from the vents now began to pour out a black and oily smoke, shot with angry red sparks.

The Cossack now knelt and took a fiddle and fiddlestick out of a black case, tucked the instrument under his chin, and began to play. It was a shrill, strange, haunting set of chords, drifting from note to note without seeming to form a tune. Yet at the same time, it sounded half-familiar.

Ami was not sure what she had been expecting, but a man in a cavalry uniform from a century ago playing the violin at the small hours in an empty warehouse yard was not it.

The strings seemed to sing of the artic winter, the shine of the northern lights on snow, and the delight of sneaking down from famished hills at midnight, where no game is, and finding a farmer's croft, where soft and frightened sons of men await to be torn and eaten.

The corpses were twitching in time with the violin music, and the dapper Cossack was dancing in the empty truck yard. He stooped and kicked and kicked and stooped, an energetic jig, dancing with his knees bent in the Russian style. His saber jumped and banged against the ground. His eyes burned as brightly as the tip of his cigarette, and his grin was as bright and white as Elfine's.

The corpses now began to twitch and jump, and their eyes opened.

The Cossack spun on his toe, twirling and playing furiously. Now, he began to laugh an insane, joyful laugh, and the smoke from his mouth made circles around his head.

Ami stood, her binoculars at her eyes, trying to see more clearly, wondering what was going on. Aloud, she muttered, "Who *is* that?"

A cold voice behind her said, "Thursday of the Supreme Council of Anarchists."

3. The Stumble

The cold voice rang strangely, for she could hear it in her head, but not in her ears, as if the words were being carried to her eardrum through the bones in her jaw. But it was a voice she had heard before. "He is Lucien Cobweb, son of Lupus. It is he who set this trap for you."

She turned. Behind her was a dark king whose crown was burning on his brow. His eyes were empty pits. The heraldry on his coat was a leafless tree.

He said, "I saw you clearly when you cloaked yourself to make your form unseen by men, at the tunnel, but I could not cross the running water and come to you then. Now you are here. Open your mouth, and I will enter you."

Her first reaction was to untwist the ring from iron to pewter. But the dark figure was but an inch behind her, opening his eyes wide, and bending his face toward her face, as if he meant to touch her eyes with the darkness in his eye pits and force her to see what was inside them.

Her second reaction was to strike, but when she did, her fingers passed through nothing but icy air, her hands went numb, and her limbs shook with a terrible, primal fear.

When he stepped toward her and off the edge of the container stack, her feet also left the edge. He did not fall but stood in the air. She fell.

Down she went, but only at half speed and landed on her feet. The four dead wolves were now alive again, breathing, and growling, and their fur was rustling, creaking, and growing over their cracked and wounded skin. They were in a circle around her. She could not feel her fingers.

Thursday threw his bow and fiddle in the air, apparently uncaring of where they might land, and gave Ami a courteous salute. "Thursday, at your service, miss! Charmed, you surely are!"

Ami felt a moment of grateful relief. A talkative one! She jerked back her head to retract her mask.

The Cossack wolf-whistled when she showed her face. "Are you not a delectable little thing! I could simply eat you up!"

Because she could not use her fingers, she thrust her numb left hand into her mouth and with her teeth, twisted the ring from pewter to white.

"Simply gnaw your lovely pink flesh and suck dry your bone marrow!"

She looked up. The dark king standing in midair was no longer visible to her, and, she hoped, nor was she to him.

"Allow me to introduce the pack and the future rulers of this city. We will keep the humans to snack on. Don't fret!"

A half-dozen wolves came from behind the roof vents. The exhaust had hidden their body heat from her infrared gaze. A dozen more wolves now slunk out of the main doors of the warehouse, and with them was the Cheyenne, carrying a compound bow and quiver, and four other bowmen with him. They were dark-eyed men with hard, sculpted facial features. They wore jeans and leather jackets and had feathers in their hair.

She was not sure if touching the dark king had permanently damaged her nerves. But she still had partial sensation in her hands, for the white ring felt warm and heavy on her finger.

A second and third group of wolves now came from out of the containers, which were unlocked, and formed a line across the street to the north of her and to the south.

There were six to one side of her, six to the other, and four immediately circling her, plus six on the roof, eleven in the yard with the great beast, and the Cossack, Thursday, grinning, hands on hips, was standing on an oil barrel. A final wolf had carefully picked up the dropped fiddle in his teeth and was casting about, looking for the fiddlestick.

The Cossack kicked both feet in the air so that his rump came down on the oil drum with a bang. "Now! What shall we discuss?"

4. The Message

Her mask was up because she needed her peripheral vision to watch the wolves circling her. She did not turn her eyes toward the Cossack, who had no weapon in hand, and seemed not the most immediate threat.

He had one of the tracers she had left inside the corpse of a wolf. He was flicking it up in the air with his thumb as a man might flip a coin, tossing it and catching it, tossing and catching, over and over.

He said, "Let us discuss matters of life and death. What is life? It is clear enough that God created the world out of mere spite, to have creatures to torment. But torture is no fun if the victim lacks some false hope to prompt her to struggle and scream. You follow me?"

Ami bowed politely, not trusting herself to speak. Had she met this frightful, crazed, smiling man before? Did he know who she was? Any wrong word might betray something crucial.

He spread his arms in a theatrical gesture, eyes turned upward. "All souls yearn for goodness, yet life forces us to do evil. We are spirits trapped in the flesh of beasts, and the beast in us must triumph. So the sadism of Heaven commands!"

As she bowed, she casually put her arm behind her back with the same motion and reached for a throwing knife with her numb fingers. She groped, brushing the knife with the back of her knuckles.

"What is the answer? How to find happiness in a world where the laws of nature say we must be beasts? The bold answer is to kill that part of ourselves which seeks anything high and noble and human. An elegant solution! By indulging each cruelest impulse and vile desire of the flesh, we find the only true rebellion; hence the only true freedom; hence the only true artistic expression of man. You see?"

Ami realized that he was not rolling his eyes upward as the theatrical gesture. She stole a glance up.

A number of white owls on silent wings were flying down and landing softly on the roof of the building above and behind. They stared down with unwinking eyes as bright as brass mirrors.

"Death is real. Death is what all art aims at. All true poetry is throwing a stick of dynamite, not just at living things, but at the idea of life itself!"

Little sparks of light crawled over the owls, and they became women, pale faced, cruel eyed, and beautiful, in feathered white cloaks and feathered headdresses with charming wands in their hands.

The Cossack saw that Ami had seen the owl women, and so he hopped from the oil drum and drew his sword. "Ah, you do see! Your escape over the rooftops is cut off; you are outmaneuvered, outnumbered, outwitted, and out of hope."

He had been speaking not, as it seemed, merely to hear his own voice, but to distract her long enough for the lid of his trap to be fitted in place.

"Now, how would you prefer to begin? Deflowered first or dismembered first? Think it over since sometimes one wishes the meat before the pleasure, but at other times..."

She tried again to draw her knife, but her numb fingers betrayed her. The *kunai* fell from beneath her cloak and clattered loudly on the pavement of the street.

The Cossack stopped, his mustache twitching. The wolves circling her froze in place, as if surprised by the unexpectedly loud noise. Their noses quivered, lips drew back, heads lowered, and ears lay flat.

Then, the Cossack stared at the dropped knife in disbelief. He threw back his head and laughed so hard his cigarette flew from his lips and landed behind him.

"Why!" he cried, "That was… really… are you still trying to *fight* us? Oh, puh-lease! Take off running. Pick a direction. Like Heaven, I will grant you false hope to help torment you. I'll give you a ten-second head start! My beasts need exercise."

Ami said, "Lucien Cobweb, I have a message for you."

"Ah! So the little teen vixen can talk!" His grin slanted sideways, and his eyebrows slanted the other direction. "A message? From Winged Vengeance? Do tell!" Then, he pouted. "Wait… How did you discover my name?"

She said, "Let all the Twilight folk know that when eternal day breaks, twilight is no more, and all deeds will be laid bare and judged."

His eyes grew wide in shock. "Who told you that? Who told you to tell me that? Who? It's a lie! It's a damned lie!" He whirled and shouted at his wolves. "Tear her to bits!"

Ami shouted, "Who wants the Ring of Mists? Here it is! Whoever takes me takes it and takes Lucien's place!"

Lucien shouted, "Wait!" and his wolves, trembling and crouching in anticipation, hesitated at his command.

She held up her fist, turned, and threw something past Lucien Cobweb's ear. He turned his head. A small, round, bright metal object clattered off the side of the oil drum behind him and went skipping off into the dark.

"Fetch!" she called.

Several of the wolves pelted after it, and then, seeing their brothers run, and greedy for the ring, more wolves broke formation and ran toward the northern part of the yard. Lucien turned his head to follow the bugging device she had tossed. "Wait! Stop, you fools! The ring is still on her fi–!"

While his head was turned, Ami took a running leap and launched herself into the air, uttering her piercing *kiai* as she did so. Lucien snapped his head back around just in time to see the side of her high-heeled boot catch him under the chin and strike his neck with the full force of her body.

Of course, her body was only five-foot-two and ninety-nine pounds. Lucien staggered back with a cough, grinned, struck her knee with one hand, took her ankle in his other hand, and threw her to the ground. She could not use her hands to cushion the blow. The wind was knocked out of her lungs, and a dazzling darkness danced in her eyes.

Lucien opened his mouth and screamed a mindless scream of rage. His teeth elongated, and his skull was pulled out of human shape. His clothing did not rip, but grew misty, changing into a colored fog and vanishing. His transition into wolf-shape was much faster than what Ami had seen his packmates do: it was done in an eye blink. The scream had changed into a howl. He fell to all fours, and by the time his hands touched the ground to either side of her, they were paws.

He was bigger than the other wolves, and his pelt was the rich and handsome silver of an arctic wolf. His forepaws were on the concrete to either side of her, pining her in. All the wolves howled with him, and the owl women screamed.

Despair overcame her. Whatever spirit it was that enabled a man to fight to the bitter end and beyond, with no hope of victory or survival, when she sought it in herself, it was not there. She had failed entirely! Hot tears stung her eyes.

Ami did not even raise her hand to defend her throat. She merely turned her head aside so that the wolf would not see her tears, and she waited for death.

When she exposed her throat, instead of striking, the silver wolf grinned the same slanted grin his man-face used, but then his ears pricked up, and his head swiveled.

He whispered, "What is that? Who is it? Who dares?"

Ami heard a trumpet blow.

Chapter 9

The Sign of the Swan

1. The Cavalry

Horncalls blowing echoed through the wolf howls. The wolves lowered their ears and tails, some whimpering but others snapping and barking in fury. The owl-women on the roof shrieked thin, high shrieks and swirled their cloaks, leaping into the air. The huge, ungainly beast reared up, bellowing.

Lucien raised one forepaw, ignoring the girl trapped under him, and stared down the dark street. Noise, howling, and commotion were coming from somewhere just beyond the stack of shipping containers on the southern side of the yard.

With her hands numb, Ami could not grip and turn her ring, and when she tried to flick her wrist to bring the wirepoon gun out of its quickdraw holster, nothing happened.

Ami did not try any precision strikes with her numb hands. Instead, she knee-kicked the silver wolf in his groin, with one leg then the other, and kicked with both legs into his ankle joint. He howled and fell to one side. She rolled to the other, driving her elbow like a pick-ax into the wolf's temple. He snapped at her, seizing her elbow with a grip like a beartrap, strong enough to break her bones. By sheer mischance, however, the elbow pad in her supersuit inflated in his mouth and tore loose of its fastenings. Ami rolled and came to her feet while Lucien choked a moment on the expanding wedge of fabric in his mouth. He spat it free.

The horn sounded again, and now came the sound of drumming hoofbeats, as if iron-hard hooves were pounding divots out of concrete. Lucien glared at her, but the noise of the horn made him turn his head.

Other wolves were more intent on her. Three jumped her. She leaped in the air and kicked one in the chest so that he landed to one side of her and failed to knock her over. But two of them grabbed her arms, one set of jaws clamping each wrist. The fabric of her suit stiffened and creaked under the pressure of those jaws, so neither arm was ripped off, but the pain was terrible, and she screamed as she twisted to strike the wolf on her left with knee and boot, and then with an ax-kick as she brought her leg back down. The wolf snarled in annoyance, yanked its head, twisted her arm, and forced her to her knees.

She cried out, more in fear than pain, knowing she was helpless before the monsters.

At that moment, a tall figure, armored head-to-foot, and riding a monstrously tall, muscular roan-red steed came pounding down the street like a thunderstorm, and the cloud of debris from the concrete exploding under the steed's hoofs was like a sirocco. The mantle of the knight flapped like vast white wings. The plumes of his helm in the night gloom shined like fire. The steed was as heavily armored as the rider, with a chamfron on the head and a crinet on the neck, a peytral on the wide breast of the horse and flanchards and a crupper to side and rear.

Wolf howls and owlshrieks erupted. The knight rode directly into the midst of the thickest pack of wolf-monsters and trampled and slew them. His lance dipped lightly as a willow wand and stuck with all the weight of horse and man, skewering one wolf after another. Then, he was past them, and the wolf corpses were tossed into the air from the fury of his passage, and the lance was red, wet, and smoking with blood.

The magnificent horse leaped into the air, graceful as a deer, while the astonished wolves below raised their muzzles and howled in awe and fear. The shadow of the huge steed passed over Ami, and she looked up, her face pale and eyes wide. The caparison of the steed spread like wings. The golden spurs on the heels of the knight caught the light and shined like red comets.

Directly atop the wolf gripping her right arm, the steed landed with all four hoofs, like a pronghorn stag trampling a serpent. Blood sprayed everywhere. The sound of bones breaking was like the noise of a tree tossed down by the wind, with every branch snapped in half. The wolf on her left arm released her, raised his maw, and vomited a stream of liquid fire toward the knight. The stream splashed off his shield.

He raised his terrible lance and gored the wolf through its burning mouth and throat. The horse neighed and reared. The knight raised the corpse on high with effortless, superhuman strength and tossed the great wolf—as large as a pony—off the spear point and a dozen yards through the air.

In the light of the fire clinging to his shield and spear, Ami could see the play of diamonds sparkling in his white armor. There was a white swan on the blue field on his surcoat, with its wings spread. The crest of a swan was above his brow, and jutting up from his temples were shining swan-wings of bright silver.

The horse neighed angrily. The knight said softly, "Yes, I know it is she!" The rearing horsemen turned his head toward her. His helm was a single piece, with a Y-shaped opening in the front where the gleaming of his eyes could be seen, the glint of his grimace. She thought the bright helm was skull-like and terrifying.

The steed came down again, landing his forehoofs on the broken body of the werewolf he had earlier trampled. The clash of the steel barding on the huge steed was like thunder.

Then, the knight shouted over the clamor of the howls and shrieks, "Little thief girl, flee this place! These dark matters are not for you! You have spoiled one clue leading us to the City of Corpses: spoil no more!"

It was a boy's voice—a teenager, perhaps no older than herself.

She shouted up at him, "What have you done with Elfine?"

"Oh? What have *you* done with Tomorrow? Avaunt this place!" He raised his shield as arrows from the bowmen standing on the loading dock let fly a volley. The arrows bounced from shield, armor, and barding alike. He steered the horse with his knee to place himself and his steed between her and the bowmen.

The Cossack leaped up into human form and onto the loading dock. His costume and gear solidified out of a cloud of mist around him. He turned and raised his pistol. But at the same moment, the dark gray wolf—the same one who had been guarding the violin case—now leaped on the man from behind and, with his jaws, tore the gun from his hand.

The gun went off, but the bullet missed the knight. Instead, there was a noise too loud to be heard, and a gush of hot wind as sharp as a blow across the skull, and the all the upper windows of the Mr. Vegetable warehouse exploded outward in a shower of glass. Balls of red flame poured out and then columns of black smoke after. Alarm bells rang. The owls scattered. Whatever it was that the Cossack's pistol fired was no bullet but had the force of dynamite.

As the dark gray wolf landed, stolen gun in mouth, he stumbled over the lip of the loading dock and fell to the concrete of the yard. His wolf pelt came off. Beneath, he was a dog, not a wolf. He had a white chest and snout, black ears, and bright eyes with circles like a raccoon mask around them. He was barking furiously, nose high, inordinately proud of himself. One owl and then another stooped down out of the black sky and clawed at his face but both of them missed.

The knight shouted, "Bad dog! Bad! You could be killed! Get out of there! Get Matthias!" To her, he turned and shouted, "Flee, miss! I shall defend you at the peril of my body, even if I die for it!"

Ami turned but she saw no direction in which to run. Several of the wolves were still circling her, hesitating, and she could not get her wirepoon gun out of her glove. She dodged one wolf who lunged at her, kicking him in the head. The others hung back, trying to get behind her.

The Cossack was staring at his bleeding hand in confusion and shock. The knight saw him, lowered his lance, and charged. The Cossack's head jerked up at the sound, his eyes bright and fierce. As before, the Cossack's splendid uniform turned into mist and vanished, and a large arctic wolf, rearing on hind paws, was in his place.

The steed's hoofs practically flew across the concrete of the yard, kicking up gouges. The silver wolf howled and leaped headlong through the air toward the knight and his deadly lance, but then the Cheyenne and two other men in leather jackets, dropping their longbows, tackled the silver wolf in mid-leap, knocking him aside, and a smaller black wolf leaped at the charging knight and threw itself bodily on the lance, sacrificing its life without hesitation. The lance was fouled, and the silver wolf was pulled by his loyal minions back into the dark doors. The Cheyenne shouted a command.

The rough necrovore reared up and grinned with its crocodile mouth, and came rushing to battle. The speed of the charge was horrifying. It seemed unnatural that so huge a beast could move so fast.

Ami saw this and screamed in fear, seeing the gigantic beast rushing on the smaller figure of the knight. The boy in armor was sure to be killed! Fortunately, she had seen the speed of the huge red steed; the horse would no doubt carry the lad out of danger.

Instead, as if life and limb meant nothing, the knight shouted a battlecry, "For God and Arthur!" bent over the horse's neck, lowered the lance, and rushed at an insane speed directly toward the vast beast.

All the wolves and owls, as if frozen, paused and stared. The great beast reared in fear as the lance darted toward its piggy eye. Instead, the shaft entered the breast where foreleg met ribcage, seeking the creature's monstrous heart. The lance shaft sunk a yard into the blubber of the monster's flesh and was torn from the hand of the knight as the tall red steed thundered past.

The beast, out of control, now trampled a line of wolves too stunned with fear to leap aside. Their bodies were scattered under the massive, galloping elephantine feet, and the other wolves yowled and fled, leaderless.

The knight drew his sword and shouted, "For Arthur! For Christ! For the Last Crusade!" The sword blade gleamed like a mirror in the gloom, wonderfully bright. And the knight set off charging after the beast. The first wolf who leaped toward the knight, he stabbed, and the sword blade erupted into bright fire, throwing shadows all along the street, and drawing reflections from all windows nearby.

By that light, in the distance, Ami saw a young man walking down the middle of the street about two blocks away. His head was bowed, and his steps unhurried. In one hand he held a book, and in the other, a candle in a candlestick.

2. Bell, Book, and Candle

As the beast rushed away and the knight thundered after in pursuit, most of the yowling wolves went rushing after the knight. The few who stayed here were circling her, their heads low, ears flattened, snarling.

She fumbled again at her belt. With her numb fingers and unresponsive hands, she could not feel which holster snap, pouch clasp, or knife handle was which. She threw down a trio of miniature grenades, which began spitting greenish-brown gas. She tossed her head to bring her mask over her face. The filters engaged automatically, and the neckpiece of her suit sealed airtight with a sharp hiss.

The tiny grenades must have been built on the same principles as her suit pouches and holsters because the volume of gas that erupted was more than seemed possible. The cloud erupted and filled the street. Her night vision was blocked, but the cloud was transparent on infrared wavelengths, and she saw the low, quadruped shapes of the wolves dancing and gyrating madly at the edge of the spreading gas cloud, trying to escape it.

Their noses were perhaps more sensitive that human noses because half of them started to stand up and take on human outlines: but these shouted and screamed even more loudly than the wolves howled, for they had no fur to protect their naked skin.

Ami ran as quietly as she could toward the edge of the cloud where the heat-shadows of the wolves were farthest apart. But there were still over a dozen wolves in the street and owls overhead despite those who had fled to chase the knight.

A wind from the river passed down the street, and the green cloud began to sink. Ami's fingers fumbled at her belt, hoping she had one more gas grenade left.

Now only a hundred yards away, she could see the boy with the book and candle more clearly. He was a young man in rimless eyeglasses with a narrow face, solemn, and grave. His hair was long, falling almost to his shoulders, and his garb was black from neck to heel. Ami was certain she had seen him before.

He was reading from the book:

...let them be excluded from the bosom of our Holy Mother Church in Heaven and on Earth; let them be excommunicated and anathematized and judged condemned to eternal fire with Satan and his angels and all the reprobate, so long as any refuse to burst the fetters of the demon, do penance, and satisfy the Church. You are delivered hence to Satan to mortify your body, that your soul may be saved on the Day of Judgment....

He then dashed the candle to the ground, saying, "So be it! So be it! So be it!" Closing the book, he drew a bell from inside the pocket of his long, dark coat, unwrapped a handkerchief from its mouth to free the clapper, and rang the silver bell with a long, high, solemn sweep of his arm.

Ami looked up. The owl women were in full flight, vanishing in the distance. Ami felt her hands tingle with pins and needles as sensation returned. Able to manipulate her fingers once again, she wasted no time but twisted the ring to pewter, shrugged the wirepoon gun into her palm, and swung quickly up to the roof of a nearby warehouse, one that was not smoldering with fumes. From there she swung to the top of a telephone pole, which gave her a good view of the street. She shot arrows into the wolf nearest the young man with the bell, and then the next nearest, and so on, until the wolves fled.

She saw brightness one street over and heard a commotion. She was eager to talk to the boy with the bell and question him, but she did not want to stand by idly while the knight was killed by the giant beast. Half-weightless, she leaped from rooftop to rooftop.

Ami landed on the roof a boathouse directly fronting the river in time to see the great lumbering beast leap from the end of the wharf and dive into the river water. Again, the ungainly beast was surprisingly maneuverable in the water, and it arrowed downward into dark depths. The lance was still sticking into the monster, and blood was trailing it as it dove.

The knight pursued it to the edge, burning sword dazzling brightly in his hand. Ami felt sorry for the lad, who was no doubt disappointed that the monster had so neatly escaped him.

Without hesitation the great red steed leaped a prodigious leap into the air, and man and rider plunged into the dark and cold waters, and were swallowed. Ami's jaw dropped. She had not realized that knights committed ritual suicide like samurai.

Then she blinked in disbelief. It was not suicide after all. She saw the light from the sword moving under the water. Whether the horse was swimming or running along the muddy bottom, she did not know.

But the knight did not give up the chase. The burning light from the sword moved into deeper water and dwindled in the distance, moving downriver toward the sea.

Ami stood, watching the water and hoping the knight might reemerge; but time passed, and the river flowed.

3. Arson

She returned to the Mr. Vegetable warehouse. She was surprised to see firetrucks and firemen already there, hosing down the smoking building. She was not surprised to see the young man with the bell, book, and candle gone. No wolves were to be seen.

However, she was more surprised—but perhaps should not have been—to see the warehouse directly opposite the Mr. Vegetable also on fire. Flame poured from the upper windows of the Catoblepas Discreet Shipping warehouse, and oily black smoke rolled endlessly out into the night.

She was still getting beeps from her bugs, which were still somewhere inside the warehouse. However, as the flames spread, the signal stuttered and stopped. No doubt the metallic parts of the tracking devices melted. The warehouse roof collapsed inward on itself.

Someone or something had cleared the wolf corpses away, taking her arrows with them.

Ami crouched in the shadows atop a roof not far away, scowling beneath a smiling fox mask. "I owe someone my life, and I don't know his name. He is the one who took Elfine unless there are two medieval knights on red horses galloping the streets of New York and New Jersey after dark on the selfsame night, which I doubt. I don't know my name. I've lost Elfine, and I have spent three mini-grenades and lost four arrows and one throwing knife, none of which I know how to replace."

Her stomach rumbled. She also had no money and no friends and no way to get a meal or a place to sleep.

Chapter 10

Werewolves and Elfs

1. Perplexing and Confusing

Ami found an all-night coffee shop run by a little old Korean man who rested a shotgun on pegs above the chalkboard where his daily menu was written. The shotgun may or may not have been loaded, and may or may not have been legal, but the two cops sitting wearily near the door of the shop were treated to free coffee, and perhaps they thought that such a weapon on display was what allowed the shop to remain open at hours when all others were locked up behind iron grates.

The officers stared when a young Japanese woman in a skintight dark catsuit, black thigh boots, and opera gloves walked into the coffee shop, her mask tucked under one arm. The cool wind of the hour before dawn gusted just as she opened the door, and her cape billowed. Both the officers, a young man and an old, had red hair. She wondered if they were Irish.

Both stared at her hips as she walked by. She was not sure if they were merely admirers or if the knives and weapons in her belt were obvious.

Ami asked the old owner if she could use the lady's room.

Inside were two stalls, a changing table, and a sink. She took out both her kimono decorated with foxes and moths, and the suit of expensive and tasteful American clothes obtained by fraud.

She set them on the countertop, one to either side of the sink, and looked at her herself in the mirror. Without Elfine around to cast a glamour, Ami did not look as pretty as she had before. Her eyes were puffy with tears and weariness. Her face was pinched with anxiety.

She looked down at the lovely kimono. If she wore that on the street, anyone seeing her, Irish or not, would notice and recall. She knew she had enemies. She did not know their numbers or tactics or long-term goals. But whether they were few or many, with agents on every street, she did not know.

Even the underwear Elfine had given her was too expensive. It looked too nice to be underthings: it was a black lace one-piece garment of a type Ami did not recognize. It might have been a bustier, or it might have been a leotard. It covered more than most bathing suits. In fact, it was more modest than what Elfine herself wore.

Wearing the kimono would, at least, be honest, assuming it was actually hers. But how much did it increase her chances of being caught? A little? A lot?

Was wearing the expensive clothing Elfine had pilfered for her excused by the nature of the emergency in which Ami was trapped?

But that question could not be answered without some way to weigh the gravity of the wrongdoing on the one hand versus the gravity of the danger on the other. It was true that if Ami remained uncaptured and alive, she had some chance of making amends for past wrongs to whomever she had wronged if she broke the law, but if she died, both she and her cause were lost.

That was a particularly painful thought since she did not know for what her cause she fought. The knight who abducted Elfine had called her a thief. And the gear she carried would certainly be useful to someone in that profession.

Ami looked in the mirror. The girl in the mirror had bright, honest eyes and thin, determined lips. It was not the face of a thief.

She spoke to herself quietly, watching the lips move on the face in the mirror. "Someone built this suit for me. It is well crafted—a work of genius. Someone trained me. I almost heard his voice in my ear when I first woke. For what purpose? What mission?"

A bewildered shrug in the mirror answered her. "I don't remember."

The girl in the mirror's lips moved as Ami said softly, "What if it was for an important purpose? A mission? A cause?"

She scowled. "I am hungry and all alone. The mission is forgotten. The cause is misplaced. If I cannot remember it, I cannot serve it."

"A misplaced cause is not a lost cause!" she said to her reflection sharply, "Just because you have forgotten what purpose you serve does not mean your life is purposeless!"

She sighed. "It does if I don't know what to do! Elfine might have been a scatterbrain, but she always had a plan."

But her face in the reflection was confident. "Someone is relying on you—someone in trouble like Elfine, but forgotten. Can't you feel it?"

She said, "Maybe so, but I don't remember who is relying on me or for what."

But the words she had heard in her dream—if it had been a dream—when first she had woken in the hospital room returned to her. *Let not the soul of thy beloved be drawn into darkness.*

But who was her beloved? A family member? A teacher? Elfine?

She looked at the ring on her finger. Was she married? Or engaged? Perhaps her beloved was husband, or fiancée. Who had given her this ring, and why?

To answer her, there was nothing. Her amnesia was a blank blackness in her soul, saying no words, revealing no past.

She saw herself straighten up in the mirror. She squared her shoulders. "Does that mean you can fail him? Let him down? Let him die? Whoever he is, someone needs your help. You are on a case!"

Her doubts answered. "And if I turn out to be merely a thief or an assassin, or if the suit is not mine? What if there is no mission, no case?"

The girl in the mirror shrugged. "There must be. That knight told you to get off the case, didn't he?"

"That means there is a case. And…"

"And?"

"And Elfine said that whenever someone tells you to get off the case, *that is when you don't*!"

She nodded, and the reflection nodded with her. "I am glad we agree. What is the next step?"

The look of determination on the face in the mirror was not as good as having Elfine come up with ideas, but it did help because, now that her mind was clear, the next step was clear as well.

2. *The Next Step*

She put on the expensive but normal-looking stockings, shoes, blouse, skirt, and jacket. Her supersuit and gear she could stow in her cape pocket, which she then carried draped over one arm as if it were a folded raincoat. Rather than return through the coffee shop and be seen by the officers, she retreated through the kitchen to a storeroom and then into a back alley.

She twisted the ring to iron, yanked it off, watched it turn clear as glass and vanish from sight, and then put it carefully back on her finger.

Hitchhiking might have been illegal in New York, but it was not as illegal as cheating the toll, and it was much more comfortable than clinging to a truck roof.

She stood by the roadside with her thumb up and smiled, and was picked up at sunrise by a sixteen-year-old boy driving a sixty-year-old VW bug.

Her worries about having to come up with a story turned out to be nothing. The boy was a talker. He told her of his past and his hopes, said he was working as an intern in an experimental theater group in Manhattan, and told a confusingly elliptical story about some sort of appliance or application having to do with cellphones or smartphones, which segued into his analysis on the growth and decline of an interpretive jazz dance artist, whose career he was debating with an anonymous user. He recited the brilliant points he had made in the argument and spoke of how he would use the pain he had suffered to improve his stage craftsmanship. Then, he complained about his girlfriend, or ex-girlfriend, who may have been the debate partner, or the dancer, or both, or neither.

Ami rode in the passenger's seat, smiling politely and nodding politely, not taking her eyes from him while contemplating what blows and holds would be most effective when fighting a man strapped into a parallel seat, with a low roof and dashboard limiting motion in every direction, should he turn into a monster.

He did not turn into a monster. Instead, no doubt encouraged by how her gaze had not left him, when it came time to drop her off at the Nineteenth Precinct building on East 67th, he jumped up, circled the snub nose of the car, and held the passenger's door for her. He asked her for her number, and she told him it was forty-nine. While he blinked in confusion, she thanked him and walked quickly away.

The precinct house was a four-story building of red brick and white granite cornices. The windows were arched, and two lanterns burned on either side of the arched door.

A metal detector whistled at her when she entered the door. An officer had her remove her shoes, and he waved a hand-held detector up and down her body while she held her hands over head. He stared at her a moment, smiled at her, the young, pretty and harmless-looking girl, and then waved her on by.

There was almost no one in the waiting room at this early hour. A janitor was mopping the tiles. A drunk was sleeping in a chair. There was a woman in uniform manning the front desk. Ami approached and bowed. The policewoman's eyebrows went up.

Ami said, "I wish please to speak with officer Dom Damiano."

"And you are…?"

"Hanako Yamada." It was the Japanese version of calling herself Jane Doe.

"And why do you want to see Lieutenant Damiano, Miss, ah, Yamaha?"

She bowed again, "It is about my sister. She is missing. She is about my height and weight—we are close enough to share clothes. At the hospital I was told the lieutenant was the man who found her. I would like to find out if he has any additional information about where was she found."

"Did you file a missing person report? I can have someone take down your statement. If you would just fill out this information…" She passed Ami a clipboard and form.

The form asked for all the information she did not know about herself, starting with her name, address, mailing address, place of work, father's full name, mother's full name, mother's maiden name, home number, day number, emergency number, cell number, driving license number, voter identification number…

While she might have been willing to tell one or two innocent lies in a good cause, she knew she would look foolish and be caught immediately if she lied about something she did not know what it was. Answering all the questions about numbers with forty-nine might lead to immediate suspicion. And what was SSN? It had nine blank spaces to be filled in, but the form did not indicate whether these were letters or numbers.

Ami bowed again and passed the form back, "I am so sorry. I cannot read or write English. May I not simply speak to the officer?"

"Lieutenant Damiano is not on duty today. That information is so we can contact you when he gets back on duty. And if you have information about a missing person, you really should give us a statement so that we can find her. It's very important that you cooperate."

The policewoman stared carefully at Ami's face. She continued, "I can have someone help you write down your information and statement. You do want Lieutenant Damiano to be able to help you?"

Ami said, "I am sorry to trouble you. Did he leave a written report I could see?"

The policewoman spread her hands, "That would be up to him or the captain. Usually, we don't share information about ongoing investigations with the public, especially those who cannot read English, but seeing as you are family, I am sure something can be arranged. Now, tell me how to spell your name, Miss, ah, Yamoto, was it?"

"I am so sorry." She bowed again. "I don't know how to spell it in Roman letters. It means mountain ricefield."

The policewoman's stare became hard and flinty. "It would be written on your driver's license, miss."

"I am so sorry, I don't have one of those."

"Your library card."

"I am so sorry. I am not from this country."

The policewoman looked her up and down. "But you shop here. Do you have a bank account? A passport? No?"

"It is missing."

"Miss, if your passport has been lost or stolen, you are required to report that. What exactly was your sister doing before she went missing? And why didn't you file a missing person report?"

"I– ah– was ill in bed and could not come here."

"And where exactly is this bed? Where are you staying?"

"I don't know the name. It was a friend's apartment. In a tall building."

"Honey, we have a lot of tall buildings in this town. Does your friend have a name?"

"Elfine Moth."

"And where is he now?"

"She."

"Where is *she* now?"

"She is gone. Away. Gone away."

"So. Your sister is missing, your passport is missing, and your friend is missing. Do you know anyone who is not missing?"

Ami was unnerved, so she bowed again, unable to think of anything to say.

"Miss, sit down right there. I think you should speak with one of the detectives."

Ami nodded obediently and sat down, folding her cape over her hands, and placed them in her lap. She waited until the policewoman turned back to typing. When the janitor left and there was no one else in the room except for the sleeping drunk, she felt for her ring. She twisted the invisible ring on her finger twice clockwise and twice counterclockwise. A dark mist rose up and surrounded her.

The lights in the room seemed dim and distant, and the walls no longer seemed quite parallel or perpendicular to each other. The sounds echoed and lingered strangely.

Ami rose and quietly walked out of the waiting room. The eyes of the officer manning the metal detector at the door did not focus on her. She stood by the door, as motionless and silent as a tree until someone came in. He was a yawning fireman from the Hook and Ladder company next door, carrying a box of doughnuts, and calling out a cheery good morning. Ami slipped through the door behind him as it was closing.

3. He Hath the Strength of an Unicorn

Outside, on the sidewalk, there was a crowned lion sitting on one side of the precinct station, shining like gold. To the other side, shining like the moon, was a bearded unicorn, larger than a stallion and more graceful than a stag.

The unicorn turned its head toward her. "In the wilderness, in whose hand is the keeping of the law?"

Ami froze in shock. The voice was like the sound like floodwaters rushing.

The lion said, "The keeping of the law is in the hand of the king!"

His roar was the cry of a brass trumpet. Ami knelt, clutching her ears.

The unicorn said, "And who shall keep the law while the king sleeps?"

The lion said, "Let the thief catch the thief, and let the vigilante avenge the blood, that when the king wakes, he shall spare you."

Ami in terror threw herself on her face, cowering. She twisted the ring on her finger from iron to pewter to silver, and the thunders of the voices fell silent. She looked up. The apparitions were gone.

A messenger on a bicycle rode by, staring at her lying face down on the pavement, but he said nothing.

4. Werewolves and Warehouses

Her first idea had been a dead end. But she was not out of options yet.

It was an eight-block walk from the police precinct to the hospital—about a third of a mile. She looked with envy at the buses and taxicabs crawling slowly by and wished she had money.

As she walked, she reviewed the conclusions formed in her mind ever since her intimate heart-to-heart talk with herself in the mirror.

The warehouse that had been burned down had been a false lead meant to trap her. The real headquarters was elsewhere, a place the truck bearing the necrovore had stopped.

There, the wolves had been removed from the belly of the beast and inspected, and her bugs had been found by the Cossack during the hour while she had been following along on foot. The corpses had been re-swallowed and the necrovore reloaded on its truck to be carried to New Jersey, with a ghost posted at the tunnel to see if she followed.

She decided that, at least for now, there was no point in looking up other offices of Catoblepas Discreet Shipping. While it was possible that the arson was meant to destroy records or equipment they wanted no man to see, it would cost them less merely to burn some stranger's place after breaking in to make it look as if their headquarters were gone. She decided that if her other leads ran dry, she could return to this one in case her guesswork was wrong.

Why select a warehouse? Obviously, they thought a warehouse would lull her suspicions. This meant they thought she should be looking for a warehouse, not some other kind of building.

So where was the real one?

Since the wild goose chase had led her out of the city, chances were the real warehouse was between the hospital and the river along the route the truck had taken. It was no doubt where Whelan and Phelan would be brought since the necrovore was still busy being chased down the Hudson River.

When she arrived, Ami saw that the alley between the dance studio and the hospital was empty of wolf corpses. Whelan and Phelan were gone. It seemed the anarchists were getting quicker on the uptake or more thorough.

Ami smiled, glad she had been thorough, too.

5. The Third Trace

She took out her utility belt, opened the belt buckle, and studied the radio controls hidden there. There were three tracer reception channels turned to zero volume. The belt tabs holding the tracers were numbered, as were the channels. Two channels belonged to the bugs hidden inside Whelan and Phelan.

The third was labeled zero-one. She had no memory of dropping that tracer. It must have been from before. Something from her previous life.

As she hoped, the radio gear was meant also to be used with the mask off. She found skintone-tinted earphone buds that fit neatly in either ear to relay the signals the mask received even when the mask was hidden in the cape pocket.

She followed the stronger first: the signal for Whelan and Phelan was coming from across the street and two blocks south. She saw the sign of the Cobbler's Club on its awning. It was, by now, almost a familiar place.

She circled the block to confirm that the signal was coming from that building. A sign in front declared it closed. No lights gleamed. The doors of the loading dock in back were shut and locked. Through an upper window, she saw what seemed to be a large dog staring out at her.

From the window of a taller building across the street, she used the binoculars from her utility belt to study the roof of the Cobbler building. There were two men on the roof, either taking a smoking break or standing watch. There was activity at midmorning: a large number of dogs, more than a dozen, were taken out by several young women for a walk in Central Park. At noon, a score of young, smiling beauties marched out of the main doors and down the street, attracting stares and whistles. Apparently, some of the showgirls or waitresses lived in a dormitory in the building. This miniature pageant traveled two blocks over to a spa and fitness club called Equinox. Two hours later, they marched back. At three o'clock, there was more activity: rear doors were unlocked, and a mixture of hard-faced men and pretty young women began arriving. Presumably, they were the kitchen crew, waitresses, bouncers, barkeep, and so on. At four o'clock the front doors were opened, lanterns raised, window drapes drawn back, signs lit, and so on, and the establishment was open for business.

Ami thought it might be too bold to join the line forming at the door to get in and go to the club, especially as she had no money. The signal from the two tracers had not moved or dropped during the hours of her patient vigil. And the mystery of the other lead was nagging her: where, or on whom, had she placed a tracer, and why? Or—it suddenly occurred to her—if she had not planted the tracer, where had the prior owner of this supersuit done so?

Chapter 11

Desecrate Ground

1. The Church of the Transfiguration

It was after midnight when she abandoning her watch over the Cobbler's Club. Ami walked down Madison Avenue, following the signal from her former life. She was tired, and hungry, and had no fare for bus or subway. The ache in her stomach reminded her that the last time she had eaten was breakfast the previous day.

On she walked. The night sky was invisible, washed out by signs and skyscrapers, and endless vertical rows and ranks of light. The air seemed warm and close despite the early season and the late hour, and the tall buildings on either hand were like the walls of a box. The hard-faced crowds on the street seemed surlier than before, and the bleating and honking street traffic ruder.

She found an open-air shopping courtyard, a semicircle of stalls with vendors crying out the virtues of their wares, surrounded by a hedge and tucked between two buildings. Here, beneath a tree, was a roofless booth for taking photos. No cameras and no clerks seemed to be paying any particular attention to it: Ami ducked in, changed into her skintight black suit, and donned her utility belt. The weight of her weapons on her hips was comforting.

She shot her wirepoon up into the tree, twisted her ring to pewter, and lifted herself out of the scene like a Greek actor portraying a departing god. From the tree, she swung to the roof of the nearest low building, and from there to a taller building.

She heard the voice of one little boy cry out in delight and awe as she threw herself lightly through the air, but if anyone else saw her, no cries followed.

Just the physical pleasure of soaring through the cool night air, far above the streetlamps, was exhilarating.

From roof to roof she dove and swung and flew, weightless as a dream.

North of Madison Square Park, she came upon an area where there were no lights. The concrete ended. Neighboring buildings loomed over a square of cedar trees and rosebushes. Midmost were several buildings, deserted and dark, connected by unlit gray walkways. The only light came from the sign on the locked gate of the spearpoint fence. Ami held up her binoculars to the lenses of her fox mask.

NOTICE: This building is unfit for human habitation; the use or occupancy of this building for human habitation is prohibited and unlawful. It was signed by the Building Inspector.

There was a smaller sign beneath the first.

Know all men by these presences that the buildings, grounds, and fixtures of this facility are deconsecrated, desanctified, desacralized, and fit for profane use alone. No further remains will be received for interment. No dead may come. It was signed by the Ordinary and the Bishop.

She put the binoculars away, frowning under her mask. What did it mean when ground was no longer sacred?

No dead may come. That ominous phrase, oddly enough, was cheering to her. Perhaps the ghosts would stay away.

The signal was coming from the fourth story of a Gothic edifice of soaring arches and frowning gargoyles. Ami swung to the steeple. She landed in the shadow of a peaked roof. Dark spaces where bells once hung gaped like toothless mouths.

She stiffened and looked upward, startled. A trio of hooded saints with drawn swords stared down at her with blind eyes. Ami relaxed, seeing that these were statues. She slid down her line to a ledge before an open window. The right-hand sash of the window was a latticework screen carved with images of ravens battling wolves. The left-hand sash hung down crookedly from a wide iron hinge cast in the shape of a grape leaf.

She twisted the ring back to white, to make herself, she hoped, invisible to ghosts. Weight returned.

She checked the window frame for tripwires and electric eyes and saw nothing suspicious. In she slid.

2. The Eight-Walled Chamber

She landed on a carpet. Dust rose into the air. With a quiet hiss, the mask sealed hermetically against the neckpiece, and bottled air from some hidden oxygen supply tickled her nose. Apparently, the supersuit was paranoid about airborne particles.

The chamber was octagonal, paneled in dark wood, taller than it was wide. Above was an eight-sided wooden dome, heavy with shadows. The wall behind her had arched windows at shoulder level covered with wooden shutters. Rays of light from the skyscrapers and streetlamps shined through the gaps in the carven window screens like a host of spears, held in parallel ranks. The rays were visible, if faint, in the dust of the air.

Opposite was an arched door with a glass doorknob. The facets of the glass glimmered in the dim light like a miniature moon. Against two walls were cabinet doors. Against the third was an old-fashioned roll top desk, but no chair. In the middle of the room was a small table next to a standing lamp. A phone sat on the table. It was an old-fashioned rotary phone.

She stepped over to door and opened it. Behind was a brick wall.

The green shadows she saw through the light-amplification goggles were confusing. The thin and parallel strands of dusty light from the carved window screens made an incomprehensible pattern of bright and dark rectangles across the obtuse angles of the walls and the door. She was not sure what she was seeing.

She doffed the mask, stepped over to the pole lamp, and, with a click, turned on the light. She blinked at the open door. The brick wall was still there. She ran her hands over it and knocked on the bricks. They were firm and solid.

She opened the first cabinet door. Behind was a panel of solid wood. The second cabinet door also held nothing but a blank wood wall. There were no cabinets behind the cabinet doors.

The roll top desk was next. The wooden slats rolled back. The desk was empty. The pigeonholes, nooks and drawers were bare.

Ami slowly turned in a circle, looking at the blocked door, the missing cabinets, the empty desk. Her eyes narrowed. There was no way to walk in or out of the chamber, and there was nothing in the chamber. It was like the set of a theater stage. What did it mean?

She knelt. She ran her fingers along the bottom of the table. Eventually, she touched something the size and shape of a dime. She inspected it without touching it. It was the missing tracer from her utility belt. That led to a next question: why had she put this here? It was not an eavesdropping device. A tracer was used to track a moving target.

Had she wanted herself to return here? If so, how had she known, before it happened, that she would lose her memory?

Not knowing why she had put it here in the first place, she left the tracer where it was.

A metallic noise, loud in the quiet chamber, erupted an inch above her head. It was as startling as a firecracker.

She somersaulted toward a safe corner of the eight-sided room, her back to no window, drawing her sword. The white blade snapped open to its full size as a *kodachi*. She crouched lightly, one knee on the floor, her fist before her and the blade parallel to her forearm. Her other hand, by instinct, without thought, had drawn three throwing stars and held them between her fingers, arm cocked back, ready to throw.

It was the phone. The noise was the phone ringing.

Her eyes narrowed. The phone ring did not cease. There was no answering machine on an older phone.

She stood, sheathed the blade and throwing stars, and stepped toward the table.

Her eye fell on the lamp, which she, of course, had lit. Her eyes moved to the windows, which, of course, were not opaque.

She stepped and peered out from between the carved wooden image of an angry crow pecking at the eyes of a lunging wolf. From which window, balcony, or roof of the two or three buildings in her line of sight, a telescope was trained on this window was impossible to say. The sensation of being inspected without the eyes of her observer being visible was the same as being watched by a ghost.

She breathed in through her mouth and out through her nose. Man did not control fate; fate controlled man. Desire was an iron chain; detachment was freedom. Only if her heart were as motionless as the dead center of a turning wheel could she act without hesitation and abide the outcome without regret. Only by desiring neither life nor death could she act without fear.

Hence it was without the slightest tremor in her hand, without the slightest quaver in her voice, that she picked up the phone and spoke, "Here am I."

"Meet me at the top of the Empire State Building."

Click.

It had been an older voice, a man's voice. Ami stood with the phone in hand, eyes wide, motionless with shock. After a moment, the dial tone came on the line.

She had heard his voice before. Something within her knew it.

Your bones are more easily broken. Your heart more easily frightened.

It was the voice of the master who had taught her how to fight.

3. Graveyard Shift

The Empire State Building was within eyesight and within walking distance. Ami swung from roof to roof until she landed on the Langham Place Building. There was no one on the rooftop at night. She changed into her civilian clothing, and picked the lock on the elevator, which she rode to the street level. From there, she walked two blocks.

The idea of climbing up the outside of the Empire State Building was one she dismissed. Visible, she would be too easily seen by men, and invisible, by ghosts, peering out from any window of the surrounding skyscrapers or up from the surrounding streets.

Even at midnight, there was a line on the sidewalk to get into the lobby to the Empire State Building. She overheard someone in line mention that there were four more lines inside to queue up in: the lobby elevator line, the ticket line, the express elevator line, and the observation deck line.

The door to the lobby was equipped with a metal detector. She remembered the metal detector at the precinct house had sensed her many metal weapons even when all were folded into the mist and hidden in her cape. Ami decided this was not the way for her.

She saw a plaque listing the visitor's hours. The observation deck was open until two in the morning. She walked all the way around the block the Empire State occupied, taking special note of back entrances for deliveries and the like. The underground ramp leading to the delivery entrance was behind a gate observed by cameras.

Despite the lateness of the hour, a truck came down the alley. When the truck passed her and she was between it and the wall of the Empire State Building, she was in a spot no eyes could see. She twisted the ring sharply to black and hopped on the tailgate of the truck as it slowed down to enter the ramp.

She found herself in an immense warehouse, stacked with crates and containers, with its own parking garage staffed by a fleet of trucks. The midnight shift apparently had a full crew manning it: there were dozens of workingmen down here.

There was one moment of tension when she dismounted from the truck. The driver saw her in his rearview mirror and called out. But when he threw open his door and leaned out, his eyes could not see her crouching an arm's length away.

There was also a large plate glass window separating the invoice desks from the loading dock and no way to cross without passing in front of it. She walked on by. One man, who was carrying an Art Deco brass sink on either shoulder, saw her in the reflection and turned, saying, "Hold on, sweetcakes, you ain't allowed to be…" But his naked eyes deceived him as she moved quietly past before his puzzled face.

No more cameras or workingmen saw her. No alarm was raised.

She found a supervisor's office, which conveniently had a private stairway leading up to the freight elevators. In the stairwell, she doffed her civilian clothes and donned her supersuit. As the snug, almost-living fabric embraced her, and the weight of the weapons was on her hips, confidence filled her.

The freight elevator doors were locked with key cards, which she had no way to pick or force. Therefore, she merely waited, silent as a fox, unseen in a corner of the corridor until two clerks in overalls, pushing a hand truck hauling a pallet of mail bags, opened the freight elevator for themselves, and, unknowingly, for her.

The elevator grumbled and shivered and rose. As they passed the sixty-sixth floor, one of the clerks turned toward the front of the elevator, where she was standing and, looking right at her, said to her, "'Tis an ill hour. The graveyard shift is unchancy. This tower is unchancy."

He was redhaired and freckled. His name tag read O'KEEFE.

Ami held her breath, wondering if he could really see her or if he were merely standing so as to face her way.

The other clerk, who was dark haired and dark skinned, muttered a sullen answer, "You're cracked." His name tag read LEROY.

"Six brothers alive elder than me at birth had I. My dad, six brothers living his elder had he. You know what that means?"

Leroy said sourly, "It means you are cracked."

"Five men went down into the grave to raise this building up. One was smeared flat by a truck. One was clobbered by a hoist. One was when a blasting cap misfired, and he was blown into the air. One fell down an elevator shaft. One from the scaffolding was plucked off by the wind. I hate working in this building. I hear black wings going past the windows."

Ami shivered, not precisely sure what this conversation meant, but not liking it. She wondered if speaking of the dead would summon them. But she dared not turn the ring to white and become visible to these living men. She was trapped in the elevator with them.

Leroy said, "You cannot hear the color of the dang feathers. There is no such thing as your wingy-thingy crow-man."

Ami's eyes grew wide. Crow-man? What did that mean?

The doors ground open. Ami vaulted upward, swung her legs up, and clung to the crossbraces of the roof of the car.

O'Keefe followed her with his eyes as she moved. He tugged on the bar of the hand-truck and carefully stepped under her, his eyes on her.

The two young men maneuvered their hand-truck beneath her and out the door. The red-haired one, O'Keefe, was still staring upward and still talking. His words held the solemn, fierce tone of someone who knows he is not being heard. "Winged Vengeance is real. The Fair Folk—that's what we call them in case they are listening close by—the Fair Folk walk among us, unseen, unheard, bent on their unknown business, fighting their silent wars, harvesting souls for Hell."

The doors closed. She was alone.

4. Observation Deck

Ami found and opened the emergency panel in the elevator car roof. A twist of the ring and she was visible again, but weightless. She resolved not to turn invisible again: it could not be a coincidence that O'Keefe had warned her of the ghosts haunting the building.

A flick of the wrist brought out the wirepoon pistol. With the softest hiss of noise, the grapnel soared overhead up the elevator shaft.

On the sixty-ninth floor, Ami clung precariously to the inward side of the locked elevator door. In the pitch blackness, she examined the lock with her ultraviolet flashlight and mask-goggles. The lock was meant to keep out intruders from the other side, not this side. It was easy enough to slide her cape hem around the latch, to stiffen the fabric to metal-hardness, and to yank the latch open.

At this hour, no one was on this floor. She picked the lock to a law firm, and entered. To her surprise—she had been planning to cut the glass—the windows could be opened and shut. She supposed the building had been raised before the invention of air conditioning.

She dialed her suit hue to a gray to match the brick of the building. Up she climbed, weightless as a wraith and quick as a fleeting shadow, in a straight line up the column of shadow created by two columns of windows to either side of her.

The observation deck on the eighty-sixth floor was empty at this hour. Up she went.

The tower grew sharply narrower. The outside of the last ten floors was coated with lights. She squinted and blinked and climbed, dreadfully aware that any hostile observer could surely see her dark suit against the wash of spotlights, like a black fox walking on snow.

Above this, it was dark. She saw spotlights positioned to light up the mooring mast, but they were not lit.

The one hundred second floor had an enclosed observatory. Again, she saw no one, but a feeling of dread touched her heart as if with an ice-cold hand. This told her that the ghosts were here, staring out over the city. She twisted the ring to white and, more cautiously, now that she weighed a hundred pounds, shot the grapnel and climbed.

She rose above a knee-high railing. It seemed absurdly low, almost as if daring someone to fall over it. Here was a hatch originally meant as the disembarkation door for airships tethered to the spire. From this hatch, to the left and right, a small balcony circled the spire.

The wind caught and tugged at her. The sounds of the city so far below were inaudible. She felt the whole tower roll and pitch like a ship at sea, but she could not tell if this were real or her inner ear playing a trick on her.

The moon was bright and half full. The lights which, earlier, had been drowning out the moonlight, now were far underfoot. A high wind was pushing scraps of silver-edged black cloud across the face of the moon. It grew darker.

No one was here. The voice had said only to meet on "the roof." What part of the roof had he meant?

There was a ladder leading up to the spire, obviously for maintenance.

Up the ladder she went.

The wind blew the moon free. Like a galleon in full sail rounding the point of an island, the crescent came out from the cloud, and silver light spilled all around.

She looked up. A cloaked and masked figure was standing, dark in the moonlight, on one of the struts of the mooring mast, arms akimbo and legs spread.

She shot the grapnel around the stanchion of one of the many transmitter dishes festooning the mooring mast and drew herself up to a strut at right angles to his. Her toes were on a beam of metal no wider than her palm. A triangle of open air with a 1,400-foot drop below parted the two of them.

5. Karasu Tengu

The black mask covered his face and came to a sharp triangle like the beak of a bird of prey. The silhouette of the cloak as it was caught and flapped in the night wind was visible. It was parted in the middle, and the hems were scalloped like the wingfeathers of an enormous black bird. To her own surprise, she realized she knew it: it was a *hagaromo*, a feathered celestial robe.

She clicked her lenses from infrared to light amplification. In the infrared, he was invisible. Something in his suit made him the same heat-wavelength as his background. In the greenish hue of the light amplification, she saw the glint of his weapon harness beneath his cloak. Underneath, he wore a black leathery body suit of the same fabric and cut as hers. A Japanese longbow, a *yumi*, was visible peering over his right shoulder. The hilts of a Japanese longsword, a *daikatana*, was visible over his left.

She raised her right fist and placed her left hand over it, inclining her head slightly. She was mute, waiting for him to speak.

He was silent for a minute, then two, studying her.

She removed her mask and cowl and tucked them away into her cloak. Her hair was caught by the sudden wind. The braid had come undone, so her locks spread like a black cloud and flew like a streaming banner, whipping in the wind.

He spoke in Japanese. "Who danced for joy on the day of darkness, when all the spirits of Heaven wept before the stone that blocked the cave where light died? Who stepped forth when none other would go to confront the dreadful spirit that stood upon the eight-forked bridge binding earth to Heaven, and opened the way? Who stood watch before the sacred grail of Sarras, from whose rim the last sacrifice at the last feast drank the last of the wine?"

Her heart leaped. Her ears knew his voice. She knew she was his disciple and she owed him absolute loyalty. She dismissed the idea of attempting any deception.

She said, "If you are asking me a password, or a riddle, I don't know the answer."

"She whose shape and appearance you mock would have known. Why should I not kill you here and now, out of memory for her?"

It took her a moment to realize what he was saying. "But I am not dead! I am here, right before you! I am she! I am… I am…"

"Your impersonation of the faithful girl you mock is preposterously unconvincing. You do not even know her name."

"I am an amnesiac."

"Unlikely."

A sense of frustration boiled up in her. She had expected a friend and ally from her former life to save her, cure her, and make all things better. She had not expected disbelief, danger, and death threats.

She cried out, "But true! My memories are stolen, along with my life! An accident or black magic robbed me. I don't know what happened to me! But I know you! I know your voice! You saved my life!"

"Did I?"

"Your voice told me what to do when I woke up in the hospital. My memory of your voice. You trained my arms and my legs and my whole body to be weapons. I fought them off and escaped. Two werewolves and a goat-monster. Redcaps."

"Oh? Where are they now?"

"Who, the monsters? All dead. I killed all three."

"Did you weep for them after?"

She drew her head back in surprise. Ah. "No. Was I supposed to? They were stronger than me. I was glad to see them die."

"Did you see to it that they were properly buried?"

She snorted in contempt. "Ha! I left them for the crows to eat."

His shoulders slumped, and the raven mask tilted downward. He said in a soft voice. "Very well. I believe you are she. Fling yourself from this tower to your death."

"What? Why?"

He straightened again, but his voice was shaking with suppressed emotion. "Is it your place to question me? I have spoken. Kill yourself."

She said, "I cannot. There is one I have been charged to save."

"You swore to obey my every word."

She said, "All my oaths were washed away by the bright lady. Why do you want me to kill myself?"

He said, "Because I am too weak to kill you as I should. I cannot see your face without seeing *her*."

"Her? Who?"

"Her to whom we both owe the greatest loyalty."

Pain stabbed through her heart. "Mother. My mother. She's dead, isn't she?"

He nodded grimly but said nothing.

She cried, "I can feel the sorrow, but I cannot remember her. I don't know her name. I don't know mine. Or yours! Who are you?"

He said softly, "I am the eyes of the night. I am the swift and deadly arrowshaft that strikes from afar. I am retaliation. I am reprisal. I am Winged Vengeance."

She felt warmth on her cheek, the sting of salt in her eye. She wiped free the tears she discovered. In a hoarse voice she demanded, "Then tell me! Why must I die?"

6. Winged Vengeance

The dark figure said, "You must die because if you are not a mist-shadow or a sending meant to deceive me, then you are in truth who you seem."

"What happened to me?"

"You fell into the hands of the Supreme Council of Anarchists. None escapes them, except by death, and, even then, sometimes death is no escape. You are enchanted, either possessed by a ghost or mesmerized by a vampire. You serve them now: otherwise, they would not have set you free into the world. No doubt even now they climb the sides of this tower. More fools they."

"How can I prove my soul is mine?"

"It is a thing cannot be proven."

"Then how do you know it is not my own?"

"The Anarchists have no reason to allow you to know you are their slave. You are more sincerely convincing if you also are deceived. The ghost within you will act when needed."

"I am true!"

He shook his head. "I expose myself to danger merely speaking to you. It is sentimentality and unwise. But the ghosts of this tower fear my bow, and they can keep the Anarchists at bay for a time."

"There is no one to keep at bay," said Ami in a weary tone. "No one knows I am here!"

He made a curt, cutting motion with his hand. "We have but a few minutes to say farewell. If you are truly my disciple, for the sake of the blood and the vendetta we serve, you would know the dishonor you have done me, as well as the danger you pose, and take your own life."

"What dishonor? I fought the Anarchists. I do not serve them! I killed their wolves. I fought against Lucien Cobweb. Do you know that name? He is Thursday of the Anarchists. He set a trap for me at a place called Catoblepas Warehouse in Weehawken. They are moving in more and more monsters. They wear counterfeit red caps. The Anarchists are moving them into the world of men in numbers too great for the Black Spell to cover."

"Why?"

"They seek to break the Black Spell of the elfs and overthrow the secret rulers of the world."

"Were that truly what they sought, none would oppose them," he said bitterly. "Where are the monster being brought?"

She said, "I am not sure. Their Eater of the Dead hauled the corpses of the wolves to the Cobbler's Club on Lexington. Is that useful information? Do you believe me now?"

He shook his raven-beaked mask slowly. "Coming from you? I cannot trust the source."

"Could I not be exorcised if I were possessed?"

"Not by me."

"I saw a boy in glasses with a bell, book, and candle. Is he an exorcist? He was with a knight. And a dog."

"He is the Ghostly Father's novice. The horseman you saw was the squire of the Green Knight. I don't know the dog. They are what remains of the Last Crusade."

She wondered at the note of bitterness in his voice.

"What if one of them vouches for me? They fought the wolves and owl-women."

"I answer nothing."

"What are the Anarchists? Who are they?"

"We should not be speaking."

She said in a shrill voice, "They know who they are! They know you know because you are hunting them! They are also hunting me! Why not tell me? Even if I were possessed, what is the harm?"

He laughed softly. "You are my little Fox-girl, indeed. Put away your claws!" He drew a breath, and his voice hardened with hatred. "The Anarchists are foes of man and elf alike: the Supreme Council is a parliament of ghosts and undead, beasts and monstrosities, and everything that most despises its own soul. They are of the Twilight. They slew mine. I slay theirs."

A cold wind blew as he spoke, and his cloak lifted and waved, and the long strands of her hair whipped past her face.

He said coldly, "I see a strange look in your eye."

"Your eyes are sharp."

"I see by night as well as by day. Your heart is turned. You no longer serve me."

A sad shudder traveled through her. Yet she would not lie, not to him. That would be disloyal. She said, "The bright lady who spoke to me in a dream absolved me of all my oaths, or so she said. I am made anew."

"Dreams are elfin things and not to be trusted."

"She said I served Heaven."

"You serve the enemy! The stench of the forces of the Night World clings about you like an odor of blood newly shed."

Ami unwittingly fingered the white ring. She remembered the unwholesome smell the ring gave off when it turned to it darker hues. Was this black magic? Her instinctive desire to tell her master all things ebbed sharply. If he did not believe her now, there was no reason to add fuel to his skepticism.

But her sense of loyalty was too strong. If she was his true disciple, she would show him obedience even when she thought him in the wrong. Obeying only orders when it suits you is not obedience.

After all, this dark man was very likely the one, the beloved soul, the bright lady had commanded Ami to save from the darkness.

She said, "I have the Ring of Mists." She held it up.

The mask betrayed no expression, and neither did his voice. "So you were successful in your mad quest, it seems." His voice grew colder. "It is a seeming that does not deceive. The Anarchists would not have let you keep so fabulous a treasure unless you were their slave."

She closed her eyes and drew a slow, long breath, seeking calm. Knowing that her only link to her past life mistrusted her, and was about to slip away, was like a dark pressure on her temples.

She must resign herself to whatever fate ordained. Removing all desire would remove all disappointment, confusion, and pain.

With her eyes closed, she said in voice as bitter as his, "You are so certain I failed? Because you think I am dead, I hear your true opinion of me. Obituaries are honest, so they say." Her eyes popped open. "Quest? How did I come to have this ring? What mission am I on? Who am I?"

The raven mask turned down. He peered at the balconies and sides of the Empire State Building below them. His mask then rose as he scanned the sky. Nothing but stars, the crescent moon, and silver-limned clouds were overhead.

She said, "No one is coming. I would never betray you."

The beak turned back toward her. "One who is possessed or mesmerized never knows. Their tricks are cruel, and deceive even the wise."

She said, "I know I would have killed myself before I allowed myself to be taken alive into their hands! Have you no faith in me?"

He said, "I once trusted a man I never saw. He was my teacher and master and leader. Why did he never show himself? Because he knew we would die at the hands of the Anarchists. He led us to death! I alone escaped."

Ami felt a flame of anger in her soul. "And now the student is the master!"

Winged Vengeance said angrily, "What do you mean?"

"No faith he had in you; you have none in me. I recovered the ring and escaped the Anarchists."

"And how did you do that?" And she heard in his tone of voice that he was asking how she accomplished the impossible. She squinted, pursing her lips. Perhaps he was asking how she accomplished what he could not.

She said, "I don't remember. Some wound or dark magic took my memory away. You are so certain that I failed?"

"I followed you. I saw you enter the Tower of Glass. You could not have escaped alive."

"Perhaps I did not. The bright lady said she restored my lost life. At first I thought that was a way of speaking. But it was literal. I was dead." Ami began shivering and could not cease.

"You are no ghost, no dead flesh revived by dark science, no vampiress."

She said, "Those things are hellish mockeries of what Heaven promises."

The dark figure squatted and rested his elbows on his knees. Now more than ever he looked like a black raven perched on a wire. "Heaven is far away, and only a deadly silence answers prayers. No miracle revives the dead once they die."

"Yet here I stand, alive!"

"You were released after being altered to their will."

"Why so sure?"

"The sleepless eyes within the glassy tower watch in every direction over the flat and blasted heath, and there is no hidden approach."

"But I was in this tower?"

"The Thirteen Treasures of Lyonesse are kept there. You tunneled in from below into to a labyrinth. There, you were trapped."

"What happened?"

"You were outmaneuvered, played for a fool. Unbeknownst to you, you carried with you a shadow door."

"A what? How did I carry a door?"

"I told you their tricks were cruel. It was one of those ancient, elfin doors, the doors of shadow, that allow one to pass in one step to any proper threshold. It opened behind you, giving a path to the Anarchists. Out poured their battalions, creatures who could not have otherwise faced the power of the elfin lords in the bright shadow of the glass tower."

The dark figure stood, and the hunch of his shoulders, the stance of his feet, was like a frown of anger. "Do you understand your folly, girl? I forbade you to go! You defied me!"

"I would not do such a thing!"

"And yet you did! From my position halfway between worlds and dreams, I was able to take up the threshold of the shadow-door and bear it away, stranding the brutes and fighting slaves of the Anarchists in the land of elfs. The Prince Brian and his wee knights were no larger than hailstones and, like hailstones, cut the invaders to bits. How the seven Anarchist Lords and their lieutenants escaped, I know not. The Tower of Glass stands midmost in the lake of their unholy blood to this hour! Tell them from me that it was Winged Vengeance who dealt to them this blow!"

"You rescued the door frame but left me to die?"

"You were beyond saving! Beyond reach! All seven of the Anarchist Lords were there and they rose up against you! Through the maze walls as clear as crystal, as clear as air, I saw the revenants lumbering and ghouls loping in. There were werewolves and shabti, yeti and vampires and ghosts, seven battalions!" He laughed a sad laugh. "More than you have arrows, boomerangs, or knives, more than that crazed lab assistant of the Mad Inventor had shots in his pistol. That intern!"

A great pang shot through her heart.

"Intern?"

"The boy whose voice drove my voice out of your ears! The fool led the Anarchists there to steal the ring and kill you! His burrowing machine had the shadow door hidden in its hold! Your own beloved!"

Her eyes grew wide. She could no longer feel any heat from the blood in her veins. Her head seemed to swim. *Beloved…?*

"My own…" she whispered.

Winged Vengeance bent his raven-beaked mask toward her. He disliked what he saw in her face. With a great swirl of his feathered cloak, he turned and called over his shoulder. "I see your heart is changed! You are the Foxmaiden no more! The revenge to which we dedicated our lives in oaths of blood is no longer in your heart. My curse is on you!"

Tear were in her eyes. She called, "I return a blessing for your curse! Behold! When eternal day breaks, twilight is no more. Your deeds will be laid bare and fall under the judgment!"

He froze. "What… When? Who told you this terrible thing?" She was shocked to hear fear in his voice. She thought he was immune to fear.

She said, "Soon! The hour is at hand! Soon! A messenger of Heaven told me!"

He laughed a laugh of scorn, and the fear was no longer in his tone. "Soon, as angels count it, is centuries hence, or eons!"

In desperation, she shouted out, "You must forgive! You must forgive your foes, and all who have caused you such woe! Show but a drop of mercy to your enemy, and infinite mercy, endless mercy, wider than the sea, will be shown you!"

"Madness!" he spat.

"It is the truth!"

"You are possessed! You would never speak such words!"

She was dumbfounded. It was true. What had possessed her to speak those words? She was not sure where they had come from.

Winged Vengeance was speaking. His voice was like a horn. "You are my disciple no longer! You have broken faith with me! Ah! But you shall do me one last service and carry my word to the Anarchists!"

The moon passed behind a cloud. It was dark.

"*Tuesday is dead and drowned in the waters!*" he cried out. "*The Abominable Snowman is dead! Six days remain! You join him soon!*"

She gritted her teeth. Must everyone give her messages she knew not where to take or whom to tell?

He spread his wings and flung himself into the dark wind. He was departing.

She screamed after him: "My name! At least tell me my name! Who am I?"

He circled the mooring mast, disappearing to the right and coming around from the left, accelerating. The wings were open but still, not flapping, yet his speed increased. Black sparks were flying from the tips of the feathers, and mist was in his wake.

She expected no answer, and yet he did. She heard his shouted words on the wind. "*Anata wa, Moth no Yumiko, Ume-no-Mikoto Moth no Shodotekiken musume, Moth no Isamu no ko!*" It meant, you are Fairchild Plumblossom Moth, daughter of Impetuous Danger Moth, son of Bold Moth.

It was like a trumpet in her ears. Her heart expanded. She knew the name! Her name!

Up he soared, high and higher. Faster he went, with no means of propulsion. She was about to lose him!

She tensed her legs but realized it was useless. Even with no weight at all, she could not gain speed or height beyond her initial jump. From the this tall tower, all other rooftops were below her, beyond the reach of her grapnel.

Too late, she cried out, “Who is my beloved? What is his name? Tell me! Tell me his name!”

No answer returned. He was far away, a mere speck against the moon.

“Where can I find my love, my own, my very own? Tell me! *Where?*”

So Yumiko Moth stood, calling upward, sobbing in grief, hot tears running down her cheeks, long after he had dwindled in her vision and was lost against the cold stars.

Here ends *Daughter of Danger*,

Book One of ***The Dark Avenger’s Sidekick***.

THE TALES OF MOTH & COBWEB continue in

Book Two of ***The Dark Avenger’s Sidekick***,

City of Corpses

City of Corpses

Now *the midnight hour draws on:*
Human form no fiend may keep
Or ever that mystic hour is told.
Lower, lower, lower it bends.
Midnight is come—is come and gone!
Down on all fours see it plunge and leap!
A human yell in a wolf's howl ends!
What gaunt, gray thing gallops on o'er the world?

Julian Hawthorne (1846–1934)

Chapter 1

The Cobbler's Club

1. Maiden of Arrows

She did not know her mother's name.

Yumiko Ume Moth showed none of the desperation and sorrow smothering her soul on her face. Without expression, without food, without sleep, without hope, the Japanese girl walked the sidewalks of the gray metropolis, her dark eyes hot with hidden turmoil. Dawn could be glimpsed as a narrow strip of gray overhead, where the sky was trapped between frowning walls of surrounding buildings.

Even at this early hour, the sidewalks were filled with hard-faced crowds. The streets were snarled with creeping cars with glaring lights and honking horns.

It should have thrilled her to have found her own name again. Instead, she felt only gloom. There was no one with whom to share the dazzling news. Her cousin Elfine had been kidnapped by a knight on horseback in the middle of modern Manhattan. Yumiko had failed to protect her.

Knowing her father's name was cold comfort. *Shodotekiken Moth* was his name, which meant: *Impetuous Danger Moth*. It was a strange name. She had no face to match it, no memory.

Knowing her own name was even colder comfort. *Yumiko*. It meant *Maiden of Arrows*. She had heard it spoken, not seen it written, and different *kanji* characters might have carried different meanings: *Beautiful Girl*, or *Brave Child*, or *Born-of-the-Evening*. But the first meaning was hers. *Ume* meant plum blossom. This was the flower of fidelity and perseverance, for it bloomed in midwinter. This also was hers.

What was not hers was the rest of her. Her home, her past, her life, all were still lost in the mist.

And her mother was lost. She could recall no face, no touch of hand, no sound of voice. That, more than anything, drained her of hope.

Yumiko had stopped at a phone booth, surprised to find one unvandalized, and looked in the phone book. There were no Moths listed in the New York City white pages, and the yellow pages listed only exterminators.

She knew of no one who would help her.

And her mother's death? She remembered nothing of that, only an echo of pain. Pain called for retaliation. She must find and kill her mother's killers. It was a duty.

On she walked. Yumiko passed the Chrysler Building. Central Park was to her left, an occasional green glimpse between gray walls. The sidewalks grew more crowded and the street traffic more raucous. The strip of sky grew bright above, but the claustrophobic streets were cold with early spring chill.

Soon, she saw the Chrysler Building again. She was going in circles. She had no aim, no destination. Her thoughts also went in circles.

To whom she could turn? It depressed her that the human world was enchanted, trapped in the Black Spell, mesmerized and mind-controlled by some sort of vast conspiracy of nonhuman, ancient, cruel, and magical beings: the *mazoku*, which the Westerners called elfs.

Was her amnesia caused by the same spell? Was there any way to break it?

Winged Vengeance had also sworn to kill the enemy. It should have solved all her needs to find again the master whose disciple she was. Instead, each word spoken atop the Empire State Building after midnight had been like another arrowshaft into her heart. Her mother was dead. Her beloved was missing. She herself could no longer be trusted since she had been captured by the Anarchists.

This strange group had declared war against both Man and Elf and sought to topple all nations, break all laws, and shatter all crowns. They were a cabal of ghosts, vampires, werewolves, and warlocks, for they broke also the laws of nature. The Supreme Council of their seven leaders were named after the days of the week. From a ghost she had learned the name of the one called Thursday, whose werewolf packs were poised to strike at New York City. He boasted that he would conquer the metropolis and keep men alive only as herds of cattle on which his wolves would feed. His name was Lucien Cobweb.

Remembering his laughter, recalling the sensation of being trampled beneath him, his hot jaws one inch from her throat, made a rush of fear and hatred, like a dark cloud, boil through her brain.

Had he been the one, himself, who slew her mother? It did not matter. He was one of the seven who had done it: the Anarchists.

Winged Vengeance said Yumiko's former life had ended when she had fallen into Anarchist hands. Therefore she must be an impostor, a hypnotized puppet, or possessed by a ghost. Winged Vengeance called her his enemy. It was an added insult when Yumiko discovered that her master truly did not believe her competent or capable of escaping from the Anarchists.

The truth was too strange for belief. An unexplained miracle had saved her from death. In a dream or vision, a bright lady had given her words to say and washed away all her oaths, all need for vendetta.

Winged Vengeance did not believe it. Yumiko was not sure she believed it herself. And so he had cursed her, denounced her, and wished her to commit suicide.

And then he departed on dark wings into the night, leaving her hollow and lost, with no tears to shed.

He did not even tell her the name of the young man she loved.

Perhaps suicide would be best. She was no coward, to cling to life when fate said otherwise! Submission to fate, and detachment from all desires, was the path to serenity. Joy was not meant for her.

Had she indeed failed to fulfill her oath, whatever it might be, to Winged Vengeance?

Yumiko found herself standing on a small arched bridge of dark brown stone in Central Park. Trees with naked branches stood bright about her, shivering in the cold March wind. She could not see how deep the stream ran. Perhaps not deep enough for a drowning.

It seemed that suicide was the reasonable and expected answer: to cast away this failed life, one of an infinite number, and to make amends in a next. Her next life would be fresh and clean of stain, and the memory of this one would be blotted out…

A noise made her stop and look up. Unlike the city noises, it was music, haunting, echoing, like a voice calling over the rooftops.

It was the chime of the churchbells in Saint Patrick's Cathedral, ringing the hour of morning prayer. The golden metal notes seemed to mock her thoughts, to remind her that there were not an infinite number of worthless lives given to man, but only one, and that one infinitely precious. The golden voice promised something higher and better than simple submission to fate.

It was hypnotic, intoxicating. A strange emotion touched her. It was a terrible emotion. She did not know if it was fear or if it was joy.

She turned north, walking away from the park, and back into the streets.

Perhaps she had tried to cast her life away, and this had been prevented, or forbidden. Who or what was the bright lady she had seen in a dream? What was the strange message she was burdened to carry?

She recalled the words well enough.

Therefore tell the Twilight people, who are neither wholly of the Daylight World nor of the Night World, that when eternal day breaks, Twilight is no more. Then will all their deeds be laid bare and judged.

What was the task she was meant to do?

Let not the soul of thy beloved be drawn into darkness.

Whatever it meant, it meant some injustice had been done, and there was none but she must right it. Someone was relying on her. Someone she loved.

With a start, she looked up. Somehow, she had wandered into the Upper East Side, past 72nd Street, to Lexington Avenue. Here, once again, was a looming sign: THE COBBLER'S CLUB. Not far away was the empty backlot where she had watched the werewolves Whelan and Phelan die. Her tracking devices that had been planted on the corpses yesterday showed that the bodies had been moved to this location. This was also the place where she had first met Elfine, who was also being attacked by the Redcaps.

As suddenly as that, all despair, all thought of suicide, all doubt quite vanished. Her feet were wiser than her head, and had brought her here. This was the only thread left to follow. Before her was her mission. She may have forgotten it, but still it was hers.

2. Gainful Employment

The second time she walked past, she saw a *help wanted* sign in one corner of a dark and highly decorated window. Yumiko raised her eyebrows. She knocked.

A dark-haired man in a dark jacket and tie with dark sunglasses opened the door. He looked Yumiko up and down. "We're closed. We don't open until four."

He spoke with the slightly wobbly precision of a fellow with a few drinks inside him, and trying not to show it.

Yumiko recognized him from the fight in the alley. He was a Twilighter who had been helping the werewolves. Apparently he did not recognize her.

She said, "You have a help wanted sign in your window."

She could not see his eyes, but his lips thinned into a sarcastic moue. "For a waitress, not a paralegal. We're looking for girls with a certain, you know, appeal to men. You ain't it, sweetcakes. Sorry."

And he closed the door.

Yumiko thought of herself as a modest girl, but this curt dismissal offended a feminine pride she had not realized she had. No appeal to men, eh? Her eyes narrowed in determination. She looked left and right and then trotted down the street to the alley where she had first seen Elfine. If expensive clothing barred her way, she would see what it took to open it.

Yumiko unbraided her hair and shook it down her back. She wished she had Elfine here to brush it magically into the shampoo-commercial shine she had earlier. Yumiko then took off the blouse, skirt, and jacket, and stood in a black lacy garment that might have been a bustier or might have been a leotard. She left on her stockings, but donned her long black boots, rolled down to the knee. She stowed everything in her cloak, which she turned into a sash, but instead of tying it *obi* style around her waist, she tied it pirate-girl-style around her hips, to add a touch of emphasis.

Swaying her hips, her heels tapping on the pavement, she went back to the door and knocked. She assumed the sultry expression she had seen on advertisements for lipstick or lingerie: chin up, lips parted, eyes half-lidded.

A different fellow answered the door, a thin and acne-scarred teen boy in a black leather hat and black jacket smoking a hand-rolled cigarette. He gawped at her in surprise, and the cigarette nearly fell out of his lips.

"I am here for the waitress job," she said, flinging her hair back off her shoulder with a toss of her head.

The youth beckoned her in without a word.

Inside it seemed dim as night after the glare of the sunny, early-morning street. There was a podium for the maître-d' to her right, a hat-check closet to the left, and before her were stairs leading down to a lounge. In the lounge were small tables crowded around a Plexiglas dance floor beneath a battery of mirrored balls, colored spotlights, and laser emitters. At the far end was a bar of white marble beneath mirrored shelves holding bottles of every shape and hue. The tables on the floor were currently empty except for three customers lingering from the previous night. The air smelled of sweat, alcohol, and opium.

The youth called, "Mr. Licho!" and this summoned the man in the dark glasses once more. He was carrying a steaming pot from which the rich aroma of freshly-brewed coffee arose.

"What is it, Blud?"

Blud, the youth, merely gestured toward the half-clad girl.

This time, he stopped and drew his dark glasses off his nose to inspect her. She now saw why he wore dark glasses: each eye had two pupils instead of one, lending a freakshow ugliness to his naked stare. He did not once raise his gaze all the way to her face, and may not have even known she was the girl he had previously dismissed.

He said to her, "You're in. Go up to the second floor, take a right, knock on the first door. Boggy is our captain of waitress staff. If she's drunk, just pour this pot over her head."

He passed the handle of the steaming pot to her. She turned to go up the indicated stairs, feeling the man's stare on her as she climbed.

She was blushing by the time she reached the first landing.

There was a mirror on the wall of the corridor at the top of the second landing. The girl who looked out at her was the same she had seen last night in the lady's room of the coffee shop, but a few hours older and wiser. "Whatever you were in your past life, you are not someone who lied to police or seduced enemies with her feminine appeal." She shook her head. As far as a woman's weapon went, this was a blade with no grip, one that cut the swordsman when it struck. She felt shamed and small. "I am not Mata Hari."

The girl in the mirror inspected her. "You might get used to it in time."

"That is what I fear." At the moment, she was the type of girl who would not cheat a tollbooth. That was a type of purity she did not necessarily want to let slip from her hand. It might shatter, with no way to put it back. "And what would my boyfriend think? I don't even know who he is or what he is like."

The eyes in the mirror narrowed. "Now is not the time for qualms. You are Mata Hari at the moment if you want to sneak into an enemy stronghold and poke around."

Yumiko shook her head, put the pot down, undid her sash, took out the blouse and skirt, and put them on. More demurely dressed, she picked up the coffee pot.

Across the hall from the mirror, the first door had a card thumbtacked to it: *Boginki Cobweb.*

Inside was a desk crowded with papers, flowerpots, and ashtrays. To the left was a sofa on which boxes of bottled vodka were resting. Three walls were crowded with shelves on which a large number of dun orchids and thin cactuses were drooping and dying. The floor beneath the shelves was littered with brown leaves and dropped needles. The final wall was crowded with framed autographed pictures of celebrities, always posed with the same portly man in a top hat and tuxedo. A four-bladed wooden fan in the ceiling was turning slowly, but the office was still hot and airless.

Behind the desk was a thin, hatchet-faced matron wearing a rather old-fashioned gown of a dark material, buttoned up to the collar. Her hair was gray and worn in a bun, but her eyes were as bright as the eyes of an eagle.

She looked up. "Well?"

Yumiko said, "Mr. Licho sent me up with the coffee."

The gray woman nodded and took a small white cup off the shelf that had a fern growing in it. She dumped the plant and soil into the neighboring flowerpot, wiped the cup with her fingers, and beckoned. She thumped the cup down on the litter-coated table. "Give it here. Big night last night."

Yumiko approached, wiped the cup with her sash, poured, put the coffee pot down carefully, turned the white cup, and presented it to the woman with both hands.

Boggy took the cup, with a scowl. "Who are you again?"

"I am the new girl. Mr. Licho sent me up here."

Boggy said, "Back up. Turn around. Let's take a look at you. How high can you kick?"

Yumiko thought it was a strange question. "How high would you like me to kick?"

"Just show me as high as you can."

Yumiko looked up and pointed at the ceiling fan. "There?"

Boggy looked surprised, then skeptical, then sarcastic. "Um. Sure."

Yumiko flipped into the air and tapped her boot heel on the ceiling between the turning fan blades, landed, spun, and did it again with the other foot, tapping the ceiling on the other side of the fan.

Boggy said, "Well, well. We are limber, aren't we? Did you bring a letter?"

"A what?"

"A résumé. A list of where you worked before."

Yumiko said, "I am new in the field."

Boggy scowled. "And Licho just up and hired you? Without checking you out?"

"Well, no, I had taken off my blouse…"

"I got the picture. Tell me no more! Iron nails! Where did I put it?" And she dug out a piece of paper. "The Magician keeps saying he is going to upgrade and computerize, but there is never enough money in the budget for it. Always funds for hiring another pretty face to smile for the marks though. What is your name?"

"Yoshiko Kawashima." It was the first name that sprang into her mind. It was the name of the Manchu princess who served as a spy for the Kwantung Army in World War II. The Eastern Mata Hari.

Boggy scribbled the name down and passed a handful of papers to her. "This is the employment form, your withholding, health insurance, and waiver. Write down your bank deposit and routing number here because we don't cut checks any more, and this is a nondisclosure agreement. You do not have to join the Actors Guild if you are appearing only in the chorus line. Well, technically you do, but the local bosses give us some leeway as long as you contribute dues. Any questions?"

"I don't have a bank account. In fact, I don't have a place to stay, so I was hoping you would give me an advance on my wages."

Boggy laughed and then took a large swallow of scalding coffee. "So you come in here with no references, no past, no place to stay, and you expect to be hired as a girl in our world-famous chorus line of Peach Cobbler Girls because you can kick the ceiling?"

Yumiko bowed. "I wish to create no trouble. If you wish to speak to Mr. Licho about the…"

An electronic noise came suddenly from the desk, a bleak squawk. Boggy looked under one pile of papers, and then another, and then found an intercom box. Boggy worked a toggle beneath a flashing bulb.

She said, "Yes, sir..?"

A rich, rolling voice issued from the speaker. "Hire her. Never mind about the paperwork. Have the wardrobe mistress outfit her with a costume and send her to my office."

There was a click.

Boggy stared at the intercom box for a moment, one eye larger than the other, baffled. Then, she took another burning swig of coffee. "Mine is not to reason why. You are in. Take this slip downstairs and go backstage. Leshenka is the name of the wardrobe mistress. Be nice to her. She is a little pixilated. She will set you up with a locker and such."

"A little… I beg your pardon?"

"Pixilated. Afflicted. Bewildered. Touched. She spat on an unlucky day and must have angered the pixies. The Goodly Folk, you know? But she knows her way around a needle and thread."

3. Stage Magician

When Yumiko stepped into the wardrobe room backstage, she saw the black ring on her finger in the reflections on the wall-to-wall mirrors there. Anyone helping her change clothes was sure to see it. She slipped the invisible ring in her pocket. Only then did she knock and ask for Leshenka.

Not long after, Yumiko found herself dressed, or, rather, revealed, in a cute but skimpy outfit consisting of a top hat, a white bow tie, a tight black-and-white corset decorated to look like a tuxedo, shiny black hotpants, and fishnet stockings. False cuffs and cufflinks circling her wrists completed the outfit even though she wore no sleeves.

Yumiko wondered if such a costume was designed as a type of subtle psychological warfare to rob serving girls of so much dignity that none would dare assassinate their superiors with pufferfish poison before committing ritual suicide. On the other hand, she was not sure how often Americans were killed with pufferfish poison. Maybe the Americans just liked pretty girls and lacked decorum.

The shoes were arch-breaking three-inch closed-toed pumps.

Leshenka the wardrobe mistress showed her the locker room and issued Yumiko a combination lock whose combination one could reset oneself. Yumiko left her expensive suit of clothing in the locker and put everything else into her sash, which she rolled up and hid in her top hat. The ring, still invisible, was hidden in the sash as well. She did not trust that the locker would stay locked.

She piled her hair up atop her head to expose her dainty neck, and used several pins driven through the hat band to keep the top hat in place perched on top of the coiffure.

Yumiko thought again of her psychological warfare theory when she was next sent to the office of the owner. The door to his office was big, the walk was long, the carpet was red, the desk was high, and the man himself was both large and tall.

The wall behind his desk was wider than the wall opposite, which meant the walls to her left and right receded the deeper in the room she walked.

He was wide of girth, but on him the bulk looked imposing rather than comical. He was dressed, despite the early hour, in a tuxedo. His hair was dark, parted in the middle, and white at the temples. His face was square. A top hat was set jauntily upon the bust of Shakespeare next to his desk. He wore white kid gloves.

He smiled and gestured her toward a three-legged barstool in the center of the red carpet. Yumiko sat. He flicked a toggle on his desk. The red and gold drapery to her left and right drew back, revealing two walls paneled in mirrors. She was rather acutely aware that he could now examine her from both sides, as well as from behind.

Yumiko straightened her poise, crossed her legs, interlaced her fingers on her upper knee, and smiled her most charming smile. She thought darkly that no one who plays at being Mata Hari can object to attracting men's stares.

Her smile froze when she noticed his eye dart immediately to the image in the mirror where her hands were reflected, first in the mirrored wall to her left and then to her right. She continued to smile, hoping her expression betrayed nothing. But in her heart she blessed whatever paranoia told her to hide the Ring of Mists in her hat.

But, like her, he continued to smile. "I am Wilcolac Cobweb. You've heard of me, I suppose? Here I am, the real thing, large as life!" He uttered a hearty laugh. "But you can call me Willy. And what exactly is your business here?"

Yumiko said, "I need a job."

He leaned back in his wide, black leather chair and looked at the ceiling. "Of course, of course. No place to stay, as I understand it? Why not stay with relatives?"

She said, "My people are in Japan."

"What part?"

"All of them."

He looked surprised and then laughed. She put her hand to her mouth to hide a laugh, and once again his eyes darted to the mirrors left and right. Lifting up one hand had revealed the hand beneath.

She said, "Sorry, I am from Akita Prefecture."

He smiled again. "Are you really? Do you come from a big family?"

She said, "No. My mother is dead."

"I am sorry to hear that," he said and bounded to his feet. He walked with an excess of energy, like a young man, despite his girth.

He crossed to the front of the desk, saying, "No, no! Do not get up!"

And he stood and loomed over her, staring down at her in her skimpy little outfit with cold eyes and a genial smile.

She suddenly realized that it was not a generic evening coat that her immodest showgirl outfit was meant to copy, but his tuxedo in particular.

She wanted to stop smiling, to fidget, to wipe away the beads of nervous sweat she felt accumulating. But she glanced at the calmly smiling girl in the saucy outfit in the mirror, and her eyes gave her a warning as if to remind her that she was on a mission, and persons unknown were likely relying on her.

He walked with his hands behind his back, circling her. The lights from the ceiling gleamed off his spats.

Willy Cobweb said, "So why did you come here?"

She had to crane back her head to look up at him. "Well, I have heard of you, of course. And the Peach Cobbler Girls are world famous."

He nodded, "Hmm. True enough." His expression was puzzled, as if he were surprised at how reasonable that sounded. "How is the outfit?"

She said, "I think I can move in it."

"Hmm. We do a winter holiday revue, where you have to dress like one of Santa's elfs. That means you work holidays at the base rate of pay. Are you fine with that? No Christmas break."

She said, "I am fine with that."

"You don't, ah, celebrate Christmas?"

"In Japan, it is treated more like a romance time. A boy might buy an expensive present for his girlfriend on that day… or make for her…" And suddenly, to her surprise, her voice choked up. Something that was more than a memory tickled her for a moment, but was gone before she could snare it.

(What had her own beloved given her? The magic ring? Or something he had made?)

Willy was speaking. She had not heard the opening of his comment. "…started in the theater as a magician. Much better than shoemaking! But the more I studied, the more I found how truly odd some of the people in this line of work were. Did you know, for example, that Houdini once commissioned the horror writer H.P. Lovecraft to pen a treatise exposing the origins of superstition as being produced by the prehistoric ignorance of mankind? Both of them made their living from bewildering and frightening people, but both urged the public to be skeptical, to be disbelievers."

She answered, quite honestly, "I had not heard."

"Pure camouflage, as it turns out. Houdini knew that the ignorance was deliberate: a cloak thrown over the head of mankind to hoodwink and blindfold us all! It was his investigations into the causes of that ignorance which led to his murder. Yes, his death was not an accident, as is often told!"

Since Yumiko had no idea who this Houdini was, she tried her best to contrive to look surprised. She was about to comment that perhaps the police should be told, but then she realized Willy might be talking about an historical character, dead for hundreds of years.

So all she said was, "I am sure the truth will come out."

He frowned, looking even more puzzled, as if that were not the answer he expected. Willy stopped pacing, stood behind her, and rested his hands gently on her naked shoulders, which Yumiko found rather menacing.

"So do you think magic is not real?" he said.

She said, "You would know better than I. You are the magician."

Willy put his fingers into one of her ears, and before she could flinch or draw away, he pulled a pearl, white, shining, and solid, from her ear.

He tossed it in the air, caught it, and pressed it in her palm. "Touch it! Stroke it! Scratch it with your tooth if you like. It is real: I just took it from your ear, where you had no idea it was hidden."

He was watching her carefully.

Yumiko said, "Since it was found in my ear, may I have it?"

He frowned thoughtfully, plucked the pearl out of her palm, and crossed around to behind his desk. With a theatrical flourish of his coattails, he sat. Then, he lay the pearl carefully on the blotter and put an empty shot glass mouth-downward atop it.

He said, "Why do you want it?"

He took out a handkerchief, waved it in the air, and draped it over the shot glass.

She said, "I was hoping for an advance on my wages. I am low on funds…"

"…and you want to be paid in pearls rather than banknotes?" he said, grunting.

She was not sure how to answer that, so she said nothing.

He said, "The first rule a magician learns is that the first rule is a trick and a distraction meant to take your eyes from the second rule."

Yumiko was not sure what to make of that. "I see. Ah. So what is the second rule?"

"That everything is misdirection and deception. That nothing is as it seems. Even the rule *that nothing is as it seems* is not as it seems."

Yumiko was even less sure how to take that. "So what is it? The true second rule, I mean. If the second rule is not what it seems?"

"The true rule is that the true rule is hidden. Stage magicians are allowed from time to time to glimpse beyond the veil, or even draw it aside for no longer than the time it takes to gasp in awe or in fear! Allowed, I say, tolerated, because no one believes our work is the work of true magic, deep magic, dark magic. Stage-tricks, they call it, illusions, done with mirrors. All that is stripes on a zebra and color on a chameleon."

"So is the pearl mine or not?"

"What pearl?" He slapped his palm down atop the covered shotglass. His hand was wide and meaty, and his glove made an enormous noise when it struck the blotter. He yanked his hand up.

"Here. Catch." He tossed a small, glinting object at her face.

Expecting it to be shards of a shattered shotglass, she flung herself backward, leaning so far back that her head was below the level of the stool seat on which she sat. She had hooked her toes through the rungs of the barstool so that she did not topple off the tiny, round seat. Her top hat was pinned firmly enough on her head that it did not fall off and give everything away.

She saw the small metal thing he had thrown flying by overhead: It was a rough-hammered iron nail connected by a keyring to a doorkey. She snatched it out of the air with her left hand and straightened up.

Willy was open mouthed.

Yumiko tucked some stray hair back into her top hat, cleared her throat, and crossed her legs again. She held up the key on the nail and wiggled it to make it jingle. "Thank you. What is this?"

He had recovered his composure. "The key to the stage door in the back. You have to come in for rehearsal at three, an hour before opening. We open at four. There is a show at seven and again at midnight. Between shows you wait tables. You are second chorus, which means you don't need to do anything other than look pretty and do a simple step-kick in time, a shimmy, a shake, and a strut. I assume you have never waited tables before."

She said, "Why? I mean, I haven't, but what gave it away?"

Willy drew a breath and let it out, and his genial smile vanished as if it had never been. He said, "It would be rare and strange to find a half-fairy serving spirits to mortals."

4. Peach Cobbler Girl

Yumiko recrossed her legs, drew a deep breath, and straightened her spine. She raised her chin and looked him boldly in the eye, "It cannot be so very rare. Here you are doing just that."

He said, "Am I?"

"You spoke of deception and misdirection," she said. "You are no magician: you are merely disguised as one. If you make a slip, and someone sees something he shouldn't, you explain it as a human doing magic, dabbling in dark forces he does not understand. But you do understand. For you are a Twilighter. A Halfalfar. A Demi."

He leaned back and smiled thinly. "As are you. What gave me away?"

She said, "You were so curious about me that you hired me before Boggy even finished the paperwork, and no one asked me whether or not I can dance. You tossed a pearl at me. It did not grow brighter, so you know I am not a mermaid. You threw a cold iron nail at me. I caught it, so you know I am not an elf. I said the name of Christ, so you know I am not a devil. You did a magic trick and waited to see whether the mist would darken my heart to disbelief when you said magic was real. So you know I am not a Daughter of Eve. And you put me in this costume first thing, before even hiring me, so you could walk around and inspect me for suckling marks. I am not a witch. Or do you want me to go into the kitchen and cut raw onions to prove my tear ducts work?"

He said, "Actually, that costume covers too much. I had Leshenka look you over for witch marks. If she had found them, you would not have made it out of the wardrobe room alive."

Yumiko gave a small nod of the head, "And also your whole carpet is red, so I assume at least one red thread in it circles the spot where I am sitting."

He said, "You are also not a vampiress because you have a reflection."

Yumiko nodded. The man was clever. He provided an explanation for the mirrors without giving away that he was searching for the Ring of Mists. That seemed to indicate he still did not suspect she was the one he sought.

She spread her hands. "If you were a man of the Day, the mist would darken your heart to disbelieve in all these things. If you were an elf of the Night, you would be more nervous about cold iron and such. That means you are Twilight. Also, your name is Cobweb. As you say, it is a famous name in the Twilight world."

He said, "But what are you? If you were a Moth, you would go to one of your endless supply of relatives. If you were a Peaseblossom, you would smell of sweet pea, and I would have scented it when I stood behind you just now. And no Peaseblossom would dare slip through the blockade between here and the Third Hemisphere. Are you a Mustardseed?"

She was about to open her mouth and say yes, but she held her peace, for he was not done talking.

"If you were a Mustardseed, then Alberec sent you, for I have never heard of one who has left his service. But what has he to do with us? Alberec's spies would not come unprepared. Dr. McGuire is famous for her care! There was no wallet in your clothing with an exquisitely well-counterfeited driver's license, no passport, no letters from home or ticket stubs, nothing."

So they had gone through her clothing in the locker. But, if so, why had not some werewolf scented it and recognized it as the package they recovered from the elevator in the hospital yesterday? On the other hand, the only two wolves Yumiko knew for sure who had scented those garments were dead, and their corpses were in this building. On yet another hand, they had a behemoth who could raise the dead, so those two might yet talk. On the fourth hand, that behemoth had last been seen just before dawn being chased down the Hudson River by the knight.

He said, "That leaves two possibilities: you might be one of the lesser clans, like the Smithwicks, Rogers, Gordons, Waynes, MacPhees, Lamplighters, or Browns. But all lesser clans are allied with a larger clan, so this merely opens up the same problem again. The other possibility is that you are a Cobweb playing some game."

Yumiko decided on a bold honesty combined with a bold lie. She said, "I am a Moth. But I am not welcome among my own any longer."

He raised both eyebrows. "That is hard to believe. The Moths are known for their family loyalty above all else."

She said, "Which makes them particularly harsh on anyone they think betrayed that loyalty, doesn't it?"

He nodded.

She said, "You must have heard rumors of recent… *events*."

Had he said no and simply admitted he did not know what events she meant, the charade would have ended in disaster because Yumiko frankly was out of ideas.

But she gave him precisely that look of confidence men of any age like to get from pretty young women, so instead he said, "Rumors, and, ah… such. There is a Moth boy that everyone heard about who created that commotion in the Elfking's hall underground during their Yuletide feast. Some of my uncles were there and saw it."

Since she had no idea what any of this meant, she merely nodded sagely. When he looked at her as if he expected her to say something, she said, "And what about the… *others*."

He sat up straight, as if struck by a shocking thought. "So there *are* others? Moths who have not sworn to the Elfking? The son of the Riddle-weaver is not the only one?"

Yumiko said, "Perhaps you have heard rumors that some of my cousins escaped this oath and also escaped punishment."

It was clear from the look on his face that he had not heard any such rumor. He said, "Well, I like to keep my ear to the soil, you know."

Yumiko did not know what to say, so she looked him in the eye and said, "I think you understand my situation."

He nodded again. "You quarreled with your elders. You do not want to swear the oath when you turn twenty-one. You think life might be better among the Cobwebs than the Moths? Why not just go to your cousins, whoever they are, who also are avoiding the Elfking?"

She said, "Finding them would require detective work I don't know how to do."

"But you come to me. Even though our clans have been enemies ever since Titania died?"

Yumiko had no idea who Titania was, so she just nodded sagely once again. Yumiko said, "Where I am concerned, all oaths are void, and all vendettas forgotten!"

He pursed his lips. "Well, the world cannot be run without oaths and promises. There are rules and laws, you know, and the lower must bow to the higher."

Yumiko said, "A friend of mine told me some Cobwebs dream of a different world. A better one."

He looked at her very carefully. "A world without rules would be… anarchy."

She said, "Would it? Some call that liberty."

He said, "Tell me the name of your parents and when and why you quarreled. If your story checks out…"

Yumiko said, "The past is the past. I've already forgotten it. Are you afraid of me changing my mind, turning around, and going back home? That is not an option for me. And what would it prove? If I actually were a Mustardseed sent to spy on you, Dr. McGee could have had some actress play the role of my hateful stepmother or whoever. Listen: I need the job, and I have no other place to stay. You need a waitress and chorus girl."

He nodded. "You've convinced me you are not a Mustardseed, at least. None of Dr. McGuire's spies would forget her name."

She nodded, looking calm and hoping that the heat she felt in her cheeks was not visible as a blush.

He said, "I am proud of my club. I think of it as sort of neutral ground. Even Moths are welcome if they behave. There was one, Rotwang's boy, used to come here now and again. But I have clients and regular customers from the Day and from the Twilight, and even, from time to time, one of the Night folk, or an old warlock out for one last fling before his turn comes to pay the tithe. But no baptized Christian is welcome here unless he has committed grave sin since his last confession. Well?"

Yumiko silently counted the number of people per day she had killed so far. She said, "My conscience is not clean, if that is what you are asking."

He said, "I don't run this place for profit, but for a deeper cause. Your purpose here is to excite lust in the thoughts of men, so you dress provocatively, you walk provocatively, you talk provocatively, and you put the drink down on the table provocatively. But you also take the food orders quickly and without error because it also serves the cause to trick Day folk into thinking good service from servants is a right they can buy. Flattery makes them ungrateful, and ingratitude is pride. Taking any person for granted is good, but taking a person smaller and weaker than you for granted is better."

"You've mentioned good and better. What is best?"

"If the smaller and weaker person a man demeans is an innocent and nubile young virgin he should be protecting from hurt and dishonor, that is best of all. Second best is for her to hate that protection, because that, again, is ingratitude."

Yumiko felt a small tickling of her pride. "What if she can fend for herself?"

He waved his hand in the air as if shooing away a fly. "That makes ingratitude even easier. Hell loves a self-made man!"

"Now, then, the trick for any of my girls, in all of this, is for her to act like she is not being demeaned. That it is normal to show perfect strangers the intimate sights reserved for the bridegroom on the wedding night. It makes the greatest gift a girl can bestow no longer a treasure, see? No longer priceless."

She nodded gravely.

He continued. "Moths are supposed to be friendly to mankind. Can you act like an elf girl and seduce a man who walks in here into committing adultery with you in his heart?"

She said, "Seduce? Adultery? You are not expecting me to… to…"

He was sincerely shocked. "Oh, no! Are you insane? I run a nightclub, not a cathouse! I am not a human! By cold iron, girl, what do you take me for?"

She said, "But you said…"

He was flustered. "I said adultery *in his heart*. By the rules, that counts just as bad. I didn't make the rules! I just play by them."

"What does that mean?"

"That means you make the lusty young men and the filthy old men *think* about it. Encourage them without encouraging them. You make them think it is no big deal for a gal to flaunt her goods and a guy to look and like looking.

Make them think it is *normal.* Sex is secular, not sacred; it is a pastime, not a selfishness-destroying ecstasy. It is just a commodity."

Yumiko remembered the billboards and clothing she had seen. "I am under the impression humans already think exactly that."

"Makes your job easier then. You just help maintain the illusion. See? Deception, distraction, misdirection." He spread his hands and smiled. "That is all we need to do, and the tithe will fall on someone else. Simple, no? Now, can you do that? I don't want your Mothish sentimentality for Sons of Adam suddenly to crop up and spoil things. Can you do it?"

She thought a moment, seeking what to say. She remembered what Elfine had said about having a crooked reputation. It brought high-priced jobs and was good for business.

She said, "In a world free of rules, everyone is responsible for himself. Right? That means I can dress, talk, walk, and act how I like, and whatever happens in the hearts of men around me, well, that is their business, not mine."

As soon as she said the words, Yumiko inwardly winced. She thought that no one could be so obtuse as to believe such obvious nonsense as what she had just said. She had tried to speak like what she imagined a wicked girl, a siren, a seductress, would sound like, but only an unconvincing caricature had come forth.

But to her surprise, Willy Cobweb merely nodded. It must have sounded normal to him.

He said, "You need a stage name. We cannot call you Kawasaki or whatever bogus name you gave Boggy. How about *Kissy Cutie* or *Wang Me*?"

"Sayori Yunomi."

Willy looked puzzled, "*Sorry you know me*? Sounds like a threat."

"*Sayori* is born of the night. *Yunomi* is teacup, but, when written, is *evening-of-beauty*. Surely a fitting name for a maidservant here." She did not mention that it also referred to an archery bow, as did Yumiko's real name. Having learned her true name so recently, she was unwilling to bury it under an alias, except at a shallow depth.

"Sorry Yunomi it is. Pretty name. Are you low on funds?"

"I have nothing."

"You need a place to stay? Give me that key back then." He took a notepad, wrote a note, and handed it to her, saying, "Okay, Sorry. Take that down to

Boggy. She will introduce you to the stage manager and the maître-d' and work you into the work and rehearsal schedule. Boggy will arrange to have you paid in cash and dock your pay for room rental upstairs."

"Upstairs?"

"The Captain owns the hotel occupying the top floors here, and some of the other chorus girls will be your roommates."

"Captain…?"

Wilcolac narrowed his eyes. "Captain Cobweb is one of my uncles. He is the owner of record here. You did not know? Well, no matter." His manner grew brusque. He clapped his hands and rubbed them together. "Boggy will explain the rules about gentleman visitors and such. No crucifixes, candles, or bedtime prayers. Some of our guests and employees are from older families and have more elf in them.

"Don't be late for anything by a second, or you're fired. Don't piss off the customers, or you're fired. No drinking on duty, or you're fired. If a customer buys you a drink, you drink from the marked bottles Boggy will show you. Customer gets too friendly, don't argue and don't fret; the bouncer will come. No blessing and no cursing, not aloud and not by runes. Don't argue with the drunks, but wait for the bouncer, or you're fired."

He smiled an avuncular smile. "You look worried. Don't be. This will be educational. Waiting tables is the one time you girls get to find out what it is like to be a guy: the customer has a right to change his mind, just like a woman does; the customer is always right, just like a woman is; the customer is fickle, the customer is bratty, the customer gets the last word; but in the end, you get what you want out of his pants, kick his hungover, sorry butt out the door, and forget his name. The only difference is that what you get out of his pants is his billfold.

"And welcome aboard. You are a Peach Cobbler Girl now. Strut with pride."

Chapter 2

Night Life

1. Run Ragged

As "Sorry" (as she was now called), Yumiko found herself no more able to spy out the secrets of the club than a goldfish in a bowl.

During the first week, she had scant opportunity to take out her radio gear and check on the source of her tracer signals. She worried that the enemy would detect the signals, or find the devices, or the little things would run out of battery power. As each hour passed, the likelihood of one or more grew greater, but all her hours were occupied.

On the first day, Polednitsa Cobweb, the staff nurse, gave her a brief but unpleasant examination, drawing blood and gathering urine in a cup. Polednitsa's little room was white walled, white floored, and windowless, smelled of disinfectant and alcohol, and was kept at a breathlessly warm temperature.

Nurse Polednitsa was a blonde who seemed too young to have passed medical school. Her eyes were so pale a blue as to look almost like the hottest part of a flame.

Her voice was sharp and dry, her accent lilting, Slavic, and aristocratic. "Listen closely. Checkups are once a month on the full of the moon. If you are found to be unclean, or pregnant, or marked with a chrism, that is grounds for immediate discharge. Use of recreational drugs, abuse of wine or spirits, or the discovery of blood not your own in your bloodstream is grounds for immediate discharge. Some of the girls here are allergic to cold-hammered iron, to flat stones with a hole rubbed in the middle, and to pomegranate seeds. None are permitted at any place on the grounds at any time. Also, some have peanut allergies, so, no peanuts. Do you have any allergies of this type?"

Yumiko could only say, "Not that I remember…"

Polednitsa handed her a questionnaire, saying, "Please write out your genealogy for five generations, back to your great-great-grandparents, with all your uncles, aunts, cousins, and second and third cousins."

Yumiko balked. "Why?"

"In case there are any genetic markers for disease, or royal blood, or a family curse."

Yumiko handed it back. "I do not know my relatives so far out. I do not even know my mother's name."

Polednitsa glared at her a moment with her hot blue eyes and then made a quick note on the paper. Yumiko casually glanced in the mirror behind Polednitsa and read over her shoulder: *Not Twilight. Day. Restrict diet. Elf food forbidden.*

There came a plethora of other questions, which Yumiko found bewildering, and which she eluded and evaded as best she could, smiling politely and bowing her head after every sentence. This seemed to exasperate the young, hot-eyed nurse.

She was then sent downstairs, where Leshenka the wardrobe mistress showed Yumiko the finer points of the Peach Cobbler Girl costume. Leshenka was a round-faced crone with wild, flyaway hair badly in need of combing, which, for some reason, she had dyed green.

Leshenka was also a full-time seamstress. She hand-stitched the front and back pieces of Yumiko's suit until it fit like a glove. The built-in corset enforced a nice hourglass shape, emphasizing cleavage while narrowing her waist sharply. The high cut of the seat likewise emphasized the length of her legs and the curve of her hips. Slouching or slumping was impossible, and striking any pose that was indelicate or unlovely was difficult.

Leshenka instructed Yumiko on how to walk and talk, how to perch on the back of a chair or railing, and how to dip when lowering a drink to the table. The wardrobe mistress rarely spoke above a rustling whisper. It was like listening to autumn leaves talking.

Two identical suits were given to her. Leshenka said, "I have made the adjustments just for you. Each of my uniforms is unique for the woman's body who wears it, so there is no swapping. You are not allowed to take the uniform off site. It takes two Cobbler Girls to put one on. Stockings on first. Bend at the hips, keeping your torso straight, suck in your stomach, and hold the suit thus and so while someone zips it for you. For bathroom breaks or emergencies, two Cobbler Girls have to be pulled from the floor."

"The waist is very tight," gasped Yumiko.

"The corset contains metal slats. Do not eat in the morning until after you don the suit. That way you know how many teaspoons you can swallow before you cannot breathe. You must stay within one pound of your current weight, plus or minus retaining water. Weigh-in is every morning. It is no harder than being on an Olympic wrestling team."

Yumiko nodded at those words, which she found soothing. Holding herself to an iron discipline was something that felt familiar. Her body and spirit no doubt remembered whatever remorseless and savage training regime Winged Vengeance had imposed on her, even if her mind forgot. This gave her the courage to face the prospect of being a nightclub hostess.

Besides, wearing a suit with metal slats seemed familiar, too.

Leshenka showed her the wireless microphone built into the bow tie of the costume. A battery pack and transmitter fit into the cummerbund. The costume not only had no pockets, but there was no other place to hide anything.

"Some of our customers do not like it if the maidservants have to write things down to remember them. The mike picks up anything spoken to you. It is recorded in the kitchen. You play back the recording to get the order."

Yumiko wondered what sort of customers objected to writing.

Leshenka continued in her dry, breathy voice, "With this system, we never get an order wrong. Also, the bouncers monitor conversations so that if the customer gets too fresh, one can ride to your rescue."

"What is too fresh?"

"New customers cannot touch you, except to put an arm around your waist to take a picture with you. Lots of the guys want a picture with a Peach Cobbler Girl, especially on their birthday. A customer who drops more than a C-note, he can pat you on the fanny or tuck a tip into your cummerbund, but can't steal a kiss or cop a feel. You never reject any advances; the bouncers reject for you. Your job is to make the creeps think they still have a chance if only they got you alone. And so you can never be alone. That is what the mike is for."

Yumiko now had some hint of how Willy had overheard the conversation in Boggy's office. Yumiko said, "How do I turn it off? Like for a private conversation or something?"

Leshenka smiled a wry smile. "No private conversations here. You'll be too busy for that."

Between rehearsals, training, waiting tables, performing in the chorus line on stage, and the half a hundred other tasks the New Girl was required to volunteer to do, this wry prediction turned out to be correct.

The sole time she was alone on the first day was in the lady's locker room on the third floor between practice sets. The locker room, showers, sinks, and toilets were together in one area adjacent to the dance studio. Yumiko trapped a strand of hair inside the hinge of her locker before closing the door so that she would know, if the hair was disturbed, that someone else had opened the door.

Then, in the bathroom, with no eyes on her, Yumiko climbed the wall above the last stall on the left and hid the wide red sash of her Foxmaiden costume (with her magic ring and hidden gear tucked away in an impossible mermaid pouch within) beneath a tile of the drop ceiling.

She was no longer terrified that her hat would fall off but now was terrified that someone would find her trove.

Even when she was not on duty, she was not alone. Meals she ate in the kitchen with the other girls, with the cost deducted from her pay. After curfew, when the twenty other dancers left for home, Yumiko bunked with nine girls in three beds, two cots, and one couch in one suite of two rooms on the fourth floor.

As it turned out, Captain Cobweb, the unseen owner, also owned the health club one block away on 2nd Avenue, and Yumiko, as well as the other show girls, were required to attend an aerobics class and to spend an hour at the swimming pool.

Allegedly, this was to keep the show girls in athletic dancing trim, but Yumiko noticed many of the same men she saw watching her doing aerobic exercises or swimming laps at the health club were later at the nightclub, so she thought that health club visits were something of an advertising ploy.

But it was also a ploy to keep her employed. Wilcolac no doubt still held her in suspicion. At least two of her roommates seemed far too eager to be her friends, and the head of the bouncer squad, Licho Cobweb, always contrived to eat his meals when she took hers and seemed to watch her from behind his dark glasses.

Krisky and Plaksy Nocnitsa, who were tall, languid blondes with eyes of piercing blue, were the two bent on being her friend willy-nilly and followed her wherever she went, pretending to chat with her. They were twins from Lithuania, beautiful as sin with voices like Slavic music, but their chatter consisted of nothing but complaints about coworkers, hypochondriac fretting over imaginary ailments, ghost stories, and plans to marry rich dotards. Both girls were morbidly afraid of owls. Yumiko could not tell if they were fully human or not.

Her other roommates were more pleasant to be around.

Xana was from Asturias in Spain and was filled with laughter and mischief; generous Anjana was from Cantabria, and her laughter was kind; Nightingale was polished, polite, honey-blonde, and from Northumbria, from which (or so she said with a twinkle in her eye) all the best-looking Englishwomen hailed; shy and sweet-faced Nariphon was from Himavanta in Pakistan, and she said she was fleeing an arranged marriage.

Hala was a Serb and spoke of the sufferings of her country in a voice of quiet ferocity. She spoke of a hero named Mark the King's Son, buried under Mount Athos, who had thrust his saber through a stone ere he slumbered and would emerge once wind and rain wore the rock and worked the great sword free because the sound of its fall would shake the hills with fear from Hungary to Albania.

Iele was Romanian with smoldering eyes and a love of gossip. She insisted the club was haunted by ghosts. She also said the mirrors were polarized one-way glass, with Peeping Toms on the other side, who paid a fee to stare.

Joan Lantern was the torch singer and was older than the other girls. She was Cornish, acted as their den mother or team captain, and fended off any male staff members who seemed too friendly. Everyone called her Joan the Wad, but the meaning of that nickname was never explained to Yumiko.

On the sill of a high window in the shared room Joan the Wad propped a pumpkin shell carved into an eerie mask in which she burned a candle by night and day. Joan claimed that the pumpkin's name was Jack and that he was her husband. Joan said Jack would tell her if any of her girls broke the rules, and therefore all the girls in giggling whispers discussed how to steal and where to hide the pumpkin or how to bake it into a pie.

Yumiko thought it odd that none of them was American, and the suspicion grew on her that some were Daylight folk, and crazy, and others Twilight folk, and sane.

Yumiko was also assigned to walk the dogs in Central Park. She had to borrow an outfit from Xana, who would only lend her something much too skimpy for the weather: a tank top and a pair of Daisy Dukes. But perhaps that was an advertising ploy as well.

There were a dozen or so large Huskies, Malamutes, and Alsatians that Wilcolac kept on the property to act as guard dogs. They had to be taken out for a walk twice a day. Even here, Yumiko was not alone. Three other girls were needed to help manage the dogs, and the old Polish handyman who kept the complex lightshow and fog-makers in order, Svarog, followed after with the pooper-scooper.

When it was time to return the dogs, the girls walked them back through the alley behind the club to the truck bay where Yumiko had saved Elfine. The kennels were a large concrete room just beyond the loading dock, down a ramp, in the basement.

The first time Yumiko was returning the brace of barking dogs to the kennel master, Jarnik, she smiled at him, introduced herself, and asked, "These are very handsome dogs. Mr. Cobweb must really like them. How long has he kept them? And so many?"

He was an older man, dark-eyed and hook-nosed with a touch of gray at his temples. Jarnik said, "The Magician? Not he. He be fearful of such hounds as these. He hates them. These belong to the Captain."

"What treats do they like to eat? Are they well behaved?"

Jarnik was pleased to talk to a pretty girl and answered at length, until she was pulled away by an impatient Krisky, who was afraid of picking up some disease from the dogs.

Why would Wilcolac keep hounds he hated? "Misdirection and deception," she muttered under her breath. Of course Wilcolac kept a pack of large, wolfish-looking hounds. Any Son of Adam who spied a lupine figure lurking near or entering the club could be convinced that he had seen a Husky in Manhattan, not a wolf.

Hand in hand with Krisky, as they sought a shortcut out of the kennels, Yumiko saw a large and square overhead door, truck-sized, tucked away behind some crates next to the kennel, leading to some deeper basement she had never glimpsed. It was marked OUT OF SERVICE. But Yumiko noticed that the handle chained to a staple in the floor was worn, the chain was scratched, and the hinges in the overhead had been recently oiled.

An out-of-service door still in use? More misdirection.

2. Lady in Waitressing

Her nine roommates plus her were the core group of the chorus line and worked ten shifts a week. The other twenty chorus girls worked five shifts on and took five off so that a score of showgirls was onstage at any one time, backing up the three main acts.

Yumiko found that not only was she able to dance, but she loved it.

The first night, as the hour for the show approached, she was almost physically ill with shyness, but the mere act of putting on the costume calmed her nerves. Even though it showed more of her than any street clothes, she felt like it was a disguise. Donning a disguise, like downing a drink, gave a person permission to live, if only for an hour, without fear or hesitation.

The whistles and commotion of the crowd were contagious, the stage lights drowned out the sight of any lascivious eyes, and Yumiko found she loved parading herself before the men. Perhaps she felt a sense of triumph when she drew the eyes of guys away from their scowling dates. There was something fearful and fascinating about it as well: it was like toying with fire.

All the dancers were athletic, but Yumiko found that she tired less easily than they, or perhaps they merely complained more after shows and shifts.

Waiting tables at first was wretched work, but eventually she got the hang of it. It boiled down to three things: the first was timing, making sure she went by each table in her area at about the time it took to down a drink or to finish a dessert; the second was organization, keeping the orders straight and menu changes up to date; and the third was friendliness.

This third thing she learned was from Anjana, one of her roommates, who took her aside after two unhappy nights of low tips. Anjana told her that this was the same job as a model, who is paid for her looks, or as an actress, who bats her eyelashes at a camera. "The marks know it is an act. Just play along."

"An act?"

"There is a hard city outside the door. In here, they want to feel the touch of softer life. In here, you play the role of a pretty girl who *wants* to bring them hard drinks and hot chicken wings in peanut sauce. They are *paying* you to make them feel like they don't have to pay you. You'd volunteer to bring them hard drinks and hot chicken wings in peanut sauce because they are so *wonderful.* Just chit-chat with them! Tell them about your past!"

Since she did not have a past of her own, Yumiko told any customer who wanted to chat with her (and most of the ones without dates did) instead about the past of Yoshiko Kawashima.

Many a man, young, drunk, sober, or old, was fascinated by her birth in the imperial clan of the Qing Dynasty and her adoption, after the Xinhai Revolution, by a Japanese espionage agent and mercenary adventurer; many a man likewise was saddened by the suicide of her mother, the imperial concubine, and by her unhappy first marriage to the son of a Mongolian Army general; and was thrilled by her role in bringing Pu Yi to the throne as Emperor in Manchuria as a Japanese puppet after the Shanghai Incident; was impressed by her brief career as a radio star; and many a man complimented her on her courage in resisting the communists after the war.

Only one asked her how a girl of seventeen had served in World War Two.

It seemed okay. The stories told by the other girls were wilder.

And the customers did indeed seem to know it was all an act. All they wanted was a beautiful girl dressed in high heels, top hat, bathing suit, and a bow tie waiting on them hand and foot, and for her to be friendly, helpful, and fun.

But she understood. It was another magic trick. The masculine appeal was misdirection: the real purpose was to separate the customers painlessly from their cash.

Her tips per night increased dramatically. She was not sure how much money the bills were actually worth because there was small chance of spending it.

After that, life was not so very hard. She enjoyed the work, loved dancing, and got daily exercise, the pay was good, and Yumiko got along well enough with the other girls.

The only hard part was that she was trapped.

She had no privacy, her costume was bugged, and at least two girls and one bouncer were watching her every move.

Maybe the mirrors were one-way glasses watching her as well. Maybe the pumpkin of Joan the Wad actually was watching her. Maybe a ghost with empty eyes and a pallid winter tree on his surcoat walked the corridors at night, fully able to see her, now that her silver ring was hidden in the locker room.

But what was happening to Elfine, all this time, assuming she was still alive? What was in the basement below the kennels?

3. Friendly Warning

On the Monday of her second week, she decided she had to find some privacy. It could not be that hard: no one could be watched every hour, every minute, without error.

That day, she skipped lunch on the excuse of going out to shop to spend some of her tip money. Krisky and Plaksy invited themselves along. Yumiko did not even try to leave them behind: she was testing to see how long the leash might be. She bought herself a change of street clothes, a slinky nightgown, a toothbrush, a dental mirror, and some other basic necessities. She bought a bag of doggie treats in a pet store. She attempted nothing overtly suspicious.

On Tuesday, she ducked into the third-floor locker room, and, finding it empty, jumped to the ceiling, balanced atop the divider of the last stall, and lifted the panel in the drop ceiling where her supersuit was hidden. She took a bugging device and a tracking device. Like her suit, the tiny disks had adjustable colors. She turned them white. The magnetic adhesive allowed her to clamp them to the clips pinching her earlobes, so she could wear them as earrings. It was not much, but it was practically the only place she could carry anything between costume changes.

On Wednesday there was a break in the routine: one of the main acts was using the stage for extra rehearsal, so chorus line rehearsal was canceled. She had four hours of free time. Again, Yumiko went out, and, again, her two roommates insisted on tagging along.

She went to an upscale clothing shop and bought a red sash that was a very close match in size and hue and fabric to the *obi* into which the Foxmaiden half-cape transformed. Misdirection and deception.

Krisky and Plaksy were at the front of the shop, trying on gloves. Yumiko casually drifted to the back of the store, where she was out of eyesight. It should be a simple matter to change into another outfit, slip out, elude the two girls, and make it back to the club unseen. Then…

When Yumiko pulled aside the curtain to step into the changing booth, Licho Cobweb was inside, smoking a cigarette.

"This is the lady's changing room!" said Yumiko.

He grunted. "I am just here to see you do not change too much."

She said nothing in reply, but smiled politely.

That seemed to annoy Licho. He said sharply, "Right now, the Magician trusts you, likes your attitude, and likes how you get along with the customers. He trusts you 'cause he's keeping an eye on you. Now a bright girl like you can find a way to sneak off without anyone seeing, I am sure. But you don't want to do that."

Yumiko bowed her head. "I am sorry to cause any disturbance."

He scowled. "You see, that's what I don't like about you. Any other girl would ask why I say you don't want to sneak off and keep the conversation going. But you! You just apologize, and it kills the tempo, and then there is an awkward silence."

She said, "I am sorry. In silence, the vanity and pain of the world makes itself known; it is a truth not found in words."

He drew back as if she gave off a bad smell, "What the heck does that mean?"

"It means you are admitting you have been ordered to watch me. This is in addition to your other duties, and the burden cannot be pleasant, so I am saying I am sorry."

"Phaugh! You are as cool as milk from a Finnish witch, aren't you, missy? You don't seem surprised."

"We are Moth and Cobweb. There is mistrust between us. Your master no doubt has foes: all successful men do. I would be a fool to be surprised."

"Phaugh! The Magician is not my master. I am the Captain's. You are also a fool if you find any blind spot I've overlooked. Don't look for one. Funerals are expensive, and so is dog food, and there is a way to save money on both if you take my meaning, little missy."

Yumiko nodded slowly.

Licho said, "You want to stay on the Magician's good side because no one else will miss you when you are gone. So stay where we can see you, see what you do, who you see. Don't go anywhere."

And with that, he tossed his cigarette butt to the floor of the store, ground it to ash with his toe, gave her a pinch on the cheek, and stalked out.

Alone in the booth, Yumiko felt as if she were in an elevator with a broken cable. The pent-up emotion, fatigue, and frustration were too much. She was sitting in the changing booth, shoulders shaking, crying, and trying to do so silently, when the store clerk came by and told her smoking was not allowed in the store.

With Krisky and Plaksy in tow, Yumiko cut short her shopping expedition and returned to the Cobbler's Club with an hour to spare before her next shift.

She spent that hour in the studio, sitting without motion before the dance mirrors, controlling her breathing, and using her patience as a weapon to scrape away the weakness in her will she now perceived had grown in her like a tarnish on a silver blade.

Yumiko told herself to wait. She must wait for the ever-present eyes watching her to blink.

Chapter 3

Envoys to Anarchy

1. Private Room

The next night, after the ten o'clock show but before the midnight show, Yumiko was handed a tray of drinks by Clobhair Cobweb the bartender and told to wait on some V.I.P.s in the private room on the second floor. There was also a small bowl of water on the tray.

She stared blankly. "Vips?"

A twitch of his lips shifted the clay pipe he forever smoked from one side of his unshaven mouth to the other. "*Very Important Persons*, me girly. See ye make no mock of them nor bring bad luck to the honor of this stout old pub." He pronounced it "auld." Clobhair was even shorter than Yumiko and stood on a raised platform behind the bar. "Recall ye that the help enters without a knock and stays until dismissed. Take a menu in case they want something from the kitchen."

Yumiko balanced the tray in one hand and went quickly and silently up the red carpeted stairs to the second floor. She entered without knocking, as instructed.

Here was an opulent room adorned in gold and ebony wood, hung with red curtains. A chandelier of cut glass was above, a smoldering fireplace with a mantelpiece of carved marble was to one side, and candles stood before the three large mirrors dominating three walls. There were no electric lights burning here.

Wilcolac in his black top hat, white bow tie, black tailcoat, and white spats sat in a tall and narrow chair of black wood carved with images of rising snakes and falling stars. Behind him on the wall were framed pictures of the major trumps of the Tarot. Key I, *The Magician*, was topmost. An uncut cigar was waiting in an open humidor on a small brass tripod at his right hand.

His left hand was at his knee, toying with a walking stick of black wood set with a silver knob. On a low table before him was a silver dish of caviar imported from Iran, set in a bed of ice and ringed by small bowls of chopped egg yolks and egg whites, lemon wedges, red onions, chives, crème fraîche, and small bits of buttered toast.

Facing him were two young men and a black dog. They were seated in plush leather armchairs with low backs, their knees almost touching the coffee table where the caviar rested. Their backs were to her as she entered and crossed the room, but she could see their reflections in the mirrors beyond.

It came as a shock when she recognized first one and then the other. Her drinks swayed on her tray, but she steadied herself in time and smiled the bright smile she had been taught.

The two young men were both in archaic costumes, seeming as out of place in the modern day as she would have seemed dressed in her Foxmaiden supersuit. She wished she were wearing it now.

The first one she knew by his face.

He was a thin, sober-faced youth in round and rimless eyeglasses that gave him a look of owlish sobriety. His dark, shoulder-length hair was tied with a ribbon at the nape of his neck. He wore a short black cloak covering his shoulders and, beneath that, a long coat of black and, beneath that, a long white tunic with a leather belt. A black hood hung down his back. On a fine gold chain about his neck was a necklace of beads set with a gold crucifix.

Yumiko wondered at the necklace. She was reminded of Buddhist prayer beads. Other necklaces (he wore several) held medallions small as coins, oval or round, set with tiny images of men, women, doves, and angels in stiff poses.

Strangely, in the mirror that reflected him, the candlelight was caught in the gold crucifix, and it blazed like a star and seemed to send a large, black shadow across the floor and up the wall behind him. But when she crossed in front of him, his shadow's size and shape were normal, and the ornament was no brighter than it should have been.

The second was a tall youth, athletic in build, broad shouldered, thick necked, and square jawed. Even though he was seated in a comfortable chair, his posture was that of a soldier stiffly at attention on a parade ground. His eyes were green as glass and bright as lamps. His gaze was disturbingly forthright.

His hair was as silvery-white as starlight, bright as a polished blade. It was thick and hale, not the thin hair of an old man. It was cut strangely, for the back of his head below his ears had been shaved.

He was dressed in a linen tunic. Atop this was a white surcoat emblazoned with a swan, and on the hem was embroidered a swan feather motif. A wide leather belt ran from shoulder to hip before circling his waist thrice. Belt and surcoat were adorned with jacinths and small diamonds. In the same way a flock of birds or a swarm of bees can move in unison and produce the illusion that it is a single organism, so here, the many flashing gems adorning his coat and sleeves made bright a field of flickers glance and dance across his broad chest when he breathed. It looked like a single living thing restlessly stirring, an elusive creature of light. His leggings were leather, and his black boots sported metal shin guards. At his heels were golden spurs.

The white scabbard at his side would have hung by his left hip had he been standing. The hilts were silver, the grip was bound in rough white leather and set with silver nails, a milky white stone was the pommel, and the light trapped by reflection in the stone beat like the heart of a living thing. In his reflection in the mirror, some trick of the firelight made a heat shimmer dance all along the sheathed sword, as if the blade within were burning with irresistible fire.

Yumiko thought the young knight was an image of splendor. Something hidden stirred in her memory but was gone before she could name it.

She had not seen his face before, but she knew the design on his coat and recognized the sword. This was the young knight who had saved her from the werewolves at Catoblepas warehouse. She was baffled to see him alive, for she had last seen him dive on horseback in full armor into the Hudson River and vanish under the water, chasing a misshapen and gigantic beast.

His dark, thin compatriot was the one who had driven the owl women away with bell, book, and candle. She even knew the dog. It had once wrestled a pistol out of Lucien Cobweb's hand with its teeth.

The collie dog was by the young knight's side, sitting, tongue hanging out. He had bright eyes with circles of black fur around them like a bandit's mask. His coat was glossy black, except his snout, vest, and stockings were white.

The dog was the only one who turned his head to look at Yumiko when she came in. His triangular black ears perked up, and he watched her carefully as she walked.

She also saw herself in the reflections as she approached: shapely dancer's legs in fishnet stockings, shining black hotpants hugging her curved hips, a corset that accentuated her hourglass shape and displayed a daring amount of cleavage, the false cuffs making her bare arms seem naked, the bugged bow tie circling her slender throat, a mass of inky black hair piled atop her head, her oval face and large, catlike eyes, and an oversized top hat above. She had been dancing earlier, and the lounge was hot and close with fumes, and so her skin was shining and flushed with pink.

Or perhaps that was a blush of embarrassment. She passed in front of the young men, wondering if either would recognize her.

She was required, when placing a drink on the table, to dip herself just so and to keep her low-cut costume in place: she had been taught to lean gracefully backward while bending at the knees, with the left knee lifted and tucked behind the right leg. It was practically a ballerina move. But this coffee table was at least a foot lower than the patron's tables in the lounge.

Yumiko steeled herself. She wished she knew whether she had ever done limbo dancing in her life before this. But her worry was needless: she bent her knees further and dipped down as elegantly as a swaying flower, maintaining her poise. (And, in fact, had anyone there thrown a punch at her head, she was in a position to block it.) She placed the napkins just so, with the hammer-and-shoe emblem of the club facing each guest.

For the first time, she glanced at the drinks and was frozen for a moment in hesitation. The barkeep had forgotten to tell her whose was whose.

The men were talking, and the tone was businesslike and not friendly, so she did not want to interrupt. Wilcolac was saying, "…was founded by Peter Stuyvesant under authority of the Dutch West India Company, chartered under the Seven Provinces. I am not sure how the writ of Arthur applies in this case."

The bourbon over ice with a maraschino cherry and lemon peel was a whiskey sour. It was a favorite drink for Wilcolac. She put the cool and sweating glass down in front of him.

The silver-haired young knight was saying sternly, "Charles V was Holy Roman Emperor and ruled and reigned in the Low Countries. The rebellion by William of Orange is not recognized as lawful by Alberec or Erlkoenig. Will you dispute with the King of Elfs and Shadows?"

That left a dark, carbonated drink and a clear drink with a lemon peel. She had a one-half chance of correctly guessing which was whose.

Wilcolac made some wry comment Yumiko did not catch. The youth in eyeglasses said, "Be that as it may, sir, the United States was dedicated to the protection of Our Lady of the Immaculate Conception in May of 1846. I will not distress the unclean spirits of your house by speaking her name. The Last Crusade has the authority to treat with you."

The silver-haired youth said sternly to Wilcolac, "We come in Arthur's name. In whose name do you speak?"

Yumiko hesitated for half a second too long. The youth in eyeglasses turned and looked into her face. His eyes seemed sad. He said softly, "The water is for me, please, sister."

She did her backward-leaning ballerina dip and placed the glass before him. Yumiko realized with a shock that his garb was not some anachronism from Elfland or a Renaissance Fair, nor was the beaded string around his neck Buddhist prayer beads. It was a rosary. He was dressed as a novice of a religious order.

This was a holy man. Or at least a holy boy.

She had been told to make eye contact with and smile at each customer, but, dressed as she was, she could not meet his eyes.

The silver-haired knight reached for the tray without waiting to be served. The novice cleared his throat and said, "Patience is a virtue, Gilberec."

Gilberec was apparently his name. He drew his hand back, saying, "Almost never got to drink this stuff when I was young. It is really tasty."

The collie dog barked. The young knight said, "Okay, okay!" and leaned back and let Yumiko serve him. He ruffled the dog's fur behind the ears. "Miss, this is root beer and not *beer* beer, isn't it? The last time I was in a restaurant, they kept bringing the wrong order…." He turned his head just as she was dipping down, so his nose was right at the same height as her décolletage.

He snapped his head away from the sight as quickly as if lemon juice had been squirted into his eyes. When he turned his head, her image was in the mirror, and the image reflected in the mirror on the far wall was a rear view of her shapely calves, thighs, and hips. He sighed and turned his eyes toward the ceiling, perhaps in prayer. He put his hand on an amber bead he carried on a thong about his neck.

The dog barked again. The young knight spoke without looking down from the ceiling. "And the bowl of water is for Ruff."

Yumiko knew she could not dip down to the level of the floor, so she knelt and slid the bowl onto the carpet before the eager dog. He sniffed her hand, licked it, and barked again.

Yumiko stood up, took up the empty tray, stepped back, and assumed the "Peach Cobbler Girl" stance: legs together, back arched, and hips tucked under.

The young knight said, "Gee, I don't know." He turned to the other boy and muttered softly. "Matthias, do you tip the waitress?"

Matthias shrugged and said, "No kind act is useless."

"All I have are my father's diamonds. Do you have any cash? Earth cash?"

"Vow of poverty, remember?" said Matthias ruefully. "Ah. I could give a blessing…?"

The dog put his nose in the bowl and began lapping energetically, careless of what he splashed on the carpet. Then, the dog raised his nose, sneezed, and barked again. The knight stole a glance at Yumiko. "I don't think she eats bones."

Wilcolac said, "Before you give any blessing, my dear young exorcist, remember that the Cobbler's Club is neutral ground! Your words might unintentionally stir up something adversarial, shall we say, which, like you, I welcomed here with promises of a safe and pleasant evening."

Gilberec said, "You promised more than that to us."

Matthias put finger and thumb to the rim of his eyeglasses, lowered them on his nose, and looked over the rims at Wilcolac. "Sir Gilberec means to say that your message proffered a most remarkable claim. We are eager to hear whatever specifics you care to impart."

Gilberec said, “How did your man find us?”

Wilcolac spread his hands and smiled a hollow smile. “Trade secret, I am afraid. As master of this house, I occupy a delicate position in the Twilight World.”

Yumiko stood in her pose, barely daring to breathe. Luckily, she had been told not to leave unless ordered out. They had apparently forgotten her.

2. *The True Knight*

Wilcolac leaned back. “Many odd rumors swirl in your wake as you walk the world, Sir Knight. They say you can detect the lies on a man’s tongue no matter how smoothly he speaks them. But you are cursed never to tell a lie.”

Matthias put his hand on Gilberec’s elbow as if silently to caution him not to answer this, but Gilberec said, “It is true. And it is hardly a curse.”

The words rang in Yumiko’s ear in a fashion she found admirable, even compelling. She believed him.

Apparently, so did Wilcolac. He said, “Is King Arthur alive?”

Gilberec said, “He lives!”

Again, the words carried an unnaturally clear sense of conviction with them.

Wilcolac said, “Then why does Arthur delay to wake his slumbering armies buried in the mountain?”

Matthias spoke in a soft but severe tone. “We did not come here to be quizzed. Your messenger said you knew a way to break the Black Spell to release mankind from thralldom.”

Wilcolac leaned forward. “I do indeed know a way!” he squinted at Gilberec. “Your curse makes negotiation quite simple, does it not? I had a long speech planned to convince you of my sincerity, but now I see I need not waste words.”

Gil said, “You speak the truth, but not the whole truth.”

Wilcolac leaned back in his tall chair, making a little temple of his fingers. “Nor do you. Who shows his hand before the wagering is done?” He waved his fingers in the air and plucked a playing card out of nowhere. “Voila!” With a flourish, he turned the card and displayed its face: the joker. With a sudden gesture, he flicked his fingers, displaying his open palm. The card was gone.

Yumiko realized with a start that she was assuming that she was seeing a mere trick, a sleight of hand. But what if it were not a trick? What if he were actually making the card materialize out of an invisible world and vanish back into it? Just because Wilcolac was dressed like a magician was no reason to assume he was not one.

Wilcolac, smiling, was saying, "But have I said enough to pique the interest of King Arthur? If indeed he is the one who sends you?"

Gil started to speak, but Matthias quieted him with a calm gesture and spoke first. "Dissolving the Black Spell is a fascinating prospect. You require something from us to proceed. But you are reluctant to ask directly, perhaps because something uncouth or untoward is involved. You need not worry. I judge no man. Our Father in Heaven sees and judges. Fear him alone."

Wilcolac scowled. "That hardly puts me at my ease."

"It was not meant to," said Matthias in a gentle voice, without smiling. "Your offer, sir?"

Wilcolac said, "Before I speak, it will save time if you tell me what you know of the origin of the Black Spell. Otherwise, you may doubt whether what I suggest will indeed operate to nullify it."

Once again, Gilberec started to speak, and, once again, Matthias motioned him silent and spoke instead. "No fear of that. We have time to spare. May I help myself to that delicious-looking caviar while you make up your mind whether to speak and how much to say?"

Wilcolac said, "Help yourself. I take delight in the comfort of guests of this house. Had I known the ages of Arthur's agents, I would have prepared some pleasant vice more commensurate with young tastes, such as malted milkshakes or hot dogs with mustard."

The collie barked and made a whimpering noise. The young knight scratched the mutt's ears and said, "There is no dog meat in that. It is fish eggs." The young knight scooped up some of the caviar on a cracker and placed the cracker on the floor. The dog sniffed it doubtfully, licked it, and then gulped it down in one sloppy bite.

"Very expensive fish eggs," said Wilcolac, one eyebrow raised. "Very. Are you talking to that dog, by any chance?"

"I talk to my dog all the time," said Gilberec, putting more crackers of caviar down on the floor.

Wilcolac said, "What does he say?"

Matthias said, "If he were wise, perhaps he would have told us to be wary of any man who makes his living by sleight of hand. We know the Black Spell cannot spread unless lamps of the Church one by one are snuffed and men lose sight and common sense. What is your offer, sir?"

Wilcolac cleared his throat and sat up straightly in his chair. He raised his voice as if he were on stage. "You are perhaps familiar with the Sybil who lives in a cave on the slopes of a dead volcano in Italy, above a poisonous lake beneath which no fish swims, above which no bird flies?"

Matthias merely said, "Go on."

"It is said she could see the future and past and wrote what she knew in nine books, but a curse of the gods, wishing ignorance on mankind, whirled the books into the air in a freak windstorm, tore them page by page, and scattered them hither and yon. Each page is now no more than a puzzle, a fragment, and a riddle.

"Some fell among the shamans of the Norse and warned them of the coming Twilight of the Gods, the Fimbulwinter, and the fall of the World-Tree; some among Aztec diabolists, predicting the coming of the white-skinned god and the downfall of Mexico; and some among the sages of India and foretold the Kali Yuga, the Age of Destruction.

"Some fragments survive to this day among the voodoo witch doctors of degenerate backwoodsmen in Louisiana and some among Eskimo wizards. The *angekok* or witch-priests of the Yukon faithfully follow the hereditary practices of six-fingered Nephilim who ruled in the New World long before the redskins crossed the Bering Strait, fleeing a nameless peril that haunted the prehistoric Siberian nights beneath the Northern Lights."

Wilcolac paused, but the other two said nothing.

Wilcolac continued in a softer voice, "Well-educated boys such as yourselves surely have heard rumors of such things? Forgotten cities overgrown in pathless jungles, abandoned with no mark of war or disaster on monument, pillar, or dome? An army of shadows who guard their own mausoleums? Monkeys seen performing cannibal sacrifices on cursed mountaintops where no trace remains of the men from whom they learned to imitate this horrid practice?"

Matthias crossed himself. Gilberec said, "What has this to do with the Black Spell?"

Wilcolac spoke in a soft voice, but made each word heavy with emphasis. "We have gathered certain scattered fragments of lore from the one place whence elfin lords never sought to remove it. In the Night World, which is their own, they can find and quell all who might know or guess their secret weakness. We of the Twilight World all vow when we come of age unbreakable oaths, intertwined with runes and curses, never to rebel. But among men, aha! In the Daylit World, the King of Shadows would never suspect the humans retain in rituals and rhymes, in old toasts or old place names, the clues of hidden things the men themselves no longer know!"

Gilberec moved restlessly. Matthias yet again raised his hand, but now Wilcolac spoke. "Your friend, my dear young man of the cloth, seems to be bursting to say something you don't want him to say. Let us hear it."

Gilberec said, "We come in Arthur's name. In whose name do you speak?"

3. The Faithful Friar

Wilcolac said, "There are those among the Cobwebs who are dissatisfied with the sneers and jeers of elfin lords and the sly looks of their ladies. The elfin blood is pure, their lives are long, and their magic is by nature what we half-breeds can only learn by art or by the crafting of bad bargains with dreadful entities. Their overthrow would please us. Do you support their reign?"

Matthias said wearily, "No one is going to give you a straight answer, Gil, not anyone who knows you are a living lie detector. You are wasting time."

Gilberec said to him, "I would rather know for sure that he will not be straight with us than to suppose he won't, without giving him a chance."

Wilcolac raised both eyebrows. "Giving me a chance…? Your cross-examination is allegedly for my benefit…? I am not willing to say who my principals are. They are not sure whom to trust. That is why they come through me: the Cobbler's Club is a bit like Switzerland. I have to be careful. If I even appeared to take sides, I would be ruined."

Gilberec said, "There could be a simpler reason why you know how to break an elfish spell than all this talk of scattered books and Eskimo wizards."

"And what might that reason be?" asked Wilcolac, assuming an innocent stare.

"You are an Anarchist. Do you deny it?"

Wilcolac took a moment to trim his cigar with a silver knife. He lit it with a spark of flame that seemed to come from the thumb of his white kid-leather glove. "A strange accusation. Here in my club, from time to time, I deal with parties on the wrong side of the law. I hear rumors of a Supreme Council of Anarchists. The oath we all swore to the elfs for some reason does not bind them. They use their supernatural powers to ruin all the institutions the elfs have erected among men as reins and chains, as hoods and horseblinkers. The Anarchists are said to have eyes everywhere, fingers in every pie, to control railways, shipyards, banks, communication nodes, and computer networks. They are said to be behind all the dark deeds that prevent the elfs from enjoying in peace their utter victory over men. But I hear rumors saying the opposite, that the Anarchists are mere agitators or died in the Great War. Supposing they were real: why would I serve them? Anarchy is bad for business."

"That is not a denial," Gilberec said to Wilcolac. To Matthias he said, "Come on. Let's go. This is pointless."

Yumiko had been listening very intently, glad that no one was looking at her.

But just then she shivered and glanced down. The collie dog had finished his caviar snack and laid himself down at the foot of Gilberec's chair, placing his furry head on the carpet between his paws so that his bright eyes were staring straight at her.

When Gil stood up, the dog growled and coughed and made a slight sniffing noise. Gilberec turned his head, saw her in her scanty, snug costume, but this time, instead of averting his eyes, he looked at her face. A thoughtful frown creased his brow.

Wilcolac said wryly to Matthias, "At this point in the good-cop, bad-cop routine, you, as the boy good-cop, are supposed to restrain your hotheaded friend to sit again, and this will make me eager to show my cards."

Matthias smiled and scooped up some caviar on a cracker. "I wish we were that organized. The Swan Knight is no hothead. He is slow to anger, but once he is angry, he is slow to forgive. He feels about truth the way I feel about forgiveness. Guilt and fear and hate tie men to their sins with heavy chains and long so that when they die, their tormented spirits remain on earth, haunting the scenes of their crimes. Without forgiveness, how can they be set free to go onward to their reward? So I have no qualms about entering the house of a Necromancer. You have more need of my services than any!"

Wilcolac said sharply, "What does that mean?"

"I saw a Jack-o'-Lantern in an upper window when I entered this house and smelled the spoor of many hounds. You flay the flesh of men for the benefit of wolves and expose the flesh of women for the benefit of men. Do you think I do not know who you are? What you do here?"

Wilcolac squinted at the young novice, and a look of true hatred appeared, if only for a moment, in his eye. "I think an innocent soul like yours cannot imagine the vices I sell, not even in your most sordid nightmares, little boy."

Matthias smiled, but his eyes were sad. "You forget. Saint Jean Baptiste is only two streets away. Your patrons come to our confessional booth. My master has heard confessed every detail of all the sins you encourage. But they have been washed away, removed entirely from the dreadful scroll no man can read. I am familiar with your works and your ways and familiar with how to undo them. You are bold indeed to invite me into your house. Unlike my knightly friend, my weapons are spiritual and cannot be bound in their scabbards. No do my weapons know any truce, nor rest."

Wilcolac's fingers tightened on his walking stick, but he said nothing.

Matthias smiled. "Invite your servant to sit and join us. Surely it is more fitting that I should wait on her than she should wait on me." And with this, Matthias stood. He turned and smiled gently at Yumiko and with a slight, almost courtly bow, beckoned her toward his empty chair.

Yumiko was paralyzed with indecision. Did this young man recognize her after all? She had been masked when they met in front of the Catoblepas Warehouse. Perhaps he recalled her from before she lost her memory. If so, what did he know about her?

She desperately wanted to hear what would be said next, but if she so much as raised her eyes to Wilcolac to see whether he wanted her to sit or to stay where she was, he might remember that she was the newfound Moth waitress whom he did not trust and send her away.

But she need not have worried. Wilcolac's full attention was now on Gilberec, who did not seem to be bluffing about leaving after all.

Gilberec had gathered his sword and his dog and taken a step toward the door when Wilcolac uttered a sad laugh and motioned him back toward his chair. "Be not so hasty, sir! I see there is no need to be indirect with you, young Sir Knight!"

The dog barked, and Gilberec paused. He turned.

Wilcolac spoke quickly, "Not all Cobwebs regard the Anarchists favorably: but I turn away no customer who is well behaved and pays his tab. I do not deny that I have had dealings with them in times past! This cannot surprise you. Certain of my experiments require access to uncouth and unhallowed substances difficult to acquire without the aid of unlawful powers. Nor would I deny to them that I have spoken with you Arthurians and that I am willing to deal with you. Come! Surely you knew this of me before you accepted my invitation! Where else could such a parley take place, but here? Will you hear this deal? A means has been found to break the Black Spell of the elfs. Does it matter who has discovered the secret weak spot? If there is no firebucket at hand to dash the flames, a chamberpot will do!"

Gil said, "Well? What are you offering?"

"Perhaps in days of old, when the elfs were strong and still knew how to walk the corridors of air and pass through the windows of Heaven, men with their gold idols and bronze spears would have been no match. But now? Only Winged Vengeance knows the high and secret path back to the toppled ruins of Sarras in the sunset clouds, and what is he but a menace? Can you tell us he is not your leader?"

Gil had seated himself. "He is not. The Last Crusade serves King Arthur."

Wilcolac said, "Then why does Arthur not walk the earth? Why is he absent from his throne in Cardiff or his seat in the Seven Hills of Rome? Who sends you forth?"

Gilberec spoke in ringing words, "Hear my voice! Arthurus Rex is king, warlord, and sovereign of the Last Crusade. To him have I sworn fealty, and my troth I keep. His laws I uphold, his words I treasure, his dreams I follow. Arthur serves truth and justice, and I serve him. Let man or elf, mortal or immortal, or the mighty demons of Hell who are the foes of Arthur know well that I oppose them with all the strength of spirit, soul, and mortal body I possess, now unto the last, so help me God. I have spoken! Who sends you?"

Yumiko stared at the young, silver-haired Swan Knight in awe. She was not sure on whose side anyone was, but, hearing such words, she hoped her side was the same as his.

Chapter 4

Truth and Half-Truth

1. Rumors of Raids and Voyages

Wilcolac said, "I am not given leave to say whom I represent. It is an interested party among the Cobwebs who are no friends to Erlkoenig nor any elf. I assure you they can break the Black Spell. But means are wanting."

Matthias said, "What means do you seek? And why do you suppose we have it?"

Wilcolac leaned back, poker faced. "I seek the Ring of Mists. Know you of it?"

"It is one of the Thirteen Treasures of Lyonesse," Matthias said, "It was kept in the Tower of Glass in Troynovant upon a baleful mead. The news heard among the elfs says that a fabulous digging machine with a drill on its nose, an Iron Mole, broke in through the foundations of the tower from below, where no eyes watched. Doctor Rotwang Cobweb, one of your clan, built that machine. Perhaps you should inquire of him where the lost ring resides? Have you spoken with him of late perhaps?"

Wilcolac sipped his whiskey a moment, thinking. "How did you know Rotwang built the Iron Mole? The factory was buried in a long-abandoned mineshaft in Pennsylvania and manned with the blind, who never saw what they were fabricating."

"A little bird told me," said Gilberec.

Wilcolac raised an eyebrow and took another sip. "Rotwang Cobweb has been known to come here to drink and watch the girls upon occasion. Most recently, he quenched his wrath in beer and whiskey, for it seems his intern, his apprentice, stole the Iron Mole and made off with it. The young man was something of a prodigy. A member of the Moth family if I am not mistaken."

Gilberec looked startled, but Matthias's bland expression betrayed nothing. Matthias said, "Doctor Rotwang is justly famous for the artificial woman he created. The elfs still blame him for the havoc she caused. That, and his earthquake machine, his counterfeiting apparatus, and his other tools of mischief have rendered him unwelcome among the elfish courts. So he had an apprentice, did he? A lab assistant?"

Wilcolac smiled maliciously. His voice was a soft purr. "You must have heard of this lad! He once flew to the moon in a vehicle of his own devising and landed in the mysterious Blue Area in the Sea of Rain, south of Plato's Crater, at the ruined non-Euclidean towers of Azathothopolis, where it is forbidden for mortals to go."

Gil grimaced, irked. Wilcolac spoke on, smiling slightly.

"Or surely you have heard of his adventures in faraway places, or his many wonderful machines, such as his supersonic dirigible, his giant searchlight, his war tank, or his amazing motorcycle which needs no refueling?"

Yumiko's heart beat rapidly in her chest, and her face was warm, but she did not know why. She glanced down at her fingers. They were trembling. Was it fear or shock? Was it joy? What did her lost self know?

Wilcolac's smile deepened. "Now, last I heard, this youth had involved himself in the affairs of Winged Vengeance and was aiding him in his ghastly crime spree. Did neither of you hear anything of the sort, perhaps, from your sources? Your birds or your confessional booths or wherever it is teenagers pick up top-secret intelligence?"

Gil started to speak, but once again Matthias held up his hand. "For a second time you mention the vigilante. Out of curiosity," Matthias asked quietly, "Why do you ask about him?"

"Why do you ask why I ask?" asked Wilcolac.

"Because it is an odd coincidence that you mention him," said Matthias.

"Odd why?" asked Wilcolac.

"After you, if you please, Mr. Cobweb." And, when Wilcolac hesitated, Matthias said, "You have to volunteer information to get information."

"You must promise not to repeat this to anyone," said Wilcolac.

Gil shook his head. "That promise is too broad."

Wilcolac smiled slightly, "Then promise you will not repeat this to the Supreme Council of Anarchists, their servants, or their spies. I fear them."

Gil said, "I will not knowingly aid the Anarchists in their work. Is that sufficient?"

"From the mouth of a man who never lies, it is sufficient," said Wilcolac. He dropped his voice. "The Anarchists until recently, very recently, had control of a dark doorway, a moon-door. The hinges are forged from iron taken from the Ocean of Storms, and the doorknob is a nugget of moon-crystal large as a fist found in the Sea of Dreams. The master craftsmen of old knew the secrets of their making. That is lost, as is so much. The Anarchists used this door to send their hordes swiftly through the mist from one hemisphere to another, directly into the Iron Mole, directly into lower parts of the Tower of Glass. Rotwang had hidden it on his vehicle before it was stolen. You see? The thing was arranged. A trap. This clever inventor's apprentice was played for a fool by Rotwang. Isn't that always the way with clever boys, book-fed geniuses cloistered in ivory towers? Too smart to realize they are rubes and chumps."

Gil stirred restlessly and looked as if he would like to strike Wilcolac in the face.

Wilcolac said, "The clever boy was allowed to steal the Iron Mole to bring the moon-door into the Tower. At the right time, the door popped open. Countless loyal fighting slaves of the Anarchists poured forth, without any of the trouble of crossing the watched and guarded grounds between."

Gilberec said grimly, "They poured forth to their deaths, or so I hear. The main force of fighting men was wiped out, and now the surviving Anarchists resort to more dangerous and desperate measures to regain lost power."

Wilcolac smiled. "They have more power than they seem. Force of arms is not where strength lies. You would not understand this, young knight."

Gilberec raised both eyebrows. "Would I not? That, Magician, is the most surprising thing you've said all evening. Not that you said it but that you believe it."

Matthias said, "Mr. Cobweb, if I may? You say Rotwang does not have the ring. Why did he not leave by the same dark door he used to enter? Why did he leave any of the Treasures of Lyonesse behind?"

Wilcolac stopped smiling. "Winged Vengeance entered the Glass Tower by an unknown means, unseen, and dismounted the door, took it, and used it to escape, leaving all the Anarchists and their armies stranded with no retreat."

Matthias said, "You say he has the ring? The vigilante?"

Wilcolac said, "No, but I say let us not rule out the possibility that he has it. Or soon will."

"Why?" asked Matthias.

Wilcolac wagged a finger at him. "Not so fast. It is your turn to answer. What is the odd coincidence?"

Matthias said, "Just that I saw the vigilante's sidekick, the Foxmaiden. In New Jersey. A few days ago. I think her master was burning down a warehouse."

Wilcolac said, "Why is that odd?"

"Because she is dead." Matthias said.

Yumiko controlled any reaction from showing on her face, but she felt the prickling sensation of sweat beginning to form on her skin. No one seemed to notice, except the dog raised his nose and looked at her.

Wilcolac picked up his cigar and inspected it thoughtfully. "This is interesting news. I know some unsavory people who would welcome it. Are you saying you can see ghosts?"

"I can see ghosts," said Matthias, "And she was not one."

Wilcolac said, "Or perhaps you did not see who you thought you did. Anyone can wear a mask."

"Not anyone can teargas a pack of wolves with a smoke pellet, swing on a wire like a trapeze artist, leap to the top of a telephone pole like an acrobat, pull a longbow taller than she is out of thin air, and then, with the accuracy of a trick-shot artist, pepper her pursuers with those poisonous arrows of red meteoric iron the police have plucked out of so many corpses so recently. I've seen her in action before."

Yumiko wondered at that word. *Poisonous...?* What had she been shooting?

Wilcolac said, "An apparition then? Some signs shown us by the hidden world seem solid. I saw one myself, a fortnight ago. It was on the evening of February 29th—a day that is between the calendar months, hence highly significant in occult matters, you understand. And as I was coming out of the Fixer's magic shop, I saw there, floating in the air above my head, a vision of a dark-haired girl who was not wearing any…" He looked at his two guests judiciously, cleared his throat, and said, "Well, I took it as an omen and hired the next dark-haired girl who asked for a job here. For luck!"

Matthias squinted, opened his mouth, but then closed it again and shook his head, looking troubled. "No apparition kills enemies with real and solid arrows."

Wilcolac said, "Why are you so sure she is dead?"

"I have it on good authority that she is," said Matthias.

Wilcolac raised one eyebrow. "Who would that be?"

Matthias said, "Trade secret."

But Gil interrupted, "Me. I told him."

Matthias sighed.

Wilcolac stared in wonder at Gil. "And how did you know?"

Gil said, "The Queen of Hell likes little black cats and lets them go into and out of her domain unharmed by the same secret back way Orpheus once used. I talked to one. A little black cat from Ulthar. She swore by Bast that the Foxmaiden had died and her shade had been seen by the riverbank, waiting for Charon."

Wilcolac had an odd look on his face, a look of envy, or jealousy. "But even when you can force a spirit into a cat, and force a cat into a Carabas cap, and get the little monster to talk in human speech, it never gives straight answers. It lies."

Gil said shortly, "Not to me. Not twice."

Wilcolac seemed annoyed.

Matthias said, "Your turn, Mr. Cobweb. Why are you sure the vigilante has the Ring of Mists?"

Wilcolac said, "I am not sure, but, as I said, let us not rule out the possibility. I know from my sources he is here in the city and the Anarchists are hunting for him. He engineered the destruction of their main host. And yet with their every resource, natural and unnatural, they cannot find him. The Anarchists can overthrow nations, wreck economies, smash rail lines, and ruin industrial combines and international banks. Everything the humans think was done by the CIA or the KGB or terrorists from the Middle East has their hand behind it! Their fingers pull the strings of all the marionettes in the world! And yet this one man eludes them. How?"

Gil said, "Every elf can summon the mist and walk unseen among men. And many a Moth and Cobweb knows this art as well."

Wilcolac made a dismissive gesture. "To be sure. But as their earthly image grows dim in the minds of men, their unearthly image grows bright to elfs and nephilim, ghosts and cats, and all night creatures! To blind the elf, one needs the Ring of Mists or the Robe of Mists. And everyone knows Sir Garlot the Red holds that."

Matthias said, "Which does not tell us why you think the vigilante has the Ring of Mists."

Wilcolac leaned back. "Simple logic. Who was present at the Glass Tower when the elfs lost the ring? If the Anarchists do not have it and the mad scientist's intern does not have it, who has it? The vigilante has it, or else someone loyal to him does."

Yumiko kept her face very still when Wilcolac said this. He was speaking of her.

She realized with a shock that, despite everything, despite her loss of memory and his master's suspicions and scorn, she *was* loyal to Winged Vengeance. She had to keep him safe also.

And save Elfine. And avenge her mother. And save her boyfriend. And not get caught, tortured, or killed.

But she realized the problem was larger, deeper, weightier. For apparently her ring held the key to breaking the Black Spell, which held all mankind in thrall. It robbed mortal men of the sight of the glories of the world in which they lived, hid whole continents, and disguised the elfish thefts and abductions. It blinded men's eyes and erased memories.

A new thought struck her. Perhaps this same Black Spell had wounded her memory also. It seemed to be a spell as wide as the sky, covering the whole globe and having many parts, many aspects.

Why was she thinking only of finding her own memories or her own cousin kidnapped by elfs? Yumiko did not remember her mission. But now she hoped, for the first time, that she was meant to fight this Black Spell and to aid in the effort to save mankind.

Yumiko closed her eyes against the pulse of anxiety that passed through her heart and lungs. At the moment, her only clue to anything was two tracers downstairs in his building she had to make an opportunity to go to see.

It was so slender a thread to follow. It might lead nowhere. More than her own life depended on it. Perhaps much more.

She snapped her eyes open, smiled, and tried to look pretty, just in case one of them looked up and wanted a drink or something. Because her only clue was so slender, and was here in this building, she also had to avoid getting fired.

2. *A Test of Spirit*

Matthias said, "You naturally want to know if Winged Vengeance is working with us against the Anarchists. Or you want our help tracking him down so that we can get the ring and trade it to you in return for breaking the Black Spell?"

Wilcolac shook his head. "Not quite. I more want to know what you will do if you become convinced that the Anarchists do not have the young inventor? You know the youth of whom I speak, do you not?"

Gil said harshly, "We do."

Matthias drew off his eyeglasses and polished the large lenses with the tail of his tunic. He said blandly, "We have all heard remarkable things of young Tom Moth, the famous son of the famous Dr. Rocket. Reason suggests that if he, and not Rotwang, were driving the Iron Mole when it raided the Tower of Glass, then the ring you seek is in his possession, or was. But I confess I am a little confused about the thrust of this conversation." He perched the glasses back on his nose and stared at Wilcolac. "Mr. Cobweb, are you offering to free the young inventor in return for the Ring of Mists?"

Wilcolac raised both eyebrows. "Free him? My principal is seeking the Ring of Mists. I was merely eliminating the possibilities. If the Anarchists do not have the ring, and you do not have it, then who has it? The vigilante? Or the boy inventor?"

Gilberec said, "Tomorrow Rocket Moth is a member of the Last Crusade, as you very well know. And the Anarchists are the ones who have him. Who else?"

Wilcolac raised both eyebrows. Perhaps forcing this admission from Gil has been his intent. Wilcolac said, "There are many dangers in the world, many strange quarters and corners where an overbold lad might go. Places which would not make him welcome."

Hearing this, the young knight grew stern. His voice grew dangerous as it grew softer.

"We will avenge the harm done to him," said Gil. "Tell your principal that. Do you think your hoodoo and hocus-pocus and pretend puppy-men mean anything to a Knight of the Table Round? I have been to the Green Chapel and returned alive!"

Wilcolac winced at the mention of the Green Chapel. Yumiko heard a voice in the distance utter a scream: she thought it was Joan the Wad's voice.

Wilcolac now stood, his round face red with emotion, and he raising his walking stick over his head. "You would dare threaten a Master of the Black Art in his own sanctum?"

As he spoke, the many candles in the chamber now blew and flickered, as if a wind that could be neither seen nor felt roared through the space. The shadow Wilcolac cast seemed to crawl up the wall behind him and swell and darken. As the candles flickered, the magician's shadow danced like vast bat wings flapping. Frost began to collect on the mirrors.

The collie dog, his hair bristling, stood on stiff legs, his ears flat, barking furiously. Gil made no move to draw his sword. He merely crossed his muscular arms on his broad chest, smiling slightly and looking unimpressed.

Matthias, who was still seated, touched his brow, belly, and both shoulders and kissed a medallion on his necklace. He folded his hands in his lap and spoke softly in Latin. She understood his words. "*Save me, O God, by thy name, and judge me by thy strength.*"

And now Matthias stood and drew out of his coat pocket what seemed like a small phial with a perforated top. From its tip he flicked a small drop of water, first to one side of him, then to the other, and then before him.

"*I beheld Satan as lightning falling from Heaven. Behold, I give unto you power to tread on serpents and scorpions, and over all the power of the enemy: and nothing shall by any means hurt you.*"

And the wind stopped. The candles grew as still and steady in their light as stars and seemed to grow brighter and brighter. The warm scent of springtide entered the room. The walking stick was jerked from Wilcolac's hand. It flew away from Matthias and across the room. It clattered against the mirror and fell to the carpet.

Wilcolac staggered and sat down in his chair again, panting heavily.

Matthias spread his arms. The bright candlelight reflected in the gold of his crucifix now blazed. "*Notwithstanding in this, rejoice not, that the spirits are subject unto you; but rather rejoice because your names are written in Heaven.*"

Matthias now stepped over toward the fireplace. Yumiko saw a playing card, the joker card, was in his hand. She could not understand how he came to have it. Had Wilcolac planted it on him secretly during the conversation? But they had not been within arm's length of each other.

Matthias held the card in one of the too-bright, too-clear, oddly unwavering candle flames until it ignited. The burning card gave off a truly vile smell. Wrinkling his nose, the young novice tossed the burning card into the midst of the logs of the fire, where it was consumed.

"Go to your reward for weal or woe, and trouble no more the earthly sphere," said Matthias in English. He continued in Latin: "*In the name of the Father, and the Son, and the Holy Ghost.*"

Matthias crossed himself. He returned to his seat, smiled, sipped his water, and helped himself to another cracker. "May I? This is delicious."

The candlelight, the shadows, and the scent in the chamber all returned to normal as suddenly as a dream ends in waking. Yumiko blinked, wondering what she had just seen.

Wilcolac wiped his face with a handkerchief. "…You will have to pardon me if I allowed a momentary burst of anger to…"

Gilberec was still standing and still had his arms crossed. "You do not fool me, Magician. You were not angry. You were afraid."

Wilcolac looked up, startled.

Gilberec continued in a cold, remorseless voice, "You are afraid because you were ordered to test us to see if any power was behind us."

Wilcolac wiped his face again, hiding his expression behind his handkerchief.

Gil said, "You did not want to do it because it would ruin your reputation. You betrayed your guarantee of hospitality. So whoever told you to do this has some hold on you, something you fear more than you love your club, your people, and everything you've built. Am I right? Just say *yes* or *no*, and I will hear the truth or falsehood in your voice. If you do not answer, that is also an answer."

Wilcolac put his handkerchief away, as apparently he was not perspiring in the slightest. He picked up his cigar, inspected it thoughtfully, and drew on it. It had not gone out: the tip turned red. Wilcolac sighed with pleasure, took the cigar out from his mouth, watching the smoke trickle upward, and spoke in a slow and even voice. "You are a very dangerous man, in your own way, Swan Knight."

"Arthur, the lord I serve, is more dangerous than I. The Lord my lord serves is more dangerous still. Fear Him. Your Anarchists raise their mutinous arms not only against unjust and just kings of earth and elfland but against the power and majesty of the almighty throne of high Heaven! You are mad. Who can fight omnipotence?"

Matthias said softly, "A clever man like yourself should not back the side sure to lose, should he? Where will you flee to escape the wrath to come?"

Wilcolac said, "The world is dangerous. None can be trusted. Mothers abandon their children; close kin will sell you to settle their debts and to save themselves. Cops are crooked, priests are phonies, and only racketeers keep their word! What would you have me do? Defy them? Defy the Anarchists? They are terrible! They are dread and fell as deadly serpents! Numberless as hailstones! They are as subtle and unseen as the night-breeze from some cursed swap where witches gather that carries the silent influence of pestilence to a sleeping village, until a passing peddler, days later, allured by the stench, finds all the houses and barns heaped with corpses black and bloated! Who can oppose such power?"

Gilberec said, "We can. We do. Leave them. Join us."

Wilcolac stared at him a moment, eyes wide. "I am bound by oath to the elfs, as are all of the Twilight Folk. You may hate the Anarchists, but who else, aside from them, dares opposes the elfs?" asked Wilcolac bitterly.

Gilberec said solemnly, "We dare. Arthur's sword is Excalibur, the Ironcleaver. The iron it cuts are chains that enslave."

Wilcolac said, "Let Arthur come out from under the mountain and speak to me in flesh, and let me look in his eyes and hear his words, and let me touch him with my hand and know I see no phantom. Then, I will serve."

"Arthur's man stands before you!" said Gil in a low and even voice. "You know the words I speak are true. You know right from wrong. If you will not hear me, you would not hear Arthur Pendragon, not if he stood before you in the flesh."

3. Last Words

Wilcolac sat, eyes downcast, sipping his whiskey sour. Finally, he shook his head. "My fate is not what we met here to discuss. What shall I tell my principals? They promise much, but you know I speak truly. I believe they can break the Black Spell and free mankind from the King of Elfs and Shadows. The Ring of Mists is needed to accomplish it."

Gilberec looked to Matthias, who had been feeding more caviar to the dog. Matthias straightened up, wiped his fingers on his tunic, cleared his throat, and said, "Tell him the Last Crusade is eager to see the end of the Black Spell, but we are skeptical that this can be accomplished. More to the point, tell him that the safe return of Tomorrow Moth is a necessary step toward the discovery of the fate of the Ring of Mists. Gil, please tell Mr. Cobweb here that we do not have this ring so that the wolves the Anarchists have hunting it will cease dogging our footsteps."

The collie barked and looked doubtful.

Gil said to the collie, "It is just an expression." To the magician, he said, "Hear me. The Ring of Mists is not in the possession of the Last Crusade, nor is the knowledge of its whereabouts, unless perhaps our missing member knows. If you do not have him, find him. If you have him, turn him over to us unharmed and uncursed. Then, we can discuss the Black Spell. Tell your principals that I bear white-hilted Dyrnwen, which slew the giants of Cornwall. Tell them not one of them will survive the stroke of this blade of fire should they work ill unto Tomorrow Moth."

Wilcolac did not reply, but frowned in thought.

Yumiko understood his frown. She often had people telling her to carry dire messages as well.

4. Leave-taking

Matthias said, “I am told elfs do not forget, nor their memories fade. Not all Moths retain this gift, as we are half human, and some are more so.”

Wilcolac smiled. “You are very politely asking if I need to have your message written down, but without bringing up the awkward question of how impure my blood is. Where do novices in cloisters learn such delicate diplomacy?”

“Wheedling a second bowl of gruel from Brother Cook during Lent,” said Matthias.

“A bowl!” muttered Gilberec. “Some people get to eat from a bowl during Lent?”

Wilcolac smiled again. “An elf once told me—these are his words, not mine—that the sadism of Heaven makes sure that the memories of the lost joys and glories carried within the elder elfs will never lose their sharp and bitter edge. While I think he was being a bit blasphemous, his comment comforts me whenever I forget something. Do not fret! All you have said will be passed faithfully along.”

Matthias said, “Any letter sent to this address will find me.” And he presented a card across the table to Wilcolac. Yumiko, moving quietly and quickly, picked up an ashtray and stepped up behind Wilcolac, as if to be ready in case his cigar dropped ash.

But she was too slow, or he was too cunning, or both. Wilcolac palmed the card and spirited it up his sleeve without pausing to look at it.

Wilcolac stood up and crossed the room behind them, moving to the door. He put one hand on the doorknob, turned, and intoned. “Gentlemen, I must see to my other guests. Order what you like from the kitchen or the bar. On the house, of course. And if I may…? Meaning no disrespect, it might prove convenient for us all if you depart discretely from the delivery entrance. Sorry!”

Wilcolac looked at her. "Wait on the gentlemen until they are ready to leave. If they need a room overnight, have Boginki put them in the Royal Suite. If they need a limo, have Licho call the service and put it on our tab. Otherwise, show them out by the back way."

Yumiko smiled and silently performed the skirtless curtsy she had been told to perform when acknowledging an order: putting her left foot behind her right and bending both knees very slightly. "If they stay overnight, do I ask Jarnik to put the dog in our kennel?"

Wilcolac scowled. "Don't ask silly questions. Of course the dog sleeps in the same bed with him! What did I tell you about Cobbler Courtesy?" He turned to the boys. "Sorry about Sorry. She's new. It has been an interesting and informative evening, gentlemen. You were not quite what I had expected." He tipped his hat with a theatrical flourish and exited.

5. A Clever Ploy

Both the young men were standing.

Matthias said, "I wonder why he apologized."

Gil frowned and said in a low voice, "For the insult to us."

"When? What insult?"

"Winged Vengeance leaves the corpses of his victims hanging from trees in Central Park, with confessions written in their own blood pinned through their hearts with an arrow," said Gil. "Does this magician think Arthur's true knight would condone such bloody barbarism? That we torture captives and exact confessions under duress or kill unarmed men? How dare he!"

Matthias said, "Don't worry. You insulted him back without meaning to. Plenty!"

"How's that?"

"Your trick with Randolph Carter's cat. You do naturally and easily what this necromancer can only do by disgusting and unnatural acts with corpses and bargains made with furies and psychopompoi. And this guy is no novice at his art: he has a ghost trapped here on the grounds, unburied, and in torment. A poltergeist, one who can touch physical objects. It put that playing card written with runes of finding in my pocket. When I burned it, I burned the fingers of the ghost holding it, but he did not let go. Some powerful curse binds him. The ghost threw the mage's charming wand across the room before I could snap it in two. This ghost is cleverer than most." They both looked toward that corner of the room, but the walking stick was not there.

"Runes of finding?" asked Gil.

"They want to find out where you sleep at night and invade your dreams. No more goons are going to be bold enough to face you fully armored and on your horse."

Gil said, "Maybe he was apologizing for wasting our time. This whole thing was a show. The Anarchists are blackmailing him. And they ordered him to convince us that Winged Vengeance took Tom."

Matthias said, "Well, it is a clever ploy. We still must explore the possibility, mustn't we? It does three things for them: First, it means we spend less time hunting werewolves; second, if we hunt him, we might accidentally flush him out into the open; and third, we at least distract him from hunting them."

"Why must we? Explore the possibility, I mean."

"Because the magician was telling the truth about breaking the Black Spell and needing the ring to do it. Which means either they don't have Tom, or Tom never had the ring."

"Which contradicts what we know," Gil said. "It is an impossible puzzle."

Matthias shrugged. "Maybe we should hire a detective."

Yumiko thought sadly that she knew just who to hire. A pang of sorrow went through her. She missed Elfine.

Gil said, "I am just glad the cat said Tom is not in Hell. I wonder where he is?"

"He could be downstairs in this building for all we know."

Gil looked down at his hip, where his sword was tied in its scabbard. "I would be happy to tear this den of vice to bits. But I gave my word this time. This time. We need more than suspicion to act on. King's law and all that."

"I wish Tom had your caution. What it is about working with atomic piles and superconductors that makes a boy reckless? Lord, forgive him for a thoughtless fool. Why did he go off by himself? What got into him?"

Gil said, "There is no answer to that. We'll keep searching. I had a very promising talk with Rat the Rat King, son of Rat the Rat King. Dick

Wittington's cat is wrong about him: I think Rat will help us. There are lots of places rats can get into in a city like this."

"If he is in this city. Or on this planet. This is Tom we are talking about," Matthias said wearily. "Well, I think we learned several things that might interest the Man in the Black Room. We should report in tonight? Or are you tired? We can just head back to…"

6. Sorry You Know Me

Yumiko instinctively put her hand to her bow tie. The young man was about to announce the location where he slept to his enemies without realizing everything he said was being overheard. "No!"

Her voice was louder than she meant. Both young men turned and looked at her curiously.

Of course, the mike meant everything she said was overheard also. She smiled the prettiest smile she could muster. "No, he was not apologizing. Mr. Cobweb, I mean. He says *Sorry* because he cannot pronounce it. Sayori is my name."

Gilberec said sharply, "That is not your name."

Her spine was like an icicle. The young knight was about to expose her. Yumiko said quickly, "It is a stage name! What I am called here!"

And before either one could say anything that might endanger her, she said, "May I interest the young gentlemen in anything from the bar?" She leaned forward and pointed at her bow tie. "Just speak your order into the hidden microphone. We record everything here. That way, we never get an order wrong."

Gil, as before, averted his eyes from her décolletage, and Matthias, as before, looked into her face. Matthias said, "Pardon me if this seems an odd question. Are you Daylight or Twilight?"

Gil said, "She's Twilight." He tapped Matthias on the elbow and pointed at the collie. The dog lolled its tongue and wagged it tail.

Matthias stepped toward her and said, "You are the lucky one, are you not, miss?"

Yumiko did not know what that meant. "Lucky?"

"Mr. Cobweb said you were the new girl, after he said an omen prompted him to hire the next dark-haired girl he saw, for luck. Do you remember me?"

She shook her head.

The young holy man took her hand in his. Yumiko was startled. His hands were large and warm and strong, not like the hands of a bookish fellow at all.

Matthias said, "Your spirit is troubled. Sister, are you in any danger?"

Yumiko thought quickly, disengaging her hand from Matthias. She said, "Mr. Cobweb is not angry with me for suggesting you keep your dog in our kennel. I should not have made an impertinent suggestion, but our kennel is very large and comfortable. We kennel dogs there. You should take a look at it. And you should look at the Royal Suite. You should stay the night."

She looked at Gil. This time, he did meet her eye.

The words *we kennel dogs there* was a lie. *You should take a look at it* was a true statement. *You should stay the night* was false.

And, of course, Licho and Boggy and whoever else might listen to the conversation her bow tie recorded had no power to hear which statements were untrue.

Gil nodded to show he understood her message. "Your boss lied about you, you know. He did not hire you for luck…"

Yumiko stamped on the toe of his boot with her spiked high heel before he could say more. She lied and said, "I did not know that. I never suspected such a thing! I am sure he was lying to spare my feelings. He hired me out of the kindness of his heart, when I was in need."

He did not wince when his toes were crushed, but he understood what she was really saying. *I knew that. I suspected it from the first. He did not hire me out of the kindness of his heart.*

"Sorry," he said.

"Yes…?" Yumiko smiled.

Gil said, "No, that time I was apologizing." He understood that she did not want Wilcolac to know she had seen through Wilcolac's deception. And, from the look on his face, he did not approve. Gil would not expose Yumiko's deceit, but he thought less of her for it.

Matthias said, "Sorry."

Yumiko looked at him. "Ah. You are forgiven?"

"No, that time I was trying to get your attention," Matthias said, "May I see a menu?"

She said, "Certainly. Does your dog bite? May I pet him?"

"My dog does not bite," said Matthias, smiling to himself. "But that is not my dog. He is owned by Sir Gilberec. We call him the Swan Knight's Dog."

The collie barked happily and wagged his tail.

Gil said, "I don't really own him. It is more like having an idiot younger brother."

The collie drooped and uttered a whine.

Gil said sharply, "There is no such thing as *Super Action Team Swan*!"

The dog yipped.

Gil said, "It is a dumb name! I don't care what Tom said!"

Yumiko knelt, petted the dog, and made much ado over him. Matthias stepped over to the fireplace.

When she straightened up, Matthias held the menu in front of her. He had written with the charred end of a stick. *I know you. I saw you floating.* He waited until he saw her eyes move over the words, and then, with a neat flip of the wrist, he threw the menu into the fireplace, where it was consumed.

Gil said, "The offer to stay overnight was generous. While Mr. Cobweb said we could keep my dog in the room, I'd like to look at the kennels."

Matthias looked at him in surprise. He, after all, had not heard which of Yumiko's statements were true and which were not. But he said, "Yes, that is a fine idea."

Just at that moment, the door opened. Boggy Cobweb, thin and gray haired and hard faced, dressed in a throat-to-ankle dun garb as stark and severe as what Matthias was wearing, stepped into the room with a clatter of heels. She spoke in a crisp voice. "Sorry! You are on stage in ten. Hop to it."

Yumiko said, "But I was to escort the young gentlemen. Mr. Cobweb himself said so."

"No backtalk, and no worries! I will see to them. Go about your business." She turned to the two youths, her face wrinkling oddly as she forced it into a smile. "Gentlemen, I am Boginki Cobweb, the concierge here, den mother, roustabout, and I do a mean juggling act. Now what do you need? Meals? Drinks? The revue is rather nice. We are doing an Easter theme, with the girls dressed as bunnies…"

Yumiko, inwardly seething at the lost opportunity, her mind suddenly bright with all the things she wanted to say or ask, swayed gracefully out the door, using the approved hip-pendulating footsteps of the Cobbler Girl Walk.

She did not dare risk getting fired, after all.

7. Three Afterthoughts

It was not until she was out in the corridor and halfway down the stairs that an idea struck her with the force of a thunderbolt.

Tom. Tomorrow Moth. The boy who flew to the moon. That was the name. He was the one. It had to be him. The inventor's apprentice. Who else but an inventor could have made all her gear and weapons?

Once the thought was in her mind, doubt was not possible.

Her fiancée. The love she had lost.

Almost, she turned around and raced back to Gil and Matthias to beg them to take her with them when they left. They could tell her all about him! They must know!

Three thoughts stopped her. First, it was clear that Gil did not know her by face or voice. She was not as sure what Matthias knew. But neither boy had reason to trust her or to speak to her.

Second, by infiltrating here, her chance of finding Tom might be better than theirs. The young knight seemed hampered by all sorts of silly rules and scruples. Yumiko had no objection to tearing down any place as need be. If only she could! But she was not a big, strong lad with a flaming sword and a huge red horse. He could throw a ravening wolf monster as large as a pony with one hand, but she could not.

Never had she felt so small and frail. She told herself that hers were the arts of frailty. Foxes did not fight hounds, but outwitted them.

She rushed into the backstage dressing room. All were bawling and bustling about. The smell of sweat and stage makeup was everywhere, and everything was a bewildering confusion of mirrors, naked lightbulbs, sequined dance costumes, and feathered headdresses. Yumiko grabbed a costume and wormed into line for Leshenka, the wardrobe mistress, to make last-minute adjustments to it. Her mind was calm and clear as a deep pond.

Because her third thought comforted her. She was no longer wearing both earrings.

She had slipped a tracer under the buckle of the collie's dog collar, where no one was likely to find it. It was number zero-four.

Chapter 5

Nocturnal Venture

1. *Ignis Fattus*

Yumiko noticed that the strand of hair she routinely left in the hinge of her locker was undisturbed. The next day it was also, and the day after, which was a Sunday. She assumed Licho, or whoever was pawing through her things, was by now satisfied that she was no threat.

That afternoon, when she walked the dogs, Yumiko belted about her waist the same red sash she had made it her habit to wear. After, she stopped in the lady's locker room on the third floor, visited the last stall on the left, and waited until no one else was in the room. She climbed the wall and lifted the ceiling tile behind which her trove had been stashed. Her groping fingers closed on the fabric. A tremor of relief swept her. It was but a moment's work to take the red, store-bought sash from about her waist and swap it with the red, mermaid-magic sash holding all her gear.

She had been wearing her store-bought red sash whenever she was off duty or walking to or from the health club. Everyone had seen it on her. When in uniform, she hung the sash in her locker with her other clothes. At night it was folded in the locked suitcase in the cedar chest at the foot of the bed she shared with two other girls.

The substitution was made. She now carried inside a mermaid pouch her suit and mask and all the tools and weapons of the sidekick of Winged Vengeance, not to mention one of the Thirteen Treasures of Lyonesse. That afternoon, as she strolled through Central Park, with Krisky and Plaksy ahead of her, and with Svarog the handyman trailing after, Yumiko fully expected a hard hand to clamp on her shoulder from behind, followed by an unsatisfying torture session (where no one would be likely to believe she had no memory), followed by saving money on her funeral bill and the kennel master's dog food bill.

But the hand never fell.

Elfine had now been missing fifteen days.

That night, the review performed two extra encores, and the celebration was extra wild. Yumiko was grateful for Licho the bouncer that evening, for a particularly lecherous drunk, a portly red-haired and buck-toothed man with enormous side whiskers and a moustache like a walrus, had goosed her.

Because she had a tray in her hand, she did not rear-kick the bewhiskered man in the shin, spin, knuckle-punch his esophagus, and follow through with a palm-strike to the nose. Instead, she hissed into her bow tie and was gratified to see Licho appear immediately and take the fellow by the elbow.

In the dim, indoor light, Licho wearing sunglasses looked ominous, and the customer did not protest when he was taken off to one side of the bar for a friendly free drink.

It was a riotous night, and curfew was an hour late. The girls were exhausted. The opportunity was here.

After the breathing of her nine roommates became even and deep, Yumiko inched from the bed she shared with Xana and Anjana. The coverlet never rustled. In an awkward position, one hand and one foot on the floor, Yumiko moved her weight off the bed by infinitesimal fractions of motion over a period of minutes so that no recoil of the bedsprings would disturb the other two sleepers.

After a nine-and-a-half minute eternity, it was done. She lay on the floor beside the bed, mouth wide, panting silently. Not for the first time, Yumiko was sorry she had lost her memory. She was willing to believe that this had been the greatest test to which her trained skill of stealth had ever been put. But without her memory, how could she know for sure?

She rolled under the bed, and from this position squirmed around in utter silence to face the cedar chest where her suitcase was kept. In the crack between the lower edge of the footboard and the upper edge of the cedar chest, she could see a narrow, child's-eye view of the dorm.

The other girls were breathing deeply, not stirring, not tossing. Even Nariphon, the sweet-faced Hindu, was sleeping peacefully, untroubled by the nightmares which so often made her twitch and mutter at night. Joan the Wad was snoring. Yumiko took that as a good omen. The only light came from the windows, which were covered with blinds. The neon lights from the street outside painted harsh horizontal streaks on the ceiling.

Only one window had its blinds open. This was a high and small octagonal window near the roof. Joan's hollow pumpkin stood on the sill, facing the window pane, staring out at the street. Its face had been carved into triangular eyes and a jaggedly grinning mouth. There was a candle burning inside, which cast dancing triangular reflections of orange light on the little window it faced. The candle never seemed to burn smoothly, but always jumped and flickered so that the eyes and teeth seemed forever to be winking and gnawing. Yumiko had been told this ungainly carved gourd was called a Jack-o'-Lantern.

Yumiko silently pulled the cedar chest under the bed. There was barely enough room to open the lid. In she reached, undid the combination lock on her suitcase, and found the sash by touch. This she silently and slowly drew out and did about her waist. Then, carefully, slowly, she relocked the suitcase, closed the lid, and inched the cedar chest back to its position.

When she looked through the crack between the chest lid and the footboard, in the darkness of the room, she saw that the Jack-o'-Lantern was now facing her. It had silently turned around. Its orange triangular eyes were now staring in toward the room. The jagged semicircle of its mouth grinned, and the guttering candle within made the grin seem to twitch and jerk.

A spasm of cold crawled through her bones. Her hands and feet felt chilled. She had to clench her teeth to prevent them from chattering. For a moment, she was lost in fear. This immobile, silent, smiling face carved into an orange vegetable frightened her more than anything she remembered.

The candle suddenly stopped flickering. Now, for the first time, the candle flame inside the hollow head was burning straight and clear. What it meant, she could not say. When a passing car outside threw bright slits of light sweeping across one side of the ceiling and then the other, the shifting shadows in the room made the one motionless shadow in the room obvious by contrast. It was as tall as a tall man, but thin. It did not move.

Then, the car headlamps were gone, and the shadows fell back into their previous angles. The shapeless shape was no longer clear. Perhaps it was standing before the dark and open rectangle of the bathroom door. Or it could have been a black dress Krisky had made such a fuss about hanging on a hanger from the pole lamp, positioning it just so in front of the air vent.

Yumiko fished the Ring of Mists out of her sash, put it on her finger, and twisted it to the white setting to ward off ghosts. The feeling of cold, the sense of dread, ebbed.

She quietly emerged from beneath the bed, passed over to the door, and stepped into the corridor. There were no motion and no change either in the Jack-o'-Lantern or in the shadow she now believed had been hidden previously in it. She eased the door shut behind her.

The halls were dark at night, but there were tiny butter-yellow lamps burning above the doors to the stairwell at either end of each corridor. It was enough for her to see by. The creaking silence and small noises that haunt even modern buildings at night were in the air. She stood on the red carpet. Facing her was a tall mirror. In the reflection, the white ring gleamed on her finger that Wilcolac Cobweb, the Supreme Council of Anarchists, and the vicious Lucien Cobweb, not to mention various werewolves, owl women, and perhaps the two boys from the Last Crusade, all desperately hunted and sought.

Twisting the ring to make it invisible to human eyes would not make it invisible in the mirror, but it would make her visible to the ghost. She stepped over to the mirror and tried to put a fingernail between the back of the mirror and the wall. She could not. Either the mirror was bolted to the wall, or else it was a one-way glass, a polarized window with a chamber beyond, just as Iele the Romanian said.

Yumiko rummaged in the slit opening of her sash. It bemused her to see two feet of her arm vanish into a nine-inch-wide satin-thin slip of red fabric. Out she drew her opera gloves from her supersuit.

Her long gloves worn over it would hide the ring from human eyes, but make it impossible to twist or untwist the collet of the ring. The sash with her weapons and gear would go around her waist. Otherwise, she would traipse around in her nightie and hope that any guard who saw her would assume she was on her way to an assignation, perhaps with a customer in one of the hotel rooms on the upper floors. This might be reported, but it would not be unusual. Because if any human saw the Fox-masked girl sidekick of Winged Vengeance skulking in her black camo catsuit, well, that would be rather hard to explain.

Yumiko noticed that her image in the mirror was looking at her skeptically. "What would your master say if he saw you sneaking about in a transparent nightgown, with your pale skin clearly visible against dark backgrounds?"

"He cursed me and told me to die."

"Well, what would your fiancée say?"

"You think he asked me to marry him? Why would I think that?" Her cheeks grew warm, and she saw her reflection blushing.

"Because I think it was serious. I remember the emotion even if I cannot picture a face. What would he say?"

"He would not like it! But what if the clue to find him is here somewhere? Or to find my mother's killer? Or whatever my mission was? Not to mention Elfine. Who may be dead by now." Yumiko tugged defiantly on the sash, drawing it snugly about her slender waist so that the fabric formed many fine pleats against her curves. "I will use the weapons nature gave me."

"You are sure?"

"No. But I am not giving up. I have forgotten my cause, but I am loyal to it. I have forgotten my love, but I will not betray him!"

Yumiko gave a brisk nod of approval to the image in the mirror, who returned this salute simultaneously.

She placed the earbuds into her ears and listened for the telltale beeping.

2. Nightcap

The signals from the tracers put on Whelan and Phelan were still coming loud and clear from here inside the building.

Down toward the kitchen, in her gloves and nightgown she walked. She ran into one of the watchdogs in the corridor. It was a husky named Batterfang.

But Yumiko had taken the trouble to feed the doggy treats to Batterfang, and to pet and befriend him, so now she merely knelt and scratched his ears, and he did not bark.

Yumiko started heading downstairs. The signals were definitely coming from some vault below the dog kennels.

On the next floor she ran into Blud, the youth who had first seen her at the door on her first day. He was pacing the corridors with a lantern. "You are not supposed to be out of bed..." His eyes were magnetized to her diaphanous nightgown.

"It's just me!" she said. She was trying to look seductive while trying to look like she was not trying. Anjana had coached her through practicing expressions in the mirror meant to show a sleepy heat in the eyes and an inviting softness in the lips; Xana had taught her how to stand and cock her hips. It was a difficult trick because it was the opposite of what Yumiko did when she meditated: she was trying to chain herself to desire, to become part of the deception of the world.

After seeing how modestly Gilberec and Matthias Moth refused to stare at half-dressed girls, Yumiko decided it was the sort of trick that only works on men who want it to work on them. But fortunately Blud (so Iele had confided in their gossip) had never recovered from the sight of seeing Yumiko so scantily dressed that first day, so apparently he wanted it to work.

He swallowed. "You know, I know who you are, Miss You Know Me. It's after curfew."

She said, "I couldn't sleep. I needed a drink, and I thought I could... I mean that you and I could... have a nightcap..."

Because, of course, if they broke the rules together, neither would dare report it.

She saw on his face he was about to refuse, so she shyly touched him on the arm, a silent plea. It was like magic. The coolness in his eyes grew warm. It was like a spark falling into the dry pine leaves of winter. A grin escaped him.

So he helped her to sneak into the bar, to disconnect the electric alarm, and to help themselves. She told him a little of her past as a Manchu princess and Japanese spy, and he took a few stiff drinks he should have been too young to enjoy. His cheeks grew red, and he grew bold and boastful and was actually sort of fun to talk to.

It turned out Blud was a handyman who helped out with the electronics of the club's communication system, the microphones in the neckties, and the special shielded phone lines running to Wilcolac's office. Yumiko was a little surprised to find herself drawn into the conversation. She found she did not have to fake her smile.

"Show me how you did that!" she cooed. "To the alarm, I mean."

"Most girls don't care about this stuff. How it works after you flip the switch."

"It is magic," said Yumiko, watching him work and making sure to crowd herself up against his back as she looked over his shoulder. "Honest magic. What is a radio but ventriloquism made real? What is a light bulb but a lamp holding a genii named electric current? And what is current but tamed lightning?" He turned, and she looked up at him with shy admiration. "And you are the lightning tamer!"

That made him grin. She stood on her tiptoes and gave him a kiss on the cheek. She could feel his gaze on her as she walked away, hips swaying.

Around the corner, she sagged against the wall, scowling at the pangs of guilt in her heart. Even the little bit she had drunk made her lightheaded, and she was angry with herself. She told herself her fiancée would understand what she had to do to save him.

But here before her was the back stairway leading down into the basement. Time was short and the opportunity narrow. She decided to fret later.

There was an alarm connecting the latch to the doorframe, which she carefully disconnected, using the tiny screwdriver she had pickpocketed from Blud during their parting kiss. She imitated what he had done to disconnect the alarm without triggering it. Her fingers were sure and swift, as if this were something she had done many times before.

3. Second Vault: Kennels

The ground level was dark except for a glowing green sign over the door to the stairwell. Here were cars parked belonging to the club. The cars of guests were parked by valets in another building: this garage was off-limits to the public and, indeed, to the staff, except when ordered here. A Peach Cobbler Girl found wandering here after curfew would be fired. Or worse.

A metal overhead door, like a garage door but larger, led to the truck bay and alley behind the club. It was now lowered and locked.

Opposite this door was a second overhead door at the top of a curving concrete ramp leading downward. The door was raised at the moment, which Yumiko thought odd. She sniffed. The musky smell of many hounds cloistered together was coming from below.

Yumiko crept down the ramp silently, making no more noise than a cat. The ramp curved in a half circle down to a lower entrance to the second vault, which was not blocked by any door.

To the right were shelves of dog food in cans and bags, jugs of water, collars and chains, protective ballistic K-9 vests, and assorted veterinary supplies. To the left were two rows of kennel cages, stacked atop each other. The cages for the two dogs currently on duty were hanging open. The other ten cages were locked and the huge dogs asleep.

To one side was a Dutch door leading into the room, or, rather, cubbyhole, where the kennel master kept a desk and filing cabinet. Yumiko remembered Elfine telling her how the daylit men liked to have everything written down.

To the other side was a door leading to a utility room which Yumiko, as the new girl, had visited many times. Here were the washing machines for hotel staff uniforms and the basins for hand-washing the Peach Cobbler Girl uniforms. A great cloth-sided bin stood underneath the laundry chute in the ceiling.

Between the two was a wide concrete floor, large enough for a vehicle to pass without touching either equipment racks or kennel cages.

In front of her was the door she had noticed before: a large overhead door marked OUT OF SERVICE, but with every sign of recent and repeated use. There was a smaller man-sized service door build into the larger metal door, like a postern in a gate. This postern door was made of metal slats just as the larger overhead door it pierced so that it could be raised with the larger door of which it was a part, but it also could open and shut independently when the overhead door was lowered.

Yumiko began walking with soft, slow, noiseless footfalls across the wide concrete space. Had she known that it was nearly impossible to walk through a kennel without waking sleeping dogs, she might not have attempted it; but since she had no memory to tell her otherwise, she crossed with a slow, careful, and calm confidence.

One or two of the sleeping hounds stirred in their sleep, or their nostrils twitched, but perhaps because they smelled no fear and instead smelled the scent of one who had taken pains to pet and pamper them, their twitches ceased, and they fell more deeply into canine slumber.

The floor was cold on her bare feet.

When she was within a yard of the postern door, she noticed that the lock was turned. It was not locked. That made her suddenly nervous.

She heard a small noise from beyond the door: an instinct told her to hide.

She did not doubt her instincts. Yumiko did a cartwheel into the utility room, grabbing the lintel of the door with her heels as she flung her body spinning into the smaller room, and swinging herself up into the exposed beams of the ceiling from which neon lights, now dark, depended. There she clung, above the lights, motionless, barely daring to breathe.

She heard the postern door open and then heard the rapid footfalls of a man's booted feet. He took three quick steps and paused. He must have picked up on some inaudible clue or scent because now she heard his footfalls approaching. He stuck his head into the utility room and switched on the lights. In her position above the lights, with the bright glare shining downward, the man was actually less likely to see her than had he left the lights off.

He was tall and broad shouldered, great in neck, bicep, and chest, but with a slender waist and graceful step. He wore a black leather jacket. His hook-nosed and high cheeked features were as harsh and brutal as if they had been carved of hard wood with sharp blows of an ax. His hair was long and straight, and he wore an owl feather braided in it. This was once of the bouncers, named Kuckunniwi, whom everyone simply called *The Cheyenne*. Everyone feared him.

He glanced left and right at the laundry bins beneath the chute and then at the industrial-sized washers and driers. His demeanor was restless, like that of a man pressed for time. She noticed that her long and flimsy nightgown was dangling down from her legs, and the hem was almost brushing the top of his head. She dared not shift her weight to free a hand and dared not try to draw up the dangling fabric, lest she make a noise.

But he was indeed pressed for time. He was blinking, but he did not even wait for his eyes to adjust to the light. Nor did he step into the utility room. Instead, with a growl of impatience, he snapped off the light and rushed back out.

She heard him retreat up the ramp at a quiet jog. The dogs were evidently used to his smell also, for none woke.

Yumiko slipped to the floor, frowning. She silently scolded herself as a fool. Why had she assumed she could sneak and spy in a nightgown? The danger of being spotted as Foxmaiden clearly was the lesser danger.

She shucked off the nightgown and tossed it in the bin marked for hand-wash only. Her suit seemed almost to jump out of the hidden compartment of the sash of its own accord. She slithered into it as quickly as a firefighter into his suit and flicked her fingers along the seams so that the leathery fabric tightened like a second skin. A flick of her wrist turned the sash into a half cape which clipped to her shoulders. The utility belt, harness, and weapons seemed eager to fit snugly into place. She donned the mask. The lenses automatically dialed themselves to a light-amplification setting, and now she was in a world of green-hued but clear shadows. She removed the glove and ring beneath and replaced them so that the Ring of Mists was now atop the fabric and could be twisted easily.

She made herself weightless, glorying in the sensation, and shot like a dark rocket across the space between the utility room and the postern door, which the Cheyenne had thoughtlessly left open.

4. Third Vault: Cold Storage

Beneath her was another semicircular ramp leading down. She kicked off the wall and traveled in a rapid glide across the downward slanting ceiling, touching the ceiling occasionally with glove or boot to propel and aim her slender body on its way.

The ramp opened up into another kennel. This one was empty, but the bars of the cages had been gnawed and clawed by something able to leave tooth marks and claw marks in inch-thick bars of solid steel. The canine smell was overpowering. Unlike the room above, there were not a dozen cages here, but scores, perhaps hundreds, stacked to the ceiling and four ranks deep. Half were piled to one side, and they were dirty with bits of straw and torn bedding, and they smelled foul. The other half were cleaned and smelled of disinfectant.

Dominating the room was one vast cage. It was large enough to hold the crocodile-headed, lion-pawed, hippopotamus-shaped chimera she had last seen young Sir Gilberec chasing along the bottom of the Hudson River, the one that swallowed dead werewolves and resurrected them from the dead. It was not back. A circus smell issued from that cage, and it had not been mucked out lately. Bags of fodder and chest freezers were along the wall behind the big cage. Apparently, a monster with a crocodile mouth, a lion throat, and a hippopotamus belly ate both meat and hay.

Also like the chamber above, there were two man-sized doors opening to the right and left and a second truck-sized overhead door dominating the wall between. As above, there was a wide lane of space for a vehicle to pass. Two forklifts were parked here, one to either side of the ramp down which she had come. Evidently, these were used to move the cages up to the loading dock on the surface level.

Lithe as an eel, she swarmed along the ceiling, and dove into the right-hand door. Inside she found a desk. Many small boxes holding files were crowded against three walls. There was no computer, no phone. She looked at the papers on the desk and discovered that her light amplification goggles could not help her when there was no light to amplify. Nor did infrared allow her to read pen marks on the paper since neither was warmer than the other. She drew her flashlight and flicked it on. In the narrow, powerful beam, she skimmed the papers rapidly.

These were invoices tracking the shipment of some good never mentioned by name. The notes for each shipment listed the pounds of human flesh and gallons of human blood consumed by each line item. The invoice material also noted how long each line item was in the cage and its weight, teeth and eye color, and general health both at the full moon and at the dark moon. That told her what was being shipped.

And there was marked how many empty cages were to be shipped on which dates to a place marked *LIs* and how many full cages were expected back; and likewise how many full cages were to be shipped to a place marked *CoC* and how many empties were expected back. The dates did not match up: there was a three-day layover period while the cages were kept here, and this was marked *R PROC.*

She guessed PROC referred to some sort of process, something that had to be done here, by Wilcolac the magician, before the caged monsters were shipped elsewhere. She recalled Elfine telling her that daylit men could not see werewolves or other monsters unless they wore red caps. Could *R* stand for *Redcap*?

She saw where each invoice listed funds due. It was listed in ounces, and the figures were high. If this were ounces of gold, then Wilcolac Cobweb enjoyed a very healthy income indeed.

Then she came across a short handwritten note: *Estimate from Empousa. She says once we have 1,000 at the City of Corpses, the performance can begin. Check Thursday.*

That might have been a day of the week, but she doubted it. CoC was an abbreviation for *City of Corpses*. Could it be the name of a ship? A haunted capital hidden somewhere beyond mortal eyes? In any case, it was the destination of the shipments. It was where the werewolves were bound. Evidently, they meant to gather a thousand of them together in that spot. For what purpose? What performance.

Then what was *LIs*? Could it be short for Elizabeth? Or a plural of the Roman numeral fifty-one?

Time was short. At any moment, upstairs, one of the girls with whom she shared a bed might turn over or wake up and notice Yumiko was missing. There was no time to read even the papers on the desk, much less all the boxes of files marked with ranges of months and years.

She unscrewed the bottom of the desk lamp, inserted a bugging device in the base, and replaced it.

That prompted her next thought. Yumiko turned on her receivers. Immediately, the beeping in her ears showed that the two tracers she had placed on Whelan and Phelan were close at hand and on this level.

In a series of long, swift, weightless leaps, she followed the signal across the wide garage to the opposite door, which was closed. It was a metal door with a heavy latch. She opened it. Within was a walk-in refrigerator. A waft of cold struck her. A vile smell assailed her nostrils.

Her brilliant, narrow flashlight beam lanced out. Yumiko discovered that she was a girl of strong constitution because her gorge did not rise at the sight, but her eyes beneath her mask narrowed. To one side of the freezer, hanging on meathooks, were corpses of huge canines that had been flayed. She saw clear plastic packages filled with brown on a shelf near them. To the other side were human corpses on hooks, also flayed, so that the muscles, veins, and bones were visible. Coats of pale leather, empty human skins, were hanging on hooks to one side. In the middle of the freezer was a rack or table with clamps to hold man or beast immobile. Scalpels, knives, and blades, curved or straight, serrated or smooth, were arranged neatly in boxes on tables or hanging in rows. There was a mass of flesh and red fat gathered in the mouths of several large drains puncturing the floor.

The tracers were in this room. She picked up a large knife from the flaying rack and poked at the mess gathered in the drains. The magnetic disks of her tracers found the metal blade and clung to it. She pried the tracers from the blade and returned it to its place. A cold and stiff rag hanging nearby allowed her to wipe the blood off the tracers.

What did it mean?

She stepped over to the shelf of plastic-wrapped packages and inspected them by the gleam of her flashlight. One was labeled WHELAN and the other PHELAN. She opened the seals and pulled out the contents, first one and then the other. The smell of brine touched her nose.

Each was a wolf pelt, with skull and paws still attached. One wolf had scar tissue around its eyes. The other had a discolored paw. This was they. Whelan and Phelan. These were two of the werewolves she had killed. Their corpses had been brought back here and flayed.

What did it mean?

Like a bubble that swells and swells and refuses to burst, some idea, some insight, was nudging at the edges of her thought, but could not make itself clear.

Suddenly, as unexpectedly as an ambush, the thought arose, "I wish Winged Vengeance were here. He would know exactly what this meant." And tears stung her eyes. She could not wipe them because of her mask, so she merely grimaced and squinted while she returned the wolf pelts to their plastic wrappings and replaced them on the shelf.

Back in the garage space, she carefully secured one tracer within the floor slats in one of the clean cages, one presumably headed for the *City of Corpses*, and then did the same for one of the dirty cages, presumably headed for *LIs*.

Then, she turned toward the garage door. As above, there was a postern door in one corner of the garage door. As before, the Cheyenne in his haste had not locked it behind him.

Down she went.

5. Fourth Vault: Lower Sanctum

Yumiko saw the leaping heat reflections in her infrared lenses before she was halfway down the curving ramp. She tossed her head to snap the mask up and to look with her naked eye.

It was firelight. Judging from the size and texture of the shadows, and the way they flickered and jumped, the light came from scores of candles thickly scattered throughout the chamber below. From the way they shivered in the still air and from the unnaturally cold air touching her face like the brush from a feather of an arctic owl, her heart told her that a ghost—or many ghosts—was near at hand.

She dropped lightly to the ground and twisted the ring to its white setting. The cold sensation receded. Her nape hairs stopped tickling.

On her belly, with her left shoulder brushing the wall, she crawled down the slope. The upper edge of the lower entrance to the ramp seemed to creep upward, revealing more and more of the room the lower her head came.

It was far larger than the garage vaults above. Lines of cast iron support beams ran from floor to ceiling, naked and ugly and showing their rivets. Yumiko could not see the far end of it. It was as if Wilcolac had purchased the basements of all his neighbors in this whole city block and then knocked down all the walls between.

At the foot of every pillar, and piled along the nearer walls, were owl pellets, the heaped bones of mice and rats, and pools of putrid decay. Perhaps the flocks of owls that made such a mess were gone by night to hunt.

On the cracked and mud-stained floor she saw a curved line painted in dull brown. Her nose told her this was dried blood. She inched further down the ramp so that more of the chamber was in view. The bloodstained line ran in a wide circle, perhaps twenty paces across, with a five-pointed star, also drawn in dried blood, inscribed within. Dozens upon dozens of candles were arranged in five clusters inside the star, some on candle stands, and some standing on the floor held upright by puddles of their own wax.

All the flames were blowing and jumping wildly even though none was extinguished. The shadows of the chamber jerked so vehemently that it was hard to focus an eye on any object without a slight feeling of seasickness. And yet the air was motionless and chilly, with no noise of wind.

Down she wormed. Lying on the ramp, her feet were higher than her head. The candlelight was only brushing against Yumiko's head and shoulders. The rest of her prone body was still in darkness.

In the wide vault was a bed or leather couch, filthy and stained, to which a portly man was strapped down. Broad belts circled his arms, legs, and body. He was naked, and his pink flesh was glistening in the erratic candlelight.

Yumiko clicked her goggles between infrared, ultraviolet, and light-amplification. She recognized the man by his overbite, his red side whiskers, and ungainly, huge moustache.

It was the lecherous customer who had poked her so rudely that Licho had led him away to mollify with a free drink.

Her bewilderment was absolute. Was *this* what was done to patrons who were fresh with the girls? They were abducted to his horrible vault?

Another inch. Now Yumiko could see above the couch what she least expected to see. Hanging from tall candlestands were an oscilloscope, a heart monitor, and bags of saline solution. It was all gear she recognized from her stay at the hospital. Tubes and wires ran from the monitoring gear to the bound man, his face, his arms, and so on.

The man stirred slightly on the bed, straining against the straps, and moaned in pain.

She thought her confusion could grow no greater, but, somehow, it grew. Was he being tortured? Or cured? But if this were a medical treatment, it was taking place in the most unsanitary environment imaginable. It was the polar opposite of the meticulously sterile hospital room where Yumiko had first awoken.

Yumiko now saw the legs and hips of a woman in a white nurse's uniform. From Yumiko's angle of view, the nurse's face was blocked by the upper lip of the entrance arch. The nurse bent over the body, and something in her hand glinted metallically in the cold and strobe-flickering candlelight, a knife or a needle.

Yumiko recognized her even before she spoke. The emotionless, aristocratic Russian accents of Polednitsa Cobweb came softly. "Your nerves are changing from a natural to a supernatural regime, so the pain centers of your brain are registering the signals as agony and death." Polednitsa made a sudden, savage motion with her hand. The man on the table screamed. It was a horrible, breathless, gargling scream, as if there were blood in his lungs.

In one impossibly smooth and rapid motion, Yumiko rose to one knee, drew the baton from her belt, and unfolded it into her longbow before she knew she had moved. Yumiko nocked an arrow and drew back the string. The Japanese longbow had a short lower haft to allow it to be used from horseback or from a kneeling position.

Polednitsa, all save her legs, could now not be seen. Yumiko's vision was blocked by the lip of the lower chamber's roof. But in the next moment, the white-clad nurse was walking around the table, moving closer. Yumiko saw her hips and then her waist and upper torso. In one more footfall, Yumiko would have a clear shot at her heart.

Yumiko regretted the fate. Killing the nurse would expose everything, ruin everything, and spoil any hope of rescuing Elfine. But she could not stand idly by and watch a man tortured to death.

Then, the man spoke in a half-strangled, gargling voice, "But it will still work, won't it? The change–"

Polednitsa said coolly, "That remains to be seen." Now all her form below her shoulders was visible. She crossed before the foot of the bed, and her back was to Yumiko. At this range, Yumiko could not miss. But she held her hand, listening.

The man said, "You have dug out my eyes and replaced them with wolf eyes, and pulled my teeth and given me fangs. The pain, the terrible pain! It was all worth it! But my skin! Why is my skin burning? I killed her, just like you said. I killed her, just like you told me to!"

Polednitsa said, "Evidently not. You were unmarried? Killing a paramour does not count. She was not your wife even if you were living with her. If you crave the unholy power, you must perform an unholy act. What about your child? Your bastard child?"

"Lives with her grandmother. Yes."

"Do you love her? Do you love the babe? That is the important thing."

"No longer! Give me the wolf-pelt. You said I could have Phelan's pelt. I will kill her." The portly man strained at the straps, yowling.

Yumiko's confusion broke like a chain breaking. This was no torture. This was some sort of reward, an initiation. He wanted to be a wolf. He craved it.

Yumiko now aimed that arrow at the man. Strapped to the table, at this angle, she could kill him in one shot. For a second time, she regretted hard fate. But if she did not shoot, it was the same as allowing a child to be murdered.

Polednitsa said, "Your flesh is not reacting as expected. I dare not inject more morphine. I have sent for the Magician."

Yumiko folded her bow into a baton and holstered it. She realized two things. First, this man was dying and likely to murder no one. Second, she was trapped. The ramp was flat and wide, with no possible place to hide, and the Cheyenne and the Magician would be coming down this way any moment.

Chapter 6

The Voice of Darkness

1. *Flay the Beast*

Before she fled, Yumiko took a bugging device, balanced on her thumb, and flicked it down the slope. It bounced, rolled, skipped along the cracked and muddy floor, and came to land right next to the legs of one of the standing candlesticks.

Yumiko retreated up the ramp. She was quietly and quickly crossing the floor between the empty werewolf cages when she saw the feet and the legs of two men descending. Their upper bodies were still hidden behind the upper entrance lip. She glanced left and right. The walk-in freezer door was shut and would make a noise if she opened it. The office door was open. She twisted the ring on her finger, became weightless, and threw herself like a slender black-clad torpedo. She snatched the edge of lintel with her hands and her momentum tossed her in a tight circle around the corner. There was a slight rustling noise as she landed feet first, bending her knees to absorb the shock, against the stacked cardboard boxes filled with invoices.

"What was that?" came the deep voice of the Cheyenne.

"Your ears are sharper than mine," answered the voice of Wilcolac. He sounded slightly out of breath, as if his chubby body could not keep pace with the young, athletic man leading him. "But let us—(whew!)—not dilly-dally. We, ah, do not want to lose—(puff!)—a paying customer."

"I heard something. Before."

"Take a moment. I will go on ahead." And she heard the noise of the postern door opening and shutting.

Yumiko was sure the vault below this was crowded with ghosts or supernatural presences, certain to see her if she stepped into their misty realm. But here? She twisted the ring to black. The room seem to distort in her vision, as if it were larger than it should be, and the angles at the corners and walls no longer seemed like right angles. The ceiling and floor no longer seemed parallel.

The Cheyenne stepped into the office. He had a handsomely decorated hatchet in his hand, whose sharpened blade gleamed wickedly. He snapped on the lights. The glare seemed freakishly bright, distorted. His eyes passed over her and did not see her. He looked behind the piled boxes, under the desk, and in the closet. As he walked, she carefully stepped behind him, silent as a doe, trying desperately not to brush against him, not to step on any scrap of paper, and not to breathe.

His nostrils flared. "I can smell you," he said. "But I cannot see you."

She touched the spot at the throat of her mask which clamped her suit airtight. Oxy-nitrogen hissed into her mask from a hidden air supply. She tiptoed slowly backward out of the room.

He got down on his knees and sniffed again. But now he looked puzzled.

A scream came from below. Then came Wilcolac's voice, calling the Cheyenne by name, "Kuckunniwi! If you please!"

The Cheyenne stood, looking indecisive, and returned the hatchet to a sheath hidden under the lower back of his leather jacket. He stepped out of the office. He had neglected to douse the desk lamp, so his shadow was spread within a triangle of light stretching along the concrete floor and across the empty cages. To Yumiko, hidden in the mist, the light seemed like a blurred and burning river.

The Cheyenne glanced up at the ramp leading out, made a small, tense grimace, which might have been his smile, and passed through the postern door. He paused to close it. Yumiko heard a key scrape in the lock and the bolt shut.

With a sense of relief, she untwisted the ring. It turned pewter. The angles of the room returned to normal, as did the distorted glare of the light. At one-sixth her normal weight, she skipped up the ramp like a stone skipping on the water. She returned her weight to normal at the last skip and slid to a halt before the postern door. Now she understood the small smile of the Cheyenne. In his hurry to get Wilcolac, he had forgotten to lock the doors behind him, but after he heard her moving around in the utility room, he had not.

She tuned her ear receivers to the bug she'd left behind, listening to their conversation, hoping to hear some warning if one of them started moving back toward her. She knelt, tossed her head to open her mask, held her flashlight in her teeth, and brought out her tension wrench and a three-pronged Bogata rake. Both were the size and shape of dental instruments. She carefully applied tension to the bottom of the keyhole with the wrench and tickled the pins with the rake to test the tension on each pin. The pin most firmly in place was the first one to prod back, and then the next…

Her hands remembered how to do this, but her brain did not, so she could not estimate how long it should take. She had no experience, no basis of comparison. How long would it take? *How long?*

The uncertainty made her nervous, and this made her hands unsteady, so the pins slid back into place. She had to start over again.

She could hear the voices of Wilcolac and Polednitsa through her earphones and an occasional sound of the Cheyenne shifting his feet. He was evidently standing very close to the bug, perhaps only inches away.

"…rejection of the tissue?" Polednitsa was asking.

Wilcolac said something the bug did not pick up. And then, either he turned his head or stepped closer to the bug. "…he deceived us, or was deceived himself, about the strength of elfish blood in his heritage. Mr. McDuffy here is less than a quadroon."

The Cheyenne said, "No. We checked. His grandfather was the keeper of the Eddystone Light, and so his father was a half-breed at least."

"Then the elfin blood itself is growing weak, and the old strength is leaving the world."

Polednitsa said, "The triannulus shows drops of divine blood in his bloodstream. He has taken the communion wafer."

Wilcolac said, "Fool! You were warned what would happen! When men eat bread, it turns into them; when men eat the bastard son of Mary, when he looks like bread to trick them, they turn into him."

The gobbling, gargling voice of the portly red-whiskered man now spoke. "Nay. Nay! Not since I was a child of seven. I had forgotten… so long ago…"

Polednitsa muttered, "How could even the smallest particle of the material still exist from years ago? It should have been digested in eight hours."

Wilcolac growled, "Heaven not only tyrannizes, but it deceives. The divine power could will anything, do anything. Instead, it tricks and toys with us, tempting us with victory to snatch it out from between our very teeth! Who can fight a foe who can change the laws of nature or raise the dead? How is that fair?"

"Sir?"

"These sneaking sacraments can spring up again, full of force, years after they should have been flushed out of body and soul. They wait like a coiled snake to bite the conscience, and even hardened killers weep like girls." He raised his voice, "Dark and adored Lady! Can anything be done?"

No voice answered him, but a coldness touched Yumiko in the ear, and a fear trembled in her heart, and she knew Wilcolac addressed whatever power it was that set all the candle flames to tremble in that dark chamber below.

Polednitsa said, "We cannot start flaying now. It will kill the subject. The skin is not soaked through. McDuffy is still awake, and the morphine has no effect. The phase of the moon is not correct! The laws of magic say…"

But Wilcolac answered, "Do not question the voice of Hell. What I know of magic, I see through the narrow bars of a gate. Lady Empousa is from beyond that gate."

This time, Yumiko did hear the voice. "*Flay him. Flay the beast.*" But she heard the words silently in her mind, not through her ears.

This horror was only one floor below her. At that moment, the last tumbler clicked into place under Yumiko's fingers. In her impatience to escape, Yumiko flung open the postern door.

A shrill electronic shrieking answered her. She had neglected to check for alarms to disarm. Through the door to the second vault, the clamor of barking from enraged dogs, startled awake by the alarm, filled the air.

Wilcolac's voice in her ear said, "Cheyenne? If you would, please?"

The Cheyenne answered, "The upper door is locked. It is the Foxmaiden. She cannot get out. Phone Licho. Have him meet me." His voice was very loud, as if he were standing atop the bug's mike. Loud, swift footsteps thundered her ear, coming closer. Then, there came an abrupt silence in her earphones. He had stepped on the bug and crushed it.

2. *Empousa*

Yumiko took a step into the second vault. It was dark here, with only small yellow lights burning near the door to the utility room and the kennel master's cubbyhole. A brighter light was shining from below and behind her, reflected from the concrete. The light behind her flickered.

Through the bug left behind in the third vault office, Yumiko could hear someone or something moving through the vault toward the ramp behind her. But it was a woman's footsteps, not the Cheyenne's. One foot clopped like a horse's hoof. The other clashed like a boot made of brass. And the footfalls were spaced too far apart: it was a giantess.

A touch of cold caressed her spine. An overwhelming fear overcame her, making her chest tighten as if she had breathed a poisonous gas into her lungs.

She twisted the ring to white, which she hoped would render her invisible to whatever titanic spirit being was coming for her. Her full weight returned.

Yumiko looked toward her escape route. A steep, concrete semicircular ramp led up out of sight. But the door at the top was sure to be locked.

It was difficult to tell with the alarm ringing and the dogs barking, but she thought she heard the noise of men and dogs also coming from overhead. Licho, and the other dogs on guard duty, must have been in the loading dock or somewhere equally near at hand. There was no escape that way.

At that moment, she also heard downstairs the Cheyenne's running footfalls trot past the shipping office door. The sound changed when his boots struck the curving concrete ramp leading up from the lower level. She could not go back.

A shadow solidified in the middle of the vault. One moment, nothing was there. The next, a twelve-foot-tall being stood there, radiating a dark majesty. The barks of the dogs all turned to howls and terror.

Here was a dark-eyed lady of regal demeanor. A hood, a veil, and sweeping black robes, which seemed to be woven of, or into, or through her living hair, draped her tall form. Her crown was a writhing circle of intertwined snakes brighter than jewels. Beneath the hem of the robe, Yumiko could see that one leg of the apparition was made of bronze; the other ended in a donkey's hoof.

This was not a mere ghost, nor even an elf, but something infinitely older, greater, more malign; something pagan men of old worshiped and adored and called a goddess, sacrificing cattle, or horses, or maidservants, or daughters.

The veiled and pallid face turned toward her. The dark, unblinking eyes swept toward the spot where she stood.

Yumiko was pinned in place by terror. Her limbs would not move. She could hear the Cheyenne's rapid footfalls approaching, and yet still she was frozen.

"Empousa of Tartarus, I am." She could hear it clearly in her mind, and the terrified yowling of the hounds did not smother or impede the sound. The cold and malicious voice was not real, not made of air vibrations like those yowls were. "To hide from me, I who am of the darkness beyond night, no elf dares. Show yourself!"

And the deadly, terrifying eyes slid past. The apparition was blind to her. The Ring of Mists could obscure the sight of more than mere ghosts.

A shiver of relief passed through Yumiko so overwhelming that she almost fainted.

But she did not faint. Instead, heedless of noise—for nothing could be heard against the sound of dogs screaming and alarms wailing—Yumiko ran toward the utility room, cartwheeling over a dog cage in her way, landing, rolling, and coming to her feet inside the room between the washers and driers. She saw her nightgown, picked it up, and stuffed it into her cape pocket. A flick of the wrist slapped the wirepoon gun into her palm. She shot the grapnel up into the laundry chute.

A spool motor in the gun spun in a whispering hum of noise. The wire tightened. She felt a jerk on the parachute harness built into her suit to which the wire was attached. A yank pulled her up out of the utility room as smoothly as a marionette being whisked offstage by the puppeteer.

3. Alarums and Excursions

She passed one hatch above the next as she rose from floor to floor. She squirmed through the last hatch into an upper-floor laundry room. Uniforms of busboys and cleaning maids were hanging in the darkened room. The alarm from below was muffled, almost inaudible. She cracked the door.

Outside was a carpeted hall, two floors below her dorm. She could see two standing mirrors in the hall, each one near a stairwell. Was it her imagination, or was there a hint of frost in one of the mirrors that looked almost like the thin, mouthless face staring out? Did a chilling draft sigh from that side of the hall?

At the same time, she heard a man's footsteps in the stairwell and a dog's claws clattering. "...some backup. Roust everyone out of the sack. This could be the big one. The one we've been prepped for. Put four men on the roof as spotters..." It occurred to Yumiko to wonder whether other hotels and nightclubs in America kept a full-time squad of bouncers and security guards who slept on-site, not to mention a K-9 corps.

Yumiko toyed with the ring on her finger; her eyes narrowed. If both ghosts and men were hunting her, the ring could not hide her from both at once. Either one might be posted behind any one-way mirror. How could she get upstairs without being detected? If the noise woke even one of her nine roommates as Yumiko crept back into the room, and into the bed... and then there was that haunted pumpkin... There was too much commotion.

Too much commotion? Or not enough?

She saw a fire alarm on the wall across the hall. A flick of the wrist, and she shot her grapnel precisely into the alarm to hook the switch. She yanked on the wire. Alarms now started whooping on every floor. Wilcolac's men could not keep everyone locked in the building, not without exposing his secrets to his innocent guests.

She released the grapnel and retracted it with a metallic hiss into her pistol, just as two men, Kudlac and Blud, and two dogs, Batterfang and Rach, stepped out of the stairwell. Doors were beginning to open in the hall. A chubby middle-aged guest followed by a svelte young redhead with sleepy eyes stumbled into the hall. Then came a man with wild eyes, still in his nightshirt, but clutching a briefcase handcuffed to his wrist. Then a tall woman carrying a lantern. Then an old hag with an eyepatch, carrying a besom, wearing yellow robes and sporting a tall, conical hat. All began uttering querulous questions. More doors opened. Kudlac called out in a loud voice that all must remain calm and move to the exits.

Yumiko made sure her mask was in place and that the seal was airtight so that no scent of her skin could escape for any dog to smell. She waited for the door opposite the laundry room to open, and the guest there, a young man with unkempt hair and a foot-long single eyebrow, carrying a bindlestaff, emerged. She stepped casually into the hall, gave a cheerful wave of the hand to Kudlac and Blud, and stepped around the young guest. In the doorframe she struck a pose, standing on one foot, the other leg bent, one hand on hip, the other raised on high, beckoning to Kudlac with her fingers.

Kudlac drew a knife, and the guests crowding hall uttered cries and shouts of confusion as he began shoving his way quickly through the guests, shouting apologies.

Blud was wrestling with the two dogs, yanking on their neck chains, not daring to release them.

She blew Kudlac a kiss from the snout of her grinning mask, and, with a pirouette, danced into the empty guest room. As she had correctly recalled, this was a room with a balcony. She stepped over, flipped the latch, and opened the French doors. She waited another moment, perched on the balcony rail in a saucy pose with her legs crossed, until Kudlac struggled free of the press, came to the door, and saw her. She tossed her hands overhead gaily and fell backward into empty air, kicking her legs up as she went. Kudlac gave an involuntary cry of alarm.

Yumiko fired her wirepoon as she fell, snagging the upper crosspiece of a telephone pole to one side. Momentum carried her through three-fourths of a great circle while Kudlac rushed out onto the balcony, staring and gasping. At the top of the arc, she released the grapnel and somersaulted through the air to land neatly on the next roof over. There came a hoarse shout from above. Men were hurrying out of the roof door atop the Cobbler's Club, and one of them had spotted her.

She braced the pistol with both hands and shot her wirepoon across Lexington Avenue. The grapnel caught a fire escape across the street. She twisted the ring on her finger and let the wire's retraction throw her now-weightless body across the avenue like a stone from a slingshot. Streetlights and headlamps passed beneath her like a bright, murmuring river. As she flew, she unlimbered her baton. The wall next to the fire escape rushed toward her like an avalanche. She snapped the baton to its full length and used it like a pole-vaulter's pole to stave off the approaching wall. Her flight path was deflected just enough that she did not ram into the corner of the building, but slid through the air past it, to soar down the narrow alley.

She snapped open her cape, and it stiffened into gliding wings. She banked and swooped around the far side of the building, going out of sight of any observer on the Cobbler's Club roof across the avenue. Then, she twisted the ring to increase her weight, cupped her wings to kill her speed, and caught a passing telephone pole in her hand. She followed a path like a barberpole spiral to the ground and landed lightly.

Then, she removed her mask and cape and weapon harness and changed the color of her suit from black to white. A girl in a pale leathery catsuit was not actually out of place among the late-night crowd of the Manhattan streets. She stepped out onto the avenue and hailed a cab. She had it drive her around the block while she changed into her nightgown, and the driver twice almost wrecked his cab trying to stare at her in the rear-view mirror. Yumiko was so pleased to have money to buy things that she gave the driver a larger tip than he deserved. "I am so sorry to have confounded you," she said with a bow.

"Don't worry, lady. It's New York."

She then scampered lightly over the fence leading to the back alley leading to the loading dock and strolled over to where the other Peach Cobbler Girls, also in their nightgowns, were gathered. The guests from the hotel were also milling in the same area. Wilcolac was not in evidence, but Boggy Cobweb was there. For once her hair was not rolled up in a severe bun, but hung to her shoulders, the hue of smog. She was calling to the guests to remain calm and cajoling them with promises and reassurances. Yumiko was nonchalantly standing with the other girls when Joan the Wad turned around and called a roll call to make sure everyone had made it out of the building safely. A minute later the fire marshal and a fire truck arrived.

And when all the hullabaloo was over, Yumiko strolled back inside with the others, pausing to pet Batterfang and praise him. The husky wagged his tail and barked happily at her. She gave Blud a shy look, dropped her eyes, and hurried past him. She glanced over her shoulder to see his eyes still glued to her. Then, she went skipping upstairs with the other girls, who were chattering or giggling or complaining as the mood took them. Closing her eyes, safe in the warm bed, a sense of profound pleasure, such as a magician must feel when his sleight of hand fools all eyes, tickled her warmly.

Chapter 7

The Red Knight

1. Hectic Evening

Yumiko was far less buoyant the next day.

Elfine was still missing. Her beloved, the boy named Tom, was still missing or dead. Her mother was still dead and unavenged.

As she stood naked in the bathroom, doing her hair and make-up before donning her Cobbler Girl outfit, and staring with unsmiling eyes at a mirror which might have been one-way glass, she fretted about the hundred little clues she had left behind on her spree. Her cover had become too fragile. A single conversation with Blud, or any of her roommates, about who had been wandering about at night could expose her, or a hidden camera, or a haunted pumpkin, or some magical watchman whose existence she could not even begin to guess.

But she still held to a thin thread of hope. The two cages marked by her tracers would eventually be shipped, one to the *City of Corpses* and the other to *LIs*, whatever that was. She had read the invoices and knew when the next shipment was due to arrive: this Wednesday. Three more days after that, it would go out. It should not be that hard to discover when a fleet of trucks was parked out back.

So she expected a hand to fall on her shoulder that day, or the next, and it did not. Perhaps this was because things became hectic then.

At first she thought this was become the shipment was due tomorrow. But she realized something else was in the air.

Some of the regular staff were absent, running errands, and no one seemed to have time to tell Yumiko what was happening. The managers were ordering everything put in order and double-checked. The janitors were doing a thorough cleaning. Wilcolac Cobweb emerged from his office and was going over the stock, talking with the bartenders, the chef, and the kitchen staff. VIP tables were set up on the lounge floor, separated from the rest by a cordon of velvet ropes.

Yumiko, wary of attracting attention, was unwilling to show any curiosity, but that night, when they were working tables before the first show, Iele the Romanian rolled her eyes at Yumiko and tossed her head with a snort. Clearly, the girl wanted to gossip: Yumiko stepped with her into the short corridor connecting the kitchen to the lounge.

2. Very Important Elf

Iele was fishing half a dozen twenty-dollar bills out of her cleavage, smoothing them, and tucking them into her cummerbund. "I have a live wire. Heavy tipper. Look over there. You can see him. The one built like an Olympic athlete. Or an Olympic god."

Yumiko opened the swinging doors a crack and peered where Iele pointed.

Wilcolac was standing at the table side, smiling a genial if subservient smile. With him was the chief chef, who was describing the main course for the evening to the guests. There were several people at the VIP table circled by a velvet rope, but only one man with the broad shoulders and muscular build of a boxer or wrestler, certainly not of any peaceful sport.

Yumiko understood why Iele was breathless: the man was handsome to an unearthly degree. His face was square and strong, his cheekbones high, his gray eyes piercing, his nose long and straight. His mouth was a thin slash that rarely flexed, and lines like calipers embraced it. His chin jutted like the toe of a boot. A grim dignity surrounded him like a dark aura.

He wore hues of sable and jet, trimmed with scarlet and gold. His shirt was silk with voluminous sleeves. A collar of lace reached from shoulder to shoulder in two broad triangles. He wore dark pantaloons like a matador. His gloves and his boots were burgundy. A chain of silver set with rubies, the copper buckle of his baldric, and a larger ruby set in the pommel of his broadsword provided a touch of brightness to his dark garb. There were gold spurs on his bootheels.

Strangely, the reflections of light caught in the shining threads of his black silk, or in the shining copper and gleaming rubies adorning him, seemed not to come from the room in which he sat. It was as if the light of stars brighter and greater than the stars in the skies of earth shone on him and shed their reflections here.

What was the most eerie about him was the grace of his posture and gestures. Every slight movement of his hand, or the tilt of his head, was fluid, strong, and precise as a dance, and this made the other men around him look as if theirs were the movements of children, clumsy and unpracticed.

The back of his neck to a line above his ears was shaved in a tonsure.

Yumiko stared in fascination. Was this the same man who had kidnapped Elfine?

The look of interest in Iele's half-closed eyes was smokier than usual. "He desires me. The fire in him, I must quench, yes? If he asks me to drink with him, you have to watch my tables, no? We'll split the tips for any of my tables you cover."

"Why me?"

"Xana would not split fair. She's crooked. You're straight."

Yumiko said, "Why is his hair that way?"

"For his helmet."

Yumiko said, "He is a knight?"

Iele gave her a curious look and a half smile. "Ah! You know of such things? I thought you were one of us. Not a sleepwalker. Yes?"

Yumiko pointed at her necktie where the microphone was hidden, "I know there are things we don't talk about. But I know about the wolves and the shadows of the dead. I know about the Moths and the Cobwebs. Not a sleepwalker, no."

"Good! It is hard to talk, not knowing who is Nighttide or Dusk, and who is Day."

Sleepwalker was evidently Twilight slang for those under the mesmeric influence of the Black Spell.

Yumiko asked again, "So, is he a knight?"

"He is. A puissant knight and dire. They bring him in to face the foe no one can face. They say he has magic, the dark art. Very costly were the gifts to bring him. Much gold."

Both girls peered out the door again at the mysterious figure. There were four other men at the table and a redheaded woman in a pointed, conical hat with a veil over her face.

The men with him were also fabulous and strange, but like stars around a central sun, the striking grace and beauty of the man in black and scarlet made the others seem to recede. A youth too young to shave, dressed in a uniform of black and red, stood at his elbow, and was armed with a longsword. He poured wine from a carafe, sipped it, and passed the cup to the elfin knight. Yumiko recognized what he was, but could not recall what the sidekick of a knight was called.

Seated at his left was a dark-skinned, squat fellow in a leather cap. He had unusually muscular limbs and unusually bright eyes and only grinned with half his mouth.

The second was a tall, beardless, handsome figure in scarlet, with the distant eye and stiff posture of a soldier. He had long, curling locks of fiery red that fell past his shoulder, a sneering lip, and six fingers on each hand.

The third had an impassive, angular face, and strange, unwinking eyes like the eyes of a lizard. On his head was a fez. Trickles of smoke rose continually from both nostrils. When he opened his mouth, he seemed to carry something like a glowing coal in his throat, whose red fire was reflected from his palate and teeth. In his hand was a cigarette in a long holder which he never brought to his mouth. He wore a jacket of sparkling sequins, as bright as the patterns on the back of a poisonous snake, which Yumiko only on second glance realized was a field of priceless diamond drops, many-colored ametrine, gems of beryl, opal, topaz, and tourmaline.

The woman sat at the knight's right hand. Her red hair fell from her shoulders, across her chair back, to pool on the floor behind her, so long were the tresses. She wore a red silk dress which hid none of her perfect proportions. Her necklace, belt, and slippers were adorned with emeralds. When she put aside her veil to drink from her cup, the face beneath was one of stirring beauty, large of eye and full of lip, a nose tip-tilted, and a fine, small chin. Her skin was as free of freckle or blemish as polished ivory. So pale of skin she was, she seemed, in the subdued lighting of the lounge, almost to glow.

Her gestures, like his, were like music made visible, infinitely graceful and smooth, and, also like him, the light in her eyes, and gems at her ears, throat, and fingers caught reflections of stars not present.

"He has a date."

Iele said, "I overhear. That is not his woman. It is his sister. She is the Captain's mistress, but unfaithful to him. It is her joy to have jealous princes fight for her possession. Bloodshed follows her. She is called the war-red war-queen. Lady Malen Ruddgochren." Iele pronounced it *Rith-gock-rain*. "She is older than time. She is to be feared."

Yumiko was not concerned with the woman. "And his name? What is he?"

"Garlot. *Sir* Garlot of Listenoise, called the Red Knight. He is of the court of the underground world, you know? The Erlkoenig, who brings the winter cold and darkness of long nights, is his liege. Garlot is of the Night World and eats nectar and drinks soma, and so even the strongest of the Twilight World cannot stand against him. Ah! But Little Willy's boss does not like it. There is much hate."

"I did not know Mr. Wilcolac had a boss."

"As in the Old World, Little Willy is a client. He has a protector. A patron. The Captain owns the club. Willy only runs it."

"Has he been around here? His patron?"

"Not for two weeks. Something came up," Iele shook her head. "We call him the Captain. He is a fiddle player and a very bad man. Not *fun* bad, *crazy* bad. Joan says he is one of the fifty sons of Lupus Loupgarou, who broke Lent seven years running."

"Does he have a name? This patron?"

"Captain Cobweb, of course. Ah! Got to run! Can you cover me?" And, with a wave of her hand, Iele was off.

Watching Iele's retreating back, Yumiko realized the distraction of Sir Garlot offered a rare chance for some misdirection and deception of her own. It would be dangerous, coming so close after her last exploit. Suspicions surely were closing ever tighter about her like some invisible net. But she dared not let it slip away.

3. Misdirection and Deception

Yumiko stepped into the kitchen for her next order up, and, as she was passing the settings trolley, where spare silverware, roses, and napkins were kept, Yumiko slipped pepper from a shaker into napkin and pulled a button off her uniform.

She then found Plaksy the Lithuanian, slinky and blonde, who had a tray in either hand. "Hsst! I have to go change! Can you cover my tables for a few minutes?"

The rule that uniforms must be spotless and in good order or changed immediately was one that had been drilled into all the girls: Plaksy could hardly tell Yumiko to stay where Plaksy could watch her without giving away that she was watching her, so she merely nodded, smiling a false smile, and said, "Yes, I am covering. Yes."

Now, Yumiko left and made for the stairs. Krisky, slinkier and blonder than her sister, intercepted her at the landing. "To where is you going, please? Yes?"

Yumiko hid her nose in the napkin as if it were a handkerchief, inhaled the pepper she hid there, and sneezed. "Cum-big due zee you," Yumiko said. "God a tewwibel gold in ma noze. You haf any stove I can tag for it?"

Had she said it without pepper up her nose, it would have sounded more like this: *Coming to see you. Got a terrible cold in my nose. You have any stuff I can take for it?* But Krisky understood the language of the sick.

Krisky shrank back in horror and covered her own mouth with a hanky. "I have a crate of vitamin C tablets in the chest. And ginger root! Boil it into a tea, and take it with honey and lemon!"

Yumiko started to explain that she could not leave the wait staff short-handed, not tonight of all nights, but Krisky, eager to play the role of advisor, healer, and life-saver, shooed Yumiko as if she were a plague victim away from the lounge floor and told her to go to the dorm room they shared.

Yumiko explained that Krisky had to cover Iele's tables if Iele got invited by the VIP to sit at his table. Krisky, alarmed, apparently forgot the rule that Peach Cobbler Girls had to be pulled off the floors in pairs, and she simply scampered away.

Yumiko trotted upstairs as fast as her high heels would allow. She entered the dorm room, which was empty at the moment. She warily eyed the pumpkin perched at its high window. The flickering candle was inside the hollow gourde, and Yumiko was aware that unseen eyes were watching her.

She did not know where in the room the ghost was standing or from what point of view it observed. For that matter, she had no idea whether the immaterial eyes of an unquiet spirit could be deceived, distracted, or blocked. The woebegone thought occurred to her that the young man she had seen, Matthias Moth, would have known exactly what to do.

But she had no choice. Yumiko knelt down before the cedar chest at the foot of the bed, reached in, and unlocked her suitcase. Inside, her fingers found the all-important sash. She glanced up at the pumpkin. It was still turned away, nonchalantly stareing out the window at the street. She rummaged around inside the sash, palmed a tracer, and then drew out from the chest one of Krisky's many bottles of vitamin C. Yumiko ostentatiously swallowed a tablet, hoping the ghost saw only that.

Closing the chest, she trotted quickly out of the room. Almost immediately, she ran into Licho and Kudlac, who were patrolling the corridor.

"Halt!" said Kudlac. "What the heck are you doing here, Sorry?"

Licho, his gaze invisible behind his dark glasses, said, "On-duty girls are on the floor. Any girls pulled off the floor must go in pairs."

She felt as shy as a deer caught in headlights. Yumiko took a deep breath, frightened, and she felt the heat in her cheeks of a blush. Her tight costume creaked inaudibly, not allowing her to draw a very deep breath. Both men stepped closer, leering down at her. With the top button of her bustier missing, her skimpy outfit covered even less than normal. Their expressions turned hungry, so different from the disciplined and modest eyes of the Moth boys.

The thought of the Moths allowed her to recover her poise. She favored the two bouncers with her warmest smile. "A big tipper just bought a round for the house. I thought of you poor boys up here, thirsty and alone, and came up to find out what you wanted from the bar."

Licho said, "Did the boss say we could drink on duty?"

Yumiko looked at him with wide, innocent eyes. "Well, I don't know. I just assumed…" And she shrugged an exaggerated shrug.

Kudlac said, "Lager." He looked at scowling Licho and shrugged. "My brother Kresnik is a monk. He says I should drink more."

And Licho's hard expression vanished. He smiled and said, "Fine. Kvass. Nothing too strong this night."

Yumiko smiled flirtatiously and swayed away flirtatiously, just as she'd been taught. Once around the corner, she trotted as fast as she could.

She reported to Leshenka, who fussed and clucked in her dry, whispery voice. "No need to switch to your spare, duckie. I have thread and needle here in the button drawer. Just take a mo'."

Yumiko gave a small shriek and pointed at the window behind Leshenka. "What is that dreadful, black-cloaked figure dressed like a raven?"

Leshenka whirled with a speed that belied her apparent age. "Where? Where?" Her voice was like a foghorn.

Yumiko said, "It might have just been a passing shadow, but it looked like an implacable avenger of evil, bent on some terrible vendetta, passing by on a dark wind. But that is impossible, is it not? Men cannot fly."

Leshenka drew a handkerchief and mopped her brow. "Of course, duckie. Quite impossible…" Her voice had dropped once more into an arid murmur. She bit off the trailing end of the thread. "There you are. Button up."

Yumiko thanked her and skipped away, leaving Leshenka peering avidly out the window, craning her neck.

Hala the Serb was manning the hat-check booth. This booth faced the atrium across a counter and had a clear view of the lounge a few stairs below into which the atrium led. Behind the counter was a walk-in closet. Yumiko entered it from behind, from the service corridor. With no customers around, Hala was leaning on her cheek, elbow on the counter, legs crossed at the ankles, fidgeting and looking pensively toward the lounge floor, from whence came loud music and the laughter of happy, hence generous, customers.

Yumiko had been going through several ploys which might lure Hala away from her duty station, but, seeing that look on her face, Yumiko knew exactly what to say. "Hala! Do you see the gorgeous man in green and black, sitting at the VIP table?"

Hala rolled her enormous eyes. "How am I not to see? He just tucked a C-note into Plaksy's garterbelt. Iele is in his lap! He puts a bracelet of fine pearls on her wrist, as if this is a trifle. Two semester's tuition for such a bracelet, easy. It is raining wine, and I have no bucket."

Yumiko said, "I'll take over here. Krisky needs help covering Iele's tables for me."

Hala eyed the lounge floor with a quick but calculating gaze. Iele's tables were near enough to the VIP table for a passing waitress to be flagged. Hala turned a narrow stare at Yumiko. "Why do you do this for me? We are not friends."

"This will make us friends!" Yumiko said. "Besides, Krisky thinks I have a cold. She does not want me sneezing on the customers."

Hala brightened. "Very well, we swap!"

"One other thing, when you get the chance—please carry a kvass up to the fourth floor for Licho and a lager for Kudlac. Here!" And Yumiko pulled some bills out from her gathered tips, enough to cover the two drinks, and pressed them into Hala's hand. Hala looked down at the bills, puzzled. But at that moment, there was a burst of laughter from the VIP table, and one of the men with Sir Garlot was calling, "Miss..? Miss..?" and he was waving a banknote in the air to encourage swift service.

Hala asked no more, but rushed away, smiling eagerly.

Yumiko was alone in the snug and dimly lit alcove, half booth and half closet, with the silent shelves and hangers of hats, mantles, wraps, furs, and coats.

4. *The Cloak of Cornwall*

Yumiko, like all the girls, had worked hat check before. Wilcolac did not have a computerized system. The hats and coats stubs were kept in a small brass Rolodex, with the check-in time logged and the owner's name written in a guestbook.

Yumiko pointed the green-shaded gooseneck lamp which hung over the guestbook down at the page. Garlot was number 11. Hanging on hanger 11 on the coat-rack behind her was a garment like she had never seen.

It seemed at first to be a gray cloak with arm slits and a hood. Then, she saw silver, blue, and dark gray threads that seemed to come to the surface of the fabric and disappear as the light played over it.

It was as beautiful as sailing cloud-banks seen underfoot from a high vantage by moonlight.

Strangely, the longer she looked, the deeper in the fabric these drifting dark and light threads seemed to be, as if the cloak were a fog bank taking the shape of a cloak, and parts were drifting almost to touch her nose, but others were yards away, reaching ever further away, drifting…

Fascinated, mesmerized, Yumiko reached out and touched the material.

…for a moment, the cloak seemed not to be there are all, but merely an afterimage… and then in the next moment, it appeared to be a cloak-shaped hole in the world looking out into a larger, emptier, darker world…

A coldness, a sense that eyes were watching her, passed over her skin, leaving her tiny hairs prickling. Yumiko yanked her hand back, alarmed.

She blinked and turned away. There was a strange throbbing in her head; she could feel the pulse of veins in her brow. For a moment, she feared she had damaged her eyes. And yet her eyesight returned to normal when she blinked. It was almost as if the fabric did not wish to be inspected too closely.

This cloak was made of mists, the same mists her ring summoned. Somehow the ethereal substance had been solidified, spun into thread, and woven. It was like seeing a cloak woven of fire, or falling water, or notes of music. It was impossible.

It was *magic*.

As the possessor of a magic ring, perhaps she should have been less intimidated. Perhaps. But she felt the same as if she had been walking past a wax manikin, or a statue of a lion on library steps, but then, a pace beyond the unblinking, unliving face, had overheard a quiet sigh of pent up breath released.

Perhaps some form of magic somewhere in the world was kind and safe. Not this. The crawling motions deep in the fabric were unsightly and unnatural. It seemed malign.

Fearful of being seen, she moved the cloak to the lower shelf underneath the counter. Removing her costume top hat, Yumiko ducked her head beneath, bringing with her the gooseneck reading lamp. Now, she took out the scissors, needle, and thread she had lifted lightly from Leshenka's button drawer when the seamstress' head was turned.

There was a brocade of silver, gray, and white thread in convoluted Celtic knots around the hems of the garment. To her relief, she found these hems to be made of normal, worldly matter, whose threads did not drift simultaneously closer and farther from the eye.

She snipped the tiny, sparkling threads of the brocade, pried open the hem at the rear of the garment, inserted her tracer, and began to sew it up again. But the nearness of the otherworldly fabric made her fingertips numb, and the sensation of misty threads receding while advancing made her eyes water, even when she was not looking directly at the foggy substance.

But she gritted her teeth, persisting until she made the last stitch. She scowled at the work, unhappy with it. Her human-sized fingers could not match the fineness of the stitches. It looked too delicate for machine work, for the spaces between stitches were greater or lesser on different swirls of the brocade curves, giving it a pleasing, living look. She wondered whether Elfine's people had made this…

"Miss?"

She heard no footfall of a man approaching. When he spoke, she was startled and banged her head on the underside of the counter.

Yumiko bounded to her feet in panic, clutching the sore spot on the back of her head with one hand, but she smiled and laughed, hoping panic would look like no more than flustered embarrassment to the customer.

Her laughter died on her lips.

5. *Hat-Check Girl*

A tall, dark man in a black topcoat and black hat leaning on a walking stick stood looking down at her. His cast of features was oriental, his eyes were slanted, deep, penetrating, and magnetic. An aura of dark majesty surrounded him like warmth from a black oven.

His eyes traveled with evident pleasure up the shapely length of her young legs and hips to the sharply narrow waist, the generous curves above, the delicate collarbone, her swanlike neck. And then when he saw her face, his expression turned to shock and shame.

The light here was dim, and her eyes were still smarting, so that even as it happened, she was not sure that it had. She blinked. But now his expression was impassive, cool, and collected.

With a quick but curiously formal gesture, he snapped the top hat into his gloved hand and proffered it to her.

She said, "You know who I am." She spoke in Japanese.

He said, imperturbably, "But of course."

He answered in the same language, but he spoke in the Kamigata dialect, which was softer and more elegant than her Tohoku accent from the mountainous northeastern part of Honshu. Her voice suddenly sounded unbearably rustic and unrefined in her ears.

"Who am I?" She switched to English.

"Why, the hat-check girl, of course." He answered in English. He had an Oxfordian accent. He cleared his throat, rolled his eyes down at his hand, which was still extending his hat toward her, looked back up, caught her eye, and raised one eyebrow.

She could not stop staring at his face. If he had known her before her memory loss, why did he say nothing? If he had not, why did he look so familiar?

He said, "When did you start working here?"

The tone of voice made her aware of how overly familiar she had been in addressing a superior. She said, "Sir! The second of this month, sir."

"I was wondering how long it takes Mr. Cobweb to instruct his staff. Here is my hat. You are supposed to check it."

To her shame, a giggle welled up in her and came out her mouth. This was very different from the times she had pretended to be giggly. It was rather horrible to have her pretense overtake her and become real.

She bowed carefully in her low-cut corset and took the hat. He proffered his walking stick, and also doffed his topcoat in a great circular flourish, to lay it on the counter as well. He wore a severe formal suit of expensive dark wool beneath, with a bow tie as white as hers.

She thought furiously while she tagged, hung, and shelved the coat and hat and placed the jade-handled cane in the numbered pigeon-hole of the umbrella stand. Yumiko pulled the guestbook up to the counter, smiled a broad smile, and said, "Sir? We are also required to take down the name and address if you would, please?"

"My name?" He looked skeptical.

"In case you forget something. This allows us to run it back to wherever you are staying. It is a free service. As a courtesy."

She tried to adopt the same alluring look she used to mesmerize Blud, but under his cold and regal gaze, her face faltered. He was repelled, not allured. The lie stumbled leaving her mouth and sounded unconvincing.

"Gladly," he said. He wrote in a rapid, perfect cursive of Roman letters. It was the type of polished handwriting no native English-speaker was likely to match.

As he wrote, she spoke. "Are you related to the Cobwebs, sir?"

"Why do you ask? Because Wilcolac and I are the only ones who know how to wear a tux? Next you will ask me if I am related to Fred Astaire." Then, looking up, and seeing the puzzlement in her face, he said, "Ah, so. He is an American dancer."

She licked her lips, wondering how openly she could ask anything before provoking trouble. "Is your family… uh… a large one? Because sometimes traveling to a strange place… ah…"

He said, "I am, in point of fact, a particularly haughty and exclusive person, of pre-Adamite ancestral descent. You will understand this when I tell you that I can trace my ancestry back to a protoplasmal primordial atomic globule. Consequently, my family pride is something inconceivable. I was born sneering."

She stared at him in confusion, understanding that she was somehow being made light of, but not understanding how, or what he meant.

"I, um, sir, um…" She stammered softly, trying to regain her professional composure, "…sure you will have a delightful evening… our staff is… aim to please…"

His voice dropped to a colder and quieter note. "I had a half-sister once. She died under tragic circumstances. Committed suicide, actually. At times I almost seem to see her still. But I know when visions are false! My other relatives disown me and call me dead. I am as alone as no man since Adam was, in that hour when all his ribs were still his own."

The small, scowling vertical line between his brows deepened. Perhaps he would have said more, but at that moment, Joan the Wad came bustling up, smiling. Joan was on hostess duty, to greet and seat the customers, but some minor emergency had called her away from the lectern, which was the normal hostess post.

Joan gave Yumiko a glance. Perhaps she had been expecting to see Hala behind the counter in the coat closet. Clearly, in the bustle and confusion of the evening, Joan had forgotten whom she had assigned to which part of the work roster and floor roster, which was unusual for her. But she said nothing, for she had kept the tall and stern Japanese gentleman waiting. She led him out onto the floor to seat him.

Yumiko, her brain pulsing with questions, was dying to look at what name he had written in the book. But first she carefully put the misty cloak of Sir Garlot back on its hanger. She saw the party at table five was getting ready to leave, so she had to pass hats, coats, and mink stoles over the counter with many a polite smile, collect their stubs, and note the numbers in the log. Then two customers, one entering and one leaving, came. And then more.

Finally, there was a lull. The dance band started playing. She clicked on the gooseneck lamp and swiveled the bulb toward the guestbook to see what the tall, dark, stern man had written. She was expecting to see some name ending in Moth.

Pooh-Bah of the town of Titipu, First Lord of the Treasury, Lord Chief Justice, Lord High Admiral, Master of the Buckhounds, etc., ad naus.; A gentleman of Japan.

6. *Unrewarding Night*

Nonplussed and disappointed, she leaned far over the counter, in a pose she had been instructed Peach Cobbler Girls never were to assume, and craned her neck so that she could better see. The dark man was not at the table where Joan had left him.

The lights dimmed. That was the signal that drink service was suspended, for the waitresses were called to the dressing rooms prior to the floor show. Joan, as hostess, took over the hat check while Yumiko rushed away.

After the show, Yumiko was sent to wait tables on a private party in an upper room in the back, which included some of Sir Garlot's men from the Night World, but not he himself. From their talk, he had retired with Iele to some other room.

They were playing a card game, wagering parts of their bodies, or that is what it sounded like. Since no actual toes, eyeballs or forearms were detached and tossed across the table at the end of every hand, Yumiko could not tell if these bets were real or in jest.

But evidently their lord was in charge of all tips and emoluments. Or perhaps they did not know the custom.

Between giving up her tables to Hala, failing to cover for Iele, and paying for the drinks for Kudlac and Licho, Yumiko made less in tips that night than anyone else.

After curfew, she lay awake at night in bed, snuggled up between Xana and Anjana and staring at the reflected candlelight on the ceiling. She wished she could climb under the bed, get her suitcase, and retrieve the earbuds from her helmet so she could listen for the sound of the tracer hidden in Sir Garlot's cloak.

She had planted a second one in the hatband of the hat of the gentleman from Japan, of course.

But she could hear Hala and Nightingale talking softly, gossiping about how to spend their extra money, and could also hear Krisky or Plaksy or both rising every ten minutes or so to go into the bathroom and take vitamins or drink cups of medicinal tea.

Were they up late because of her? They had been assigned to watch Yumiko, but had lost sight of her. Had either of them told Wilcolac yet? Were his suspicions roused?

Yumiko felt a sense of claustrophobia, but also of choking urgency. She could not stand still. Elfine had no one else looking for her. But each time Yumiko moved, she took risks, she made little mistakes, she left little clues, and the pattern of her actions and absences must be growing clearer to the hidden eyes that sought her.

A sense of dread grew deeper, hardening into conviction. Wilcolac must know! He must have figured it out by now!

With these thoughts tormenting her, it was many weary hours before she could force herself into sleep.

The next morning, just at the onset of morning dress rehearsal, Yumiko was pulled out of the chorus line by Licho and told to report to the Magician's office.

Wilcolac wanted to see her.

Chapter 8

Hob in a Bottle

1. Death Warrant

Once more, Yumiko Moth found herself in high heels, seated on a high stool in the red and gold private office of Wilcolac Cobweb. As before, the walls to her left and right were full-length mirrors. Before her was the massive desk of Wilcolac Cobweb, with its green blotter and gold pen set. To one side of the desk was a bust of Shakespeare, and to the other, a tripod holding an ice bucket in which an amber bottle rested. Before her and above her loomed Wilcolac himself, square-faced, bulky, and stern.

She was dressed in the wasp-waist corset, hot pants, and stockings of her Peach Cobbler Girl uniform, a white tie circling her naked throat, white cuffs at the wrists of her bare arms, and a top hat pinned precariously atop her oversized raven-black coiffure. She wondered darkly if Wilcolac had waited until dress rehearsal before issuing his summons, not just for reasons of psychological warfare but also for the practical point of putting her in awkward shoes, with no place to hide weapons and hardly a way to bend or inhale.

Wilcolac had been scratching with a quill pen on butter-yellow parchment when she entered. He had silently gestured for her to sit, and she waited in silence for him to address her.

As if pulled on a torture rack, the minutes while she sat elongated painfully.

She watched the delicate motions of his huge and meaty hands as he dipped his pen in an inkwell or blotted up stray ink marks, and she wondered, not for the first time, why elf and half-elf seemed so hesitant about modern conveniences and technology.

It was not as if he did not also have a ballpoint pen set on his desk and a phone, and his private secretary owned a typewriter for which it was apparently impossible to find replacement parts. This secretary was an ill-favored youth in the adjoining office with the apparently impossible name of Skrzat Czart.

The thought occurred to Yumiko that Wilcolac was writing out something fraught with ceremonial significance, a document which had to be done in just the way it had been done centuries ago. A death warrant? *Her* death warrant?

It was a silly idea, but difficult to dismiss once it was lodged in her head. Yumiko cleared her thoughts and concentrated on her breathing, patiently waiting until the waves disturbing the waters of her soul grew calm and still.

Hence it was with an unusual degree of serene detachment that she saw Wilcolac clean his pen, salt his document, put them aside, and raise his eyes to her.

This was it. He knew who she was. Questioning, torture, and death were before her. Yet she was calm.

Their eyes met. Her gaze was like a bottomless well, pure, cold, and unruffled. His gaze was puzzled, but he masked his puzzlement under a layer of bonhomie.

"Well, well!" he said in a voice of brassy and unconvincing joviality. "No doubt you knew this day would come! A little frightened, are we?"

Yumiko met his gaze without flinching. Her life as she remembered it was less than a month; she had achieved nothing, saved no one. And yet no quiver of fear disturbed her. "I am ready," she said.

"Ah, good!" he said clapping his hands together and rubbing them. "Well, your two week trial period is over. You've missed no rehearsals, spilled no drinks on any customers, and you've kept your uniform tidy and presentable.

Polednitsa gave you a clean bill of health on your blood tests. You were worried? Everyone is. Congratulations!"

Since no one had told her even of the existence of a two week trial period, the news failed to elate her.

But Yumiko wondered if this were some particularly cruel psychological torture, meant to make her feel relief and relax her guard so that the command to have her dragged in chains down into the bone-strewn underground vault would be all the more shocking by contrast. Therefore, she merely smiled and said, "Thank you, sir."

Unexpectedly, a glint came into his eye. Had she herself not felt the selfsame mood three days ago, she might not have recognized it. It was the victorious glee of a magician whose sleight of hand fools the chump.

He had fooled her. How? What had he done?

"Good, good!" he said, nodding. "This being the case, the time has come for you! You, see, I have discovered something about you…"

At that moment, in mid-sentence, just as Yumiko was about to find out what he had discovered about her, the phone rang.

Wilcolac snatched the handset up to his ear with comical haste, "Yes? Yes! *Yes?*"

She realized the hectic confusion of last night was still in effect. Wilcolac bellowed, "Don't let him leave! Don't let him kill any mortals! I'll be right there!"

Wilcolac startled her as he bounced out of his chair, coming toward her. Moving with surprising energy for one so stout, and pelted across the room.

Yumiko by reflex leaped to her feet when he jumped. He rushed past without noticing. The door slammed. She stood blinking, breathing heavily. He had left his top hat on the desk. She looked down and found herself in a half-moon stance: Feet spread, legs bent, left foot forward, toes turned slightly inward, left forearm up to block, right fist at her hip. She glanced at the mirror, frowned, and adjusted the position of her rear foot slightly. Sloppy. The stance did not feel correct in high heels, and they made her backside stick out too far.

When was the last time she had actually drilled? It was outside the range of her remaining memory. So, more than two weeks ago. But she could not have practiced her *katas* while she was here in the Cobbler's Club, being watched.

She glanced at the mirror again and remembered what Iele the Romanian had told her. She suddenly felt as if eyes were watching her. Yumiko cleared her throat and straightened up, tugging and tucking her tight costume back in place.

The sensation of being watched did not ebb. Yumiko casually glanced over one shoulder, slowly scanning the room, while trying to school her face to convey an air of idle nonchalance.

Humming a leisurely tune, she allowed her drifting steps, as if by pure chance, to carry her over to Wilcolac's desk, and she rolled her eyes here and there, and again, as if by merest happenstance, allowed her gaze to come to rest on the desk top where the parchment lay.

It was partly covered with blotting paper. Only the lower part of the page was visible:

> *...that Arthur lives. His voice I heard, and I know he speaks the truth. Your assurances have proved false: Sir Gilberec is no poseur, but a true knight of the Table Round. In his hand is the sword you spoke of.*
>
> *Allow me to be frank. No force of yours can defeat him. Send as many wolves or monsters as you may. Shades will not approach him while he walks in the company of the second, his cousin Matthias. He burned the hand from my dead Lantern. My mighty specter is now one-handed due to this. Must I lose more before you are convinced? No one as powerful a ghostly father since Dominic Moth I have seen!*
>
> *However, at great expense in bribes and gifts, I have lured to my house a knight equal in puissance, or more. He is bound by no code of honor, but is a caitiff and treasonous and will strike down the youth from behind, unseen, for the Cloak of Mists is his. Of course, I speak of Garlot Lackland, the Exile of Listenoise.*
>
> *I have gained means to send a message to the elusive Matthias Moth. All is in readiness and awaits but your nod. My reed you have in this.*

The text ended there.

To whom was it sent that it had to be written with a quill pen on parchment? The salutation would be at the top.

She offered another casual glance at the mirrors. For all she knew, any might have men behind them, or cameras, or ghosts, watching her every move. Did she dare push aside the blotting paper to see the upper half of the letter?

It was unsightly to lean over dressed in this uniform. Instead, using the same poise as if she were lowering a drink to a table, Yumiko tucked one leg behind the other and bent her knees, keeping her upper body upright. She kept her face half turned away, masked in an innocent expression, and only turned her eyes down.

She peeled up the merest corner of the blotting paper:

To the venerated and dreaded Thursday of the Supreme Council of Anarchists, Lord of Wolves, Captain Lucien Cobweb, my patron, greetings and salutations. Dread Sir, two Arthurians met with me…

Tears of fear came into her eyes at that moment and made her vision swim. The Captain! She had heard the title of the absent owner of the club once or twice but had not made the connection. Lucien Cobweb had been wearing a captain's uniform from some antique and Napoleonic army when she had seen him. And Iele had called the Captain a fiddle-player. Yumiko had seen him playing it.

This was the house of the master of the werewolves, Thursday, one of the seven Anarchist lords. This was not neutral ground, but a stronghold of the enemy.

Lucien had already once lured her into a deadly trap in the warehouse district across the river. Perhaps this room was a trap. Perhaps this letter had been left for her to find, and Lucien stood behind the one-way mirror, savoring her shock.

She breathed and let the fear subside. She had forgotten her former life and mission, but it had not forgotten her. To increase the dangers she faced by panic was shameful. Yumiko blinked and forced herself to concentrate on the words in the letter.

…two Arthurians met with me in parley on the evening of Friday the 13th, a day my art shows to be auspicious for acts of darkness. As you commanded, against my better judgment, I put them to the test.

The first is as honest and bold as rumored and is a true knight of the Lost King. Sir Gilberec vows that Arthur lives...

The sensation of being watched grew and became overwhelming. Her fingers, as if by themselves, dropped the corner of the paper with a guilty start. Yumiko straightened up, brushing at imaginary dust specks, darting her eyes left and right.

There. A face was staring at her. A tiny, whiskered face with glittering eyes. He was looking at her through the glass of the bottle perched in the ice bucket next to the desk. He was not behind the bottle peering through it. He was inside.

2. *Old Overholt*

For a moment, she thought it was Elfine, and she gasped. But, no, this was a man's face. He was shirtless and shaggy, and his hair was like a tiny lion's mane. His beard spilled across this chest like an open fan. He wore what seemed a loincloth of hair. He looked for the world like a miniature caveman. He even had the tiny bone of some small beast thrust through his topknot.

He was kicking his legs, keeping afloat in the alcohol. She saw his legs were deformed in their lower extremity. Kicking was evidently hard for him.

Despite resting in an ice bucket, this was not a champagne bottle. It was amber and square. The label held a cameo of a stern old man, or perhaps it was an ugly old lady, wreathed in barley stalks, and also the words

Since 1810
OLD
OVERHOLT
STRAIGHT RYE
WHISKEY

She bent closer, puzzled, wondering at the sight. Why did the magician keep a little man in a bottle of rye?

Even as she watched, the little man at the neck of the bottle thrashed. He pounded, or, rather tapped, his tiny fists against the brown glass. Then, with an expression of panic, he slipped below the surface of the liquor. Now he was near the middle of the bottle, waving his legs feebly, both little hands to his throat, eyes bulging.

The label was off the cork, and the bottle was not full, so it had been opened previously. She pulled at the cork, but her fingers slipped. She wound her fingers around the bottle's neck and pushed with her thumbs. The cork came free. (She was half expecting it to pop and fly in the air, but, of course, it did not. Whiskey is not carbonated.)

Now what? She could not reach a finger into the neck of bottle to rescue the drowning swimmer. She opened one drawer and then another, hoping to find a glass. She found a set of files in one drawer, an elaborate makeup kit with wigs and latex prosthetics in another. The next held a book of dark leather bound shut with three chains which moaned and trembled when light struck it. She shut that drawer quickly. The next held a set of chains, fetters, and trick handcuffs, such as an escape artist might own, as well as hoops, ropes, candles, cards, crystals, and a hat with a false bottom.

There were two cupboard doors below the drawers. Behind the right was a control panel with labeled switches sitting atop a rack of silently turning reel-to-reel tapes. Behind the left was a miniature bar with several bottles shelved before a mirror, a nook containing lemons and limes, and, above that, a row of cut crystal tumblers.

She set out the tumblers and poured them one by one. The little man was caught in the neck of the bottle. He narrowed his body strangely, as if he had no bones, and shot out of the bottle to land in the final glass. He sank to the bottom. Yumiko put her fingers in the alcohol to fish him out, fearfully wondering if there were any way to start his breathing again.

But her fingers came back dry. The little man opened his mouth and stood up, and what should have been, to a man his size, a bathtub full of whiskey, now was in his mouth. He did a headstand, slurped up the last bit remaining in the bottom, righted himself, and jumped up to stand with one foot on either side of the rim of the glass.

He raised his hand in an airy salute. "Top o' the morning to ye, missy!"

His voice was very loud. Instinctively, her hand flew to her collar, whose bow tie held a hidden microphone, which she smothered with her fingers. At the same moment, she realized that Wilcolac would never allow the kitchen staff to overhear his conversations with any of the Peach Cobbler Girls.

Her eyes darted to the control panel. The door in the lower desk was still open. She could see each label next to a toggle had a name penciled in. One read *Sorry*. The toggle was off and the light next to it dark. Wilcolac had turned it off before she entered, of course.

The little man, perhaps irked at being ignored, made a trumpet of his fingers before his mouth, and shouted, "Top o' the morning to ye, I said! Is it deaf as a post, ye are?"

"I hear you quite well, thank you, sir. But I don't know what that means. Please?"

"Aha! 'Tis an outrageous and orgulous Oirishism which no real potato-eating Irishmen would ever dare say, 'faith and begorrah!" He rolled his R's with a trill so that last incomprehensible word came out something like *begorr-rr-rr-rrah*. "Cream rises to the top, so he who says the same be wishing the sweetest part of the day to you."

While he was talking, she undid her collar and stowed it under the empty tumbler, hoping that would prevent the sound from being picked up. "Well, then, top of the morning to you." And she bowed slightly.

"And the bottom of a sweet lass!" So saying, by some means unseen, he propelled himself like a miniature rocket away from the tumbler, across the desk, and into the plush leather chair behind it. He rebounded from the pliant surface, yodeled, and swan-dived toward her fanny, arms out. He intended what could be called either a pinch or an embrace, depending on whether one used his size scale or hers.

He was fast, but she was faster. She turned and neatly caught him in midair with one hand.

"Mercy!" he cried, now blubbering. An abnormal, impossible amount of water came from his eyes, far more than his body size could account for. "Mercy, great lady!"

"Don't worry. I will not hurt you."

"Mercy, O lady with the sweet, luscious, peach-shaped–!"

"Or, if need be," she interrupted, "I may hurt you."

He kicked his legs. Her fingers entirely circled his small form, pinning his arms to his sides.

She brought him near her nose. "Are you drunk?"

"Oi, aye. Drunk as a lord. Drunk as a house of parliament full of lords, and a long parliament session at that! Willy meant to keep me poor old bones locked tight in the bottle, so I would be too addled with strong drink to gather my wits and remember the runes and sleights, riddles and couplets, to work me mighty charms. Your lips, from this angle, are huge and wonderfully lush! How 'bout a kiss?"

She gave him a shake. "Why were you in that bottle? Tell me!"

"I was saving it!"

"What?"

"A prisoner am I! Out of my right wits! Strong drink will do that! And bonny, buxom lasses. Tell me! Keep you your keys or hanky in that fair bosom? I ask only because if you need me to fetch anything you've tucked away…"

She dunked him headfirst into the first glass of whiskey. Bubbles flew from his nose, and he writhed and kicked his legs and made outrageous faces through the transparent wall of the glass, but he did not actually seem to be drowning. She waited, eyes narrowed, wondering how much lung capacity someone only ten inches tall could have.

After a while, he stopped kicking, opened his mouth, and sucked half the glass into himself. Perhaps he knew the same trick as whatever seamstress who made the pouches of her suit, for his body was too small to hold the volume of alcohol he had just imbibed.

She pulled him closer to her eyes once more, squinting. "Why does he keep you here?"

He expelled a stream of alcohol toward her eye. This was not like a man spitting. It was more like a carnival mask through whose mouth a firehose has been threaded opening up a blast. But she had half expected such a thing and parried with a quick motion of her thumb. The beam of fluid splashed back in his face, harder and harder as her thumb came closer. He yelped. She clamped her thumb over the lower half of his face.

She turned and saw where melted ice water had collected in the bottom of the bucket. She plunged her hand and her prisoner in.

She held him under the freezing water until he stopped squirming.

Now, she drew him out and deposited the little man on the blotter. "Are you sober?" she asked. "Speak respectfully to me."

He shook his limbs and wrung his long locks like a woman wringing a washcloth.

"Hah! You coyless colleen! Why should I rule my tongue for you? I am of the Night World, vast and dark, and what are you but a halfway lass, a by-blow? My blood is better than yours! And I– I... what's the accursed word? I *outrank* you!"

"Then speaking to an inferior will be all the more humiliating. First you must bow."

"Hoo hah! Must I, now, says she? You've let your hand away! I can put a girdle round the earth in forty minutes or ere a leviathan can swim a league! This bone I hold can shrivel the spots off a giraffe and fold his long bones into a cockleshell! If I take it in my lips, I weft invisible and unseen! Or waft? Is it waft or weft?" He raised his hands to the bone stuck through his topknot, but his fingers seemed lax and rubbery, and he could not dislodge it nor undo the knot. "Higher magic is mine! Dire magic is mine! What have you? What can you do?"

"It is a fair question." Reaching across the desk behind him, she snapped her fingers sharply with her left hand, and when he whirled drunkenly to look, she snatched him up with her right hand.

"Good reflexes you got there, missy." He said, mournfully.

She put him headfirst back into the ice water and looked at the gold-plated clock on the desk. Her lips grew thin. Eventually, she pulled him out again. He sputtered and snorted.

"Water! Foulest element! No one can drink that stuff!"

"Time is short. The Magician returns at any moment. Tell me..." And she was paralyzed for a moment by the sheer number of questions she desperately needed answered.

"What would you have of me, beautiful lass? A kiss?"

Only for a moment. She knew her top priority. "...Tell me where Tomorrow Rocket Moth is!"

"Seek him in the City of Corpses, for he is among the dead." And the horrid little man laughed.

Her eyes narrowed again, and her lips grew thin. There was little actual change to her expression, but a dark fire glinted in her eye to make her face seem like a mask through whose eyeholes the Gorgon gaze of a long-necked ghost were blazing.

Yumiko pulled the little bone out of his hair. The topknot had been tightly knotted indeed, and his scalp tender, for he started to yowl something horrible until she submerged him once more.

Up she brought him again. "I am Japanese," she said. "We invented all the truly hideous tortures."

"I am a fairy of the Springtide lands, beholden to the May Queen. Neither truth nor gift am I compelled to give thee! But only lies and curses, half-blood dipsy doxy! Curse your absurdly gorgeous figure and that sweet, warm scent from your hair. What is that, by the bye? Perfume or just hair soap?"

"Sweat." She had been in the chorus line before she was summoned here.

"Smells nice."

"Thank you. I am about to crush you to death if you don't answer."

"You're welcome. What was I saying? Oh, yeah. You are a half-breed halfwit! A really, really, very attractive one though. All the Moth girls are lovely."

"Thank you. How do you know my bloodline?" But she frowned as she said it because the little man might have been in the room during her first interview and heard everything she had said then. Not to mention any conversations between anyone taking place in this room thereafter. Plus anything his magic charms might tell him.

He writhed in her grip and gnashed his teeth, "Prepare to receive the curse of the Goodly Folk! The curse of Nebuchadnezzar romping on all fours and chewing grass will be the least of the plagues I will visit on you! The curse of Zahack and his arms twisted into venomous snakes is second! Next, I'll put a hump on your back that will grow its own mouth and sing crass limericks! Give me my magic cat-bone so I can cast these evil charms!"

"Have you no sense of right and wrong? I saved you from the bottle. I shall free you from the Magician."

"Right and wrong! Prose and song! High and low! To and fro! A fairy heart is a wild harp plucked whither way the mad winds blow, never chary and never still, and it flits as flitting will. No conscience can compel us, but only the charm of names enspell us."

She sniffed again. Whiskey. In the Magician's office. In the very building she had seen Elfine depart, back when first they met. "You are a house hob."

"That I am!" The little creature seemed to deflate. He said in a voice that tried to sound brave, "But– but– It does not mean my magic is any less ferocious! I can mess up your bookkeeping!"

"Ah? So?"

"I can put dirt in your casserole, mud in your pillow, or… or… I can have important bills get lost before you pay them! And see your guests are irked with any divertissement… musical groups double-booked…"

"So you only do, what, again? Housework magic?"

"Erique Claudin had a hob who could make stars in his opera house succeed or flop. He dropped a big chandelier on the audience. Hob authority extends to any kind of house with guests, public or private! But you still cannot compel me! Go ahead and try! Try to grind me between your teeth! Or, better yet, rub me against your–!"

"Your name is Sly Jack Crookshank." At least, that was the name Elfine had said. Yumiko blessed her memory that had recovered that scrap of information out of all the confetti of comments and quips Elfine was wont to speak. Maybe Yumiko's ancestors, whoever they were, on the elfish side of her family had given her a touch of the photographic memory Elfine had mentioned. Yumiko giggled at the thought.

She had to cover her mouth when she laughed, so she had to let go of the wild little sprite in her hand. But the little man seemed to deflate before her eyes at the sound of his name and her laughter.

And he bowed low to her.

3. The Magic of True Names

He said, "The ancient rule I cannot escape. My name you have. One wish I grant, no more."

"Why not three?"

"Elfin blood grows thin and stale. Only the greatest and most ancient grant three. I command no terror in the hearts of men. One wish is yours. You must claim it now or count it lost! Speak!"

"Return Tomorrow Moth here and now safely, hale and whole, with no evil coming with him or following!"

The little man raised his hands, "That is not a domestic matter! It is beyond my authority!"

"It is not your… genre?"

"That is one way to put it."

"What *can* you do?"

"I arrange the house. I do not even clean and cook, but merely make such chores come out well or ill. All the success of Wilcolac is trapped in me. Do you really think a magician knows aught about running a restaurant, hotel, theater, gambling hall, bar, and more? Him? A snake charmer? A thimble-rigger? He counts stars and reads cards! He torments the shadows of the dead! By freeing me, you've ruined him, robbed him of house luck, no matter what else you wish or do not wish."

"You suddenly seem sober now."

"Life suddenly seems sobering now."

"What happened to your Irish accent?"

"It immigrated."

"What?"

"That voice was for play. This is toil. Ask! And be done with you!"

"Tell me where Elfine is."

"Do not ask that. I sent her to the tower where you slept your first night here back on earth. I know less than you."

"Then you know who I am."

"The girl sidekick of Winged Vengeance, the Archeress, the Ghost-slayer, the Foxmaiden. Of course I know. You are of this house, and I am its *lares*."

Ghost-slayer. What an interesting title. But she did not ask about that. She said, "Crookshank, can you restore my memory?"

"No. I do domestic tasks. Arrange parties. My blessing can grant a good review in *Theater Weekly*."

"Does the Magician know who I am?"

"How could he? You are about to free me."

She shook her head. "I am not. Your powers are worthless."

"I am a sprite of the May Queen's realm! Magicks most dire! Hire! Fire, um–!"

"But nothing I desire. I do not need clean plates or a comfortable bed."

He raised one finger, and suddenly the tiny bone that had been in her hand was in his. He smiled. "But I arrange *this* house, or I did. I arranged you to be called to the office. Wilcolac means to punish you for some error of yours, some misstep. But I arranged to have him called away on the phone. I am arranging it so that he is being kept away while we talk. There is no hurry. Take your time. Ask wisely."

She said, "You have something in mind?"

"I do. Something you want very badly, something you need most of all. Because you might think you can creep and sneak so subtly that even Jack-o'-Lantern, the Widow Joan's sad bridegroom, will not see, but he is one of the most famed ghosts still trapped on our side of the veil. He did not see you, but he saw the bed you left empty during that crucial hour before the fire alarm was pulled, and the men all saw the Foxmaiden swing away on a wire."

"Why hasn't this watch ghost reported this to his master already?"

"Time between the living world and the dead world is not coherent. There is no ratio, no fixed rate of exchange. Besides, I arranged for the Magician to be very busy since one of his special guests, someone he had to truckle and bribe and call in favors to lure into this place, just so happened to arrive."

"Not to mention the shipment arriving today."

The little man looked surprised and then impressed. "So the Foxmaiden knows about that, does she? You are quick."

"Thank you."

"No doubt you want to see where that shipment is heading, don't you? But you are kept too busy, watched too closely. You see, the one thing you really want and need is a way to escape from the people watching you that arouses not the slightest suspicion."

She said, "How?"

"Pour all the whiskey back into the bottle, and I will show you why my leg is crooked."

Yumiko did so. Crookshank took the bone in his hand, and it elongated to the size, compared to him, of a hiking staff. He struck himself in the leg. Immediately, his foot swelled up to twice and thrice its size. The big toe swelled up faster, like a balloon, and the swirls of his toe print formed into the crude shape of a face. The second and third toes stretched like spaghetti and became crude arms. The pinky toe and the one next to it puffed out and became caricatures of legs, and then they migrated along his foot to the heel to take up a position opposite the crude arms. Crookshank's leg was now no longer reaching to an ankle. Instead, his ankle was thin and entered the small body which once had been his foot at the navel.

"Happy Birthday!" shouted Crookshank, and he drove the magic bone into his own heel, severing it with a crack. There was no blood. The foot, now shaped something like a hairless monkey, something like a cartoon, and something like a potato, opened its mouth and began to cry.

"Quick! Feed him whiskey! Booze! Booze! No time to loose!" shouted Crookshank. Yumiko proffered the whiskey bottle, unsure how to get so wide a bottle mouth up to so small a creature's mouth. But the new creature clung eagerly to the mouth of the bottle, and Crookshank solved the problem by kicking the new creature sharply in the rump and toppling him into the interior with a splash.

Yumiko said, "Does he need alcohol to live?"

"Not a bit! I just want him to grow up with the same vices as mine, so he will not look down on me. Now! Put cork in bottle and bottle in bucket. I will dance the great dance of growing pain and weave my charm, and when all is done, this will be my very brother."

Yumiko watched with mingled amusement and disquiet as Crookshank hopped and jigged on one foot in a circle around the rim of the ice bucket, chanting blasphemies and calling on old names of pagan goddesses. Inside the bottle, the homunculus twisted, expanded, and grew like a balloon being puffed up. In a short time, the creature in the bottle was exactly the image of Sly Jack Crookshank.

He said, "You must give it a name."

She said, "Let it be called *Bakemono,* for it fakes another's shape."

"That is not a proper name! I was thinking something like Wee Jon, Hairy Knob, or Darkheart Dick! Why did I ask you?"

"Why *did* you ask me?"

Crookshank shrugged irritably. "You have more of Adam's blood in you than I. Adam is the namer of names."

The new little man, Bakemono, now tapped against the glass. "Wait! Aren't you going to free me, too?"

Yumiko was caught by surprise. "I..."

Bakemono said, "I can cut off my foot and make a copy to replace me, so no one will see that I am gone!"

Sly Jack shouted, "Silence, Fake! When you wake, you will think and say, and, indeed, play my part in every way!"

Sly Jack pointed his bone wand at his twin in the bottle and uttered a word Yumiko did not hear. Bakemono fainted and fell to below the surface of the whiskey.

"He will not drown?"

"Not if he knows what is good for him!"

"And where is your escape?"

He said, "Take me over to the window."

Yumiko looked around. "I see no window."

"Step over to the wall behind the desk. Notice the seam in the wainscoting and the similar seam between the wall panels. On the floor near the corner, see the tiny carved design of the Mock Orange bloom, which is Deceit. Fifty-eight inches above it, which is the exact height of Wilcolac's walking stick, amid the line of bloom designs carved into the seam, is an Acacia, which is Concealment. Touch them at the same time. Since you do not have a walking stick, use your finger on the wall and the pointy toe of your shoe on the floor."

She looked. Stripes of wood, as broad as her thumb, ran along the wainscoting where floor met wall and similarly ran vertically up the wall panels. They were carved in a variety of floral designs, but eventually she found and touched the two Crookshank described.

She did not feel any button or latch under her finger. Nonetheless, a panel of the solid wall retreated three inches and then slid silently aside. There was no noise of gears, so it might have been magic.

Behind was a full-length window, a French door, opening out onto a sheer drop.

4. Windows and Mirrors

Yumiko blinked in the sudden dazzle. The street, so far below, beneath the bright morning sun was like a forgotten world. It seemed like ages since last she had seen crawling cars and strolling pedestrians, garish signs, and lovely storefront displays.

The little man hopped up and lit on her shoulder. His severed foot had grown back but was more deformed than before, bent at an uglier angle than it had been.

He sat with a sigh and rubbed both hands over the tiny patch of skin between her shoulder and her neck, like a man might do to smooth couch cushions. "Nice! You have nice skin! We should do something unnatural together. What do you say? The Dark Powers would like it!"

"No, thank you. I belong to another."

He grimaced. "The Darkness does not like that kind of talk! You have to be more independent! And much more impolite!"

He put his feet together and, with a cheer, made as if to slide down into her cleavage, like a child sledding down a hillock.

She snatched him into her hand before he traveled an inch.

Yumiko opened her palm and looked down. "Why me?"

He stood up on her palm, brushing back his wild caveman hair with both hands. "Why you what?"

"If you can arrange for Wilcolac to be called out of his office, and arrange for staff or guards or girls to be called in, then you arranged for your bottle to be opened by me. So why me?"

"Who else? Should I trust a Cobweb? Boggy would keep me if she knew what I was and become the mistress of this place herself. The Cheyenne is a man-wolf. And the chorus girls? Nightingale would make me have her be the star of the show. Hala would be the winner at the gambling tables. Joan would have me free her husband. But none of them would dream of freeing me. They would wish for frivolities. Not you. You want no power over this house. No power over me. You keep your word like an elf."

She was not sure if that were a compliment. "So what is it exactly you are suggesting I wish for from you?"

He said, "Open the window, and I will tell you."

"You'll fly away."

"Not from one who knows my name. You see, in magic, if you owe someone, that someone will find you again. Not until I discharge my debt to you, and I am sure of getting free from you to a place you will not find me."

She opened the narrow glass door. The smell of the city, the mutter of traffic, came into the room.

He said, "I can make the sleepless eyes watching you sleep. I can make the unwinking eyes wink. I can make it so that you can escape unobserved from this house and return to it, for as many hours as you need to do your errands beyond, or report to your master, or whatever else you'd like. And when you return here—if you return—no one will suspect a thing. Wilcolac, instead of any punishment, will send you out himself, with his blessing and an expense account. If that is your wish, then wish it."

"How can you do this?"

"Magic! I am Night even though I am small. Wilcolac is Twilight. He has human blood in him! Do you think he is immune to the Black Spell? To all of the twists and turns and clinging tendrils of that mighty mesmeric spell? Speak! Is this your wish?"

She hesitated, suspicious.

"Or I could have you get a raise in wages instead or have whoever you like trip down the stairs and break a leg. Speak! And return my name to me."

"How can I return your name?"

"How can a bride agree to be wed, or a judge condemn a prisoner to death, or a gambler accept a wager? Saying so makes it so."

"Very well. I wish the wish and return your name. Sly Jack Crookshank. It is yours again. Is there anything else, or is that enough?"

He tossed back his head and laughed. "More than enough! And now I must away! A thousand evil pleasures before me lay! And every wicked deed I do, blame me as you will, the blame goes back to you!" He took the bone in his hand and touched it to his lips. And at once he was gone.

Yumiko showed none of her disquiet on her face. Was this good fortune or bad? Had she been foolish to free him?

No matter. She turned back to the desk. For a moment, she wondered if her eyes deceived her, for the tiny stains of spilled alcohol were gone, and all the tumblers put away. All was as before. More magic? Was this part of the spell Crookshank had promised?

The unread letter was still on the desk. But as she was reaching for it, the fear touched her that, if Crookshank was no longer arranging business to keep Wilcolac away, the Magician might return at any moment. First things first.

The little man inside the rye bottle was asleep. But what if something else were watching her?

She stepped over to the mirror. Looking closely, she saw how the panels in the wall mirror were separated by the same strip of decorative wood as the back wall. It took only a moment to find a Mock Orange bloom fifty-eight inches above a decorative Acacia bloom on the floor. She touched both. One pane of the mirror moved back and silently slid aside.

Inside was a dark corridor, carpeted with rubber mats, extending to the right. Large square panes of glass showed Wilcolac's office beyond. The dark corridor ended in a stairwell landing. No one was there.

She turned. The telephone was a multiple line office phone with a rotary and large, square push buttons. Perhaps it was fifty or sixty years old. She had no time to take it apart and do a thorough job. Instead, she unscrewed the earpiece from the handset and unscrewed the mouthpiece. Beyond one was a speaker; beyond the other, a mike. Both were connected to the thick cord by copper wires. Into the one cavity she put the bugging device she had been carrying all this time, disguised as her right earring. Her left earring she put in the other.

She replaced the phone and was straightening up just as she heard the doorknob of the office rattle. To her horror, Yumiko realized she had not closed the panel in the wall mirror. She flipped one handed across the desk, somersaulted in midair, and landed before the open panel. Her toe and finger touched the spots on the wall and floor simultaneously. The glass began to slide shut.

There was no time to return to the stool. The office door was already swinging open. So Yumiko merely raised her hands to her hair as if she were adjusting a stray strand or toying with her hat.

In the mirror, she saw behind her that Wilcolac was locking the door. He was fumbling with his key. His image slid before her nose as the panel returned to its place. Behind her, she saw Wilcolac turning. His face lit up when catching the sight of a pretty girl primping in the mirror, without a care in the world.

He clapped his hands and rubbed them together. “Well!” he called in a hearty voice. “Where were we?”

She turned as if only now seeing him and smiled gracefully. “You had discovered something about me.”

He bounded over to his chair, threw out his coat tails theatrically, and seated himself.

Chapter 9

The Red Lady

1. Empowerment

Wilcolac said, "What I found out is that Hala brought drinks up to Kudlac Obors and Licho Lampasma last night while they were standing watch outside the Royal Suite. A lager and a kvass. And you paid for them out of your own money. I know you don't have much money because I know how much you have."

Yumiko, not sure what to say, and wondering if Sly Jack had actually cast a spell at all, crossed over to the stool, and seated herself again. She noticed Wilcolac's gaze traveled up and down her silk stockings when she crossed her legs, and she realized she was getting very weary of being Mata Hari. Why couldn't she just have a silent flying cape, hide in the shadows at night, and shoot evildoers from a safe distance, like an honest dark avenger?

So she said, "Thank you, sir. I am happy to help."

He leaned back. "You do not see my point. That is very interesting. Very."

Yumiko smiled, waited, and tried to look pretty.

"Here is my point." Wilcolac templed his fingers. "It is an old trick, a hazing thing, they sometimes play on the new girl. She brings drinks that were not ordered, and then she gets stuck with the bill. Comes out of her pay. Teaches her to get the orders right. Everyone laughs at her. But you were not tricking Hala. You paid. Now, as best I can piece things together, that happened right before the second show. But Sir Garlot did not announce he was buying drinks for the house until after that show was over."

Yumiko wondered if the next thing out of his mouth was going to be the order for her to be dragged to the lower vaults, where Empousa waited. Or perhaps Crookshank's spell had blinded him to the obvious, and she would suffer nothing worse than being sacked, which would cut off her hopes of finding Tom or Elfine.

Not for the first time, she wished she had been born a man so that instead of this smiling and looking pretty, she could have grabbed Wilcolac by the collar, slammed the back of his head against the wall, and demanded answers. Maybe while threatening his face with his own broken whiskey bottle or giving him a mean poke with his quill pen.

She could think of nothing to say. So she put her palms on the sides of the stool on which she sat, which gave her shoulders a bit of a shrug, and she tilted her head, smiled some more, shifted her weight, and recrossed her legs. Satin whispered, silk rustled, and leather creaked when she moved. She did her very best to look innocent, sweet, alluring, and harmless.

It must have worked because now a genial smile broke out on his features. "What I discovered is that you anticipate customer demand, you care about the morale of the staff, and, rarely enough, you are honest. You could have rooked Hala out of the drink money, and no one would be the wiser. And so, as a reward, you are to be empowered—yes, *empowered*, that is just the word—with an additional expansion to your duties. You are hereby appointed *Special Executive Liaison of Visiting Dignitaries, Women's Auxiliary Division*."

This certainly sounded better than being dragged down to the lower vault. "A splendid title. I am surely unworthy of it. Ah… What does it mean?"

"It means you are the new kid, and any annoying jobs that no one wants and anyone can do, you will do. You'll take it and like it. Lay back and think of the Cobbler Club. You are volunteering!"

"I am happy to volunteer. For what, please?"

"Her ladyship Dame Malen Ruddgochren is a high-born and pure-bred elf of ancient lineage. She has rarely come into this hemisphere or seen the daylit mortal men at their toil, certainly not this century. She has taken it into her head to go to the market fair to shop."

"The market fair?"

"So she calls our stores and shops. While she is here in New York, she wishes to shop. And she has straightly forbidden me to send any men along to escort her. The problem is that she does not know the way to Macy's, Saks, or Bloomingdale's. She has never been in a horseless carriage before, much less a limousine, and I am not sure she knows how to use a telephone to call our limo service. Or use an elevator. Or knows whether to walk out of a shop without paying. So you are to be her official assistant."

"Assistant?"

"Carry her packages, say 'yes, ma'am' when she talks, that sort of thing. Make sure she does not walk into the men's restroom. Make sure she does not sing a song to make police horses rear up on hind legs and dance. Make sure she does not kill any Daylight men. At least, not while any cameras are around. And everyone has cameras these days. Questions?"

"I am not allowed to wear my Cobbler Costume outside…"

"Go change!" said Wilcolac brusquely. "See Boggy, and she will give you a company credit card for your expense account. It will all go on Garlot's tab anyway. If you make it back in time for the first evening show, fine. If not, no problem. Before curfew or after is equally fine. You will escort her back to her dwelling place and return here. You will get time and a half for this duty."

"Time and a half?"

"Consider it hazardous duty pay. Now shake your pretty little fanny! One does not keep a high-born elfin lady waiting." Wilcolac pushed a button on his desk which unlocked the door.

Yumiko rose and curtseyed and took her leave.

She realized what this meant. Crookshank had performed his promise to the letter. Once Lady Malen released her and sent her home, there would be no one around, no one to check on her or note her movements until she returned at whatever hour she chose.

In her heart, she blessed Crookshank.

2. *Instructions*

Yumiko donned her kimono. This was for three reasons. First, that it was the nicest thing she owned. (The expensive American-style businesswoman suit

Elfine had gotten for her was nicer, but it was stolen.) Second, any onlooker seeing the strange sight of a lady in medieval costume would surely think it less strange if the girl following her were also in costume. An onlooker might conclude they might be actresses on the way to a dress rehearsal or something. Third, it allowed her to visit the lockers, fold the red sash into an obi, and wear it so as to carry her suit, mask, gear, and weapons with her.

After that, she dashed to Boggy's and received the credit card she was to use on the elfin lady's behalf.

Boggy quickly recited a set of rules to follow: "Do not speak until spoken to. Answer direct questions directly, and do not be familiar. Say *My Lady Malen* when introduced and *Ma'am* thereafter. Walk two paces behind and to the left unless she indicates otherwise. Cover your mouth when you laugh. Do not raise your eyes to meet her eyes unless she asks a question. Speak no curse words…"

These made sense to Yumiko and seemed to be common politeness. But then the rapidly listed instructions started to sound odd.

"Say no blessing, not even if she sneezes. Never say the name of the Savior. If you must refer to a certain holiday in December, call it *Yule* or *the Winter Holiday*. If you go into a restaurant, do not touch the salt or refer to it. Do not touch her with anything made of cold, hammered iron or let her come in contact with such material. Do not allow any crows or birds of ill omen to land on her. If they try, shoo them away. Do not let her come in contact with broom, lupine, or gorse, peony seeds, or freshly baked bread…"

There was more. Yumiko fretted she might not remember it all.

"…don't let her kill any mortal men. And don't keep her waiting!"

Yumiko took the elevator up to the top floor, where the Royal Suite was. The carpeting in the atrium was green and gold. The electric lights had been switched off, and candles in white and citrine glass holders twinkled instead. Only two doors opened from the atrium, one into the service stairs and the other into the suite. There was no corridor on this floor as the entire floor was taken up with the suite.

There was no number on the door, but a small brass plaque bearing an R under a crown. One of the hurried instructions given her was that she was not supposed to knock but should wait for the lady's servant at the door, a footman, to knock for her and to introduce her to the lady. Once the lady accepted her, and not before, she was to enter and leave unobtrusively, without knocking.

However, there was no footman here. Yumiko narrowed her eyes at the stubbornly footmanless door. She was not to keep the lady waiting but was not allowed to knock until she was introduced and accepted, but neither was she allowed to enter without knocking.

She put her ear to the door, but no noise penetrated. There were no mirrors in the atrium, and so she had no one to talk to about her decision. Finally, she decided that the lady might be offended at the intrusion, but would at least know Yumiko was present, if she entered uninvited. One the other hand, if the lady were offended by being kept waiting, the lady would have no way of knowing Yumiko was standing silently outside.

She twisted the knob. It was unlocked. In she slipped.

3. Royal Suite

Before her was a sitting room, luxuriously appointed. Gold furnishings on squat massive legs stood on a plush carpet of black. A table whose top was a single immense geode of polished quartz was midmost. Tapestries embroidered with hunting scenes hung from the walls, hiding whatever the original décor had been. There was a large archway to the left, framed by two marble pillars leading into other rooms in the suite. Facing her were French doors leading to a tiny, well-kept rooftop garden looking down on the avenue. A second archway, framed by two wooden pillars, to the left opened up onto a large hall with a stone floor, lit by a walk-in fireplace.

Before the huge fireplace was a chair of ivory, sitting in a bright circle shed by a spotlight directly above. Here sat a red-haired woman in scarlet finery trimmed with ermine and adorned with emeralds, staring into the fire. Her skirts reached to her feet. Her ornate bodice left her shoulders bare. She wore a snood into which her braided hair was gathered. Atop this was a tiny red cap, smaller than a French beret. At her feet were a knife and also a silver platter on which many bones were piled. This was the same woman, unusually beautiful with skin unusually pale, whom Yumiko had seen last night with Garlot: Dame Malen Ruddgochren.

Yumiko took a soft footstep toward the figure, wondering whether she should clear her throat. The elfin lady seemed to be asleep even though her eyes were open.

Yumiko took another step, and a strange, dreamlike sensation crawled over her. A pressure was in her nose and ears and behind her eyes. Nothing in the room changed shape, but Yumiko suddenly saw the scene anew.

First, the light shining through the French Doors was the dim pink of early dawn, not the bright light Yumiko had just seen through the windows in Wilcolac's office on this same side of the building.

Second, the pillars to either side of the second archway were not wood. There were two mossy oak trees growing here with thick roots, rugged bark, and twisted branches. Their roots penetrated the floorboards, and their crowns reached higher than normal perspective could explain, as if a thirty-foot tree was beneath a twelve-foot-high roof. The arch was formed by two limbs growing together.

The stone-floored hall beyond the arch, Yumiko now realized, was larger than it seemed. It was vast. It was too large to be in this hotel. There were an encircling balcony and buttresses reaching to a vaulted ceiling that would have extended beyond the hotel roof. It would have stretched out over the avenue had it been real. She realized she was looking into something like a dream. But it was a dream she was seeing with her eyes open.

She took a third step. The sensation of being trapped in a dream grew more powerful.

Yumiko saw more details: The flames in the fireplace were not flickering and moving as fire on earth would burn. The tongues of yellow and red waved languidly, hypnotically, like the swaying of seaweed in a current, and the sparks hung in the air, almost motionless, and neither flew nor winked out.

The circle of light in which the lady sat was shed by a white candle that hung unsupported in midair above her head, in blithe contempt for the laws of gravity.

The stillness of the lady suddenly, with no cause, seemed nightmarish. She was neither blinking nor breathing. Was she dead?

However, several of the leopards and stags in the forest scenes in the tapestries along the walls had turned their long, strangely human faces toward her and were regarding her through stiffly woven fronds with sad and solemn eyes.

The sensation grew more terrible. Yumiko felt as if she were choking.

4. Twilight and Night

Yumiko closed her eyes, held her clamoring thoughts into silence, and concentrated on her breathing. Slowly, calm returned.

When Yumiko opened her eyes, the scene was altered. All the dreamlike dread was gone. She felt awake. The pounding in her head was gone.

The proportions of the stone-floored chamber were still impossible, but the chamber was smaller, and the fire in the fireplace now kept pace with the normal rate of time. The ceiling now seemed to be merely painted with a cunning image of a ceiling balcony and shadowy vaults whose perspective was meant to fool the eye. The far walls, which were no longer far enough to reach across the street, were hung with mirrors, making the hall merely seem longer. The beasts in the tapestries had ducked their heads back to their former positions and were holding still.

The red lady was now standing and facing her, and the white candle was no longer hovering in the air, for the lady held it in her hand.

The lady stepped forward, holding the candle high. As she crossed the archway, the scene behind her changed again and shrank, becoming more solid. Now it was a room carpeted and decorated just as the sitting room. The ivory chair was still present, as were the platter of bones at its foot and the silver knife, but the fireplace was of normal size and shape. The ceiling was dark plaster. The trees to either side of the archway were no longer growing through the floor. Now they were saplings standing in tall brass urns.

Yumiko remembered to drop her eyes.

The red lady was tall. Seen close, her neck was white as paper, an unearthly white. The red lady's lips were red as blood, but they were not painted with lipstick. It was their natural color. The top of Yumiko's head did not reach her bare shoulder. The lady reached down with a pale white hand with blood-red nails, took Yumiko's chin between her fingers, and lifted her face to inspect it.

The lady's eyes were gray as tarnished silver, gray as storm clouds before the storm, and deep. To look into them was to peer as if through two pellucid windows into a sea of shadows without bottom, memory beyond memory, older than Babylon, older than the Flood.

Her voice was a sighing of woodwinds. Yumiko both heard the words in her ears and, at the same time, not with her ears. It was as if some part of her brain were asleep and Yumiko but dreamed that she heard this voice.

"To draw back from the night-shadow so quickly and cleanly is unusual," said the lady thoughtfully. "You are not fully a Daughter of Eve. Subtle ichor of nobler ancestry is mingled with the dross of mundane blood. You are a beauty and no Cobweb."

Yumiko kept her hands at her side. She did not allow her fingers to form into a fist but kept her expression mild and her thoughts silent.

"Tell me your true name, the day and hour of your birth, and the names of your native and conniving stars."

It was a direct question. Yumiko said, "Please let all be well between us, Dame Malen Ruddgochren. Please call me Sayori. I do not know the names of the stars that looked on my birth."

Malen said, "Speaks she the truth?" But she had raised her strange eyes and was looking over Yumiko's head at a point behind her.

A voice that was neither male nor female spoke. The tones had a peculiarly dry timbre. From the sound, the words were not formed in a mouth with damp tongue and palate, and there were no lungs made of warm, moist tissue behind them. "At times. She reveals and conceals the truth by speaking and by not speaking."

Malen evidently understood this riddle, for she nodded thoughtfully. She spoke again. "The scent of high and distant stars clings to her, silver and gracious with forgotten grace. But also the scent of the grave and the foetor of the noisome worm."

The eerie voice answered. "She has been washed clean of all oaths and curses, fresh as an eight-day-old child at baptism."

Malen was still holding her chin, and so Yumiko could not turn and see who or what stood behind her and spoke these words.

Malen's gray eyes narrowed, and strange light was in them. "Speak you of uncouth things to me? Begone!" She turned her gaze to Yumiko again. Her fingers tightened on Yumiko's chin, and her face drew near. "I see dark deeds in your eyes and murders without remorse. And yet you are unstained and fresh? The starlight is closer to you than any starlight that falls to Earth. You are a strange one, girl! Explain yourself!"

"I cannot explain myself, Ma'am. I wish I could. Ma'am."

Malen let go of her chin and straightened up. Her long red hair now unwound itself of its own accord from the snood and parted and swayed as if there were a wind blowing in the chamber. But there was no wind. The candle flame fluttered in her hand.

The lady said, "I see but one full moon in your eyes and no winters. Where is the winter in your eye? You are less than a month old. Mayhap you are some newborn changed by charms into a ripe young woman in an hour? Or if not this, some other trick as merry and cruel was played on you. Listen! Listen?"

Yumiko looked attentive, but Malen said nothing more.

"Ma'am..?"

Malen now leaped back, lightly as a doe, and turned on her toes swifter than a ballerina. She flung the candle away to one side, heedless of where it fell. It left a thin trail of blue smoke behind it. "Listen! Can you hear the music? Can you hear it?"

And now Malen, with eyes blank yet shining, began to whirl and caper, her toes not fully touching the carpet, her body swaying like the branches of the birch tree in the strong spring wind, her arms like floating scarves, her hands like bright green birds soaring and circling, her red hair following her like the bright tail of a torch in a gale.

A sudden jolt of sorrow passed through Yumiko. Tears were in her eyes, and a sob caught in her throat. Yumiko somehow, in some strange fashion, knew that the emotion was not hers but was coming from somewhere in the room and passing through her. She ducked her head and, again, controlled her breathing. The sensation vanished as if it had never been.

Malen now stood before her, looking down. "You are no witch. That is sure. Do you hear the voices lamenting? The song troubles you?"

She said, "I hear no voices, ma'am, no song."

"Your ears are held. Your brain is clay. Why did the Magician send you to me? His mind is a maze, and I cannot see past the first twisted winding."

Yumiko was now puzzled and beginning, despite her best efforts, to grow frightened again. "Ma'am? The Magician said you needed a girl to wait on you when you went shopping. To the, ah, market fair. Here in this hemisphere."

Malen now turned her back to Yumiko, but then slowly tilted her head and looked over her shoulder. "That was long ago. Long and long. Fifteen minutes. Half an hour. What is that in elf-time?"

Another direct question. "I don't know, ma'am."

Malen sneered. "Of course you do not, foolish virgin, until I tell you! In dreams, a man can live three lives and more between the time he rolls from bed and ere he smites the floor. Empires of the instantaneous creatures who live in the flickers and wisps of dreamland could rise and fall and the ruins be covered by creaking and malignant trees in that time." But now she smiled brightly, clapping her hands in joy like a schoolgirl. "So you are my maidservant? We shall have fun together!"

Yumiko bowed. "The Magician places me at your disposal with his compliments. Ma'am."

"I remember my ambition from long ago. From this morning. The dawn was fair to see, and I bade it linger. I wish to see their shops and stores. Is their wealth more glorious than ours? I must see the Daylight Men!"

And sudden passion overcame Malen, for her fair limbs grew stiff, and her head was thrown back.

"I must see them in their false lives and corruption, worshipping false idols or none at all! The Galilean is dead. He must be! He was tortured! He must be afraid to return! Why is he not afraid? Arthur is dead. Merlin is dead. Do the dead arise again, like a man waking from sleep?"

Her hair began to sway and flutter so violently that trickles of smoke came from it.

"I must see the men of the sunlight in their swine pens, rooting in sin, wickedness, and mutiny, and this will prove that none will come to save them, no high judge forgive. I can tolerate the fires if I know they will go before me."

Whirling suddenly, she grasped Yumiko by the shoulder and gazed down into her face. Her fingernails, bright red, bit into Yumiko's shoulder.

The music of Malen's voice became strident. It was out of step with the words appearing inside Yumiko's head. This formed a jarring double echo. "I have an enemy. He means to burn me with fire, trapped within immortal flesh unperishing, so that I will burn more and more, forever! He has prepared the Lake of Fire for my masters. I have seen it. Is it not right that I hate this enemy? Is it not right that I hate his servants? I am afraid of fire! Prometheus stole it. It should not serve them!" But with her mouth, she said only, "Why do they worship him and not me? Am I not worthy of worship? In older days they did, you know. The Sons of Adam bowed and served and sacrificed to me."

Yumiko was frightened and tried to keep her face blank and her eyes down. She was not sure if any of these questions had been meant for her, so she resolved to say nothing.

Or so she thought. To her surprise, she heard her own voice come softly but sternly from her throat, saying, "Fairest daughter of fairest Ernmas and Delbaeth of the Storms, surely the dead can be risen. I was risen. Take heed. You cannot place yourself beyond the reach of your judge by dying nor make your soul too dark for him to see. Even if you make your bed in Hell, he is there."

Malen let go of Yumiko's shoulder. Her hair fell back down around her shoulders and ceased to smolder. Her eyes seemed like the eyes of any woman who has known sorrow. Her mouth was hidden behind her fingers.

"The music ceases. Mercy speaks from you, but there is no mercy in you."

Her fiery hair braided itself like dancing snakes and folded itself into the snood again. The unearthly beauty returned to her tones. "You are a puzzlement! The Magician has chosen well. Were you easily known, hence dull, I might forget you, and perhaps you would cease to be. At times, I think many I have forgotten have vanished away without trace, by hundreds, by hosts and nations. But I cannot be sure." She pointed behind her. What had been an archway between two trees was now a mirror between two potted plants, and what had seemed a chamber was but a reflection of this one. The ivory chair, however, still existed, but it was on this side of the mirror, facing the French doors.

The red light of early dawn was still pouring in through those doors. If this was a dream, Yumiko was still in it.

Looking down at Yumiko, Malen raised one eyebrow. "Why did you come into my presence without being announced?"

Yumiko bowed. "I was told not to knock. There was no footman at the door."

"I consumed him." Malen spun in a circle, and a long red cloak which had not been there a moment before clasped her shoulders. Now she smiled. "But you and I shall walk arm in arm, chattering and laughing gaily, like childhood friends, and old gossips! You are pretty for an under-creature, and the smell of mortal bread and wine is not obnoxious on your breath. We shall be friends, and I shall preserve your life! Is this not a kindness of mine? Am I not kind?"

"Most kind, ma'am."

"Show me the finest treasures of the city! Let us go!" And she took Yumiko by the arm, and she strolled grandly out the French doors and into a garden that had suddenly grown larger and darker than was possible, with many orchids and tropical blooms which had not been there a moment before.

5. An Elf Hour

The rooftop jungle was rich with strange perfumes beneath red clouds. Flowers with the faces of young maidens, or orchids like leprous crones, gazed at Yumiko with wide eyes. In the distance, albino elephants stalked the clearings in eerie silence.

Yumiko concentrated on her breathing and recited verses from the Diamond Sutra silently in her mind. *There is neither form nor emptiness. There is no passing away and no coming into existence.* The jungle grew smaller, and the trees grew less with each breath. A sensation of drunkenness, which had crept upon her so subtly she did not notice it, gradually receded.

Malen led her down a vine-cloaked fire escape to the streets of New York.

It was difficult leaping from landing to landing in her kimono, but there was no other way to keep up with Malen, who went sailing down the stairs without touching them as if she were sliding on an invisible glass ramp.

Down on the sidewalk, it was day, and the sights and sounds seemed normal. On the final landing, Yumiko looked up. The vines and jungle trees had vanished, but a single baby elephant, white as snow, was peering curiously over the roof of the building down at them.

Yumiko released the safety-catch on the final length of metal ladder. It slid open. She rode it downward as it fell with a clang and a clash to the pavement of the alley. She landed, rolled, and came to her feet lightly. Then, she straightened, adjusting her kimono, smoothing the fabric, and stepping quickly after Malen. The Red Lady had left the alley and stepped into the middle of the avenue, and she was making imperious gestures at the honking cars and buses. Yumiko was unable to persuade her to return to the sidewalk.

The Cheyenne darted into the traffic. He was dressed in a buff leather jacket with two rows of shining brass buttons on his breast, and a cap with a bill was on his head. It was a chauffeur's uniform. He saluted. "Your limousine awaits, milady! This way!"

Malen said, "That man there swore at me. When he wakes tomorrow, his teeth shall hatch with infinite pain into scorpions and asps, and sting his mouth and throat with lingering poison! So I decree!"

The Cheyenne darted a dark glance at Yumiko and said, "Please don't. It is bad luck to kill humans, ma'am. You really shouldn't rile them up. They belong to the Winter King."

"Oh, very well," she pouted. "I shall instead have him slumber twenty years."

A moment later they were in the back of the limousine and driving slowly to Bloomingdale's. The Cheyenne spoke over his shoulder without turning his head. "Will you agree to leave the humans alone? They can be dangerous in groups. Your brother would not like it if you were to get hurt."

Malen raised an eyebrow. "Of what order am I? We harm. We are not harmed."

"Humans are easily startled," the Cheyenne said, unimpressed. "They might stampede. Don't you read the papers?" He passed a rustling gray sheaf through a slot in the glass separating the compartments.

Yumiko looked at photographs of rioters in ski masks skirmishing with rioters in hoods while police in riot gear stood in the distance, looking on indifferently. The photo showed a dumpster fire and black-clad figures dancing around it. Under their feet was a blonde girl, being kicked and beaten. The caption read: *Protestors Blame Mayor.*

The headline read MURDER SPREE CONTINUES. Minorities, women, hit hardest. *Fifty-first victim found torn to bits in public pool.*

Yumiko's eyes skipped down the paragraphs. "A largely peaceful protest is ongoing for the third straight day… over the last fifteen months… wild dogs killing women, children… victims consumed… remains… by some large animal… peaceful protestors demanding… cops pelted with rocks, fireworks, Molotov cocktails… smashed cars… arson fires burning since… firetrucks unable to enter… streets barricaded by protestors… police criticized for harsh tactics… the possibility of declaring martial law…"

Malen said, "Shall we see them fight? It is the only thing I like about the Sons of Adam. They fight dirty."

The Cheyenne said, "Please stay away from any bad neighborhoods, ma'am."

Malen pouted. "It has been a long time since I saw the gladiators at the circus. When they closed the last one, I so hoped they would reopen! A curse on Saint Telemachus! It has been over a thousand years."

The Cheyenne remained with the limo when the red lady and Yumiko went into shop.

The next hour passed without incident. Malen seemed subdued by the sight of so many human beings, by their electric lights, escalators, telephones, and water fountains.

More than once, as they shopped, Malen wondered aloud about the absence of woodland animal noises, birdcalls, and leaf-whispers. She did not seem to be able to adjust to the traffic noise or elevator music. She was impressed by how many floors there were and insisted on going to the top. Yumiko found a door leading to the roof. It was locked, but it flew open of its own accord when Malen commanded it to.

The wind was blowing here. The surface was gravel. Malen sailed over to the low railing and stood peering down at Lexington Avenue. She suddenly said, "The Magician's dog displeases me. Let us leave him behind. I see a bridge across the air to the stores across the boulevard from us. You have shown a liking for pulling yourself out of my dreams at odd moments. Do not pull now, or you will fall to the street."

And the two of them walked across a smooth semicircle of an airy substance that looked like rainbow when they began to walk from roof to roof and looked like planks of crystal when they finished. A Victoria's Secret, a Gap, and a Banana Republic were below.

Nothing untoward happened to any humans as Malen glided from clothing racks to jewelry counters, ignoring lines, and barking commands at clerks or other shoppers. She did not notice which side of the counter was meant for shoppers or why doors opening into the back were forbidden. She ignored queues and doormen alike. Something in her great height, flowing hair, and rich garments streaming like red banners in a wind that touched only her made people get out of the way on the sidewalk as they strolled from one shop to the next. Malen jaywalked across streets, ignoring traffic lights, but then again, so did everyone else, so this did not make her stand out.

Only once, as they were walking, did an oddness occur. Malen climbed up from pot to lantern to an ornamental gargoyle in a keystone above the door of a highrise and caressed one of the Art-Deco faces carved there. The face grimaced and tried to bite Malen's finger. Yumiko gently urged Malen to come down.

Aside from that, Malen was unexpectedly well behaved. When they took a taxicab, for example, and the driver would not take Yumiko's credit card, Yumiko was able to persuade Malen to undo her charm and restore the man's braying donkey head to human shape.

The red lady insisted on buying Yumiko a red parasol with an ivory hilt at Saks Fifth Avenue. Yumiko was glad for it and used the parasol to shoo crows and ravens away, which otherwise tried to alight on Malen.

They were walking down an alleyway without enough room for both to walk abreast, and Yumiko was carrying hatboxes, parcels, and packages, not to mention her parasol. Yumiko spoke in a voice of alarm. "My lady! Back! Back the other way!"

With glacial dignity, Malen turned. "What did you say, girl?"

Yumiko said, "Some danger is near. I am not sure what."

"I am of the elder ones. I am of the Night. No danger threatens me. Put your burden down."

The dirty alley seemed an odd place to store parcels, but Yumiko placed them quickly on the stained macadam. She looked up in time to see Malen striding regally around the corner.

Biting back a cry, Yumiko yanked up her kimono with both hands and sprinted after her.

6. *Stampede*

The sun was directly overhead when Yumiko came from the dim alley into the bright street, so she was dazzled for a moment. She heard a terrible noise. It was a noise which, once heard, can never be forgotten, like the roar of the sea, like the voice of a waterfall. It was the sound of a large crowd of men screaming and bellowing in rage and hatred.

Yumiko blinked. For a moment, the street seemed empty. There were two or three deserted cars in the middle of the street and a line of police cruisers, lights flashing, parked in a line. Yumiko saw behind the police the shining highrise where she and Elfine had slept that first night.

But the street was not empty. Before the line of police cruisers a group was listening to a speaker with a bullhorn. He stood beneath a banner and addressed the crowd through a bullhorn. A line of policemen in heavy gear stood to one side, in a narrow rank along the stairs of the hotel. The roar came from elsewhere.

She spun. Malen was standing in the middle of the empty street gazing without curiosity in the opposite direction.

From this direction around the corner suddenly came a mob. Those in the vanguard hid their faces behind balaclavas or bandanas. Some held signs taped to metal poles. Others flourished baseball bats or bludgeons or heavy bike locks. Some held bottles stuffed with burning rags, the flames pale and half-invisible in the bright sunlight. A figure in the forefront wore a black hood and waved a fire ax. The sound was like a physical thing, roaring. The sharp noises of glass smashing and the shrill bleating of car alarms added to the din.

The rioters were charging the gathered crowd at full speed. The police line raised large, square shields. It was amazing how quickly the empty street was suddenly full of human figures, all running toward Yumiko and Malen.

Malen neither moved nor flinched but looked with disdain at the flood of men about to sweep over her.

Yumiko ran toward her. Whatever words of warning she shouted at Malen were lost in the uproar. The surging mob was immediately in the way. She saw fists, a blur of running legs. Some were boys as young as she, or younger, but taller, huge, strong, with arms that outreached hers. A girl fighting men was like a man fighting a troop of apes: a single firm blow would defeat her.

She could not see over their heads. Yumiko dashed up over the hood and on top of one of the abandoned cars. Before she knew what she had done, Yumiko flung herself heedlessly through the air at the hooded man with the ax, who was swinging at Malen.

Yumiko screamed like a falcon, a shrill, high scream. The man turned. She was smaller and slighter than he, but when she struck him in the face with her forward foot, her one hundred pounds of weight was behind the blow. The ax went spinning from his hands. He fell supine. *If the foe cannot breathe, he cannot fight.* She landed with her knee at his trachea. *If he cannot see, he cannot fight.* She drove her thumbs toward his eyes.

But the voice of her master in her memory was not the only voice there. *You shall serve the purposes of Heaven.* Something more powerful than instinct turned her hand. Instead of gouging out his eyes, she struck his nose with her palm, breaking it. And for how long did he need to be blind? She spat in his eyes. He blinked and screeched.

Because he was neither a werewolf nor an ape, merely a boy acting as savagely as one.

At that same moment, instinct made her leap and roll aside. An obese man behind her, screaming obscenely and aiming a baseball bat at the back of her head, missed her and struck the supine man in the stomach, folding him in half.

Yumiko plunged her hands into the seam of her obi, seized the first weapons to come to her fingers. One was a barblike throwing blade called a *kunai.* The other was a mini-grenade. Again, her instinct was overcome by something higher, and her fear was replaced by giddy amusement.

She threw the mini-grenade instead of the knife into the obese man's temple. He staggered, dazed, and inhaled the plumes of the erupting cloud, which smothered his next obscenity and hid his face.

Yumiko realized that, even among the other dancers who had elfish blood mingled in their veins, she had better hand-eye coordination and sharper reflexes and tired more slowly than they. No Daylight man, mind mired in the Black Spell, could match even the grace and glamour of the Cobbler Club

Girls. And an untrained, leaderless rabble of ruffians was even less a match. She laughed aloud.

A young hooligan at the fat man's elbow raised his boot to stomp Yumiko in the face. She braced the butt of the kunai on the pavement next to her ear. The blade was longer than the diameter of her skull, so the youth drove the knife through his boot sole into his foot rather than breaking her head. "Watch your step!" she warned as she kicked his other leg out from under him.

From her prone position, Yumiko put her legs over her head, kicked, and threw herself upright. The mob was about to run over her. She stiffened her fingers into a knife hand and drove them into the ribs of the man directly in front her. "Pardon me!" she cried. When he doubled over, she used his back, and then used the head of the rioter behind him, to vault herself through the air again and to rebound from hood of the abandoned car onto the car roof, which trembled under her footstep.

Now she was tall enough to see over the crowd. The skirts of her kimono were awry, her hair was wild and loose, her face was pink with battle-joy, and her red mouth was bright with laughter.

Yumiko suddenly wondered what she was doing. What instinct had urged her to save the Malen from harm? If the humans tore one of their elfin tormentors to bits, that would be simple justice. Her eyes darted through the crowd. There was no sign of Malen.

There was no sign of the police wading into the fray. The police line was retreating in an orderly fashion, not interfering with rioters. They clashed with the first crowd. There was a confusion of raised fists and clubs and curses, gangs of three and four pulling attackers to the street and stomping them down. It was awkward and ugly and none of the beauty of well executed blows was present.

The next thing Yumiko fished out of her sash was her baton, which she unfolded into a staff. She whirled and spun the staff into the insanely screaming faces and blocked and bruised the hands and arms that reached for her from all directions. The weapon was like a ghostly disk of metal, so quickly did she spin it.

Then, she realized she was wasting energy. The humans were slow and stiff in their movements, like lumbering creatures of clay. So she switched to a long-front stance, spread her grip, and began to move the staff in sharp, controlled strokes and thrusts, more precise and more painful while perhaps less damaging.

She was taken by surprise at how much more harm she committed on opponents who did not know how to take a blow or to fall. One eager boy climbing up the fender with a knife, when she dislocated his kneecap, plunged backward, arms wind-milling, and landed on his head, where he lay in a daze, swearing. No one in the crowd behind raised a hand to break his fall.

Despite her Twilight speed and their Daylight slowness, numbers mattered, and she was hard pressed. She needed time and chance to draw her wirepoon pistol and teargas pellets to cover a retreat. Time and chance she did not have.

She assumed Malen was more than capable of fending for herself. Indeed, Yumiko's main fear was for what Malen would do to the throngs of men. She stole another glance behind her. The police still had not moved. The Black Spell, or something just as wicked, held their hands. They let the riot roar on.

A moment of good fortune came when those standing farther off, seeing Yumiko atop the car, now began pulling rocks and bottles from their knapsacks and throwing them. Men who had climbed onto the hood were hit by rocks from behind. When they scattered and ducked, these men were easy to trip and topple back into the crowd.

She narrowed her grip, spun the staff, and found it was easy to parry these unaerodynamic, inaccurate missiles and redirect them toward the upturned, masked faces of screaming rioters trying to climb the car. The bottles shattered with startling noise on the pavement rather than on her staff if she deflected them correctly, and her attackers would draw back, frightened.

The rocks were painful but not deadly. Breaking a nose or bruising a throat was enough to take an amateur out of the fight. Even a black eye would discourage the more timid.

The best thing thrown at her was a bottle filled with gasoline and sporting a lit rag from its neck. That one she tapped with her staff so that it shattered on the car trunk. The mob recoiled from the splash of flaming oil and glass splinters. "You can have this back; thank you!" she cried sweetly.

The front rank pressed back into the oncoming second rank, creating a tangle, and now the flood of rioters suddenly had an eddy in it, a spot of blank pavement. It was her path of retreat.

She waved her farewell, smiled, unfolded her staff to twice its length, and used the force of the expansion to pole-vault over their heads. From there, she landed on the canvas roof of a sidewalk stand selling newspapers and drinks, which the rioters were busily looting. From there, a utility pole was within reach. She began to scurry up the rungs.

This was not unnoticed. Men were roaring and reaching for her. But only one man at a time could come up the rungs of the utility pole. She lined up her shot as carefully as a billiard player with a pool cue, whistled sharply, and when the man looked up, she shot the staff tip out to double length. Down he fell, taking the man below him along to the pavement.

All around the pole a double circle of raging men raised clawed fingers, trying to grab her legs and pull her down. The mob seemed a single beast, a horror from Greek myths with a hundred hands.

Suddenly, a strange, nightmarish sensation plucked at her soul. The hands reaching for her grew dark and darker. The brown of human skin turned into the brown of tree bark. Each man screamed in panic, horror, and pain, a terrible sound, as twigs emerged from ears and nostrils, and hair of head and beard turned green. Their toes emerged from their shoes and were driven into the concrete of the pavement.

In a moment, there was a circle of trees around her.

The greenery was spreading. Rioters farther away where twisting, cursing, calling out, and trying to run. Their steps were slow and slower, and their shoes burst asunder, as feet and toes became writhing roots of wood driving into the suddenly soft and yielding street surface.

One young man, perhaps too young to shave, threw himself to his knees, clutching an ostentatious gold crucifix on a gold chain at his neck, and cried out a simple children's mealtime prayer. *God is great! God is good!*

The curse passed him by without touching him. He opened his terror-wet eyes, saw his arms and legs unaltered, jumped up and ran like a jackrabbit, leaping over the roots and slipping past the crooked, leafy grasp of his shrieking, cursing friends.

In a moment, as swiftly as it had come, the roaring sea noise of the riot dwindled and vanished. The mob was routed. Yumiko looked toward the end of the street, wondering where Malen was. Surely this was her work. But now the crowns of the trees were tall, and she could see nothing but leaves in that direction.

She jumped from the pole and swung on a tree branch and then to the ground. The branch broke under her hand, but she landed in a roll and came to her feet, unharmed. Human blood came from the broken ends, and a voice of woe cried out in pain from beneath the trunk. She threw the branch from her with a shiver of disgust.

Yumiko saw scarlet fluttering between the trunks. She peered fearfully around the bole of a tree.

Chapter 10

The Hollow Hill

1. *The Ivory Chair*

Here was a clearing set with grass. A group of rioters, now unmasked, was down on hands and knees, chewing the grass contentedly, their expressions blank. Dame Malen Ruddgochren was sitting with her hair unbound, spilling through the air like a red cloud.

She was seated on the selfsame chair of ivory Yumiko had last seen back in the royal suite of the Cobbler building. Yumiko now saw it was made of human bones. Malen had a femur in her hand, which she was carefully fitting into a slot between the radius and the ulna of an arm bone amid the struts of the chair arms. The other bones creaked slightly, and stiffened, to clamp the femur firmly in place. Now it was part of the design.

Yumiko was horrified. "You are not supposed to kill them."

Malen did not look up. "Who speaks to me?"

"I mean, ma'am. My lady. You are not supposed to kill them, ma'am."

"That is better. Mind your tongue, lest it haply turn into a poisonous adder. Why are you allowed to kill them, and I am not?"

Malen now turned her head and stared at her. Her gray eyes reflected a silvery light from a source that was not present anywhere in the environs. Apparently, she meant it not as a rhetorical question, for she said, "Well?"

Yumiko should have said something flattering, but the truth leaped angrily out of her lips. "I was trying to save you!"

"You? Little un-bred half-breed? The mongrel bint means to save me? When I told you I was in no danger? Such presumption on your part. And *look* at your clothing! I shall do the Magician an evil turn because of this, for loaning me so insolent a draggletail! What shall it be? Ah! I will not tell him who you are." She smiled and clapped her green hands together, delighted with herself. "A delicious revenge! And to compass it, I need do nothing."

Yumiko was startled, and perhaps some wisps of the drunken, dreamlike sensation that surrounded the red lady caught her off guard, for she blurted out, "You know who I am?"

Malen threw back her head and laughed.

2. Discovered

Malen covered her smile with her fingers. "I should not laugh. Elfin mirth when overloud drives mortals mad as well as those whose blood is weak.

"Know who you are? Pretty as a Moth, but with slanted eyes, dark locks, and ivory skin like a daughter of Amaterasu Omikami? Two weeks ago dead? Perfumed of the towers of starlight of Sarras before their downfall? Hah! I should have known you immediately, except that no one looks at half-breeds, or drudge girls, and everyone knows you are dead. But even then, I did not think on you until you betrayed yourself."

She lowered her fingers. "Girl, I just saw a crowd stoning you, and you took the stones in mid-air aside with a stick without looking and flung each one back in their faces. One pitched a bottle of Greek fire at your head, and you deflected it back to shatter at the feet of he who threw it. No mortal man of the Daylight world can do that, nor Moth, nor Cobweb, nor cunning Mustardseed from the Twilight, nor any of the wise Peaseblossom clan, save for one and one only."

Yumiko said, "If you please, ma'am, who?"

She raised an eyebrow. "Interesting. The Peaseblossom was at the club last night. I would say he was in disguise, but is it called a disguise when one removes, rather than dons, a mask?"

"Winged Vengeance was at the club?"

"You pretend not to know your own master? How droll."

"But– Did you expose him to the Cobwebs?"

"Cobwebs?" Her voice rang with disgust. "Bastard sons of harlots! Have you any idea what sort of filth it was to whom Cobweb mated his daughters to produce so many abnormalities and half-humans? Why should I care how many wolf-men of the Anarchists your crow-man kills? Lucien can do his own cleaning up!"

"But– I heard– Is not Lucien Cobweb your beloved?"

"Hardly, my dear girl! A child in pigtails who is weary of her spotless Sunday frills might sit in a puddle and make a mudpie, but not to eat for luncheon. Besides, if I need someone to fight my suitor at the elfin court, Hafgan, when he grows tiresome, who better? And more than that, Lucien is a card I can let drop from my sleeve if Erlkoenig attempts to arrange another political marriage for me. No one takes a bride who dallies with the hounds-keeper. How much less one who lies down with hounds?"

"You are not with the Anarchists? Not against them? They mean to overthrow the elfs! Overthrow you!"

"So let them." Malen looked a trifle bored. "I know little of these tiresome affairs. I would not know of *you* at all, would never have even heard your insignificant name, had you not come into our lands to rob our Tower of Glass to lead an army against us."

"An army?"

"You were there. King Brian's men were upon your men like wasps."

"What men? I have no men. Ah. Do I?"

Malen waved her hand in the air, as if to brush the question aside. "Men or monsters, what difference? Werewolves and clay statues, abominable snowmen, blood-drinking vampires, and other deformities and abortions. All of them led by shades of the dead who hold no terror for us, we who are the pure-bred children of Air and Old Night."

"What? I did not send them! *Me?*"

"You were in the burrowing vehicle made by one of the Anarchists, the one called Saturday. If you are not his, why were you in his machine? You had the shadow door the Anarchists stole from Sarras. It was an antique."

"But why would I have–?" Yumiko started to ask. But then she stopped, for she realized that while she had heard about the raid on the Glass Tower, she herself had no memory of the event. Onlookers had seen her there. They had seen on whose side she had seemed to stand. But she was acting covertly now, wearing a false name, deceiving onlookers. Why not then?

Upon seeing Yumiko's hesitation, Malen allowed her cruel smile to take on a sharper angle. "All you Twilight people squabble among yourselves right enough, but you drop your quarrels readily if the opportunity arises to deal the purer blood some hurt, do you not? It is in the nature of the lower orders. You are all anarchists at heart. Lawless. You have no discipline. That is why we rule you, and that is why you need us to rule you."

Anger made Yumiko blush. "We are not like that! I am not like that!"

Malen stood up. "Are you not? A line of policemen are sleeping yonder, but will soon wake. You are a murderess several times over. Turn yourself in."

Yumiko shook her head a rapid shake.

Malen said, "No? Return the ring you have stolen. It is a precious relic of the elfs. No one of your world has any right to it."

Yumiko shook her head again, but now with a slow and deliberate movement.

Malen laughed. The echo of laughter inside Yumiko's head was louder and harsher than what ears carried. "Very well then. Keep it! The ring will bring you to Hell soon enough. Let the Anarchists undermine Erlkoenig. Nothing has been right since Alberec grew soft and traded thrones with his son. I don't like the way the king treats my brother. Why is Listenoise no longer in my family's hands? Can you answer me that, girl?"

Yumiko bowed. "I know nothing of such affairs."

"Nor I of yours." Malen said, "Nor care. I resent that in the crystal perfection of my elfin memory, I will carry your name a thousand years after you are dust, and then ten thousand more. How to make the memory more pleasing?"

Yumiko found her body shaking with fear. Once again, she had the clear intuition that this was a mood being put upon her from the outside. She closed her eyes.

The voice of Malen was malicious music. "Suppose I turn you into an eel and throw you in the sea? There you would be without hand or foot, mute and ugly, and unable to step on land. What vengeance could you work on me then, disciple of Winged Vengeance? Well, girl? What would you do?"

Yumiko opened her eyes, and there was no fear in them. "Pray for your immortal soul." And this answer surprised her, for she had meant to say something else entirely.

Malen subsided, and some of the pale beauty of her face departed, and her eyes were sad and reflected only the sunlight here.

"Elfs cannot return to paradise. The Second Adam undid the evils done by the First Adam," Malen said softly, "But we have no part in either. We did not fall with the first. We will not rise with the second. Your filthy human blood grants you some advantage after all."

Malen raised her hands. The men crawling at her feet, eating grass, now stood, but their eyes were still blank. "In courtesy to Erlkoenig, I shall allow the sun to end their bovine dreams."

Yumiko said, "And the trees?"

Malen looked at her sidelong. "You said not to kill them. They are not dead. They live! As trees."

Yumiko fell to her knees, put her hands on the grass, palms down, and bowed her head to touch her hands. Her shining black hair spilled across the green grass. "Please restore them, milady."

Malen's voice was no longer in her head. It sounded almost like a human voice. "Why do you plead for them? You were maiming them a moment ago. They are not your race. They are not your blood. And yet you humble yourself to me… for them? You are not the disciple of any Winged Vengeance, or any vengeance, winged or afoot. What is wrong with you? Explain yourself!"

Yumiko looked up. "I fell in love with a boy. He is missing, and I must find him. All these young men here, they sought my life, true! But if they do not return to their sweethearts, then why should mine be returned to me?"

Malen began to laugh. "You cannot be the girl I thought you were. She served revenge and was bound by vow. There is no returning from the dead. She would have known her own master's face. Someone has played a trick on you, or on me, or on both of us!"

Now Malen laughed more. "Yes, yes, I will let the sunlight burn the charm away, and the trees will be a mob again, and all will forget this day. It is within my jurisdiction, for the great streams and currents of the Black Spell concerning bloodshed and battles are all mine to command. I do it as a courtesy to Erlkoenig! I do it as a courtesy to you! For you have fooled me utterly as I thought you were the Foxmaiden, the sidekick of the dreadful vigilante! Or whoever enchanted you fooled me."

"But I am she. I am!"

"No! No more! The jest has run!" said Malen, clutching her slender stomach and still swaying with mirth, rolling her eyes here and there. "It was a diversion, an amusement. Rarely does a masquerade or well-woven illusion hoodwink me. I will not regret to remember this in ten thousand years! The little drudge at the dance hall, who flourishes her bosom and shakes her bottom for coins! In the very building Lucien owns! I thought *you* were the disciple of the deadliest fighter in three worlds! Well played! Well played."

Malen made a gesture. A sensation like a fading dream which slips out of memory touched Yumiko as swiftly as a stolen kiss and was gone. The wrinkles and stains in Yumiko's silk kimono vanished. The fabric was clean and pressed, the rips neatly stitched. Her face and hands were cool, freshly bathed, and her hair was shampooed, dried, and brushed. Someone had mended and washed her clothing. Yumiko wondered about the instantaneous creatures dwelling in dreams Malen had earlier mentioned. Perhaps Malen had maidservants there as well, who could perform an hour of chores in an instant.

The trees and grass were gone. The street was as before, and the men also, save that they stood swaying on their feet, eyes open, fast asleep, many of them snoring.

"So I have seen the daylit men," Malen was saying. "So what? What changes I was promised! Nothing changes. I saw the plebeians rioting for bread in Rome, the Blue and Green racing factions rioting for games in Constantinople, and the pagans in Alexandria in tumult against the followers of the Galilean, rioting over nothing. Only their toys are different. Why my brother Garlot meddles with these herd animals… ugh! Why not nap a hundred years until the matter settles itself?

"It is nothing to me!" she continued. "Let Garlot slay whom he must. I will return to Is-Elfydd." She pronounced it *Iss-Ailveeth*. "I shall return to the fairest Land Beneath the Land, and be done with you. Gather up my parcels. Quickly, now! I will summon steeds. Can you ride a stag?"

3. The Doors of Is-Elfydd

As stately as kings in procession, two deer of a breed Yumiko did not know carried them through the streets of New York. Malen rode a snow-white stag, bareback but side-saddle, and Yumiko rode astride a dappled black, with her skirts demurely parted. Despite it being March, these bucks had not yet shed last year's antlers, but instead had magnificent twelve-point prongs.

Yumiko had the parcels and boxes of the lady's purchases bound up and piled between her and the steed's neck, and she steadied the stack with both hands. The beast she rode had no rein, no bridle, no bit. Malen, cantering ahead, had unbound her hair, so that it fell from her shoulders to the rump of her steed like a scarlet pelisse, and when any people stared or flourished a camera, the strands stirred, and the glamour of the elfin lady spread forgetfulness where she passed. Only one drunk in the gutter and one soapbox preacher wearing a Salvation Army uniform followed the sight of the two deer stalking past and did not blink or have eyes go blank.

They entered Central Park from Fifth Avenue, between the pond and the zoo, but as they rode, the trees grew taller, and the city sounds grew more distant. The path underfoot changed, becoming cobblestone, and then a pavement made of luminous crystal that tinkled and hummed under the deer hoofs. By the time they reached Belvedere Castle, it was as immense as the Forbidden City in Peking, and black and silver banners adorned with leafless trees rose from the ninety turrets. Umbrageous silhouettes in silver armor with peaked helms stood watch, but Yumiko's eyes were prevented from seeing their features, for a shadow hid them. The outdoor theater near the great lawn was larger but also had stands, stalls, and lists for joust and melee as well as a floor for dance and opera.

The great lawn had grown. Instead of six baseball diamonds, now six great mounds or hills loomed there, with dolmens like stone tables or archways opening into nowhere crowning their green tops. The trees here were taller than any ash, fir, or redwood known to man and soared nine hundred feet into the heavens. Platforms of glass holding cottages made of malachite bricks were in the swaying branches, and larger platforms holding mansions and palaces of emerald, chrysoprase, and green aventurine were nestled to the trunks, and the towers and minarets of these treetop palaces were carven of solid sapphire adorned with blue quartz. The bridges connecting these several outbuildings to the manor houses were ribbons of silk, without handrails.

Yumiko noticed one eccentricity about the towers growing from the treetops. Each tower top on the side that faced the sun was elongated into a triangular sail which draped like a hood over the balcony, so the tower top resembled a Jack-o'-Pulpit flower.

Malen, seeing her gaze, turned and called over her shoulder, "Are not the towers of elfland more fair that the skyscrapers of men?"

"Very fair, milady. Why are they empty?"

"They are not. Many of the Fair Folk are above us, but your eyes are unfit to see them. Do you know the name of those towers, girl, or why their crowns are shaped like spathe?"

Yumiko did not know that word, and said, "No, ma'am."

"It is in imitation and memory of the cloud towers raised in Heaven by Mulciber before he plunged from the crystal scarp of Heaven in the roaring wake of the route of black angels in their fall. In Sarras, the City of the Grail, the spathe or hood of the tower allows the archangel of the sun to pass by close above the golden streets, but his view of the tower beneath is blocked, and he does not accidentally sanctify mews, dovecotes, bridal chambers, or other tower rooms set aside for profane purposes. The elfs use the same architectural device to shun the gaze of vexed or angry stars, who otherwise would shed an adverse influence. Stars have long memories. But I see you have not heard this lore erenow?"

"No, milady. This is new."

Malen smiled. "Then your imposture is incomplete."

"I beg your pardon, ma'am?"

"The wings of Winged Vengeance come from Sarras. It is where all swan robes and raven cloaks are woven. The vigilante was unknown before Sarras fell, so he clearly knows that walled city, at least well enough to yearn for retaliation against the Seven Lords of Anarchy, who arranged for the overthrow of those fair walls and contrived to bring the Prince of Giants so high into the cloud-lands. The vigilante's disciple in the fox mask is from that city as well, or was. It is obvious enough who she is."

Yumiko asked casually, "Who is she?"

"What do you care?"

Yumiko said, "As I have only this day discovered that I was ensorcelled or enchanted to believe I was her, I am naturally curious about who I am impersonating."

"During the battle in the Glass Tower, one of the miniature knights of Brian, riding a dragonfly, saw the Foxmaiden raise a bow and shoot and slay a ghost who beset her."

"I don't understand."

Malen clucked her tongue. "You have no education! Ghosts cannot be touched by arrows flung from any bow of earth. Hence this girl is one who carries the far-famed ghost-slaying bow of Yorimasu, named in song, Hamayumi. Twenty years ago, it was taken by Impetuous Danger Moth to be the bride price for the hand of Dandrenor, the Widow of the White Hands, but after called Dandrenor the Grail Queen. Danger Moth had no son, so who else can avenge the Queen? Who else can find the Grail?"

Yumiko was electrified. "Then this is her mother? The mother of the Foxmaiden, I mean." But the grief welling up in Yumiko's heart was answer clear enough. She almost did not hear what the Red Lady was saying.

Malen was staring at the sky, her eyes filled with bitterness. "The Grail is the vessel which caught the blood of that drunken Galilean. Now they cannot stop his blood! It is everywhere, in every cathedral! His shed blood should have been our victory! How did it become venom to us, unceasing vexation, an unquenchable fire? We were promised that the Galilean would go into Hell! Promised! The sign of his tortures should have given us power over him. By every proper rule of magic, it must! Why does it give the lesser orders power over us?"

"Pardon me, my lady. But you were telling me who killed the Grail Queen. Who is responsible for her death?"

Malen drew her eyes down and cast an indifferent glance at Yumiko. "I care little for the doings of Twilight and hear less, but even I heard of the downfall of the towers of Sarras. I drank a toast when she died. Hail the death of Dandrenor, daughter of Pellinore." Now Malen favored her with a half-lidded gaze. "You can see why I have an interest in this tale."

"No, milady."

"Her father is Pellinore! Pellinore son of Pellehan. Pellinore of Listenoise."

"I don't understand, my lady."

"Then you are dull of wit, are you not? This usurper rules my ancestral seat. If Listenoise were Chryseis, then Pellinore would be Agamemnon, and my brother would be a baser sort of Achilles, without the good sense to go sulk in his tent." Malen growled in her throat, her voice made musical with disgust. "Instead, Garlot slays the Arctic giants with gay abandon, fells Iotuns like trees, and places all the Winds of Winter under Erlkoenig's ambitious scepter! Erlkoenig buys Garlot's heart with trinkets, the Mantle of Mists, which hides his evil deeds, and the Crystal Cauldron of Youth, to which he flies whenever he is wounded any slightest scratch, the vain boy! He keeps it in a locked treasure chamber whose walls are carven amber, lit by his collection of girls in bottles. But Garlot has done me a good turn at last and visited the pleasure house of my lowborn lover Lucien, as I asked."

Yumiko was not interested in this. "Then who slew Dandrenor?"

But Malen did not hear the question or did not care to answer. "Yes, I am the one who arranged this pass. Soon the City of Corpses will be filled, their number complete! Then, the promise of my mistress, Empousa of Tartarus, will be done, and the Black Spell be torn entirely asunder. It is beginning already. The threads fray! Did you not see the chaos, the glorious chaos? Tumult, riot, and strife? Such is the effect on the kine called mankind when the Black Spell is yanked violently from their brains. Humans are escaping control. What keeps them tranquil grows weak. Reckless hate, vile crimes, and mob violence will become ever more common."

"Tell me of this Dandrenor! Who slew her?"

Malen gave her a withering look. "Should I know? Should any elf? A Giant slew a Moth. One baseborn miscegenation slew another. A trifle. Let dog kill dog!"

Yumiko licked her lips. "Milady is so wise. She knows much that is hidden. A giant slew Dandrenor, you say? But then why does Winged Vengeance hunt the Anarchists?"

"Sarras was trampled by the giant Ysbadden, who was sent by the Anarchists, who rose by profane vessels to that high and sacred place. He agreed to seize by force for them the Sangreal, the sacred cup of Him we name not.

Ysbadden betrayed them and kept the Grail. The giant dwells in the Third Hemisphere, and it is said no traveler can come upon the giant's tower except when that traveler is lost. His tower moves like an unanchored ship and is never seen above the same hill twice. That is why they seek the ring the Foxmaiden took. Without it, the tower of Ysbadden, Caer Nevenhyr, forever eludes them."

Malen smiled down at her. "I will guess the riddle of your making," Malen continued. "The vigilante hired some elf of my generation, in whom the old blood is not diluted, the old fire not dimmed, to make homunculi, or more than one, each thinking herself the Foxmaiden, and skilled with her skills. These he sent into the world in several places, to confound huntsmen and to draw those seeking her astray. That would explain why a grown maiden is but a month old. You look so real! The craftsmanship is skilled! I'll wager it was Maeve of Orberica or Morgan le Fay.

"I had no part in the fall of Sarras, but the mischief of the Anarchists pleased me, so I seduced one and arranged an introduction between Lucien Cobweb and the Owl Princess, Lachusa of the Strega. Lachusa is a witch of darkest craft. She introduced him to Empousa of Tartarus. Lucien hired Wilcolac, for whom you dance and flirt and pour."

Malen's laughter was a beautiful silver glissando. She continued: "Your role in Hell's design is small, but every customer you please earns a reward for the Necromancer. He buys his herbs and essences, rare substances pressed from the glands of the unborn, and calls upon Empousa. So it is arranged that foolish and ambitious pooka-dogs from Elfland become something darker: werewolves of Tartarus to inhabit the bodies of men who slay their own! Each dog, each man, each murderer, each drunk whose downfall you thus aid, is written in a fearsome scroll of judgment no power of earth or underworld can unwrite."

Yumiko was so taken aback by the malice in Malen's eyes, that she forgot her own sorrow and asked, "Then you– you are behind all of this? Why?"

"To do Erlkoenig, who awarded my lands to another, a hurt from which he will not soon recover."

"Then you seek to undo the Black Spell? The Anarchists will keep faith with the Last Crusade and free mankind?"

Malen turned away. Her stag now stood still. One of the tall green mounds was before her. Malen raised her hand, and a trumpet note from a horn unseen blew dim but clear from below the soil. At once a doorway opened in the mound, and a tongue of ground, grass and all, reached down into the dark, gem-studded depths. A faint melody, but fair to the ear, whispered up from below, and there seemed to be little winking lights in the far distance of the passage sloping into the heart of the hill.

A delayed thought reached Yumiko. She said, "Wait! Garlot keeps girls in bottles? How is this? Who are they?"

Unseen hands now plucked Yumiko from off the back of the black stag and flung her roughly toward the grass. She somersaulted in midair and landed on her feet. The parcels and packages, now weightless, swirled like autumn leaves into the air, spiraling high and low, and then danced into the corridor. The black stag pranced after, following music Yumiko could not hear.

Malen was still on the white stag. She gazed down at Yumiko. "I release you from my service. You have bemused and amused me this day, worked without complaint, and so I let you keep your human shape, as I agreed with the Magician to do. I will grant you this favor, and answer your two questions, and one more. Three in all. Hear me.

"Yes, my brother keeps a treasure chamber where he lolls in comfort on rugs of slain smilodons and tigers after he had boiled himself in the Crystal Cauldron of Youth, which closes all wounds and restores all lost blood. There he keeps the fairy maidens he has captured from Troynovant. They are not half-breeds like you, but true fairies, but who were caught trespassing into the human world. And there is one little Moth, whom Garlot caught for Lucien but decided instead to keep for himself. None is bigger than a pinky, and he hangs the bottles from the top of his amber-walled chamber and uses them as lanterns. To shed the light that keeps them small surely strains and pains the poor dears, but they cannot come to full size again, caught in such strait vessels, so what else can they shed, but tears?

"As for your other question, the world was designed to grow continually as man multiplied, but the elfs steal the new lands that arise shining from the sea and wall off the new hemispheres to expand into new directions, crowding men into ever more claustrophobic and violent and narrow spaces. Like rats crowded into ever smaller mazes, their bloodlust rises. My power grows.

"The Black Spell can be overthrown in two ways, one by adding light and the other by adding blood—namely, by adding a horror too great for the human mind to dare to cover with amnesia. Half a hundred have been slain by wolves in New York, shocking crimes unnatural, in ways that touch man's most ancient fear, and so the sleepwalkers stir and murmur in their sleep. Soon they wake! Ask of me a third question."

Yumiko said, "Why would the Anarchists free the humans?"

Malen laughed in scorn. "Why would jackals crop grass like oxen? They would not. The Anarchists free no one. When the leash is yanked from Erlkoenig's hand, do not imagine the Sons of Adam will slip the collar. A stronger hand will take his place. That is all." Now her smile became so dreadful that Yumiko felt queasy. "Does Euhemerus Cobweb imagine his wispy fingers will be that? Or Rotwang's metal prosthetic? Or what Zahack has in place of hands?"

Yumiko realized that these were the names of the Supreme Anarchists. Malen was so contemptuous of the doings of Moths and Cobwebs that she truly did not care whose secrets she spilled to whom.

Malen was still talking, delighted with herself. "The Anarchists are fools. Mere pawns. As if Twilight could overthrow Night! I am one of the eldermost of the Night. So we name ourselves in sorrow and self-scorn because once, long ago, before nightfall, light was with us. But there is a darkness deeper than mere nighttime in which all memory of light is lost."

Yumiko stammered, trying to grasp the implications of these terrible revelations, of treason within treason. "Then the Last Crusade..."

"Are fools to think an Anarchist keeps his word! What faith, what fealty, what honor does anarchy not seek to break? Fools twice over to think the Anarchists will surrender their captive once they have the Ring of Mists!"

Yumiko's heart leaped. "The captured Crusader is alive?"

"Yes, but in the City of Corpses, among the dead. And the Last Crusaders are fools thrice over to hunt Winged Vengeance, and unwittingly lead the Anarchists to where he hides! The moment the vigilante is found, and the crusader no longer useful, Sir Garlot will strike down Sir Gilberec from behind, unseen, by ambuscade and stealth. The wolves will cease to be slaughtered! The wolves will multiply. This great, gray city will drown in blood; the Black Spell will break, shattering human brains as it shatters. Then shall all the human world go slowly mad to see all their nightmares real and solid and standing in the sun."

Malen smiled again, evidently pleased at Yumiko's expression of horror.

"But I have shocked you, poor dear! We cannot have that! Three gifts I granted, in answering answers three: and now in turn I take one gift from you to me. I take your memory. Let all you have heard from me and seen, fade when we part like a passing dream!"

Yumiko was unable to move or blink. She was trapped by the gaze of Malen's terrible gray eyes.

Malen leaned closer. "Do you think I share my confidences with a serving girl? But it is pleasing to gab and gossip, and so I asked the Magician which of his girls needed fewer memories."

And still laughing merrily, Malen kicked her white stag, and down into the world below the green mound she went. The stag leaped in great bounds, but the elfin lady, sidesaddle and bareback, did not even bother to put out a hand to steady herself, for gravity did not dare to dislodge her.

In sudden silence, the hillside door closed, and the slope was only grass.

4. The Charm of Forgetfulness

Yumiko found she could move again. Trembling, she walked away from the mound. The strange, terrible eyes of the Red Lady were an afterimage before her; the eerie, cruel music of that beautiful voice echoed in her ears.

At first, nothing happened. She remembered the conversations clearly.

It was when she reached the edge of the great lawn and came into the shadows of the trees that it began. As silently as venom in wine, Yumiko felt the charm of Malen spreading fog in her mind.

It was like small and silent flakes of black snow in her thought, and wherever any snow landed, it covered and benumbed the memory beneath so that it was lost to sight. Yumiko forgot what Malen had told her about the albino elephants while the two walked in the rooftop jungle. She forgot why Malen had given her the red parasol or what had become of it. Then, she forgot

Malen asking the stone face on the wall for directions to the riot and then forgot what Malen had told her about the ravens and their part in her quarrel with her sister, the Morrigan.

Yumiko stepped from the path, knelt on the grass, cleared her mind, and made her soul quiet and still. She concentrated on controlling her breathing until her awareness of her breathing faded away.

The trees were no longer taller than redwoods, and if any villages, mansions, or towers were among the leaves and branches above the great lawn she had just left, they were hidden. The mounds crowned by monoliths were gone. The baseball diamonds were back. The sense of being trapped in a dream was gone. Never had she felt so clearheaded and awake.

Yumiko emptied her mind and let her soul grow utterly quiet.

She found that she was losing no more memories. Any thought she did not think could not be taken from her. The evil charm was held at bay.

Yumiko stood. She moved as carefully and slowly as a girl balancing a vase of burning acid on her head, for a sense of lurking, patient malice was still all around her, almost palpable, cold as an unseen snow cloud.

Did she dare to put on the Ring of Mists here, right at the gate to a buried elfish kingdom? For she was apparently in the middle of an invisible crowd of elfs. Malen had said who dwelled in these towers, but as soon as Yumiko recalled her remark, it was gone. Yumiko put her hand in her sash and fished around. She found the ring and slipped it on, turning it with her thumb. Perhaps if it fended off ghosts, it could fend off this. But she kept her hand hidden as she did.

The sense of being ringed by unseen eyes faded, but the sense of being inside a cold cloud did not. How could she think or concentrate to plan a strategy if whatever recent memories the thought brought with it were erased from her mind?

A silent inspiration entered her mind without thought, without concentration. She remembered the boy who had escaped when all around him had turned into trees by saying a simple prayer. This memory did not fade. *God is great; God is good...* And the charm did not remove these words from her head. The memory of the frightened boy praying did not vanish.

She said the words aloud, reciting them as if they were a mantra, merely a focusing point for her mind to unleash some power inside her. A clear intuition told her this was wrong, backward. These were not magic words. The thing could not be done by reciting phrases without meaning.

Silently, she said the words again, and, this time, she thought of the several things the Red Lady had said about the Galilean, about Arthur and Merlin, and about the shed blood which turned the roaring victory of darkness into their greatest defeat. Was not the power of Heaven which saved that unknown boy from the charms of Malen the same power which raised the dead? It greatness and goodness were beyond measure.

The cold cloud was gone. The memories were no longer fading. Nothing like black snow was any longer blotting out the words she had heard or the scenes she had seen.

Then, she remembered the words of Matthias Moth, the young blackfriar. *In the name of the Father, and the Son, and the Holy Ghost. Behold, I give unto you power over all the power of the enemy: and nothing shall by any means hurt you.*

She said this as well. Before she finished, indeed before she even began, she knew she was free.

In the distance, above the traffic noise beyond the trees, she heard the bells of the cathedral tolling the hour.

A feeling of awe, of puzzlement, but also of a childlike willingness to accept everything given her without puzzling over it, flooded her. She had defeated Malen's invincible magic! Easily, almost without effort, she had overcome one of the older powers of the Night World.

A sense of gratitude bubbled up in her heart like a well from underground, like a geyser, like a volcano. Because it had not been her, had it? Something had come to her aid. Or someone, rather. Someone great and good.

Usually, Yumiko hid her mouth when she smiled. Usually, she showed no expression on her face. Now she spun in a circle, gay and giddy, and laughed until tears of joy trickled down her cheeks.

She danced and spun until she came to a little arched bridge above a stream. Looking down, she saw her reflection. Yumiko leaned over the railing. Her hair had come loose of its ribbon while she danced, and it hung down like a waterfall of shining night, framing the narrow oval of her features. In the reflection, she saw her resemblance to a fox indeed in her high cheekbones and the sharp chin.

"I remember my mother's name." She said down to the face looking up.

Dandrenor. The lips of the smiling image below her moved as she said the name. The face was smiling and lit up with immense joy. Yumiko had never seen so pretty a face.

Except for one. Like a light bursting into brilliance in a dark room, a fragment of memory, clear and sharp, rapt her.

Yumiko saw her mother's face.

Chapter 11

The City in the Summer Stars

1. In Memory

Because the sight was in her memory, the sudden sting of tears in her eyes made the scene of tree and park, bridge and stream blur and swim, but it did not blur her mother's face.

Her mother's face was unlined, and her skin was smooth and clear, but her eyes were filled with the serenity and sorrow of wisdom not found in youth. Her face was oval, her features were clear cut, and her chin came to a delicate point. Her eyes were the color of the sea.

A wimple covered her hair and shoulders, held in place by a silver fillet at her brow and a silver broach beneath her chin in the shape of a fish. The trains of the white robes fell in long curving lines to the floor as did the flowing sleeves like great white wings. Embroidery as delicate as dewdrops seen on a spiderweb strand was woven through the panels made of ivory, milky, and silvery threads, and the pattern of images could not be seen when looked at directly, only from the corner of the eye. The hems and lining were red. Yumiko knew this red fabric was not a sign of joy and celebration as it would have been in her father's home in Japan. It was the sign meant to honor the memory of martyrs. Neither was the white robe a symbol of mourning, but of purity.

In the memory, Yumiko stood with her mother at the intersection of two colonnades. The pillars were so tall that their capitals were lost in the bellies of the clouds above. These clouds were dark and lowering, wonderful shades of slate and spun wool and charcoal. In the breaks of the cloud could be seen stately planets like colored lanterns dancing the rounds of their cycles and epicycles.

Between the planets hung a two-tailed comet, bright as a torch, perplexing astronomers, which presaged the doom of the high and sacred city of Sarras.

Above all this curved the vaulted azure dome of the chamber, which was more vast than any chamber of earth, more vast than earth itself. Images of crowned and haloed martyrs, each holding the weapon or tool that had tortured or slain him, as if robed in sunset-colored clouds, stared down through the constellations decorating the lower reaches of the dome. Now and again one who was not an image peered down also.

Yumiko and her mother stood atop the dais reached by three steps. The bottom step was white marble clear as a mirror, the second black onyx, the top porphyry red as blood. Atop the dais was a cupola held up by four white posts. Midmost was an altar. Atop this was a cup of white gold, and all the lights in the chamber were gathered to it.

Light came from this cup. It must have just that moment been uncovered by the cloth of gold folded behind it because in Yumiko's first memory of the scene, she was still blinking, her eyes not acclimated to the blaze. The inner surface of the small, flattish cupola dome was hammered silver, and these mirrors cast the cup's light back at it, redoubling its brightness.

Yumiko recalled her mother's voice. Dandrenor was saying, "The Sangreal was brought to England by Joseph of Arimathea, whose sister, Enygeus, wed Bron the Fisherking. He fathered Mordrain the Hermit King, who was the father of Merlin the Thaumaturge. Yglais, the sister of Merlin, wed Phanes, the son of Malen the Red War Queen. Phanes fathered Pellehan, who fathered Pellinore, my father. Ere she was wed, Enygeus was the first Grail Maiden and kept the watch. After her came Sarrasintë, Yglais, and Esmerée the Fair. Now I keep the watch, and I have not been relieved of that duty."

Yumiko said, "I will not be apart from you, Mother! Not again!"

Dandrenor seemed not to hear. "Here it is. Behold the source of your woe."

Yumiko looked. Despite herself, she was awed by the beauty of it, the loving craftsmanship. Never had she seen so fair a thing.

The bowl of the vessel was a hemisphere carved from a single monstrous ruby, nine inches across. The million facets sparkled and blazed as a hemisphere of red fire. About the mouth and down the sides of the bowl ran bands of white gold wide and thick. A massy stem of white gold connected this red bowl to its foot, a ruby hemisphere so lucent that the cup seemed to stand stop a dome of flame.

Celtic knots of rose gold wire intertwined images incised into the white gold bands. Red against white shined figures of a lamb, an ewer, an ear of wheat, a torch, a grape leaf, a door, a shepherd's crook, a crown. Above and around were letters in three languages: *Yod*, *He*, *Waw* in Hebrew; *Alpha* and *Omega*, *Chi* and *Rho* in Greek; *INRI* in Latin. These gold bands formed curving crosses reaching from stem to mouth. At the crux of each peered a cameo of ivory outward in four directions: the head of a bull, a lion, an eagle, a man crowned with rays. The cup mouth was hidden beneath an ornate gold lid topped with a tiny cross.

"It is very precious," said Yumiko. In the memory, her point of view was closer to the ground. How long ago had her mother died?

"The seen is but a visible shadow of the unseen," Dandrenor said as she tilted open the lid of the cup. "It has no luster save what is granted to it." Yumiko now saw that the diamond and gold vessel was not the cup itself, merely a container to hold it.

The real cup was a drinking bowl made of glazed clay nestled in the mouth of the diamond vessel. It was plain and dun.

"It is just clay."

"As are you. Look again. Look with your heart."

When she looked again, it seemed different. Now Yumiko saw what she had thought was clay a substance finer than ivory, more pellucid than mother of pearl. Heat as gentle as a kiss hovered over it. Yumiko realized it was alive.

"What makes clay so white?"

"The fire in the heart of its master was hotter than any kiln or star. This cup caught its master's blood as he was dying, and the blood is the life."

"If this is the cup of life," said Yumiko, "why is it hidden?"

"It is life to those who are washed, penitent, and prepared, who have put the old life by. But who drinks of this cup unworthily, drinks to himself damnation."

Yumiko scowled. "I missed you. Every day. Other children had a mother to tuck them in, to kiss their hurts, and to take them to the festivals of O-Bon and Christmas and to see the fireworks. Father said you were living in the clouds. The village boys said that you were dead."

"I visited you in your dreams each night."

"It was not enough. I remembered only scraps and bits when I woke. Why did you let him take me? Uncle Hosshin and Uncle Mubo taught me to pierce targets, not to arrange flowers. I was raised by three soldiers who lived in a quarry at the mouth of an abandoned mine next to pools of blue poison, hunting goblins and ghosts who escaped out of the mineshaft! In the village below the mountain, in school, or in motion pictures, I would see beautiful girls in their finery, with their gentle laughter and graceful steps. All the boy's eyes followed them. No one's eyes were on me. I was invisible! A mother seen in dreams was not enough. Not enough! Why did you let Father take me from your arms?"

"Ah, my child," she said most gently. "He feared that if you lived with me in this place, you would take my duties and become the next Grail Maid after me."

"You did not come take me?"

"And disobey my husband? He is lord over me."

"But you did not obey him! He ordered you to come down to earth, to live on the haunted peaks of Shinzan and Honzan, with us, to send him out to hunt the *namahage* with bow and spear by night, and to welcome him home!"

"I also am sworn to obey a Lord greater far than your father, who bids me stay and watch this cup and revere it. Do not blame your father. How could he know that I was to be the last?"

There came a noise like an earthquake from without. It was the sound of a tower falling, if a tower were as tall as a mountain.

Dandrenor said "The stones of the rubble will burn up in the atmosphere before they strike ground, or so I pray. I do not want the death of this city to slay the unsaved before their time."

The floor beneath their sandals shook, and the flagstones cracked.

2. A Stiffnecked Child

Dandrenor said, "I am sorry that your father's death was what brought you back to me. I am the Widow of the Grail once again as I was when he won me. Our months here together were too short. You are still too heavy with the sins of earth for the wings you wove to bear you upward. But consider the flying squirrel, the cobego, the Chinese gliding frog, the Paradise tree snake. None of these fly, but none die by falling."

Yumiko said, "I will stay and guard the cup of life."

Dandrenor shook her head sadly. "I am given to know that my task is to stand fast at my post, and watch, and wait. Heaven ordains this."

"Why did Heaven overlook to post a warlord here with ten thousand men?"

"Ten thousand are nothing against Ysbadden, for he is the greatest of all giants, their chief and champion. His life is charmed. Only Dyrnwen might slay him."

"Where is this Dyrnwen? Why is he not here if he is so mighty a hero?"

"Dyrnwen many years ago was lost."

"And were no other heroes available for Heaven to put here?"

"It pleases Heaven to guard its treasures with meek and gentle hands, lest any man boast. But I have no hope in swords."

"Then you will be saved? By a miracle?"

Dandrenor spoke softly. "It is not given to me to know whether I shall live or die this hour. All I know is that the Grail cannot suffer desecration while it is watched faithfully. Nor can its power be perverted to unholy use unless the watching is betrayed. To be slain at my post is no breach of my faith. I can fall, but I cannot flee."

"They will kill you and then pollute the cup!"

"This is not like your father's eight million little gods and the fastidious purity rules they hold."

"You mock the gods of Japan?"

"I married one of them. Another is my mother-in-law, whose sire and dam are brother and sister. Should I worship such in-laws? That would not be seemly. In any case, their purity rules and pagan rites are turned downside-up by Christ. The blood of martyrs does not pollute holy things, but sanctifies."

Yumiko said, "Then let me stay and die with you! Let my blood be spilled!"

"That is your father's pride speaking. You are unbaptized. The life in you is human life, not the higher life we are given, and so your blood has no power to bless."

"Let me stay and die for honor's sake!" In her memory, Yumiko saw that her younger self was dressed in a tunic of white fox fur, cut like a man's tunic, and when she spoke, she held up the longbow in her hand. It was *hamayumi*, the ghost-slaying bow. Arrows in an ivory quiver rattled at her shoulder.

Dandrenor said, "There is an honor higher than the honor of the warrior's code and a mercy deeper than justice."

Yumiko said stiffly, "It is the duty of the strong to avenge the weak!"

"And justice is a fine thing," said her mother. "But it is not the final thing."

"I will stay!"

"You shall not. My sister Ygraine of the Wise Reeds, Ygraine of the many counsels, was shown your fate by a night vision from Heaven. She spoke to me in riddles, but I have unwound them. All this shall accomplish the purposes of Heaven."

"What purposes?"

"In the time of Pellinore, darkness rose, and the Grail was removed from the circles of the earthly world and brought here. Now mayhap the violent hands of the Prince of the Giants will tear this cup from its resting place and return it down below."

"Why?"

"This cup alone restores the lost memory of Eden, which all the Sons of Adam and Daughters of Eve carry like a whisper in their hearts. Whose life overfills the maw of death? Whose light enters the darkness, but the darkness cannot encompass it? What memorial is not to be forgotten, even beyond the end of days? Those were the riddles my sister asked of me."

"I don't care about Aunt Ygraine and her riddles! Everyone says she slept with a hairy monster, killed her misbegotten boy, and fled for shame into hiding!"

"Many often repeat lies unaware, dealing wounds of words no power can gather back up again. Therefore it is better not to gossip. Ygraine has never done a shameful thing, nor ever will. Her wisdom says…"

"I care nothing for her wisdom!"

"Hush! If you cannot be wise, be obedient. Listen to your mother. All the strength of Heaven is mirrored in this cup, and against it no mists of Everness, no charm of elf, no curse of fallen angel howsoever mighty, can prevail. One day you will forget me..."

"Never!"

"The sight and image of this Grail will perish last of all you forget and will return first of all you call back out of the mists, for it is potent against the Black Spell and will break it. The Black Spell can be broken only by blood, which drives men mad, or by light, which makes them hale. This is the light, hidden under the appearance of blood. By this the Sons of Adam will be saved. And more beside."

"The Sons of Adam in the village below us mocked and teased me because our strange mansion was so fine and fair but had no running water, no electric light, no radio, no telephone. Why were all these wonderful things, useful things, forbidden to me? The Daughters of Eve teased and mocked me for I was seen dressed in the skins of animals my uncles caught, running up and down the mountainside beneath the moonlight, and they called me a cavegirl! What do I care for them? A curse on them!"

The heat from the Grail now was stronger, hot and scalding on Yumiko's cheeks, and she stepped back, her hand before her face, frightened and angry.

3. Ill-Said Words

Dandrenor said sadly, "Use no heavy words so lightly, not in this holy place." She closed the golden lid. "Because you have said this thing, an ordeal will be set before you before you are fit to serve."

"I will not serve!"

"Those are the very words of the Archangel of Darkness." Now Dandrenor did looked frightened, and sorrow was mingled with her fear. "Oh! My child! My sweet child! That you should say such words! You will fall far before you rise again, but I will pray that gentle hands will help you aloft once more."

"We are alone. None hear."

"Foolish child! You do not see the thousand potentates and powers thronging this place, warrior angels adorned in the panoply of stars! Your lightest word they never forget, save what the confession takes away." Dandrenor raised her hand and slapped her smartly across the cheek.

Yumiko staggered back, shocked. The anger and insanity within her broke. She had no more wild defiance to say.

Her mother spoke in a calm but terrible voice, "Let that be the beginning of your penance! Do you imagine you can thwart the purposes of Providence? If not through you, the Lord of Hosts will still provide a way to save his people, but you will not be saved. Cease to kick against the goads! Say nothing more, lest a heavier burden fall on your head!"

Yumiko, greatly ashamed, but forbidden to speak, merely bowed.

The sound came again like a mountain falling. And in the mighty chamber where they stood, the pillars swayed, the clouds parted, and the planets beyond trembled in their orbits. Cracks were all through the azure dome, marring the faces of the saints.

Through the cracks were visible the heavens beyond the dome, galaxies and clusters of galaxies, small and clear, a scope of heaven so wide even the boldest astronomer would have been dazed to take in so many splendors, so far distant, so ancient, at a glance, undimmed by the deceptive fogs and mists of Earth.

A peculiarity of the air in this place so strengthened the visual ray of the eye that distant astronomical wonders, long walls and superclusters of galaxies, seemed within arm's reach. Near galaxies were magnified into fans and disks and shields and clouds of diamond dust. Trails of farther superclusters curved across the black heavens like the arms of a writhing kraken, or the spiral shape of narwhal horns.

The floor bucked like the deck of a ship. Dandrenor was unmoved and showed no further sign of fear or anxiety.

Raising her voice above the din, Dandrenor said, "Here is my tear which I wept when you were born, for the travail was long. This tear I bathed in the Grail, and it came to life and keeps its own shape, for now it touches Eternity."

Dandrenor lifted a fine chain, from which hung a teardrop shape of lambent crystal, and she placed it about her daughter's neck.

"Keep to yourself this memento of your mother's love, for the Grail light is in it. Keep it with you, lest the fumes of Earth confuse and confound you. Keep it in memory of me."

Another shock rocked the chamber. Pillars fell. Planets went careening from their courses, colliding. The comet was snuffed out. The azure light flickered like a candle in a storm. Great slabs of the ethereal dome above now fell, but fell upward, into intergalactic space.

Dandrenor said, "Take your arrows in your hand and grip them tightly."

Yumiko again did not speak despite not understanding the point of this command. She shrugged her shoulder to put the mouth of her quiver in easy reach, and she put her fist about the gathered shafts, just below the fletching.

It was well that she did so, for at that moment, the floor gave way. Great rocks and boulders of the azure floor substance fell with her, and dust that glittered like diamond powder mixed with pearly starlight. She was weightless, falling. The clouds were far below her, and far below her reeled the earth and the sea like a carpet of blue and white and green and brown, wrinkled with many textures.

She saw above her what seemed walls and towers rising above the fog, and around it islands like green hills where houses, windmills, and farms rose on snowy hillsides. The terraced farms were overgrown with hydrangea, iris, orchid, hyacinth, and the orchards and walled gardens planted with some species of fruit tree whose leaves were blue. But these islands were the suburbs surrounding a city in the air, and the fogs on which they rode were clouds.

Her younger self must not have found the sight odd, for Yumiko had no memory of staring at the sight of windmills atop puffy clouds and wondering how the wind which pushed the clouds could turn the windmill arms.

The farms were burning. In the moat and canals of clear air between islands of fog stood vessels like ironclad zeppelins, flying a sable banner without any charge or device. Grappling lines ran from the airship to the cloud bank, and a motley combination of stiffly moving armored figures, loping shaggy shapes, lumbering corpses, and slinking ghouls swarmed across narrow gangplanks from ship to shore.

Yumiko was seeing them from below, like a mermaid staring upward at the peaks of icebergs. The largest was directly above her, and she could see the fog-surrounded blue crystal foundations of the celestial city as a fish might see the planks of a sinking raft.

Her mother's voice reverberated in her mind. She could hear her thoughts as clearly as if a ghost no larger than a ladybug were sitting on her ear. "With my blessing, and all my love, depart and face your trials. You are as brave as your father taught you to be. Alas that I had not time enough to teach you mercy. You have given me the gift of allowing me to save my daughter's life alive."

Through a gaping crack in the blue crystal, Yumiko glimpsed her mother, unhurriedly raising a hand as a last farewell, and unhurriedly turning back to kneel in prayer before the altar holding the Grail.

Yumiko remembered falling like a dustmote in a searchlight beam in the column of light shed by the Grail through the break in the floor. She extended her cloak, which snapped into the form of gliding wings. But the moment she passed outside the beam of light and entered the thicker cloud, all memory stopped.

4. Things to Come

Yumiko stood for a time bent over the railing of Gapstow Bridge in Central Park, watching her tears fall in the water, and replaying the scene again and again in her mind.

What had happened to the teardrop talisman her mother had given her? Yumiko had no notion.

How had the longbow, once made of bamboo, been changed into a strange metal that could alter its length? For it was clearly the same bow, her bow, and it felt right and familiar in her hands.

And the cape was hers; and evidently it was older than the rest of her Foxmaiden suit. And these other things, her weapons and devices… she unsheathed a metallic boomerang and stared at it blankly… whence came these? From whose forge?

Who else? It had been Tom, the inventor's apprentice. All these things were gifts of love.

Two realizations, like firecrackers that banished startled demons of ignorance, ignited in her mind. The Red Lady, Malen, was her great-grandfather's grandmother. A squabble over some tract of land had caused the enmity between Malen and the Elfking Erlkoenig, and so Malen had stirred up the

Anarchists and brought them hellish powers. All this was done by Yumiko's ancestor, whom she should honor. But how did one honor an ancestor who murdered her own great-grandchildren's posterity?

The second realization was that Sir Gilberec, the young knight of Arthur, was her only hope of revenge now. Dyrnwen was not a hero. It was a hero's sword. Ysbadden the Chief of Giants could not be slain save by that sword.

Sir Gilberec had spoken the sword's name when he had uttered his threats, and his oath, against the Supreme Anarchist Council, and flung those words into the face of Wilcolac the Magician.

She looked down, "At least I remembered my mother's name."

The reflection was smiling at first, and then scowled. "Elfine is in a bottle, remember? Hob suggested you report to your master, remember? Garlot will strike down Gilberec from behind, remember?"

More firecrackers went off in her mind. She did not see yet how it was to be done, but her task was to rescue Elfine, thwart Wilcolac, save Gilberec, and find Tom.

But she still had no memory of Tom's face, no echo of his voice, no touch of his hand in hers. The sorrow of that held her for a moment. But the moment was brief. The memory of the light to banish the Black Spell was brighter, and it filled her with stern resolve.

The green park she left behind her. The tall and gloomy buildings loomed ahead.

Yumiko Ume Moth showed none of the resolute conviction enflaming her soul on her face. Without expression, without fear, without doubt, the Japanese girl walked the sidewalks of the gray metropolis, her dark eyes hot with hidden hope.

Into an alley walked a slender figure in bright silk. A moment later, overhead, swinging on an unseen wire shot a slender figure in black, her masked fox-face grinning. Out snapped her wings. Rising air caught her. Upward she circled.

Here ends *City of Corpses*,

Book Two of ***The Dark Avenger's Sidekick***.

The Tales of Moth & Cobweb continue in

Book Three of ***The Dark Avenger's Sidekick***,

Tithe to Tartarus

Tithe to Tartarus

'O see ye not yon narrow road,
So thick beset with thorn and brier?
That is the Path of Righteousness,
Though of it few inquire.

'And see ye not yon broad, broad road,
That lies across the lilied leven?
That is the Path of Wickedness,
And leads away from Heaven.

'And see ye not yon bonny road
That winds about the ferny height?
That is the Road to fair Elfland,
Where we must go this night.

'But, Thomas, ye shall hold your tongue,
Whatever ye may hear or see;
For who speaks word in Elflin-land,
Ne'er sees more his own country.'

Traditional

Chapter 1

The Mask of the Foxmaiden

1. Nightfall over the City

It was dusk in Manhattan, and Yumiko Ume Moth sat atop the Chrysler Building combing and braiding her shining hair of raven-black and brooding blackly on vengeance.

For now, at long last, out of the mists of amnesia, Yumiko finally knew about her mother's murder.

Yumiko knelt atop the spire. The crown was seven radiating arches mounted one atop the other, clad in stainless steel. Below her was the observation platform on the 61st floor of the Chrysler Building. Gliding weightless, she had followed a flock of pigeons riding a rising thermal to reach that height. Here, impressive Art Deco eagles glared out in all directions, facing Central Park, Times Square, Grand Central Station, and the East River. In the bay was the Statue of Liberty.

The sun in the west was smothered in clouds as orange as flame. The towers of the city were bright on one side, dark on the other, and threw long, horizontal shadows across the rectangular texture of lesser buildings. Windows running up the western sides of long-shadowed skyscrapers shined like upright swords whose mirrored blades reflected the pyres and burnings of conquered castles.

These lofty buildings were below her. Only the Empire State Building was taller. No workingmen had died in the construction of the Chrysler Building, and so Yumiko had no need to worry about ghosts.

She knelt atop an arch in her skintight gray supersuit, with black opera gloves and thigh-high boots. Snugly about her form was cinched her weapons harness with all its pouches, sheathes, and holsters. There was no wind; the air was still.

Yumiko did not know the elf-trick of having hair braid itself, and so it had been hanging down to the small of her back in a ponytail. The long ponytail was only a bit in the way of her quiver, only mildly likely to be snagged as she swung from rooftop to rooftop, and only partially inviting for an enemy to grab while wrestling to twist her head into a helpless posture.

She frowned and combed and brushed and frowned, wrestling with memories of sorrow and loss and trying to gather the scattered threads of clues and plans into a single braid.

One tiny fissure in the black wall of her amnesia had parted, and one glimpse alone had been shown her. She had recalled strange sights of iron-clad airships flying the black flag of anarchy attacking a walled city in the clouds, Sarras, from which the sacred and ruby-red Grail by robbery was ripped. Yumiko's mother Dandrenor, the Grail Queen, had died at her post.

Yumiko knew that Winged Vengeance, a survivor of Sarras, sought revenge against the Anarchists who had arranged that attack. She had been his sidekick and disciple before her memory loss. He alone truly knew who and what Yumiko was and had been. But now he mistrusted her and cursed her as a traitor.

Despite his mistrust, following a clue she had revealed to him, he had visited one of the secret strongholds of the Anarchists, the innocent-looking nightclub run by the magician Wilcolac Cobweb and called the Cobbler's Club. She had seen him there, a man about town in top hat and tails, not a shadowy vigilante in his celestial flying robe of black.

The Supreme Council of Anarchists were seven men, or creatures, who took the days of the week as code names. Yumiko had discovered Lord Thursday to be Lucien Cobweb, the chief of a pack of werewolves, who were being smuggled into New York City by the hundreds. When the number reached one thousand, the wolves would emerge, immune to any weapon of man, and fall upon the city in slaughter and blood.

Two things opposed them: one was Winged Vengeance, who was hunting and slaying the Anarchists. The other was the Last Crusade, who were hunting and slaying the werewolves.

Lucien, the Lord of Wolves, working through the magician Wilcolac, had attempted to win the aid of the Last Crusade against Winged Vengeance. The Last Crusade consisted of Sir Gilberec Moth the Swan Knight, a young man whose tongue could speak with animals but could not speak untruths, and Matthias Moth, a Dominican novice and exorcist, whose eye could see ghosts.

Their third member, Tom Moth, an apprentice inventor, was missing.

And he was apparently Yumiko's fiancé. Or something of that sort. She was in love with a young man of whom not the slightest memory remained in her mind. She had lost even the memory of her loss.

But Lucien had also hired Sir Garlot the Red, a knight of Elfland, possessor of the ancient and potent Cloak of Mists, to challenge and kill Sir Gilberec once he was of no more use to them. This same Sir Garlot had abducted and imprisoned Yumiko's only friend and ally in this world, her scatterbrained cousin Elfine. Garlot was keeping the fairy girl in a bottle in his treasure chamber.

Yumiko had been working in the Cobbler's Club in disguise as a waitress, dancer, and hat-check girl. This allowed her to place bugging devices in Wilcolac's phone and tracking devices in the hatband of Winged Vengeance, the collar of Sir Gilberec's dog, and the hem of the cloak of Sir Garlot.

Eventually her raven-black hair was braided and gathered into a snood, which was tucked, in turn, into her cowl. But by that point, her mood was lighter. Her next step was clear. She had placed the threads carefully. Now it was time to follow where they led.

"I must be a vain girl after all," she muttered wryly, smiling for the first time. "Any reasonable adventuress wears a bob or pixie cut."

Night had fallen. She donned her fox mask.

2. *Electric Spoor*

She took the time to check carefully each control in the mask, discovering features she had not noticed before or not remembered from her previous life, including how to turn on the airtight seal and the oxynitrogen supply.

To her delight, she found one of the settings of the eye lenses would superimpose a stereoptic gridwork and a dot of light on her view to give her the distance and direction to each tracer currently being tracked. A second feature opened an inset map. A third feature could allow status-alert lights from her electronics to appear in the corner of the her view and open status messages.

Yumiko summoned the inset map into the lenses of her goggles. The city spread below was overlaid with a grid of green lines. She confirmed that the tracer *zero-five*, the one she had hidden in the hem of the misty cloak of Garlot, was close at hand, in Central Park. Apparently, Malen's brother had gone home to Is-Elfydd.

Rescuing Elfine might be a quick matter for a girl who could turn invisible. Yumiko spread her wings and launched herself into the night. Central Park was one long block away past Rockefeller Center and Carnegie Hall. The Chrysler Building was tall enough for her glider to carry her into the park, past the zoo and the meadow and the lake. She landed silently in the upper branches of a tree.

She twisted the ring to summon enough mist to render her invisible. Gliding and swinging from tree to tree, she came to the baseball diamonds of the Great Lawn.

Yumiko studied the little green numbers twinkling in her view as she peered down from her perch, wishing the suit had come with an instruction manual or that she could remember exactly how it worked.

Then she realized. One number was longitude. One was latitude. The third was elevation. It was a negative number. Yumiko had been maintaining the hope that perhaps Garlot's treasure chamber was in a tower or treetop mansion. That thread of hope snapped. The tracer was below ground.

Yumiko twisted the ring back and forth, hoping against hope. When she twisted the ring until the band was shining black and the face in the intaglio that of a desiccated corpse, the tall hills crowded with monoliths rose above her, and the impossible mile-tall trees rose above that. The whole landscape seemed strange and out of proportion, as if objects both near and far were no longer obeying the normal geometric rules of perspective. But no gateway to the buried city was visible, and she could not recall under which hill it stood.

Before, when Malen had led her into this version of the scene, no watchmen had been seen. Now she saw what seemed to be corpses impaled atop sharpened posts of extraordinary length. The poles were gathered thick as reeds and spaced in a circle at the feet of the prodigious trees.

As one, all the bodies raised their heads. The empty eyes fixed on her. The pressure of their gaze smote her heart; a coldness like a flock of myriad needles tickled and pricked her limbs. The jaws of the empty mouths opened, and a cry of shrill misery, rising and falling, filled the air.

High above her, emerging from glass and jasper towers and stronghouses perched among the tall and thick branches of the impossible trees, now strode forth shining elfs in armor bright as silver, carrying bows and bright spears, and with the light of arctic stars gleaming in their eyes.

A silver trumpet sang: the note of music was so beautiful that it made her feel faint and elated, as if she had been injected with morphine. It was a soporific, benumbing. She twisted the ring to its pewter setting.

She could no longer see the trees, but the sound of the fair horn and the cold terror in her heart from the eyes of the dead still gripped her.

She retreated quickly. Her panicked heartbeat did not slow until she was perched atop the Chrysler Building once more.

Yumiko was surprised at the sensation of helpless anger. At first, she could not put it into words. It was not just that the trail led underground, where she could not follow. There was a touch of deep sadness, and of longing. She wanted strong arms about her, the arms of a protector she trusted, a man smart enough to outwit even the elfs in their ancient, ageless scheming and to surprise them.

Then the mingled thoughts and feeling came clear. *Tom would have known what to do*. Tom would have built or stolen a burrowing machine and simply dug down there, guns turrets blazing. That he was the type to put gun turrets on a burrowing machine, she had no doubt.

She cherished this thought. It was like finding a fragment of a page torn from a lost volume of a missing library. But the library containing all her thoughts, feelings, ideas, traits, triumphs, and losses was lost.

3. A Magic Shop

The next closest tracer was *zero-six*, the one she had placed on the top hat of the Japanese gentleman at the club, named Pooh-Bah. She suspected that this was not the real name of Winged Vengeance, who she knew to be of the Peaseblossom clan. It did not sound like a real Japanese name. Maybe it was Ainu?

In any case, she needed his help and now had more to tell him. How she would overcome his suspicions, she did not know.

She followed the signal to a spot between Lexington and Park Avenue. Here was a shop with three golden balls over the door. **We Fix It!** one gleaming neon sign declared. **AL_ HOURS _PEN!** flashed the red sign above the first, in blithe contradiction of the boast below.

Other hand-printed signs were thumbtacked to the door. *Restorer of Reputations. Astrology. Palmistry. Love Philters. Checks Cashed. Souls Pawned.*

Finally, there was a small brass plaque on the door. *We Are Many, Proprietor.*

When Yumiko peered through the smaller of the two windows, she saw what looked like a cluttered museum. Here were long-eared and spike-nosed goblin masks, skull-masks, and wolf-masks, and there were whips and chains and an iron maiden. An idol of Shiva, blue as a corpse and dancing on the back of a cowering dwarf, was on a pedestal midmost, and in each of her eight hands she held a weapon. There were mummified skulls hanging from the ceiling, inverted crosses and pentagrams, a stuffed alligator with a human head, and other things more grisly or disgusting.

The other window was larger. Here on display were a cabinet for holding a sleepwalker, a glass tank into which a wax dummy in a straitjacket was suspended by his feet, and a box on sawhorses for sawing a lady in half above a heavy grating meant to catch the blood. In the far corner of the window display was a wax dummy in a tuxedo, a wand in his hand. On his head was the top hat from which the tracer signal came.

From this second window, she could see the rear of the gloomy, unlit shop. There sat a shape dressed like a Franciscan friar. The hood hid the upper half of the mummified face. Its lips were sewn open into a wide clown-grin, displaying teeth of black iron. It sat on a seat shaped like a metal rib cage, with steel skulls adorning the arms. Behind this throne was an old-fashioned door of dark planks waxy with age with three huge hasps of wrought iron and a doorknob of blood-red cut crystal that glittered like ruby. It was as tall and wide as a gate.

Oddly, it was not the corpse of the friar that made Yumiko's heart contract with fear and sent nightmarish, shapeless images of horror swimming behind her eyes. It was this tall door. What it meant—and where it went—she did not want to know.

She felt the evil gazes before she saw them. Fear like an ice-cold blade pierced her. The human-headed stuffed alligator was looking at her, as were the long-eared South Sea Island masks, the shrunken heads, and the statue of Shiva. The wax dummies had not moved, but now their painted eyes seemed alive, piercing her. The sleepwalker in the cabinet was not a wax dummy, for it had turned its head toward her without opening an eye, and held at a tilt as if listening.

And an intuition or a buried memory told her of the delight Winged Vengeance took in leading anyone seeking to follow him into traps and dead ends or into the arms of enemies worse than he. She knew that this was a place of power of some dark and malign entity. Whatever was inside this shop was worse than any elf of night.

This was a second dead end.

She twisted the ring on her finger, became weightless, and shot her wire-poon pistol overhead.

Perched on a flagpole many blocks away, she panted, doffed her mask, and mopped her brow. Did her old master think he could outsmart her? She may have forgotten her lessons, but her quality of character was surely the same.

Donning the mask once more, she tuned to *zero-one*, the tracer she had left in the octagonal room in the ruined church, where she had made contact with Winged Vengeance not long ago.

A warning light blinked amber, red, amber. *Out of Range.*

She had not known the tracers had a range.

4. A Vanishing Chamber

Twenty minutes and two miles later, she was down Fifth Avenue and past the Empire State Building, a block from Madison Square Park. Within an unlit area surrounded by cedar trees rose a square tower of red brick beneath a roof of tarnished copper. She landed on the roof between pale, weather-worn statues of saints and sought the window she had entered before.

She pulled the lopsided shutter open and saw nothing. She clicked from one lens setting to the next. Tossing her head to retract her mask, Yumiko drew and pointed the narrow, powerful beam of her flashlight within.

Vertigo touched her. She had been expecting to see a floor a foot or so below the sash, and on the floor, a table with a phone inside an eight-sided chamber. The table was not there. The floor was not there. The chamber was not there. Instead, she saw a dusty, empty space like a well, plunging down past the reach of her flashlight beam. The wheels and rafters from which church bells once hung were above her head, and the old chains, corroded with disuse, dropped down beyond sight.

She shone the light on the sides of the belltower. It was the wrong shape and too small. The eight-walled chamber she had seen here before could not have fit inside this space.

The sense of disorientation passed. She smiled wryly. Yumiko thought that a girl who carried more arrows, throwing stars, knives, boomerangs, and mini-grenades than would fit into a hope chest was the last girl with the right to complain when someone else used a similar trick to hide a secret room.

And the elfs hid towers in treetops and hills in ballparks. If Elfine were to be believed, there was a third hemisphere in addition to the two men know, where mountains and islands and whole continents were hidden. But how could a globe have three halves? In three dimensions, it could not.

Yumiko lit a flare and dropped it. Down and down into the dark it fell. It came to rest on a broken floor, where there were no pews, no baptismal font, no altar, merely empty niches. Yumiko donned her mask and inspected the barren interior with her magnifying lenses. Discolored bricks, brackets, and small square holes in the walls showed where fixtures had been torn out.

But as she leaned in the window, an alert light flickered in the corner of her gaze. A motion of her chin touched the control to bring the display to the center of her view.

The tracer *zero-one* was green.

Little numbers in green fire showed the distance and direction. Another touch of the chin-plate brought up the inset map. The source was off the edge of her map, but the signal was strong, and the bearing was clear. It was past Morningside Heights, somewhere in Upper Manhattan on the West Side.

Puzzled, she straightened. When her head was outside the window, the signal strength faded sharply. A step or two away, and the alert light turned amber. *Signal lost.*

5. Many Dimensions

Yumiko pondered. How could the inside of the window of a deserted church be within range to pick up the signal from a bug seven miles away but outside the window be out of range? How could farther be nearer than nearer?

In three dimensions, it was impossible.

Suppose a two-dimensional creature, like a living square, thought his universe were but a flat plane, but it actually occupied the surface of a sphere. To him, the third dimension would be as invisible and unimaginable as the realm of the elfs. If he ventured near an open shaft piercing through the core, he would hear sounds from the other hemisphere as closer and clearer than sounds traveling to him the long way around the curve of the equator.

Some side effect of the disappearing eight-sided room had left open a path or crack through which radio waves could pass. It was only a guess, but she had nothing better.

It was too far to travel by rooftop, and she was in haste. She slid down a wire into the deserted building, changed into her kimono, neatly vaulted out a broken upper window, rolled, came to her feet, and walked out of the shadows onto the brightly lit and crowded sidewalk. Seven minutes later, she was at the subway station.

A minute after that, she was seated in a crowded car, sitting between a bald girl wearing a large gold hoop as her nose ring and a man wearing a mohawk with Maori tattoos all over his face. Yumiko decided she would not look too out of place in a kimono, wearing a grinning black fox mask with gold ears, not among the night crowd of Manhattan.

It might have been swifter to travel north gliding and swinging along the rooftops rather than in this noisy machine with its frequent stops, but the leisure allowed her to study the other files recorded on the computer memory of her mask.

6. *The Ears of the Vixen*

The listening devices had settings for recording either on a continuous loop, at set times, or whenever sounds of certain volumes or types impinged on them. The feature, as best she could tell, contained a voice-recognition program, so the mike would turn itself on for certain voices but not for others. That seemed more magical than some of the magic she had seen, and a good deal more convenient.

Menus tracking the files of the recordings could appear in her lenses. The file for the bug labeled *alpha* showed a red light. *Unit no response.* Alpha was the one she had dropped in the lower vault of the Cobbler's Club and which the Cheyenne had stepped on.

7. *The Fangs of the Wolf*

Beta was in the lamp on the desk of the invoice storeroom in the third vault. The mike came awake when what sounded like groups of workingmen entered the kennels, swearing and shouting and hauling heavy loads. There were bumps and thuds and the sounds of engines roaring and whining. After a pause, more sounds, this time of wild barking, howling, cursing.

Next came a hideous scream, "My arm! My arm!" She recognized the voice. It was Blud, the boy infatuated with her.

The boy's cries were greeted with a roar of laughter and more curses. Then came the voice of Jarnik, the kennel master, cursing Blud for a fool. "No human meat for three days! Such is my order! Would you undo my work? Get him out of here! The scent of blood drives them to frenzy."

"You want I should put a tourniquet on his stump? Blood is getting all over everything." That was the voice of Svarog, the handyman.

She heard the creak of the chair and a footstep, a thud. Whoever was seated at the desk rose and slammed shut the door shut with an impatient bang. The noise level dropped below the mike threshold sensitivity, and the recording stopped.

The shipment of werewolves had arrived.

8. Four Calls

The final listening device was in the phone on Wilcolac's desk.

The first file contained a recording of a call from his supplier protesting innocence over a missing shipment of aquavit while Wilcolac uttered increasingly dire threats in a voice of decreasing warmth and volume. She tapped the fast-forward control impatiently.

Next was someone named Svevid, evidently an accountant. He and Wilcolac discussed how to comply with new health coverage regulations for full-time and part-time workers, including Leshenka the seamstress, whose wages were paid in cabbages. Yumiko could not tell if this were slang, or a joke, or a custom of certain Twilight men.

The next call was from a police detective, asking about a missing person named Fred McDuffy. From the description, this was the same overweight man Yumiko had seen dying from a failed magical experiment. Wilcolac blandly denied any knowledge of the man.

The next file held an elderly female voice Yumiko did not recognize. "I am very worried about you. You know your time is near… when they are coming for you… the bargain you made…" said the voice broke off sobbing.

Wilcolac replied in soothing tones. "It will go as smoothly as it went seven years ago! I have made arrangements and can offer a choice morsel when the Dark Door opens. A true prize for them! Do not fret, please… All is well…"

Yumiko wondered who this might be. His mother? It seemed strange that he could have such a thing, some sort of normal life outside the orbit of his criminal career. His mother was alive to worry over him, when hers was not.

9. Captain and Magician

The next file held a voice she knew: the words were quick, the pitch was tenor, the tones light and mocking, the accent hovering between a lazy drawl and an angry snarl. A shiver of hatred traveled up her spine before she consciously recognized it as the voice of Lucien Cobweb, Lord of Wolves.

"Your letter came down my chimney just now and almost splashed in my soup!"

Wilcolac's smooth baritone answered. "Dear master, I meant not to disturb. But events move quickly, and I know you want to keep apace."

"Arthur is dead! You need worry your fat-cheeked, tiny, pointed head on that point no longer! This Gilberec is a charlatan!"

"Of course, dear master. I would not dare contradict you, even when the truth was obvious, and obviously not in your favor. How impolite it would be to warn you of the overwhelming danger you so heedlessly court!"

"You dare toy with me, palm-reader?"

"Sir, you came to me after the disaster of the Glass Tower. You were the military arm of the Anarchists but had no more troops to command. You yearn to regain the respect you have lost, lest they turn on you and rend you!"

"The conversation is as fresh as raw meat in my mind! I am still waiting for you to pull the promised rabbit out of the hat and saw the lady in half."

"Have I not arranged for wolves to supply your want?"

"Wolves I had! Merely not where men could see. But speak. Say your say."

"Master, Sir Gilberec Moth is a true knight of Arthur! The blood of victory touched his tongue. I heard his voice, and the enchantment of truth is in his word. It is an old spell, an ancient spell, but its like has been heard on earth before."

"But a hypnotic charm that merely makes you *think* you hear the truth is not a lost spell, but a common one."

Wilcolac's voice grew cold. "If my master thinks I am so easily chant-caught by a Moth untrained in any Dark Art, let him tear out my living heart this very day, for I am worthless as your practitioner."

"Well... Ah! The young friar might have cast a hex on you."

"What? Does he perform the Black Mass before or after he goes to confession? I told you what happened to Jack-o'-Lantern. Or was I deceived by enchantment about that also? For Jack is yet shy a hand."

Lucien snarled, but the noise turned into a barking sort of laugh. "Hoo-hah! So the boy sincerely *believes* Arthur lives and says so! And his magic tongue forbids he tell a lie! That merely means someone in a wax mask, or some ghost wearing a corpse like an old suit of clothing, has deceived the young fool. Arthur is dead! Merlin is dead! I was there when Nimue so said! There is no High King to bless such knights. Their power and pomp long ago burned away to ash, and treason cracked the Table Round. My hounds need fear no boy pretending to be of Arthur."

"And if I am right? If Arthur lives? If he blessed the boy with victory? How many of the werewolves I so thoughtfully prepare for you have you spent against him? Is he even wounded? I saw no wounds on him. Have you killed his horse? I have seen a pack of your wolves outrun an armored car and rip it to bits. If he is just a fake, your creatures should have at least been able to kill his horse."

The file ended there, but the next file was time-stamped within the same minute. Her mike had automatically shut down during Lucien's long pause of angry silence, only to resume when he spoke again.

Lucien said, "No matter. Arrange the match."

Wilcolac said, "Yes. Matthias Moth left an address where he could be reached. Sir Gilberec will not refuse. His sense of honor makes him blind. But, master, if I may: I am curious. What changed your mind?"

"The Foxmaiden was under my paw. Right under me! The Ring of Mists was on her person. I smelled the smell of darkest magic. But lightly she slipped away from me, and now the others take me lightly! Once, I had battalions to threaten them! What have I now? A few pookas and spooks. Some werewolves. Some owl women. A magician. Bah!"

"I don't understand why that convinced you…"

"Saturday, that lying filth, told Sunday that I will not find the ring. I must prove him wrong."

"How will this duel allow you to gain the ring?"

"It will not. But I will gain the cloak of Garlot."

"Garlot is not likely to turn his cloak over to you, master. It is one of the Thirteen Treasures."

"Not while he lives, no. The duel is merely meant to throw dust in the eyes of Malen."

"Surely you do not mean to slay the brother of your mistress!"

"She must not see my hand is in this. He must die that same hour so that it will seem his wounds killed him. The profession of arms is fraught with peril."

"No wound can kill him, master!" objected Wilcolac. "His is the Crystal Cauldron of Youth."

Lucien's laugh was a giddy chuckle. "Well, that is too many treasures for one man, is it not? Besides, I need the cloak and want it. In a lawless world, what other reason do I need? I am a spontaneous spirit. Mine is a soul of fire! The cloak has the same powers as the ring, and so my promise to Sunday will be satisfied."

"Not precisely the same, sir. I am not sure such a substitution would be welcome by the…"

"Yes, you see the brilliance!" interrupted Lucien. "I feel an inspiration tingling in my lower back! I will tell my assassin to wait until after Garlot kills Gilberec with sword and lance. Malen told me he bathes in his accursed crystal pot after every fight, whether he is wounded or not, and toys with his collection of tiny women. My assassin will sabotage the pot to make it deadly, slaying Garlot at the very apex of his celebration, when he thinks himself most safe! Within his very treasure room! The irony will be delicious. I am an artist. Do you not see? You perform your tricks on stage, but I perform mine on the stage of the world, with life itself as my masterwork! Art is death! Death is art!"

"As you say."

"You think me mad. I sense your disdain."

"Believe rather that it is envy, my master," purred Wilcolac smoothly. "Your thoughts reach deep and unlit places far beyond my meager wit."

"Your words are true, even though you mean them for mockery. But you only become so buttery in your flattery when you want something. Speak!"

"What of Tomorrow?"

"A perfect time for the duel! Make it noon, and I will have the assassin strike as soon as Garlot returns to Is-Elfydd."

"No, sir. I meant the Moth. What of Tomorrow Moth?"

"He passed the Ring of Mists to the Foxmaiden. You made windy promises to me, magician, about your abilities. Where is she? She was in the club, and you lost her."

Yumiko smiled. Lucien must have heard of the time Yumiko let the bouncers spot her in costume before swinging away from rooftop to dark alley faster than any pursuit. She allowed herself a moment of glee, knowing how cleverly she had returned to the club, disguised as herself, unobserved, unsuspected, to take up her job as a humble waitress.

Wilcolac said, "Let me play out the hand. I have more than one card up my sleeve. The Cheyenne will not fail me."

"I want more magic ring, not more talk."

"Tomorrow Moth must know her hiding place or how to reach her. Any man will break under torture."

"Any man, yes. Any Moth? If we wake him from his enchanted sleep, he need only open his mouth and call on names which we cannot withstand. The fragment of the celestial cerulean dangles about his neck."

"Ask a virgin to defile it. A human girl, able to touch holy things."

"By what illusion or clever lie can we have a pure maiden willingly remove and mar such a thing in a way that the trick will not backfire? If she does it unknowingly, or unwillingly, the gem will not abandon him."

"My master is wise. But if Tomorrow wakes?"

Yumiko was gritting her teeth. One thought ran through her brain, like a mantra, but a mantra whose repetition brings misery, not peace. *Say where he is. Say where he is. Say the smallest hint!*

Apparently, neither man was influenced by her unspoken wish. Lucien spoke in sarcastic tones. "Has he wife or lady who fills his drinking horn, or mother who girds him on his sword?"

"He has friends who seek him."

"Necromancy is men's magic. Women's magic might undo it, yes. But the Swan Knight and the Ghostly Father's novice? Do these boys command any art to break the spell and glamour laid on him? I doubt it. Even Arthur alive and hale, with Excalibur in his hand, could not battle the unseen, unfelt influences conjured by Sunday, Lord of Ghosts, and Monday, Lord of Vampires. All the powers of every outcast hated by the laws of Heaven is ours to command! What is Arthur to that? What are Arthur's knights?"

"Yet no man has seen the Leader of the Last Crusade, the Man in the Black Room! Who is he?"

"Who cares? The Tithe to Tartarus will solve all of our problems with Tomorrow Moth, and with a satisfying finality. Once he is one with *them*, and *they* enter him, all he is will be theirs, and all he knows will be ours. The torments we could bring to flesh and nerve are nothing compared to that."

"And if something goes wrong... We should be careful, master, and take all precaution..."

"I move as my inspiration demands! I have the heart of a poet, wild, mad, and free! Why do you think I can kill without remorse and drink blood like wine? Poetry breaks chains! Art shatters worlds!" Lucien laughed a weird, high, crazy laugh. And then, as if one personality had been switched off and another switched on, his voice was calm, soothing, rational. "You need not fear. The Lord of Wolves will not break faith with you. A wolf is loyal above all else! You will see Tomorrow Moth with your own eye, at the Tithing Ground, even if you do not see him. The whole cavalcade will escort him! You will be seated among them! I can arrange this with Erlkoenig, who thinks me no more than his hounds-keeper. And then, for you, peace of mind. For seven more years."

The recording ended. Yumiko was rapt with delight for a moment to learn that Tom was still alive. Then fear, terrible fear, was like a nest of snakes in her stomach, or winding through her limbs from within. The echoes rang in her mind of strange phrases: *the Tithe to Tartarus... the Tithing Ground... you will see him, even if you do not see him... once he is one with them... the torments we could bring... are nothing compared to that... and then, for you, peace...*

Each thing, no matter how horrible, she feared these words meant, her imagination conjured another, even more horrible, a moment later.

How could she be so afraid for a boy whose face she could not recall, whose voice she could not remember? But her heart remembered, and she wept.

She gritted her teeth so that no sobs escaped her. She doffed her mask and wiped her wet cheeks, scowling angrily.

The girl with the huge gold nose ring patted her shoulder and said, "There, there, honey. It will be okay! Don't let them stinkin' rat finks get you down!"

Yumiko, bleary-eyed, stared at the stranger in confusion, wondering what she knew. "What rats?"

"Any of 'em! They're all *rats*! Ya can't give 'em the satisfaction!"

The man with the full-face tattoo silently offered Yumiko a tattered handkerchief.

Yumiko thanked him and daubed her eyes, and decided she liked the sons and daughters of the Daylit World far better than the beautiful and long-lived folk of the Night World.

Chapter 2

The Lair of the Vigilante

1. Abandoned Factory

On a high rooftop near the train station, she donned her dark suit and fox-mask and swung with simian grace along the skyline, a black shape flitting in the gloom above the street lamps. For the signal was now strong and clear.

About a mile later, she reached a run-down section of the city. Few were the lights in the windows, and few were the windows on the ground floors that were unbroken. It was quiet here. There were no cars moving on the streets, no people on the sidewalks.

The signal came from a windowless factory building of red brick. It had a slanting roof of black so that it was three stories tall on one side, four on the other. From the higher corner fronting the street a round chimney of red brick loomed, huge and tall, pointing at the black sky. Once letters had been painted on the chimney; they were now faded and inscrutable. The chimney seemed tilted, for the slant of the roof fooled the eye.

The front of the factory was a windowless, lopsided slab pierced by a large overhead door for trucks and a smaller door for people. Both were painted over with jagged, angry graffiti. The look of the weeds cracking the pavement before the two doors, and the tarnish gathered on the padlocks, showed that neither had been opened in years.

She landed and circled the factory on foot.

An abandoned lot was to one side, a place of cracked pavement, weeds, and more graffiti. In the lot, pushed up under the eaves of the slanted factory roof, were three dumpster bins filled, not with trash, but with nightsoil and mulch. Two of them had been undisturbed for so long weeds and little pale flowers were growing from an unhealthy greenish crust. The third sat under the mouth of a chute protruding like a rainspout from the factory.

The rear of the factory boasted a few sickly trees and a chain-link fence topped with barbed wire, as torn and bedraggled as the trees.

The remaining side of the factory was flush against a flat-topped two-story structure of pale concrete. Its doorways had been boarded over, and the boards had been scrawled with graffiti and then kicked in, leaving rectangular gaps like missing teeth. A single broken window stared out of a pale concrete wall.

The factory on this side was twice as tall as its neighbor. For some reason, a metal door coated with peeling orange paint was planted in the midst of this otherwise blank brick wall that loomed over the flat roof of the pale building. This orange door had no landing, and no stairs led to it.

Yumiko was standing in the middle of the road, peering upward, when a traffic light dangling over the intersection nearby changed from red. The green glass was broken, so a sudden white light shone on her, startling her. She looked around the street warily.

It was eerie to see the streets so empty and to see so many buildings without lights. In the near distance she heard the muted roar of a single motorcyclist speeding down the barren streets, but when she swung herself high and landed on the broken traffic light and looked, the engine noise died away, and she saw no one.

From her perch, she looked again at the broken boards covering the doorway to the flat-topped building, and looked more closely at the single broken window. From this angle, she could see a ledge and a drainpipe which would have allowed any moderately athletic man to mount the flat roof with only modest effort.

Frowning beneath her grinning mask, she looked back and stared at the orange door. Why was it there? If there had once been stairs leading to the top of the flat building, no sign of them remained. If Winged Vengeance meant to have an airy opening only he could reach, this door was not high enough.

Then she saw an extending ladder, rusted and worn, lying on the gravel of the pale roof. If it had been sporting a pretty pink bow, the lure would not have been more obvious.

2. *The Other Way In*

Yumiko lowered her weight, unlimbered her telescoping bowstaff, and used it to vault herself up from the broken traffic pole. She sailed over the slanted black roof of the factory, shot her wirepoon to snag the lip of the huge, high chimney, and swung to the rim.

She looked into the dark depth. Why would a winged man use any door? The orange door was an obvious trap. On the other hand, using an obvious trap to lure the unwary into a subtler trap was not obvious. Perhaps this chimney was the real trap. Perhaps Winged Vengeance came and went by another way she had not yet seen.

She did not like the idea of lowering herself into a factory chimney, even one years dead. Ash or residual fumes might be lurking down the dark shaft. Or bad smells. She sealed her mask and turned on the oxynitrogen before fixing her grapnel securely into place and descending into the gloom.

Down she went. She lit no lights because the reflections escaping the chimney mouth above might be visible. There was no heat here, insufficient visible wavelengths to amplify, and no ultraviolet, so she was blind with all her lenses.

Her nerves jumped when a red light flickered in the corner of her vision. *Toxic environment.* A second message reported that her suit integrity was good.

Some residue from chemicals burned here long ago? She might have believed that, except that when she landed in an ash heap at the bottom of the shaft, something cracked under her foot. She left the wire in place to allow for a quick escape. Now she risked a light. In the ashes underfoot, she saw the smooth curve, the eyeholes, and the upper jaw of a human skull.

The burning chamber was punctured by a fuel vent leading in and a set of clogged slats underfoot originally meant to allow ash to fall out. To one side was a large metal hatch for introducing the material to be burned.

In the flashlight beam, she saw that the fuel vent had particles of ash dancing before it. She holstered the flashlight and clicked her lenses to infrared. The gas entering through the fuel vent was slightly warmer than the bricks behind it, so she could see colored plumes like ghostly smoke pouring silently in.

There was no lock to pick on this side of the hatch, nor any hinges. And she had not seen a hacksaw anywhere among the many useful tools in her belt, or a crowbar. However, her kunai-blade could serve. The ring in the knife butt could be rotated, and the bowstaff tip fitted to it like a bayonet. (Yumiko was once again impressed with the modular cleverness of her weapons.) The point of the stubby throwing blade she wedged into the hatch jamb. Then, she braced her bowstaff against the far wall of the chimney. The powerful force of the telescoping bowstaff expanding drove the knifepoint hard enough into the crack between jamb and frame to create a gap. The blade of her kodachi was narrow enough to slide through. Eventually, she found and dislodged the bolt holding the hatch shut.

She put her shoulder to the hatch. The rusted hinges groaned and refused to move. She dismounted the knife, braced the tip of the staff against the stubborn hatch, and expanded it. Under this battering ram, the hinges screamed, and the hatch banged open with a strident clang.

Yumiko sighed, wondering if there were any passersby on the street or in nearby rooms who had not noticed. Next time, she would just ring the doorbell and present a calling card to the butler: *The Foxmaiden will do you the honor of furtively and surreptitiously breaking into your secret base after sunset. Please take no notice.*

There was no help for it. She retracted her grapnel, cutting herself off from a quick exit, and slid out nimbly through the hatch.

Outside, her flashlight beam showed the crawling clouds of poison slithering out of the hatch with her. The clouds did not rise, but poured like water, clinging to the ground. She oiled the hinges with oil from her sword cleaning kit, put her back to the hatch, braced both of her feet against the brick floor, straightened her legs, and silently forced the hatch shut. Then, she threw the bolt. The seal was tight, and no more poison escaped.

3. Aside from the Poison

An open grillwork of supports upheld the slanted roof. She shot her grapnel into one of them, rose up, and twined her legs around a brace. Her flashlight beam could not reach the floor. She shut it off. It was dark as a tomb. Saying farewell to all hope of stealth, Yumiko ignited her second and last flare.

Below was a wide, empty factory floor, ankle-deep in poison gas. Protruding pipes, metal braces, and empty holes showed that whatever equipment had once been here was long since gone.

She drew one of her folding boomerangs and affixed the flare to a clear clamp that apparently had been designed just for this purpose. She threw.

The spinning boomerang cast brilliant light across the scene, and the shadows looped and spun in answer. One lopsided wall was pierced with the larger overhead door. This was the street side, the front wall. Nearby loomed a set of wooden platforms like giant shelves, evidently a warehouse storage area. It was adjacent to a roofless walled-off area one-story tall. From her high perch, she could see office spaces bare of furnishings, a short hallway, and the smaller door from the street.

The factory space was wide enough for the boomerang to fly in a circle and return. She swung out on her wire to catch it and to hurl it in the opposite direction.

The rear wall of the factory was broken into little bays and inlets. Whatever utility rooms, motors, plumbing, lockers, or other fixtures which had been there were also gone.

A second time the boomerang returned to her hand. Now she threw it to one side. In the spinning glare of light, she saw a catwalk clinging to the taller of the two long side walls. This catwalk was twenty feet off the floor and ran the whole length of the factory. It reached from the brick chimney at one end to an enclosed loft at the other. The loft clung to the slanted ceiling like some bulky, square version of a swallow's nest.

The boomerang passed over the catwalk and became embedded with a clang. The light was now motionless over the wide empty place.

Yumiko looked up and down. Aside from the spreading cloud of poison, nothing in the surroundings seemed unusual for an abandoned building.

Or almost nothing. The boomerang was sticking into the side of what looked like an elevator car. This block-shaped feature stood at the midpoint of the catwalk. She estimated this was the spot where the orange metal door pierced the wall. In the brilliant light from the flare, this elevator car seemed rust free, the paint fresh. It was more recent than its surroundings. The catwalk passed before it. But there was no elevator shaft above or below. From the floor of the elevator car, a large, long, square, sloping metal shaft ran parallel to the slanted ceiling. This shaft ran to the point in the shorter wall where, from outside, she had seen a rainspout pouting over the dumpster bin of liquid filth. Perhaps it was part of the ventilation system. It looked like a laundry chute.

With the flare motionless, she saw details previously missed. Where the catwalk met the brick chimney, twenty feet off the ground, a second hatch penetrated it. This second hatch was directly above the one she had broken open. It had new hinges and showed marks of recent use. There was a wheel to turn instead of a latch.

Yumiko groaned with understanding. Anyone able to fly down the shaft who knew where the upper hatch was, instead of dropping into a well of heavier-than-air poisonous gas, could simply turn the wheel, exit the chimney shaft, and walk on the catwalk.

There were no stairs from the catwalk to the factory floor. Not that a winged man needed them. The catwalk ran to only one spot. Yumiko swung through the roof supports toward the loft. Once, large windows had been here, overlooking the factory floor, but now all were boarded up with plywood. That was not the strangest sight.

Where the catwalk touched the loft, the metal walkway ended in an old-fashioned door with a large doorknob of blue glass. It gleamed like a vast sapphire. The wood was held by large metal hasps, and the door and door-frame came to a peaked arch at the top.

Before the door was a brown mat, sitting on the iron grillwork of the catwalk.

Yumiko was unwilling to step onto the catwalk because she could not see why a winged man would use one to reach a door four stories in the air. Instead, she swung gracefully in and used her glider wings to break her speed just enough that she could drive two knives, one in each hand, into the plywood boards covering the windows. Weighing less than a pound, she could hang from one hand or flip herself up and balance on her boot toes on the knife hilts. The dizzying drop to the empty factory floor was below her. The railing was next to her, as was the odd, archaic door.

She had seen such a door in the magic shop where Winged Vengeance left his tuxedo. It was similar in shape, but it was not the same wood, the same size, or clasped with the same ornate hinges. The knob was sapphire, not ruby. But it was clearly a brother to that other door.

She looked down. The brown mat had letters on it. They spelled out GO AWAY.

4. The Inner Sanctum

Yumiko put on boot on the catwalk handrail and reached out with her hand.

The glass doorknob turned. The door was unlocked.

A thrill of suspicion trickled up her spine to her neck. What sort of vigilante left the secret door to his hidden sanctum unlocked?

Warily, Yumiko drove another knife into the plywood further away and perched on it. With her back to the plywood, she expanded her bowstaff, extended to twice its normal length, and used the far tip to prod the door open.

She waited warily for an explosion or an attack by poisonous asps. Neither came.

Closer she crept again, clinging weightlessly to the plywood, and peered around the doorjamb.

At that moment, the flare was exhausted. The light fluttered and failed.

Darkness closed in. Yumiko drew her flashlight. In its beam she saw the eight-sided chamber beyond the strange door, paneled in dark wood, dark beneath a high, octagonal dome.

Weightlessly, she swooped into the chamber, landing in a crouch with no more noise than a falling cherry blossom petal. Here on a table in the middle of the carpet was the same phone on the same table she had seen before.

She waited, wondering whether it would ring.

The phone remained silent. She sent the flashlight beam left and right to inspect the eight walls.

Last time, the arched door had opened, not onto a catwalk inside a deserted factory uptown, but onto a brick wall. Last time, the arched door had been opposite three windows in three walls looking out on the churchyard of a deserted church downtown. The three walls were there, but now two of them were pierced by narrow doors. The wall between them was a niche holding a photographic portrait draped in black. To either side of the photograph were flowers in vases and twigs of incense in holders.

Yumiko shined her beam on the picture. Her sob caught in the throat, heavy with emotion, before her brain consciously recognized the clear features, green eyes, raven-black hair. It was her mother.

Stepping nearer, she saw that these smaller doors both sported brass handles, but neither knob nor lock. Behind each was a blank brick wall.

Next, she looked at one of the cabinets. It was also unlocked, but, as before, it also opened up on a blank wall. She pushed back the top of the rolltop desk. Empty.

She walked a circle, slowly inspecting the eight walls. Then, she turned her flashlight up. A wooden dome made of eight curving panels was above. As when last she stood here, the chamber was like a stage setting, not a real room. What was she overlooking?

She directed her beam downward, seeing how obvious were the trail of triangular prints her boot toes made in the thick dust and the tiny, sharp imprints of her heel. Her brow creased. Did Winged Vengeance never sweep the carpet? Perhaps that had been her job. But where were his boot prints?

Kneeling, Yumiko ran a finger along the fibers. She inspected the dust on her fingertip. It was a white powder. The alert light in the corner of her vision flashed. *Toxic environment.*

Yumiko shivered, remembered that her supersuit had clamped shut, air-tight, the last time she had entered this chamber. At that time, she had not known how to turn on the warning messages from the suit's hidden instruments. Despite this, the suit, or whatever thoughtful paranoiac had designed it, had saved her life.

But she also remembered taking off her mask during her last visit. Why had the toxin coating the carpet not acted on her then? She tried to remember the exact order of events. Yumiko stood, stepped over to the pole lamp, and switched it on.

In the bright light, the dust stain on her fingertip looked dull gray. The warning light in her lenses winked out. The air registered as safe to breathe. She turned the pole lamp off again. The dust turned from gray to white. The warning flashed. *Toxic environment.*

What kind of material could change its properties when struck by light and turn from lethal to harmless instantly? Whether it was elfin alchemy or human super-science, it was astounding.

And astoundingly stupid to use. How did Winged Vengeance make sure, when he left the room and stepped into a dark place, a closet, unlit corridor, or out into a moonless night, he had no small gray stain overlooked on his elbow, or boot sole, or clinging to the hem of his cape which would instantly suddenly turn white and lethal again? In fact, how had she left this room of death safely?

She could not remember. But surely she had twisted the ring to render herself weightless before exiting since there was no other exit but the window. Could the mist of the elfs disperse the dusty poison?

Yumiko twisted the ring twice widdershins.

5. Hanged Men

The mist thickened about her, rendering her unseen to human eyes. Immediately, her hands began to tremble. Her fingers were cold. She bit on the switch inside her mask to increase the oxygen flow, but she still seemed unable to breathe. Yumiko turned the flashlight left and right, wildly, looked for the source of the threat. No one was here.

Then, she switched the flashlight off. There was a man hanging by his neck from a rope descending from the shadows of the eight-sided dome. An arrow pinned a note, written in blood, to his chest, and protruded from his back. His eyes were terrible pits of emptiness opening into a universe larger and darker than the universe of stars the Earth's tiny globe spun through. A second man, eyeless, bound, and hanged, was next to the first, also impaled by an arrow. A third man, hanging by the neck, arrow-stabbed, had his wrists tied behind him by his bootlaces. A fourth hung head downward.

She looked over her shoulder. There were more behind her and more to either side, like grisly fruit hanging from a rich tree. One looked as if he had been run over by a truck before being hanged and impaled. Another, as if he had been burned. Yet another had huge bites torn out of his bound arms and legs, as if he had been lowered into a pit of savage animals before dying.

With a creak of ropes, the corpses now all rotated so that their bloated, blackened, torn, and desiccated faces all faced her.

Yumiko screamed in shock and terror. She had let go of the flashlight and covered her mask with her gloves. Gritting her teeth, she forced her cold fingers to move. She grabbed and twisted the ring. Once, twice, thrice, and once more again.

Her longbow and short sword snapped out to their full length, and her cape unfolded into glider wings, knocking the phone off the table. Bolo and boomerang and dozens of knives, barbed and throwing stars jumped out of their belt pouches and fell to the carpet.

The metallic clamor of the dropped weapons rang in her ears. The echo hung in her ears a moment, and silence came.

Fear vanished.

The ghosts of the slain were gone.

A light as clear and subtle as starlight was streaming from the ring in all directions, glinting like Procyon on a clear winter night.

Yumiko stared at the ring in awe, but this time, it was the awe of wonder, not of terror. The woman's face in the intaglio of the ring had changed again, and now her features were those of a stern and bright-eyed angel crowned with rays.

Chapter 3

The Face in the Glass

1. Starlight

She stood. The chamber now seemed airy and clean. The dust on the carpet had also vanished. The suit indicated no toxins were in the air. Yumiko unsealed and opened her mask. The air seemed fresh and clear.

She had to undo the harnesses of her wings. Cutting blades were now visible at the toes of her boots and running along her forearms from wrist to elbow. An elbow pad and two kneepads made her motions less limber.

But she did not twist the ring to banish the starlight yet. It seemed to have banished the mist that had been in this chamber, unseen and unsuspected, and to reveal yet another level of hidden things.

She stepped over the rolltop desk. It was no longer empty. One of the pigeonholes contained a radio apparatus; another held the five-sided element charts and astrological calendars for a type of divination called *on-myodo*; the tools of a chemistry set occupied others and a compact but thorough forensics lab; the drawers held groups of notebooks. She opened one; the page was blank. She held it near her nose and sniffed. There was a faint odor from the page, as if ink were present, but unseen. She closed her mask and went through the various settings of her lenses and flashlight, hoping the ink was visible in the ultraviolet or infrared. It was not.

She opened other notebooks at random. All were blank. Here was the desk of her master, crammed with his secrets, years of journals and diaries, and she could see none of it.

2. Celestial Collection

Next, she opened the cabinet door on one of the walls. This time, bathed in the silver light of her ring, instead of a blank wall, the cabinet held a large and obvious handle. It must have been invisible before, hidden in the mist. She pulled it.

On the other side of the chamber, the blank wall behind the rolltop desk sighed and slid open. Beyond was a walk-in closet. Three walls of the closet contained a set of glass shelves behind smoked glass panels. The shelves held what seemed at first to be a collection of gems that blazed with white fire. A dial could adjust the polarization of the panel to darken them and to make the blindingly bright shapes visible.

A touch of the finger moved the glass panels to bring more into view from below and to hide those above. The rear of each shelf was mirrored so that the things displayed could be seen from front and rear.

But the materials glittering in the collection were not gemstones. One or two she recognized, such as an awl or fork, an inkwell or arrowhead. Other objects were curved or pointed or hollow, like fishhooks or drinking bowls or sets of linked rings; but not quite of the right size and shape for any of these things. Here was a sets of cubes and prisms forming a hollow pyramid; there a group of what looked like miniature sundials or crystal toadstools; and the next shelf held what might have been spiral horns of fabled beasts, except that they were crystalline and transparent.

Some held liquids but were not shaped like bottles. Some emitted light but were not shaped like lamps.

All were as beautiful as works of art but looked like nothing in nature, and so they might have been decorations of pleasing shape. All were made of a crystal that seemed to fool the eye. One moment the object seemed smaller and nearer to the eye than the cabinet around it, and the next, it seemed larger and farther. Most of the objects burned solemn blue or pristine white, but there were, now and then, gem-like gleams as red as Antares, as blue as Bellatrix, as golden orange as Capella.

Looking closer, she saw that nearly all were chipped, marred, or asymmetrical as if bits were missing.

Then, she gasped, for she recognized one of the artifacts: it was a silver scarf-pin shaped like a fish, with azure chips for scales, and the light of Arcturus for eyes. Yumiko had seen her mother wearing it, holding the folds of her wimple at her throat. Yumiko's eyes, in her younger days, must have been different from her eyes on Earth, for she had not remembered the ornament as so beautiful, so bright.

When she turned the dark glass entirely transparent, Yumiko found her naked eye could not look upon her mother's pin. Yumiko saw no way to open the case to touch the pin. Nor was she sure the touch would not burn her.

She turned the dial and darkened the glass once more. Now Yumiko understood what this was: litter recovered from the rubble of Sarras, the fallen city of the stars.

Silently, she closed the cabinet door.

3. Armory

A second wall of the eight-sided chamber also contained a cabinet, in which was a switch previously invisible. Pulling it open made the blank wall opposite the desk slide open. A second hidden closet was directly opposite the first.

This second closet contained weapons. Two weapon racks faced each other, one filling each closet wall. The first held black blades and dark weapons, massive and heavy, and quivers of red arrows cut too long for her bow. The other held weapons of silver-white, slender and more graceful blades, shorter arrows. Gratefully, Yumiko re-supplied the arrows and throwing blades she had lost.

Between the weapon racks was a chest of glass drawers holding other supplies. The upper drawers held arrowheads of different shapes: leaf shaped or trefoil, broadhead or bodkin-point.

One drawer held flint-napped arrows of stone. A label read: *For nephilim.* The next higher drawer held arrowheads of fire-hardened ash for vampires and, above that, silver arrowheads for werewolves, all neatly labeled. The uppermost drawer held red metal arrowheads. These were labeled: *Meteoric Iron from Sarras. For elfs.*

There was also a single arrowhead made of a black substance that seemed to be neither metal, stone, nor wood and was bitterly cold to the touch. *For the Dragon.* She wondered about that label.

From the lower drawers she replenished her missing miniature grenades, flares, and so on. There was even a cubbyhole holding a pad of metallic cloth to replace the one a wolf had torn from her elbow three weeks ago.

She found a small box containing a hacksaw, needle-nosed pliers, and other useful tools her utility belt had been lacking.

Yumiko twisted the ring and banished the starlight. The eight-walled chamber seemed smaller than it had a moment ago, and the air hot and close. Like her other gear, this toolkit was a mermaid pouch. With the starlight gone, she could flatten the toolkit to an impossibly small size. Nonetheless, she had to remove and leave behind the pouch of weapons from her utility belt to make room. Evidently, her previous self had thought carrying an extra dozen throwing daggers, a trifork spearhead, and a brace of climbing claws was a better use of space.

4. *Locked Doors*

Next, she went to one of the two interior doors and opened it. With the ring no longer shedding starlight, the brick wall was still there—or seemed to be. But now she was sure that the brick wall was merely a trick, a thing of colored shadows. There was a switch or lock hidden in the mist, invisible. She reached toward her ring but then hesitated.

Winged Vengeance did not have the Ring of Mists to command the mists to draw back. How did *he* open his door? He no doubt went through the rooms of his lair many times a day, including while burdened with laundry bags. Or, more likely, body bags.

She pushed on various bricks at hand level or eye level, but nothing moved. The bricks felt solid.

Perhaps he used a key or a remote control. But, if so, it would be something he carried on him at all times. Wings? She flapped the hem of her own cape against the wall. It was a celestial flying robe, at least, of a sort.

The bricks remained bricks.

Or rather, the elfin illusion of a wall of bricks remained. What would Winged Vengeance carry on his person at all times which was proof against elf magic?

Then, she laughed, reached over her shoulder, drew out a red arrow whose head was made of meteoric iron from Sarras, and touched it to the so-called brick. As suddenly as if waking from a dream, she realized she had been staring at a door that was merely coated with red wallpaper printed with a repeating pattern of rectangles. She rapped on it with a knuckle and heard a hollow, wooden echo. The doorknob was plain to see. She opened it.

Beyond was a barren cell, such as a hermit might use. There was a sleeping mat on the hard floor, a lamp, a trunk that contained a man's clothing, a chamber pot, and a wash basin. Winged Vengeance certainly did not coddle himself.

There was only one decoration in the hermit cell: a standing screen of black rice paper. It was a triptych of three panels. Calligraphy was painted on the screen in energetic but controlled strokes of red ink. One panel read: *Those who flee the light adore the dark.*

In the center, it read: *Let me be in the dark and bring my terrors, and dark they will no more adore, for it is become their foe.*

The final panel was two bold ideograms, which meant: *In the darkest night, there must be vengeance.*

There were two archways on the far side of the cell opposite the rice screen. These opened into even smaller chambers. One was paneled in mirrors and held a stationary bike, weightlifting equipment, and a wooden practice dummy called a wing-chun. The other was paneled in cork and held a chair, a music stand, and a violin in a climate-controlled glass case. The sight of the violin stung her eyes with tears and troubled her heart, but no memory surfaced to tell her why.

She returned to the main chamber and opened the other door. This one also seemed to have a brick wall behind it until she touched an arrowhead to it.

The door now opened into a room with white walls and floral wall screens. Midmost was a pink bedspread. At the walls were a chair, a desk, and a wardrobe.

In she walked, arms spread, and she spun in a circle, smiling. A stuffed white teddy bear with a bow about its neck sat cheerfully on the pillow. She picked it up and hugged it without knowing why.

Beyond the fluffy pink bed were two archways. One led to a miniature kitchenette. The other held a door, behind which was a luxurious bathroom where an old-fashioned tub crouched on claws clutching glass marbles beneath a gas-powered brass water heater.

She bounced on the bed, leaped up, spun on her toes again, and flung the wardrobe door open. She knew without trying anything on that it would all fit. She plucked up her favorite wide-brimmed straw hat, doffed her mask, and pushed back her cowl so that she could wear it. Yumiko smiled at herself in the mirror above the vanity bureau and tilted the straw hat at a rakish angle. She turned again and looked at herself in the mirror over her shoulder, striking a pose.

There were two photographs tucked into the frame of the mirror. One was a slightly blurred black and white photo of a dark-haired woman with two children. It had the stiff quality of a photograph taken with a box camera long ago.

The children were a young girl and an older boy. The little girl was tall and seemed almost too old for her mother to hold in her lap. The young man sat to one side and behind the mother. He had dark, intent eyes. All three had the black hair, ivory skin, and epicanthic eyefold of the Far East.

The other photograph was in color. It showed a clean-shaven freckle-cheeked redheaded youth in an aviator's leather jacket. Goggles were pushed high on his forehead, making his orange forelocks stand up at wild angles. On his back was some sort of metal backpack with wings, only part of which could be seen protruding from behind his shoulders. In one hand was what looked like an electric crossbow. It had ruby lenses at the tip of each arm and thick electrical cables running to the stock. His other hand was raised in a thumb's-up salute.

His eyes were as blue as cornflowers.

An emotion too large for words possessed her. She drew the color photograph out of the frame and stared at the boy's face intently. This must be the one. It was he. Tomorrow Moth, the young inventor. Her fiancé, supposedly.

It was the first time she had seen his face.

She looked up and saw herself staring at her. She said to the image of herself in the mirror, "This must be my room!"

The image in the mirror said back, "It is. Welcome home."

5. Riddles

Yumiko hesitated for a moment between puzzlement and fear, wondering whether she had finally gone mad. For she had spoken to herself several times in the mirror, whenever she was troubled. It had never answered back before.

Yumiko, embarrassed, removed her straw hat. The image in the mirror remained wearing hers.

"I beg your pardon? Can you talk?" Yumiko asked. "Are you real?"

Her face in the mirror tilted her head to one side. "Does anyone ever answer that question by saying *no*?"

"What is your name, please?"

"Yumiko Ume Moth," said her face.

Yumiko scowled, and her face scowled at the same time, imitating her. "That is my name!"

Her face said, "No, your name is the Foxmaiden. Your name is *vengeance*."

Yumiko shook her head, but this time, her face did not imitate her. Instead, it nodded slowly, insistently, staring her deeply in the eye with a knowing look.

Yumiko said, "Who are you, really?"

"Your shadow in the glass."

"Are you a spirit? A ghost?"

"The ghost of a living girl?" her face asked impishly. "As Tom would say, *That would be a slick trick*."

"Then how can you talk? What are you?"

"I am a diary, if you please." The other smiled. "Your diary."

"What? I mean, I beg your pardon?"

"I can talk because you needed someone to confide in."

Yumiko's heart leaped. "Then you know all my past! Tell me! Please!"

"That would be my pleasure," said the diary. But then she said, "Who danced for joy on the day of darkness, when all the spirits of Heaven wept before the stone that blocked the cave where light died?"

Yumiko scowled, and her shoulders slumped. The talking mirror was asking her for her password. Of course a girl would keep her diary locked.

6. Family Photo

Yumiko's eyes fell on the black and white photo. She drew it out of the frame and brought it close. The lady wore a dress of a style Yumiko did not recognize, a fair garment of many silken pleats falling in smooth lines.

It was her mother. Which meant…

The diary said, "Who stepped forth when none other would go to confront the dreadful spirit that stood upon the eight-forked bridge binding Earth to Heaven and opened the way?"

Yumiko inspected the two children carefully. They were dressed in summer kimonos called *yukata*. Hers was decorated with a pattern of moths; his with ravens.

Even as a little girl, Yumiko had possessed something of the rangy limbs of an athlete, the narrow features and high cheeks of Akita Prefecture.

She stared narrowly at the youth. The man into which he would grow was clear in his features. It was the face of Pooh-Bah of Titipu, the tall and impressive Japanese gentleman she had seen so briefly at the Cobbler's Club.

Why was a youthful Winged Vengeance with Yumiko and Dandrenor in a family photo?

The diary said, "Who stood watch before the sacred grail of Sarras, from whose rim the last sacrifice at the last feast drank the last of the wine?"

Yumiko jerked her eyes up from the photo and stared at her reflection's eyes in the glass. "I know that one. Dandrenor. Dandrenor is the Grail Queen." She turned the black and white photo and showed it to the mirror. "Now I have a question for you: Who is this little boy?"

The diary's eyes narrowed. "You do not recognize your own half-brother? That is rather odd. You answered the riddle right, but Nyctalope warned me not to trust anyone wearing your shape."

"Nyctalope? Is that his name?"

"He said you fell into the hands of the Anarchists and so might be a clone grown from the cells of the real you, or possessed by a ghost, or just a dead body animated by an electronic brain. They do things like that."

Yumiko grimaced. "Please! How do I prove I am the real me?"

The diary bowed slightly. "I am sorry, but you prove yourself by answering the riddle correctly and by knowing who your own brother is, or so I would say. You've done one of those, so it may be permitted that I recite you the final entry I was given. But the other entries must stay locked, I'm afraid."

"Wait! That is not fair! I am the real me!"

"How do you know?"

And Yumiko had no answer for that.

The diary shook her head. "If you were the real you, and not just some shadow or reflection like I am, you would not want me to take the chance and tell someone who might be a stranger or enemy about your private thoughts and feelings, would you? If you were the reflection of me, rather than me of you, would you not do the same?"

7. The Final Entry

The reflection in the mirror was now seated and no longer wearing a straw hat, but she was dressed in her skintight black supersuit, with the cowl pushed back. Over her shoulders was flung a long, sleek, black trench coat with padded shoulders and a pinched waist.

But the expression was different from her normal reflection. There was a bitter look in the narrowed eye, a harsh set to the jaw, a frowning coldness in the crease of her brow and tilt of her pretty head.

"Personal log. Day 1,441 since her death. She is still unavenged."

Her voice was like the voice of a stranger, stern of tone, joyless, fierce. It seemed like something from another life.

"Komobo questioned me again about the nature of the mists of Everness…"

Komo meant red-haired person. *Bo* was a diminutive to show affection, like using a baby name for your boyfriend.

"…but then he insisted on doing test after test, trying to find how it affects kinetic energy. I told him the reason why pistol bullets do not work in the mist but sling bullets do is that guns are not things of the world beneath the mist. Why doesn't he listen to me? For some reason, he thinks his laser pistol will still operate. He says there is light in the Otherworld, so it has to work. I told him it is a realm of darkness."

A sigh of exasperation sounded in the glass.

"So pigheaded! It is the same argument we had when I told him any disguise would deceive anyone from the Daylight and all but the greatest of the Twilight. He thinks my mask will not fool anyone. Even though he practically made it! All that new gear he put in! I don't have to carry that stupid huge radio around in my hand any more.

"He said that I am the same height and have the same voice and the same walk when I dress up. He says people will recognize my bottom when I walk. In the suit, everyone can see my bottom perfectly well. I think he was saying that to tease me. He is so mean sometimes!

"I told him! Even a tiny little mask around the eyes is enough. A pair of glasses is enough. It is one of the conventions of the Black Spell. He worries about me too much!

"He exposed a group of white rats to the mists in higher and higher concentrations. The rats lost visibility, growing less visible to light and more visible to darkness. After that, they lost gravity, solidity, location, and then memory.

"I saw his rats floating in their cages and others walking right through the walls.

"I could hear the squealing of the one that had no location. It sounded scared until it suddenly fell silent. After a while, the mangled body rematerialized.

"The one with no memory never recovered. It could not go through the maze it had been trained to run through. It did not recognize its littermates or its mate. The effect does not wear off.

"So he is convinced the Ring of Mists is not just a story but would act the same way. He says he knows why Saturday wants it. But he would not tell me. He just grinned at me.

"Obviously, Saturday already has a way to sneak past the guardians, enter the Third Hemisphere without permission, and smuggle creatures out. He has been doing it for months. So that is not why Saturday wants the ring.

"We had the same argument again. I said I have to kill Saturday, so he has to show me where the hidden dockyard is. Komobo told me that the prince of giants killed my mother. How was I going to fight a giant who has a charmed life? He says his cousin will kill the giant. With a magic sword. It is what knights do. And that Saturday has to stay alive long enough to finish work on his machine.

"I asked him what his friends thought of all this. He has not told them his plan. The squire would not let him steal the ring if he knew because theft is dishonorable. The novice would not let him because theft is a sin.

"I don't know what to do!

"I cannot tell Nyctalope. Nicky-chan would not understand. I am loyal to him! I am loyal to Mother! But I love Komobo! I love him! I think he is about to propose. He has that look."

Her cheeks were pink, and her eyes were bright. The bitterness was, for a moment, gone.

"I will go with him." Now her voice was solemn. It sounded to Yumiko's ear like her own voice, not the voice of a stranger now. "When he steals the machine, I will go with him. He does not know how to sneak and steal. I do.

"I will go. Whatever you believe with your whole heart, even if it means your death, cannot be wrong!"

And with those words, the reflection was her own real reflection once again.

The diary would not speak again. Nothing else Yumiko said elicited any reply.

She saw an ornate clock on her desk. It was now after midnight. Her cousin, Gilberec, was due to be assassinated today at noon. Today she had to rescue Elfine, by hook or crook, before Garlot was assassinated in turn. Tomorrow the wolves currently hidden under the Cobbler's Club would be shipped to the City of Corpses, where Tom was hidden, and she had to be back there for that to follow them and to find him.

There were other secrets in the lair of Winged Vengeance, but she had no time.

8. Farewell Note

Wishing for some garb less conspicuous on modern streets than a black super-suit or a kimono adorned with a Moth family crest, she took a moment to peer through her clothing in the wardrobe. There, she found the black trench coat she had just seen herself wearing in her diary: she folded it neatly into the pocket of her cape next to the kimono.

Her emotions were disturbed as she rose to depart. Should she take that stuffed bear? Or the music box? These things were hers, but if she left, she might never see them again. If she did take her belongings, where could she put them? A rented bus locker? There was a figurine of a ballerina poised on one toe next to her calligraphy set. Had it once had some special meaning to her? The memories hovered just beyond her reach.

With a sigh, she closed the door on her old room and its forgotten treasures. "I am an exile," shee whispered. "I have no mother, no home."

Taking a paper and pen from the rolltop desk and a bottle of blue ink she found there, she wrote: *Dear brother, Euhemerus Cobweb is of the Supreme Council of Anarchists. He has wispy fingers. Rotwang is also and has a prosthetic. Zahack has something instead of hands. The final shipment of werewolves leaves the Cobbler's Club for the City of Corpses on Friday, March 20th.*

By way of signature, she drew a little cartoon of a grinning fox face.

After a moment, the ink faded from view, and the paper seemed blank again. She thought that was a good sign. She pinned the note to the center of the desk with a knife so that he would notice it.

Carefully avoiding laying a foot on the catwalk, she departed the loft and used the upper hatch to enter the tall brick chimney above the poison layer. Weightlessly, she soared up and out into the night.

Chapter 4

In Darkest Night

1. Below Street Level

When the train she wanted began pulling away from the platform, lightly, Yumiko dropped to the metal roof of the car. She figured that, having purchased a ticket like a proper human being of the Daylight World, she could ride whichever part of the train suited her.

Whenever a low tunnel roof threatened, she slipped over the back of the caboose. This was an older car, and there was a metal step or hitch protruding from the rear where she could perch while remaining below the level of the caboose windows, and the track would speed by, a blur of ties and a sinuous stream of rails, mere inches below the heels of her boots.

The signal for tracer *zero-four*, which she had planted on the collar of Gilberec's dog, was downtown near Grand Central Station. The signal was emanating from below street level.

Yumiko thought it might be dangerous to mingle with the crowd while invisible, so she clung to the ceiling of the train platform at Grand Central Station, weightless, and passed from the lit areas to unlit ones while trying to find some buried hall or service stairway leading to the point from which the signal came.

Down she went, and further down, to dark corridors and tunnels where no one was. She drew her flashlight from her belt and tuned it and her goggles to ultraviolet. The sensation of cold might have come merely from being in a cold, empty, unlit tunnel, but then again, it might not. In the pitch darkness, there was no point in being invisible. She twisted her ring to silver to escape the gaze of ghosts.

Eventually, she found a utility door whose padlock she could pick, leading to a narrow metal stair leading down to a metal balcony.

On this balcony was a diesel engine with a chain belt running to a wheel of iron affixed to a yard-wide pipe that murmured and thrummed with flowing water. The engine was throbbing and warm to the touch, idling. Here also was a spotlight on a pivot, switched off the moment, and other levers and clutches for other chain-drums connected to the engine. Down from the platform reached a ladder that could be lowered by turning a drum. She pulled the clutch, engaging the engine, and the chain played out, lowering the ladder. The hum of the engine and the clanging rattle of the ladder segments unfolding echoed loudly from the spaces below.

Down she went and found herself in a dim but empty tunnel. It looked like a dry sewer line. In the near distance, she saw a brick archway sloping down from the main tunnel. It was lit with a carbide lamp hanging from a rusted hook.

Closer, she could see this arch led down into a sluice or spillway. The far end was round and covered with a set of louvers, like giant metal Venetian blinds, that could be opened or shut. The louvers were open at the moment, allowing the coal-red glow of the clouds above the skyline to enter, along with a dark glimpse of the East River and cold, clear air.

On the floor of the spillway, the beam from the hanging lantern caught something small, square, and white and made it shine like a ghost. The stone arch leading to this spillway had a sluice gate that could be lowered on chains. She did not like the look of that, but she was curious about the white gleam.

She took a few steps down the slope. The concrete surface was slick and wet underfoot. Lying on a square stone in the middle of the mud of the tunnel floor was a white envelope, with a fragment of brick lying, as a paperweight, atop. The beeping of the tracer was loud in her ears. She clicked on the tracking grid and saw a dot of light resting on the envelope. The tracer signal came from there.

She did not touch it. This was a trap. She started to back away.

A rattling, sliding metallic clamor came from overhead. The trap was closing.

2. Spotlight

Yumiko cartwheeled backward up the slope. She landed on her feet before the archway, in time to see a barred gate fall down over the mouth of the spillway and the louvers at the far end downslope grind heavily shut. Had she been a hair slower, she would have been trapped in the slanted spillway.

The ladder leading up to the balcony was rising.

Yumiko leaped lightly to a point just beneath the balcony, where the ladder no longer was. She landed silently and crouched down. At the same moment, the spotlight on the platform came on, brilliant, blinding. The beam of light stabbed down and shined through the bars of the grate into the spillway. No one was trapped there. The spotlight swung in a puzzled fashion left and right, peering curiously down the dry tunnel.

However, the balcony floor was a metallic mesh, not solid planks, and would not form a shadow, should the spotlight pivot straight down. She shot her wirepoon to snag the railing of the platform and triggered the retraction spool motor so that she was jerked upward rapidly.

The spotlight did not swing toward her but instead shut off. It was pitch black. Her infrared lenses showed a heat source on the balcony, but it was too small to be a man and too low to the ground. Perhaps that was the residual heat from the engine. She somersaulted over the railing. She clicked her lenses and flashlight to ultraviolet. There was no one here but a dog, lying down with its head on its forepaws as if half asleep. She could not see its coloration by ultraviolet, but it was a collie. Someone had put an archer's cap atop the dog's head and had left a pair of gloves on the floor of the platform next to the dog.

She turned the flashlight left and right. There was no one here. She saw a small round hatch she had not seen before, covering a crawlway. She knelt down and shone the flashlight in. She saw cables and wires strung, but no one on hands and knees was crawling rapidly away.

That left the narrow metal stairs leading back up to the utility door. She scampered up the stairs. Even under her light footfalls, they clanged and rattled. The utility door was open, unlocked, just as she had left it. She switched her flashlight to visible light and examined the threshold and the floor beyond the door, which she, clinging to the ceiling, had not touched. The dust here was thick and undisturbed.

Like a silent explosion, the brilliant light from the spotlight on the platform now lit up. The beam caught her and threw her shadow across the ceiling. Startled, she turned, but instinctively raised her elbow to block her eyes.

"Freeze! Hands up! Hands up!" came a gruff voice from below. Bewildered, Yumiko obeyed, squinting against the blinding light and raising her hands.

She was caught.

3. Cornered

"Drop it! Drop it!"

She opened her fingers. The flashlight dropped away and clanged against the metal balcony before toppling to the tunnel floor. She wondered at the voice. It did not sound quite right. It was too deep for a child's voice but very gruff and scratchy.

"Ha ha! Thought you'd sneak up on me, did ya? Did ya? Yup! Yup! But now who's sneaked who? I sneaked! I sneaked! I am the sneaky one. Yes, I am. Yup! Yup!" This was followed by a breathy noise like an animal panting, as if the man, or the boy, had trouble breathing.

Slowly, Yumiko lowered one hand to let the shadow of her forearm fall across her eyes. She squinted. The scene was washed out by the brilliant spotlight. She could see nothing.

"I liked your other uniform better," said the gruff voice.

She squinted down at the light. "What other uniform?"

"Can't hear you."

"I said, what other uniform? When did you see me before this, please?"

"With the top hat. You were almost naked. I liked it."

"You mean the Peach Cobbler suit? You saw me in the club?"

"Can't hear. Take off the mask! Not very realistic. Couldn't fool me. Nope! Nope! For one thing, those eyes don't blink. I am very smart."

This was more puzzling. Yumiko tossed her head, and the fox mask slid up. The chin hung over her eyes like a visor. There was no point in hiding a face he had already seen.

The voice was saying. "You bet! You bet! Can't fool me. Nope. Gil did not know you, and Matt did not know you, but I knew. Because your arms and legs were bare."

That was puzzling. "You recognized my arms?"

"Armpits. And your bottom. I sniff bottoms. I always know bottoms."

Sniff what? Then Yumiko's confusion abruptly transformed into astonishment. "You are the dog! The dog that was with the Swan Knight!"

"Yup, yup, that's me. That's me. Swan Knight's Dog."

"Who are you?"

"My name's Ruff. Like in Ruffle, but with no L. Rhymes with *tough*, and *gruff*, and *takes no guff*."

She scowled. "It also rhymes with *bluff*. You have no gun trained on me, have you?"

"What? What? Gun? Course not! Guns don't like shooting elfs. They try to miss. You must know that. 'S why you carry weird old weapons. Right?"

She slid down the stairway and landed at the bottom. The reflected light from the upturned spotlight showed the dog. He was sitting on his haunches, a green archer's cap perched on his head, a white owl's feather in the brim. His forepaws, which were covered in green gloves, now looked like the forearms and hands of a human. His was scratching his furry belly thoughtfully with his human fingers.

His tongue hung out one side of his grinning jaws.

4. Carabas Gloves

Seeing the direction of her gaze, he raised his hand, waved, and said, "Look what I can do." He proceeded to interlace his fingers, raise both index fingers, and twitch his thumbs while chanting, "*Here is the church, and here is the steeple. Open the doors, and see all the people*! Wait. I did it wrong. Fingers go inside. Lemme try again. Oh, that is no good. Here. Want to see me hitchhike? Look! Look! Aha!" He made a fist and extended his thumb. "See?"

"Most impressive. How can you talk?"

"How can you turn invisible?"

"Magic. I have a magic ring."

"Hah! Thought so. Me, I wear a magic hat. Also, I am a pooka."

"I don't know that word."

"Pooka are friendly *yokai*. Except for the unfriendly ones. Not them. My old name is Sgeolan, but I serve a new master now. I am a Dog of the Table Round. And a member of Super Action Team Swan."

"Who am I?"

"Why ask me? You forget?"

"Yes."

"Oh! Well, you are the girl who vanished when Tom vanished. The Winged Vengeance's Sidekick, Foxmaiden. You go around shooting Cobwebs to death with arrows, and then shoot their ghosts. Kinda scary, actually. I saw you throw a boomerang once. It came back to your hand. Right back! That looked like fun. I wanted to chase it. I have one, too, but I cannot throw it so good. In my spy kit. Oh! Oh! And I saw you fighting werewolves in New Jersey. You were outnumbered. Your name is not Sorry. That is a silly name."

"Do you know my name?"

"Of course. Tom would not shut up about it. Yummy Cutie."

"Yumiko."

"Nope, you're saying it wrong."

"But it *is* Yumiko."

"Nope. Tom said *Yummy Cutie*. He said it a lot. A whole lot. Ah… Where is he, by the way?"

"What does he look like?"

The dog tilted his head to one side. One ear stood up, and the other flopped over. "You don't know what he looks like?"

"No. I saw a photo I hope is his. I want to hear if your description matches it."

"His pelt is red, but it only grows in patches. The rest of his skin is naked. Kind of freckled, like a strawberry. So he wears clothes. A long white coat. Or a flight jacket."

"Patches?"

"Top of his head, armpits, like that, you know? Maybe a little bit around his lips when he has been working in the lab and going without food and sleep for days, but I think he usually scrapes it off."

"What color are his eyes?"

"I dunno. Dogs don't see color."

"How did you know his hair color then?"

"It smells red."

"There are many red-haired men. How will I know him?"

"He is the only one I've ever met who eats liver, onion, and peanut butter sandwiches. Ugh. I wouldn't touch that! And I eat from garbage pails. So you can smell it on his breath."

"I cannot smell that well."

"Hah! I knew it! Dog noses are better than Fox! Dogs are number one!"

"No, I am not really a fox."

The dog tilted his head the other way and perked up the other ear. "Yes, you are."

"How will I recognize him?"

"Tom? He wears goggles. And a labcoat. And a jetpack. Carries a laser pistol."

Her heart was pounding in her chest. Her cheeks felt warm. "So he has a rocket pack? And a spaceship? Is there really any boy who can build such things?" Tom had been wearing a square metal bulk on his back in the photo, but only now did she realize that this must have been part of a jetpack peeking over his shoulders.

"Wrecks them, too. You should see the mess left over when he tried to pull an Immelmann with his dirigible. He was dogfighting a Roc over the ruins of Nan Matal. There were not any dogs involved. I don't know why they call it that. No dogs."

Strange feelings, but with no memories, no images, attached to them, came and went in her brain.

Yumiko did not hear Ruff's next remark. He repeated himself.

5. *The Boy with the Rocket Pack*

"So… Why are you here, Fox? You were trying to sneak up on me. Why?"

"Please! I want you to take me to the Swan Knight. There is a plot against him."

The dog seemed unimpressed. He yawned. "Someone trying to kill Gil? Must be Tuesday."

"You mean Thursday. He is involved. Malen Ruddgochren, the Red Lady, is ultimately behind it. She brought Garlot here from Elfland. Sir Garlot the Red Knight. He has the Mantle of Mists, and this allows him to strike down valiant knights unseen."

The dog said, "No, I did not mean Tuesday the Anarchist. I mean *it must be Tuesday* because it happens all the time. It is like a phrase. I picked it up from Matt. But before we talk about Gil, let's talk about Tom."

"Ah, yes. If you say so. I'd love to hear all about him!"

"Do you… ah… have anything to say?"

"What do you mean?"

"Anything to say about his location? Where did you take him to? Where is he?"

For a moment, she did not understand the question. "Where is who?"

"Tom. Tom Moth. You must know who I am talking about. He is your second cousin three times removed on his father's side and your third cousin once removed on his mother's side."

"A hob in a bottle told me he is at the City of Corpses. I don't know where that is. I want to find him. Do all the elfs remember their family trees this way? In so much detail?"

"If you hang out with Moths like I have, you'll pick up the habit. I did not know what a third cousin was until I was following Gil."

"And do you know my family?"

"Not really. I know your Dad is the grandson of Susa-no-O, which is why he kicks so much butt in such a major way and why he can fight giant centipedes and stuff. And everyone knows your Mom. But I don't know you, and you were the last person to see Tom alive. So why are you saying you don't know where he is?"

"Because I don't." The implication of what Ruff the dog had said sunk in. "Wait a moment! You cannot believe I had anything to do with his disappearance!"

"Nope? I think I can. Why can't I?"

She stuttered but had no answer. She pressed her lips together.

He said, "I mean, he vanished without a note. So did you."

"When was this?"

"We were keeping an eye on Saturday of the Supreme Anarchists' Council, and he vanished at the same time. Next I heard from my old friends in elf court that you led a bunch of Anarchists to attack the Tower of Glass and rob the place. And you have the Ring of Mists. You just said so."

"I did not lead the Anarchists there to the Glass Tower. I mean, I led them there, but I was not leading them." She pouted. "That was not worded in the best way. I was tricked. I think."

"You think? Uh? That slips your mind also?"

"I am an amnesiac."

"An amnesiac? Is that like an Anarchist?" There was a hint of a suspicious growl in his voice.

"No. Nothing like."

"They sound a lot alike."

"An amnesiac means I cannot remember. I have forgotten everything."

"How come you can speak English without an accent?"

"I cannot remember how. I must have learned it."

"So you don't work for the Anarchists?"

"No!"

"But—now wait a minute. If you don't remember, maybe you *do* work for the Anarchists, and you don't remember working for them? Because you don't remember. How 'bout that?"

"I would never betray Tommy-chan."

"How do you know? Maybe you did betray him, and—see if you can follow where I am going with this—and you don't remember betraying him! Because you don't remember. See? How would you know? That is a pretty clever question, you know, right?"

"I know!"

"Yeah, I know, right?"

She sighed. "No, I mean, I know I would never betray him. I do not know how I know, but I know. There are some things the heart knows even if the mind is covered in fog."

"Like what?"

"I beg your pardon?"

"Like, tell me something a heart knows when your brain is fogged."

"Will you ever betray your master? At any time in the future?"

The dog bristled.

She said, "See? But you cannot see the future any more than I can see the past. But we know. You know right from wrong. You know fair from foul. You know what is natural and what is corruption. You know that life with all its snares and glamour is false and cannot be all there is. We all know these things, but none of us can say when we learned them."

6. *Kind of Sneaky*

"That is a good speech."

"So you believe me?"

"Nope. Nope. Not a bit," he said happily. "I am a dog who does not believe you, not one bit."

"Why not? It's the truth!"

"You strike me as being kind of sneaky. Yup! Yup! Sneaky! *Sneeee-keeee…*" He said this with a growl. "You did not knock when you came in, and you did not like it when I shined a light on you, and you slipped a bug on me when you were petting me. That took advantage of my good nature."

"But I did that because I needed to! Not because I wanted to!"

"So? So? Maybe you are telling me this cock-and-bull story now because you need to, not because you want to."

"But why would I work for the Anarchists?"

"Dunno. Maybe you were sick of that crazed loner who kills people and hangs them on trees, and you wanted to get in with a whole group of crazed loners who kill people. Foxes are really sneaky."

"I am not a fox! This is a mask! A mask!"

"So if you are not sneaky, why wear a mask? Why go around shooting people from the shadows?"

"Well… I have enemies."

"Uh-huh. Uh-huh. Hey, listen, ponder this one. Maybe you have enemies because you wear a mask and go around shooting people from the shadows!"

"But I hate the Anarchists! They killed my mother!"

"The Grail Queen?"

"Yes!"

"Sarras was destroyed by the giant Ysbadden."

"The Anarchists helped him."

"How did they help him? What did they do?"

"I– I am not exactly sure about that. They had troops. They brought them on airships."

"Let's see. You hate the Anarchists because they helped the giant destroy the high city of Sarras, and so they were indirectly involved in your mother's death. Because they had airships. But you do not actually remember your mother, or her death. Am I right? Or how they helped? So why do you hate anyone?"

"No, I remember my mother's last words and the attack on the city. I saw that. Part of it."

"I thought you said you forgot everything."

"I forgot that also, but it came back. I hated the Anarchists before I lost my memory."

"But you don't hate them now?"

"I am pretty sure I do. They seem like horrible people."

"But not as horrible as a man who dresses up like a crow, and crouches on rooftops at midnight, and puts a lariat through the window of a guy in bed, and then pulls him out of bed by the neck and out the window, and everyone on the street sees the guy strangled to death in midair, kicking his legs in the light of the moon, and everything. Not horrible like that, eh?"

Yumiko was surprised. "Did Winged Vengeance do that?"

"Last Thursday."

"He did that last week?"

"No, it was months back, but it was Orgoglio Cobweb, who was the Thursday member of the Supreme Council of Anarchists. That was before the new guy got the job. The last Thursday before him."

"That does sound pretty horrible. But maybe the man deserved it."

"Sure. Maybe. Maybe not. But it was not like there was any trial, or the guy got to have his say, or even say a prayer and get shrived before he died, so who knows? Willy Cobweb is a necromancer, and he could summon up the last Thursday's shade and talk to him and find out, but you shot the ghost. You shot the ghost of Orgoglio Cobweb with your magic bow. You kill dead people. That is your job. Kind of a freaky job if you think about it."

Yumiko said, "I am an enemy of the Anarchists. They are hunting me to kill me."

"Really? Then how come Wilcolac has you working in his club? And dancing? Aren't you his servant girl? He really kind of talked down to you. I was there. I heard. And you stood in a corner and did not say anything."

"I am spying on him. In disguise."

"No, no. That's just dumb."

"Dumb? Why?"

"Because it is! Don't you know who that guy is?"

"Wilcolac? No, not really."

"He is famous. He is a magician, a master of tricks and traps and sneaks and slippery cons! If I can figure you out, he can."

Yumiko frowned, remembering her own clear intuition from earlier that morning, before he sent her out with Malen, that Wilcolac had indeed penetrated her disguise. Malen had done so easily enough, and so had Sly Jack Crookshank.

"Don't you think his wolves can smell as well as me?" Ruff said, snorting. "The werewolves of Thursday, his whole pack, their scent was all over that place. It was coming from the basement, but that green-haired tree sprite, Boggy Cobweb, would not take us down there. I think she was trying to get rid of us. And here is a second question—how come you were with the Red Lady all afternoon? Carrying her packages? If you hate the Anarchists so much? Don't you know who she is?"

"She is Lucien Cobweb's lover."

"That is kind of like saying Arthur is Sir Kay's younger brother. She has lots of lovers, and they all hate each other."

"Ah. I don't know who she is."

"She is the Red War Queen. Moth's second wife. Moth, your ancestor. The ancestor of the whole Moth family. She is the mother of Phanes, who married Merlin the Magician's sister, Yglais, who bore Pellehan."

"I see. And who is this?"

"Pellehan is the father of Pellinore, who is the father of Dandrenor, who is your mother. So you spent the whole afternoon with one of the three wives of Moth, who is your own great-great-great-grandmother. Unless I missed a great. And she did not know you?"

"She did. She deduced my secret identity."

"And—?"

"And then she let me go."

"Why did she do that?"

Yumiko said slowly, "The magician told her not to hurt me."

"Why did he do that?"

She frowned in thought but had no answer.

He said, "Think this through. Willy could hire or buy a girl to replace you. Malen is one of the Elders. Like Vivian, like Nimue, like Maeve. Even great lords and barons are careful around them. We call them Antediluvians. They remember the world before the Flood, and their parents remember Eden, and remember helping Eve tend the flowers and Adam dress the vines. If Willy wanted you alive, why put you in danger by sending you to her? And if he did not want you alive, why tell her to spare you?"

"I think he wanted me out of the place. A shipment came in today."

"Which means he knows you are spying on him. He knows."

She had nothing to say.

"So you see why I don't really believe your story. You sure look like you are working for the Anarchists. Or you are a chump, and Wilcolac is conning you. If Wilcolac let you into his house and out of it again, it is because he has someone following you, and he wants you to lead him somewhere."

"Where?"

"At a guess? To your master, Winged Vengeance. That is what Willy was trying to get my master and Matt to do, when they went to visit your club."

"Is there anything I could say to make you trust me?"

"Sure. Just get Winged Vengeance to come by and tell me you are on a mission for him, infiltrating the Anarchists and only pretending to dance and carry packages for them. I understand all about that. I used to be in the intelligence-gathering business myself. I was in bark-ops."

"Black-ops?"

His ears drooped, disappointed. "That was a joke! Tom always laughed at it."

"Winged Vengeance does not trust me."

"Oo-kay-yy... Why do you want me to trust you, again, please? I mean, I don't know you."

"How did Tom meet me?"

"I'm not sure. Winged Vengeance and you would sometimes show up in the same places we were."

"We?"

"The Last Crusade. We are hunting for the same people, but not for the same reason, so your boss and my boss would get in each other's way. The first time, it was kind of friendly, sort of a rivalry; and the second time, it was less friendly because Gil tossed your crow-man out through a plate glass window for something he said; and the last time, it was not friendly at all because you put an arrow in a guy that Gil had promised safe conduct, and he was talking him into defecting. Left us with no leads. He was pretty pissed about that."

"How many people are in this Last Crusade?"

"Fox-girl, are you out of your cottin-pickin' mind? I am not giving you any free intel."

"I would really like you to trust me."

"Well, fine. Give me the Ring of Mists, I'll give it to Gil, and he can swap it to Willy in return for getting Tom back."

"I don't think that is wise."

"Thought so. If you really wanted Tom back, you would have swapped the ring for him the moment Willy made us the offer. So you going to give me the ring?"

"I think I better keep it."

"Okay. Let me ask you one more question. I may just be a dog, but I see things, you know? I keep my nose to the fewmets, as they say."

"Who says that?"

"Dogs. We sniff fewmets. It is a dog thing."

"I will answer your question."

"Remember when we visited your club?"

"Yes."

"That wasn't the question. That was just set up. This is the question: Ready?"

"I am ready!"

"That wasn't the question either. That was me asking if you were ready for the question. Here it is: Why did Willy call you into the room with me and Matt and Gil? Just to stand there?"

"You ordered drinks. He did not order me to leave."

"Why not?"

"He overlooked me." A slight smile touched her lips.

"You think you outsmarted him? Him?"

The smile left her face. "No?"

"No. He does not overlook things. He is not an overlooker. He wanted to see if you would show some sign of recognition to Gilberec, who is your cousin. Your first cousin because his mom is your aunt."

"But I don't have any memory!"

"Or if Gil would recognize you."

"Why didn't he?"

"Dunno. Maybe 'cause he was raised alone. Because you lived in the clouds, where no one who does not have wings can go. Because you wear a mask and hide in the shadows. Why do you do that, by the way? Why not fight fair and square, out in the bright sun where everyone can see, honorably?"

She remembered the wall screen in the hermit cell where Winged Vengeance slept. Yumiko repeated it, but changed the last word. "Those who flee the light adore the dark. Let me be in the dark and bring my terrors, and dark they will no more adore, for it is become their foe. Even in the darkest night, there must be justice."

Chapter 5

I Am a Sneaky Fox

1. Good Faith

The dog scratched himself behind the ear, first with one gloved forepaw and then with his hindpaw. "Heh. Not sure what to make of that. But let us say we did trust you. What do you want us to do for you?"

"If Gilberec fights him, Garlot plans to cheat and use his Cloak of Mists to strike down Gilberec from behind. So I want you to call off the duel. Call it off."

The dog made a snorting noise that might have been a laugh. "He's a guy. He is more of a guy than most guys. He's Gil. Call it off? That's not going to happen."

A shiver of frustration ran through her. A half-buried memory of a thing she recalled having once said surfaced: that her father had lived on the haunted peaks of Shinzan and Honzan, venturing to hunt the *namahage* with bow and spear by night. Into such a life he commanded his wife should descend from the solemn peace of the celestial city to join him. Yumiko wondered what defect in the masculine spirit prevented men from understanding that danger and bloodshed were undesirable states of affair.

Yumiko said, "Then he has got to throw the fight or back out after making an excuse. Garlot must remain alive."

"Heh. Heh. You are pretty funny. You want Gil to take a dive? To tell a fib? That is not going to happen. So you want Garlot to survive the duel to the death, do you? What? You put a wager on him or something? You don't want Malen, the lady whose packages you tote on shopping trips, to be sad when her brother gets killed? What is it?"

"A friend of mine was kidnapped by Garlot. I need him alive to find her."

"But if you forget everything, how come you remember your friends? And who is this friend?"

But then Yumiko remembered Elfine confessing to being a smuggler and how the little blonde had been wary of the police. From what little she had seen of the young Swan Knight, he was not the type who would wink at violations of the law. Yumiko's intuition was to trust and talk, but her sense of caution told her not to spill secrets whose repercussions she could not guess.

Instead, she said, "Something bad will happen if the two of them fight. When Wilcolac calls, tell me where the duel will be."

"He did not call. He wrote. A challenge letter."

"Please tell Gil not to accept!"

"Too late. He wrote back straight away."

"Garlot will kill him!"

"Nope! Garlot is going to lose and lose in a bad way!"

"Garlot will cheat!"

"Then he will fight in a bad way and lose in a bad way."

"Tell me where the match will be."

The dog wrinkled his muzzle skeptically. "I am not sure you are cleared to know."

"Please tell me! It's important!"

"Why? What are you planning?" He made a snorting noise in his nose.

And when she did not answer, he said, "So how does this work? I am supposed to trust you and answer your questions, but not the other way around?"

She said, "What if I told you something you want to know? As a sign of good faith?"

The dog said, "Faith is good. That is what Matt says. Good faith must be even better. So what do I want to know?"

Yumiko said, "Well, what do you want to know?"

"Tell me what you are planning?"

"Not that. Something else."

"What else?"

"I don't know!"

The dog yawned, gaping his jaws and curling his red tongue. "And I do? You're the one making the offer. Go ahead and offer. Offer away! Offer your mouth off."

"Tom is alive and going to be at the Tithing Ground."

The dog's head jerked erect, and his ears stood up. "When?"

"I don't know when. Wilcolac will be there also. And a whole cavalcade will escort him. He will see Tom but will not see him. It will give Wilcolac peace of mind for seven years."

"What's that mean?"

"I don't know. These are some things I overheard. Tom is in an enchanted sleep. Lucien Cobweb is not willing to wake Tom and torture him because he is afraid Tom will open his mouth and call on names which they cannot withstand. Tom has a fragment of something called the celestial cerulean around his neck, but Wilcolac does not know how to get a virgin to defile it. How am I doing? Is this something you wanted to know?"

"You are doing good, Fox. This is all good stuff."

"What is the celestial cerulean?"

"You know how mermaids sometimes collect treasures from sunken ships?"

"Ah. I'm sorry, no."

"The sea-dwellers don't have fires, so they don't smelt ore or blow glass, and the only time they see things like gold coins, steel swords, or green bottles is from shipwrecks. Well, the fall of Sarras was like a shipwreck. Cerulean is to land-dwellers like gold or glass is to a mermaid. The word just means any sort of trinket that falls out of a castle in the clouds—any sort of stuff the wind-dwellers make."

"Do you know where the Tithing Ground is?"

The dog cocked his head so that one ear stood up. "I do not know where the Tithing Ground is. I know *what* it is. It is the boundary between the Night World and the World Which is Darker Than Night. It only appears once each seven years."

"I was hoping you knew. It would have been easier."

"You are going to go back to the Cobbler's Club, aren't you? And put on your other costume? Even though I told you not to? You think you are so super sneaky, you can sneak after the Magician when he leaves to go see Tom? Or not see him. Whatever."

The dog's tone was accusatory. Yumiko felt her pride prick her. She snapped, "So! Is Gil going to fight the Red Knight even though I told him not to? He thinks he is so super knightly that he can win even if Garlot uses magic and cheats?"

The dog's ear drooped. "Gil is not as interested in winning as you would think. There is this guy he wants to impress, a guy he has never seen. If he lives, if he dies, that does not matter as long as he lives and dies just like this guy wants him to."

"A guy he has never met? You mean King Arthur?"

"Nope. Some other guy. Your Mom kept his cup."

2. Betting A Limb

"Will Gil kill the Red Knight?"

"Sure! He is really good with a lance. Were you thinking of betting a limb? I think you humans should have tails. That way you can have something to wag when you are happy. You bare your teeth when you are happy, and that just looks weird. And I saw you dancing in the club. You were trying to wiggle your tail, but it did not look right."

Yumiko felt her cheeks growing red, and so she pulled down her mask to hide her face. The dog was apparently getting the better of her in this conversation.

"Are you covering your face because you are embarrassed? I can smell embarrassment, so there is no point in covering your face."

The dog was very definitely getting the better of her in this conversation.

She said, "I am not sure what else I can offer. Let me ask. If I were a trusted member of Super Action Team Swan, what would you have me do?"

"You told me who Thursday was. That was helpful."

"When did I do that?"

"In front of that warehouse near the river that smelled like canned broccoli and carrots. The one Thursday blew up." The warehouse opposite Catoblepas Shipping in Weehawken had been called Mr. Vegetable. It seemed that Ruff remembered the smell but forgot the name on the sign. "You blurted out his name in front of everyone. I laughed about it later because I bet it hurt his feelings. I bet. I bet. But not my tail. I am not betting my tail, no. Gambling is stupid!"

She said, "I know other names. Euhemerus Cobweb is Sunday, Lord of Ghosts, for it is in his name that the shadow of the Hunter King, named Le Maudit in life, was summoned. A man named Zahack is one of the Anarchist Lords. He has twisted snakes instead of hands. Another one is Rotwang."

The dogs ears perked up. "Rotwang Cobweb? You know him?"

"Yes. He is the one who built the Iron Mole Machine that Tom and I rode to break into the Tower of Glass. Tom stole it from him. He has a prosthetic for a hand. Is that the one?"

The dog shook his head. "Tom is apprenticed to Rotwang. For years, Rotwang has been teaching Tom how to be a mad scientist and to use both unnatural magic and dangerous technology together, mixing the two in order to meddle with nature is ways man was never meant to venture, combining them into an abomination of awesomeness!"

"Did you say abomination of… awesomeness?"

"That is how Tom described it. Did you know he made his own crater on the moon? Sort of by accident. A big one. He said he named it after you."

"That is so sweet!" She clasped her hands together before her bosom, wondering at the pounding of her heart. "He named it after me?"

"Sure did!" the dog nodded. "Yummy Cutie Crater."

"Is it normal for an amnesiac girl to want to kill her boyfriend she does not remember?"

The dog said, "If it is Tom, then, yeah, I think it is. It really is. Anyway, don't go around telling people that Rotwang is an Anarchist. That is pretty top secret stuff."

"But he *is* an Anarchist. He is the one who hid the moon-door aboard the Iron Mole. Wilcolac told you so!"

The dog scratched. "And Gil says Willy was telling the truth. That let you off the hook."

"Off the hook? You think I smuggled the armies of Anarchists into the Glass Tower?"

"Yup. Or we used to. You were the obvious suspect."

"But—but that's insane! Winged Vengeance is the one who closed the moon-door and cut off their retreat so that the elfs would kill them all. Why would I have smuggled an Anarchist army into the Glass Tower if I am the disciple and sidekick of Winged Vengeance?"

"What do you mean? Why would you be sneaky, and trick Tom into taking you along, and be sneaky, and trick the Anarchists into following you, and be sneaky again, and trick the Anarchists into a spot where they would be cut off from all escape, and die? You really don't remember what you and the vigilante are like, do you?"

Underneath her mask, she scowled. "I seem not to have been very admirable."

"It's because you are a fox. They are mean and sneaky."

"I am a girl."

"You don't act much like one."

"What does that mean?"

"Crawling around in the dark killing people from behind! It is ugly when girls fight. Turns them mean and sneaky, like foxes. It is almost as if you don't like it. Now, Gil, he likes fighting. Got him kicked out of school and everything! You should get a man to do your fighting for you."

"I am trying to find mine. I wish you would help me. Where is this duel taking place?"

3. Choosing a Side

"Well, well. I should not tell you, but I will. Atop the Brooklyn Bridge. Noon tomorrow. Which is today, I guess, since it is after midnight."

"The Brooklyn Bridge? You're kidding me."

"I am dogging you. Only goats kid."

"What?"

"They have to pick a famous spot because the Black Spell is weaker there. The Anarchists are expecting Garlot to win, and they want the rumor that no one can beat them to be spread far and wide across the Twilight World in story and song."

"What about the traffic? All the Daylight folk?"

"They will remember some other event, like a bomb scare or something. And if the Anarchists cannot arrange for the city of New York to close a bridge, they should give up being secretly in control of the world."

"I thought the elfs were secretly in control of the world."

"Well, the elfs are kind of like evil cowboys herding mankind into the slaughterhouse door, and the Anarchists are kind of like evil foxes preying on the livestock, trying to start a stampede."

"What about the half-and-halves? People like me?"

"The Mustardseeds are on the side of Alberec, the Cobwebs are on the side of Erlkoenig, the Peaseblossoms are not allowed to leave the Third Hemisphere, and the Moths are not allowed to enter. The Anarchists are mostly Cobwebs, but not all of them, and they are not on anyone's side."

"Who is on the side of mankind?"

"Gil. Me. Matthias. Tom, if we can find him. Whose side are you on?"

"Tom," she said. "I want to be at his side." She pushed back her mask and wiped her cheeks with the palm of her glove.

"Are you crying? You did not used to do that. I mean, I only saw you three or four times, but I am a good judge of character. You are not the type who cries."

"What type am I?"

"The type who shoots people from cowardly ambush, watches them die without offering them a drink or a mercy killing, then leaves the body to rot without so much as a polite note to the widow. Pretty cold, really. You are not a nice person. Are you different? What happened to you?"

"I died. I was dead."

"What? For real? Or is this like a figure of speech?"

"Yes. Both. Maybe. I am not sure."

The dog rose to all fours, shook himself, and said, "Brr! Well, at least I know now what Tom sees in you."

A giddy sensation passed through her. "Really? What? Tell me!"

"Same reason he likes atomic piles, and walking on the moon, and strapping a rocket to his back. He likes everything weird and dangerous."

4. *What He Sees in You*

She scowled. “He likes me because I am *weird* and *dangerous*?”

“And you are nubile, fertile, and fecund as well as being youthful, virginal, voluptuous, and luscious. I am sure the skintight black suit helps, too. Next best thing to having black fur. Also, you have bright eyes and white teeth. That is a sign of health.”

She rubbed her temples, angry at the sensation of warmth rising in her cheeks. “I really have no memory of why I liked this guy. Are you sure he liked me? Aside from my teeth.”

“And your hair!” said the dog cheerfully. “A shiny pelt is also a sign of health. He talked about your hair a lot. Because it is long. Men do not have hair like dogs do, and so you miss it. Human psychological problems are related to you being bald all over. That’s my theory. Also, he is in heat. He is a boy. Boys are always in heat year round. It means your litters come at all seasons, which I frankly think is a mistake. What if you have whelps in the winter, when food is low? I betcha never thought about that; I betcha. Huhn! Did you ever think about that?”

“No, I honestly can say I have no memory of ever contemplating that particular aspect of human reproductive tactics. Thank you. Did he say anything else about me?”

“I was going to be the best man.”

“Wait—so he did ask me to marry him?” She began breathing hard, clutching her throat. “What did I say? Did I say yes?” And then she blurted out, “I knew it! I *knew* it!”

“Uh. Uh. What was the question again?”

“Am I married? Am I engaged? What happened?”

“Gee, I dunno. He was going to ask you, but then he disappeared. But he was serious about it. He drew up plans for your honeymoon cottage. He never told anyone but me. I was sworn to secrecy.”

“Where is this honeymoon cottage?”

“On the drawing board.”

“What did it look like? Did it have roses?”

“Nope. No roses. It was round. Round like a ball. But it did have had graviton-powered mass drivers evenly spaced around the hull. Each one could both produce thrust and act as orbit-to-surface megaton-strength kinetic bombardment weapon. It was sweet!"

"Pardon me? Did you say *hull*?"

"You cannot have a honeymoon on the moon without a space-traveling bathysphere. It's got to be airtight. There is no air there. On the moon. The hull keeps the air in."

Yumiko gritted her teeth. "I have to find him. Just to prove that he is real. No one could do what he does."

"Funny. He said the same about you when you two first met."

"How did we meet?"

"I was not there. I only heard about it. You crashed in through the upper window of a restaurant on top of a skyscraper and shot a bunch of gangland crimelords with arrows, and you stuck knives into a few more. And there was a lot of tear gas, but Tom keeps a breathing apparatus in his fountain pen. He was handcuffed to a chair but cut his way free with the rotary hacksaw hidden in his wristwatch. I don't know the details, but you and he got trapped in the kitchen from the gunfire coming from the military helicopter gunship circling the skyscraper, and he made an explosive out of kitchen cleaning chemicals and blew open the locked elevator door, but you went up the shaft to the roof, and he went down using his magnetic shoes, and he was kind of mad at you for not thanking him for saving your life. At least, that is how he told it."

"Why was I killing gangsters?"

"I dunno. It's kind of a thing you do."

"Why was Tom handcuffed to a chair in the same room with them?"

"He thought they were supplying the Anarchists with contraband, so he went in to go talk with them without telling anybody where he was going. He's crazy like that."

A sense of impatience seized her. This amazing man, her fiancé, was missing, and she did not know if Wilcolac was going to the Tithing Ground later, sooner, or now. There were more questions she had for the dog, many more, but they would have to wait.

Yumiko asked how to find him again without being led into an underground trap. "Do you have a phone?"

"You mean like a dog phone in my doghouse? No. Elfs don't trust phones because it is too easy to fake voices, but on parchment you can write protective runes to prevent forgeries. There is a walled graveyard behind Saint Jean Baptiste Church on Third Avenue. Leave a note in the stone pot atop the grave of Dominic Amorth 1898-1961. He'll see that Matthias gets it. Do you know ciphers?"

"None that I remember."

"This one is pretty easy. Write your message in Morse code. The first ten consonants in the alphabet are dots; the second ten are dashes; one vowel is a space between letters; two vowels together is a space between words; and the letter Y is the end of a sentence. Spaces and punctuation, just put where you'd like. Takes four times as long to say anything, but good luck trying to use frequency analysis to break it. So to say, 'I am a very sneaky fox,' you would write down something like, *'Claim tons! I act eel chrum act dot! Mr. Touch Latham of to shreth! Treach the Strathcray!'* Got how it works?"

"You enciphered that in your head just now?"

"You kidding? I worked on that for hours before you showed up. Anyway, nice talking to you. I gotta go. Don't do anything stupid, okay? Don't get me in trouble for talking to you."

The animal exited through the small round hatch and into the crawlway beyond, where nothing as tall and bipedal as she could follow. Yumiko worked the engine to raise the grate and open the louvers of the spillway leading out. She expanded her glider wings, swooped down through the dry tunnel, and dexterously darted through the metal louvers, and then she was out over the river. The starless cloud-glare of a city night was above her.

5. *Sleepless*

It seemed wiser not to return to the Cobbler's Club. Yumiko's delight at having money to spend among the Daylight Men turned sour after the third hotel she attempted turned her away because she could produce no credit card, driver's license, or identification. Telling the desk clerk that her number was forty-nine, as Elfine once had instructed, did not mend matters.

She found a hotel that charged by the hour. To judge by the décor and the furtive aspect of its patrons, it was used only by adulterers and their paramours.

She doffed her mask. Her snug black leather catsuit attracted stares from the clerk, but not puzzlement, for she was one of the more modestly dressed women in the lobby. She did not like the looks of the place, but at least it seemed safer than sleeping in a bus station.

Chapter 6

Hastilude

1. Heraldry

By noon, all approaches to the Brooklyn Bridge were blocked by cars. Apparently, it was commonplace in New York City these days for traffic jams to turn into mob scenes since the riot police were out in force, wearing heavy gear and lugging large shields. Police barricades occupied all the ramps near the Manhattan entrance to the bridge, and more barricades were placed along South Street, FDR Drive, and even the East River bike path. A line of police boats prevented river traffic from passing under the bridge.

Yumiko, since dawn, had been perched, invisible and motionless, atop the Manhattan-side bridge tower. Hours passed. She was as patient as a cat watching a mousehole.

Below her, in the middle of the elevated pedestrian walkway in the middle of the empty bridge, now rose two brightly colored tents or pavilions, roughly two hundred feet apart.

One was blue and white and displayed the pennant of a swan. The other was red and black. The device on this pennant was a fish with tusks and dorsal spines of gold. A throng of men surrounded one tent, and a pair of figures was at the other.

When these pavilions were being set up, Yumiko nimbly made her way down one of the suspension cables for a closer view. The wooden fence meant to separate footpath from the bike path had been draped over with colored fabrics. The warhorses were positioned on opposite sides of the opposite ends of this fence. Yumiko knew they were the warhorses because they were taller and larger than the geldings or mules gathered behind each pavilion. The warhorses were armored and caparisoned, one in blue and silver, the other in black and red, adorned and splendid and terrible to the eye. Both horses had cloven hooves like those of a deer, the lashing tail was like a lion's tail, sinuous and long with a puff of hair only at the end. These were steeds from fairyland. Both were roans. They were as alike in build and height as brothers. Small wonder Yumiko had once confused them.

Neither knight had mounted as yet.

Sir Garlot stood by his steed, and his shield and spear and helm were yet in the hands of his squire.

The shield was black with a blood-red emblem of a tusked sea-monster bent and diving. The upper part of the shield was adorned with a crescent poised with its points upward. Images of this fanged fish were also on his surcoat and steed. A gilded statuette of the same figure peered from the crest of his dark helm, goggle eyes low and staring, tail held high.

Half-transparent, ghostlike, and baffling to the eye, his wide fog-hued cloak streamed from his broad shoulders, sometimes lifted by the whispering winds of earth and sometimes by silent winds from other realms.

Yumiko recognized from the Cobbler's Club the vassals of Garlot standing behind him. The first was a burly dwarfish creature in a black coat and rimless metal cap, armed with a warhammer. The second was a man-at-arms whose coat was gemstones and whose tongue was as bright as a coal of fire. Smoke rose from between his teeth. The third was a ten-foot-tall six-fingered warrior with scarlet hair. He was clad in mail and bore a two-handed sword great enough to hew a horse in twain. She cursed them in her heart as bad tippers.

Yumiko saw no men at Sir Gilberec's tent, but she did see dogs. At least two dozen mutts and strays of various stages of unkempt savagery were seated in a semicircle on their hunches behind him. None was small. None wore collars.

In addition, strange sounds from his tent hinted that living things were swarming there, but from above, she could not glimpse them.

Sir Gilberec himself was standing at the lists. He was in blue and white, and his helm was adorned with swan wings. His cloak was blue. The sign of the swan was on his shield, surcoat, and crest. His armor was silver, and adorned with diamonds, and was like white fire were the sun touched it.

He had no retinue, save for one figure with him no taller than a child. This one was dressed like a pageboy in a tabard adorned with the device of a white swan. His throat was hidden by a wide ruffed collar. In one hand was a trumpet. His gloves and boots were green, and a wide-brimmed cavalier's hat with a white plume hid his face from Yumiko, who was above him. But when he raised his voice, she recognized the scratchy, growling voice of Ruff the dog. How he contrived to stand on his hind legs or carry a trumpet, Yumiko was not sure.

"...and do you also swear to use no unknightly ploy nor devising, nor spell, chant, charm, trick, or unworthy sleight to gain any advantage? That you allow the fallen opponent gentle right to rise again and if he be unhorsed, also to dismount and continue the melee afoot?"

"In no wise," called Garlot. Yumiko heard him clearly. His voice was like deep music, and the magic of the elfs was in it. "I denounce yon fool as a half-breed, a Moth, common and a sure dastard, born of nothing: his titles and dignities are lies. No knight he! Neither gentleness nor courtesy use I. I will slaughter him as I would a swine or a slave, by fair means or foul as please me. Here is mine oath!" and he spat on the deck of the walkway.

Gil was armed, with shield and spear in hand, and his head was hidden in his helm. This helmet was sleek and strange to see, not like the heavy helm with a pointed visor the squire of Garlot held. Gil's voice seemed harsh and commonplace after the eerie baritone of Garlot. But his words were dignified: "Wise not to speak false oaths in my ear, Sir Knight. I will offer you the gentle courtesies you denounce, that my victory be more worshipful."

"Swagger and preen, my cockahoop!" sneered Garlot. "Is your half-mortal strength fit to fight an immortal? What is Twilight? Dying Dusk surrenders ever to Night!"

"As does Night to Dawn," said Gil. "Weary my ears with no more boasts. Arms, not words, shall decide."

And he used his spear like a pole to vaunt into the high-backed saddle in a strong and fluid leap, without releasing spear or shield from hand, as lightly as if he did not bear forty or fifty pounds of war harness on his frame. The great red horse reared and curveted, and Sir Gilberec flourished his lance on high. Sir Garlot's men murmured their applause until Sir Garlot turned and scowled at them with dark brows.

Yumiko did not fully understand why Sir Gilberec's effortless leap into the saddle was so impressive until she saw Sir Garlot mount up, his motion ponderous in his heavy armor. In his hands he took up the reins and also a stout cord to tie himself in the saddle. Only after he was ahorse did he don his helm and then take up the lance and shield.

The two men moved as if on parade, horses stepping with high gait and slow dignity down the lists. The two saluted as they passed each other by lifting their lances. Then, at the far end, each man near the tent of his foe, they turned. The horses stomped and fretted, snorting. In the distance, honking horns from the endless traffic jams clearing the great bridge had caused were like the voices of geese far away.

2. *Tilt*

Ruff stood near a rack on which several lances were propped. He lifted his trumpet, and so did the lizard-eyed Eft. A braying note that split the air issued from the bell of Ruff's trumpet; a louder note and a gush of flame came from the other.

The warsteeds were like arrows seen flying from the bow before the singing of the string is heard. Like falcons in flight was their swiftness. Their skirts rippled like white-capped sea-waves in a gale, snapping in the wind of their speed, and the barding clanged and rang.

The hooves of the red steed of Gil cast up divots of wood out of the walkway, and the detonation of noise was a jackhammer. The uproar of clatter from the steed of Garlot was no less, but as his steed flew, the cloak of Garlot left a trail of fog in the air behind him and spread left and right like the wings of a storm spreading.

Both men, at first, rested the butt of the lance on thigh, and the small pennants near the sharpened blade fluttered gaily. Closer they thundered.

Each was in precise control of his steed; each man's kneecap was only an inch away from the wood of the fence separating the steeds. Both now raised their shields, one blue as heaven with a shining swan midmost, the other black with a blood-red sea-monster writhing on its surface. Closer yet, and as one their spears dipped gracefully and ominously, tips weaving and ducking lightly like the tips of fencing epees, but with force of man and horse in full career behind the threatening blow.

Each held the heavy spear in his prone palm, resting the weight on forearm and clamping the shaft against body with elbow. Garlot held his dark shield high, as if to protect his head; and Gilberec held his bright shield low, as if to protect his thigh. Both leaned forward in the saddle, stiffening their legs and clamping knees firmly to the heaving sides of their mounts.

Just before the shock, each knight lifted the lance from beneath his arm and brought the tip up. The mist from his cloak exploded silently from the shoulders of Garlot, and he was hidden from view.

The shock of the crash was deafening.

Yumiko could still see Garlot. He had taken on the strange wrongness of perspective ghosts displayed. He and his horse were monochromatic, like a black and white photo. The spears shattered into flinders as they passed, and each man now held merely the truncheon in his hand. Both were reeling in their high saddles like stunned drunks.

It had happened almost too quickly to see. Garlot had driven his invisible lance blade directly toward the helm of the Swan Knight, who, even though blind to his foe, raised his shield and parried the blow.

Meanwhile, Gil, without seeing his target, had raised his lance in a feint toward Garlot's eyes, who straightened in the saddle. This brought the eyeslit of Garlot's heavy jousting helm up out of harm's way but also blocked his vision. He raised his shield as well. But Gil in the same motion dropped the tip again, struck his foe glancingly along the leg, and drove the spearhead under the rim of the shield and into Garlot's midriff. The blow was of such force that the spear shaft bent in a half circle before exploding into fragments.

Garlot's steed ran on. Garlot was slumped in the saddle. Now Yumiko saw Garlot was stained with a black fluid coming from his side. She realized that this was blood but that the mist had robbed it of the appearance of color.

Gilberec's steed galloped past, headed toward the far end of the lists. Although the Swan Knight was still far off, Ruff was holding up a fresh spear, proffering it butt-first toward Gilberec.

Yumiko noted that the squire of Garlot was not making any move to hand his master a new spear. At first, she thought the reason was that the squire could not see the unseen man. But then she saw a wonder. The broken lance of Sir Garlot was burning with many tiny sparks. It was healing, growing, mending itself. Yumiko wondered if this were the same magic Malen had once used to mend a torn robe, something from a dream world were lifetimes could pass in an earthly hour.

Gilberec was also swaying, jarred by the shock, but he kept his saddle. Garlot recovered himself first, straightened in the saddle, and now turned his horse sharply. Like a steeplechaser, Garlot leaped over the cloth and wood barrier separating the horses, and charged toward Gilberec, whose back was to him. Gilberec had only the broken fragment of a spear in hand.

All of a sudden, the two dozen dogs sitting in a semicircle at the blue and white tent now began barking. A black cloud issued from the tent flap. It was a flock of bats, strange to see by day, flapping and chattering.

Gilberec stirred himself at the clamor. He did not turn but called out, "Steed from Erlkoenig, sired of Arion, your master disgraces you! Throw him!"

The horse of Sir Garlot must have heard and understood, for the beast now reared and bucked. More black blood spread across the belly and legs of Garlot. The Red Knight drove his spurs into his steed and sang a strange, loud, deep note, as a song from the roots of the world heard echoing in a dry well. His voice brought his beast back under control.

The bats were circling Garlot's position, and their chirping and shrieking became a shrill frenzy.

Meanwhile, the feral dogs ran down the lists. Some had their noses to the deck; others had their muzzled raised, baying. But the dogs by scent closed in toward the unseen Sir Garlot.

Sir Gilberec did not continue toward the end of the lists where Ruff was barking excitedly and waving the spear butt in the air. Instead, he cast the broken shard of spear from him and drew his sword. Angular letters in a language unknown to Yumiko blazed in the blade, and pale fire, half-invisible in the sun, radiated from the edges and tip. Gilberec stood in his stirrups, elbow high, sword outstretched before him, and he charged toward a foe he could not see: a foe who had a whole spear in hand and could slay any swordsman before ever he would be close enough to strike.

Either he did not know his enemy was armed, or else Gilberec was insane.

Yumiko raised her bow and shot three arrows in rapid succession into Sir Garlot. These were not her red arrows, whose iron heads were poisonous to elfs. These were bodkin heads, meant to pierce armor. None did; all glanced off without penetrating. Her fourth arrow was one of the red ones. It struck Sir Garlot in the thigh, penetrated the metal cuisse, flesh and blood, and pinned his leg to the saddle.

Sir Garlot's men, when they saw Gilberec releasing hounds onto the field, ran to their riding horses to mount up, all except the Eft. The dragon-eyed Eft tossed his helmet aside, ran forward, and breathed out an arching gout of fire of prodigious length. This reached many yards down the lists, falling among the dogs, and causing Sir Gilberec's horse to rear up and whinny in anger. Yumiko shot the Eft in the open mouth, and the arrow head emerged from this back of his skull in a spray of blood that caught fire when it touched air.

The Eft crumpled and fell, and the fire from his wounds spread as a pool spreads.

Sir Garlot cried out in a loud voice. His squire blew a trumpet blast. Sir Garlot and his men turned and fled the field. He had had enough.

Garlot threw his enchanted lance aside. He cut the straps of his heavy shield with a misericorde, and this let him clench his forearm to his belly to block the bleeding wound with his forearm.

Yumiko shot her wirepoon grapnel into the deck and slid down it, using her bowstaff to hang from it. She mounted up on the riding horse of the Eft, which was startled by the weight of an unseen rider. This horse, seeing all its fellows fleeing and scenting their panic, whinnied and chased after them.

A great wall of fog erupted from the shoulders of the Red Knight as he swirled his cloak and cast it over his men. They faded from view and lost all colors. The pack horses and mules followed after Garlot as he ran.

So did the horse to whose neck Yumiko clung.

3. *Flight and Fog*

Down the bridge they galloped, with Sir Gilberec, alone, in pursuit, one youth chasing three armed men and a squire.

But Sir Gilberec shouted, calling on the horses to halt. The riding mounts of Garlot's men became ungovernable, rearing and plunging. The two dozen dogs and more entered the foggy cloud hiding the invisible Sir Garlot and his unseen retinue, sniffing and baying, coming closer.

Through the fog, clinging to the neck of her rearing horse, Yumiko could see the bright silhouette of Sir Gilberec on his strong, swift steed, calling out the names of King Arthur and Saint Michael the Archangel. The light from his flaming sword made a rainbow in the foggy mists around him.

Yumiko realized that Gilberec was not insane, but had a clear advantage over any mounted foe if the mount could hear and understand the word of the Son of Adam and know them to be true.

But it did not serve her purposes that Sir Garlot be slain this day.

With a swift motion of her hand, she fitted half a dozen microgrenades into the slot on one of her folding boomerangs and threw it. The whirling metal weapon became visible when it left the cloud of fog, spinning toward Sir Gilberec. He raised his shield and deflected it into the deck, where it skipped along like a lopsided wheel, exploding into stabbing flashes of light, tear gas, and dense clouds.

The second boomerang he did not see until it rebounded from his helmet, which rang like a gong. Both boomerangs looked like miniature crop-dusting planes doing tailspins, putting out smoke to blind his eyes, pepper spray to pain the noses of his dogs. The delay of even a moment allowed Garlot and his vassals to open a lead.

4. *Into the Night World*

Over the police cars barricading the bridge entrance, the elf-steeds of Garlot and his men leaped as lightly as deer. For about a hundred yards, no more than that, the horses picked their way among the motionless and honking cars gridlocked about the entrance ramp. Garlot raised his hand and sang. A flurry of sparks flew up from his fingers and spread like ripples in a pond. All the humans on the street slowly sank down and slept, the car engines sputtered and died, and the lights of traffic signals went out. The silent cavalcade raced on. Yumiko did not see whether they trampled any slumbering men, women, or children trapped in their spell, for the fugitives were fleeing with all haste, and the calls of Gilberec were behind them as they fled, and all four winced and cursed when he said the name of Christ.

Yumiko was fearful that Sir Garlot would be able to see her as easily as she saw him. But it proved to be not so. Garlot's frog-mouth-shaped jousting helm was not a battle helm, and the eyeslits were placed too high for him to see around him, except when he leaned forward in the posture of a lancer ready to strike. Whether he was awake or had fainted in his armor, Yumiko could not say, for he lolled and swayed alarmingly in the high saddle, and only the rope binding him in place prevented his fall.

The squire lad came alongside the Eft's horse to which Yumiko clung. Without slowing his gallop, he dexterously snared the trailing reins with his spearhaft, took them up, and tied them to his saddle pommel. It was neatly done. On the two horses ran. Neither he nor any other saw her.

In the second hundred yards, they turned and went down a slope. The change was gradual, and the horses were galloping, so Yumiko did not see and did not after clearly recall how it had been done, but suddenly they were among buildings that looked like the buildings of New York, but were not. These had no glass in the windows, and their facades were overgrown and draped with grapevines and ivy, and plants filled all the sidewalks in wild profusion: deadly nightshade, henbane, mandrake, datura, felonwort, and various bright mushrooms gleaming with fungoid light.

The road under their hooves was not macadam nor concrete, but a crystal that gleamed in the shadows.

There were no people here, no street signs, no automobiles. Between the skyscrapers in the harbor, she saw a colossal statue of a stern and kingly bat-winged being, crowned in rays, holding aloft a mace to smite, not a torch to illume.

The sound of Sir Gilberec and the gleam from his sword were lost behind them, for the pursuer could not see nor scent them. Yumiko did not see any bats flying after.

Sir Garlot reined his steed and gathered all the fogs of his cloak to himself. With the help of his squire, he broke the arrow shaft from his thigh and mounted a palfrey. This let his warsteed gallop after with no other burden but the horse's barding. But the red arrowhead must have penetrated the great steed's side and must have pained him, for the footfalls were not as strong as they should have been.

The squire said, "Sir, let us have the harness off you that I might bind up your hurt."

But Garlot kicked the palfrey into a trot, not pausing to undo his helm or heavy armor. He said, "The Cauldron of Youth awaits in Is-Elfydd. If but one blood drop or strand of hair of mine yet lives, all life will be restored to me."

The horses were swift and not allowed to rest. Quickly, they arrived at a place that was not Central Park. Yumiko had seen this landscape before. Here was the palatial fortress in the place of Belvedere Castle; this time she clearly saw the fair-featured and cold-faced elfs with silver spears and black silk surcoats standing watch, their eyes as bright and regal as the eyes of falcons.

Past the jousting grounds at the Great Lawn's outdoor theater Garlot and his men galloped. Bloodstains were all along the side and flank of the palfrey Garlot rode. Here, three other elfin knights riding strange split-hoofed steeds with a horse's head and tails of a lioness came riding alongside, calling out and asking the news.

The Nephilim cried back, "Woe and treachery! Sir Garlot was struck unmannerly a blow most dolorous! Make way! Open the gate! Open wide the gate!" And these three other knights raised ram horns to their lips, and blew a blast, and added their clear and penetrating voices to his.

Other riders came running alongside or went before. Now they approached the tall hills, crowned with stone tables and standing stones, looming in the shadows of vast trees up from whose branches villages and towers of bright glass, transparent stones, and shining ceramic rose.

Soon a brightly colored cavalry was all about them as an escort, and two gold-eyed young maidens in cloaks of owl feathers soared along just above their heads, calling out blessings, healing chants, and kind words. And still no one saw Yumiko.

The ground opened, and a corridor as broad as a tunnel dove into the ground. The air was bright and dancing with a myriad of colored lamps, scented with soft spring winds, and haunted by soft echoes of a silvery music that had no name.

Her horse trotted on the heels of Garlot's squire's. Into the underground realm she passed, and nothing hindered her. The cave mouth closed behind her, leaving the surface realm behind.

Chapter 7

The Cauldron of Youth

1. Unwatchful Guards

The lamps grew brighter as the underground ramp passed through three gates, one faced with carven slabs of copper, one of bronze, one of a reddish metal Yumiko did not know. Archer's slits like squinting eyes peered from the walls, and murder holes shaped like gargoyles with dangling tongues glared down from the roof.

The inner panels of the gates, which had been flung open to receive him, were coated with polished silver. As the cavalcade passed through, she saw many knights and squires, Elfs and Efts, Nephilim and Nibelung, all with plumes and cloaks and banners and torches crowding around Garlot and his retinue in the reflection. She also caught a glimpse of a slender white figure with a white fox-face visible in the reflection. It was her image in the mirrored gate, but the glimpse was lost in the crowd of superhuman and semi-human faces, bodies, steeds, stags, leopards, and feathered riding beasts.

Only one officer attempt to halt the rush, a tall elf in a black surcoat wearing a wreathe of mandragora and amaranth. He stood in the path, calling that all must be inspected lest a shape-taker or evil ghost smuggle itself in. But the six-fingered Nephilim riding at Garlot's shoulder, without slowing his galloping steed, shouted, "Garlot is the son of Phanes! Whose son are you, under-creature?" and he flourished his mace at the officer, whose head was turned instantly into the head of a frog and was thus rendered unable to answer.

Thereafter, no one barred the way.

2. The Stable

Past the third gate, the corridor opened into a vast cavern. In the middle of the air were three great lamps like moons of crystal holding silver fire. The cavern floor was a valley shaped like a bowl. Gardens, grape arbors, and groves of cedar trees were here along with groves of giant mushrooms and gleaming fungi with puffballs of phosphorous; all were watered by small, bright, rippling streams that led to a central pond of water clear as air.

Ignoring all the winding pathways, Garlot and the cavalcade raced directly down the slope, trampling or leaping over rosebushes, fungi beds, short hedges, or garden walls whose bricks were mother of pearl, green smaragds, or black onyx. Yumiko saw no huts or houses in this underground garden, but the booming hooves of their horses ran over doors and windows set in the ground like trapdoors and skylights.

They came to the central pond and dove in, horses and all, without slowing. The water was around them, but it felt neither cold nor wet. Down they drifted, and a blood cloud rose up from the stomach of Garlot like a plume. The lakebed of the water gave way beneath them, as insubstantial as an illusion, and the horses passed without pause below and were in midair, with a vast well dropping underfoot and the waters like a roof above. Yumiko felt dry, and the coat of her horse was not wet.

A bridge made of gossamer film, writhing like a live thing, swiftly and gently reached from the balcony at the side of the vast central well gaping beneath them, and the many horses found its crystal surface under their hooves. Without pause the cavalcade continued to run. Down the slope of the gossamer bridge they ran.

The beams of the colored moons above came through the rippling lake as if through a lens.

The horse Yumiko rode landed on a balcony whose wide and pointed archways facing inward looked upon the vast shaft of air. There were ranks of archways, each beneath the next, reaching downward as far as the eye could see.

Flitting like motes through this shaft were winged servants, bug sized or doll sized or child sized, toting mops or yokes of buckets or baskets of laundry, going from lower balconies to higher or back again.

Yumiko craned her neck. It was all one balcony, winding down like the groove in the horn of a unicorn. The beam of silver from the lake overhead reached down like a finger of moonlight. From far below, she heard the sound of thousands of hammer blows on anvils: an army of smiths busily at work.

They passed gates and doorways opening into arsenals, barracks, and underground stalls or kennels or mews where steeds and hounds and hawks were kept, or creatures odder yet, smilodons and woolly mammoths, Tasmanian tigers, Irish elk, shining hippogriffs.

They came to a stall where Garlot dismounted. The floor was straw. He said, "Batraal son of Barkayal! Into your hands I place my destrier, brave Tachebrun. He is of the blood of Arion, steed of the wind. See to his wound!"

The six-fingered man was apparently named Batraal, for he answered, "Sir! This is the work of Winged Vengeance. For see! The red arrow is his sign."

But the stout, squat creature in the black coat said, "Let the elfs stand back! Nibelung hands can touch the iron unharmed. This work is Vig's. Ither! Hale you the master to his cauldron."

Ither was the elfin squire. He came forward, and only now did he undo and remove the awkward helm and heavy breastplate of his master. Sir Garlot had made no complaint before; but now he screamed and swore terrible blasphemies as the pain of motion when his habergeon was pulled over his head tore at him, and the sticky red undercoat of linen cut away. Red blood now ran freely down Garlot's legs and splashed on Ither. The cloak of fogs took on a pink hue as particles of blood floated in the airy fabric.

Garlot said, "Ither! Your shoulder to me. Batraal! To my treasure house. Let none else come."

Ither said, "Sir! A surgeon of skilled hands is nigh. Let us pull the spearhead from your wound before it gets worse."

Garlot spat blood and uttered a proud laugh. "The Cauldron of Youth is at hand. What matter if the wound is better or worse?" And he yanked the lance head roughly from his own guts. Now blood and more doubtful fluids gushed in earnest from the wound, and he fainted away as one dead.

At the same time, two bald grooms with faces like monkeys came and led the horse Yumiko rode to a stall. She nimbly jumped up into the rafters and clung to a roofbeam.

The grooms undid the saddle and furnishings of the dead man's mount and began brushing it. From her high angle, she could see into the next stall. The wounded warhorse of Garlot had been freed of barding and saddle and was lying on his side. Its belly rose and fell as it panted. A veterinarian in white, wearing a wreathe of healing herbs on his head, stood peering over the head of Vig the Nibelung, who was drawing the arrow, telling him how to do it. They were preoccupied and did not see what Yumiko saw. A gush of black water came from the throat of the coughing warhorse and spread across the straw.

Two black mice came out of the steed's mouth with the water. Their motions seemed stiff, unnatural, unliving but quick, like toys whose mainsprings were tightly wound. Their whiskers did not twitch, and their eyes did not blink. The two black mice scampered into the straw, along the baseboard, and through a knothole in the wood.

3. *The Great Balcony*

As Garlot swayed, Ither caught him in his arms. The squire spoke in a loud voice, ordering the throng of well-wishers and onlookers out of the way. He then called for linen. Batraal the Nephilim came and helped Ither bind their master's midriff. Batraal insisted they tie the cloak of mists about their master. He was not willing to have any other touch so rare a treasure nor to bear it himself.

Then, the two each lifted Garlot in their arms and ran quickly out the archway and down the balcony with him. Yumiko followed, running along the tops of the walls of the stalls to reach the door without brushing into anyone in the throng.

Batraal and Ither were already moving quickly down the spiral ramp of the great balcony, but the heads of all the crowd of elfs gathered before the stable door blocked Yumiko's way. She shot her grapnel to snag one of the countless pillars lining the balcony rail and swung across the dizzying emptiness. She struck no flying servants but overtook the running pair as they circled the balcony.

She joined them, running silently behind the two. Down the vast spiral they ran. The doors opening up onto the spiral balcony here were narrow and mean, unadorned. But as they descended, they ran past finer doors, adorned with carvings, hung with painted signs. Farther down, larger doors of finer make were surrounded and supported with statues, bas-relief work, tapestries, and banners. Farther yet were wide gates leading into presence halls and ballrooms lit by gems or miniature moons. Past nicely appointed chambers they went as well as past arched gates revealing indoor lakes of strange fluids beyond, or museums, libraries, shrines, ballrooms, and other chambers whose purposes could not be guessed. At various gates stood sentries, who presented their pikes in salute of Garlot.

At last they came to a courtyard like a semicircle cut out of the wall and golden doors supported by tall statues of the fanged sea monster with tusks and dorsal fins of gold like unto the crest of Garlot. Elfs and Nephilim in black-and-red livery stood guard.

4. The Hall of the Red Knight

Rumor must have flown ahead. Worried scowls sat on the brows of Garlot's houseguards, but no surprise. The doors were open, and eft linkboys with glowing eyes or burning tongues lined the passage to light the way. At the door stood a squat, round-bellied, and black-skinned Nibelung in a fur-lined cap. His luxurious white beard reached past his belt, and his rich white curls past his shoulders. His coat was red and trimmed with black mink. Yumiko thought he looked like a miniature and sinister Santa Claus. A chain of office was around his shoulders and a key ring at his gem-studded belt.

Batraal the Nephilim called, "Althjof! Is all ready?"

The whitebeard answered, "The wood is lit; the elixir is boiling. I have the amber key in hand." And he turned. He trotted briskly on his stubby legs to keep ahead of the long and rapid strides of the elf squire and longer but slower gait of the tall Nephilim.

They passed through a wide entrance hall, where tusked fish of flesh and blood sported in a fountain of black marble above a floor of blood-red jasper. Above was a dome of aventurine, carnelian, and red agate held on the tailfins of fanged and frog-mouthed sea-beasts made of stone and standing on their heads. Into a narrow corridor they went.

Whatever marvels or riches filled the apartments of Sir Garlot were not seen since this narrow corridor had each door shut, and each archway was either covered with a curtain of hissing snakes or a curtain of flames, hotter than a fireplace. Such fires were the only light. No servants were here.

The way was blocked by three doors. The first was a cedar door adorned with pearls and painted runes. The second was a door of black iron which Ither, the elfin squire, was warned not to touch. The third was a door of solid fire whose latch and hinges were made of living snakes, unconsumed, petrified, and held in place, agony in their eyes. They held the door shut by biting each others' tails.

Althjof opened the first with a touch on the correct rune, the second with a key, the third with a word whispered to the burning serpents, who released each others' tails from their fangs and hissed. Each time, he held the door for the pair bearing Garlot, and, each time, Yumiko had to slide or somersault nimbly by him and then cling to the carven roofbeam when he trotted swiftly past her underfoot to overtake the others.

Beyond the door of fire, the walls to either side fell away, and the roof rose beyond sight. The floor of the corridor continued three more paces, as a tongue extending to nowhere, and ended at a brink. Underfoot was black abyss. At the far side of the chasm, a bowshot away, was a wall of cyclopean blocks of black marble. Each block was two yards on a side. In the middle of this wall was an oval door made of amber planks bound with hasps and hinges of silver.

Althjof put one of the keys of his keyring to his mouth and blew. A shrill whistle issued from the metal. At this noise, a gossamer scarf, thin enough for light to pass through, unfolded from the threshold of the amber door. It reached across the abyss as lightly as a spider's thread might reach, to touch the brink of the tongue of floor.

5. The Gossamer Span

Althjof went first across the filmy bridge, trotting swiftly, and he took out a key whose wards and shank and bow were carved all of one piece of yellow amber. Ither went next, carrying the wounded Garlot on his back. Batraal came third, his hand on his master's back, helping to steady the burden. Yumiko came after.

The flimsy gossamer trembled and swayed under their footfalls. Althjof reached the far end before the others. "Light!" he called. "I must have light to work the lock!"

Two thin, high cries of pain echoed in the air, and suddenly two glass vessels, no larger than wine bottles, one hanging on either side of the amber door, lit up with bright light. Inside were miniature women sporting butterfly wings. They were clad in short tunics that left their limbs bare, and the hues and patterns matched their wings. The light was shining from their hair and skin.

In that light, Yumiko saw two small and swift shapes dart by underfoot. It was a pair of black mice, clinging to the underside of the gossamer bridge, visible only because the surface was so thin. She saw their paws and bellies, their motionless eyes, as they scampered by, quick as birds in flight.

Yumiko stopped on the gossamer bridge long enough to draw her baton, unfold it into a bowstaff, and string the bow. The others were drawing away. She ran to catch up.

There came a chime of noise like a ringing bell when the bolt of the amber door was drawn. The door opened by parting in the middle and sliding aside. Within was a blaze of light. Yumiko saw in the middle of the chamber beyond a crystal orb, larger in diameter than a man is tall, hovering above a fire blazing in an open hearth of veined red marble. There was no smoke. A nest of snakes were living in the burning wood and consuming the smoke in their mouths as the wood burned. A fluid clearer than water was in the orb, roiling and boiling.

The chamber walls were umber, auburn, fulvous, citrine, and translucent. To every side were panels, panes, niches, and walls of amber, reaching from roof to floor, every hue of yellow from goldenrod to lemon. The amber walls were carved into nooks and shelves and arabesques. Bound chests and caskets made of glass or amber stood there, the coins and bars of gold, rare wood, bolts of cloth, or phials of essence visible through the smoky yellow. Also on the shelves, or dangling from each arm of the chandelier, a glowing, miniature winged girl in a bottle was weeping.

Yumiko redoubled her pace, hoping to see Elfine. Ither stepped forward to enter the treasure chamber, but Batraal slowed his steps so that Ither was ahead.

Batraal whirled and drew his greatsword. Batraal was coated for a moment with many small sparks of light. Yumiko had seen such lights gather around Elfine just before the girl dwindled to miniature size. But the Nephilim did not shrink. He grew. First, he was ten, then fifteen, then twenty feet tall. His brigantine and broadsword grew with him as he grew. The light from the open door behind him cast his black shadow across the gossamer bridge.

Yumiko, caught by surprise, coming too quickly, skidded to a halt and stepped back a step. The gossamer trembled under her footstep, and she realized how she had been discovered.

The Nephilim cried, "Your arrows I know! That you have the Ring of Mists I know! Your weakness I know!"

Batraal lifted his sword in both hands overhead and then raised his head and stared into the blade. Yumiko could see his ice blue eyes reflected in the mirror-bright blade. She saw them focus on her.

The gigantic warrior called. "I see you!"

6. Shooting and Plummeting

Behind Batraal, she saw Althjof and Ither had unbound the Cloak of Mists from Garlot and were hurrying to put their unconscious master into the fluid boiling in the crystal orb, which she realized must be the Crystal Cauldron of Youth.

A ladder of three oversized amber steps rose next to the cauldron, and the youth and the dwarf were wrestling the limp, heavy body up them. They pulled him up the first step.

But she saw something no one else was in position to see: a black mouse was in the treasure chamber, just under the amber steps. Streams of black smoke were issuing from its tiny mouth. The thin thread of black mist was rising up, looking like a rip in the tapestry of the universe.

Through that rip a pale king with empty eyesockets protruded an arm and a leg, as if he were stepping out from the curtain severing seen from unseen. She knew him: about his neck hung a hunting horn, and his surcoat showed the sign of a pale winter tree.

Ither and Althjof pulled their master up the second step.

And the pale king was putting his hand into and through the crystal side of the cauldron. The hand and arm passed through the substance as easily as a beam of moonlight through glass, without touching it. Scars at his wrist, such as suicides are wont to wear, now parted, and a fluid blacker than night entered the bright fluid boiling in the cauldron.

All this she saw in the moment it took the Nephilim to grow in size, to raise his great blade, to peer into its reflection, and to see her.

"Wait!" she cried. "The cauldron is poisoned! Garlot is in danger!"

Ither and Althjof pulled Garlot up the third step. She drew an arrow and nocked it.

"Throw down your bow!" roared the Nephilim. "I am Batraal son of Barkayal, who taught man how to observe the stars, and a daughter of Cain. I am of the elder line of Adam and by rights should rule. Throw down your bow, Winged Vengeance, or die!"

All the shrill voices of the girls in the bottles rose up in a clamor when the name of Winged Vengeance was spoken, crying and shrieking. Ither and Althjof, hearing the commotion, did not look up, but redoubled their efforts, hastening to plunge Garlot into the boiling fluid.

Yumiko realized that no one there could see the ghost. Perhaps they could not see the dark and ghostly blood he was shedding into the liquid boiling in the cauldron.

She called out, "I am not Winged Vengeance! Your master is about to die!" But the first three words of what she said was lost in the uproar, and, unfortunately, the last six were clearly heard.

But at the same time, she drew two arrows from her quiver and in one motion knelt and nocked and shot the first, turned the bow sidewise, went prone, and shot the second.

Both shafts passed between the legs of the twenty-foot-tall giant and went through the open door to the treasure chamber.

The first struck arrow Althjof, the dwarf, in the leg and passed through it. He stumbled and fell into the cauldron with a splash. Ither, unbalanced and scalded by flying water, lost his footing, but he fell backward down the amber stepladder, bringing Garlot's bleeding body with him. This first arrow was not red, but had a bodkin head.

The huge blade of Batraal swung. He missed her head, perhaps because she moved, or perhaps because he had no other mirror to use to keep her in his sight. Or perhaps he was not aiming for her at all. The blade cleaved neatly through the gossamer surface, and it parted. The half on which he stood remained rigid and supported his weight. The half under her feet collapsed and disintegrated, suddenly no more solid than a puffy cloud.

The second arrow flew swift and sure a mere inch above the floor and struck the black mouse through. The mouse was struck, but it was the shadow figure of the dead king who fell back, a shaft protruding from his chest. Ghost and arrow together shimmered like objects seen under rippling water and evaporated.

This was a white arrow, called *haya*. It was male, the first ghost arrow, and it spun clockwise—deasil—when shot. In her hand was *otoya*, the female, the second ghost arrow, which spun counterclockwise—widdershins—when shot. To her credit, it did not fall from her hand when she fell.

It is startling how fast a body falls. To Yumiko, it seemed as if the Nephilim was yanked upward like a puppet on an unseen string more swiftly than an ascending rocket. Without losing her grip on the bow shaft or arrow, she twisted the ring sharply, making herself weightless, and shrugged her wings into place. But now she was visible. Her speed of descent slowed, thanks to air resistance, but she was still traveling down.

She could not fold the bow away while it was strung. She slung the bow over her shoulder. A flick of her right wrist slapped her wirepoon pistol into her palm. She fired, but the grapnel rebounded from the slick surface of the marble blocks of the cyclopean masonry of the vast and bottomless chasm down which she fell.

Did she have time for one more shot? She steadied the pistol in both hands and aimed at the Nephilim, hoping to grapple the gossamer bridge on which he stood. The grapnel penetrated the transparent fabric of the bridge, but the tall man knelt and swept his sword. With a high-pitched shock of metallic noise, the wire parted under the blow, leaving the grapnel head behind.

She was falling only as fast as an autumn leaf, but falling she was, and with no way to climb up. No convenient warm updraft was likely to rise from below and give her altitude. She yanked a pair of needle-nosed pliers out of her belt and stared at them. "No climbing claws!" she muttered. "What kind of superheroine ever leaves her climbing claws behind?"

She had only a moment before the Nephilim, the door, and the two small bottles burning like lamps would be too far above her and out of range. She and all her gear were weightless at the moment. She was not sure how this would affect performance. But she had in hand something with a much longer range than the wirepoon pistol.

She kicked her legs so that she was supine in midair, put her feet up, caught the bow shaft between sole and heel, nocked a judo-point arrow, and shot.

This time, she aimed not at the wall or the warrior but at the lamp. A judo-point head is blunt but has hooks to snag the surface it hits. In this case, Yumiko used such a head hoping it would snag the glass it shattered, slowing its speed and doing no harm to the girl inside the bottle.

A moment later, bright as a falling star, a brunette with wings like an Eastern Tiger Swallowtail, wearing a brief and sleeveless tunic of matching yellow and black, came speeding down the shaft and landed on the nose of Yumiko's mask.

7. A Small Boon

"I am Fayline," she said with a curtsey, fluttering her wings to keep her footing on the nose of the mask of the slowing-falling girl. "Daughter of Lorilla of the band of Zurline of Burzee. You have freed me! Ask of me what boon I may grant."

"I would like to go back up, please," said Yumiko.

"Up? Up where?"

"From where I fell."

"When?"

Yumiko was puzzle. "I do not understand."

"You want to go up to the spot from which you fell. When did you fall?"

"Just now. A moment ago."

"Ah! That I can do!" So saying, the fairy girl grew until she was the size of a doll. A frown was on her face. "Or maybe I cannot do. You seem rather gigantic, and you smell like the realm of woe. I cannot turn into a bird any who bears this scent."

"Appearances can deceive," said Yumiko. "I am light as a feather at the moment."

"Ah! Your weight is in the land of the dead! That is a clever place to stow it."

And she wrapped both arms about the nose of Yumiko's mask and beat her wings furiously, shedding many sparks and glittering motes as she did. Slowly, but surely, Yumiko's descent halted. For a moment she hung while Fayline strove. And then the tiny impulse from the girl no larger than a dove prevailed, and Yumiko began drifting upward.

Higher they came. The Nephilim was kneeling on the gossamer, but he had sheathed his terrible sword. The fairy girl tugging on Yumiko's grinning fox-mask made her clear to see against the backdrop of unrelieved darkness.

Yumiko said, "I think we should avoid him. Follow near the wall and get above him."

The fairy laughed. "Ah! No! That is not what you asked! The spot from which you fell is even with his toe. There is no bridge there now, of course."

"You are not willing to carry me a few yards higher than I asked?"

The doll-sized girl wagged a tiny finger. "Tsk! Tsk! You could have used different words if you wanted something different. I thought you wanted me to carry you all the way back to Sarras or the hospital room window where the holy saint put you. This is easier! I would have liked to turn you into a bird if you forgot to ask beforehand to be able to turn back. That would have been funny, too!"

"Funny?" asked Yumiko, incredulous. "What of gratitude? I saved you!"

"I am granting you your boon! You get one! Just one! And as soon as I am done, I can forget all gratitude and the pain and danger I was in and flit away free! You do not think I am cursed with memory, like an elf, do you?

My ancestors discovered how to live without regret, here in the land of tears, among the exiled children of Eve. It is like your amnesia!"

"Exiled? From where?"

"Don't remember, don't know, don't care."

"From Heaven?"

Now the little face crumpled in sudden, sharp sadness, and Fayline cried, "Why did you say that? Why did you say such a terrible thing?"

At this point, Yumiko came back to the spot in midair where the gossamer bridge had been. Fayline flew away without a backward glance, straight up the shaft.

The Nephilim, frowning, stepped to the broken end of the remaining half of the gossamer bridge, measuring the distance to Yumiko with his eyes.

8. *Another Small Boon*

Through the legs of Batraal the Nephilim, Yumiko saw that the amber doors behind him had been pulled shut.

Yumiko was not used to shooting the bow while weightless. She stiffened her cloak and spread it, and her legs rotated slowly until her spine was pointed at the target. She wanted to keep the line of the shot near her center of mass. She flexed her spine and craned her neck like someone shooting an arrow directly overhead.

The blunt arrow flew sure and true into the other bottle by the door, shattering it. A moment later a glittering fairy girl was hanging in midair before Yumiko's eyes, and she curtseyed politely. Her wings and tunic were patterned like a Monarch butterfly.

"I am Luel, daughter of Ereol of the band of Ozga the Rose Princess of Oogaboo. Ask of me what boon…"

"Without maiming or slaying me or anyone, immediately open as wide as they are designed to be opened the amber doors there leading to the treasure chamber of Garlot if that is where Elfine daughter of Iolanthe is kept, and keep them open until the moment I say otherwise, to allow me to shoot arrows into more of the bottles currently kept there and free more captives."

Luel smiled charmingly, clapping her little hands with joy. "That I can do!"

Just then, Batraal gleamed with a firefly swarms of lights, swelled up to twice his size, reached out, and caught Yumiko between his palms. She threw a knife into his nose, which made him laugh, since, at his size, this was smaller than the sting of a bee to him. Then the pellets of tear gas and pepper spray hidden in the slots of the hilt of the knife ignited, and an immense volume of noxious gas erupted directly into all the nasal and throat cavities of his head. When he yelled in pain, tear gas blew from his throat. He jerked his hands toward his burning face, releasing her. Now she was tumbling in an irregular spin, flying toward the black wall with no weight but great momentum.

Luel, still smiling brightly, landed on the back of Yumiko's glove, clung there, reached out, took the Ring of Mists in both hands, and twisted it sharply. The ring darkened from pewter to cast iron to shining onyx, and the face in the intaglio went from drowsy to sleepy to dead, a corpse face with lips sewn shut.

Yumiko felt eyes on her, many gazes filled with hate. The sensation was far more potent than she had felt it before: she was paralyzed, unable to move.

Luel twisted the ring yet again. The shining onyx ring turned black as soot, and the face collapsed into a skull. The mist around Yumiko was thick and dark, so she lost all sight of the Nephilim, the amber door, the gossamer bridge, the stark and smooth walls. She was nowhere. She could see nothing.

9. Nonbeing

And within the nothing was a deeper nothing, visible like black against gray. The shapes of dead men, their empty eyesockets turned toward her, empty mouths gaping in mirthless hunger, painful hunger, infinite hunger. They envied her for being alive. They wanted life, but never, not for eternity, not ever would the smallest drop of it be theirs. It was a terrible, burning, thirsting envy, a malice beyond madness. They lusted for her life and envied her for having it. There were dozens here, scores, hundreds, reaching out toward her.

Below and behind these dark shapes was a figure even darker, as if darkness could turn from a mere absence of light to a positive force that destroyed light.

The ghosts were the size of men and fluttered like bats in the gloom. This one was the size of a tower, or a hill, and the featherless wings that opened from its shoulders were greater than the sails of a mighty ship. They were the wings of the leviathan.

And beyond and beneath this tower of darkness were hills and mountains of shapes vaster and deeper, leviathans wallowing, not in the sea, but the depths of uttermost blackness darker than the bottom of a sea trench and at a pressure even more massive and relentless.

Yumiko heard a voice she had heard before. She had heard this voice in the lowest vaults of Wilcolac's establishment, where he conducted his black sorceries. It was the voice of Empousa. Yumiko heard it in her mind, not her ear, and her mind went as if deaf with fear. *The little vixen we seek is there, plain and clear to see. After her! Upon her! Bring the ring to Wilcolac, damned spirits!*

Twittering and screaming like bats, with many a jerking, angular, and ugly movement of flying and falling, tossing their limbs this way and that, the dead by scores and myriads came through the darkness toward her.

Chapter 8

The Treasure Room

1. Amber Chamber

Then came light.

The world turned solid around her, as firm as a mother's arms about a baby. Warmth was here, and brightness, and beauty of three dimensions, and the solemn symphony of her living heart, beating a rapid tattoo, proving time was passing once more. Even the beautiful sensation known as sound was here again, coming in the way nature intended, through the ear, not like a needle thrust directly into the brain. But the sound itself was not very pretty. It took her a moment to realize it was the sound of a woman screaming. It took her another to realize it was her own voice.

She leaped to her feet, staggered, stumbled, and fell to her knees. She blinked her eyes free of tears. Where was she? What was happening?

She was surrounded by the gleaming yellow, brown, and gold of slabs and screens of amber of Garlot's treasure chamber. It was larger than its seemed when seen through the amber doors. The huge crystal cauldron was midmost, but here also were chairs, a writing desk, a book cabinet, all partly or wholly hewn of polished amber. In addition to being a bank vault and an infirmary, this was Garlot's library or sitting room. There were miniature girls along the shelves and in the chandelier, and also in a lantern on the desk and atop a candlestick. There were too many tiny, glowing, woebegone faces to take in at a glance. She did not see Elfine.

The body of Althjof was inside the cauldron. She saw it through the glassy walls of the cauldron and wished she had not. Althjof was curled like a dead insect, fist raised as if ready to ward off a blow, and the body was slowly rotating as the agitated bubbles boiled over crooked limbs. Each inch of skin was pale, bloated, and blistered with severe burns.

Ither the squire was kneeling at the foot of the cauldron, prodding the snakes that lived in the fire with a fire poker. His back was to Yumiko, but he turned at the sound of her screams.

The bleeding body of Garlot was propped up in a chair at the foot of the amber step ladder leading to the cauldron mouth. His eyes were open, but he was unconscious. The gray cloak was draped over the chair back behind him and had clouds and splotches of red floating through it.

Like a fire arrow, like a shooting star, Luel darted from Yumiko's trembling hand toward the amber doors of the chamber. The key had been left in the lock. The brightly shining fairy girl thrust her foot into the bow of the key and whirled about it like a ballerina executing a spin. There came a chime of noise when the lock opened.

Luel raised her other foot and placed it between the leaves of the door. There came a spray of sparks, like the tail of a skyrocket, which pushed against the other leaf of the door while sending her shooting backward, and this forced both leaves wide open. Then, laughing and kicking her legs, she broke the key in the lock, so there was no way to turn or fasten it again.

Ither stood and drew his dirk. "Surrender! Yield!" he shouted.

Yumiko said, "I yield. I have no wish to–" but her voice was weak and thin, her head was light, and shadows were pulsing at the edge of her vision, threatening to drive her unconsciousness.

But at the same moment Luel swooped down, swelled from insect size to doll size, picked up the bow and arrow Yumiko had dropped during the moment of darkness, and thrust them into Yumiko's hands.

Ither, seeing the bow in her hands, roared and leaped. Yumiko was shocked at how swiftly he moved. He slapped the longbow out of her hands and pinned both elbows behind her back with one arm. She squirmed, trying to get her feet under her, to find some leverage. The blades in her shoes popped open, but she was in no position to slice or cut his feet. Blades along her forearms opened, and stiffened, and cut his silk sleeves, but they scraped against the mail sleeves underneath. Now he put the dirk at her throat. She struggled, wild with fear, but the teenage elf held her as easily as a grown man would a child.

Her earlier fight with the human men had deceived her. She was as strong and fast as they were, but she was not as strong and fast as a male of her own race. And the elf was not her race. He was a thoroughbred whereas she was but a half-breed. For the first time, she wondered if the arrogance of the long-lived elves toward the Moths and Cobwebs and other half-humans was justified.

2. *Fairy Nicety*

Yumiko brought the wirepoon pistol out of its hidden wrist-sheath and shot the barb of the grapnel into and through Ither's foot, pinning it to the floor. At the same time, she clicked the tongue control inside her mask to deploy the snorkel, which came out of the top of her mask with a rubbery pop of noise and struck him neatly in the eye.

The knife blade scraped against the collar of her suit, but the young squire did not use enough force to penetrate an unexpectedly metal-hard resistance in what had been soft as leather a moment before. She flexed her shoulders, deploying the glider wings into a stiff, metallic shape. Retracting the forearm blades also made her arms suddenly thinner in his grasp. His grip slipped, and she writhed out of it, sleek as an eel.

Across the chamber she somersaulted, but landed in the palm of Batraal son of Barkayal, who had grown to an even larger size, and thrust his hand up to the elbow into the chamber.

He closed his fingers, crushing wings against back and arms against sides. Her legs were kicking in midair below his pinky. Her shoulders were trapped in a shrug in the circle of his forefinger. He put his thumb with menacing gentleness on her crown between the pointy fox ears of her headgear. He need only straighten this thumb to snap her neck.

Luel once again darted across the room, picked up the dropped longbow, and came to where Yumiko's pinned hands were wiggling and scratching against the thighs of her boots. Luel hovered at her left hip and thrust the bow into Yumiko's surprised fingers.

Yumiko gasped to Luel, "Help me! Get me out of this!"

Ither was kneeling, yanking at the barb impaling his foot. He gasped to Batraal, "Slay him! Slay Winged Vengeance!"

Batraal said, "Feels kind of soft and slight to be him… I do not think this is Winged Vengeance. For one thing, he looks like a crow. For another, we are alive."

Luel landed on the nose of her mask and curtseyed. "I have helped you, just as you said! I have neither maimed nor slain you or any; opened the doors specified in the time and fashioned specified, nor can they be locked shut again, and your bow is in your hand. You are allowed to shoot and have my permission. It is no doing of mine that you lack the present ability to act on that permission. No more was asked." She ticked off each item on her fingers, and when she was done, she clapped her hand with her fingers spread and jumped up and down on the mask nose.

Ither and Batraal continued to argue.

"Smash the other bottles!" gasped Yumiko.

Luel pouted. "I did what you said! You said you wanted to shoot arrows into the bottles with the door open! There is the open door! There are all the bottles with my sisters in them! There is your bow! You said nothing about smashing before. What is *wrong* with you?"

"Free them! Free Elfine!" cried Yumiko.

"I *hate* the daughters of Eve!" Luel clenched her fists and clenched her teeth. "They *never* want what they ask for! Even if you listen carefully, with both ears, and do everything exactly as they say!" Luel gave an energetic dance of frustration on the nose of the mask, as if she were about to kick Yumiko in the eye, and this made Yumiko by reflex jerk back her head, and this snapped the mask open and flung Luel overhead and back out of sight.

Luel circled back like an angry wasp, glowing red like a ruby star. "I did as you said and just as you said! My debt is gone! I have already forgotten you!"

Ither yanked the grapnel out of his shoe, and the bloody metal hook retracted, hissing back into the pistol in Yumiko's right hand. He took up his knife and came limping across the floor toward where she hung in the Nephilim's fist.

Yumiko said desperately to Luel, "Wait! I said you had to wait until I specifically said to close the doors again!"

The light surrounding Luel turned a brighter shade of crimson. "You did *not*! You said I had to make sure they stayed open until you said *otherwise*. Since I broke the key off in the lock, they will stay open forever up until the moment you say that word and thereafter. I have done all! No changing your mind! No taking back what you said!"

And with that, she dwindled to a mote, a speck, a bright atom, and she was no more to be seen.

Ither came near and flourished his knife. "Flick your thumb, Batraal! We can use the assassin's head for a hurling ball! Why do you wait?"

A low and solemn voice said, "No. Hold your hand. Slay her not."

Yumiko craned her neck to turn her head and peer through the crystal sides of the cauldron. Garlot was seated on the far side. He had not moved, but now his open eyes were awake.

3. Vengeance Is a Girl

Ither was now just below her, looking up. "Batraal! Winged Vengeance is a girl! Most unexpected. Look! There is a light caught in her eyes. She is of the lineage of Amaterasu of the Sun. Her face is bright and full of passion. Hold her nearer! Hold her still! I will kiss her."

Garlot said, "Do not kiss her."

Ither looked over his shoulder. "But, master, she is so pretty, she must be a Moth. They are said to be sweet on the lips."

"Would you shame my name, squire? Take no untoward advantage of any lady."

"But she is a Moth, not a lady! And she stabbed me in the foot."

"She is the Foxmaiden, who slays the women Winged Vengeance is too proud to slay. She no doubt has a spring-loaded poisoned switchblade hidden under her tongue and will stab through the roof of your mouth into your walnut-sized brain if you molest her. Prepare the hook and winch to fish Althjof out of the cauldron. Batraal, place her in the chair facing me."

Yumiko was pushed in the chair. The huge hand held her there. The amber substance of the back and the armrests turned to liquid for a moment, and came about her like lariats of glass, and solidified again. A chair leg snared her ankles.

4. *The Red Knight*

Garlot turned his bloodstained eyes toward her. As he spoke, his words were slow and labored, as if his wound pained him. He never stirred so much as a finger but held completely still as he spoke. "I offer you a trade. You will forgive the discourtesy of my affectionate chair, and I will forgive your trespass into this chamber, where none of your race may come. Do you accept?"

"Yes."

She spoke without hesitation. She was not sure what penalty or curse normally accompanied any trespasser caught in an elfin treasure chamber. No doubt it was worse than anything she could do to him in retaliation for trapping her in a magic chair. It sounded like a good bargain to her.

He said, "Are you here to free my collection of fairies?"

"Yes."

"That is unwise. Two of them granted you boons to repay your kindness. Were you satisfied?"

Yumiko said, "Pardon me. I do not know what that question means."

"Heaven punishes mortals by letting mortal wishes be granted to instruct each fool to know that earthly life has nothing an immortal soul craves. Heaven punishes fairies by letting them recall their old obedience. This is to instruct them in thanksgiving, a source of joy unknown to melancholy elfs."

"I was not satisfied with the boons they granted. What obedience?"

Garlot said, "In the first days, before the Tree of Life was felled, the sons of Adam were sovereign over nature. Storms grew calm at the command of Cain;

Seth trod on scorpions and dragons unhurt; Abel the Just ascended up on high, beyond where eagles fly, and builded him an altar in the clouds. Rumor says Sarras once stood on the same spot in the middle air."

This seemed to be saying that fairies and elfs originally were made to serve mankind, not to rule them. Yumiko said, "If I command you to release me, will you?"

"Interesting question. In whose name would you ask if you were to ask?"

"In the name of Arthur."

"He is king no longer. He died."

"They say he sleeps."

"Do they? Do they really?" A hint of amusement hid in his voice.

"In the name of Christ then."

"Even more interesting. Are you baptized? By what right do you call upon that name?"

She stared at his impassive face. His eyes were heavy, his lids were half closed, and he showed no expression, nor did he blink. She found this unnerving. She twisted her wrists and ankles but could not dislodge them.

She said, "I don't know if I have the right."

He said, "Then I don't know what will happen in this place if you call on that name. I hear he killed the Great God Pan, and this was not long after he drove a host of fallen ones out of their house and into a herd of swine, which drowned themselves in the sea. That host, or some horde of evil ones doing work in their name, is in this city. But I notice you do not think to ask me in the name of Erlkoenig, who is my liege and master. Why is that?"

She said, "Erlkoenig did not send you to fight Sir Gilberec the Swan Knight. Would he be displeased to learn?"

"You know much," he said, and his eyes narrowed slightly. "If he learned you have the Ring of Mists, that might well bring on you more trouble than your current playmates, bandits, cutthroats, and Cobwebs with delusions of grandeur. I offer you another trade. You keep my secret from Erlkoenig, and I keep yours. Do you accept?"

"Yes."

"You answer with alacrity. Most folk would ponder longer or be wary of unspoken conditions, clauses, or assumptions. Most would ask to consult their lawyers."

"Elfs have lawyers?"

"Elfs invented lawyers. It is one of the few inventions humans copied from us, rather than the other way around."

Something moved in the depth of her buried memory at these words and caught her attention. It was as if something important, something forgotten, was hidden behind the idea. "Elfin life is copied from human life? Why is that?"

For the first time, he showed expression. His brows moved upward infinitesimally. "All know why."

"I do not. Tell me, please."

"The Sons of Adam were made in the image and likeness of the Creator, and so they are creative, even in their fallen state. Sons of Air are made in the image of Adam, and we copy him."

"But you copy only the Middle Ages?"

"What do you mean?"

"You have swords and sailing ships, but no atom bombs or moonrockets."

"Our hearts delight in the forms Man invented when he was at his finest. When holy saints and chivalrous heroes walked the earth, even the lordliest of elfs feared to meddle with them. Arondight could have destroyed us all, but no atom bomb could."

"Who is Arondight?"

"The blade of Lancelot du Lac, given to England just as Kusanagi was given to Japan and Joyeuse to France. It was struck from his hand by the good fortune of his adultery and his treason to his best loved friend and liege. Praise be to whatever devil tempted him! Do you think these pale and sickly modern men could resist a woman one-tenth as fair as Genevieve? Do you think they would bow the knee to Arthur? Only to gather stones to stone him. Modern man is mostly matter. We are mostly spirit. Only what is deep in dreams is solid to us, and high, fine, and ancient things gather dreams about them which do not die. We do not copy the art and artifacts of dim and dismal days like these, lest our houses look like homes in Hell."

"I don't understand."

"You saw the proud towers in whose shadow we rode to come here. Desolate, arrogant, empty. That is the true appearance of the soul of New York.

The spirit of the city is dead, and elfs know the art of walking alive into the dreams where the ghosts of those not yet called to judgment wander."

Yumiko was a little miffed at his dismissive tone. "What about moonrockets? Merlin never built one of those."

"Men of this day went to the moon but did not go back. The rockets rot, and the engineers forget their lore. Whereas Arthur did not build half a tower at Camelot, nor fight half a battle at Badon Hill, nor did Saint Patrick drive half the snakes from Ireland. These little men of these little days have conquered more of nature and less of spirit until they have not enough spirit to rule what they conquer. We are long-lived folk, long in foresight and long in memory, and we do not forget. But who are you?"

Yumiko was surprised. "I thought you knew. I am the Foxmaiden."

5. *The Maiden of the Moths*

"You are the servant and disciple of Winged Vengeance? He has the last cloak from Sarras, and he flies, not swift and high like a bird, but as a dark angel. If you are she, how can you not know what every child knows?"

"There is much I have forgotten."

"Are you a Moth?"

"I am. Why do you ask?"

"I was expecting the minion of Winged Vengeance to be a Peaseblossom."

"Why?"

"Because he is alone. You are alone. Moths flock."

Yumiko said, "Elfine Moth is in this chamber. You must release her."

"Must I?"

"Yes."

"You seem quite certain."

Yumiko did not know, and had no guess, as to why he had not slain her instantly, but she assumed he wanted something from her he could not gain by force or magic. So she did not answer but merely assumed a relaxed posture, that is, as relaxed as a girl can assume when she is pinned in place. She could cock her head to one side with an air of nonchalance and stare at the ceiling.

He said, "What would you have of me?"

That was an unexpected comment. He must be in a very bad bargaining position, pressed for time, desperate.

She said, "All your prisoners in this chamber released, starting with Elfine Luminiferous Moth."

"So many fairies in Manhattan? They will cause mischief and madness. It is the high will and command of Erlkoenig that such as these remain in Troynovant, in the Third Hemisphere men never see. By coming here, they trespass. I am in my rights to keep the king's law. It is finer here than the dungeons of Mommur."

"As each is freed, she will offer a boon to her savior. Is there no place where they could be free and happy, free of mischief, and Erlkoenig also be happy? We have ten thousand spirits in Japan. We have room."

"There is a colony in Cottingley, England, and another in Boxerwood, Virginia. Will that do?"

Yumiko said, "Unlike the fairies, you understand the spirit in which I ask."

"I do not. Sending a Moth to free a Moth—that I understand because you hang together and side with no one. By why do you care about these diminished ones? They will never be grateful. They will not remember. You will gain nothing."

"Your boy wanted to molest me, and you stopped him. You gained nothing. How is this different?"

His eyes narrowed. "You are a vigilante. You live for vengeance. I am a knight. I live for honor, just as bards live for truth and philosophers live for beauty."

"You strike men down from behind, unseen. How is this honor?"

Ither was occupied in erecting a large tripod over the cauldron. Batraal had resumed his former size of merely ten feet or so and was steadying the structure with one hand while Ither lashed the beams in place.

Looking down from above, Ither said, "Hoy! What *molesting*, you saucy half-breed wench? A privilege never forgotten! A single elfin kiss makes all mortal kisses afterward more unbearable than kissing a dog!"

Garlot turned his bloodshot eyes but otherwise did not move. "Silence. The life and death of Althjof hangs in the balance pans on the whim of this Moth lass. If she asks for your head, I will give it to her."

6. Well Water and Wine

Then, the eyes turned back toward her and grew narrow, as if he winced in pain. "My honor is much stained, for I am a bad knight, and where is the flood of the fountain that can wash the stains from my soul, the blot from my escutcheon? Elfs do not forget.

"But still a knight I am!" he continued, bitterly. "Erlkoenig has no Winged Vengeance to terrify his foes with sudden death swooping from dark clouds. But I am the next best thing. If I am feared rather than honored, then this is drinking well water when the wine is gone. By why free my collection? I am within the law. They are not of your blood."

"I dare not seek mercy unless I grant mercy."

Now his eyes narrowed further. "Mercy? What word is this? Who are you?"

"I am the Foxmaiden."

"Impossible. I saw the body of one her victims. Parts of the body. She does not know that word. You are an imposter."

"I died and was reborn."

"Impossible! Neither elf nor necromancer can raise the dead alive again, nor can the proud spirits of Hell, despite their deceptions. No one can do it."

"The fountain you seek is real. Something washed away my vendettas and oaths. A lady told me."

"Where is this fountain? Show it to me, and I will believe."

"I cannot show it. I did not see it."

"Then how do you know? Ours is a world of deceptions and deceits like hollow Russian dolls, one within the next, and no core, no solid doll at the heart. How do you know?"

"Why should I doubt? Despair is the last deception. It kills the thirst for truth."

For the first time he showed expression, for now he gritted his teeth in pain and tears came from his eyes.

Yumiko said calmly. "Release me. I command it."

"In whose name do you ask?"

"Your name! In the name of Garlot, the Red Knight, whose life I saved from certain death twice this day. I will save Althjof if you tell me what to do."

The arms and legs of the chair relaxed as she spoke that name, and she was free. She stood.

Garlot said, "I offer you a trade..."

She said, "No!"

A spasm shook him. He clutched the pink bandages that wrapped his midriff. He coughed and caught blood from his mouth in his handkerchief. "I offer... in return for..."

"No!" she snapped. "No trade. I will save Althjof. But I do not know what you would have me do. Tell me. Freely I will do it. This is mercy."

Ither, the squire, swung down from the tripod to the top step of the amber step ladder, shouting in anger. "How dare you speak so to the master, you lowly drudge! His blood is of the highest and most ancient line!"

She turned and scowled coldly at the boy. She could feel her heartbeat in her face of some high emotion, perhaps anger, perhaps fear. "What blood? The blood of servants. In my veins is the blood of Eve, the mother of mankind. Go pick up my bow and hand it to me."

Ither was startled by the sheer effrontery of it and sputtered. "We are smarter than mortal men, wiser, older, more beautiful. Our memories fade not. We are lucid in sleep! Time and seasons are our servants; plague and pestilence dare never draw nigh to us! We can see hidden things afar off or hidden in the heart! The least of us has written poetry sweeter than Dante, songs bolder than Orpheus! I could put your feet on backward or give you a hedgehog's head!"

Yumiko drew herself erect and spoke in a voice more stern and regal than his. "It is not for your wit or wisdom or age or any other great gifts that you have the right to rule mankind. You have no such right at all. Those gifts were meant to be placed at his service. The fairies spoke of exile. Where are you from? Where is your home?"

The young elf's face grew pale as ash. He stammered, and his eyes swam with a strange look of pain and loss.

Garlot said, "Do not torment the boy, Moth girl." Then, he said, "Ither, fetch her bow as she asks and do her all good service. Do not blame her if she yanks our chains. We forged the fetters ourselves, saying at first how little one mere link more would matter, one mere foot, one mere fathom."

Ither picked up the white, red, and black great bow and then stared down in surprise. "The spirit in this is ancient! It smells of high Heaven!"

Galen said, "You have not paid mind to your lessons! That is the ghost-slaying bow of Yorimasu. Danger Moth gave it to Pelenore of Listenoise, my half-brother's half-witted son, who sits in the high seat in Ruddystone, which my sister wishes for me. It was borne up to Sarras and lost to lore."

"How comes she by it then?" demanded Ither.

"Silence, willful squire! Hand it to her on your knees." And Garlot said to her, "Shoot the widdershins arrow into the brew. Do not hit my steward. You may stand on the top step if you wish."

7. *The Left-Handed Arrow*

Yumiko understood now why Garlot was so solicitous. She took her position, and in one smooth motion, nocked the white arrow, raised the bow high, and drew back the string as she lowered her arms. The string sang, the arrow sped, but it shimmered and vanished after entering the water before it struck the bottom of the cauldron.

Immediately, the fluid seemed brighter, cleaner, clearer, as if a very light film of darkness had been banished.

Had her irreplaceable arrow been so suddenly obliterated, with no trace left? Wondering, she reached over her shoulder, opened the quiver, and felt the feathers of the two white arrows. Unlike her others, these two returned with dreamlike swiftness to her quiver. A more convenient magic for an archer could not be imagined.

Within the cauldron, the fluid thickened about the motionless body, and little white dots, no bigger than snowflakes, fell into Althjof's torn and boiled skin from every direction. He stirred; he thrashed; he put his head above the water and gagged and gasped for breath. His face was now smooth and youthful, and his long white beard was now short and black and thick, as was the hair of his head. Ither hauled him out of the cauldron with a rope and pulley running through the tripod.

"No worse torture I have ever known!" the now-youthful old steward said, shaking his head gravely. "It was a mercy when all the outer parts of me died, my eyeballs perished, and I saw my disintegrating flesh no more, my nerve endings cooked, and so I felt nothing but boiling water in my lungs. Is it like that for you every time, my lord?"

Garlot said, "A ghost possessed the spirit of the cauldron and silenced its charm so that the elixir of life was merely oil, and the boiling was merely boiling. A clever way to turn the best of medicines into the worse of deathtraps in an instant, with no change in appearance. The unclean spirit was banished back to Hell by this girl, who seems to be dressed as the Foxmaiden of Winged Vengeance but speaks strangely and unlike her. You owe her lauds and thanks."

The steward bowed. "How may I repay this?"

She said, "Show mercy to the next fifty folk who need mercy."

He straightened up, looking surprised. "Fifty?"

"Is your life worth fewer? Forty."

Pride and confusion warred on his face. "Fifty then. But mercy is not in my nature. I am a child of the Svartalfar, a son of darkness and stone and the fire at the earth's core."

"My nature changed. Yours may yet." She turned to Garlot. "Wilcolac the Magician sent the black mice at the command of Lucien Cobweb. The spirit within was called Le Maudit, the Hunter King. Lucien is Thursday of the Supreme Council of Anarchists and your sister's lover. She is aiding the Anarchists in the hope of weakening Erlkoenig."

Garlot raised his hand, and a glittering swarm of sparks flew from his fingers.

8. The Sons of Air

The eyes of his three servants, Elf, Nephilim, and Nibelung, all went blank. They were entranced.

Garlot regarded Yumiko narrowly. "You are acute one moment and obtuse the next. You spit out dire secrets without checking the eaves for eavesdroppers. One of these is my sister's creature, and another is Erlkoenig's spy.

Why does Wilcolac conspire against me? He is famed for being neutral in all disputes and welcoming to all."

"The club is the headquarters for Thursday, Lord of Werewolves."

"Why should I believe this tale? How could you possibly know this?"

"Look at my face. Do you have a perfect memory, like other elfs do?"

"I don't recognize your face."

"I was the hatcheck girl. I waited on your men when they went into the backroom. They are bad tippers."

"Ah. One of the magician's dancing girls? I did not look at your face."

Yumiko blushed. She said sharply, "Release Elfine and all these imprisoned here."

Again, a shiver passed through his frame, and again he clutched his side. "Let us set out clearly the terms of the trade..."

"I told you. There is no trade!"

"That is not the way of the elfs. We were strictly instructed by the fallen angels in Hell. They are not blinded by the light; only they see reality clearly. *No one is free, no two are equal, and no three can be one!* That is their motto. It means all gifts come at a price."

"What comes at a price is not a gift, but a purchase."

"The fallen angels say otherwise."

"If you wish to be damned, follow the damned. But I will not swap with you. Your life has infinite value! So does the freedom of those you pen here."

"You broke the door of my treasure house. No locksmith will dare mend a lock a fairy has broken, lest he be cursed. Do you owe me nothing for that?"

"I owe you an apology for being a rude trespasser. You have already forgiven me the trespass. I ask for forgiveness for the rudeness." She bowed.

"Why should I grant it? And do not say for mercy's sake!"

"I have shown mercy to you."

"Gilberec Moth is your blood and my foe. How can you show me mercy? It is wrong! My race despises and abuses mortal men, but we despise you half-mortals even more. Am I to be in debt to you? Would you heap coals of fire on my head?"

"You can never repay this debt to me. Only to Heaven."

"You killed my dwimmerwurm. This was plain murder."

"I do not know what that is."

"My eft. The dragon newt that looks like a man. The one who breathed fire."

"Oh. That one."

"That one. His name was Pheleg, son of Belphegor. You cannot claim the death was self-defense as he was no threat to you. You cannot claim it was honest combat since you struck without warning while concealed. You cannot claim a duty to defend the Swan Knight since you are no vassal of his, and he clearly did not know you were there."

She was silent and bowed again.

"Where is your mercy now? You saved my life but took his. What words of Heaven will you speak to shame me now? You are a murderess! I curse you and your mercy! To avenge my loyal eft, I am in my rights to arrest, enchant, or enthrall you or execute you swiftly or slowly. I could put the Ring of Mists on my finger, as a trophy of war, and put the ghost-slaying bow in my arsenal until I find another virgin fierce enough to wield it. What stops me?"

"Honor."

"So? I am already the least honorable knight in the land. There are tax gatherers and panderers and coiners more honest than I! With a soul so black, what is one more stain?"

"With a soul so black, why add one more stain? But please release my friend and all these others."

"You did not save me from the Swan Knight for mercy's sake but because you wanted to follow me here and loot my treasure chamber."

"But I shot the first black mouse for you. And I shot your steward to prevent you from going into the cauldron and being boiled to death. I did not mean for him to fall in. You have my apology for that. I am sorry."

He said, "And if that is insufficient?"

She said, "I also saved the life of your steward, the dark dwarf."

"Ah! But you tell me life is infinite in value, and one cannot be swapped for another. Do you espouse heavenly words only when they suit you?"

She had no answer for that but bowed deeply. "Then I am at your mercy."

"Again with that word! You are in my power. Do you understand how entirely within my power you are, you silly little girl?"

She answered nothing, and her face was blank. He evidently interpreted this to be insolent boldness on her part, for now he became animated in his gesture and fierce expression, and this set his wound to bleeding.

"I am within my rights, as a keeper of the elfking's law, to lock you in a cell, or a dream, or a book, or turn you to stone, or chain you to a hearth as a kitchen drudge, or feed you to the Questing Beast inch by inch! Nor is your soul safe. I am within my rights to charm you with chanted spells and make you the willing paramour of my horsegroom, or of his horse and make the unspeakable crimes of Pasiphaë your own!

"And I am not even the most skilled or most terrible of my kind at songs and spells and invocations from the substances of dream."

Still she had no answer. The longer her silence grew, the louder his anger grew.

"Elf is paramount over Man and Moth alike! The Sons of Air are masters of all Creation! Did you think your toys and weapons would save you? What are your gizmos and gimcracks compared to the high sorceries of the Night World? How did you imagine you could come here? What makes you think I should accept your hateful mercy! If you are dead, what thanksgiving do I owe then? And… And… what do you mean, *first* black mouse?"

9. The Second Black Mouse

Now she spoke in a soft voice. "Sir, there were two. I assume one ghost was in each of them. The dead mice were in your horse's belly. Not the little one, the big horse with metal clothing."

"The word is *destrier*. His name is Tachebrun. Horse armor is called barding."

"Did you stable your horse at the Cobbler's Club at any time? Then that was when Wilcolac introduced the mice into Take—Tacky—I am sorry. I cannot pronounce it. I mean no disrespect. Into your horse."

"Why two mice? One was to poison the cauldron. What was the other one's task?" He winced and clutched his side and turned his head. The back of his seat was empty. No garment was thrown over it. "And where did my cloak go? Where is the Cloak of Mists?"

Yumiko smiled and waited.

Garlot turned his bloody eyes back toward her. "What mirth is this? Do you mock me?"

"I smile for sake of the joy which comes from the further mercy I shall show you this day."

He slumped in his chair wearily. "Speak!"

"Since your men are asleep, I will help you into the cauldron. After all your prisoners are freed and you escort me back to the surface, I will tell you where the cloak is. Even if it is moved or hidden, it cannot escape me."

"How could you come by such knowledge?"

Her smile grew brighter. "What are the high sorceries of the Night World compared to the science and technology of the modern age? My beloved is a wonder worker. And his spirit was equal to the task of returning to the moon! I mean to save him, and so I mean to emerge from here alive and well. And not all the elfs in the underground realm nor all the omens and fiends of night will dissuade me!"

Garlot spread his hands in surrender and nodded. "You exasperate me into submission. In mercy's name, I accept your gift of my life. For mercy's sake, I grant you and all whom you would, liberty and free passage from here, safely. You will find the Day World, where men live, in the same year and day you entered this realm.

"Your terms I accept meekly, with one emendation: I will return Elfine Moth to your hand when you return my stolen cloak into mine. But for the sake of Pheleg, whom you have slain, when we meet next, we meet as enemies. Look to it. Now help me up, please. I am not accustomed to pain."

Chapter 9

Fire and Shadow

1. *The World is Marred*

The promise to return Yumiko to the surface within the same day as her descent was not strictly kept. By the time Sir Garlot, atop his magnificent roan charger Tachebrun, sped like a roaring wind up from the secret gate of Ys-Elfydd, night had fallen. Yumiko's own sense of time was confused, and she did not see any clocks on banks or hear any church bells. From the look of the streets, it was after midnight, in the small hours of the morning, which, technically, was the next day.

Yumiko was sitting side-saddle behind his high saddle, her arms tightly around his broad shoulders, her cheek against his back, her knuckles white.

Misgivings fluttered in her rapidly beating heart like moths in a dark closet. She did not like that the rump of the steed was too broad for her to sit astride; that Garlot would not permit her yet to see Elfine; and that Garlot had emerged from the cauldron younger and more virile than before, gleaming elixir dripping from his mighty, naked limbs.

He rode now with his helm tied to his saddlebow, and the hairs of his head, blown by the wind, tickled the crown of her head, and his alluring musk tickled her nose. Had she been in a posture peacefully to meditate, she could have cleared her mind from the heated, wild, dreamlike images her close embrace of the villainously handsome elf sent dancing through her.

Instead, the wild ride down the streets of New York was intoxicating, and she yelped and clung more tightly to his warm, strong body each time they overleaped a honking automobile, startled a pedestrian, or jumped from street to stair to elevated track to the roof of a moving bus and to the street again.

Her misgivings increased when they passed fire engines, their sirens wailing and lights flashing, crawling through the intersection. Ahead, the light of leaping fires beat against the knees of the surrounding towers. They turned a corner and raced down the street. As abruptly as if she had opened an oven door, heat beat Yumiko's face.

Ahead was the Cobbler's Club. Arms of fire billowed from the second and third story windows, and a nodding cowl of smoke rose above, the billows dark and solid in the light of the surrounding streets and shops. A crowd of onlookers had gathered around the police cars and ambulances. A police officer with a bullhorn bellowed at Garlot as his great steed leaped from the hood of his police cruiser and over the yellow sawhorses forming a barricade.

Garlot looked over his shoulder at Yumiko, raising one eyebrow. "Here? Truly?"

"Here."

"Your oracle must be mistaken."

Yumiko tossed her head to lower her mask and called up her inset map. The red dot centered on a window on the fourth floor. Wilcolac's office. "No mistake. Where is Elfine? I need her help for this."

He said, "You will remove whatever mark or rune you placed on my cloak, hatcheck girl, ere you return it to me in my hand. Your heart's desire will be returned to you when mine is to me."

"Whole and unharmed!"

"Whole, unharmed, unmolested, in her right wits, unenchanted, well and happy and alive. Yes. You have the oath of an oathbreaker." He scooped her up in one strong arm and, bowing at the waist, lowered her from the saddle.

Her tiptoes were touching the pavement, but he had not yet released his arm from around her, when a hideous scream of terror echoed from overhead, louder than the bellowing of bullhorns, the scream of sirens, the roar of flames. Yumiko looked up.

She recognized Licho by his dark suit and fluttering tie, the dark glasses whose fragments spun off his face into the night air. He was flung off the roof and went plunging down and down, shrieking as he fell, legs kicking in midair. Two arrows, one from either eyesocket, protruded from his skull, and two streamers of blood, like red ribbons, followed after him in the air.

There was a line of Peach Cobbler Girls in top hats, corsets, and silk stockings, quailing and hugging each other, between Yumiko and the spot of pavement Licho struck, so while Yumiko heard the shrill screams of those who saw the grisly impact, she did not see it herself. One of the girls, Anjana, pointed upward and cried, "It's him!"

There, atop the roof, silhouetted against the flames, his cloak of black feathers streaming in the rushing heat, his elongated mask like that of a plague doctor, or like the beak of a carrion-eating raven, loomed a black and sinister figure.

He had a violin in hand and was playing a wild, mad tune she recognized: the *Danse Macabre* by Saint-Saens. He was using the back of a short, curved blade as his fiddlestick, with the catgut stretched between the tip and the hilt.

Death at Midnight plays a dance-tune,
Zig, zig, zag on his violin…

The firelight caught a glint of this goggles as he turned his mask, looked down, and met Yumiko's gaze. There she stood, still on tip-toe, still with her shapely hands on the broad shoulders of Sir Garlot, who still had one arm about her.

Three wolf-shaped monsters on the roof came leaping out of the flames toward the dark figure. The dark figure calmly slung his violin behind him and took his Japanese longbow from his shoulder. Vast black wings opened, and the flames reared back from him, and he was carried smoothly upward into the billowing clouds of ash and smoke, bringing one of his attackers with him. A moment later, whining pathetically, a wolf fell from the cloud, blood gushing from its jaws, struck the corner of the building, and toppled downward, leaving long red streaks against the stones. The other wolves yowled, biting insanely at the arrows now protruding from neck and spine and flanks.

Then, her view of the building roof was blocked, for Garlot had raised his shield overhead with the arm not encircling her. She looked at him. Garlot was smiling down at her. It was the gloating smile of a man who likes having his arm around a pretty girl. Fretfully, she extracted herself from Garlot's arm and stood on the pavement.

Garlot straightened in the saddle and displayed toward her his shield. A red arrow was protruding from it. "Meant for me, I hope. I would hate to think your famous partnership had been fractured. Now see to your business. If my cloak burns, I will burn your little friend."

"Are we back to that?" She scowled. "What of mercy? What of thankfulness?"

"What of idle fancies? What of all airy, unreal things? The world is marred! Blame not me, but the ill will of the Maker who foresees all evils and prevents none, slothful in omnipotence! Will you stand idly, doing nothing, like him in whose likeness you boast you are made?"

And from his saddlebag, he drew out a small cylinder of blue glass. In it was Elfine Moth, half crumpled in a ball, dazed or half asleep. The volume was too small to allow her either to sit down or to stand erect. When her prison bottle moved, Elfine stirred and straightened, straining against the glass walls confining her. Seeing Yumiko, her face brightened, and her wings lit up. She pounded against the glass with her little fists. "Ami! I've been elf-napped! Save me!"

Garlot drew back his arm as if he were about to cast the bottle into the hottest part of the burning building. "Not all the floors seem lit yet," he said mildly. "Which is it to be? For you are going into the fire either way, either to retrieve my treasure or yours."

Instead of answering him, she said to Elfine, "I am coming back for you!" Yumiko shot her wirepoon toward an upper window and was yanked swiftly upward and away.

2. *Iach and Iohanna*

Yumiko twisted her ring to return her weight just before her boot heels struck the window. She crashed in through the glass. Her supersuit went momentarily stiff and tough to deflect the razor sharp shards, and her foot hit the exact spot in the wooden panels beyond to spring the latch. She fell into the room awkwardly, did a shoulder roll, and came to her feet in time to fetch up against the desk, strike the edge with her belly, and fold in half with a dazed gushing, elongated grunt of air from her mouth.

The room was as she remembered it: red carpeted, wedge shaped, with the two walls receding from each other as they ran from door to desk coated with full-length mirrors. The difference was that it was dark, the room was filled with smoke, the electricity was out, and the only light was a line of fluttering red glowing around the threshold and jambs of the door. The paint on the door was blistering and peeling from the heat.

Light also came from the small man, dressed like a miniature caveman, trapped inside a whiskey bottle lying on its side on the desk. He was floating motionless in the fluid.

A touch of cold traveled down her spine. A voice spoke in her ear. *Open the door. I am so alone.*

She straightened up in shock. "Who is there?"

Save her.

At the same moment, the little man inside the bottle stirred, and his eyes opened. He saw her and screamed, "Don't hurt me! He forced me to do it! I would surely have done anyway 'cause it was right funny, but that doesn't count! I was temporarily insane by reason of permanent drunkenness! You deserved it anyway!"

Yumiko saw shadows break the line of light gleaming under the closed office door. Someone was standing there. She heard the pounding of little fists on the door, a sob, and a voice cursing. Then, "Open this door!"

It was Joan Lantern. She had not made it out of the building.

The little caveman shouted. "Don't open! She's insane! Never open doors during a house fire!"

Yumiko saw the button on the desk which unlocked the door. She pushed it. The door swung open. A red glare of leaping flames jumped into the room, and a roar like a beast as oxygen from the room gushed into the anteroom and stoked the flames there.

A woman was staggering in the doorway. She started to fall, but, strangely, impossibly, something unseen caught her and pulled her in. A gust of wind pushed the door shut with a sudden slam. Darkness and smoke were within. Joan took another step, staggered, and fell.

Yumiko leaped over the desk, caught Joan in her arms, and lowered her to the carpet. In the dark, her lenses could not deliver a clear picture of how severe Joan's burns were. Thinking quickly, Yumiko pushed back her mask (which made the room dark to her), turned up the oxygen gain in her suit, knelt, and put her throat on the nose and mouth of the other woman. Fresh air rushing from the suit played over Joan's face.

Another tremor seized Yumiko. She shivered with cold.

A voice spoke. *Wake! Wake, lest ye die!*

The little man cried out, "Don't let her near me!"

The band of red light from the door threshold was falling across Joan's face. Joan's eyes fluttered open. "Jack? Is that you?"

Yumiko said, "Sorry. It's Sorry Yunomi. Don't stand up. There is smoke in the room."

Joan said, "Find the hob! I am so alone. Save him."

The house hob, at that moment, was gyrating madly inside his bottle so that the sideways whiskey bottle began to roll across the desk. Yumiko, without moving, shot her wirepoon, flicked her wrist, caught the bottle in a loop of the wire, and yanked it to her hand.

"This house hob? Him? Is this who you want to save?" Yumiko asked. "Let's get you out of here–"

A sudden memory came to her. Sly Jack Crookshank had said he had selected Yumiko to save him because the other girls would have demanded things presumably less to his liking: *Joan would have me free her husband.*

Yumiko pushed the bottle into Joan's hands. "Here he is. Make him free your husband."

With surprising strength, Joan reared up and slammed the bottle into the carpet, smashing it and cutting her hands on the glass. "Free him!"

Yumiko tossed back her head to lower her mask. In her lenses, she could see the little man lying in a puddle of broken glass and rich-smelling whiskey. He coughed in the smoke. But the little man said, "Fie on thee! Queen once, now thrall! Speak to me my own true name! Or else devil a foot I stir at all!"

Yumiko said, "*Bakemono* is his true name. I know. I named him."

But Joan said, "Seanglic Coscam, Sly Jack Crookshank, is thy name! Damn your eyes, my boon I claim! My love release from ward and debt! All that he owes this house, forget!"

The little man shrieked like a steam whistle and clutched his face. "Not my eyes! Not my eyes! I grant it! Be free! Jack! Thou art clear and clean of me!"

Yumiko said, "Wait. What is going on? The real Crookshank is gone. You are a copy!"

The smoke in the room suddenly drew back, and frost gathered on all the mirrors. In the middle of a building on fire, the mirrors were turning pale with cold.

Yumiko twisted her ring. She saw a headless body of heroic proportions, painted blue with woad, with designs of owl, lions, and jackals in colored inks painted on his chest, belly, and thighs. A rude loincloth of buckskin hid his loins. In one hand were two javelins with heads of napped flint. But he held his own severed head in the other hand, long of locks and long of mustache. The empty eyes were dripping tears, the neck stump dripping blood. Above the shoulders, where no head was, burned two pearls of luminous fire, and the jagged grin of a disembodied mouth. The links of broken fetters fell from his wrists and ankles. He replaced the head on his neck stump, and now the eerie flares of light shined from the holes of his eyes and from beneath the mustache.

Joan could see this apparition in the mirrors. She rose to her knees. "Iach! Iach Lochrann! My love! Your Joan has not forgotten you! I have been true! A thousand years are gone, and your lady has not wavered!"

He answered nothing. Joan raised her hands. "Beloved! Tell me, O, tell me wither you go! If to Heaven, I will run to the cathedral, break my wand and all my dark oaths, and be baptized! If to Hell, I will curse the Holy Spirit and fling myself from yonder window and be buried at the crossroads as a suicide!"

Now he turned the terrible pale lights of his eyes toward her. "I cursed Heaven and was accursed of Heaven. Now in woe I wander the earth to expunge my evils but also to work thy good. For look! Here is the handmaiden of Saint Barbara, who brings the host to those who die unshriven and unrepentant, or suddenly from thunderbolts, and whose mercy steps into the moment between when the heart stops and the soul flees the body."

There came a flash of lighting and a thunderclap as loud as a field gun when the ghost spoke the name of Barbara. Crookshank, scrambling along the damp, glass-strewn carpet, screamed and tripped and fainted away.

The shade continued speaking. "When this handmaiden presents the destined cup, be contrite ye then. Forswear the Dark Lord and all his trumperies and hollow pomp. His promises are lies. Seek me no more by the unlawful ways of necromancy, nor sell yourself again as slave to a magician. He will be here soon."

"Tell me what to do!"

"As yet, you have no soul to save. That, and all other ills, will be undone and mended. Aid the handmaiden once she has her mother's cup, and by her repentant prayers and yours, gain you the grace of kindly Heaven. I linger in this formless limbo of unlife to speak these words of hope. The living waters that issue in a flood from the foot of the throne of the Kingdom of Light rise and rise to welcome you. You have forgotten how to thirst for them."

Joan said, "For me? For me alone? Or for us both?"

The ghost said, "It is not for you to know what Heaven wills but to rejoice in it."

"If not for us both, then I curse Heaven! Your embrace I want, not some pale Nazarene! Your wife am I, not his!"

"Wife of mine no longer: greater joy awaits than connubial."

Crookshank stirred and came awake, croaking, "The living should not heed the words of the dead! Ignore him! Seek your good only in yourself!"

"Seek ye the greater joy and gain all, and more than you dared ask. Foreswear to seek lesser joy, lest ye lose all." The ghost grew in size and filled the room. The inaudible voice was like a trumpet inside their skulls. "Rare indeed is granted the gift to speak from the beyond to one's living love, albeit we all crave this with our dusty hearts. Will you not hear what I have said? Will you not save the soul I love more than mine own, my dear Iohanna?"

The ghost vanished. The heat returned, and the smoke closed in. At that same moment, the beam from a spotlight shined through the window Yumiko had broken open and splashed across the ceiling, blindingly bright. Joan saw Yumiko in the mirror, saw the black, bat-winged suit and ginning fox mask, and screamed in terror.

Yumiko twisted the ring to make herself visible. "Joan! I am a friend!" Of course, once the dark figure materialized just next to her, Joan screamed yet again.

A loud voice, amplified through a bullhorn, called up. Joan, moving more swiftly than any woman of the Day World, dove over the desk and out the window. Yumiko leaped after her, snatching at her legs. Her fingers closed on nothing. Yumiko grabbed the jambs of the broken window lest her momentum carry her out into midair.

Looking down, she saw Joan, bewildered, land in the net the firemen were holding.

Crookshank was standing on Yumiko's shoulder, leaning casually against her ear. "Faith! An odd thing, that. Certain death to leap from so high a window, save in one and one hour only: when the building is all afire. That is an irony, eh?"

3. The Rule of Debts

Yumiko snatched him up into her hand.

"Not this again!" he groaned. "By the eyeball of Balor, woman, you do have lively reflexes, don't you? Are you part rattlesnake? 'Twould explain much."

Yumiko said, "Why are you back here?"

"I live here. This is the house I mind. Just because you lit it afire don't mean I leave my post. We are not all like you, after all. By the bye, where *is* that grail you are supposed to be looking after? Shouldn't you have taken up your mommy's work by now?"

Yumiko shook him until his teeth rattled. "Why are you back here?"

"Ah! Agh! I never left, you stupid bint. Willy knew you from the moment you walked in, wiggling your hot hips like a slattern! The Captain, he wanted to torture you straight off, but Willy, he likes tricks and sleights and subtleties. That is the way magic is. It never works on you until you have been told. That is why the elfs tell the magicians so much of the dark lore, and the magicians in Hollywood and New York put these things in stories and books. The vampire bite can't bite unless you hear about them as a child. Why else would we not use the Black Spell to sponge all memory of us away? Why would we let anyone remember the name of Jack o' Lantern? He is as old as the Picts, older than Caesar." Crookshank shivered and looked around nervously. "Don't mind me! Go back to what you were doing!"

She narrowed her eyes and shook him again. "So you told me how it works. Because you had to."

"Don't you wish you had a memory like an elf? Now, can you bring to mind the exact wording I said? No, no, you cannot. Poor thing."

He put his little hands on her finger and thumb and pushed them open. She strained, but in vain.

The tiny creature, less than nine inches tall, now twisted her thumb so painfully, she was forced down to one knee, wincing. He threw back his head and laughed. "Girly, did you think to overmaster me? I let you grab me. I wanted it. Your hands are soft and fair, and feeling you caress my body lights up my love-lamp. And when I anger you, how brightly you blush! How your bosom heaves! Your eyes, how they flash! Every time you changed clothes, I watched you! Do you really, truly think a half-blood Daughter of Eve can outsmart a true-blood Son of Air and Old Night? Pshew and Pshaw! I let you start this fire because I mean to build this house back bigger and finer than before after Wilcolac returns from the Tithing Ground with all the bounty the devils will pay for the soul of your Poor Tom Moth. He thought he could outwit Rotwang, poor Tom, who had him outwitted nine ways from Saturday! Heh, heh. Get it? That is sort of a joke."

"I did not light this fire."

"You or your master. What does it matter? He has only stopped the last shipment of wolves from going out. There are nine hundred in the City of Corpses! Numbers enough to raise havoc even if the Black Spell will not be broken. It will warp and weaken, and then men will still go mad! And then your boy goes to the Tithing Ground!"

"Where is that?"

Crookshank released her thumb and hopped up onto the broken window jamb, looking down at her. "Hah! Hah! If I knew, I would tell you, for then you'd be damned certain to be certain damned. None can find that dark soil save he who walks through the Devil's own door!"

Yumiko rose to her feet, scowling, troubled.

He cawed. "And now are you here to steal back what Willy has rightfully stolen? The Cloak of Mists is hidden, and in my house, as long as I am here, I ordain that you will not find it. You will never find it!"

Just at that moment, the signal from the tracer hidden in the cloak stopped. On another channel the two tracers hidden in the crates downstairs also stopped. It was not hard to guess why. The electronics were not designed to pass through a furnace level of heat unharmed.

Crookshank laughed, a sound like that of jackals yapping. "What now, serving wench? You have lost all, and I have won! All! All, I have won!"

"Not all," she said, "Not what you want most from me."

"Eh? What's that?"

Yumiko opened her hand and unzipped her suit front, showing her cleavage. She said, "You have conquered me and won my heart! Take your reward!"

Crookshank was taken by surprise. He clung to her wrist, eyes goggling. "Wait. Is this some trick you ply on a poor old house hob?"

She pouted as alluringly as she could and began to tug the fastening back up. "Well, if you don't want me… and after I saved myself for you!"

The little man leaped with great alacrity toward her décolletage, but she was quick enough to get the fastener shut. He clung like a miniature monkey to the bosom of her suit, trying to find the hidden fastener. She turned the ring on her finger four times widdershins. She turned weightless, invisible, and insubstantial, and found herself in a realm of utter darkness. The black shadows of the dead, twittering like bats, began to rise up from below. But at her elbow was a blue shadow.

4. The Rule of Deaths

Yumiko said, "Jack, is that you? Help me."

"In whose name do you ask?"

"Saint Barbara! In the name of Saint Barbara. You and I both died unforgiven. We are in her keeping."

The blue shadow reached out with a hand and plucked the little figure of Crookshank off her bosom. Crookshank screamed until black shadows gathered and hardened around him. Then the little man's screaming, wailing, and cursing grew dim and faint, as if they came from far off, but he never ceased nor paused to breathe.

The ghost said, "I will help you."

He pointed with the two javelins in his hand at the fluttering, shrieking shapes of hungry shadows rising up from below. They flew in jerky, ungainly motions to reach them, but they could not grow closer, for adverse winds drove them back.

The ghost asked, "Does any memory of my kingdom remain on Earth? Is any word spoken of fair Dal Riata? Do the druids yet revere the kingly names recorded on the Drosten Stone?"

"I don't know."

"Is Iach son of Uradech, Iach the Strong, remembered only for the carved gourd his foes propped atop his headless corpse to mock it? I won the hand of the Queen of the Shee of Cornwell in nine great wars, answering the nine riddles of the salmon, and wrestling the nine runes of the wind gods from the nine worlds. Ere Brutus, ere Eochaid, ere Gann, or Sengann, I ruled and reigned. Are none of my deeds recalled?

She said, "I don't know. My memory is lost."

"It is in the land of the dead."

"May I have it back?"

The ghost said, "The dead have no art to raise the dead."

"Who can?"

"You know better than I, Daughter of Dandrenor. Nor may I keep this imp of evil here with us if you cannot name his crime."

"Well… I am not sure how exactly he did it, but he put me in his debt. He told me the rule. *In magic, if you owe someone, he will find you again.* And I saw later how fairies and elfs are so quick to repay a good turn with a boon. But the boon I thought I was giving him—I thought I was freeing him from Wilcolac—did not exist because he was no slave, no serf. He was the senior partner. He was the one who runs the house. Wilcolac only lives there. Did someone follow me? Did I betray Winged Vengeance? Will my debt to him continue and let him find me later?"

"That ring you bear was given to you that you may lead those who are called to come into the land of ghosts. But your time is not yet. Dark powers are hunting you. Each time you use the ring to enter the darkness, you grow clearer to their dark sight."

"You did not answer my question!"

"Nor you mine. What is his crime?"

Then, she remembered what she had been told of the purpose of the Cobbler's Club. "Lust. It that enough to condemn him?"

"It is enough, for now."

"I am not innocent. I mean, I helped him. I dressed up and danced and... I did not think there was any harm in it. What is wrong with a girl attracting the eyes of men?"

"Whose eyes?"

"I don't understand."

"For whose eyes did Heaven shape your charms? For yourself? For a crowd? For pay? Or for the one other for whom you are intended?"

"Crookshank's crime was not against me, was it? It was against Tom."

"This imp is larger here than in your world, for here he is a mighty spirit, but it is given me to exact from the living a term of service sevenfold as harsh and long as I served. I was his watchdog and spy. Now the hounds of Hell will take him for their sport, and I shall take his eyes. He will await the judgment here."

"Await? Isn't this Hell?"

"This is Earth!" The cold voice of the ghost held, for once, a note of surprise.

"How can this be Earth?"

"It is a dark part of Earth, deep in the Mists. Here we shadows who have not yet crossed the dark river linger for a season. Do not return to this dark place without the Father Dominic. Next time, I cannot be at hand to protect you."

And he reached and took her hand and twisted the ring clockwise until it turned white.

"But I do not know any Father Dominic!" she said. But there was no one there but a dark room, filled with smoke, and the wash of bright searchlights illuminating the broken window.

Yumiko remembered the final boast of Crookshank. His curse that she would never find the cloak had been strangely worded. *As long as I am here.*

He was not here now.

She brought up the last known position of the tracer. The cloak had not been moving. The red dot floated on the mirrored panels of the wall to her left. Or, rather, it floated behind them.

Yumiko found the mock orange bloom decorating the mirrored panes four and a half feet above a decorative acacia bloom on the floor and touched both.

A mirrored pane slid back and then whined and jammed. She took out the hacksaw she had so recently acquired and made short work of cutting through the sliding hinges holding the panel in place. The panel fell with a crash and broke. Beyond was the secret passage she had seen before. On a hook right at hand was the tenebrous and supernal Cloak of Mists.

5. *Elfine, at Last!*

One moment later, Yumiko was swooping through the night air weightlessly to where Sir Garlot stood next to a dazed and blank-eyed police captain. This captain was shooing others away with stiff gestures and stiff words. "Mounted police business! Move along!"

Two moments later, she had the bottle with Elfine in her hand, and Sir Garlot was trotting away. Whatever words of cold farewell he spoke, she did not hear. Yumiko touched the blue glass to one of her red iron arrowheads, and the substance, which was not glass after all, popped like a bubble rather than shattered like glass. Elfine grew up to normal size as fast as she fell out of the bottle, so her wondering eyes, bright with joy, were the same level above the ground before and after she resumed her full size. Her wings vanished. She was wearing her green bodice and short shirt with her pom-pom slippers.

And then in the next moment, the two girls were crying and hugging. Yumiko had her mask raised. Both were talking at once, and when Yumiko fell silent, Elfine spoke enough for two.

But once Sir Garlot had left, whatever influence he had over the eyes and minds of mortal men left also, and so now firemen were pulling the two girls back from the scene, medical technicians were handing them bottles of salty juice and telling them to drink up to stave off dehydration, and a bewildered police captain demanded to know what was going on.

"I have got three corpses, one of them a nurse, hanging from lampposts at the intersection. They have little notes on their chests. Notes written in blood! And they are pinned there by arrows in their hearts. Even weirder, there are two large dogs hanged by the neck and dangling out of upper-story windows of the building. Who the heck hangs a dog? We cannot get in because of the fire, and all the evidence is burning away! What can you tell me about this?"

Yumiko said, "I do not think I can tell you anything about it, officer!" and then, to her horror, a giggle rose in her throat and erupted from her giddy, happy face, and there was nothing she could do about it but cover her mouth with both hands.

6. You Remind Me of the Babe

The police officer said, "Everyone here saw you fly up to the window and fly back down. You shoved one of the survivors out the window. She says you are the one who lit off the explosions in the basement. And what about all this gardening? Yards and yards of lavender flowers spread all over all the doors, and garlic and onions are on the windows."

Elfine said helpfully, "That is wolfsbane, Mr. Copper Flatfoot Man!"

The officer glowered at Elfine and then glowered even more forcefully at Yumiko. "What kind of outfit is that? What is with the cape? Why did you bring a bunch of dogs up on the roof? What about all those people you shot? I have two witnesses who say it was you!"

Yumiko said, "Not I! It was my master."

"Your what now? People saw you! Up there! A moment ago!

"I am a fox," said Yumiko. "He is a crow!"

Elfine said, "Let me explain it to him."

Yumiko, bubbling with laughter, could not speak, but gestured to Elfine, inviting her to explain it.

"Officer, I am a fairy detective from fairyland. But sometime I do crimes here, too. I come from across a sea that you cannot see, but I was seized by ne'er-do-wells, and I was held in a well by ruffians who roughed me up and made me unwell because, well, I well knew where their new base was. I got shipped around and around in a crate until I ended up in Willy's basement... It was a basement base. But I do not mean the elf knight who nicked me! He netted me with a net! His base is base under a baseball diamond. All these things are all around you, yet you are blind to them. Blind as a blind cop who cannot see! See?"

The officer said, "See what?"

"See you! You cannot see anything, practically, because your brain is stupid because it is covered in mist. You must have missed seeing whatever the mystical mist is misting, mustn't you? It musses your eyes. You men are as helpless as babies! You remind me of the babe!"

He said, "What babe?"

Elfine clapped her hands and cheered. "The babe with the power! What power? The power of hoodoo! Who do? You do! Do what? You remind me of the babe!" She leaned close and whispered to the police officer. "That is something *human beings* say. Shirley Temple said it to Jareth the Goblin King. It is from a movie about Bobby Socks. And bachelors. One of them did not have a mate. Either it was the sock or the bachelor. I learned about it from human school when I was studying humans. You are an endangered species."

Yumiko, by that time, was laughing too hard, too elated by joy, to care or to warn Elfine.

And so a few moments after that, both girls were locked in the back of a police cruiser with their hands cuffed behind their backs.

7. Moths in Chains

Elfine was still talking. "Yumiko Moth? What kind of name is that? You solved the mystery without me! *The Case of the Confused Crimefightress* is over and done! You should have waited! I wrote down notes and everything!"

Yumiko said, "I still have to find the City of Corpses. Unfortunately, that man that the police are shooting at is my old master, and I think he just burned up all my leads. And I have to find the Tithing Ground, but no one knows where it is, except someone who has been there before or walked through the Devil's door, whatever that is."

"My nose itches." Elfine said, "I know where the City of Corpses is. It is a necropolis, a graveyard. That is just a fancy word for it."

"They are hiding werewolves in a graveyard? Nine hundred of them?"

"Where else?"

"Which graveyard?"

"Calvary Cemetery in Queens. There are stairs that lead down. The entrance is hidden beneath a mausoleum. It had a dome with a statue of Saint Joseph on the top. I think a man buried his son there. I saw them go in with their crates. I would have to show you."

"Then we have to go."

Elfine said, "I'd love to, but look!" She turned her back to Yumiko and wiggled and jerked her hands in her handcuffs, so that the links tinkled. "These are made of iron. I cannot shrink. I mean, I can a little bit by ducking my head and hunching up, but that does not really count."

"I will handle it."

"And I don't have any magic for escaping. I could not get away from Sir Garlot either. The world won't bend the rules for me for escapes and things like that. It is not my genre."

Yumiko said, "I said I will handle it. Thank you."

"Do you have magic now? You seem more sure of yourself that you did three weeks ago."

"This is my genre."

Yumiko waited until the police cruiser was stopped at a stoplight. She leaned back and tapped with the toe of her boot on the glass separating the front seat from the back. "Pardon me, officer. May I?"

The officer who was not behind the wheel turned and slid open a small clear slot. "What is it, miss? I am not taking you for ice cream shakes, so stop asking."

Yumiko said, "Thank you for the hospitality. We enjoyed ourselves, but it is time to go."

But the officer did not answer. The slot was narrow, but it was large enough for one of the hypodermic arrowheads from her utility belt, fitted with an ampoule of tranquilizer, to be shot from the magnetic accelerator in her derringer and to pass neatly through to strike the officer in his neck. It was a difficult shot, with her gun hand pinned behind her back, but she was flexible enough to twist and bring her hand around her hip. The other officer turned, startled, and so was at a bad angle, therefore Yumiko had to ricochet the second dart, this one blown from her helmet snorkel as if from a blowpipe, off the rear-view mirror to strike him at an exposed part of his neck.

She left both pairs of handcuffs lying neatly on the back seat of the cruiser but took her hypodermic darts and made sure the rear doors were once more locked from the outside before departing. The light turned green, and the shouting and honking behind the motionless police cruiser began. The two girls skipped across the crowded sidewalk in the confusion and hurried away from the scene.

Yumiko was surprised to hear birds twittering and to see the pink light of dawn striking the eastern faces of the gray towers high above. What had seemed at most an hour spent in the elf-mound of Is-Elfydd had been twelve hours or more. Yumiko felt grateful it had not been longer.

Chapter 10

The Lass from Elfland

1. *Tailors and Giants*

The two girls walked, or rode the train or bus, for fifty-eight minutes all told. They spoke as they went.

During the first leg on the train, Yumiko told of the events since Elfine's kidnapping: how Yumiko had been drawn into a trap by Lucien Cobweb the Wolflord at Catoblepas warehouse but had been saved by two boys named Gilberec and Matthias Moth; how Yumiko had taken a job as a dancer for Wilcolac Cobweb at the Cobbler's Club, but this was yet another trap, one intended to discover the hiding place of Winged Vengeance; how she had put a bugging device on the collie dog of Gilberec Moth, now revealed to be a servant of King Arthur and acting in his name. Tracing that bug had led her into a trap the dog set; how she had interfered in the duel between Gil and Garlot so that Garlot would lead her back to his treasure vault, unsuspecting. But her footsteps had betrayed her, and once again she had been detected and trapped.

Yumiko was quite glum by the end of this recitation, and she rested her head wearily against the window of the train, watching the light of the streets underfoot go by.

Elfine put an arm about her and gave her a hug. "Don't worry! Just because you are a failure at everything you try does not necessarily mean you will fail!"

Without moving her head, Yumiko slid her eyes toward the other girl's cheerful face. "Technically, I think it does mean that."

"No!" insisted Elfine, squeezing her tightly. "You don't understand how these things works."

"How do they work?"

"When the giant fights the little tailor, the giant trusts in his own strength. But the little tailor always wins in the end. He does not trust himself. He knows he is not strong enough. He asks for help."

"From his friends?"

"What friends can help against a giant? Don't be silly. From angels!"

"What?"

"Terrible angels shaped like wheels within wheels, and storms and staring eyes and swords of fire turning in each direction! And when the little tailor wins, he gives thanks because he is not all puffed up with pride like a giant. Giants do not know how to be thankful."

Yumiko murmured, "Thanksgiving is a source of joy unknown to melancholy elfs."

"Don't fret! All your horrible, embarrassing, clumsy failures are in the past!" Elfine bounced up and down on the seat. "You saved me! You'll save What's-his-name!"

"Tomorrow Moth."

Elfine tilted her head and stopped bouncing. "Wait. I know him. The son of Dr. Rocket. He is my third cousin four times removed. He ignited the Mount Sinabung eruption in Sumatra. Are you sure you want to save him? He is kind of dangerous."

"Dangerous or not, I know he was going to ask me to marry him. But I do not know if he actually did or not. I cannot remember!"

Elfine put her hands to her mouth and bit her nails. "I cannot stand the suspense! When do we find out if he did? Can I be your maid of honor?"

Yumiko smiled and patted her on the knee. "Yes."

"Oh! What colors should we have? If the bridesmaids have winter complexions like yours, they should wear icy tones rather than pastels. Are you going to invite any elfin relations to the wedding? It had better be a Unitarian ceremony because they cannot go into churchyards. Also, don't serve ham at the reception."

"Ham?" asked Yumiko, wondering if she had missed a comment.

"There is an ancient race that lives among Christian and Paynim that often hides their lineage. They were told the secret name of God, and for this reason all other races hold them in jealousy and suspicion, and every few years mobs rise up in fury and butcher them without cause. And they cannot eat ham."

Yumiko said, "Let us save the bridegroom first before planning the reception."

"Why? He is not going to have any say in the matter."

Yumiko said, "Because there is another thing to discuss first. You say the City of Corpses is in Queens. How do you know? And why were the Anarchists after you? For that matter, why did you come here?"

"Here on the elevated train? To make the bus connection at Lexington."

"Here in the Daylight World."

2. The Book of Ayre

Elfine told her story:

"Before his exile to Troynovant, my father once took me aloft in a hot-air balloon at the summer fair in Cranston, which is nigh to the northernmost lighthouse on the Isle of Man. He showed me a book he had brought aloft with him, a precious book that could only be read on holy mountains or at high altitudes, far above the Mists of Everness, for the ink was starlight, and each page glowed and shined. It was a very old book, for the last chapters were written in Greek, and before that, in Mycenaean, Voynich script, runes, and hieroglyphs, and the oldest parts were plates showing the dancing men of the cave painting script of Bhimbetka.

"He had me trace the letters and repeat the staves. Now, all the older elf generations suffer no loss of memory, and so they never inscribe words and letters save to cast a spell. This spell was to imprint into my memory words neither age, nor chants, nor drugs, nor mists, nor time could ever make fade."

And Elfine sang these words:

"*The great creator made his creations with a love of creation. But none can make who is not made free. Freeborn were born each tongue and tribe and nation.*

Creation is marred by marring order, balance, harmony; but none can love who loves not freely.

"*Justice miscarries, and mercy goes astray when love, true love, has not its proper say.*

"*Free are we to know life and bliss; free to know death and woe; free to ascend to the joys endless, free to fall into darkness below. The lonely soul, alone, lacks power to fly. The lonely soul, alone, has power to die.*

"*Truly alone is none; even the One who is One alone is Three in One.*"

Yumiko said, "I don't understand."

Elfine said, "Ayre Moth saw what happened to my ninety-nine sisters. Father did not want that to happen to me."

"What happened?"

"I told you this part. Did you forget? To swear the oath of fealty all Twilight swears to Night, which renders rebellion impossible. But some Moths have found a way not to swear. That is why I want to find my cousins. To find out how they did it."

3. *Aboard the Ironclad*

"Do you want to know how I smuggled my way into New York? I was quite clever about it. After father was exiled to Troynovant, he brought his library with him, and I read detective stories from the human world. Humans cannot simply enchant one another to get what they want, so they commit crime and they fight crime in ways the elfs don't know to watch for.

"My opportunity came when Erlkoenig had returned to Troynovant for the Wintertide Court. Snow buried the fields and roads in honor of his coming, and all the trees and towertops were white and bright with ice beneath the moon. The whole city was alarmed with the rumor that one of the ancient vampires of the Northbrood was at large. The Northbrood can drain a man's life as a basilisk can, merely with the fell light of his eyes, drinking not a drop of blood. It was Monday of the Anarchists, the Lord of Vampires.

"He was gathering barghests and cooshee and other hounds of elfland and offering to turn them into werewolves, to give them the bodies to wear of humans who were kinslayers.

"Tongues wagged, and rumors flew when the Winterking did not ask his own champion, or any of his own knights, to hunt down the Vampire Lord. Instead, the Winterking called upon Sir Bertolac the Golden, the Summer Champion, to hunt through the city and the coasts round about to discover the vampire's nest, or the hideout and smuggler's cove of the werewolves. It was thought that Erlkoenig did not wish to involve his own knights either because he did not trust them to be willing to overcome the Vampire Lord or, worse, did not trust that they were able. Nothing would darken their repute if Alberec's knight failed.

"But the Summer Knight did not use proper modern police methods. He just did not read pulp magazines, I guess, or get a proper modern education like mine.

"Well, I could work undercover where he could not! It was not hard for me to find a pack of whist hounds of the low and villainous sort, scofflaws and scoundrels. I kept pulling the tails of the horses of the knights or men-at-arms following Sir Bertolac, trying to get their steeds to buck them into the mud, or dropping beehives dripping with honey onto their helmets. One knight chased me right into the den of some bad hounds. And when those bad hounds got into dog fights with other packs, I went with whichever of the two was worse! So I wormed my way deeper and deeper into the dog underground."

Yumiko said, "So easily?"

"It was not easy. It took a long time. But I am close enough to fairy blood to pass for one. No one knows I have a memory. No one bothered to watch his mouth around me. So I soon heard where and when the Vampire Lord was recruiting his dogs. I do not need to give off light when I am small: I just do that to show lightheartedness, which helps with levity.

"I followed the first dog, and lost track of him, and then a second, and lost him also, but the third led me into a cave south of the city where there were a dock and rowboats waiting.

"With them were *shabti*, the men of clay brought to life by Egyptian magic. They can neither speak nor think nor betray. With muffled oars and smothered lamps, they rowed out into the bay. Below us in the deep was a giant manta ray, coated from wingtip to wingtip, mouth to tail, in armor. And it had a narwhal horn or lance it used to tear holes in ships.

"But it was not armor. This was a machine, large as any galleon or schooner, and there was nothing like it in the Night World. Its horn was no tooth but a ramming prow.

"I knew the Day Men had submersible vessels, but none like this. It was a thing of Twilight. It may make me sound bad, but my heart leaped when I saw it. I had always been told that I was second best, a dim copy of an elf. And here was something the elf world did not have.

"It was neither a motor vessel of the Day nor a magical galleon of the Night. It was a magical motor vessel. It was ours.

"The iron was scary, but I was able to keep away from it. Most of the ship was made of wood or copper or brass. Once I was aboard, I made friends with some rats living in the hold, and the rat's nests were in the wooden decks, not the iron hull. Not friends, exactly. I helped the rats pilfer food, and they did not eat me. They helped me. I could tell when someone was coming long before I saw or heard anything because the rats would get all stiff and quivery.

"This ship was the biggest machine I had ever seen, and the sound of turning wheels and terrible energies was always in the air. The decks were lit with gaslight. I crept along corners during the dog watch, looking.

"I saw the great brass wheel the helmsman used to steer and the two ports like eyes in the conning tower that showed the black waters streaming by overhead.

"I saw the smaller, eight-man submarine gunboats like remoras clinging to the sides of the ship, inside half-shells that could be pumped full of water or air to allow them to come and go at will.

"I saw the galley and the workrooms and engines, the bunks for the men, the quarters for the officers.

"Once I crept into the captain's cabin, and I saw Monday, the Vampire Lord, in his high-collared black cloak and wide-brimmed black hat, playing Mozart's *Requiem* on the pipe organ. He was playing *Dies Irae*. Sadness was in his terrible eyes, and he did not hear me, and turn, and look at me, and kill me. After that, I stuck to the rat's nest.

"Under the sea is the perfect place for him to hide. You would think more vampires would take advantage of it. There is no sunlight in the deep, not way down below the continental shelf, and even if the air bottles failed, he would be safe.

"Once we fought with a great squid. The ship rammed the monster and ran it through with our prow, but it wrapped the hull with its tentacles, and the hullplates groaned. We shocked it with lightning from the ram, but it did not let go. We blew all ballast and rose to the surface into a tempest, dragging it up with us, and all its phosphorescent skin turned red with anger. The captain, a fierce, red-faced man with an iron hand named Saturday, sent out stout sailors with harpoons to battle the beast. The ship's mast was struck by lightning, and this recharged the weapons enough to slay the beast. The great corpse was lashed to the starboard side of the ship. During the watches that followed, we sailed on the surface while the corpse was flayed and butchered. The sailors had to drive the sharks away.

"Another time, we were pursued by a tall, strange vessel that showed no running lights, flew no flag, and moved without sail or screw or wheel. We dove, but she sank and followed us. Down and down into a crevasse in the sea we went and lost sight of her.

"We put in for a week at Back Cup Island, where they have a dock and shipyard hidden in the crater lake of a dead volcano cone. We took on water and supplies, including pineapples, and men let the dogs out six at a time to be exercised. But I was not discovered.

"How the ironclad submersible got around the Great Wall of Mist between the Third and Second Hemisphere, I do not know. Maybe we dived under it while we were sailing under the ice cap.

"All I know is that one day, there was a lot of noise and banging and carrying on. The sailors were cursing like sailors. I could smell fresh air. So I hid in a crate and waited for it to be unloaded.

"I peeked out and saw we had made port. I saw the man ordering the *shabti* around. He was tall and dressed like a pharaoh, in white linen, wearing a gold death-mask to hide his face, and a pschent covered his hair. He had both men of clay and of wood to serve him, and he ordered them with gestures of the flail or the crosier he had in his hands. His mask spoke for him, but he never spoke. Men called him Wednesday of the Anarchists, or Lord of Mummies.

"The whole vast dockyard and kennel warehouse were underground, but I flew up through a vent. Guess where? Bedloe's Island."

Yumiko said, "I am afraid I do not know where that is."

"It is the one the Statue of Liberty is on."

The first shipment point was LIs. It was not a Roman numeral for fifty-one. It was an abbreviation for Liberty Island. Yumiko was startled, "How can this be? There are tourists. The island—how big is it?"

"Fourteen acres. But they could have had mermaids help them hollow out the caves beneath, in which case it might be bigger on the inside than it looks on the outside. And if you have a base buried in the bedrock below the river, what does it matter how big the island is above it?"

"But the tourists! And the police! How can you run a smuggler's shipyard right under the toes of a famous monument?"

"What makes you think the police do not all work for the Anarchists? The tourists could all be actors or wax dummies just pretending to be tourists. All their bases have to be in famous spots. In case they are discovered. It makes it harder for the elfs to erase all memory of the place from everyone's mind."

Yumiko remembered Ruff saying the same thing about organizing a duel on the Brooklyn Bridge. "It seems insolent. A monument to liberty hiding anarchists."

Elfine shrugged. "If you ask them, the Anarchists will say they like liberty, all the liberty, and nothing but liberty."

"What happened next?"

"There is not much more to tell. I hid in a crate with a whist hound with red ears named Shuck. We talked, or, actually, I played dumb, and he talked. He seemed to think eating a man and taking his place, his memories and so on, would be great.

"The human involved—if Shuck was right—apparently thought he was going to get werewolf powers, something he could take on and off like a cloak, and no one told him that he was just going to be possessed by a dark spirit and be the horse carrying a rider.

"Our crate was hauled in the back of a truck to an underground place full of dead rats that smelled horrible. Then, two days went by while some men took Shuck out of the box and did horrible things to him. I think the men were Cobwebs.

"I flew out once or twice and looked around, but there was evil, powerful evil, all over the place, and the doors were locked without even a keyhole for me to slip thorough. I was hungry.

"So I just hid in the crate, and then on the next day, Shuck was shoved back in. He was kind of dazed and not talkative. Men moved the crate to a truck and then to the cemetery.

"I got out of the truck before it actually passed the gate and went onto holy ground. I was still curious, though, so after a bath and a meal made of bird's eggs, I went back to the cemetery gate. I could see them on the hilltop in the distance. They were still unloading. I waited for the same truck to go back out through the gate. This time I just followed it from the air, or I hung on to the antenna and let it pull me.

"It went to a place that dogs like Shuck might like: gambling and swearing and lots of drinking hard liquor. I kind of liked it because it had humans and half-bloods and elfs all in the same place, just laughing and losing money and dancing. Everyone was getting along! It was just what I had heard America was like.

"I poked around, and I fiddled with the roulette wheel so it would spin better, and then I talked to the house hob and paid my respects.

"He gave me an idea on a nice place to stay while I was in the city since he said I could pass for a human, too. I asked him about the underwater ship, and he said its name was *Nautilus*. He seemed really interested, and I told him all about her. I asked him about my cousins, and he said they would be coming by the Friday after next, so why shouldn't I stick around?

"But I said, no, I did not want to do that. And then a pumpkin and some evil men tried to catch me to make me stick around.

"And I almost got away, but I did not. I ran outside, but one of them snared me. And then you came down out of the night sky wrapped in the American flag to save me!"

4. The Angels Stopped Coming

They walked from the train station to the bus stop. Yumiko wore her black trench coat with the collar turned up and the cowl tucked away. She hid her mask in a cloak pocket, which she turned into a sash and wore about her waist. She bought a green poncho from a street vendor selling umbrellas and rain hats and gave it to Elfine in the hope that the blonde half-fairy would be less conspicuous. Elfine declared that she loved her gift and ran excitedly down the sidewalk, flapping her arms to make the poncho fabric flutter.

They took the bus across the Queensboro Bridge past Sunnyside to Flushing. Yumiko found seats in the back, hoping to avoid attention. Elfine swung from one hand-strap to the next and led the bus driver and passengers in singing a rousing chorus of "Take Me Out to the Ballgame" and then "We Are off to See the Wizard".

The girls got off at Roosevelt and 51st in Flushing. Elfine waved goodbye to the bus driver and to every passenger whose child had recently lost a tooth, whose names, for some reason, she knew.

They walked for ten minutes or so. The immense green slopes of the cemetery were visible in the near distance, dotted with headstones, obelisks, monuments, and mausoleums. The skyline of famous buildings rose across the water, looking ominously like a larger version of the same scene.

"No skipping when we enter the graveyard," warned Yumiko. "And no singing show tunes! I was surprised you did not get knifed by the big boy in the ball cap. The BAM shaved into his skull is his gang sign."

"He had a nice baritone! *Katie Casey was baseball mad! Had the fever and had it bad!* Besides, even the worst man was once a baby, and every baby can see the fairies who come to dance around his crib."

Yumiko glanced at Elfine sidelong. "Why do fairies dance around cribs?"

"Newborns tell us news of the paradise in whose gardens they were so recently formed. But then they grow up, lose the second sight, forget paradise, and forget us." Elfine sighed wistfully and pouted. "The world is so sad! Men would be happier if you could just remember things."

"There is little hope of that, in my case," said Yumiko without expression. "But I will gather up what broken fragments of my life as I may and save my love." She shrugged, smiled at Elfine, and spoke again. "Strange that you say 'us' and 'you.' You talk as if you are a fairy and I am a human, but we are both Moths. Both half-and-half."

Elfine scowled and stamped her foot. "And the other fairies in Garlot's bottles never let me forget it! They *teased* me! They were so *mean*! Just because I am not as dainty and fine as they are! And they were always surprised to see me the next morning, and so they said the *same* mean things again! For three weeks!"

Yumiko nodded and put a gentle hand on the other girl's shoulder. "I never got over finding out that I am not full-blooded Japanese. I must resign myself to the shame."

"Shame?"

"Of being a mongrel. Of having mixed blood."

Elfine giggled and clapped her hands. "But you don't have to worry about that any more! This is *America*! We are in America. Here, it does not matter what you were born. It only matters what you make of yourself. That is why I came. My Dad says it is insane for elfs to boast about being pure-bloods, considering."

"Considering what?"

"Considering where they come from. The Night Folk, before the Great Flood, could change their appearance, size, and hue, so you could not tell who was what except by how he acted. Back then, there was no big difference between elfs and efts and pooka and sprites, except one looked after men, and the others looked after fires or fauna or flowers."

"What happened?"

"The world got old and wicked. Elfs got weary. The ancient privileges diminished, dried up, and died off. The angels stopped coming."

Elfine pouted sadly as she skipped along, kicking a pebble down the sidewalk as she went.

She continued, "The Night People are generally now stuck in one or two shapes or sizes. You see? Leprechauns are shoemakers; fire-breathing efts are fighting-men; banshees are washerwomen and corpse-dressers; and Nibelungs are blacksmiths. The different shapes were once only their work clothes, but now they are stuck in them. And their children take after them. Some of the older ones, like Nimue or Malen or Morgan, can still do the old tricks."

Yumiko was puzzled. "Are elfs and fairies the same race or different races?"

"Same race but different jobs. Different *genres*. I guess we are different races now, but we did not use to be. Elfs can get tiny, and I can get big like this, and we look a lot alike, but the fairies never agreed to the deal, so we never have to pay the tithe."

"Tithe? Is this the same tithe?"

Elfine nodded energetically but then said, "Same as what?"

"Tell me about this deal."

"Once upon a time, the proud, dread, and darkest Prince of the Fallen Angels, whose name it is dangerous to say, convinced the fairies that the waters of Lethe, the River of Oblivion, would sponge their memories of our old home away, so they could be happy again.

"Instead, the fairies forget everything, and now they are *too* happy.

"But the Queen of Heaven took pity on the fairies and sent guardian angels streaming down from windows in Heaven, with crowns of light and swords of fire. You cannot see them because you would turn to ashes if you did, but sometimes they whisper things to the fairies, things no one knows, which is why fairies sometimes know things for no reason. It is to make up for everything they forgot. So that is the difference. Elfs do not have anyone to watch over them. So they get in trouble."

"But what was this deal?"

"I told you about this before. You don't remember? Maybe I skipped the details. The first High King of the Elfs, Asagrim son of Aer, was taken to a tall mountain and promised all the fair kingdoms of the Earth spread below if he would bow and worship the Prince of Darkness. As a sign whereof, every seven years, the elfs give over one tenth of their produce and profits and the firstborn of their flocks, and their firstborn sons are made to pass through fire."

Yumiko's face went blank and then went pale. Her steps became slow and mechanical. Elfine, skipping along, wrapped up in the telling of her tale, continued heedlessly:

"Asagrim, who was childless, agreed at once. But then he fell in love with a daughter of the North Star, and was wed, and had a child, and did not want to give him up, and so he asked if a willing victim could be substituted in the child's stead: and this was done. Asagrim went to live in Tartarus in his son's place, and Uther was raised to the throne of the High King. Uther refused to pay the tithe, and the Prince of Darkness cursed him and hurled him from the throne, and no one knows his whereabouts to this day."

Yumiko's steps grew slower. Her eyes had an unfocused look. Elfine, dancing on ahead, continued speaking.

"The Night world feared the Darkness and did a wicked thing. The son of Uther, when still a babe in swaddling, was placed in a coracle and abandoned to the mercy of the sea. Wave after wave, each mightier than the last, carried him away from the shores of Elfland, until a ninth wave slowly rose and plunged, roaring, and all the wave was flame. At the crest of the ninth wave, seen by the sharp-eyed against the rising sun, the babe arose, stood on his legs, and raised his hand in a sign that he would one day return. And so he was borne away toward mortal lands. The second born was Alberec, who came to the throne of the High King in his stead. You are probably wondering what the name of the firstborn is…?"

5. *The End of All Tales*

Yumiko halted. She swayed. She sat down heavily on the small strip of green grass between the sidewalk and the wall of rough, unhewn stones. She sat with her back to the wall, facing the four noisy lanes of traffic passing by on the boulevard.

Elfine now looked over her shoulder, eyes wide and mouth quirked to one side. She turned and scampered back and gazed down silently. The raven-tressed girl was seated in her black trench coat, head bowed, arms wrapped about her knees, huddled into a frail, dark shape.

Elfine pouted, as if annoyed her friend had not been listening to her tale.

Yumiko spoke in a dull voice. She sounded much like one who has been struck in the head by a mallet and is still numb in the tongue. "The people tithed to Tartarus. You said they are taken alive. They are not simply killed? Sacrificed?"

Elfine said, "Killing them would allow the baptized people to escape."

"You said it had to be a willing victim." Now she did look up, a terrible, tiny ember of hope in the desolation of her blank eyes.

Elfine rolled her eyes and cocked her head, staring fretfully at the clouds. "Well, what counts as a sign of willingness is open to interpretation. Proserpine is a girl who was starving and ate some pomegranate seeds, and eating the food of the dead counts as accepting their hospitality. Or signing a contract in blood saying you will serve a familiar spirit for seven days in return for seven years of his service if one of those seven days is the day the familiar spirit is due to go back down below. Or if a damned magician disguises himself as a man's wife, and the man agrees to go in her place, thinking he is saving her. Or they get him drunk, or enchant him, or tell him it is temporary. It is all very tricky and unfair. Not every legal system is as fair as what they have in Merry Old England."

As Elfine spoke, the ember of hope faded and died.

Elfine squatted down next to her friend, and put her arm around her shoulders, and stroked her hair, and said, "There, there, it will be all right."

Yumiko said, "My fiancé is going to be taken alive to Hell. He may have been taken already. How are you so sure it will be all right?"

Elfine said, "All tales have happy endings."

"That is not true. What about *Romeo and Juliet*?"

"Only the middle part is sad. Juliet was condemned by Minos to be whirled about on dark winds in the Second Circle for centuries, and Romeo was turned into a bleeding tree in the Seventh Circle. And they forgot how to pray. But the prayers of Laurence and John reached Saint Lucia. The Prince went down to Hell and brought up Adam and Moses and Elias and John the Baptist. When the Prince was weary from fighting demons, he rested in the shade of a tree, and this was the tree where Romeo was, and Romeo asked not for himself to be saved from damnation, but for Juliet. Romeo said it was his suicide that drove Juliet beyond grief, which means her death was his to blame, so that he is a murderer, not she a suicide. And then again, when he was weary from battling demons and devils, the Prince stepped into the blowing winds to cool his brow, and Juliet came whirling down and asked that Romeo be forgiven for his suicide since it was mistake, not malice, which drove him to it.

"And all the peoples of their families and city who would have died before their time had the feud continued came to the Prince and prayed, saying that the deaths of these two lovers was not suicide, but sacrifice, from which the peace that blessed fair Verona was born.

"Perhaps for these reasons, or perhaps for a reason known only to him, the Prince had compassion and took the foolish lovers by the hand. Not without travail, he led them up the cornices of Mount Purgatory and gave them the opportunity for salutary repentance. And the angels were amazed with the Prince, for one and all said suicide was unforgivable. But the Prince commanded Heaven and Earth to pray for those who have taken their own lives.

"As for the lovers, together they entered eternity. Romeo is within the star Castor and Juliet within Alhena, and they dance together in the constellation of the Twins, clothed in brightness, on the azure floor of Heaven."

Yumiko scowled. "That is not part of the story."

"Mortals only ever tell a small part of any story because they only see a small part of the world: the part on this hither shore, where evil reigns, time rots, and death rules all. On the thither shore is more to tell and the true end."

Yumiko calmed herself and controlled her breathing. She murmured in Japanese, "*Thus shall ye think of all this fleeting world: a star at dawn, a bubble in a stream; a flash of lightning in a summer cloud, a flickering lamp, a phantom, and a dream.*"

These were the words of the Enlightened One from the Diamond Sutra. But Yumiko did not want to find the windless peace of Nirvana, the peace of non-self-being, if it meant surrendering her beloved, whose living face she had yet to see.

Yumiko was confused. It seemed to her then that Joan the Wad, who was willing to defy Heaven or Hell or both at once, whatever the cost, to be with her lost love, was more enlightened than any girl who failed to defy Nirvana to be with hers. She was certainly spunkier.

Was love merely one more illusion in a world of illusion? It seemed to Yumiko then, at that moment, like the fundamental and infinite truth of all truths was love.

But then a voice spoke. *Don't listen. Elfine is lying. There is more to all stories, much more. But it is worse, not better. Far worse. Beyond the grave are sorrow, pain, and emptiness without end.*

Yumiko leaped to her feet, and this startled Elfine, who erupted into a conflagration of sparks and shrank to the size of a dragonfly, leaving her poncho on the sidewalk.

Yumiko shrugged out of her coat so that she could draw her weapons. She stood with a *kunai*, a heavy throwing knife, in one hand and her *kodachi*, a shortsword, in the other.

All tales ending happily? Don't make me laugh. All songs end in lamentations. All end in endless screams. There is no pleasure, no feast, no wine, no warmth, no light, and nobody forever.

For this was the voice of Kuckunniwi, the Cheyenne.

Beyond life is death. Beyond death, pain. Pain, hunger, cold, darkness, loneliness.

6. Saint Calixtus's Gate

The Cheyenne must have seen her at the Cobbler's Club during the fire and followed her here. She had, after all, taken no steps to shake any pursuit. Yumiko's eyes darted up, left, right. But where was he? Where was the voice coming from?

Some children in a station wagon on the boulevard, seeing her in her skintight black suit with knife and shortsword drawn, waved and cheered as their vehicle went by. Yumiko saw that the stone wall had a corner. She ducked around it.

Here, the wall was interrupted by a tall wrought-iron gate. A long avenue stretched before her, bordered by trees, into green slope after green slope thick with headstones, obelisks, winged statues, monuments, and mausoleums like windowless and miniature palaces. At first, she saw no people. Perhaps visiting hours had not yet begun, for the gate was shut.

She saw no sign of the Cheyenne, but he must be near. It was difficult at her full weight and with her hands full, but Yumiko lithely jumped, kicked off the gate posts, helped herself with a second kick against the crossbars, and sailed upside down over the top of the gate, her head, shoulders, hips, and thighs clearing the ornamental top spikes by inches. She clenched the knife between her teeth and took a bar in her free hand to slow her fall. She slid and somersaulted to an easy landing on the grass beyond, coming to her feet in a crouch.

Next to the wall, at an angle which had been invisible from the gate, near a marble statue of a fireman, was an immense red warhorse, wearing barding. A riding horse, slenderer and smaller, was with it. Both were cropping the grass.

A third horse, this one laden with burdens, including long lances, stood near. With them was a white donkey. A collie dog with a white vest and a raccoon mask around its eyes was trotting proudly back and forth around the horses, barking loudly.

Standing between her and the horses, with their backs to her, were two youths among the stones, talking in low tones. One was broad and tall and dressed in white linen with a blue surcoat, and a sword was at his side, hilts glittering with diamonds. The other was thin and long haired, wearing rimless glasses that gave him an owlish look. He was dressed in a white tunic and scapular with a black hood and cloak. It was the Swan Knight's Son and the Blackfriar's novice. Gilberec and Matthias Moth.

Both fell silent in mid-sentence, turned, and looked at her.

Yumiko looked back, as startled as they.

For a moment no one spoke. Gilberec eyed the blade in her hand and the knife in her mouth. He made no move to draw his sword. "So are you a ninja? Or a pirate?"

Chapter 11

The House of the Dead

1. Four Cousins and a Dog

Yumiko took the knife out from between her teeth. This *kunai* had a hoop in the pommel, into which she thrust her forefinger, and she began to flick her wrist to spin the knife blade. The motion formed a blurred disk of metal. "We've met," she said.

Matthias stared at her face. He said in a voice of slow surprise, "Is that you? You are the dancing girl who waited on us in the Cobbler's Club."

Gil said, "That girl was a redhead."

Matthias said, "Not the one who brought the caviar. She came in later and brought drinks. The one who stood in the corner and would not sit down."

Gil said, "The girl who is not Sorry. The one you saw floating through the mist on Leap Day." Gil said to her, "The last time we met you stepped on my foot."

Yumiko was a little surprised and glanced at the collie dog. "We've met since. You did not see me."

Matthias said slowly, "Gil. The shadow says this is the Foxmaiden."

"What makes him think so?"

Matthias looked meditative, as if he were listening to an inaudible voice. After a moment, he said, "In life, he was a bouncer at the nightclub where she was a dancer."

Gil said to him, "I told you she works for the magician."

Matthias said, "And I told you not to judge in haste. His job was to follow her when she went out to report to Winged Vengeance. They had penetrated her disguise."

Gil crossed his arms and scowled down at her. "So you really are the Foxmaiden? Now you are showing your face? I did not see you last time we met. Here." And he stepped over to the pack animal, drew out her two boomerangs, and tossed them into the grass at her feet. "Are these yours?"

She nodded. "They are mine."

Gil said, "I am happy, Miss, to hear whatever explanation you want to give. If you were a boy, I would break you in half."

Yumiko said, "I did it to save my friend, Elfine." Yumiko waved her hand behind her, as if to beckon the other girl to present herself.

Elfine, from behind her, called out, "Hi there! Wait a minute! I remember how to do this!"

Yumiko glanced over her shoulder. Elfine, full sized and dressed only in her green bodice and skirt, was pushed up against the gate, one arm through the bars, waving.

"I am the daughter of Iolanthe daughter of Ellyllon, and Ayre Moth son of sun-bright Pururavas. Ayre is the founder of the Manx branch of the family. He is legally considered a mortal even though he is as long lived as an immortal. Ayre's mother was Urvashi, who was born in this wise: Indra of the Thunders saw Nara-narayana meditating and sent a curse in the form of two *apsara* to distract him, lest his meditation unlock the enlightenment Adam lost and regain mastery over nature and the elements! Instead, Nara-narayana struck his thigh, and Urvashi came forth, and danced, and distracted the two of them, and they were put to shame. My name is Elfine."

Gilberec said, "I am the son of the Swan Knight and Ygraine of the Riddles. She is the daughter of Pellinore of Listenoise and Danaë of Arcadia. Of the Swan Knight, I can say no more. I am Sir Gilberec, vassal of Arthur."

Matthias said, "How do you do? I am the son of Carabosse the Maleficent and Malthus Moth. Malthus is the son of Mabon the Enchanter, son of Parlan, son of Phanes. Mabon is brother to Malagigi. I am Matthias."

The two boys looked at Yumiko, expectantly. Gil glanced at her sword and spinning knife and crouched stance and sighed in annoyance.

Matthias said, "If you wish to introduce yourself, please feel free. I don't know your real name."

The collie dog trotted up and sat down between Gil and Matthias and barked happily. This was Ruff, without his hat.

Gil said, "Is your name really Yummy Cutie?"

Yumiko frowned terribly at the dog. "Tell him to stop that! My name is Yumiko!"

Through the bars, Elfine said helpfully, "She is the daughter of Dandrenor the Grail Queen and Danger Moth! Danger Moth is the son of Bold Moth and is the brother of Fearless and Reckless, names they earned while searching for their missing mother, Kasumi-himi no Mikoto, who was struck three times by her husband, once for disobedience, once for weeping at a feast, once for laughing at a funeral. This broke the promise Bold Moth had given her, and so she returned to the hidden world. Reckless descended into Hell and became a necromancer and exorcist; Fearless circumnavigated the globe, slew giants in Patagonia, and earned a fortune in trade; and Danger, in the company of Cyrano Moth, ascended to Heaven in an engine shaped like a locust and impelled by gunpowder. There, he met Dandrenor. By the way, I have been looking for you."

The two boys looked thunderstruck and exchanged a glance, a shrug, and a wordless roll of the eyes.

Gil said to Yumiko, "So you are a cousin of ours? After all this time? You sure do not act it. Moths are supposed to help each other."

Matthias said, "I certainly would not have guessed. You are something of a figure of mystery to us."

Yumiko was not sure how to answer this, so she turned and said over her shoulder, "Why don't you shrink down and come through the bars?"

Elfine said, "I think this is holy ground. I– I am not sure I can come in. I may not be welcome."

Yumiko said, "Please, you must! I don't know what we are looking for!"

Gil said to Matthias, "Matt, go see to that, please."

Matthias nodded and went back to the gate.

2. A Requirement of Knighthood

Gil stood with his arms folded and his legs spread, his head tilted forward, as unselfconsciously as a prince. He bent his gray-green eyes upon Yumiko and said, "The relics of the departed are underfoot, awaiting resurrection. It is an ill place to draw a weapon. Put yours away. It would grieve me to put my hands on you."

Yumiko straightened up and sheathed her weapons. She rubbed the palms of her gloves against her thighs nervously, but, of course, no sweat was wiped from her hands.

Gil said, "Come over here, please."

She took a few steps and bowed nervously.

He said, "I am not going to hurt you. I would never strike a woman. But I would like an explanation. Sir Garlot is a wicked and faithless knight, and victory over him was put into my hands. Yet you shot him with arrows and blinded and nauseated me and my horse, Rabicane, with smoke." The red war steed neighed and prodded Gil in the shoulder with his nose. Gil said, "This greatly offended his pride since he was sure he could outrun and overtake Tachebrun, and for many a year, he wished to make the attempt."

Yumiko cast her eyes down, "Elfine was his prisoner. I needed Garlot to be wounded but survive the fight so that he would return to his treasure house, where his cauldron can heal his wounds. Malen the Red, his sister, told me he kept his fairy girls imprisoned there."

Gilberec said, "We are first cousins, you and I. My mother is your mother's sister. Why didn't you come to me?"

She looked up. "What do you mean?"

"Once I defeated him, I could have demanded the release of your friend, or all his prisoners, without any tricks, or cheats, or deceptions. To be allowed to ransom one's life is a requirement of knighthood, in honor of the one whose red blood ransomed us. Why not ask me for help?"

Yumiko was taken by surprise by this suggestion. "I– I don't know. It never occurred to me. I was alone. I had no one to trust. I thought you might arrest Elfine for smuggling. She's a lovable rogue. I don't know you."

Gil's eyes widened slightly. Now it was his turn to be surprised. "Of course you know me! You were there when I threw your master out the window of that rooftop restaurant where we met for tea when he shot his mouth off. We've talked at least twice, maybe four times. You know I would not lie to you."

Yumiko said, "I don't remember that. I don't remember anything!"

The collie barked and wagged his tail.

Gil said, "Why are you here? In this cemetery?"

Yumiko said, "This is the City of Corpses the magician shipped all the werewolves to once they were prepared. He is not neutral at all, but the sworn servant of Lucien Cobweb, who is Thursday of the Anarchists."

"Who told you that?"

"A ghost named Le Maudit. I shot him." Yumiko said, "Where is the Cheyenne? I heard his voice. And where is Elfine?" For neither she nor Matthias were in sight at that moment.

The dog barked. Gil said, "The Cheyenne is dead, and Elfine is around the building at the water fountain. Are you looking for Tom?"

"Yes."

"You think he is here?"

"Yes."

"Why? Who told you he was here?"

Yumiko said, "The house hob of the Cobbler's Club, named Sly Jack Crookshank. He was the one actually running the house. Or was. It is burned now. The magician was just a front."

Gil shook his head, "A tiny sprite that lives in a whiskey bottle? I am afraid he's been deceiving you, cousin. How did the Cobbler's Club burn down?"

"I– I don't know."

"You remember that I can hear it in your voice when you shade the truth?"

"I mean I do not know for certain, but I think it was Winged Vengeance."

The muscles in Gil's jaw twitched as he silently ground his teeth. "What, again? He has to go and destroy all our leads? All our evidence? What is his problem? Whose side is he on?"

Elfine came flying out from behind the corner of the gatehouse, circled Yumiko like a dragonfly, landed, and swelled up to full size. Matthias came into view and quickly trotted over. Matthias was smiling, "We hit the jackpot, Gil!"

3. Breaking Fast

Matthias stood grinning, and Gil said, "Out with it. What jackpot?"

Matthias gave Elfine an affectionate pat on the head. "Our cousin from Troynovant here knows where the *Nautilus* docks. That must have been why the Anarchist asked Garlot to catch her."

Gil said, "Where?"

Elfine said, "Bedloe Island."

Gil said, "Where is that?" But the dog barked, and Gil said, "You mean Liberty Island? Where the Statue of Liberty stands?" And the dog barked again, and Gil said in a ponderous tone of voice, "You mean where the statue stands called *Liberty Enlightening the World* but no one knows that except for some know-it-all dog because everyone else in the world calls it the *Statue of Liberty*? That island?"

Elfine hopped up and down and clapped her hands. "That is the one! It is made of copper. So it is elf-friendly. We can come to America too and be free. May I?"

Gil said, "May you what?"

Elfine said, "Be free! My daddy said you knew the secret. That is you! That is you two! You are called the Last Crusade. Are there only the two of you?"

The dog barked and raced in a circle and barked again. Gil said, "No, we are not called Super Action Team Swan. And there are three of us. Four, if you count Ruff."

Yumiko said, "Tom is the other member. He is here in the cemetery. You have to show us where."

Elfine pointed. "It is up the hill a ways."

Gil said to Elfine, "I cannot make you an American if that is what you are asking. There is an ordeal all must pass. A trial by paperwork and years of waiting. If you are asking to join the Last Crusade, that is not in my hands either. The Man in the Black Room selects us. Frankly, I am not sure if any willing volunteer is turned away. Nothing but a willingness to serve is required. Your aid now will display the willingness is present."

Elfine said, "I'd be happy to help! As long as I do not have to drive a long stick like that through people's bodies." She pointed at Gil's lance. "It looks messy and horrible."

"It is not a thing any girl should see," Gil agreed. He turned to Matthias, "Release the ghost and send him on to his reward. We have no more need of him." He turned again. "Matthias will require a little time to complete his work. Have you ladies had breakfast yet?"

Yumiko could not even remember the last time she ate. Was it during her shopping expedition with Malen? She had not ordered any room service in that hot-sheet motel, but she had stopped for a croissant and green tea at an open air café the morning before the duel on the Brooklyn Bridge. Which had been noon yesterday.

Yumiko said, "Actually, thank you. I am a little hungry. And Elfine has been kept in a bottle."

Elfine said, "Garlot's vassals fed us gruel, bean curd and yogurt, salads and salty tea, and made us exercise and do ballet twice a day. And then there was choir practice. As prison life goes, it was not so bad. We were kept in trim like fighting cocks."

Gilberec opened his saddlebags and drew out a brightly colored cardboard box. "I have some cold tacos from Taco Hut left over here and half a two-liter bottle of warm root beer that's gone flat. There is no cup, so you'll have to drink out of the bottle."

Elfine wrinkled her nose. "Boys eat such interesting things for breakfast!"

Yumiko bowed. "We are very grateful for your generosity."

Elfine looked nervous when Gilberec handed her the box and the bottle. He knelt, crossed himself, and clasped his hands over the fast food. "Bless us, Lord, and these, thy gifts, which we are about to receive from thy bounty. Through Christ, Our Lord, Amen." And he made the sign of the cross a second time. Elfine heaved a sigh of relief and laughed nervously.

"I suppose it did work!" she said. "But I don't feel any differently."

Gil handed her a cold taco. "The more mortal food you eat, the better you will be able to allow memories of past wrongs done you to fade, and the less things like music and the motions of the planets will influence your thinking. You will find yourself able to decide to do or not to do things that are now fixed in your character. If you start eating ambrosia and nectar again, however, you will return to a more dreamlike state."

Elfine wrinkled her nose again. "So eating a taco will make me more human? Who designed this world and its crazy rules?"

Gil said, "The designer is the same one who bids us eat his flesh and drink his blood every Sabbath, that we may consumed by him. The freedom you seek is found there. Looking for freedom in any other place puts you under the Black Spell. The fair enchantments of the elfs or the ugly malice of the devils will fix fetters on you."

Elfine said, "How are you immune from the oath that binds all of the Twilight folk?"

Gil said, "I swore to Arthur. That oath prevents Erlkoenig from demanding my fealty."

Yumiko said, "Where is the Cheyenne? I heard his voice."

Gil looked impressed. "You have good ears. He is in the land of the dead. As we would be if Matt has not seen him hovering near the booby trap that killed him. It turns out the rats in the city did know where Winged Vengeance was hiding—or one of his hiding places, at least. An abandoned factory in Harlem. The Cheyenne saw you going into the chimney and, much later, coming out."

Yumiko said, "I think I heard his motorcycle. Following me."

"Then he was sloppy. He could have kept his distance. He had a dowsing rod given to him by Sly Jack Crookshank that was pointed at you. The Cheyenne tried to break into the factory after you left. He found an upper door one can only reach from the roof of a neighboring building. This door opened into what looked like an elevator. But when he stepped in and pushed the button, it electrocuted him, and the trap-door in the floor opened and sent his body sliding down a long chute and into a dumpster filled with liquid filth sitting in a vacant lot on the other side of the building. We were not fooled by that trap, but we almost stepped onto the catwalk and would have blown ourselves up with limpet mines. The ghost warned us in time. Warned Matt. I cannot see him."

Yumiko said, "Where is this divining rod now?"

"We buried it with the Cheyenne."

"You buried him?"

"You sound surprised. You think we were going to leave a dead man lying in a garbage dumpster filled with sewage?"

Matt came walking back at that moment, looking weary. He doffed his eyeglasses and rubbed the tail of his tunic over the lenses with thumb and forefinger. "Well, his shadow is no longer cast on Earth, but unless our good cousin Elfine can help us, I am not sure where the entrance to the underground installation is. The Cheyenne mentioned the name, but with so many headstones here..."

Elfine pointed at a tall dome, perhaps the largest one in sight, dominating a nearby hill, rising like a smooth white mountain above the peaks and crags of obelisks and memorials. "That one there. The Johansson Mausoleum. That huge monument one on the hill there, with the marble dome and the statue of Saint Joseph on top."

Gil thanked her, and took the reins of his palfrey, and walked through the headstones rapidly toward where Elfine had pointed. Matt, who had been eating a taco, now strode after. The dog barked at the white mule, which only slowly stirred into motion. The red war steed trotted along at Gil's shoulder without being led. Yumiko followed.

Elfine skipped from headstone to headstone, chatting merrily. "It says Johansson. I thought maybe a man name Johan buried his son there. And there is a statue of Saint Joseph. He is the man who carries Baby Jesus. Have you heard about him? He was a humble carpenter, but his ancestors were kings."

Gil did not break his stride but answered and said, "His story is well known among mortal men. He breathed his last on Earth with the Virgin to one side of him and the Christ to the other, so all men wish to have such good company at death. To Saint Joseph I often pray since I wish my own father, whoever he is, to have Heaven's favor and protection."

Matthias said, "Before we go in, let us commend ourselves to his powerful intercession. Those whom Saint Joseph watches shall never die a sudden death, nor shall they be drowned, nor shall poison take effect on them, neither shall they fall into the hands of the enemy, nor be burned in any fire, nor overpowered in battle."

They came to the mausoleum. A dolomite dome rested on the intersection of four pavilions whose ornate entablatures in turn were held up by Corinthian columns. The pediment and frieze were decorated with grape and ivy leaf patterns. The entrance porch held great bronze doors molded with grape trellises. Beneath the architrave and between the columns on each face were three evenly spaced windows, each with a lattice of bars. The bronze doors stood open. A low ramp of wood covered the stairs. The doors and the ramp were large enough to admit a small truck.

In they went.

4. A Prayer before Battle

Within was cool and gloomy. The ceiling of the dome was a mosaic of colored glass showing Hercules battling Cerberus. Two archways opened up to the left and right into deep recesses, where angels in niches stood peering over sarcophagi with brass plates inset into the walls. A barred grate of heavy bars, shaped like curled acanthus leaves, blocked a third archway. A dark stair beyond led steeply down. At the top of the stair was a block and tackle for lowering weights. Mats had been placed on the marble pavement to protect it unsuccessfully from scars and scuffs caused by moving heavy bulks, no doubt crates.

The collie dog sniffed at the barred grate blocking the dark stair leading down and made a low growl. Gil said, "This is the place. They are here."

Elfine, craning her neck and staring upward, said, "How can they be here, where it is so quiet and pretty? This is holy ground, isn't it?"

Gil answered Elfine, "To hide. Elfs of purer blood cannot approach sacred things to desecrate them. The Cobwebs are half-mortal men, as we are."

Matt said, "In the holiest Church the most wicked evils will be found. Devils do not war with lukewarm believers, but with the saints."

Elfine got on her knees next to the door, put her nose to the locked grating as well, and sniffed. She said, "There must be another exit. Men or Cobwebs carrying werewolves in crates might go in or out this way, but not werewolves walking on their own feet. Besides, even a groundhog is wise enough to have a second escape exit out of a burrow."

Hoofbeats muffled by the mats laid here, Rabicane the war steed came stomping into the mausoleum. Sir Gilberec took the gleaming breastplate, leggings and helm of his armor from the saddlebag, and began to dress himself in his armor. His armor was cunningly fashioned to be donned by one man, without the need for a squire.

Matthias prayed aloud to the Trinity and asked for the intercession of Good Saint Anne to aid his prayers, and Saint Cyprian of Antioch, and the Cure de Ars. Elfine stared at him in wonder, every now and again asking who these people were and how good their hearing was. Matthias answered her questions with a smile. Gilberec asked him also to pray to Saint George, Martin of Tours, Joan of Arc, and Demetrius of Thessalonica.

Yumiko plucked on Matt's cloak hem. "If you please," she asked. Then, she stopped, overcome by a mingled sense of caution and humility. The eyes of Matthias within the circles of the lenses of his spectacles were mild. "Yes, cousin?"

"Is it possible for the dead to come again to life?"

He nodded and crossed himself. "If not, then all we believe and know is folly, and all in which we hope is vain. But not by any art of men or occult practice of devils can the thing be done, nor by elfin glamour, or any kind act of nature."

"Then how?"

"All mortal things are condemned to pass away. Mother Nature is the royal headsman. Only the pardon of the king can suspend or reverse her death warrant."

"I saw a bright lady. She was dressed in white with a red cloak. A great sword was in her hand, but she also held a lily and a palm leaf. And she offered me a cup. In it was not wine, but a golden fire."

Matthias said, "Did you see her with your eye?"

"In a dream. I think I was dead. I woke up in the hospital."

"The white robe and the white lily are her virginity, the red mantle and the palm are her martyrdom. She was slain by the sword for her faith. It might be any number of saints."

"A ghost called me the handmaiden of Barbara."

Matthias nodded. "If your vision was of Barbara, the cup she held was the host. Saint Barbara visits those who are struck dead suddenly—killed by lightning—and offers them last rites and a last chance to confess and repent.

Between the moment the lightning leaves the cloud and before it falls to the earth is time enough."

Yumiko stared at Elfine and then looked back at Matthias. "What did you do to her? She was unwilling to step on holy ground before and could not say prayers or hear them said."

Matthias said, "I baptized her. Normally, it is done by a priest, in a proper rite, with godparents at hand, and after due instruction. But in an emergency, in the middle of mortal peril, any layman can baptize any willing soul. If done in the name of the Father, Son, and Holy Spirit, the sacrament is valid no matter who performs it."

Yumiko felt a shock of emotion run through her. She had been alone since the moment she woke, alone and lonely with none to help her, no ally, no friend. Now, the very day she had freed Elfine, Elfine had joined *this*, whatever *this* was.

Yumiko knew it was unfair for her to feel jealous, but the feeling persisted. Elfine had exited the world and entered a rich mansion, and now the mansion door was closed, and Yumiko was on the wrong side.

Yumiko remembered hearing Gil's ringing words to Wilcolac. *Arthur serves truth and justice, and I serve him.* Those words had lodged in her heart. In a world of greedy beggars and crass liars, the urge to serve a high and noble cause was mystical, magnetic, and irresistible.

Yumiko had seen the wicked power of Malen fail only once. She had seen an attempt to corrupt a willing victim into a werewolf also fail. What was this power that stood against the Black Spell and prevailed?

The bright lady, Saint Barbara, granted Yumiko new life and freed her of her old oaths and hatreds. The bright lady served the same high and holy name whom Arthur and his men served. Yumiko's own mother, Dandrenor, had died in this service, slain by the enemy. This enemy had not ceased to hunt and harass and deceive Yumiko since the first hour she woke in the hospital.

Elfine had just joined.

And Tom was with them. What more did she need to know?

Yumiko dropped to her knees. "Then you must do this for me."

Matthias looked troubled. "Now, wait. Elfine had no need of instruction because she knew all the Church teaching at least as nursery tales. And there were other, ah, circumstances…"

Gil said, "Father Dominic appeared to him in a dream last night and told him he would do it today. Baptize Elfine, I mean. We did not know her name, but we were actually expecting someone to show up."

Yumiko said, "Tom is down there! And a great host of monsters and evil dogs. I may die in the attempt. Will this not aid and strengthen me?"

Matthias said, "Well, cousin, it is not magic. The baptism is new life, spiritual life, that calls an end to all mortal things. When this is done, you are no longer of this mortal world. You cannot get it because it is useful or to get something from it."

Gil stepped over to his palfrey and drew out one of the lances stowed on the creature's back. He was splendid in his shining armor and had his proud helm tucked under one arm. A coif of links covered his head and neck. He said, "You will be in no danger, Cousin. You and Elfine shall stay here."

5. *Knight and Ninja-Girl*

Elfine heaved a sigh of relief. "I'll watch the horses."

Yumiko raised an eyebrow. "Why am I staying here?"

"I have enough trouble trying to protect an unarmed novice and a crazy dog," said Gil. Rabicane the war steed snorted proudly, and the dog barked leaped up to Gil, putting his paws on his surcoat. Gil gently pushed the dog down, telling him, "Yes, very useful. Could not do a thing without you."

Yumiko said, "What has your spirit-dog told you of me?"

Gil said, "You put a bug on him, and he set a trap for you…" (Ruff barked.) "… he set a trap for you because he is a smart dog…" (Ruff barked again.) "… a very smart dog. He decided to trust you and tell you where my duel with Garlot was, and then he was sorry he did that because you threw a boomerang and hit me in the head."

Yumiko said, "Nothing else?"

Matthias spoke up, "I know that in recent months, you had been following Tom around. I know you have been keeping an eye on him. He is a reckless boy, and you saved his life at least once."

Gil looked surprised. "Saved whose life? When was that?"

Matt said, "When we went upstate to hunt down the giant rat of Lake Carlopa. Remember that Tom went to Shopton that night? He was searching for radiation traces of a hypothetical matter-amplifier he thought might be causing the problem. He ended up chasing a water-breathing ape in a motorboat."

Gil said, "Wait. Was Tom in the motorboat chasing an ape? Or was the ape in the motorboat with Tom chasing him? And why do Tom's stories still always sound crazy to me, when I fight monsters from Elfland for a living?"

"The ape was piloting. Tom was chasing him with those ridiculous rocket-propelled water-skis that snap out of his boots."

Gil said, "Better than those rocket-propelled, telescoping stilts that snap out of his kneepads."

"Anyway, he told me his shoes exploded. This girl pulled up in a black speedboat running without lights. Her boat had a prow shaped like a crow and crow-wings as part of the hull design. She hauled him out of the water and gave him mouth to mouth."

Gil scowled. "And what happened to the water-breathing ape?"

Matt said, "You can ask Tom when you see him."

Gil looked at her. "Why were you up around Lake Carlopa?"

Elfine clapped her hands. "Oh! Do you really have a crowboat? And a crowmobile? What about a crowcopter?"

Yumiko answered both of them. "I don't remember. I don't remember anything. But you cannot stop me from going down into the City of Corpses to find Tom."

Gil said, "I could certainly try, Cousin. Tell me, please, what you would do if you were stuffed you into one of those coffins with the lid wedged shut or tied to a tree by your hair or something?"

Elfine was scandalized. "Knights don't treat ladies that way!"

Gil to her, "*Ladies* do not need to be. Ladies do not put themselves into harm's way without regard for who must pull them out again."

Matthias said. "It's true. Knights are allowed to manhandle ninja-girls."

Yumiko said, "It is said that you can hear the truth in anyone's voice. You will not stop me. I have the means to escape all traps and to elude any guard set over me. Nothing you do short of death will stop me."

Gil frowned.

Matthias said, "She is boasting, right?"

Gil said, "No boast. She is telling the truth."

"A means to escape all traps?"

Gil said, "The magician told us. She has the Ring of Mists. One of the Thirteen Treasures of Lyonesse. And I, for one, am not going to try to pull it off her finger by force."

Matthias said, "No doubt that is wise. Imagine what your sword would do to someone who tried to take it from you by force."

Gil said, "So how do we stop her from following us?"

Ruff chose that moment to romp around at Yumiko's feet, to leap up, and to lick her in the face. She ineffectually tried to fend him off while simultaneous rubbing the wet off her cheeks.

Matthias said wryly, "You could always have your vicious dog stand guard over her, with orders to rip out her throat if she moves. That will work."

Gil said, "Are you going to make jokes, or are you going to be serious?"

Matthias said, "Both at once. Serious is not the opposite of funny. Unfunny is the opposite of funny. A little levity will ensure we do not act in haste or anger."

Gil raised his eyebrow higher. "Anger? I think that, considering she murdered a witness to whom I promised safe conduct just last winter and, just yesterday, threw a metal boomerang into my face and spirited away a villainous and recreant knight out of my hand, I am displaying remarkable courtesy. I called her 'miss' and said 'please' and everything."

Matt said, "There is something really odd going on here."

Gil said, "What? That Winged Vengeance or his sidekick has shown up yet again on a case we are working on to mess things up? That is beginning to seem kind of routine by now."

Matthias said, "But why should she care what happens to Tom?"

Yumiko decided it was time to ready herself. She removed her sash and snapped it so that it transformed into a cape. From the flat inner pocket in the cape lining she drew her mask and put her trench coat away. She then connected the cape to her shoulder clips and felt the fabric move of its own accord as the struts of the (at the moment, unextended and unseen) wings connected to the parachute harness hidden beneath the suit. She drew her cowl and donned her mask and shrugged her baton into her hand. A flick of the wrist extended the baton to his longbow length, and she bent and strung it.

She said, "I have vowed a vow. Nothing will deter me."

Ruff barked. Gil glanced at the dog and then stared at Yumiko. "Merry Christmas! You're right."

Matthias said, "What did he say?"

Gil said, "The thing she just did with her cape. The trick longbow. Tom built that. It looks like his handiwork anyway. Smart metal. Like the rocket skis in his boots."

Matthias said to Yumiko, "Please tell us what is going on. What, exactly, is your interest in Tom?"

Yumiko said, "He is my fiancé. I think. I love him and he loves me."

Gilberec and Matthias stared in silence, flabbergasted. Matthias shrugged, as if silently to ask if she were telling the truth. Gil slowly and gravely nodded, a look of astonishment growing ever larger on his face as he did so.

Eventually, Matthias took off his glasses and rubbed his nose. "Of course. I should have known. It was obvious. It all fits."

Gil stood stock still. He looked at Matt. He sputtered for a moment. Finally, he found words again. "It was not obvious. It is not obvious now. How was it obvious? Nothing fits!"

Matt said, "Everything. The way he talked whenever she came up. The way he was acting weird, even for him. He was in love with her."

Gil said, "What? How can you tell the way he acted was any different from the way he normally acted? Weird was normal for him!" He turned toward the dog. "Ruff! You must have known this. Why didn't you tell me?"

The dogs ear's drooped, and his eyes grew large and wet with doglike emotion. He put his head down on his paws and whimpered.

Gil said, "That is no excuse! Well, wait a moment. I suppose it is an excuse." He sighed and knelt and petted the dog between the ears. "It's okay. Good dog."

Ruff thwacked his tail once, mollified.

Yumiko slid her mask back on her head and peered down. "What did he say?"

Gil said, "Ruff is showing you and Tom that he can be trusted. He did not spill Tom's secrets to me, nor yours." Ruff barked again. "He says you are a sneaky fox, and so you have a lot of trust issues."

"Uh…" Yumiko took her gaze off his face and looked sidewise at nothing in particular.

Gil was still on his knees petting his dog. He looked up at Yumiko. "So how long has this been going on? You and Tom?"

Yumiko said, "I don't know. I have no memory. I lost all my memories in the mist. An old entry in my diary said that Tom's experiments show there is no cure for mist poisoning. Do you understand now why I must find him, and save him?"

Gil stood. He was tall and broad, and he gleamed like cold fire in his silvery armor. "I understand Tom would shoot me if I got his girlfriend killed. And you are my first cousin."

Matthias said, "No, she has to come with us. Or, rather, we have to go with her."

Gil looked skeptical. He did not speak but his expression spoke volumes.

"Think through everything we know now, Gil. We asked your mother about the Ring of Mists—what it does and who is looking for it—and we have already figured out most of what her answer meant. Tom brought Yumiko with him to break into the Glass Tower after stealing Rotwang's Iron Mole machine. So she has the ring, and you know she did not steal it from Tom. I am assuming he pushed it onto her finger."

Gil said, "You mean Tom planned this."

Matthias said, "He certainly had something in mind. What do we know about the Tower of Glass? What do we know about the Crows of the Dismal Fell? Why did Tom not simply slip an arm around his ninja girlfriend, walk through the walls unseen, and float out of there like a ghost? Because, save for seven, no man comes back from Caer Sidi. The only way out was deeper in. He put the ring on her finger and stayed behind. Why?"

Gil said, "Out of chivalry."

"Chivalry is your thing. His is quick thinking. What was he thinking?"

Yumiko answered, "That if he and I were separated, I would come looking for him. But if there was something I was supposed to do, some way to save him, I don't recall. I don't remember a thing. He could not have known I would lose my memory."

Matthias said to her, "Tom is crazy smart. You said he was experimenting on mist effects, studying them. He knew overexposure caused amnesia. So maybe he did know." Matthias turned to Ruff and said, "What do you think?"

Ruff barked.

Matthias adjusted his glasses on his nose. "See? Even your dog agrees with me."

Gil said, "You don't know what he said."

Matthias said, "I cannot understand dog talk. That does not mean it is not obvious he agrees with me. Ruff is a good judge of character. Besides, you do not have to protect her. No one is going to lay a hand on her because no one will lay an eye on her. I might have to help her, but not you."

Ruff wagged his tail. He barked again. Gil looked weary and stared at the heavy metal grating over the stairs leading down into darkness. "My own dog turned against me!"

Matthias said, "Okay, so I don't know. What did he say?"

Gil gestured solemnly toward the heavy bars covering the stairhead. "Ruff pointed out that Yummy Cutie is the only one who can pick the lock to open the gate."

6. Two Boons

Yumiko said cheerfully, "I have but two demands! Two boons you must grant me ere I unlock that gate! First, you, Gilberec Moth! Never call me Yummy Cutie again!"

Gil raised his hands as if in surrender. "Granted."

Yumiko said, "And you! Matthias Moth!"

He said, "Yes?"

Once more she sank to her knees before him.

Matthias said, "I have explained that it is not a thing done lightly, or for gain, or for any reason other than the deepest. Even the bond of marriage is less than this, for Christ's word is a sword that can and will sever friendships, families, nations."

She said, "I have seen the power of your Christ. I have seen the elfs quail in fear at his name. His is the power that brought me back from death. I do not despise the teachings of the Buddha, the World-Enlightened One, but they do not comfort me. They do not feed me. To what else should I give my life? To vengeance? To vendetta? That is a nightmare. I wish to wake."

Matthias said, "You are joining a host that marches with a war banner raised. Scorn, suffering, and martyrdom are what we gain in this life. Our sign is the dead tree on which the world crucified and cursed him. The Black Spell will be redoubled against you and all who are under its sway. Your pay is hate and scorn from all who love the world. Do you understand?"

"I am the daughter of Danger Moth, who slew the Monster Centipede of Seta-no-Karashi, and of Dandrenor of the Grail, who kept her watch faithfully unto death and thereby saved the Cup of Christ from stain. The blood of gods and true samurai flows in my veins. I know what is being asked of me."

Matthias nodded. "Very well." To Elfine, Matthias said, "Take that cup from my mule's saddlebag, and go fill it up with water from the fountain. Come back here. You are going to be her godmother and be responsible for her moral instruction."

Elfine smiled brightly. "I always wanted to be a fairy godmother!"

To Yumiko, Matthias said, "Do you renounce the Devil and all his works, the pomp and vanity of this wicked world, and all the sinful lusts of the flesh?"

Chapter 12

The Devil's Own Door

1. The Underground World

The pack horse, riding horse, and mule were left behind.

The weight of the earth seemed to grow ever more massive and oppressive above them. Ruff was in front, sniffing. Gilberec tramped down the dark stair, flight after flight of them, as the air grew still and stale. Rabicane was surefooted on the stairs as a goat on a crag and moved with remarkable silence for a beast so large and covered with mail and plate.

Gilberec carried no light and seemed to need none. Yumiko had her flashlight, but it was tuned to ultraviolet.

Matthias was in the rear, with a silver lantern burning holy oil in one hand and an aspergilium of holy water in the other. This was a silver instrument, shaped something like a miniature mace, designed to sprinkle holy water from a reservoir in the handle though a perforated orb at the tip. A clamshell cowl covered the orb at the moment to prevent drips.

A time came when Gil froze, Rabicane neighed in alarm, and Ruff growled, his ears flat. Gil said, "Matt, I think there is something here on the stairs. Ahead of me."

Matthias said, "It is someone who needs our help. He says that he was pulled out of his grave from underneath, through the bottom of the coffin, and that the wolves are mauling and despoiling his body."

Gil said, "Ask him to lead the way."

Yumiko twisted the ring on her finger. The dark stair grew darker, and the lines of perspective of the flights leading down no longer seemed to converge correctly, as if the geometry were somehow askew. Standing on the stair was a young man in a coat and tie. It was not until he turned that Yumiko saw the massive wounds tearing him nearly in half. His entrails spilled out his back and dragged along on the ground behind him.

Nauseated, she turned her head. Behind her, on the stairs leading up and up out of sight, were packs of dogs. These dogs looked like shadows, with lamps for eyes, and made no more noise than a fog bank rolling over the countryside as they walked.

Yumiko twisted the ring on her finger back to white. The dead man and the shadow dogs were no more to be seen. She whispered to Matthias, "What is behind us? There is something following us down the stairs."

Matthias said, "These are the shadows of all the dogs who ever killed a carrion-eater that despoiled a man's corpse or dug up a coffin. They are called the Hounds of Saint Anthony the Anchorite. He is the patron of gravediggers. He often fought demons that assumed the shapes of beasts of the desert. May he help us now!"

"Did you call them?"

Matthias laughed. "Not I! I am but the student. My Master, Father Dominic, sends them with his blessing because the enemy has been foolish enough to despoil holy ground. Without their help, we would stand no chance."

The stairs emptied into a cave. The floor was uneven, and still pools stood in certain places, glinting in the light of Matt's lantern. Great mouths and vents opened to their left and right, with pits and slopes in further caves rising or falling. But underfoot was stone, and here and there marks in the surface where heavy weights had been hauled. In places a line of boards or pallets or ramps had been laid to allow workmen to pull loads over uneven rock.

The cave led to a series of tunnels. There was no clear path there as the wooden boards now forked and forked again. Apparently, many workmen had been busy for a long while hauling crates from several entry points into this underground world.

They came across a chimney in the roof worming upward. Directly beneath was a broken coffin, which had apparently been pulled down from its resting place. The labyrinth path swerved here, and came to a second chimney, and a third, all with crawling channels leading upward to the broken bottoms of despoiled graves. There were many more forks and tunnels leading left and right to other fresh graves.

It was a labyrinth. They would have soon been lost, but Matthias calmly pointed out the turns as the ghost told him.

They came suddenly on another flight of stairs, leading down and down through a wide gap into a great open space. The walls to either side opened wide, and the stairs grew broad. The roof was left behind. Below was a cavern akin in size and shape to the one Yumiko had seen in Is-Elfydd.

2. *Mists and Magic*

Yumiko gasped at the size of the cavern and at the width of the buried valley it held. As they began to descend the stairs into it, Matt said, "You are probably wondering how such large, empty places could be below Queens without the roof collapsing or the river seeping in. All these caves were carved out by the sea long ago at the command of the mermaids, and they are only partway resting in our world."

She said, "I was not wondering. I assumed it was magic."

He said, "It is magic indeed, but magic is bound by rules as iron hard as the rules of physics or ethics but hidden from the eyes of men. Do not think these things happen for no reason or as in a dream."

Yumiko said, "I meant I thought it was magic as in my ring, which can reduce mass."

He said, "Very much like your ring or Gil's sword."

"His sword? It does not seem anything like my ring."

Matthias smiled. "They work on the same principle."

"What principle?"

"That the Creator made both seen and unseen, and it cannot be unmade. Matter or energy can be combined or changed in form but neither created nor destroyed. Sins can be atoned by another in your place but not merely wished into nothingness. Where do your visual elements go when you turn invisible? Or where does your mass go when you turn weightless? Is it destroyed?"

Yumiko decided that Matthias had the spirit of a schoolteacher. She said, "It goes into a realm of mist. Nothing is destroyed."

Matthias said, "So it is with Dyrnwen. The sword makes visible and palpable the unseen fire of the spirit, for the blade glows more brightly the nobler the hand who wields it. The blade pulls fire out of that world into this."

Yumiko was doubtful. "I have seen no fires in the mists."

"Then you have seen only the lower parts, where sad ghosts linger. There are high places there. Bright beings dwell in them."

3. The Infernal Lake

Down they went. A reddish glow, dancing and rippling, could be dimly seen in the distance, and the tall black shadows of some intervening columns of stone blocked their view.

Like a furnace under bellows, the red light suddenly turned orange and bright and leaped upward. Before them was a wide circular cave, interrupted with many columns where stalagmites and stalactites had grown together. Midmost in the cave was a lake of burning black fluid. Fires danced and smoldered here and there across the surface, which was boiling. From this the light came.

The lake was large, interrupted by many stalagmites that rose like islands in the black fluid. A shoreline of pebbles and black sand reached to the left and right in a great circle around the lake.

At the far side of the lake, opposite them, were a dozen or more pavilions with banners. Only one of them had a lamp inside, casting a glow through the silk tent walls. The rest were dark. An area to the left of the pavilions had been fenced off as a corral wide enough to hold a dozen horses but empty now save for palfreys.

Beyond the pavilion, set in to the wall of the cave, was a tall door. Yumiko had seen this door, or one like it, not long ago. It was as big and broad as a gate in a castle wall, peaked at the top, with massive hinges and hasps. The doorknob, even from a distance in the bad light, gleamed and glittered like a ruby larger than a softball, winking with red fire.

There were two arrow slits piercing the cave wall, one to either side of the door. Bright light shined through the slits. The horizontal slit was near the bottom of the vertical slit, which gave them the aspect of upside-down crosses.

Before the pavilion was a trestle table. Human skeletons red with blood and gnawed remnants of haunches of meat were piled on the table, amid many black candles.

Between the feast table and the fiery lakeshore was a narrow space of sand and rock, where many hulking, furry, lupine shapes lounged. One or two stirred, or paced, or lashed a tail or flicked an ear, but most were still and silent, as if torpid with sleep after much feasting. In the flickering shadows of the stone columns, it was hard to estimate the numbers, but it was easily over two hundred.

To either side of this shore where the werewolves were gathered stood a tall line of Egyptian statues in stiff postures. Each was twice the height of a tall man. They wore narrow beards and carven headdresses or miters or crowns either bulbous or peaked, and hieroglyphs were incised down torso and leg. The stone hands held wooden flails or curved bronze swords like sickles.

Firelight glittered balefully in the blank eyesockets of the statues, and Yumiko understood that these were alive and malign.

4. The Watchman

Down the final flight of stairs went Ruff, Gil, the warhorse, Yumiko, and Matthias. The column of agitated flame dancing across the infernal lake died down, and the orange light returned to a sullen and scattered red glow. The great cavern was lost into shadows. The light from the fiery lake was visible in patches. The lamp from the one occupied pavilion, the candles on the grisly feast table, and the glowing arrow slits near the tall door were as dim as stars on a foggy night.

The stairway passed between two tall stalagmites rising like boar tusks from the uneven floor. Yumiko saw a heat signature coming from one of the stalagmites. She raised her bow and shot. The shaft slid hissing through the air to the right of Gil, who flinched in surprise, raising his shield. A man wearing a wolfskin cloak, many gold necklaces, and an expensive pair of running shoes, now swayed into view. His chest was painted blue with woad. A Tommy gun was in his hand. An arrow was protruding from his neck. He fell to the ground with a sigh.

Ruff inched forward and sniffed. Gil bent down and pulled out the arrow. He stared at the hypodermic needle in the tip. "What is this?"

"Tranquilizer," answered Yumiko. "I am trying not to kill as many people."

Gil said, "Well, Cousin, you and I do not think alike. You rob him of his chance to fight me. I cannot slay a sleeping man, nor is it wise to leave him alive behind me."

Yumiko pointed with her bowstaff at the ram horn the guard wore on a strap about his shoulder. "I did not want him to give the alarm."

"I am not come like a thief in the night." Gil took up the guard's ram horn in his hand. Gil had a lance strapped to his steed. He took the lance and sprang lightly into the saddle. "What does our guide say? Is this the place?"

Matthias looked at a point in midair where nothing was visible, and said, "Yes. But there were more wolves here before, and a magician, and a cavalry of strange knights. He says that the dark door appeared as the Lord of Wolves performed the black mass and feasted on raw human flesh. He calls it the Devil's Own Door."

Yumiko said, "I saw that door inside a magic shop on Park Avenue and Lexington. A hob in a bottle told me its name. The Tithing Ground is beyond it."

Ruff barked. Gil said, "Ruff says this is their way out. The wolves are going to use it to go up into the city."

Matthias said, "It is a moon-door. In the same way a mermaid pouch makes more space fit into a narrow volume than should, a moon-door remove the space between two points."

Gil said, "I used to have one leading to my attic. Why haven't they used it yet?"

Yumiko said, "Can a moon-door point at different targets?"

Gil said, "My attic door would follow us from house to house across country, so, yes, I guess they can open into more than one spot."

Yumiko said to Matthias, "Ask the ghost who passed through that door last?"

Matthias said, "Our guide says that thirteen strange knights came, and one was posted here to guard the door, but that nonetheless thirteen went through the door."

Gil said, "Thirteen minus one does not equal thirteen."

Matthias said, "In elfish math, it does."

Yumiko said, "The thirteenth man was Tom. They disguised him. Tom went through that door. The wolves are waiting here because that door, at this moment, does not open up into the magic shop. The door opens up on to the Tithing Ground! Today and now Tom is being tithed!"

Gil said, "Then you have to get to the door, Cousin. Hurry! I will lure or drive the Red Knight away from the door. I go right; you left. Go!"

Now Gil turned to Matthias, and leaned down from his saddle. "If I do not make it back alive, here is a letter to give my mother, and here is one for Nerea." Ruff barked. "And tell the Green Knight to tell his dog that Ruff died bravely, too. Follow her. She may need your help."

Yumiko sprinted off down the dark sands. Matthias made the sign of the cross and ran off after the girl in black.

Gil saluted them with his lance and rode the other way down across the black sand at the edge of the fiery lake, going counterclockwise, blowing a blast that rang and echoed from the unseen cave roofs above.

5. *The Wolf Pack*

Gil now threw the ram horn away and readied his lance and shield. Rabicane trotted, then galloped, and then charged.

Not scores but hundreds of the round, humped shadows gathered around the feet of all the stalagmites or resting on the black sand now stirred, and stood, and reared up, eyes blazing. Hundreds more of the lupine shapes, eyes glinting, began to appear between the columns near the cave wall, where folds of rock or tricks of shadows held dens and tunnels driven back into the stone.

Howls, terrible howls, split the air and smote the ear.

There were werewolves gathered on the sand before her, but Yumiko twisted the ring, rendering herself unseen. These wolves, one and all, hearing the horn call and seeing the armed and armored knight on his huge steed running along the far shore, dashed into the fiery waters. They were licked by flames, but their werewolf fur was unburnt and unhurt.

Yumiko was terrified, certain he would be killed. She glanced back, wondering where Matthias was. She saw the Hounds of Saint Anthony, a great and invisible host of shadows, pouring down the stair and across the black sand, following Gilberec. It was like seeing a black cloud of some gas heavier than air rolling out from a spigot and spreading to fill a volume. Some hounds ran on the cave's black sand, some through the cave's black air.

Gilberec encountered the first wolf and impaled him neatly on his spear. The monster did not die, but snapped at the wooden haft with his teeth, yowling and yammering. Gil yanked the bloody spearhead free and plunged it in again, but the monster, undaunted, pressed forward, snapping. Gil with Herculean strength hoisted the spear up, hauling the living animal aloft, overhead, and sent it spinning and screaming from the tip of his lance and into the lake of fire.

Two and three and a dozen wolves were leaping upon Gil in the next moment, but Rabicane jumped over them and trampled them with mighty hooves while the spear of Gilberec darted left and right, as swift and deadly as the horn of a unicorn in wild wrath.

Splashing through the red mud, Gilberec reached a spot where the beach was narrow, and only three or four could come at him at a time. But the werewolves were not afraid of fire and were not burned by the boiling lake, and so half a hundred came swimming and wading and splashing through the black and boiling liquid, surrounding him.

His spear lodged between the jaws of a dreadful wolf and was lost to his grasp. Now he drew his fair white-hilted sword, born in the forges of elfs. The blade, which burst into flame, white hot, was as bright as the flames from thirty torches. The wolves yowled, dazed and maddened by the light.

Ruff climbed to the top of a stalagmite. He had donned his green hat and green gloves, so now he had hands like a human. Tail wagging, tongue lolling, he lifted up the Tommy gun the watchman had dropped and opened fire. A roaring, shattering staccato of thunder gushed from the gun. The werewolves were annoyed, as if by bee stings, but the bullets were not silver and hurt them not.

Yumiko ran on. There were no wolves between her and the dark door. But a line of tall and impassive statues stood along the wall to her left, and she saw their bleak eyes moving, following her.

Ahead, standing before the door itself, was a knight in red, fully armored, and on his horse, his lance above him, pennant dangling. His helm was lighter than what he had worn to joust, but his shield and coat were the same. The heraldry on the shield she knew well: *Sable, a dolphin uriant embowed Gules dented Or.* This was Sir Garlot. On his back, writhing and blowing in unearthly winds, was his great Cloak of Mists.

She hid behind a stalagmite, fearing that his cloak gave him the power to see her. But his helm was turned the other way, where the armies of werewolves were chased by and retreating from the Swan Knight. Smoke and fire came from the wounds of many wolves, and dozens had fallen. Scores and hundreds more remained, and more and more poured up out of openings and crevasses in floor and walls.

The dogs of Anthony the Anchorite descended like a crashing wave. The wolves near Gil now twisted, and shuddered, and screamed in madness. Yumiko could see the shadowy dogs pulling the dark wolf-shaped spirits out of the spines of the possessed men or yanking them out of their throats. A dozen of them and then a score, two score, more, suddenly turned from wolf creatures into naked men wearing wolf pelts or wolf cloaks.

Their eyes were dazed and bestial, and their mouths were spitting foam and shouting wordless shouts. The dreadful intelligence of the werewolves was gone, the power which allowed them to assume the shape and strength of wolves was gone, and their immunity to wounds and fear was gone.

The ones Ruff had previously shot now fell down dead, slain by the self same bullet wounds the werewolves had ignored, but, to which mere human flesh was not immune. The hundred or so wading through the burning lake had all their human flesh turn red and black in the surly fires. They screamed and floundered, inhaling flame directly into their lungs. When those near the shore, coated with the boiling and burning fluid, ran out onto the sand, the sticky black fluid clung to them, and flames lashed out at the hair and skin of those they stumbled through.

Had they been able to coordinate, to rush at Gilberec with their hands, or to pick up stones from the cavern floor and hurl them, their numbers would have surely prevailed.

But a human being running on all fours, naked, armed only with the puny fingernails and puny teeth of a human being, was no match for a fully armed and armored knight on horseback no matter their numbers. And these were not all young and athletic men either but included many thin and weak and sickly who yearned for the potent bodies of wolf monsters.

As for the true werewolves, those dread spirits forced to relinquish their human hosts, Yumiko could see the terrible battling in the middle of the air. She heard the snarls of dogs and the howls of wolves.

Spirit was fighting spirit, and shadow was fighting shadow. She could see the shapes reflected in the smoke above the burning lake or reflected in the leaping shadows dancing across the crags and cracks of the walls and cave roof. It was horrible.

The great sword of Gilberec rose and fell, and burning men in wolf cloaks ran in circles, their blood catching on fire, fire billowing from their mouths and spurting from their eyesockets. The beach was narrow. Many fell into the lake of fire, and, as they did so, flames from the disturbed surface shot into the air. First one, and then many columns of fire rose up, roaring and blisteringly hot from the black surface. The heat began to crack the pillars holding up the cave roof.

Yumiko frowned up at the cave roof, for little streamers of dust were beginning to sift down through the dark air.

Now a great chunk of roof came whistling down through the air and struck the lake. An immense gush of fire, yellow mingled with white, rose up from the splash.

6. *The Red Knight's Squire*

In that light, Yumiko saw Sir Garlot drive his spurs into his steed. At his shoulder was his squire, the one who had wanted to kiss her. They were only twenty or so yards ahead, and the fires from the burning lake and the glory of Gilberec's bright sword lit the whole scene bright as day, sending black shadows leaping across the rough and broken ground and walls.

The squire raised his trumpet to his lips and blew. The men in wolf pelts shrieked in reply and drew back from Gilberec, some crowding near the cave wall, others crowding and whimpering near the shore line. This left an empty lane between the two crowds.

Into that lane now came Sir Garlot, riding atop Tachebrun. Seeing Gilberec had no spear in hand, Garlot cast his spear aside and drew his sword. The two men saluted each other by flourishing their blades.

Yumiko ran toward the dark door, furious at herself for having paused. But the squire was still in the way. She shot an arrow at him, but the hypodermic head did not penetrate his coat of rings. The youth drew his dirk but could not see his attacker. She whirled a boomerang toward his head, catching him in the throat and meanwhile spun a weighted chain from her *kusarigama* around his knees. She yanked, he fell, and now she was able to impale his exposed calf with a throwing knife carrying a hypodermic of tranquilizer clamped at its point.

Now she saw a strange thing. The stone statues had seemed not to move, but now more than one was positioned in front of an opening or cleft in the wall, preventing the yowling werewolves behind them from entering. Several statues had dead werewolves at their feet, with blood upon their hands or flails or their crooked, sickle-shaped swords. All this was hidden in the mists. Had she not been in the mists herself, she would not have seen it.

Whatever it meant, there was no time to ponder mysteries. Yumiko reached out her hand toward the red crystal knob. Before her hand touched it, the arrow slits to either side blazed brightly, and the door groaned and began to open.

7. The Northbrood

Two figures were standing at the door arch. A cold as fierce as a curtain of iron thorns fell across her. They were slender, pale, and narrow-faced figures with long black hair falling past their shoulders. Both wore low-crowned and wide-brimmed black hats and long black cloaks. Beneath the cloaks, their narrow feet were naked.

With one slow and coordinated motion, both raised their heads. She saw their mouths with pale lips.

Both smiled. Their fangs were like the fangs of serpents and unfolded from their upper jaws as their dreadful smiles widened.

With nightmarish slowness, both took a silent step forward. They were drawn forward more quickly than a single slow footstep could account for, or perhaps the shadows about them were growing in size, or perhaps perspective and distance were collapsing.

Their eyes were like distant stars, and a cold like that of the arctic midnight reached from those eyes directly into her heart. A wave of weakness burned away her willpower and ate up her strength like fire among dry leaves. She knelt; she fell. With her last strength, she twisted the ring on her hand from iron to pewter to silver to argent. White starlight spilled from her hand. The two cold figures raised their hands, squinting, and hissed in annoyance.

Yumiko heard Elfine's shrill cry in the near distance behind her. This was the last sound she expected, and her reaction was one of terror for her unarmed friend. "There she is! There!"

Then, she heard the voice of Matthias, calm and even toned. "*Kyrie eleison*. God, our Lord, King of Ages, All-powerful and Almighty, you who in Babylon changed into dew the furnace flames and protected and saved the three holy children…"

Matthias stepped into her view. In one hand he held high the silver lantern. In the other was the aspergilium. The silver lantern suddenly blazed brighter, and he flicked his wrist to close the hood. The hood of the lantern was perforated with the image of a cross. A beam of light shaped like a cross fell across first one of the pallid men and then the other.

Matthias raised his ringing voice above their thin, shrill, and wretched screams. "We beseech you to make powerless, banish, and drive out every diabolic power, presence, and machination; every evil influence, malefice, or evil eye, and all evil actions…"

The two pale men screamed and tried to flee. Both raised their arms. Shadows gathered and spread from armpit to elbow and down their sides to their thighs, and they assumed the forms and features of two gigantic black bats. With a swirling gust of wind, they clawed their way into the air.

"...Burn all these evils in Hell, that they may never again touch me or any other creature in the entire world..."

Large creatures could not take off swiftly. Matthias flicked his aspergilium, and drops of holy water fell across their wings and brought them crashing to the floor. Where the drops touched, shadow and substance, flesh and bone, were torn apart, and sizzling white flames shot up.

"...where they will be bound by Saint Michael the Archangel, Saint Gabriel, Saint Raphael, our guardian angels, and where they will be crushed under the heel of the Immaculate Virgin Mary..."

Both bat creatures changed their heads back to human heads and began speaking in effeminate voices, blaspheming, cursing, threatening, squealing. Matthias flicked his wrist to send tiny and gentle sprinkles of water across their cheeks, which made their screaming faces collapse inward, their skulls implode, and their heads evaporate into black ash. The batlike bodies shrank, burning, legs and wings bent at crooked angles.

A suction force reach up through the floor dragged them below and out of sight.

"The Lord is my salvation," said Matthias solemnly. "Whom shall I fear?"

8. The Living Creatures

Yumiko had risen to her knees. Elfine landed on her shoulder.

"What are you doing here?" Yumiko was angry.

"I got bored." Elfine rolled her eyes. "The horses are fine."

"But–"

Elfine tugged Yumiko's hair braid to try to pull her upright, "Save Gil!"

Yumiko got her feet under her, stood, and turned her head. On the black sand halfway around the circumference of the lake from their current position, Sir Garlot was exchanging blows with Sir Gilberec, but the gray vapor from Garlot's cloak rose up, and Garlot was visible only as a shadow of motion seen from the corner of the eye or not at all.

The sickly, twisted men in wolf coats, and the werewolves as yet untouched by the shadow dogs, who stood in two columns watching the combat, were cheering, jeering, and mocking Gil with howls and curses.

Gilberec swung again and again at the unseen foe, but his blade cut through rock, or cut through air, or glanced from an unseen shield. He could not parry what he could not see. In half a dozen places, his bright armor was pierced, and crimson blood stained his silver surcoat, leggings, sleeves, and saddle. Yumiko could see that Garlot was now behind Gilberec and had taken his sword in two hands, readying to strike at the other knight's unshielded back.

Yumiko saw that the starlight her argent ring shed could not reach so far. Even if she entered the black world of the ghosts, she could not reach Gil before Garlot's blow fell. And she had been warned not to enter that world again.

In desperation, she twisted the ring deasil one more time. The metal changed from argent to a brilliant alloy of solidified brightness, an ethereal metal with no name on Earth. The angel face in the intaglio turned into an archangel. The starlight gathered and grew bright and brighter until it seemed the noonday sun was on her finger.

The scene changed. She saw no wolves. The men who stood looking on all now were handsome, bright, and beautiful, but foul raiments, rags, and tatters of filth clung to them, as if they swam in sewage. Maggots and loathsome insects covered their beautiful faces.

A titanic living creature now stood behind Gilberec. A second was behind Elfine and a third loomed over Matthias. The three living creatures were armed with spears and great round shields the hue of a beryl stone. Their flesh burned as brightly as brass seen in a furnace. Each had four faces, as of a man, a bull, a lion, and an eagle, which could turn in any direction. They had six wings, two folded over their bodies as cloaks, two entwined about their midriffs like skirts, and two spread and displayed. Their feet were round hooves cloven like a bull's hoof. Their whole bodies and backs and hands and wings were full of eyes.

Energy like burning coals or balled lightning moved up and down and among the living creatures and shot from their countless eyes, and the fires were bright, and out of the fires came bolts of lightning.

These creatures were not merely tall, but they seemed to reach upward into infinity so that nebulae and gathered galaxies formed crowns around their fourfold heads. How it was that their bodies were within this tiny underground chamber, which could not have held even the smallest finger of arms longer than the arms of spiral galaxies, was something her eyes could not tell her. Her thoughts scattered like startled fish, unable to see what she was seeing.

The flares of light also issued from behind her. She turned. A fourth living creature was standing over her, and she was in the shadow of its shield. The countless eyes of its wings and body and terrible fourfold faces regarded her with gazes of all-consuming fire.

Yumiko screamed in utmost terror at this apparition. She threw herself on the ground.

One of the lightning bolts issuing from the countless eyes now reached down and smote Yumiko in the head. To her surprise, she did not die, but instead had a clear and sudden thought. She yanked the ring off her finger.

The four-faced living creatures vanished.

As before, the ring kept the same aspect and shape as when on her finger, so the bright sunlight continued to pour forth.

Elfine must have had the same inspiration occur to her at the same moment, for before Yumiko even opened her mouth to speak, Elfine had taken the ring in her two doll-sized hands. The brightness from the ring touched the brightness shed by Elfine's wings and ignited them. Her speed became like the speed of an arrow, a comet, a thought. Between Gilberec and the descending sword she flew, carrying the ring, leaving a streak of dazzling light in her wake. The mists of Garlot's cloak were no more. Gilberec saw, and turned, and blocked the cowardly blow, and then he laughed a great laugh. Garlot uttered a moan of fear. Elfine hovered above Gil, far out of any reach, and drew circles and loops and figure eights in the air.

Elfine danced and laughed at the sight of Sir Garlot unable to vanish or escape. She banged the ring against her hip like a pretend tambourine, danced or wore it like a glowing crown, at other times spun it about her waist like a hula hoop, and shimmied in midair, changing her size to match.

As one, the Egyptian statues ground into motion. They fell upon the werewolves from behind with flail and sword, and methodically, silently, began to kill and maim them and to hurl the huge wolflike bodies into the central lake. The fury of the lake grew, and flames erupted, and more debris fell from the ceiling. The wolves, in a madness of wrath, attacked the statues, breaking stone fingers and toppling one of them, which then stood up again, face impassive.

"I don't understand what is happening!" exclaimed Yumiko.

Matthias pulled her to her feet. "Tom is beyond that door. Do you understand that?"

In they ran.

9. The Tithing Ground

They found themselves not in the back of the magic shop but in a strange landscape. The sky above was starless and black as a midnight sea beneath storm clouds, and the air was heavy and oppressive. A full moon, silver and huge, hung above the scene. But this was not the moon as it looked when seen from Earth's surface. One small ocean like the eye of a Cyclopes was in one quarter of the pale face.

Yumiko wondered if this were the far side always turned away from Earth. Tom would surely know.

She and Matthias stood in a land of silvery dust, fine as fine ash, and here and there rose square-sided columns. These looked like headless Egyptian obelisks—or perhaps something older than Egypt. In one place the columns stood in pairs, and a crosspiece or capstone made them into tall and narrow structures like gates. Yumiko thought they looked like the *torii* of a Shinto shrine but cruder, simpler.

Matthias was climbing as quickly as he could up the sliding, sandy slope of the nearest silvery ash heap, coughing. Yumiko sealed her mask and followed him, wishing she had her ring with her. Her lighter footfalls stirred up less dust.

He pointed. The fine dust was making him cough, and he did not speak. Yumiko looked. From this vantage, she could see that each flat-topped obelisk was carved into a weeping mask that stared forever upward toward the black heaven, mouth open in despair. The capstones of the dolmens were placed directly atop these masks; the brow or the chin was visible from beneath the capstones.

Yumiko saw that the dolmens formed a line, as if the stones marked a straight path half hidden beneath the silver sands. In the distance, perhaps a mile away, perhaps two, she saw a line of slim steeds and cloaked figures riding, with little lamps like fireflies—or serving fairies—hanging near their heads and keeping pace.

Behind the horsemen came loping three score werewolves, with caparisons of linen thrown across their backs, trotting in order. The wolf paws kicked up silvery dust, and their paw prints reached behind them in a line. The hoofs of the steed stirred up no dust and left no tracks, and by this, Yumiko understood these were elfin steeds.

She could see them sharp and clear against the black sky as they crossed a rise. She counted. There were thirteen horsemen.

Yumiko began to run down the slippery hill of silvery ash and kicked up a blinding cloud. With each step, the soft ashy surface sucked on her feet and clutched her ankles. She halted before she toppled downslope.

Matthias came stepping and sliding after her. He coughed and said, "This ground is not meant for anything as heavy and clumsy as man or Moth."

Yumiko said, "I left my ring behind to save Gil. How do we catch them?"

At that moment, from beyond the distant hills, came a sound of bright and haunting trumpets. It was the horn call of the elfs.

It was answered by a shrill, thin wail, rising and falling, of an inhuman voice. The lingering cry contained no words but was filled with bitter hatred, pain, and malice. It was the voice of Hell.

"They greet each other," said Yumiko. "Have you some power to carry us across the mile between? Across these dunes?"

Matthias was rubbing his thumb against his fingers. She saw a trickle of the silver ash falling. He said, "This substance is human dreams and hopes, ground into powder. This is a realm of dreams, but we are not in the part where human dreams reach. The kings who ruled before Adam are trapped in this place."

She said, "How can that help?"

"The laws are different here." He took off his glasses and put them carefully in a pocket. "I can assume my true form without harm. I will be naked, but it should not embarrass you." Then, he lowered his hood and spread his arms, pulling his cloak up like wings. Shadows gathered around him, and his body shivered and shrank.

A moment later a batlike creature made of solidified darkness shook itself free from Matthias's cloak. It was larger than a condor, larger than a pterodactyl. A fearful coldness came from the black creature. The dust in the air about its nostrils and mouth was not disturbed by any breathing. It was not alive.

Yumiko stepped back. "You are a vampire!"

The big-eared bat skull shrank, and stretched, and formed Matt's head. "Well, yes and no. It is sort of an interesting case, really..."

But the sight of the shadows around him, altering his form, suddenly brought a buried memory to the surface. It was not something she remembered with her mind, but there was a tingling in her fingers and toes, almost as if her flesh and blood were trying to remember something.

He said, "Don't be afraid..."

She wrapped her arms around him, wings and all, and hugged the monstrous shadow form to her bosom.

"...or, um, on second thought, perhaps you should be *more* afraid than this."

"Turn back into a boy and then back into your spirit form."

"I'd be naked."

"Quick! As quickly as you can! I have to feel what it feels like."

The bat creature gave a shrug. "Okay. This is what confession is for."

The shadows dispersed from him. For a moment, she was holding a tall and naked young man in her arms. His unfocused eyes were averted, staring upward. The black shadows again swirled around him.

She could feel what was happening. She felt his human flesh sinking and rotating into another direction, another type of reality. His spirit, which was a higher condition of being, swelled outward, came to the surface, and solidified.

She held him tightly so that he had to strain and push to bring his batlike form into solidity. And she let her own flesh get pushed by the strange pressure in the opposite direction, the opposite condition.

Her suit and mask were tighter than his and took her a longer moment to grip the collar with her snapping jaws to twist and win free. The grinning fox mask lay in the silver ash, staring up.

The vampire Matthias swirled his batwings of darkness and shadow around him and cocked his head to one side.

The white vixen was larger than any natural fox, and a white pearl hovered near her in the air. More by instinct than memory, she rolled the pearl over her shed suit and mask and watched them be pulled inside.

"You don't seem surprised," said the she-fox.

He said, "Well, I lost a bet with a dog. That will show me."

She said, "Should I try to carry your gear? What can you do without it?"

"Drink life, smother joy, strangle laughter. Nothing good. But my gear might blast your fox-spirit pearl if you touch it. Make for the cavalcade as fast as you can! I only fly slowly in this form, so do not wait for me."

"I do not really have a plan," she admitted.

"Plans are overrated," said Matt. "Faith is sure. Did you think your will, or mine, arranged all this? Go! You will know what to do when the time comes. And may Saint Herve guide you!"

The ash was now firm underfoot. Like the elf steeds, she left no footprints as she ran. With labored and pumping strokes the bat-winged monster pulled itself into the dark air and flopped after her. She soon outdistanced him.

The sound of many small silver bells chiming came over the dunes.

Chapter 13

The Gem of Memory

1. The Cavalcade

She topped the rise and saw where the dunes and hills of silver ashes petered out, got lower, and came to an end. The landscape beyond was a level plain of broken slabs and flakes that looked like salt flats, if salt were black rather than white or shattered mirror of black glass.

Beneath the spiderwebby and broken surface were dim skull-shaped shadows, half visible beneath the bright moon, of giants trapped below the surface like flies in amber.

In three places along the horizon the unearthly flatness of the landscape was broken by the silhouette of a giant hand or arm half-pushed out of the glassy surface, fingers half closed as if still clawing for freedom, each finger taller than a skyscraper.

Nearer, a great well had been carved down into the glass, reaching down past the lips and fangs and into the throat of the huge, half-seen, motionless form. Two vast eyes like lakes of jelly quivered under the surface.

In a semicircle about this well stood twelve hooded figures, each three times the size of a man.

A tongue of silver ash reached out toward this well and nearly touched it. Above this tongue or walkway of ash, the final dolmen in the long line rose.

The elfin cavalcade was even now trotting quite silently down the line of dolmens leading here. One square gateway of stone the thirteen steeds passed by and then another. They approached the final dolmen.

Beneath that final dolmen, but standing on the dark glass, not the bright sand, was a thirteenth hooded figure. Even from a distance, Yumiko recognized her. One of the feet beneath the robe was a leg of bronze. The other was the hoof of a donkey. Issuing from the hood were the heads of the serpents woven about her head as a crown. It was Empousa of Tartarus.

Yumiko raced across the silver sands. She could not feel her paws, nor did she breathe any breath, so great was her speed. No dust was kicked into the air behind her.

Then she was between the last two dolmens. The last dolmen was black stones, and the dolmen before it, a few yards away, was dark red. Only a few grains of silver were scattered on the dark, glassy, cracked surface underfoot. Her tongue lolled; she panted.

The elfin lords on their beautiful steeds were riding toward her. On the other side, behind her, the veiled and hooded face of Empousa was lifting up, and dark eyes that flashed with regal pride gazed silently down on the little white she-fox.

The elfin lords were passing beneath the red dolmen. Each wore a bright cloak of green, woven with patterns of leaves from different trees and plants. The cloaks were voluminous and fell across the flanks and withers of the steeds. These were much like horses but with the hooves of deer and tails of lions.

The steeds were caparisoned in bright lozenges or diamonds of silver against black, green against gold, or green against silver. Four of the riders held standards emblazoned with heraldry. The steeds wore no barding, except, oddly, on their skulls. The chanfron covering each mount's head was engraved and etched to look like a fanciful human face: ragged beggar or crowned king, jester in coxcomb or veiled priestess, soldier in helm or poet in laurels. Each hooded rider likewise wore a mask engraved to be a fanciful equine face, as a horse, unicorn, or hippogriff.

The first rider in the line, seeing the white vixen before him, reined and halted. His cloak was birch leaf, and his mask was a destrier. "By wood and welkin, what sly diversion have we here? Phadrig Og, what say you?" The voice was musical lilt, a man's brogue.

The second rider bore aloft a standard of a gold harp on a sable field. His cloak was rowan leaf, and his mask was a hippocamp, with gills at the equine cheeks and fins for ears. He reined his steed and bent his masked head toward the first rider. "Noble Majesty, no doubt some ill-wisher seeks to hinder the payment of the tithe. Let us blast the intruder with nine deadly songs and ride on."

Yumiko looked back and forth along the line of riders. Which one was Tom? When she found him, how could she free him?

The third rider came forward, and the first two were forced to fall back and make way. He wore the mask of Sleipnir, or some mythic horse with four ears, and his cloak was the leaf of the ash tree. There was no eyehole on the right of his mask. Within the left-hand eyehole, his eye glinted a greenish gold. "King Brian, tell your vassal to stay his voice! We ride not now on Elfin ground, and the mouth of Hell is but a pace away. In this place, no weapon of silver nor weapon of song may be raised. Puck! What is this creature?"

A fourth rider carried a banner of a she-lion of gold on a green field. His cloak was alder leaf, and his mask was the face of a jenny. A male voice, his tones sly and wicked, came trippingly forth. "The gleam of starlight dances in the vixen's fur and the scent of Sarras fallen. But see how the passing seconds and minutes pass through the creature's eyes. No highborn elf is this, but a filthy half-breed. The blood of Eve the Accursed muddies her veins. Some Moth or Cobweb, this."

Yumiko opened her mouth to speak and then closed it again. She lowered her head warily and looked back and forth, whiskered nose twitching. She thought it better not to speak, not in this place, not if no one here knew who or what she was.

Now came a fifth rider, masked as a unicorn, whose robe was willow leaf. A regal feminine voice seeped from her mask. "Trample her. That is neither drawing a weapon nor singing a rune."

The sixth rider was also a woman. She was masked as a hippogriff with a beak of gold, and her cloak was hawthorn. Her banner displayed a white tree of seven branches on a green field. "Queen Ethne, the eyes of Empousa glint strangely at us. It may be unsightly to shed blood so near the Hellmouth. It would be like spilling wine into the sand a pace away from a man parched with thirst."

Yumiko now grinned. Six riders had spoken. Six had not. It was likely Tom was among those six. She held perfectly still, eyes darting, hoping the others would speak. Whoever did not speak was Tom.

Empousa now raised and lowered her brass leg. The glassy ground boomed like a hollow drum.

The seventh rider was masked as Pegasus, and his cloak was oak leaf. Streaks of crooked shadows shaped like the tines of antlers passed through the hood of his cloak without touching it and spread over his broad shoulders. In cold and ringing tones he spoke. "Silence, Fand! Silence, all of you, on peril of your lives! The beauty of elfin voice reminds the dark angels of old sorrows. Let us not try their patience lest the tribute increase. Lucien! Attend me!"

The foremost wolf of the pack now came forward, crouching and whining. He was large as a pony and silver like an Arctic wolf.

The horned and masked rider said, "Your voice is not fair enough to offend the dukes and counts of Hell. Speak. Who is this? Why is she here?"

The wolf said, "Imperial Majesty, this is the Foxmaiden, the sidekick of the vigilante who pesters the Anarchists, your enemies, who of late have caused commotion in your realm. She is here to hinder the tithing."

The horned rider now leaned from the saddle and breathed. A plume of cold air issued from the mouth of his Pegasus mask and smote Yumiko.

At once the cold penetrated her flesh and touched her heart. Her spirit form slipped away, and now she was a girl sprawled on her knees and forearms on the black ice. A trifle of fox fur clung to her breasts and hips, no larger than a bathing suit. Her black hair, unbraided, spilled down to the left across her neck and shoulder and arm onto the icy surface like a shining river delta. Her warm fur was gone, and she was shivering with cold and fear, but her dark eyes blazed brightly.

2. *The Finding*

The horned rider glared down at her. His eyes were like distant stars. "Speaks he the truth, little Foxmaiden? Are you here to hinder the tithe?"

She stood up. "Lucien Cobweb does not speak the whole truth. Under the name Thursday, he is a member of the Supreme Anarchist's Council. He conspires with Malen the Red and Empousa of Hell to undermine and overthrow your rule."

A gasp came from one of the riders behind. It was a woman's voice. Her cloak was patterned with vine leaves. Her mask was of a hayagriva, a blue-furred and gold-crowned *yaksha*, known to roam the jungles and mountains of India. Something in the tone of voice, or the set of the shoulders, told Yumiko this was Malen Ruddgochren herself.

Yumiko spread her arms wide. "I am here for my one, true love, Tomorrow Rocket Moth. I returned from the dead for him. He will go back to the lands of the living with me."

The horned rider in the Pegasus mask said, "There is no man here who will answer to that name. That name is quenched in the wine of oblivion and lost in the woven songs of Elfland. His face, his form, his fame, are now as elfs decree. He is not yours, but ours."

The elfin lords and ladies now removed their masks. The faces beneath the hoods were none she knew. Yumiko blinked, and all the faces changed. No one she looked at directly changed, but when she turned her head, whatever face she was not looking at, male and female swapped appearance with one another; old and young; dark and pale; man and elf. Some faces turned into skulls or masses of warts. Some turned to the visages of hawks or hounds. One hood held nothing but the stars of Ursa Majoris.

The silvery, heartless laughter of the elfs now chimed in the air. Whispering voices seeming to come from overhead or underfoot or from behind her head or inside her stomach, taunting her. "Riddle me this!" "Love thou me, or another?" "Which is he?" "Pick me!" "Come to my arms!" "My kiss will slay you!" "Foxmaiden, I am your love!" "Know you me not?" "Poor Tom's a-cold!"

The mockery fell silent when Empousa again raised her brass leg and stomped it against the ringing ground. This time, vast voices from underground moaned in pain.

The elfin lords and ladies donned their masks again, and the horned rider raised his hand and gave the signal to ride on. The slender steeds in their bright caparisons began to pass by Yumiko to the left and right.

Yumiko, half-naked and cold, stood with her fists clenched. She had no weapons, no magic ring, and no idea what to do. If eyes and ears could be trusted, there were five yet who had not spoken. But could they be trusted?

Of the remaining five, one held a banner where a black wolf reared on a white field, and, behind him, two riders were slender and sat sidesaddle. Yumiko doubted that the proud elfs would disguise Tom as one of their standard-bearers or one of their ladies.

The second to last rider wore a kelpie mask and was cloaked in hazel leaf. The last rider in line wore the mask of a backahast wreathed with seaweed and was cloaked in the leaf of an elder tree. He seemed stouter than the others, less graceful in his posture. Surely the last position would be the position of least honor in the cavalcade?

Yumiko grabbed the stirrup of the last rider as he rode by, and clung. "Tom! Tom! Is that you?"

"Sorry! Get away from me! Haven't you done enough?" The man in the backahast mask kicked her.

An elf would not apologize. He was calling her by the name he knew because he could not pronounce Sayuri. The voice was altered in timber and accent, perhaps by magic, but his words were his.

The one in the backahast mask was Wilcolac.

Spurned by the kick, the girl rolled rather than fell, bounced to her feet, and leaped nimbly onto the back of the steed before him in line, the one in the kelpie mask. She pulled aside the mask and pulled down the hood. Here were the round and cruel features of Wilcolac the magician. Every nuance of expression, the look in his eyes, the shape of each hair on his head told her eyes that this was Wilcolac. But she was not looking at his face. She remembered what she had overheard: *The fragment of the celestial cerulean dangles about his neck.* Lucien had been afraid to remove it.

Yumiko dug her fingers into the collar of the stranger's cloak.

Her fingers found a slender chain, such as a woman might wear. She yanked. The pendant was a bit of blue-white crystal shaped like a teardrop, glowing with a clear and piercing inner light that brought tears of wonder to her eyes.

It was he. It was Tom. She had found him.

3. The Last Gate

A clamor rang in her ears. The cavalcade was crossing under the final dolmen, the final gateway of black stone. The first eight passed beneath, led by the man masked as a destrier, with the hippocamp bringing up the rear.

The surface underfoot was broken black glass. Yumiko could see the reverse image of herself, her black hair almost like a hooded cloak falling to her hips, with both pale arms about the mantled figure atop his handsome steed. She had her arms around a man who looked like Wilcolac. In the mirror reflection, he looked like Tom.

The star at his throat was much brighter in the reflection. Thunderstruck, Yumiko recognized it.

Keep to yourself this memento of your mother's love, for the Grail light is in it. Keep it with you, lest the fumes of Earth confuse and confound you. Keep it in memory of me.

It was the same pendant her mother in the last hour on her last day had bestowed on her. The light from the pendant seemed to pierce like a lance straight into Yumiko to her core. A great smoggy darkness of confusion and forgetfulness began to stir and quake and break.

All riders save the last two had passed the final dolmen. But here stood Empousa, who raised her hand. The steed beneath Yumiko faltered, fell, and died. Yumiko wrestled the man she held out of the saddle and fell to the ground with him. She had acted in time: no part of him was trapped under the dead horse.

Empousa spoke. Her voice was inside Yumiko's head as well as outside. As the outward shout of the hag's hellish voice hurt her ear, so too did the force of the silent words burn inside her skull. "Who dares bring this pure and sinless virgin to the very lip of Hell?"

The shout of Empousa was painful to the others there as well, for all the elf lords shrieked or flinched, and many clutched their brows.

The real Wilcolac in a false voice now spoke from behind the backahast mask. "Surely she has committed some sin! No one serves in my nightclub who has not. I see to that!"

Yumiko said, "I have been baptized this very day."

Wilcolac said, "Perhaps the form was incorrect!"

Yumiko raised her voice, "I was baptized in the name of the Father, and of the Son, and of the Holy Ghost! Get away from me, you things of Hell!"

At the sound of these names, even though her high-pitched, girlish voice seemed very small and frail in the wide and starless landscape of cracked black glass and dunes of silver ash, the thirteen gigantic figures fell groveling as if deafened by thunderbolts. The dukes of Hell were shrieking and howling, cursing and uttering blasphemies.

Empousa recovered first, rose up, and spoke. "Do you mock us, loathsome Lords of Elfland? Wish you to have the kingdoms of the world be dashed from your pretty hands? We have prepared kingdoms of pain here in our realm to receive you instead!"

Now it was the turn of the elf lords to wince and cry, for the shout of Empousa was pain. Yumiko clung more fiercely to her man and clenched her teeth.

The horned rider wearing the Pegasus mask spoke in solemn tones. "Dread and divine Empousa, the Sons of Air and Daughters of Night approach in solemn fear to render the tithe and tribute due the august and infernal realm and your great sultan."

Empousa inclined her head with regal nod, and the snakes woven in her crown hissed and shook their rattles.

The horned rider turned and said, "The tithed one must step over the final threshold of his own will. That is the bargain. See to it."

The rider in the hayagriva mask addressed the rider in the backahast mask and said bitterly, "You should have let me kill her, as I asked, you stupid little magician. You know who goes in the mouth if your puppet does not." She did not disguise her voice. It was Malen.

The rider masked as a backahast dismounted. Mask or no, his bouncing, energetic walk was the walk of Wilcolac. He went to where Yumiko clung fiercely to the motionless man. Wilcolac said, "Thrall! Stand up! Cast that girl from your arms! Walk through the last gate!"

The empty-eyed young man obeyed and rose. His movements were slow and clumsy. With a potent twist of his arms, he shoved the half-naked girl roughly to the broken glass of the ground. She whirled in midair and landed in her feet in a crouch. With ponderous steps, he strode forward. She pounced. Yumiko found it easy enough to throw the blank-eyed youth over her hip to the ground, and drop, and grasp him in a tight hold.

The chain at his neck glittered and flashed. She saw into the depth of the stone. A wisp of clinging fog lost its grip and rolled away, revealing a lost memory.

4. *Darkness and Light*

The recollection took no time to unfold into her memory.

He told her words to say something important, some phrase she was supposed to utter if the elf threatened to kill her. But his voice, his words, were still mingled in forgetfulness. It was on the tip of her tongue, almost clear.

She and Tom were standing in a corridor of transparent glass. The maze reached several levels above and below them, and, far above, clearly visible through the intervening yet transparent floors, was the circle of stone forming the foundations of the tower above. The tower itself was invisible. Only the spiral of unsleeping watching things, the hideous masks of the guards, and the dark, winged shapes at the crown betrayed the outline of the tower.

At the same moment he was done telling her the words, the Anarchists found the turn leading into the dead-end corridor where Tom and Yumiko stood. With a roar, they rushed forward.

Tom took the ring, knelt, and put it on her finger. "Marry me. Be my bride. I promise you, we will live through this! And when you see me again and you see this pendant, you will remember."

He twisted the ring sharply on her finger as he spoke, turning it once, twice, thrice. "Now envision a safe place! Your thought will carry you there. Distance means nothing. Concentrate! You will see ghosts. Stop for nothing. Do not speak to them. Do not listen to their promises. Go!"

The ring darkened from silver to pewter to iron to obsidian. With the fourth twist, she could not longer see him. She was in another world, a cosmos of darkness.

Had he heard her answer? Had she said it in time?

How her eyes could see, she did not know. The darkness was visible. How she moved, she did not know. The wind was palpable and bore her weight aloft. The black shapes of ghosts she expected, and she knew her longbow would protect her.

But a darker shape, as massive as a sunken continent returning to the surface of the sea, she had not expected to be here, in this ghost world. Yumiko fled the vast fallen angel on the dark winds of the unlit cosmos like an autumn leaf before a hurricane.

Then, a hideous voice from below her called out in mocking tones. She looked. The fallen angel held up the shrieking soul in its palm, a torn and tormented figure that danced and trembled. She ceased fleeing, but stood in midair and peered.

For she knew him. In life, it had been Guynglaff Cobweb, Lord Tuesday of the Supreme Council of Anarchists, Master of the Abominable Snowmen. His apelike face had been one of the many Winged Vengeance demanded she memorize. Who had killed him?

For here he was, dead, a small speck of darkness screaming in the vast and scarred palm of a spirit older and darker that loomed in the black world. But her arrows could abolish ghosts and curse them never to return to Earth. Dead was Lord Tuesday, but she could harm him yet.

Prudence told her to flee; love of vengeance told her to slay. Hatred drove out fear. She drew her bow and dove like a falcon.

The peak of the hood of the fallen angel was larger than a mountain. Past it she fell, deep and deeper. The hand holding Lord Tuesday was like a black lake fed by five rivers. The fallen angel, without a word, and not even smiling, cast back his hood when she came close and revealed his face.

She recalled the horror of the shock, and the blood gushing from her eyes and ears, and the constricting, white-hot, branching pains shooting through her chest as her heart burst. She recalled desperately trying to mouth the words Tom had told her to say, but there was no air in her lungs. The words! What were they?

She found herself in a blinding light that did not blind her. It was a dozen times brighter than sunlight, but restful to her eyes, filling her with golden warmth… A bright lady was coming closer to her in the midst of this light, reaching out…

5. The Runes of Deceit

She wound her legs around his midriff and locked her ankles. His breath was driven from his body; he gasped like a sleeper in a nightmare, but he did not change expressions. Her elbow was behind his head, driving it forward, and her arms were locked around his elbows. Despite his greater strength, he had no leverage to rise.

The horned rider glared down at the young man and woman rolling and writhing on the glassy ground at his steed's hoofs. In a dry voice, he said, "These antics detract from the dignity of the day. If we are tardy by one tenth part of one second beyond the time agreed for tender of payment, our kingdoms and our children suffer. Make haste."

Yumiko, while pinning the arms of the man she held, saw a playing card tucked into the fold of his fancy cuff. She pulled it out with her teeth and crossed her eyes to stare at it. It was the joker. Angular letters had been written all about the margin of the card.

The last time she had seen such a card, it had carried runes of finding, meant to expose someone in hiding. Could not the same magic be used to hide someone?

Yumiko tossed her head and spat the card away. It fell to the glassy surface. The man she held shrank, losing weight and age, and his face melted and reformed. He no longer looked like Wilcolac. Instead, here was a freckle-cheeked young man with startling blue eyes and a mop of uncombed red hair atop.

The sight was like the blast of many trumpets heralding a victory parade in Yumiko's heart. Heat and cold pulsed through her veins. Her world spun. This face was at the center of it. She knew each freckle. She knew him.

His eyes were blank and dull: he was as if asleep.

With a cry of anger, Wilcolac drew a long dagger with a curving, snakelike blade. He knelt, clawing frantically, picked up the playing card, rose, and came toward her.

Yumiko caught sight of the gem glittering on the necklace, the one she gave Tom in the desperate hour when they parted. The light again flared into her, parting an inner darkness. She remembered giving the pendant to Tom. And she remembered more.

6. The Glass Maze

The floor, ceiling, and walls of the labyrinth were as clear as air. Only the splatters of blood, torn corpses, and shattered weapons showed where the halls and stairs were. To their left were the mighty doors of silver, set with many runes and charms. Tom's laser-howitzer had burned away the hinges on one side, just enough for Yumiko to use her wirepoon grapnel to snag and drag the ring to them. But the hinges were alive and groaning and growing back together, and the doors were pulling themselves back in place after having maliciously fallen onto the laser-howitzer and shattering its delicate lenses.

The hordes of attackers, men in dark suits, werewolves, vampires, men possessed by ghosts, and statues large and small seemed nearby but were kept from them by the glass walls.

"Listen," said Tom. "No time to explain. Give me your pendant. Lord Saturday means to send me alive to Hell. These creatures will have to take me alive and keep me alive. Come find me. I won't look the same, and I won't be the same, but anything wearing this pendant is me. Your passage through the mist will make you forget, but if my calculations are right, you cannot forget this pendant. You can use the ring instantly to find me again at any time, merely by concentrating on the sight of the pendant. They will not dare take it. When you find me, just grab me and hold on. As long as you hold me, I am safe. No matter what, do not let go. No matter what they turn me into, do not let go. Say my real name to me to wake me up. Now, can you do that?"

"I swear," she said softly.

"And if they threaten to kill or hurt you, say these words..."

7. Quills

Wilcolac reached down, and took Yumiko by the hair, and drew back her head at a painful angle, exposing her throat.

But she called out the words Tom had told her. "In Christ's name I dedicate the blood I shed to mingle with his. My death I give to the glory of the Holy Ghost. To the Father, I commend my spirit!"

It was the same thing she had said to the demon in the midst of the dark world before she died. She wondered what it meant.

A great wail came out of the gathered dukes and counts of Hell.

The horned rider said, "Stop! Touch her not!"

Wilcolac hesitated.

The horned rider said, "The spot where a martyr dies is holy, and her bones would blast us. The anger of our hosts who summon us here would be without limit. She must release him of her own volition."

Wilcolac stepped back. He said, "My lord, I can change his face and name. This august company can do more. Lady Malen, if you would?"

The voice of Malen came from behind the mask of the hayagriva. "Thrall! Be thou a porcupine! When she releases you, cross the threshold and be damned!"

Immediately, Tom's body, cloak, garb, and all darkened, shrank, and changed, and a new form swelled into being in Yumiko's tightly straining arms and legs. The porcupine was twice or thrice normal size and writhed and turned and snapped at her. Barbed quills, sharp as needles, entered her tender flesh in a hundred places. Her every instinct told her to open her arms and to fling the monster from her.

But he did not claw and drag himself over the threshold. Those were not his instructions. Yumiko tightened her grip, driving the terrible barbs into herself. She was slick with blood.

She cried, "Tom! Tom Moth! Tomorrow Rocket Moth! Wake! Wake! Hear your name and wake!"

The creature thrashed. Barbs struck her in the face and pierced her cheek. With immense pain, she continued to cry out his name. He did not wake.

The pendant had not changed. The fine chain was still around the neck of the porcupine, glittering. The elf magic left it untouched. The piercing light from the teardrop smote her again.

8. Ballroom

Yumiko on her featherless batwings dropped silently down from the shadowy ceiling of the ballroom. Seven men in formal suits and ties lay toppled among the broken tables and overturned chairs near the punch bowl. Arrows had pierced gunhands, necks, lungs, and hearts.

She turned one of them over. It was her target. With a cleaver she cut off the hand, wrapping it in plastic and stowing it in her pouch. Winged Vengeance could check the fingerprints later to confirm the kill.

The sound of the elevator chiming interrupted her thought. She moved quickly, overturned a table, knelt behind it, and nocked a red arrow. She had a second arrow in hand with a different head in case what came through the door was man, not elf.

It was neither elf nor man, precisely. It was a youth with an unruly head of bright red hair, whistling a merry tune and skipping. He wore a lab coat over his clothes and a pair of goggles over his eyes. He had a yo-yo in his hand, which he spun to the left and then to the right and then back again. The yo-yo was beeping, and little lights at the hub winked.

He hopped over one of the dead bodies, paused, looked down, and clucked his tongue.

Yumiko drew back. In his dim light, no one would spy her. The red-haired youth looked up, smiled at her, and waved. "Yoo-hoo! Ollie, ollie, oxenfree!"

She stood and drew her bowstring to her cheek.

"No shooting," he said, "My doctor says puncture wounds are bad for me. Is that arrowhead made of a ferromagnetic alloy by any chance? If so, fire away. I'll be invulnerable."

Yumiko gritted her teeth. "What is that?"

"Ferromagnetic. The kind of magnetism displayed by iron and associated with parallel magnetic alignment of neighboring atoms."

"And if my arrowhead is not? Not ferro—what you said."

He smiled sadly. "Well, I will be less than invulnerable. Say cheese!"

"Why should I say–" but then she was blinking in blindness, for a silent eruption of white light had emerged from his belt buckle. She heard a whistling snap of noise pass just before her nose, but when she tried to backflip out of the way, her hand tugged her bow. The bow was snagged on something and did not move.

She blinked the floating spots free and focused her eyes away from where she was looking, so she could see the scene with her side vision.

The youth was now seated atop the table next to her. His legs were crossed at the knee, and his foot was pointed at her. Out from his boot, a length of thin white metal had extended. It was about as big around as a walking stick. It reached from his leg to her bowstaff, passed between her bowstaff and bowstring, and then had embedded its tip in the floor. She could still move the bow and draw it, and she could point an arrow at any target anywhere in the room, except for the spot where he sat.

"You are annoying!" she cried.

"Yes," he said.

"And very annoying!"

"Yes," he said.

"And, and, uh–!"

"Fun. Unpredictable. Persistent. Smart. I always get the desired result in the end."

Beneath her mask, she scowled. The last of the blue dots floated out of her vision. She spoke in a quieter voice. "How did you follow me?"

"The first time we met, I decided I simply had to see you again. So I whipped up a harmless radioactive isotope my Geiger yo-yo here could detect and tagged you with it the second time we met. Varying the antennae length helps me triangulate." He did an around-the-world and a walk-the-dog, and then pulled the yo-yo back to his hand, and tucked it away in a pouch at his belt.

"How did you follow me just now? I disabled the elevator," she said.

"I re-enabled it. And improved it a bit. Now it can shoot through the ceiling. I can take you for a ride. Kind of a short ride, sort of a parabola, but it will be fun. Want to come?" He looked down at the floor. "You have to stop killing people by the way. Someone from the heavenly city of Sarras should have better manners."

She said, "How do you know who I am?"

He said, "Your ninja outfit is not airtight, and you leave clues and traces where you go, especially if you get wounded. A drop of blood contains your whole genetic code. You are my first cousin, four times removed, counting through my father Vidric, but counting through my mother, Dr. Rocket, you are my second cousin once removed. I am…"

"Tomorrow Moth. The boy who flew to the moon. Everyone knows your name."

"Boy, then. I've grown. I don't know yours. Name, I mean."

"My father is Danger son of Bold. My mother is Dandrenor daughter of Pellinore. I am Yumiko Ume-no-Mikoto Moth."

"Take off your mask," he said.

"No," she said.

"Yes," he said. "I can see through it anyway with my X-ray goggles."

He must have been fibbing about his goggles having X-rays because he stammered and stared when she removed the Noh-play fox mask she wore, shook her hair free, and looked up at him.

"Wow," he mused. "You really *are* yummy cute!"

"Yumiko."

"How about that elevator ride? I want to see if the disintegration bomb timer will work properly and blow the roof before we hit." He twitched his foot, and the length of metal hindering her bowstring now retracted and slid into a sheath hidden in his boot. He hopped to his feet. "Shall we?"

She said, "How can you hide a twenty-foot pole in your boot?"

"You mean my gyro-stilts? If you have lived your life in the clouds, you probably do not know about mermaid pouches. There is a lot you can do with space compression that the mermaids never dreamed of. Including storing compression energy more efficiently than any spring. Speaking of which, your outfit is really pretty clumsy and unclassy."

"W– what?"

"You could do better. What say we go to my flying lab and kick around a few designs?" He stepped closer and grinned an alarming grin.

It was too close. She threw a knife at his leg, but an invisible force made it wobble and spin away harmlessly. But the smoke pellets she flung in his face were not deflected. Evidently, they were not ferromagnetic.

She left him coughing in a cloud, and leaped out the window, and so escaped. That ended their first date.

9. Venom

Yumiko did not release the porcupine. The twelve figures now departed from their positions surrounding the mouth in the black ice and began walking slowly forward toward the black dolmen.

Wilcolac was trembling, but so very slightly that it could only been seen in how the reflections of the firefly lights above this head shifted and shook in the curving blade surface. He said, "King Brian, if you would?"

The Irish brogue issued from the mask of the destrier. "Who am I to discomfort a fair maiden, poor wee thing but half an elf? Lady Nimue is crueler than me. Let her do the deed."

"With pleasure, Your Majesty," came a smooth voice from behind the mask of Embarr, a steed famed for running on water as well as on land. She threw back her cloak, whose leaves were those of the water reed. She called, "Thrall! Be thou a serpent to constrict and bite, and let thy tooth be deadlier than an asp! When she unhands you, cross the threshold and be damned!"

Immediately, the porcupine became a great serpent of no type seen on Earth, larger than a boa constrictor, but hooded like a cobra. Yumiko seized it by the throat before it could sink fangs into her neck, and she forced the great head back, but powerful coils now wound around her punctured, bleeding body and began to crush her bones. Fangs sank into her wrist. The pain was like a scalding burn traveling up her arm. Dizzy black spots crowded her vision. Her finger grew swollen. Her forearm was turning blue. The coils of the snake clamped her tighter than a vice. She could drawn no breath. Her eyes grew dim.

She could only whisper and croak his name, again and again. He did not wake.

But she could still see the pendant glancing and gleaming around the serpent's throat. And she did not let go.

10. Theater

Yumiko swung from rooftop to rooftop using her *kusarigama*. Whenever the hook did not catch properly, she fell and snapped out her batwings. She glided to the top of a lower building.

A rushing gush of noise thundered from the dark sky. Down from the low-hanging clouds, riding three narrow columns of exhaust that issued from his winged backpack, dropped Tom Moth, grinning. His roaring backpack grew muted, whined, and fell silent. He dropped lightly to the roof. He was wearing goggles and a heavy leather flight jacket, with the wool collar turned up.

"Let's go around again," he said. "Race you to the top of the Flatiron Building!"

She did not answer but threw a handful of pellets at him. The wings of his backpack tilted, and a blast issued from the vents at the tip of either wing. The jet exhaust dispersed her smoky attack handily.

"Stop following me!" she cried.

She swung and soared again. He rocketed past her underneath, his face turned upward, and his arms and legs imitated a slow backstroke. He was waiting on the rooftop where she landed. He was lounging in a Morris chair.

"Where did you get a chair?" she asked.

He stood up. "Aw. I was sure could you figure this one out." He stood, and folded the chair into a segment as small as a handkerchief, and stowed it among the many pouches and holsters of his belt. "It is smart metal. An alloy made with the folding space folded directly into it. I could do this to any of your gear. Here!"

And he tossed her what seemed a small pistol. She thought about shooting him, but instead pointed it at a chimney pot, and pulled the trigger. It was a wire-harpoon gun.

After a moment or two of playing with it, she said, "How did you make the retraction spindle so small, so powerful, so silent?"

He said, "Same as my stilts. I use the force of the compressed space when it unfolds to drive it. In this case, the space fold is torsion-wise. Wound rather than compressed. You can have it along with the parachute harness that goes with it. On one condition!"

Her longing for so useful a device warred with her suspicions. "What condition?"

"Go out on a date with me."

She said, "I am not going into your lab! You would strap me to a slab and do terrible things!"

"Don't give me any ideas. We will go some place public, with a crowd. To see a motion picture."

She frowned. She would have to return to the sanctum and find something nicer to wear. "What kind of motion picture?"

"It's science fiction. All the best films are science fiction!"

Later, seated in a darkened theater with a soda in one hand and a bag of popcorn in the other, Yumiko decided she did not really like science-fiction films. There were too many explosions, for one thing, and the space princess ended up doing all the work and saving the spaceman. Why bother keeping him around? The swordfighter's stance was wrong. And why did the magic swirling space vortex bring only one character back from the dead? It dishonored his self sacrifice. Yumiko did not like stories where the heroine had to do the rescuing or where characters did not stay properly dead.

Yumiko also did not like the taste of the soda pop. It was so sweet it almost tasted metallic.

Tom leaned close to her to explain some plot point or to say why the alien first officer could not fall in love with the pretty ship's nurse. He put his arm across her shoulder as he did, and his breath was in her ear. When he straightened up again, he left his arm in place. Under her lashes, Yumiko looked sidelong at his profile. In the gloom, the flickering light from the screen played across his face.

She took another sip of the metallic soda, relaxed, snuggled back into her chair, and put her head on the young man's shoulder. She did not like science-fiction films. But she decided she really liked going to see science-fiction films.

Chapter 14

Who Speaks Words in Elfinland

1. Shock

The horned rider said, "Do not permit her to die in this place." Nimue raised her hand again, and the fiery pain of the venom in Yumiko's blood flooded her arms and legs but avoided her chest and heart. Still Yumiko clung.

The twelve hooded giants had gathered, six to one side of the final threshold and six to the other. Empousa stood midmost, one step beyond the dolmen. Ten of the riders reined their nervous steeds. Five were to Empousa's right and five to her left, with the tall dukes and counts of Hell looming over the elfin lords and ladies. The wolves that had come with the elfin cavalcade were still on this side of the threshold, glaring down at Yumiko with yellow eyes.

Yumiko could hear Wilcolac's teeth chattering. "My lord, if you would be so kind..."

But the horned rider said, "Am I less than Brian? Maeve. Do this work. Time is short. Something swift."

One of the figures riding sidesaddle wore the mask of Aethon, one of the horses of the chariot of the sun, and an arabesque of curling flames surrounded the eyeholes and nostrils of her mask. Her cloak was the leaf of the ivy. She now spoke. "Thrall! Be thou an eel, and sting her with shocks. When she lets you go, go over the threshold and be damned."

The creature was larger than any eel on Earth. These pains, if anything, were even worse. She felt her heart stop and start again. Her lungs could not inflate. Yumiko was forced to hold the slippery body with hands and feet and grip it with her teeth, lest it escape her.

Her vision faded in and out. But she saw the gem of memory winking.

2. The Lakeshore

The two of them sat by the shore of Lake Carlopa in upstate New York, far from any eyes to see. Yumiko was feeding the ducks by throwing them breadcrumbs. Tom was feeding the ducks by throwing a slice of bread in the air and using an energy instrument to blast it into freshly toasted crumbs that rained down like fluffy brown snow. The instrument was a wand with stops or keys something like those on a flute. He did this one-handed since the instrument could also emit a suction ray to pick up the next slice of bread and a pressure ray to hurl it high. For once, she could see his eyes, which were the most remarkable shade of blue.

His other arm was preoccupied by being wound around her shoulders. Beneath a light robe, she was wearing the skintight supersuit he had designed and redesigned.

Allegedly, they were here to test the latest improvements to the breathing gear and the automatic air quality sensor.

But for now, they fed the ducks.

She admitted how hard her life had been after her father's death, when she was taken up into the clouds. "Mine was the only bow in the city, the only weapon of any kind. I knew it grieved my mother that I practiced every day and neglected all she wished to teach me. I thought I was honoring my father. And yet would he have wanted me to vex her so? He still loved her."

Yumiko spoke of her mother's passing. "…She did not abandon her post for him. For me. For death. How angry I was when she died! She left me! Again! And now I am ashamed. Where is the respect and obedience I owe her? To hunt down her killers is all I can do."

Tom had a similar story. His parents were still alive, but only in a way. "When I returned to the cabin, everything Winged Vengeance told me in the dream had now come to pass in the real world. They were both simply sitting in their chairs at the kitchen table, mouths open, staring at a lantern that had gone out. They could speak, and react, and everything seemed normal.

"But it was not. The spark of genius was gone from my mother, the zeal and drive from my father. They could no longer hear music except as sound vibrations. They could not change their habits or make complex decisions.

"They had no memory of me.

"They had no love for me, a little boy they regarded as an intruder. They threw me out of the house and electrified the door. Every day for a month, I tried to break in. Through the windows, at night, I could see them going through the routines of their former lives like clockwork.

"I kept myself alive by doing odd jobs for the neighbors, repairing lawn-mowers and electronics. I used the money to buy rice. I did not have a pot to cook it in, so I folded a leaf into a crude cup, filled it with water, and used that to cook. I used the plastic bag and the water to make a magnifying glass to start a cooking fire, but this only worked on sunny days.

"Eventually, relatives found me. Halloway and Lightningrod Moth were brothers who ran a traveling carnival. They would follow the Cobweb & Dark Pandaemonium Shadow Show around the country, trying to undo the aftermath of Mr. Dark's eccentric pranks and cruelties and disfigurations. So at age seven, I ran off to join the circus. I would be there to this day if I had not set the circus train on fire. A lurch of the caboose where they let me keep my chemistry set broke my bottle of yellow phosphorous and exposed it to air.

"I vowed to find a way to restore my parents."

She did not weep when she told her story, but she did when he told his. Afterward, as if it were the most natural and right thing in the world, he pulled her close, and leaned over, and kissed her.

Perhaps it was the most natural and right thing in the world. It certainly felt like it.

3. Fire

The voice of Empousa echoed in the minds of all present. "The time is come. Present the tithe, or be forfeit."

The horned rider said, "Wilcolac Cobweb, I hereby in law and solemn oath take and adopt you as my firstborn son. Step over the threshold and be damned."

Wilcolac fell to his knees. "My lord, Erlkoenig, I beg you…"

Erlkoenig nodded his horned head. "Call me father, dear son. Mine own father once worked my salvation by substitutionary atonement. I accept you as my personal savior, little magician. You wanted to have magic arts akin to ours. Now pay the price. Do your legs fail you? Your father can amend them."

Erlkoenig raised his hand, and an unseen force pulled Wilcolac upright. His legs moved like stiff boards, unbending, and marched him toward the threshold. Wilcolac still had control of his arms and hands, however, and so he bent and slashed at the muscles and sinews of his legs, trying desperately to cease their mechanical motion. The elfin lords and ladies laughed and applauded this display.

Wilcolac stumbled and fell to the black mirrored surface, which clanged under him. Blood flowed down both legs. Hurriedly, he scooped up his blood with his fingers and drew some angular marks on the black glass with it. "Thrall! Become a fiery salamander! I call upon Chaos, and Old Night, older than any created thing, older then the Devil, to hear my words and aid my work!"

And words in a language Yumiko did not know, which her ears seemed not to be able properly to hear, gushed from the throat of Wilcolac. Red phlegm also gushed out, for to utter these words tore his tongue and his lungs.

Wilcolac's magic made a deeper change to the form she clutched, for now the creature went beyond nature and was worse than all that had come before.

The eel in her hands grew longer, became covered in red diamond-sharp scales, and then burst into flame. This was not the small lizard creature called *salamander* but the otherworldly monster of fire for whom it was named. The flames were blue hot at its scales and yellow and red in concentric blankets around it. Yumiko was clinging fiercely to the hottest part of the creature.

Wilcolac screamed, "Cross the threshold before me! Crush that Sorry girl, and cast her aside, but you must cross the threshold first!"

The fiery and sinuous body of the monster also had all the strength of a constricting snake. It felt like red-hot chains wrapping her bare flesh. The flames hurt worse than any electric shock. The scales were hard and barbed like the skin of a shark. Many scales darted out thin jets of blue-white fire more painful than quills. The venom of the jaws ignited once inside her bloodstream, burning along her veins the cord of a fuse.

The wounds were shocking, terrible. She felt bones break and ligaments tear.

The burning ate her flesh. The venom ate her bloodstream. If she lived, she would be maimed for life, unable to walk, unable to move. She knew she was not dead only because of some magic charm or force of will from Erlkoenig, who wished her to die elsewhere, not here. Every fiber of her being screamed that she should let go.

But Yumiko, in the midst of the flames, could still see the glint of light at the salamander's throat.

4. The Dark Sanctum

It was Nyctalope's habit to speak with her in pitch blackness. His eyes allowed him still to see her. She had taken to the habit of keeping her mask on during these interviews. It amused her that the lens system Tom had built into the Noh mask allowed her to mimic her brother's power of sight.

His real name was Yakanshiryoku Peaseblossom. He was the son of Sarutahiko Peaseblossom, Dandrenor's first husband. But in Western lands, he called himself Nyctalope. He was the Eyes of the Night.

This time, she was almost sorry she could see him. The sinister crow-mask with its long, metallic beak and headdress of sharp feathers had been pushed back, and his eyes were weary, his handsome face careworn. He leaned on the staff of his bow, staring down at where she knelt. His shoulders sagged. The black-fletched arrow reaching over his shoulders seemed somehow less ominous. She imagined he might fall to the floor if she kicked the bowstaff out of his grasp.

He said, "I worry that I can trust you. Is not your oath an oath of iron? I have forbidden you to see this boy! He is not to be trusted! He is apprentice and intern to the mad inventor, Rotwang Cobweb. I have received messages from two of my agents. Henry Arnaud has traced Anarchist money into Rotwang's coffers, and Fritz the Janitor sends me a report from the Nineteenth Precinct. Officer Don Damiano traced the disappearance of a blind hobo from the local shelter to an abandoned mine owned by one of Rotwang's dummy corporations."

Yumiko said, "There are four dozen abducted blind men working in the mine. They are given an electrical apparatus that allows them to see some objects and not others, and they work on Rotwang's construction project. He is building an Iron Mole to dig underneath the barrier to arrive in the Third Hemisphere in an unprotected spot."

The look on his face, when he thought she could not see his face, was very rewarding to her. He said slowly, "So you knew the boy was a spy, and you are practicing counterespionage on him?"

"I know he is good and kind… if quite annoying. And brilliant! He is deceiving Rotwang, letting the inventor complete the machine. He has already made spare keys and vacuum tubes needed to regulate and guide the atomic engine."

Nyctalope Peaseblossom shook his head sadly, wearily. But no weariness was betrayed in his voice. Had she been unable to see, his mood would have remained hidden.

"There was once a man in a dark room whom I served loyally. For his sake I joined what he called the Last Crusade, the final effort needed to overthrow the reign and realm of darkness on this Earth. I never saw that man, never learned his true name, but I loved him then. Now I curse him in my heart each day. I and all my brothers in arms in that crusade were ordered where an ambuscade waited. We were wiped out…."

Yumiko said, "What did the man in the dark room do wrong?"

"He did then what you do now. He trusted too easily. Rotwang Cobweb was a member of the crusade. I objected to the others that he could not be trusted. I was ignored. He betrayed us, and the enemy was waiting. I alone was taken alive and brought to the Tithing Ground. By the sheerest mischance I escaped: I had a gem Mother gave me they could not remove, and it spoiled their ritual. I turned my back to the world and donned my wings, though they had turned dark from all my dark deeds. Back to Sarras I flew, but there was no comfort there. Do you see the error of trusting?"

Yumiko said, "But he trusted me!"

"Who? Rotwang?"

"No. Tom. He told me his real name is Sylvester. Tomorrow Moth is a name he uses for publicity, for his engineering company, and the children's books written by Appleton Moth about his adventures. You see, he did not want to be called Sly Moth."

5. Substitution

Yumiko was burned and wounded inside and out, bones broken, limbs swollen, blood poisoned. Her arms and legs had no more power to move and could grip nothing. The salamander was writhing free. Her voice made a gargling, scratchy, horrid sound. "Sylvester! Sylvester Moth! Sly Moth!"

She shouted it. Despite the pain in every part of her lungs, throat, tongue, and lips, she shouted the name.

He heard. Somehow, somewhere, he heard. As quickly as in a dream, the salamander changed into the redheaded young man. He cried out in grief and horror at the condition of the girl he held in his arms.

She stared in wonder. He whispered, "Don't worry, darling. I know what is going on. I won't let them hurt you anymore." Tom's eyes glinted dangerously as he crouched over the wounded girl, glaring at their enemies all around.

The pain had not made Yumiko cry. But her relief at those words, her feminine joy at hearing a male voice, a confident and dangerous male voice, assuring her that he knew what to do, was overwhelming. She could hear the love in his voice. And so, despite the danger all around her, she suddenly felt safe.

Empousa raised her hand, glaring at Erlkoenig imperiously. No word need be said. Time was up.

Erlkoenig gestured to the huge arctic wolf. "Lucien! Drag that sad magician over the threshold and be done with this charade."

The werewolf grinned. "Gladly!" And he stepped, and lowered his terrible jaws, and gripped Wilcolac by the neck, and backed up across the threshold, pulling the chubby magician after him across the broken glass.

Once the white wolf had his rear paws over the threshold but before his head or the burden he dragged crossed it, Wilcolac twisted sharply in the monster's jaws and drove the snake-shaped dagger he had never released up and into the back of the neck of the wolf.

The wolf howled in wrath and staggered back. All four paws were over the threshold. Lucien turned and turned again, snapping, but the knife was impaled into his mane too near his skull for him to turn and grip it. Red blood spread over the white fur.

Yumiko saw that the playing card, the joker, was not in Wilcolac's hand. It was pinned by the knife blade to the wolf's neck and coated with blood.

And then Lucien turned into Wilcolac Cobweb. There he was, romping on all fours, dressed in a military coat and fur hat like what Lucien was wont to wear. And his voice did not sound very much like that of Wilcolac, but it did match his pitch and accent a bit.

The Wilcolac who was face down on the last few bits of silver sand, on this side of the threshold, bloody in both legs and bleeding from hand and neck, spoke without looking up. "Lady Empousa. I present the tithe. There is Wilcolac son of Erlkoenig, the king's firstborn son."

"It is not acceptable." Empousa said, "We cannot touch him."

"Damn it!" screamed Lucien. He looked like a man, but he was still on hands and knees, turning and twisting like an animal, trying to bite at the protruding knife hilt. "Someone pull this damn thing out of my damned neck! God damn it! Damn me, but that hurts!"

"Now, it is acceptable." Empousa said, "With his own mouth, he has said it."

Yumiko saw Erlkoenig and the other masked riders turn their hoods away. The Dukes of Hell drew themselves up and cast their cloaks aside. Vast beings, winged and many-limbed and many-headed with many staring eyes, began to rise in their places. But these were scarred and maimed, faces and limbs burned by lightning bolts and hellfire, the magnificent and majestic glory which once had been theirs was turned to horror. Their scarred and scabrous wings were larger than thunderclouds. In some impossible way the eye could not see or the mind not comprehend, the dread living beings were larger than the landscape on which they stood and seemed ever to grow larger. Their fingers elongated dreadfully, reaching down to where Lucien cursed and kicked, for he had not yet noticed his peril.

The yawning mouth in the glassy ground behind them now gave forth a peal of horrific noise. Yells, screams, laughter roared out of the underground places. The ground shook. Cracks formed in the glass surface, and fires burst like bombs, sending jets of flame leaping into the sky.

Yumiko closed her eyes, unwilling to see more. She heard the sound of Lucien struggling and cursing, screaming in earnest now. It grew shrill, panicky, hopeless. The sound traveled a little ways away and then downward, echoing off the sides of the well as he was dragged below. It mingled with the laughing and shrieking and sobbing from underground and the roar of the fires. His voice turned into a long, thin, endless wail. It was the scream of a being who is not allowed the moment of rest a creature that must pause to breathe can find between sobs.

She heard crackling noises, as if glass slabs were moving. The heat and roar of the flames was cut off abruptly. The horrid clamor from underfoot fell silent. She heard the grinding of immense teeth breaking through the glass well which held the giant throat open. The mouth shut. Then came earthquakes, clamors, vibrations, and crashes. Still Yumiko did not look, but, from the sound, she knew the face of the giant whose esophagus was being used as the door to Tartarus was being pulled farther down underground, and the strange black mirrored substance of the surface was being piled in the wake of that subsidence into the pit thus formed.

The noise of a mighty wind came and lasted for many minutes. Then, it died into a whisper and faded.

An eerie hush fell over the landscape.

6. *The Tear of the Grail Queen*

She felt Tom wrap his cloak gingerly about her.

Malen said, "Wolves! Fall upon these two and tear them to shreds."

But Erlkoenig said, "Heap no more wrath upon yourself, traitress. For your treachery, in seven year's time, you will come here again. The Moths must be saved alive for my interrogators to question."

She heard Tom call out, "In my hand is the tear of the Grail Queen, bathed in the light of the most holy Sangreal. She is alive in Heaven, a martyr, and I call upon her, upon the cup she watched, and upon he whose cup it is. In his name I ask you to gaze at this crystal and recall the bliss of Heaven you so rashly and ignobly forsook. Look! See how the light shines!"

Through her closed lids, Yumiko saw the light grow bright and brighter.

She heard the gasps and cries from the company gathered there: Brian sobbed, and Puck swore. Ethne, Malen, and the other women hissed.

Other years and seasons now floated up as if from the bottom of the sea, rising like sunken continents restored to their own places. Her childhood, girlhood, and youth. Much of it was sad or silly, and many things she regretted.

But the pain in her body began to fade. Perhaps it was shock. Perhaps the flames had burned her nerve endings away. Either way, death was near.

She heard Erlkoenig's voice. "Very well, young inventor. The elfin lords depart. We of the Night World have no dealings with the light you bear. But the wolves are not so awed by lost things as are we nor as delicate to avoid Christian blood. May they slay you for this insolence."

7. Rest

With great pain, Yumiko willed her eyes to open. There was Tom, bending over her. Oddly, she saw hanging in the air over his head the glowing white pearl that had appeared when she assumed her spirit form as a fox.

Of the elf lords, she saw no sign. The only remaining sign of the black landscape was a single huge hand thrust up into the air from the ground, motionless. Even as she watched, a wind blew dunes to cover it over. The silver sand now stretched to each horizon. The black glass was buried. The whole was elfin domain again, with no well, salt flat, or valley openly beholden to hell.

As for the werewolves, Yumiko saw they were running in circles, leaping and snapping, attempting to pull down a great black batlike form. Pools of blood were splattered all along the silver ash.

Whenever one wolf would leave the chase and turn, and run at Tom or Yumiko, the batlike form would swoop, and gather the running monster into his wings, and tear at his throat. Then, the bat would fold itself into the wound and enter the wolf body, whereupon the wolf would turn and rend its brothers, falling upon them with tooth and claw until it was torn apart. Whereupon the batlike shape would pull itself out of the maw of the dying beast and flap its way heavily into the dark air again.

The wolves never seemed to understand what was happening, for they never ran at Tom in pairs or as a pack. Or perhaps they enjoyed the sport, not minding who killed whom. Or perhaps they saw how desperately the vast bat struggled since the circling and leaping pack came ever closer to where Tom cradled Yumiko in his arms.

Whatever force had been holding her death at arm's length was gone. A floating numbness was creeping into her. It was nice to feel weightless again. There was not the least trace of fear in her: only sadness.

Yumiko whispered. "Tom. Don't cry. I am happy. To see you. One, last…" But pain closed her throat, and she spoke no more.

Yumiko could not focus clearly on Tom's face. He was saying something, earnestly and urgently, but the words faded into and out of existence.

Now it was time to rest. Yumiko wanted to explain to Tom that she was happy, very happy. She need only sink down now into the softness of nothingness awaiting her and enjoy the rest. Sweet rest.

She closed her eyes and let her head drop back.

8. Red Wine

She could not rest. Something was bothering her. Had Tom heard her answer? Had she spoken it in time?

Yumiko pried her eyes open again. She croaked and could not speak. She was very thirsty. The silver ash was everywhere. It was choking her.

She saw a little dot of light in the dark heaven, like a firefly. Down it darted rapidly. Here was Elfine, still carrying the white ring. Elfine called out in horror when she saw Yumiko's wounds and burns.

The nine-inch-high girl landed near Yumiko's motionless, limp left hand. This was the hand that was not swollen. Without a word, Elfine thrust the ring on Yumiko's finger and twisted it. Starlight, and then sunlight, burst forth.

Four vast and terrifying living creatures were then looming over them, larger than galaxies, light years tall, but somehow compressed by some impossible quirk of perspective to became visible to the eye. Now their wings were entirely folded, their bodies cloaked, and three of the faces out of four were not seen. The remaining face was like the face of a man, bright as the sun. To stare directly at it was to go blind.

A half dozen of the braver werewolves turned, yammering, and ran toward the nearest of the four living creatures. They approached the huge ox hooves of the creature's feet, which were glowing like ingots in a forge. Fire came from the many eyes in the feathers of its wings, and lightning came from the fires, and the six brave wolves were whirled into the air and lit ablaze. The wolves were destroyed so swiftly that no yelp escaped. They were consumed so utterly that no scrap of fur or splinter of bone remained.

The others wolves, not as brave, then ran away, yammering. It was in vain. Fires from Heaven fell down among them. As when a candle flame is blown out and leaves no trace, they were gone.

Now from underneath the eagle feathers of the wings, one of the living creatures raised a hand and spread its fingers. In the light shed from the living creatures, the heaps and dunes of ash suddenly faded away and were no more, and the dark surface beneath grew bright as ice, and all the cracks were mended. The white light from the mirror surface became like flame, but the flickering flames were albino grass and gentle white reeds and pale brush. The standing stones and obelisks turned into trees of many fair shapes, oak and ash and hawthorn, slender birch and many types of fruit trees, but each one white as snow. The dolmens became trellises for white rose or pale grape. The eyes in the wings of the living creatures flew up into the dark and empty heavens, taking fixed positions, and becoming stars.

Tom, staring upward, slack-jawed, uttered softly, "By Schroedinger's cat! What the heck was *that*? What *happened*?"

Elfine tugged on the ring on Yumiko's finger. She said to Tom, "It is stuck! Turn the ring! Or else the priest vampire boy cannot get near us."

Tom said to Elfine, "And just who are you?"

Tom took Yumiko's hand in his. The light from the ring dimmed, turning from sunlight to starlight to metal. The band went from brilliant to argent to white. The archangelic face became angelic and then a visage of an open-eyed woman. The vast beings looming over them shedding lightning bolts disappeared from view.

The pale colors in the landscape turned to green grass, brown trunks, wooden trellises, and flowers with as many hues as the rainbow.

"What *were* those things?" asked Tom. "Where did they go?"

Elfine tilted her head and rolled her eyes. "I think they are still here. They are always here. They are angels. If you look at them wrong, you die."

Tom said, "Those things are *what*? I thought angels wore dresses and played harps and looked like King Vultan of Mongo, but girlier. If those bad boys are around all the time, why don't they help us? In battles?"

The batlike shape landed heavily on the white grass near Tom and Yumiko. The head of Matthias replaced the triangular batlike skull. "They do. But only the eyes of faith can see the result."

Elfine said, "Or a magic ring!"

Tom said, "She's dying. Can you do anything?"

"Fear not," said Matthias. "I can. We are in the dream realm. It is a very old and solid part, and we are physically present, but all of this around us is dream stuff nonetheless. Find me a cup."

Elfine picked up a white acorn cap and grew suddenly to her full size, expanding the acorn cap with her. "Will this do?"

Tom said to Elfine, "Just who are you again?"

Elfine had dimples when she smiled. "I am going to be the maid of honor at your wedding!"

Matthias opened his mouth, and fangs as long as switchblades unfolded from his upper jaw. He shook his wings, and they became human arms. He tore open his wrist with a vicious slash, and squeezed his fist, and poured his living blood into the white cup.

"This would not be lawful on Earth," said Matthias. "I hope it is allowed here."

Yumiko murmured. "Yes. Tell him. I said. Yes. I do."

Matthias said soothingly to her, "Do not worry. Once I was a vampire, who drank life from others. But now I can draw upon those selfsame evils as a source of strength. You see, holy unction cures it. Vampirism is just a disease, a spiritual plague rather than a physical one… and…"

But Tom said, "That is not what she is asking about." He bent his head lower. "What is it, darling?" But Yumiko was too weak to answer.

Matthias said a prayer over the cup, and made the sign of the cross over it three times, and presented it to her. "Hold her head up. Let her drink."

Yumiko was very thirsty but did not want to drink blood. The idea was nauseating. However, the cup at her lip smelled of red wine. It was cool and refreshing on her tongue and went like warm and cozy fire down her throat. She was surprised the nerves and muscles in her lips and mouth were hale enough to sip and taste and swallow.

She stretched her limbs and sat up. Her flesh was pink and whole, and her bones unbroken, and not even the smallest cut or bruise marred her. The hair on her head was not burned, nor was there even the smell of smoke. Yumiko laughed in breathless joy and cast her arms around Tom, who looked surprised to the point of shock.

Matthias, meanwhile, smiled, started to speak, turned pale, fainted, and fell. The batlike form was entirely gone: he lay naked on the grass.

Chapter 15

Ne'er Sees More His Own Country

1. The Waking World

Tom turned toward Matthias, startled. Yumiko stood and drew the green cloak embroidered with holly leaves around her. Elfine said to her, "Welcome back! Say! Is this really the dream realm? What happens if the people dreaming about this section of landscape wake up?"

Yumiko said sharply, "Where is Wilcolac?"

Wilcolac's voice came from all directions at once. "I am here. I have cast a word of power from myself like a falcon from my wrist to wake those very beings and restore me to my place."

And Yumiko looked and realized that she could see him. The fat man was still wounded, bleeding from mouth and nose and from both legs. The long green cloak still draped his portly form. Beneath he was dressed in eighteenth-century formal gentleman's wear, complete with cravat and waistcoat. He was seated on a headstone, swaying, grimacing, and the blood from his wounds had stained the marble pink in places. From somewhere, for he had not had it before, he had summoned his walking stick. He leaned on it wearily, murmuring words to it. Perhaps it murmured back.

All around was the Cavalry Cemetery of Queens. Yumiko squinted and blinked, for the day was dazzling bright. The morning sun was still near the horizon, which surprised her. It felt like many hours had passed. But, from the look of things, the cemetery was not yet open for business. The dolomite dome of the Johansson Mausoleum rose from the crest of the hill above. Headstones and statues were crowded around.

Yumiko looked left and right. Matthias was nowhere in sight. Nor was Elfine.

Yumiko moved toward Wilcolac. The voluminous green cloak fluttered about her with the agitation of her walk. "You tried to toss my beloved into Hell to save your own wretched soul."

Tom stepped forward, put his arms around Yumiko, and whispered, "There, there! It is bad form to take vengeance on my evildoers until after you say hello to me!" He bent his lips near hers.

But then he saw Wilcolac watching. Instead of kissing the girl, Tom turned and squinted at the magician. "Wait a minute. I know you. You are the club owner. Of that place Rotwang used to take me when he wanted to get cross-eyed. The Crummy Club. Right?"

Wilcolac smiled sourly. "Cobbler's Club. Winged Vengeance has burned me out, but the dim vigilante seems not to know how modern society works. My insurance is well paid and covers acts of arson, and since my friends control the insurance industry as well as the legal profession, I foresee no difficulties."

Yumiko had tilted her head back and parted her lips, but when no kiss was forthcoming, she twisted a bit in Tom's arms, just enough to express annoyance, but did not pull free.

She turned her head to scowl at Wilcolac. "But your master is dead. Thursday."

Wilcolac said, "Alive. But burning slowly in Hell. Forever. As I sit and contemplate my future, I am trying to reckon the ways in which this disadvantages me, if any."

Yumiko said, "You serve him. You must be loyal."

"Must I? Lord Thursday forced me out of a comfortable neutrality and friendship with all sides. Excitement and calamity became a daily routine. He invited his dreadful girlfriend into my place, whom I hope is rotting in an elfin jail in Troynovant, or languishing in an enchanted sleep, or trapped in the shape of a sapling."

Wilcolac smiled at her and continued. "Spare him no pity. It was at his behest I took you into my service, but I saved you from him. He wanted to torture the location of the vigilante's lair out of you. I knew we could find it with a little psychological pressure, an obvious tail for you to spot and shake and a smoother tail for you not to, and a little patience. The Cheyenne sent me the signal to indicate you led him to your master's hidden lair, or else I would not have given Garlot the go-ahead to duel with Gilberec. I assume the foolish young knight is dead..."

Yumiko was surprised when Tom released her and stepped away. A cheer from his throat interrupted Wilcolac's speech. The red-haired youth was jumping, waving both arms overhead, and hallooing.

Through the forest of headstones came a jingle of spurs and a clatter of armor. Gilberec atop Rabicane came into view trotting down the slope, leading his riding horse, his pack horse, and Matthias's white mule. The truncheon of a broken lance was in his hand, and his shield was dented. Ruff the dog came running pell-mell down the slope, barking excitedly, then he ran back up the slope toward Gil, barked more, and ran down the slope again.

2. A Noble Offer

Wilcolac looked up at the young knight approaching. "And to think, Lucien called me foolish when I told him it was likely Arthur's blessing was on the boy."

Yumiko could not resist an arch smile. "I know. I heard. I had you bugged."

He gasped in surprise and coughed in pain. He wiped blood from his mouth onto a handkerchief. "Resourceful. But you were a creature strictly of fifteenth-century samurai weapons and ninja tricks, or so I heard. When did you enter the electronic age?"

Yumiko smiled again, eager to boast about Tom and his cleverness, but Wilcolac did not wait for her answer. "No matter! The affair is done. You have no more business with me. My ties to the Anarchists are cut. If anything, I am grateful to you. And I am glad, very glad, Lord Thursday is in the inferno, luxuriating in each one of the punishments laid out for me."

Yumiko said sharply, "That is disgusting! To let another suffer in your place!"

He smiled a crooked smile. "So says a young woman baptized just today. How droll of you."

Gil arrived, doffing his helmet and tucking it under one arm. His silver hair in the sunlight looked as metallic as his breastplate. He looked down from his seat in his saddle to the wounded man.

He spoke without preamble. "Wilcolac Cobweb, do you wish to escape from the Anarchists? Another Thursday will be appointed in time, or another Lord of Anarchy will see that you were useful once. You did not have the strength to oppose them then. Join us. Serve Arthur! My sword will protect you."

"And you make me this most noble offer… why?

"To save your mortal life and perhaps your immortal soul," said Gilberec grimly.

"Oh? And not because you wish my particular talents to serve your cause rather than theirs?"

"Quite the opposite," said Gil. "You must forswear all magic, break your wand, release your familiar spirits, and cast any books of hidden secrets into the sea."

Wilcolac smiled. "And give up show biz?"

Gil scowled.

Wilcolac waved his hand in the air as if to shoo away a fly. "No, my lad, I have made many grisly sacrifices to win what I have won, and many a dreadful secret I have unearthed, things known to no others. And now I have been to the maw of Hell itself during the tithing of the elfin kings. My reputation among the other practitioners in the field will soar!"

Yumiko said, "Your hob, Crookshank, is gone. Your ghost, Jack-o'-Lantern, is gone. I killed one and freed the other. Joan the Wad said she was going to be baptized."

Wilcolac's smile became a little stiff. He said to Tom, "You know, young inventor, while you were languishing in the grip of the pharmaceuticals and enchantments I plied you with, your girlfriend was dancing for tips at my club. Truly sleazy and uncouth old men would tuck grimy bills of high denominations into all sorts of intimate crevasses. She was not entirely naked."

Tom said, "Schroedinger's inconsistent *cat!* You are so going to die now!"

"Am I?" smirked Wilcolac. He squinted up at Gilberec. "Well, Sir Knight. Your ears are keen. Did I speak any untrue thing?"

Gil's face darkened. The look of steel in his eyes was not pleasant to see. He threw down his truncheon at the magician's feet. "As easily as that spear was broken, your enemies will break you."

"Fortunate for me that I find myself in better company then, is it not?" Wilcolac spoke on in an airy and carefree tone. His smile was smug. "Will you kindhearted young folk with your foolish high ideals be content to watch me bleed and die, or will you call an ambulance for me?"

Tom said, "We may need to call an ambulance for Matthias in any case."

Gil said, "Why? What happened? Where is he?"

As if summoned by his name, out from between two angelic statues, leaning on the five-foot-tall form of Elfine, Matthias came walking into view.

3. Anti-vampirism

He was dressed once more in his Dominican habit of white beneath a black hooded cape. His steps were slow and unstable.

As he drew near, Gil said, "Have you checked yourself for wounds?"

Matthias said, "I am well."

Gil said, "What happened?"

Matthias said, "Nothing unlawful."

Gil scowled. "A vampire trick. Those are not good for you."

Matt said, "A vampire drinks blood and drains the life of another. I gave of myself that another might drink and shared the life within me." He smiled sadly. "It sounds mildly blasphemous when I put it that way, I know, but the grace of Heaven allows some of us, in some small way, to participate in the work of Christ even though we all participate in the sin of Adam. I can do nothing of myself."

"Spare us yet another theology lecture!" Tom said, "What happened?"

Matt raised an eyebrow. "You were there. You saw."

Tom said, "I mean, just now. You vanished."

"The magician's spell, for which I suppose I am grateful, deposited me back in the waking world near my things. Elfine found me and Yumiko's pearl."

Elfine brought the pearl over. Yumiko twisted it in her hands and was able to shove it in the same imaginary direction her vixen body had come out from. The pearl vanished, and her suit, boots, gloves, and other gear solidified into her hands. The green cloak was so voluminous, and the smart material so plaint and convenient, that she was able to draw on the suit without any loss of modesty, as if in a tent. The boots and gloves followed a moment later. The mask vanished into the pocket of her cape because she had no time to brush and braid her hair.

Matthias hobbled closer. "Thank you, Magician, for bringing us so neatly back to Earth. But there are things you may not bring on holy ground."

"Now, wait a moment…" Wilcolac started to say.

Matthias raised the little silver crucifix dangling from his rosary and said a blessing. The black walking stick in Wilcolac's hand moaned, vibrated, jumped, and then exploded into a mess of splinters. The larger fragments began to turn red and give of little wisps of blue smoke.

"How dare you!" Wilcolac was red faced with fury.

Matthias said, "When I was in your house, I said nothing to disaccommodate you. But now you are here. This ground is consecrated. I am no knight, who sheathes his sword on the Sabbath, or in parley, or when peace is made. You are forever at war with Heaven, Necromancer. You are the slave of those who just this hour sought your life and soul. You have escaped from Hell by less than inches, less than seconds, and your life will lead you back there. Escape from them. Choose life, not death. Save yourself."

Wilcolac heaved himself painfully to his feet. "Never," said the magician with finality.

"Schroedinger's unprintably uncertain and acausal *cat!* You are *so* going to die," declared Tom, glaring steadfastly into Wilcolac's condescending smirk.

Wilcolac stiffened, gargled, swayed. The life went from his eyes. His body fell backward across the headstone, quite dead.

4. *The Eyes of Night*

Gil glared disapprovingly at Tom.

"Not me! I did not do anything!" Tom protested. "You think I can cuss someone to death? With a cat?"

The body slid off the headstone and turned toward them as it struck the grass. Now all could see where a red arrow was imbedded in the top of his skull up to the fletching. The arrowhead and shaft protruded a foot out below the chin. Death had been instantaneous.

Ruff barked. All looked up.

Dark against the bright morning sky, passing from cloud to cloak, slid a dark shape on wide wings, black as a crow and silent as an owl. The longbow was visible as a thin horn issuing from his head, reaching in the direction of flight.

The distant figure was sideways to them, one wing foreshortened and hard to see. He reached both arms above his head, almost as if in a swan dive, before drawing them sharply but smoothly down and apart, which was the Japanese style of archery.

This time they heard the whisper of the arrow fly. The second arrow struck the fallen body square in the chest, passing through the heart and pinning the corpse to the ground. There was a scrap of paper bound around the shaft. A little wind pried the paper open and set it to flutter. Yumiko could see some of the words listed: *black magic, abduction, murder, rigged gambling, purveying lewdness…*

Gil made a fist and raised it at the wide-winged black shape as it dove smoothly into a cloud bank and was lost to view. "Another lawless slaying. No trial, no mercy, no hope. Why does he mar our work?"

Yumiko said, "I can answer that."

Gil looked down. "Will he be in the factory if we go back?"

"I doubt he will connect the moon-door to that threshold again now that it has served its purpose."

Gil looked puzzled.

Tom said, "She means thresholds. Winged Vengeance stole Rotwang Cobweb's irreplaceable moon-door right out of the wreckage of the Iron Mole. So it acts like the door to your attic, Gil, or the gate to Mommur. Sometimes the entrance is in one place, sometimes in another. But the attic, city, or room is not actually behind the door."

Gil said, "No, I knew that, I was wondering what purpose."

Yumiko said, "I assume the factory was meant to kill whoever Wilcolac had tailing me. Nyctalope must have suspected you would find the ghost and force it to bring you here; otherwise, he would not have been hiding in the clouds overhead, waiting for you to bring any surviving Anarchists out from the Tithing Ground. He knew where it was, for he escaped from there."

Tom said, "He and I should form a club."

Yumiko said, "He is not one for joining clubs."

Gil said to her, "You said you could tell us why he hinders us."

"The hindrance is not deliberate. He acts as he does because of who he is."

"Who is he?"

"He is Nyctalope Peaseblossom."

Gil said, "He was in the previous Last Crusade. But I was told they all died."

Tom said, "Should have been called the *Not Quite the Totally Last Crusade*."

Yumiko said to Gil, "Two lived. The other was Rotwang Cobweb, who is an Anarchist."

Tom said, "Lord Saturday, the Master of Revenants. He told me before he gave me to the Werewolf guy, Lord Thursday. We should discuss with the Man in the Black Room why he never told us that the man for whom I was interning, and was later hired to spy on, was an ex-member of the same crusade I served."

Gil said, "Don't interrupt. You and I will discuss your private expeditions into danger zones with unvetted allies later."

Tom said, "Unvetted? She's my second cousin once removed!"

Gil ignored him and turned to Yumiko. "You were saying, Cousin?"

"I was speaking of Nyctalope. Your fight he condones—indeed he fights it himself—but he trusts neither the Man in the Black Room nor any living being."

Gil said, "Where is his sanctuary? The Magician tricked us into looking for it, and we were nearly killed by the deadfalls."

"It cannot be found," said Yumiko, "He carries the eight-sided chamber on his person."

Elfine said, "Is he allowed to do that? It is not fair if detectives cannot find villains!"

Yumiko said, "He is no villain. A dark mermaid helped him. I do not know which one. It takes up nearly no space. Anyone who steps into the sanctuary is actually in his pouch. That was the destination I had in mind when I tried to use the Ring of Mists to return from the Third Hemisphere."

She sighed and said half to herself, "How am I going to get all my outfits out of my closet? And get my diary?"

She turned to Elfine, "Which reminds me, I now remember something. Damiano was the name of the police officer who brought me to the hospital. He is also one of the agents of Winged Vengeance. When I arrived unconscious in the eight-sided chamber, Nyctalope had his agent put me in the hospital."

Elfine said, "With all your weapons and supersuit and such?"

Yumiko said, "All redesigned by Tom. Nyctalope did not trust them. He thought I was a trap as well." She pouted. "As it turned out, he was right. I led an enemy to his door."

Matthias said, "Why didn't he bring you to one of the Moth houses? We have one in every city. You could have found help there."

"He is not a Moth. He is solitary."

Elfine said angrily, "He could have parked you some place safer than a hospital were werewolves could find you! And a goat man!"

Yumiko said, "He did not know the Ring of Mists was on my finger and that its scent calls ghosts when the band is black. Euhemerus Cobweb, the Lord of Ghosts, had no trouble finding me."

5. *Experimental Results*

Yumiko turned to Tom. "I can report the experiment in intercontinental teleportation was a total failure. The dark part of the world of mists—the part the lost ghosts haunt—is watched and guarded just as well as the upper parts. The mist barrier between here and the Third Hemisphere is impenetrable."

Tom said, "You told me the ghosts could not stop you. That is why you were the logical choice to go."

"The demons stopped me."

"They should not be able to come up in the mist that high. It is not their layer. Insubstantial beings exist at a higher strata than non-dimensional beings"

"I dove down."

Tom looked shocked. "What? But why? What could possess you to do that?"

Yumiko said sadly, "What possesses anyone who dives into the arms of a demon? A flaw in me made me so crave some trifle in the demon's hand that I fell willingly onto his palm. He but closed his fingers. But I have learned a hard lesson."

She reached down and shut the eyes of the dead man. "Many things have gathered to convince me that reckless slaughter betrays my mother's memory and does not avenge her or honor her."

6. *The Announcement*

Yumiko turned to the others. "I have an announcement. Saint Barbara told me to tell you that when eternal day breaks, twilight is no more. Then will all the deeds of the Twilight Folk be laid bare and judged. She said that this hour is at hand."

A look of astonishment and joy overcame the face of Matthias. His eyes behind his spectacle lenses seemed large. Now they seemed larger still. He called to Gil, "Did you hear that? Did you hear?"

Gil said warily, "It might not mean what you think it means."

Matthias said to Yumiko, "Was there anything else? Did the saint say anything about the Grail?"

Yumiko said, "No. Nothing about that. She only told me not to let my beloved be drawn into darkness." She put her arm around Tom and smiled up at him.

Matthias said to Gil, "It means we are destined to succeed!"

Gil said, "Or those who come after us, inspired by our brave deaths, will succeed. Or it means the Second Advent is nigh and has nothing to do with the Black Spell at all."

Elfine said, "What are you talking about?"

Gil said, "The Last Crusade. We are not crusading against the paynims or to free the Holy Land. We will free all the lands. We will break the Black Spell."

Tom said, "Which reminds me. I also have an announcement."

Yumiko's face lit up. Elfine clapped.

Tom threw out his chest. "I have figured out how to enter the Third Hemisphere, recover the Grail, drive back the Mists of Everness, and save Mankind from the domination of the elves!"

Yumiko's face fell. Tom looked at her, startled. "What? What is it?"

Yumiko bowed. "Nothing of importance. I just thought–"

"She just thinks you are an idiot!" said Elfine.

Tom said, "And who are you, again, exactly?"

Elfine grinned. "A lovable rogue girl detective."

Tom said, "Wait. Does that mean you detect the girls of lovable rogues, or that you are a rogue girl who detects, or…"

"All of that, of course!"

Matthias said, "Elfine knows where the *Nautilus* docks. So you see what our next step will be."

Gil said, "Before that, the next step is getting this body properly buried and our reports squared away with the Man in the Black Room."

Yumiko said, "And I must meet him."

Gil said, "Oh?"

Yumiko said, "If I am to become a member in good standing with the Last Crusade."

Gil looked skeptical. "Well, Cousin, I am not sure how to put this, but you do not make a very good first impression, and there are some real drawbacks in your history."

Matthias said, "And there are drawbacks in our histories as well. That is why we are so eager to give anyone a chance to turn over a new leaf. Also…" He turned to Gil. "Tom will insist she come."

Tom said, "I will?"

Matthias said, "Because of your big announcement!"

Elfine jumped up and down and clapped again. "Announce it now! Announce! Announce! Pronounce the announcement!"

Gil said, "What announcement?"

Tom said, "Yeah, what announcement? That I figured out a way past the–"

Elfine shook her head and gestured meaningfully towards a silent Yumiko. Tom looked quizzically at her. Finally, a look of enlightenment came to his face, but was immediately transformed into an expression of sheepish embarrassment.

Tom cleared his throat. "I would like to announce… Well, wait a minute. I am not sure if I can. I wanted to ask… that is to propose… Wait a minute."

And he got down on one knee.

"Yes," said Yumiko before he could say anything. "I do. I accept."

Tom stammered. "But you don't even know what I–"

"I do," said Yumiko. She raised her hand and displayed the ring on her finger. "You already asked. I accept. I am yours."

"I mean, I am asking you to be my–"

"Yes," said Yumiko. She smiled shyly, and bowed politely, and took his hand, and urged him to his feet. "My answer to you is yes."

Tom stood and sputtered. "I mean… what I… uh–"

Ruff barked impatiently. Gil sighed and shook his head, "You said it, boy."

Ruff barked again. Gil laughed and translated. "Shut your trap, Tom, and kiss her already."

Here ends ***The Dark Avenger's Sidekick***

THE TALES OF MOTH & COBWEB continue in

The Mad Scientist's Intern

Science Fiction

The End of the World as We Knew It by Nick Cole
CTRL-ALT REVOLT! by Nick Cole
Pop Kult Warlord by Nick Cole
Soda Pop Soldier by Nick Cole
Back From the Dead by Rolf Nelson
Mutiny in Space by Rod Walker
Alien Game by Rod Walker
Young Man's War by Rod Walker

Fiction

Turned Earth: A Jack Broccoli Novel by David T. Good
An Equation of Almost Infinite Complexity by Peter Grant
Brings the Lightning by Peter Grant
Rocky Mountain Retribution by Peter Grant
The Promethean by Owen Stanley
The Missionaries by Owen Stanley

Fantasy

Summa Elvetica by Vox Day
A Throne of Bones by Vox Day
A Sea of Skulls by Vox Day

Military Science Fiction

Starship Liberator by David VanDyke and B. V. Larson
Battleship Indomitable by David VanDyke and B. V. Larson
The Eden Plague by David VanDyke
Reaper's Run by David VanDyke
Skull's Shadows by David VanDyke
There Will Be War Volumes I and II ed. Jerry Pournelle
Riding the Red Horse Volume 1 ed. Tom Kratman and Vox Day

Non-Fiction

Jordanetics by Vox Day
The Last Closet by Moira Greyland
4th Generation Warfare Handbook by William S. Lind and Gregory A. Thiele
Appendix N: A Literary History of Dungeons & Dragons by Jeffro Johnson
The Nine Laws by Ivan Throne
Compost Everything: Extreme Composting by David the Good
Grow or Die: Survival Gardening by David the Good
Push the Zone: Growing Tropical Plants Beyond the Tropics by David the Good

www.ingramcontent.com/pod-product-compliance
Lightning Source LLC
Chambersburg PA
CBHW020948310726
48980CB00001B/101
* 9 7 8 9 5 2 7 0 6 5 2 6 6 *